# Brother Fish

Books by Bryce Courtenay

*The Power of One*
*Tandia*
*April Fool's Day*
*A Recipe for Dreaming*
*The Family Frying Pan*
*The Night Country*
*Jessica*
*Smoky Joe's Cafe*
*Four Fires*
*Matthew Flinders' Cat*
*Brother Fish*

The Australian Trilogy

*The Potato Factory*
*Tommo & Hawk*
*Solomon's Song*

Also available in one volume,
as *The Australian Trilogy*

# BRYCE COURTENAY

# Brother Fish

MICHAEL JOSEPH
*an imprint of*
PENGUIN BOOKS

MICHAEL JOSEPH

Published by the Penguin Group
Penguin Books Ltd, 80 Strand, London WC2R 0RL, England
Penguin Group (USA) Inc., 375 Hudson Street, New York, New York 10014, USA
Penguin Group (Canada), 90 Eglinton Avenue East, Suite 700, Toronto, Ontario, Canada M4P 2Y3
(a division of Pearson Penguin Canada Inc.)
Penguin Ireland, 25 St Stephen's Green, Dublin 2, Ireland (a division of Penguin Books Ltd)
Penguin Group (Australia), 250 Camberwell Road,
Camberwell, Victoria 3124, Australia (a division of Pearson Australia Group Pty Ltd)
Penguin Books India Pvt Ltd, 11 Community Centre,
Panchsheel Park, New Delhi – 110 017, India
Penguin Group (NZ), Apollo Drive, Mairangi Bay, Auckland 1310, New Zealand
(a division of Pearson New Zealand Ltd)
Penguin Books (South Africa) (Pty) Ltd, 24 Sturdee Avenue,
Rosebank, Johannesburg 2196, South Africa

Penguin Books Ltd, Registered Offices: 80 Strand, London WC2R 0RL, England

www.penguin.com

First published by Penguin Group (Australia) 2004
First published in Great Britain by Michael Joseph 2007
1


Jacket photographs by Getty Images
Maps © Alan Laver



Printed in Great Britain by Clays Ltd, St Ives plc

A CIP catalogue record for this book is available from the British Library

ISBN-13: 978–0–718–15142–3
ISBN-10: 0–718–15142–9

# BOOK ONE

# CHAPTER ONE

## *The Anzac Hotel – Launceston, 1986*

I'm standing at the Gallipoli Bar waiting to meet Jimmy Oldcorn in the Anzac Hotel in Launceston. Jimmy and I meet in this particular pub on the 9th of August every year regardless of where we happen to be in the world. It is a tradition that goes back a long, long way to a cold and bitter war most Australians have forgotten. Thirty-four years ago I invited Jimmy home with me from Korea – for he was a Yank with no place in his native country he could remember with sufficient affection to wish to return.

Jimmy and I had been taken prisoners of war and had spent almost two years in various establishments initially under the North Koreans, and subsequently the Chinese. We'd both been wounded, though not in the same battle, and each had a leg badly broken when we'd been captured. Even the best part of two years into captivity, with the bones knitted, our bad legs still gave us a fair amount of pain. Close to the time of the cease-fire and armistice, we'd been released in a prisoner-of-war exchange with the Chinese and were subsequently taken to US 121 Medical Evacuation Hospital in Seoul for assessment of our injuries. Here they gave us the good news and the bad news. The bad was that, in both our cases, they would need to break the crookedly knitted leg and reset it. The good news, for me anyway, was that the comfort bag the Red Cross gave me included a large bar of chocolate.

Compared to the bad, the good news must sound pretty trivial. But it just goes to show, even in extremely emotional moments, life often comes down to trivial things. This simple gift of chocolate was a symbol of great importance to me. Asians don't eat chocolate – it is not a taste they've acquired. On the other hand, for a poor Australian kid growing up in the Great Depression and the lean years that immediately followed, chocolate was the ultimate luxury. As a prisoner of war it had come to represent all that was good about our way of life. When the pain and the beatings became really bad I'd dream of tasting chocolate just one more time before I died, although I knew the likelihood of this happening was extremely remote. A prisoner of war with a broken leg and multiple wounds had virtually no chance of surviving the primitive conditions of a North Korean field hospital. When we did survive the various field hospitals, the POW camp that followed promised to finish us off. Now, almost miraculously, we'd made it! Here I was, the personal possessor of a bar of milk chocolate and safely ensconced in a military hospital bed, a fair-dinkum bed with springs that squeaked, all sixty-five pounds of skin and bone concealed beneath crispy white sheets.

With trembling hands I tore away the top quarter of the outer wrapper, peeled the silver foil from a corner of the chocolate bar then carefully broke off an individual square. Then, postponing the grand moment when it would contact my tongue so as to better anticipate the experience, I examined the brand name pressed into the tiny portion. Its calligraphy, so precise and assured, belonged to a world where sanity and order always prevailed. At last the warmth from my finger and thumb began to transfer into the tiny square and it started to soften, so I placed the chocolate in my mouth, closing my eyes to savour its exquisite creaminess. The initial flavour was everything I'd dreamed about. Then, after a few seconds the richness hit my stomach. It was as if I had been punched in the solar plexus, causing me to double over in the bed so that my head slammed against my knees. This was followed by an irrepressible surge which rose from my lower regions and threw me backwards. I started to retch when, just as suddenly, my torso was hurled forward, sending a spray of watery vomit over the snowy sheets. The unfamiliar chocolate had been too much for a stomach accustomed to a diet of boiled millet and thin rice gruel. I had come full circle, back to an experience that began on the night I was taken prisoner by the North Koreans.

On the night of my capture I had been dragged unconscious from the snow into a partially demolished hut. I awoke in great pain, and pleaded with my captors to fashion some sort of splint to support my shattered leg. While they nodded their heads acknowledging that they could see my leg was broken, they seemed unconcerned. They spoke no English and seemed more interested in going through my pack than attending to my condition. Soon enough one of them came across a small bar of army-issue chocolate, and after removing the wrapper seemed not to know what to do next. Thinking it might be a good way to ingratiate myself I attempted a smile and indicated, by bringing my fingers to my mouth and making a chewing then swallowing motion, that he should eat it. The soldier broke off a square and placed it into his mouth. Instead of allowing the chocolate to melt on his tongue, he did as I had indicated and chewed, then immediately swallowed. I waited for the look of delight to cross his face. To the enormous amusement of the others, his face screwed into a grimace of disgust and he began to spit furiously. Bent double and clutching his stomach he started to heave, and then vomited over his canvas boots. His comrades, delighted at the practical joke I'd played on him, were convulsed with laughter, congratulating me with their looks and smiles. When the soldier finally recovered, I could see he was furious. I had caused him to lose face in front of his mates. He advanced on me and, without warning, snatched up his rifle and smashed the butt into the side of my jaw, breaking several teeth. I had just discovered the hard way that chocolate wasn't an Asian thing.

From the Evacuation Hospital in Seoul, after the briefest of goodbyes, Jimmy was evacuated to the Tokyo Army Hospital while

I was to go to the British Commonwealth Hospital in Kure, the port we'd departed from when we'd first embarked for Korea.

At Iwakuni Airport the Red Cross had put on a posh meal for the Commonwealth prisoners before we were to board an ambulance train to the military hospital. As demonstrated by the chocolate episode, my stomach wasn't yet ready for such a generous gesture. All I could eat was a couple of forkfuls of vegies, using my paper napkin to wipe the glaze of butter off the baby carrots, although, as a special treat, I took a chance with two dessertspoons of mixed-fruit jelly. Yet, despite not having the stomach for the meal, to this day I remember the entire menu. This first Western meal I'd encountered in two years gave me additional assurance that I was back in safe hands. In my imagination I ate every scrap, slowly, savouring every morsel.

*Cream of Tomato Soup*
*Roast Chicken and Bread Sauce*
*New Potatoes and Parsley Sauce*
*Fresh Vegetables*
*Mixed Fruit Jelly and Whipped Cream*
*Cheese, Bread and Butter*

I also recall thinking that roast chicken was something you only got at Christmas, and just for a moment my mind, which had long since given up counting days and months and only recognised seasons, became confused, and I thought *this must be Christmas Day*, the only day of the year almost every Australian tasted roast chicken.

After three and a half months in hospital the authorities took the opportunity to bum a ride for a dozen or so of the Australian walking wounded, myself included, on a chartered Qantas flight taking some of the military top brass back to Melbourne.

It was decided that I would do a further three months' convalescence in Australia before being discharged from the army. With my left leg in plaster up to the hip I was still very much dependent on my crutches, and it had taken a fair bit of persuasion on my part to convince the army doctors to let me go home. Crutches notwithstanding, I was going back to the island – the war was over for me. Before leaving Japan I'd been given two years' back pay and a couple of medals to wear on Anzac Day. It was more money than I'd ever possessed in my life, and I got scared just thinking about it.

The arrangement was that I was to remain in Melbourne to await Jimmy's plane from Tokyo due in two days' time. How he'd persuaded the US military to let him do his convalescence in Australia I'll never know, except that Jimmy could persuade most people to do most things.

My chartered Qantas flight had been the first plane into Melbourne that morning and, after I'd taken the airport bus into town where the driver dropped me off at a boarding house in St Kilda Road, one that he personally recommended and that turned out to be owned by his auntie, I took the tram into the city and bought myself some civilian clobber. The usual stuff – sports jacket, a couple of pairs of daks, one brown and one grey, three pairs of socks, though I only had need for one sock in the meantime, two white shirts and a decent pair of shoes, though again, only one shoe being useful in my present predicament. Then I bought a cheap suitcase to carry my army uniform and slouch hat.

I was still sixty pounds under my normal weight and I'd been careful to buy everything miles too big, with the result that I looked an awful fright. I'd put on a few pounds in the hospital but was still in a pretty emaciated condition and reckon I could easily have been mistaken for a dero who had been shaved head and beard to get rid of the lice, given a good scrub down and then issued with a new set of one-size-fits-all charity handouts from St Vincent de Paul.

I don't suppose it mattered much, I knew nobody in Melbourne. After all the fussing about in the hospital and the military debrief, where they took us through the propaganda to which we'd been subjected by the Chinese, I was happy enough to be left on my own.

I spent the remainder of the morning taking several short tram trips for a bit of a squiz at the big city. Around one o'clock I got off the tram at Flinders Street Station and bought a meat pie, which the bloke behind the pie cart smothered in tomato sauce without being asked to. I guess an Australian who didn't want tomato sauce on his meat pie was unimaginable. Earlier in the day, crossing the bridge in the tram going down St Kilda Road, I'd seen several ducks gliding on the Yarra, so I bought half a loaf of bread and, with the pie and the bread stuffed inside my shirt, I headed towards the Botanic Gardens across the bridge. I only just made it; the pie in a brown paper bag was hot as buggery and left a blister on my skin, a small price to pay for your first meat pie in three years. I found a bench beside the river, ate my pie, fed the ducks with the bread, watched the lazy brown Yarra go by, basked in the sunshine and soaked up the calm and peaceful world around me. Calm was something I hadn't enjoyed a lot of for what seemed to me to be a very long time.

Melbourne in the summer of 1953 was just trying to get its head around hosting the Olympic Games in three years' time and the city fathers were busy painting and repairing buildings, knocking down the odd one, and planting a few extra street trees to give the metropolis a veneer of sophistication when the world came to visit. A row of a dozen or more cranes stretched along a street near Flinders Street Station.

Though I wasn't much of a judge of big cities, four days before I was due to leave Japan I'd been given a forty-eight-hour leave pass and took the train to Tokyo to meet up with Jimmy, who I hadn't seen since we'd left the hospital in Seoul. We'd chatted on the phone a couple of times and sent the odd postcard to each other but, having been together cheek and jowl through hell and back for just under two years, I was naturally anxious to see how he was getting along. One thing was certain, Melbourne was no Tokyo – that much I can tell you.

With both of us on crutches, Jimmy and I had gone to the Ginza strip where we took in several of the honky-tonk, neon-and-noise girlie bars, beer halls and strip-tease joints. They all seemed much the same, the Japanese girls wearing too much lipstick, their short, stocky legs in PX nylons and high heels, hitching up their skirts to show a provocative glimpse of suspender as they hoisted themselves onto the bar stool beside you. 'You buy me drink, soldier.' The pitch, like Johnnie Walker whisky, never varied.

Later we headed for Shinjuku, the red light district. It was awash with beer and bourbon and the dull roar of humans trying to have a good time. The bars were seemingly endless, most with tricked-up American names such as the Golden Horseshoe and Alabama Annie. I especially remember two, Hound Dog Hotel and the Memphis Maiden, though in the latter instance I imagine very few of your actual maidens ever stepped through its sliding bamboo doors. All of them existed for a single purpose: to attract the homesick GI with a pocketful of Yankee dollars and a determination to get laid before going home to Mom's apple pie and the waiting arms of a Mary-Lou, a bobby-soxer when he'd left and now a lovely young woman waiting glory-boxed and teary-eyed to become a bride.

After almost two years in the grim surroundings of a POW camp the glamour and glitter of Tokyo's Ginza strip and the blatant sexuality of Shinjuku seemed totally surreal. The fact that we were drinking alcohol while pumped full of antibiotics no doubt added to the bizarre experience. It was all becoming too much: the blazing lights, flashing neons in pinks and reds, electric blues and acid-sharp whites, the noise, especially the noise, the painted faces of the girls with their hard, obsidian eyes, began to physically overwhelm me. It felt as though I was being bashed over the skull with a baseball bat and I could feel my heart beating like a voodoo drum. I was suddenly possessed by an almost irresistible desire to screw up my eyes, hold my hands cupped to my ears, squat down onto my haunches and go into a blithering funk. My senses were completely overloaded and I knew I was very close to breaking down. When Jimmy turned to me and said, 'Brother Fish, let's get the hell outta here, I can't take no more, man,' I was damn near tears and, in my haste to put my beer down I bumped the base of the glass I was holding against the edge of the bar spilling what remained into my lap.

Now, less than a week later, here I was in Melbourne where the pubs shut at six o'clock when the city settled into an almost sepulchral quietness. It seemed entirely appropriate that the dozens of construction cranes piercing the pre-Olympic skyline gave the impression of a city playing host to a convocation of bishops, their arms stretching out to bless the buildings kneeling beneath them. I was to learn later that they were there to remove the Victorian verandahs from many of the buildings, a modification that the city fathers believed would improve the city in preparation for the Olympics. Melbourne was tarting itself up, determined to show the world it was not some colonial backwater, but a modern and vibrant city.

I'd decided to buy myself a slap-up dinner on my first night home as a quasi-civilian and so I took the short tram ride up Swanston Street, then hobbled up Bourke on my crutches. It was just a little after six-thirty but the city already had its shutters down. I eventually discovered a restaurant but found myself suddenly reluctant to enter. Looking through one of the windows I could see the small square tables covered with snowy tablecloths and matching serviettes, each folded into a Pope's bonnet. A single red rose in a small cutglass vase was the only colour on the tables. Gleaming cutlery lay pristine, softly glowing as if presented for display in a jewellery-shop window, and the wine glasses, two at every place setting, sparkled as they reflected the light from an enormous crystal chandelier that dominated the centre of the room.

I'd never tasted wine, it wasn't the sort of thing a bloke drank in those days. Maybe if you were taking a girl out and wanted to impress the pants off her you'd order a bottle of Porphyry Pearl, but you'd drink beer and she'd drink that and you'd hope it had the desired effect. It was the wineglasses more than anything that told me this was the wrong place for my sort. It hadn't been long since I'd frantically grabbed at rice gruel from a communal dish hoping to get two fistfuls into my mouth before it had all disappeared. I'd dreamed of one day sitting at a table with a clean cloth, cutlery and a plate of my own, but slap-up dinner notwithstanding, this didn't appear to be the sort of restaurant I'd have instinctively chosen to eat my prodigal son's return dinner. The menu stuck into a little frame in the window left me further confused.

*Canapés Riche*
*Cream of Asparagus Soup*
*Fillet of Sole Meunière*
*Chicken Maryland*
*Bombe Henri*
*Welsh Rarebit*
*Coffee*

What the fuck was *Canapés Riche* and why was it necessary to *Bombe Henri*?

I was hungry and tired and my leg hurt. I'd barely slept on the plane coming over and except for the meat pie, hadn't eaten all day. So I summoned up the courage to enter.

I'd hardly taken a step inside when a waiter in a penguin suit loomed above me. 'Good evening, sir,' he said.

'I'd like to dine,' I replied, hoping that by using the word 'dine' I'd make the right impression. He gave me the once-over, slowly, starting at my feet, noting the crutches and plaster cast sticking out of the end of my trousers. He appeared to be passing silent judgement on my new clobber, which hung like a Charlie Chaplin outfit on my skinny frame, and finally he brought his gaze up to my pale, freckled face and shaven head. His expression was not welcoming.

'Do you have a reservation?' he asked, omitting the 'sir'.

'Well, er, no. As a matter of fact I've just flown in from Japan,' I said, smiling pleasantly in an attempt not to appear nervous. I felt less assured in front of this jumped-up kitchenhand than when the Chinese had interrogated me.

Maybe it was his attempt not to laugh. I guess, in 1953, not too many people dropped into Melbourne from Japan on crutches, in oversized clobber, sporting a haircut of the type usually undertaken at His Majesty's expense in Pentridge Prison. His expression changed into a sort of half-sneer, not the full disdain, but more a '*Don't take me for a bloody fool, sonny boy!*'

'I'm sorry, we're fully booked tonight.' Again the 'sir' was absent.

I nodded towards the empty room behind him. 'But there's nobody in the place!'

'People are inclined to dine late at the Society Restaurant,' he replied haughtily.

After two years as a prisoner of war under the Chinese my self-esteem wasn't up there with Laurence Olivier's. 'I could eat quickly,' I offered, inwardly cringing at the pleading tone my voice had assumed without my permission.

One eyebrow shot up. 'That is not the purpose of this restaurant – sir!' Except for the pause in front of the 'sir' he pronounced each word as if it stood alone.

I knew I was beaten neck and crop, though at least the 'sir' was back. Feeling piss-weak, I hobbled away grumbling to myself, '*Welcome back to civvy street, Jacko, real nice to be home from the war, mate.*' Then, in the middle of the street I turned back to face him. 'BASTARD!' I yelled, then again, 'BASTARD!' But the restaurant door was shut and he'd disappeared.

I hobbled back to Swanston Street with my crutches burning into my rubbed-raw armpits and waited for a tram. With the help of the conductor I climbed aboard, and when he came to take my fare I asked him to let me off somewhere so I could find something decent to eat.

'Fancy a nice feed o' fish, mate?' he asked.

'That'd be great.' After the stuffy waiter, his vernacular was familiar and comforting.

'Righto then, know just the place. It's a sixpence fare to get there, but, I promise, it's fair dinkum.'

After an excellent plate of flake and chips and a cup of hot sweet tea on St Kilda Pier I felt a whole lot better. During the course of the meal I had decided I'd had enough of the big city. Instead of our hitting the bright lights of Melbourne (*Ha, ha! What effing bright lights?*), I'd try to persuade Jimmy that we ought to catch the *Taroona* directly to Launceston. Melbourne had nothing to offer two Korean veterans on crutches, and the sooner we got to the peace and quiet of the island the better.

I also decided I'd spend the following day buying presents for Mum and my sister Sue, something girlie, like talcum powder and perfume, Chanel No. 5. While in Japan I'd already purchased my main presents, five harmonicas, one for each member of the family. They were made in America and had a real nice tone. Then, if I could find a shop that sold fishing gear, I might buy my two younger brothers, Cory and Steve, some good nylon fishing line.

Jimmy's plane came in late the following afternoon. 'Let's go home to the island, leaving tonight,' I suggested at the airport. I indicated our crutches, my wooden ones and his fancy new lightweight aluminium Yankee extravaganzas. 'No use hanging around here on these, is there?' Then, to slot the proposition home, I added, 'Anyway mate, Boag's, the Tassie beer in Launceston, is miles better than the local piss.'

'Hey! Mel-borne, da young lady on the aeroplane she tol' me it got lots o' green trees like Central Park an' a big brown river run clear through da middle.'

'You don't want to know, mate,' I replied. 'Bloody good place for a funeral.'

Jimmy laughed. 'You da boss here, Brother Fish, ain't no big deal, I's seen Central Park and da Brooklyn River. Dis yo' country, man. What you pro-pose suits me fine – I been hurt bad from dat war and dis nigger in need of nourishin' and yo' mama's cray stew just da medicine I needs.' He pronounced it 'med-des-seen' in a way he had of separating and often stretching the syllables in a long word.

Of course, today, in the context of hip-hop music and in current

African-American street talk the word 'nigger' is used in a prideful way, much as the derogatory word 'wog' in our culture has become a badge of honour when used by the children of Italian and Greek migrants. But in 1953 it was a very different America for an African-American cove like Jimmy Oldcorn. In the South they were still lynching Negroes and elsewhere they still openly used the pejorative 'nigger'.

Moreover, in the Korean War, Negro recruits were initially segregated as they had been in World War II. This was done with the patronising excuse that they preferred to be 'with their own kind'. While there were coloured combat units, in the eyes of the senior staff officers coloured men made poor soldiers. They were thought to be cowardly, unintelligent, afraid of the dark and only fit for labour battalions, though there was no evidence to substantiate this point of view and the coloured combat units fought as valiantly and intelligently or, on occasion, as poorly as the white. Despite a Presidential decree in 1948 promising equal opportunity in the armed forces, this perverse view persisted. The senior army brass in some instances came from the Southern states and they feared desegregation in the army would make the nigger too big for his boots when he returned home to the South and it would lead to demands for desegregation in institutions and facilities in civilian life.

In fact, in mid-1950 when things started going wrong for the Americans in Korea, Jimmy's unit was thrown into battle where on the 10th of July 1950 it recaptured an important road junction at Yechon. But that was to be a one-off victory. Like the rest of the American units committed from the occupational forces in Japan, they were under-trained, under-strength, under-equipped and most certainly under-motivated.

Some time after coming home I recall reading an account of the early days of the war, and came across this paragraph concerning Jimmy's unit:

*Defeat and constant retreat lowered their morale and men withdrew in confusion and haste, often abandoning their dead, their weapons and their equipment as they struggled in disorder to the rear.*

Although all the regiments committed in those first months were found wanting, the failure of Jimmy's 24th Infantry Regiment against the North Koreans was put down to it being a Negro unit. The equal failure of the other units was not ascribed to them being Caucasian, but instead was blamed on the fact that they were ill-prepared and poorly equipped.

As it happened, Jimmy did not take part in the debacle that followed the US Army's entry into the war or in the ignominious retreat known as the 'big bug out'. He only arrived in Korea in early 1951 where, shortly after, he took part in a successful skirmish against the enemy rescuing a white unit under difficult circumstances. Nevertheless, he felt the need to defend his regiment. 'What you expect, Brother Fish, when dem honky units did a bug out to save dey asses, dey say it 'cos da enemy is overwhelming! When we outta der like a jack rabbit wid a pitchfork up his ass, dey say dat because we is cowardly niggers!'

There is another interesting aspect to the 24th Infantry Regiment and, it is true, it was not a happy outfit and had problems other than poor training. The unit contained both black and white officers but the American army would not allow a black officer to command a white officer. For example, if a white lieutenant was posted to a company with a black captain as 2IC, the black captain had to be posted out and a white captain replace him. As a result, each time this happened it sent a clear message to the Negro troops that they were seen as inferior. It is not difficult to see how this would have affected their fighting morale. In October 1951 the US Army was finally desegregated and the 24th Infantry Regiment was absorbed into racially mixed units and ceased to exist. But by this time Jimmy was in the hands of the Chinese.

Jimmy Oldcorn's reason for being with me in Melbourne began in a North Korean field hospital situated in a cave somewhere deep in the mountains that form the inhospitable spine of the Korean peninsula. We'd been chatting together, me talking of home and the island in an attempt to forget our miserable surroundings, when suddenly the idea struck me. 'Hey, Jimmy, when this is all over why don't you come home with me, mate?' I'd repeated the offer on several occasions and did so again when our release looked like being a real possibility, though on that occasion I was quick to add, 'Mind you, you'll probably go a bit stir-crazy, there's bugger-all to do except lie in the sun, fish, surf, dive for crayfish or go duck or roo shooting. But my mum cooks real good cray stew.' Sounds funny today, but at the time the qualification wasn't intended to paint a picture of halcyon days spent on an idyllic island. I honestly felt the need to warn him in advance that things were pretty slow-moving back home.

But, of course, he took it to mean an invitation to paradise. He'd tut-tut and shake his head. 'I don't know, Brother Fish, that I can endure such hardship. It ain't easy when you're accustomed as I is to da cos-mo-pol-itan life of Noo York city, man!'

We were both badly wounded and slowly rotting in the freezing, stinking, dark, wet, dirty, overcrowded cave that passed for a North Korean field hospital. While he always agreed to come, adding some amusing protest such as the one above, we knew it was just talk, a way of bolstering our despairing spirits. We both had badly broken left legs that hadn't set well and our wounds in several other places were infected and suppurating under the now filthy bandages we'd applied ourselves, mine being a couple of field dressings every Australian soldier carries and Jimmy's from the first-aid pouch the Yanks carried. We fully expected to be shot, as the Korean soldiers, used by the Japanese as POW guards during World War II, had a well-documented reputation for senseless brutality. In the chaotic early stage of the war, they were known to shoot their captured wounded. I guess we were lucky – they certainly weren't the friendliest mob, and why they hadn't put a bullet through our heads and put us out of our misery was a complete mystery. Nevertheless, they seemed determined to let the consequences of neglect do the job for them. We were clearly not intended to come out of the cave alive.

Later, prisoners became a valuable negotiating tool in the cease-fire talks. We were half dead and by now happy to receive a merciful bullet to the head when the North Koreans handed us into the care of a Chinese field hospital. Although their conditions proved just as primitive as those of the North Koreans, as our captors they were somewhat more benign. Moreover, they attempted to set our broken legs, though the doctor who did mine injected too little anaesthetic, leaving me in agony for the last part of the process. In any event, both Jimmy's leg and mine were badly set and encased in a carelessly made plaster cast that would cause us both a great deal of grief in the months that followed.

Time, more or less, heals most things, including badly knitted bones, and if you don't die you get better. The pain in my leg eventually got to be tolerable, though it never progressed much past that stage, and the filthy plaster cast remained on. Thankfully our mobility increased. Though we were still on crutches, we began to entertain the idea of an escape. It was all pie in the sky, of course, just another fantasy like Jimmy's coming to Queen Island. For a start we had no idea where we were, and while we may have been able to head south by reading the night sky we had no idea where the front lay. Furthermore, while I may have managed some small distance on my bamboo crutches, Jimmy's barely reached his waist and made movement for him very difficult. He'd utilise the crude crutches as if they were twin walking sticks. It was a slow, jarring and painful form of locomotion and he couldn't sustain it for more than a short period. Eventually I managed to steal a length of field telephone cable and, fisherman style, lashed his crutches together to form a single support that allowed him to move about more efficiently in the manner of a pirate with a peg leg in a kid's pantomime.

We were in the depths of a North Korean winter with night temperatures down to minus thirteen degrees Fahrenheit. Escaping under such conditions would have been a forbidding task for the fit and healthy, never mind two coves more than half-starved with only one pair of sound legs between them.

Spring saw our legs liberated from their plaster casts. The cutting away of the plaster is a memory that will be with me for the remainder of my life. For months I'd endured not only pain but an incessant itching under the cast that very nearly drove me crazy. Nothing I did seemed to help. I would poke a thin piece of bamboo down into the cast and cease the itching for a few moments before it would resume. Sometimes I would use the bamboo stick so frantically that eventually blood would trickle out of the bottom end of the plaster cast. When eventually the cast came off it liberated a vast colony of lice that swarmed in their tens of thousands over my emaciated left leg and thigh. It was such a bizarre sight that the orderly yelled happily to anyone standing close to come over. The tiny, disgusting grey creatures swarmed over the wooden pallet I was lying on and dropped to the earthen floor where the onlookers gleefully stamped on them. It was the best joke all day and the noggies marvelled at my leg, which the lice had picked to raw meat – in some places to the bone. Thankfully, in return for this unexpected sideshow, the orderly powdered it with a sulphur compound and bandaged it up. Two days later they reclaimed the bandage. I hope they washed it for the next cove, but things were that primitive it would have been unusual if they had.

With the removal of our casts we were officially cured, even though we continued to die slowly of malnutrition and the pain in our legs was seldom absent. From the last of the many field hospitals we'd been in we were sent to a POW camp on the China border. What followed was a further twelve months on legs that never quite healed and our wounds, while finally closing, remained tender to the touch. We were also introduced to Chinese methods of interrogation and their attempts at brainwashing, which were often funny though sometimes decidedly not.

So, you can imagine our joy when a cease-fire was called between the United Nations Command and the North Korean/Chinese Alliance and a prisoner-of-war exchange was arranged. We lined up with a bunch of Yanks, Brits, Turks, Canadians, South Africans and, of course, Australians, as well as nations I don't rightly recall. It was August the

9th, 1953 – a day I shall never forget. We waited on the 38th parallel at the exchange point at Panmunjon and I remember turning to Jimmy and saying, 'We made it, mate, and I have you to thank. I don't reckon I could have done it on me own.' I tried to smile, to make the remark sound a tad flippant, but it didn't work – my lower jaw became unhinged and I found my mouth wobbling and I started to weep.

'Nosirree! Brother Fish, we done made it together, man! Da one brother without da udder ain't worth a pinch o' sheet.' He gripped me by the shoulder, his large hand still strong. 'Dat what it mean to be brothers in arms.'

We were then taken to US 121 Medical Evacuation Hospital in Seoul for an assessment of our injuries. We were safely tucked up between clean sheets, our heads and beards and the other hairy parts of our bodies shaved clean, where I noticed for the first time that my pubic hair had turned grey. We were then de-loused, showered, had our open sores dressed and commenced the tricky business of holding down small amounts of meat and milk. I was troubled at the thought of leaving Jimmy Oldcorn for our respective hospitals in Japan. I decided not to mention Queen Island before we parted in case it embarrassed him now that we were free again. I wondered if I'd ever see him again, and this thought really played on my mind. The thought that I was about to lose the best mate I'd ever had kept me awake all night and I became profoundly depressed.

When we'd taken our departure from each other I'd tried to sound cheerful and I could see he was trying to do the same. Men are such silly buggers, they joke when they want to cry, and finally all I could think to say to prevent myself breaking down again was, 'Go on, piss off you silly bugger!'

Jimmy laughed. 'I always knew you had no good manners, Brother Fish. I's gonna miss you playing da fish tune.' We shook hands when we should have embraced, but those were different times and men didn't show their feelings as easily as they do today. There was no mention from him about coming to the island.

To my surprise and delight, three weeks later, my leg re-broken and in a decent cast, and while sitting rugged up in a wheelchair in the compound of the British Commonwealth Hospital in Kure, a nurse arrived. 'You've got a call from Tokyo,' she said, breathlessly, obviously having run from the phone to find me. She took hold of my wheelchair, laughing.

'What's the joke?' I asked, as she began to wheel me away.

'Oh, nothing, just your caller. At first I didn't know who he wanted. This deep American voice kept saying, "Put me through to Brother Fish, ma'am!" It wasn't until he described you that I realised who he meant.'

I became excited, Jimmy had called. 'What did he say, I mean, how did he describe me?'

The nurse stopped the wheelchair and giggled, embarrassed. 'I can't say.'

'Go on, nurse, I can take it,' I grinned.

She started pushing again. '"Little runt. Ginger. Millions of freckles. Leg's broke bad, ma'am."' She laughed again. 'It still didn't entirely click until he added, "Plays da mouth organ like he an angel."'

I shall always remember her name because it seemed so appropriate to the colour of her eyes and wasn't the sort of name sheilas had in those days. Skye Morrison had dark hair, a trim figure and a lovely little bum that apple-shaped the rear of her khaki pants, though I should quickly add my libido at the time was nonexistent. We'd arrived at a phone affixed to a corridor wall, the receiver still open and dangling from its cord. I grabbed it, grinning like an ape. 'G'day, Jimmy,' I yelled.

'Well, Brother Fish, when I'm gonna have me some of yo' mama's dee-lish-ous cray stew?'

He would later tell me that my persistent invitation to visit was the first time anyone, other than an institution and the army, had allowed him to share in their life. Life on an island in Bass Strait was probably as much beyond Jimmy's imagination as his life in New York was beyond mine. I felt pretty certain that a bloke who'd grown up in what I knew from the movies was the world's largest concrete jungle would soon enough grow weary of island life. It was sufficient to hope we might share our convalescence for a short time. Rest, sunshine and good home cooking with the added tender loving care Gloria and Sue would lavish upon us was what we both needed to mend our broken bodies and restore some sense of normalcy to our lives. The island may have had its shortcomings but I felt sure it would supply all these prerequisites in abundance.

Our friendship had developed seemingly against all odds. When you are locked up with other men, sharing the stench of their rotting flesh and their constant moans and cries of despair, craven as it may seem, you soon lose any sense of compassion and become deeply preoccupied with your own survival.

All you can think about is release from hunger and pain. Staying alive becomes everything, a primal instinct that comes to possess and separate you from the fraternity of your fellow prisoners. While you may occasionally bond with them against the common enemy, it is merely another survival mechanism kicking in. You sense that you are going to need all the selfish strength you can muster to stay alive. Affection is pointless, emotional energy wasted – if you're not careful it will kill you all the sooner.

Hate and anger are emotions that attach to pain and starvation as a means of survival. Pretty soon your fevered imagination turns the bloke dying beside you into the enemy who is stealing the food from your mouth. That is to say simply by receiving a similar mouthful to your own, your share and therefore your chance of survival is diminished. This is a vile sentiment to which, in retrospect, few men will admit. Moreover, it is completely irrational. The North Koreans in particular – or even the Chinese – would not have increased my ration by a spoonful had all the men around me perished. But logic plays no part in one's sensibilities when pain and starvation conspire to rob you of life.

In such circumstances, where each wounded man in captivity is in great pain and hanging on for grim death, conspiring to keep himself alive at any cost, it takes a strong leader to hold men together and to prevent them from descending into a dog-eat-dog environment. I regret to say that leader wasn't me. At twenty-five I was the oldest among the equally ranked prisoners of war and, as veteran of another war, I should have done better. My gammy leg was no excuse, I should have assumed control. Instead, Private Jimmy Oldcorn, three years my junior and with a leg as bad as my own, was the man who pulled us through. He gave us the leadership we so badly needed and, in the process, forced us to keep our collective nerve while giving us hope when death seemed a far more certain outcome than the prospect of staying alive.

For reasons I shall never understand he chose me as his offsider. It may simply have been that he was a coloured man from a segregated regiment and his fellow American prisoners were all Caucasians. Perhaps he feared racial prejudice would forbid any of them acting as his offsider. I was the stray dog without a collar – by choosing me he avoided confrontation. Whatever his reason, I count myself fortunate. Despite my own self-preserving instincts, Jimmy forced me to behave rationally and with a concern for the welfare of our fellow prisoners. In the process, the leader of a New York street gang turned a pack of near-animals back into humans and undoubtedly saved my life and the lives of a great many others.

You see, humans are essentially tribal. Such is the strength of tribal bonds generated in the military system that soldiers will conform to the hierarchical demands of their army unit even in the face of probable death. The wanton slaughter of the 8th and 10th Light Horse regiments that took place at the Nek on Gallipoli is a classic example, the charge of the Light Brigade at Crimea yet another.

Captors intent on destroying the morale of prisoners in order to crack their resistance must first break up the tribal structure by separating the officers, senior noncommissioned officers and soldiers. They must also break up any sub-units they may have captured intact. Without the leadership to organise and direct and the solidarity created by time and habit, soldiers suffering mistreatment become more vulnerable to capitulation and death.

Even when rank is present and taking responsibility, in circumstances where men are constantly harangued, neglected, weakened and dying of their wounds or starvation, it takes a very talented leader to keep them mentally steady and determined to hold out. That Jimmy, a buck private and coloured soldier from a segregated regiment, had the fortitude and character to step forward and take control rather than give in to his own self-preserving instincts was, to say the least, unexpected. He'd endured a lifetime of discrimination, was very much a loner and with his orphanage and reform-school background, where initiative and original thinking would have been beaten out of him, he might have been expected to just look after himself. Yet, here he was, taking control when we needed it most. I found this little short of remarkable.

By the time we were transferred to the POW camp, the bond formed between Jimmy Oldcorn and myself had grown very strong. I had come to trust him like a brother. More than this he was my mate and, in the arcane and inarticulate way Australian males have of expressing their emotions, your mate is for life, come hell or high water.

This is how we might have been described when we first joined our respective armies. In the red corner, Jack McKenzie, K Force, 3rd Battalion, the Royal Australian Regiment (3RAR), five-feet five-inches in his size-six army boots. In appearance all sinew and bone, wearing a blaze of copper-coloured hair, deeply freckled and, at twenty-five, already irreparably sun-damaged. Fighting weight, 125 pounds when fully fit.

In the blue corner, Jimmy Pentecost Oldcorn, 24th Infantry Regiment, 25th Infantry Division, American Negro, six-feet six-inches in his khaki army-issue socks, weighing in at 260 pounds of solid muscle with fists the size of soup plates.

This was not how we looked when we departed from the hell of the North Korean hospital cave and were handed over to the Chinese. Despite losing a mountain of weight Jimmy remained a big man, around

180 pounds. While I, reduced to sixty-five pounds in total, could have been knocked off my feet by a healthy sneeze.

Jimmy was the colour of bloodwood honey, which at the time was disparagingly known in America as 'high yella', while I came from a long line of redheads who seem to have been born minus a layer of skin. His hair, grown long in prison camp, would at a later time become fashionable and be referred to as the 'Afro', while his dark beard sat naturally and evenly attached to his jowl and chin as if carefully worked up by a clever make-up artist. By contrast, I carried several months of uncut, filthy, matted red hair and a ragged beard, both crawling with vermin. I must have looked like one of those long-limbed Indonesian ginger-coloured apes. What are they called – orang-utans!

Even when we'd been liberated and cleaned up, the disparities between us remained. We were both emaciated, heads shaved, eyes over-bright and set into deep dark sockets, the difference being that he still looked like a Nubian prince while my hollow, bruised-eyed appearance and pale, almost translucent skin speckled with a firmament of ginger freckles suggested that I'd been subjected to several bouts of chemotherapy long after I should have been mercifully left to die.

I'm not sure what it takes for two blokes to become the sort of mates who will willingly die for each other. It can't simply have been gratitude. Jimmy had little reason to feel grateful to me and while he had undoubtedly saved me on more than one occasion from throwing in the towel, he'd done the same for the American prisoners. Yet, apparently they didn't feel the same way about him. I asked him on one occasion whether they'd come to see him in the Tokyo hospital to which they'd all been taken. Jimmy just laughed. 'Ain't like dat, Brother Fish, in Uncle Sam's mil-it-tary. Coloured soldier do a white soldier a goodly deed, pick him up when he fall down, dat white guy he gonna hope his friends ain't lookin' on, man.' It seemed that not one of the Americans he'd helped pull through had come to thank him.

On the contrary, they'd appeared without Jimmy on a movie newsreel they'd shown us in the hospital, where they'd all been transformed into individual heroes. They were now men of enormous internal fortitude who had survived the worst the Chinese could throw at them and, in the true spirit of the American fighting man, triumphed over adversity. I have no doubt whatsoever that these mostly whimpering, frightened little boys with conveniently short memories will wear their Purple Hearts and campaign ribbons with pride for the remainder of their lives.

Perhaps, unlike me, they didn't feel the obligation to be grateful. It is my observation that when men are dying they hate in a more specific way and haven't the energy required for gratuitous racial hatred that only seems to reassert itself when an ethnic type finds itself in the majority or back in firm control, as they may have felt once we'd been liberated.

If the other Yanks weren't exactly salt-of-the-earth types, then nor was I. On the racist issue, when a law such as our own White Australia Policy existed I had little cause to feel superior. Though, I confess, back then I wasn't even aware such legislation existed. Around eighty-five per cent of Australians live in one or another city on the eastern seaboard where it is not common to see a full-blood Aborigine; that is, someone who is actually black in colour and not someone of mixed race who is basically unrecognisable from the white population. Often the children of a black–white relationship will be as white as the Caucasian parent; moreover, the second generation will be indistinguishable from the general population. In any case, there weren't any Aborigines of any caste on Queen Island so that, like most of my fellow countrymen, I had no experience of people of a different colour. The first time I really became aware of racism in my own country was after I'd joined K Force and we were sent for training to Puckapunyal, the military base just outside the town of Seymour in Victoria.

We'd all but completed our training and were given a weekend leave pass before returning to pack up and get ready for embarkation to Japan to join the remainder of 3RAR. The island was too far to travel home and so I'd spent the weekend with Jason Matthews, who lived in the Melbourne suburb of Fitzroy. We'd left Melbourne to return to camp and arrived in Seymour at ten-thirty a.m. with three hours to spare before we were required to report. Naturally we made for the local pub, which was already crowded with K Force troops. I joined a mob where I knew most of the blokes except for one of Rick Stackman's mates named Dave McCombe, and an Aborigine I'd seen previously at camp but hadn't yet met. Rick introduced me to McCombe, a real big cove, and then I went over to the black guy. 'G'day, Jacko McKenzie,' I said, sticking out my hand.

'Johnny Gordon. 'Ow ya goin', Jacko?' He had a chest full of campaign ribbons and looked a fair bit older than me, perhaps in his early thirties.

We proceeded to get stuck into the grog and it didn't take long before the beer loosened our tongues and the usual subject came up – our personal reasons for joining K Force. Some blokes admitted it was to get away from their wives, but most, like me, simply couldn't settle down after the Second World War. When it came to Johnny Gordon's turn he seemed a bit hesitant, and took a quick gulp from his glass before speaking. 'I was brought up on a mission outside Condabri. That's in Queensland, up north some. It's one of those places with whites-only toilets – a one-pub town that doesn't serve blacks except out the back next to the rubbish bins and the boss's pig pen. They won't let you in the front door but they'll take your money, no worries. First thing I found out as a kid, money don't have no skin colour.'

'You fair dinkum?' I was genuinely surprised. While the others may have heard of Australian pubs that didn't allow black people to drink on the premises, it was a first for me.

Johnny nodded.

'So this mission – like a hostel, was it?' I asked.

'Nah, we had a house – two rooms, kitchen outside. I lived with me granny.'

'And yer mum and dad?' Jason Matthews asked.

'Me mum got the polio and . . .' he paused, and grinned self-consciously, 'me daddy was someone I didn't never know.'

'Sometimes that's better, mate. Me old man was an alky, come home pissed and beat the crap outta me most days of me life,' Dave McCombe said in an attempt to cover Johnny's embarrassment. Then he asked, 'How'd yer live? You know, make a crust?'

'Me granny got a permit.'

'What, that like the dole?' Tiger Anderson asked.

Gordon shook his head. 'They called it a Certificate of Exemption, and it meant she didn't have to get special permission every time she wanted to leave the mission to go to work in town. Without it, if they seen her on the streets at night, the police would pick her up and throw her in the slammer 'til mornin'. She'd walk the four miles from the mission each day, get treated like shit as a cleaner and get paid about half what the whites got doing the same yakka, then she'd walk home again at night carrying the groceries she'd bought.'

There was silence all round, then Tiger Anderson said quietly, 'Why didn't she bugger off, I mean, go somewhere else?'

'Couldn't,' Gordon replied, 'it was against the law to leave the mission.'

I was finding all this hard to believe. People who couldn't leave, go where they wanted like other Australians, was an entirely new idea to me. I wondered for a moment if Johnny was conning us, but he didn't seem the sort of bloke who'd bullshit for a bit of gratuitous sympathy.

'Your grandad, where was he?' Jason Matthews asked.

'Dead, when I was a little kid. He was a TPI – totally and permanently incapacitated, something he got in the First World War, my gran never said. He coughed a lot, probably his lungs were buggered from the gas. He fought with the Light Horse in the Middle East. I reckon he must have been a pretty good soldier – he was mentioned in dispatches twice.' Johnny Gordon then gave a bitter little laugh. 'On Anzac Day my granny would arrive at the ceremony wearing Grandad's medals and for that one day a year she was treated like a whitey. "Mrs

Gordon, would you like a cup of tea? Do have a scone." I get real agro when I think about it, but my gran glowed with pride.' He took a pull from his beer, and continued. 'Next day they crossed the street to avoid her. To them she was a twenty-four-hour once-a-year white and then, at the stroke of midnight, she magically turned into a dirty black lubra again.'

We were all silent – I wanted to ask if his mother died from the polio, but I mean there wasn't a whole lot you could say. I reckoned we'd asked enough personal questions.

Then Rick Stackman spoke up.

'That's pretty crook, but it don't explain why you joined up for World War II, Gordie.'

Gordon grinned. 'What do you reckon, mate? Anything to get away from bloody Condabri! You join the army and they gave you an exemption certificate.'

'Yeah, exemption to get your balls shot off!' Rick Stackman joked.

Johnny Gordon lifted his glass. 'The army was a different world for a blackfella like me, for the first time in my life I was an equal. I remember writing home to Granny saying how we'd wear each other's shirts, eat from the same plate, wash in the same water, shit in the same toilet – wonders would never bloody cease!' Johnny laughed, recalling. 'She wrote back and said that was very nice but if I ever used a word like that again she'd take a stick to me.'

We all laughed. 'Righto, Gordie, from now on we're gunna treat you like a boong so you don't get too bloody uppity with us white guys!' Rick Stackman jested. He was the one among us who always had a wisecrack at the ready.

Rick's joke seemed to clear the air a bit. 'Yeah, them were the bad old days, all right. Must have been a bit different though when you got back, you know, from the war?' John Lazarou suggested a bit clumsily; Lazarou had been made a lance corporal only because everyone else had refused the job and he was too dumb to work out that as a lance corporal he'd end up being everyone's dogsbody. Predictably enough he was known as 'Lazy', which wasn't a bad sobriquet for a bloke who was by nature energy deficient among other things of a dilatory nature, but who had been stupid enough to be elected lance corporal of our platoon under the mistaken impression that the added authority was going to give him an easy ride in the army.

'Nah, worse. I'd just gone through a colourblind war with my battalion, we'd fought our way through Syria, Kokoda, Gona and Shaggy Ridge. When I got home the RSL had a reception for the fifteen veterans who'd returned to Condabri, only there were sixteen – they forgot to count me. Not only did they not invite me to the reception, but I was not allowed to use the RSL club. On Anzac Day though I was invited to have a beer in the keg room out the back.' He gave a bitter little laugh. 'The president said it was a special dispensation in recognition of my service record.'

'So you told him to shove his beer up his arse, the whole bloody keg?' Dave McCombe suggested.

'Nah, I might be a blackfella, but that don't mean I'm an idjit. I'd made it through the war alive, I wasn't about to become a peace-time casualty with a posse o' drunken hoons coming after me in the back of a ute one dark night.' He raised his glass. 'Here's to K Force. When they asked for volunteers to go to Korea I reckon I must have been the first veteran to put me hand up.' He drained his glass. 'Drink up, fellas, my shout.'

It was the first time I'd ever heard anything like this. Here was a guy with a chest full of ribbons who'd fought for his country and whose grandfather had done the same and he was copping shit from the town he lived in. Baldwin had its share of misfits, bastards and no-hopers but I was pretty certain this wouldn't happen in the island pub.

Later when we got to know each other a bit better, after a drink or seven, Johnny would get a bit maudlin and then someone would say, 'Garn then, Johnny, give us yer Abo poem.'

***Anzac Day, Living with Granny (Cherbourg)***

*Grandad died when I was three*
*My mother called me in explained to me*
*I had to live with Granny from now on*
*I said why because Grandad's gone*

*I helped Granny from daylight until sundown*
*Later she sent me to school in this black town*
*Grandad was a returned soldier went to war*
*Middle East Light Horse Battalion seen his medals when I was four*

*Granny used to work in town four miles away*
*She would have had permission to go to work each day*
*Condabri town was racist to the core*
*Natives Only sign on the toilet door*

*Black people not allowed in pubs sell bottled wine out back*
*Not allowed in the streets after dark if you were black*
*Every day Gran was the old black woman working here*
*Except this special day Anzac Day every year*

*Granny wore Grandad's medals and smiled with pride*
*Tears in her old eyes she didn't try to hide*
*Mrs Gordon this Mrs Gordon joins us at the Town Hall*
*After the Anzac march lunch together colour didn't matter at all*

*Granny was treated like a Queen Anzac Day*
*See the shiny medals flashing from far away*
*Next day they crossed the street racism was back*
*Didn't treat her equal just because she was black**

**I'm grateful to Cec Fisher for the use of his original poem – B.C.*

At the conclusion we'd all clap and then one of the blokes might say, 'Okay, you silly bugger, we've suffered enough. It's your shout!' We'd all laugh and, good-naturedly, Johnny would call for another round.

Johnny Gordon was the first person I'd met who'd been subject to racial persecution. I knew, of course, in the historical past, the Aborigines had been treated badly by the white settlers. But even that was a fair way from home. The Tasmanian Aborigines and those on Flinders Island, isolated from the mainland for 8000 years, had lost the knowledge of making sea-going craft, so Queen Island, in the middle of Bass Strait, apart from visits by sealers and a few convicts who'd escaped from shipwrecks and who were rounded up from time to time, remained unpopulated until white settlement in 1888. Furthermore, the traditional owners on the other two islands had either been murdered, bred out or eliminated by various diseases brought in by white settlers more than a century before I was born. It was something you learned a bit about at school but when you asked, people would say it was in the dark past and better left alone, that lots of things happened in them times which were different from ours. I guess us white people didn't want to be reminded that we'd pretty well murdered a whole race of people.

At home the subject of racism never came up in discussion, except for an occasional mention of the yellow peril just waiting to invade us. In my imagination I saw them as a plague of human locusts coming in, yellow as the sunset. Our grandpa, father of my father Alf, had warned us about them. 'They're the Chinese and they're coming to get the abalone. Eat anything that mob, beetles, caterpillars, even cockroaches – if it moves, they eat it, even puppy dogs. But their favourite is abalone, of which we've got heaps. Filthy stuff, tough as old boots, can't do nothing with it. The buggers love it. They can have it far as I'm concerned, bloody rubbish.' Then he'd add quickly, 'But we can't have them comin' here to get it.' So, by virtue of a geographical accident, I grew up with no real preconceptions about colour except for the brilliant yellow Chinese who were less a colour in my imagination than a sort of perpetual feeding frenzy threatening to come out of the sunset.

True, I'd served in New Guinea at the war's end and for the first time met people of a different colour to myself, but this didn't mean they were inferior. The fuzzy-wuzzies, as we termed the near-naked native population, were a happy and likeable people who helped us survive the difficult terrain by acting as scouts, porters and general dogsbodies. While they outwardly appeared more primitive than us – some they said were still head-hunters – I didn't think of them as lesser humans. Sure, they seemed childlike by our standards and some villagers still used the bow and arrow to hunt. We soon learned that they were much better adapted to their own environment than we were, and under the prevailing circumstances were clearly superior to us. Thinking back I'm sure we would have treated them in a somewhat patronising manner, but at nineteen and very naive in such matters, I wouldn't have seen this as a form of racism.

Nor, for that matter, could I feel superior to the Koreans or Chinese. We termed them noggies, chinks, chows, chonks and gooks, but I accepted this as the usual deprecation of one's enemy, a part of the process of taming them in our imagination. Colour – yellow, black or brown – as a notion of inferiority seemed pretty bloody stupid to me, so the colour of Jimmy's skin was irrelevant.

There was a fair bit of panic in the US after the Korean War over the performance of their prisoners. If some Americans in captivity behaved less honourably under pressure than their trainers expected of them, it should be remembered that they were just frightened kids, while I was a man of twenty-five and ought to have behaved a lot better when confronted by the enemy. Your average Yank grunt was around five to seven years younger than the Australian K Force soldier, and most were still decidedly wet behind the ears. I certainly couldn't claim the same excuse.

Also, I have to say that one of the wounded Yanks with us was one of the bravest men I have ever known. Fifty years later I still think of him with deep admiration. His name was Chuck Ward, the tail gunner on a B29 shot down over China. He'd managed to bail out when the bomber crashed, though the rest of the crew were incinerated. Bob landed deep in snow-covered mountains and managed to elude the enemy search parties for five days. But in the sub-zero weather his feet became frozen and he was forced to give himself up to a Chinese patrol. The Chinese then forced him to walk the thirty miles to our medical hut on his frozen feet. I still recall the day he came to our hospital shed. Long before he arrived we could hear his cries and screams of pain echoing across the icy landscape. Dr Wong, a truly decent man, even if he was a gook, did his best to save the airman's feet, but, in the end, was forced to amputate.

So, if I appear to be slagging the Yanks, then I'm giving the wrong impression. Men simply don't come any braver than Chuck Ward. But the other prisoners were just kids – some were conscripts who didn't want to be there in the first place, young lads just out of high school, though many, like me, hadn't completed their education. The odd bruise or a broken collarbone from a football game was probably the worst pain they'd experienced. Some looked as if they hadn't yet had their first shave and, generally speaking, had very little understanding of the reasons for the war.

The prisoners who were volunteers looked even younger. Many of them had joined the army lured by large colour posters along the major roads promising 'Have Fun in Japan'. It wasn't entirely a lie, not like the First World War poster with General Kitchener pointing a finger at Australia's youth and instead of the English version that said, 'Your Country Needs You!' our version read, 'Join the Grand Picnic in Europe'. The American poster kept its promise and young American armed-forces personnel had a ball in Japan, where most of the work they did was ceremonial. One young bloke from Louisiana confessed to me, 'I was the best in my company at rifle drill, I did all the ceremonial duty, only one problem: I couldn't shoot!' Another admitted to me that they were soft and when the South Korean army crumbled much sooner than expected, and with the marines on the other side of the Pacific, the regiments stationed in Japan as occupying forces were thrown into the battle entirely unprepared and with no time to even reach full strength.

As the war turned nasty for the Americans, so desperate did the situation become that reinforcements were thrown into battle with only six weeks' basic training, ten weeks short of the usual requirement to turn a civilian into a fighting man. Passing through Japan on their way to Korea, these reinforcements were issued with rifles and carbines. But so urgently were the troops required at the front that there was no time to fire their weapons so that they might be correctly calibrated. These were mostly city and small-town kids who knew little or nothing about weapons, and they went into battle as indifferent shots armed with rifles and carbines that couldn't be relied on to fire accurately at any distance.

A lot of shit has been shovelled onto the Yanks in Korea and if I seem to be making excuses on their behalf, it's because the real circumstances are never explained. There was another thing – members of the Australian ground forces were all volunteers and if we were a bit rusty we'd initially been very well trained, while so many of the Yanks were ill-trained conscripts who deeply resented being forced into a war they neither understood nor wanted. This happened again in Vietnam. Anyway, this wasn't the sort of military mix you would expect to become a bunch of Hogan's Heroes in captivity. Nor, for that matter, could you expect them to have the experience or motivation to stand up to North Korean brutality or Chinese interrogation.

However, Jimmy Oldcorn, the only member of a coloured battalion among the Yank prisoners in those field hospitals, was different. He wasn't much older than any of them, but he never kowtowed to the enemy. He didn't bait or defy them but he was obdurate and persistent when it came to what he believed to be our rights. I guess, in one way or another, he'd been at war all his life and didn't scare as easily as we did. In fact, the presence created by his huge blackness and deep *basso profundo* voice seemed to intimidate Mao's little yellow soldiers, who usually modified their high-pitched yapping when they attempted to interrogate him and generally treated him with more circumspection than they did the rest of us. If we were all foreign devils then Jimmy was the devil wrought bigger, darker and more dangerous than the rest of us. In any man's army he would have been the bloke you'd want beside you when the shit hit the fan. But, despite his humour and his calm strength, I sensed that underneath Jimmy was a loner. I guess I wanted him to feel I was the one bloke he could trust.

Make no mistake, by proffering my friendship I wasn't offering Jimmy Oldcorn any big deal. I've scrubbed up a fair bit over the ensuing years, mostly from reading widely and having a good ear and better-than-average memory, which, to my advantage, some people have mistaken for intelligence. To this has been added a good tailor, and a penchant for silk ties and handmade shoes. Most of these phoney appurtenances I've picked up from wealthy conservative Hong Kong Chinese with whom we do a lot of business and who have a preference for bespoke English tailoring, French linen and Italian leather. While it may be different today, in most of the boardrooms I've frequented in life, it was important how you dressed. The American CEO of a large corporation once told me that a gold Rolex on your wrist would generally get you over the line in an important interview, though diamonds around the perimeter would immediately disqualify an applicant. Anyway, over a period of time my grammar corrected itself, a process inadvertently started earlier in my life by our town librarian.

But, when I first met Jimmy I was a pretty knockabout sort of bloke, your regular ocker who didn't amount to much and who might well be expected to spend the rest of his life on a fishing trawler. Fortuitously circumstances changed for me and I found myself mixing in elevated business circles, which, in turn, led to being accepted at a social level requiring some semblance of culture. A few quid in the bank and the status that goes with it does a whole heap to tune up your vowels while allowing people to see you for what you ain't. I make no apology for this, I was poor a long time and I've never tried to conceal my background. On the other hand, I haven't, as some do, felt the need to announce my common-as-dirt beginnings with every word that comes out of my mouth sounding as if it's been fashioned with a pair of tin snippers.

That's what being Australian is all about. You can stay put and nobody thinks any worse of you, or you can have a go and, if you've got the determination and are prepared to work you can be what you want to be, rise to any level in life without being prevented from doing so because you happen to come from a working-class family. Although today, with so many Australian families on some form of welfare it's a lot harder for the bottom to rise to the top.

My family were fisherfolk and when I was a kid on the island, 'fisherman' was very close to being a dirty word. Fishermen were on the bottom rung, and the sea was one of the last frontiers where you could hunt for food you didn't need to pay for. Access to the sea is free to those willing to take the risks involved. The way things were, we seemed never to have fully recovered from the Great Depression. There wasn't a lot of work about other than on a fishing trawler or a cray boat – a hard, dirty and dangerous way to make a crust. The interior of the island's Anglican and Catholic churches boasted almost as many memorial plaques carrying the names of fishermen who had disappeared at sea as there were headstones in the churchyard.

Queen Island, set slap bang in the middle of Bass Strait, is subject to sea mists and furious gales, and over the past hundred years many a sailing ship has been wrecked on our notoriously dangerous coastline. The small fishing craft that met their end smashed against the reefs and cliffs or lost in a sudden storm were simply too numerous to count. Everyone knew fishing was a mug's game, nevertheless it was the only game in town a poor family could play.

In those post-Depression years most Australian working-class parents dreamed of their sons growing up to be something a little better. On the island this hope was simply defined in a mother's prayer: *'Dear God, please don't let him grow up to be a fisherman!'* If you couldn't read or write you could always work on a fishing boat. As a fair number of men on the island fell into this category, including my old man, the cruel sea was how we scraped a precarious and always dangerous living.

Alf, my old man, was a rough sort of cove, what some might call an ignorant man. But if he couldn't read or write he wasn't a whinger or in the least resentful of those who may have been considered more fortunate than him. He'd give you the shirt off his back if you needed it and he'd always provided for his family. Even during the Great Depression when he couldn't get work on a trawler he'd go out in a skiff and set craypots or bring home a snapper or a couple of bream. Our clothes were made on the faithful table-top Singer from the same sugar bags we used as towels, but I can honestly say Alf saw to it that we never went hungry. He was as honest as the day is long, even though honesty wasn't a virtue much discussed on the island – it was simply taken for granted that people didn't steal from each other, and crime against property was thought to be something that happened on the mainland or the big island where people thought they were better than us but whom we knew were a bunch of crooks and shysters, or as my mum would say, 'People who'll steal the wax out of your ears to make communion candles'.

That was the curious thing: while, like us, most of the island's inhabitants came from convict stock who'd moved in from Tasmania in 1888, there was virtually no 'conventional' crime on the island. When we were kids the community did have a policeman who carried the grand title 'Bailiff of Crown Land and Inspector of Stock' but whom we all knew as Mike Munro or 'The Trooper', who got just as pissed as everyone else of a Saturday night. But if you wanted some documentation done that concerned the law you went to see Nicole Lenoir-Jourdan, the bossy-boots librarian and local piano teacher, who also acted as justice of the peace and who somehow managed to scare every schoolkid on the island and not a few of the dimmer adults into believing that she had infinitely more power than any policeman when it came to matters of upholding the sanctity of the law.

The words 'justice' and 'peace' were a powerful combination that came together in our imagination to mean that if there was no peace, then the justice meted out by Miss Lenoir-Jourdan would see it soon restored, with dire consequences for the bloke who'd had the temerity to disturb it. While there appeared to be no immediate evidence that the offender had been punished, we kids sensed this was done in such a deep and covert manner that the offender would carry the inward scars for life and never again dare to repeat the offence. Little did I know at the time that this fearsome justice of the peace was going to have a large influence on my life.

In other matters where an adult needed sorting out for an undeserved act of violence against a member of the community, if he was a Protestant, his mates saw to it; if a Catholic, then Father Crosby would summon him to the church and take him out the back and make him put on a pair of twelve-ounce boxing gloves, whereupon the Irish priest, the ex-cruiserweight champion of County Cork, would give him a damn good thrashing and then haul him into the confessional. With a bloodied nose and a fistful of 'Hail Marys' as penance he was forgiven, and life on the island returned to normal. One way or another most things got sorted out. Looking back, this rough justice may seem little better than a kangaroo court, but I tell you what, it worked a treat.

Like all his mates off the trawlers and cray boats, Alf would get thoroughly pissed of a Saturday night. But to be fair to the fishermen, most of the other blokes on the island, with far less cause to drink the miserable week right out of their heads, were also down at the pub nudging elbows and getting equally legless.

Like many a small man before him, and a redhead to boot, Alf McKenzie was of a fiery temperament and quick to take offence; moreover, he couldn't hold his booze. It was a deadly combination and he was apt to get into regular blues, usually over some imagined insult and, with disquieting regularity, he'd pick on someone way above his own fighting weight, a fox terrier taking on a rottweiler.

Although, in his defence, unlike a lot of other men on the island, when pissed he didn't become a wife-beater – one of two crimes, the other being incest, that seemed to go unpunished in the community. This was probably because the former was too common to be remarked upon except as women's gossip, and the latter too shameful to be admitted under any circumstances by anyone. It's only now, decades later, that I realise that incest was not uncommon in many an island family.

Alf would occasionally take a half-hearted smack at us kids, though more out of a sense of duty than from real malice. For a bloke who could pick a fight at the drop of a hat I can't remember him ever seriously beating any of us boys, and he never laid a hand on my sister, Sue, either in anger or the other hidden and secret thing.

I recall how at Monday-morning roll call at school there'd be dozens of kids with black eyes, thick ears, split lips and multiple bruises who'd supposedly run into the doorknob or fallen off the chook-house roof or some other such euphemism for getting the tripe knocked out of them by a drunken father. By the time they were teenagers most of the boys had flattened noses that hadn't come about as a result of fights behind the school dunny.

As for the other, I dare say the female children and some of the males will carry the scars, secret guilt and shame for the remainder of their lives. In recent years the priesthood, Anglican and Catholic, has come in for a hammering for child abuse and with just reason, but, at least on our island, their parishioners were often just as guilty. Not that I think Father Crosby was up to no good. Certainly nobody has come forward and nothing untoward has surfaced over the ensuing years. As for Reverend John Stephen Daintree, our Anglican rector, he was nearly eighty when he came to the island and could barely raise an arm above his head to invoke a blessing, much less anything else. But then again, when you scratch the surface of any society, island paradises included, you're certain to find a darker side.

Of course, there was no such thing as child welfare at the time. Island folk, as they'd done since settlement, kept to themselves and resented any sort of bureaucratic interference, even if it proved to be in their own best interest. My mum would say we were a three-monkey society: see, hear and speak no evil, even if, plainly, there was a fair bit of it going on around us.

Alf McKenzie, a small man on an island of predominantly big ones, was considered a part of the Saturday-night entertainment where half-a-dozen serious fights usually took place at the back of the pub. Pound for pound he was a half-decent fighter, but his stubborn refusal to take on anyone around his own weight made his contribution to the evening's fisticuffs the curtain-raiser with all bets off. If he looked like getting the tripe knocked out of him a fellow fisherman would step in and pull him away from his opponent, always to Alf's loud protests that he should be allowed to finish the mongrel off.

If he wasn't a contender in the brawls behind the pub, nevertheless, as a drunk, Alf was the scourge of Baldwin. After closing time, when everyone had stumbled home to beat their wives and children or to sleep it off, his caterwauling would keep half the women in town awake. He'd be banging dustbin lids together, serenading the female population at three a.m. on his harmonica and generally making a bloody nuisance of himself. As the husbands of the wives he took to serenading had long since passed out from the grog, he had the women of the town to himself. The odd bucket of water or the amber contents of the occasional chamber pot seemed only to freshen him up for further mayhem. If he wasn't a good drunk, you couldn't fault him as a stayer.

He'd come home at dawn usually with one ear torn and wearing a shiner or evidence of an earlier bloodied nose or all three, buttons missing off his shirt and his person cut and bruised from falling on his arse, still pissed as a newt as well as toothless. His missing teeth were by way of precaution. He'd leave them in a tin mug on the mantelpiece above the kitchen stove prior to departing for the pub, his real teeth having been singly and collectively knocked out, the last three on the night of his twenty-first birthday party. When you're forced to be a fish-eater all your life teeth don't assume the same importance as they do to the carnivores in society.

You could hear him coming a mile off and my little mum would be standing on the front verandah in her pink chenille dressing-gown, felt slippers with the left big toe sticking out, the barrel shapes of her hair curlers visible through a matching pink chiffon scarf. She'd be standing grim-faced with her arms crossed, cigarette hanging from the corner of her mouth, squinting through the half-light waiting for his shambling, stumbling, falling-down self to appear through the early Sunday-morning mist, shouting, 'Gloria, I'm coming, lovey! I ain't deserted yiz!'

'No such bloody luck,' she'd sigh, as she waited to grab him by the scruff of the neck and lead him into the washhouse in the backyard where, clothes and all, winter and summer, she'd shove him under a cold shower, requiring him to stay put until he'd shown some semblance of sobriety. When she judged the time right she'd chuck him a well-washed sugar bag to dry himself off and then put him to bed to snore away the rest of the day until he rose in the late afternoon to a plate of fried eggs and toast and a cup of scalding sweet black Bushells tea. Later in life, after she'd embraced the Catholic faith, she'd put him under the shower and haul him out when she returned from mass, usually some two hours later.

As the children of Alf and Gloria McKenzie, we were the fourth generation from convict stock on both sides of my family. Today that passes for some sort of status. When we were kids and had done something we ought not have, my mum, who usually got things in perspective, would sigh and say, 'Four generations of McKenzies and Kellys and we still haven't produced anyone worth a pinch of the proverbial!' Though, in a thousand years, she would never have admitted to it, we all knew what the substituted word was. We were crap, a family at the bottom end of the social heap, and that was that, there was no point having tabs on ourselves. Sometimes though, by way of conciliation she'd add, 'Although one thing: God, in His infinite mercy, gave us a good ear on both sides of the family that, until your father got his disgrace ban, has saved us from being total no-hopers.'

What she was referring to was the harmonica, or mouth organ as we all called it. It seems, going way back in time, we've always been a musical family. John McKenzie, my convict great-grandfather on my dad's side, played the fiddle, though my grandpa, Cliff McKenzie, took up the mouth organ when it first came out from Germany and was known as the *aura*. As a young bloke of eighteen in Burnie, where John McKenzie had settled after gaining his ticket of leave, Cliff quit fishing to join the 1860 gold rush on the mainland.

He soon discovered that he didn't much care for digging and, after staking several useless claims, he found he was marginally more successful with a pack of cards than sluicing for ore. While playing poker with an American prospector, he won a *harmonicon* known as the Prairie Queen, an instrument far superior to the *aura*. It was all the encouragement he needed to quit and become a bush musician.

This new career inevitably led Cliff McKenzie into country pubs, picnic races, bush celebrations, weddings and wakes, enabling him to continue the family tradition on two fronts: as an expert in making music and a proclivity for getting drunk, and to this he added an addiction to gambling. He eventually grew tired of the itinerant lifestyle and when, in 1888 he heard that Queen Island was to be opened for land settlement he came to the island at the age of forty-six where he received a grant and took up farming. He married a girl from Burnie, a cousin twenty-five years his junior. My grandmother, Maud Jasmine, gave him six children and died giving birth to Alf.

Of course my grandfather, despite his career as a bush musician where he should have picked up a thing or two about rural living, knew nothing about tilling the land or keeping livestock. He soon got into debt with the bank, which eventually foreclosed on him. With the change he got after the bank had sold his farm, Cliff McKenzie bought a small house near the harbour and resumed life as a fisherman, one of the first on the island.

He never bothered to marry again but, with his background and the social graces he had acquired as an entertainer, the mouth organ wasn't the only instrument he employed to charm the island ladies. In the process he succeeded in scattering his seed widely and generously. Two generations along, a good few kids at school possessed our red hair and pale freckled skin and, moreover, had a distinctly McKenzie look about them.

On my mum's side, also an original island-settler family as well as convict stock from Hobart, there appeared to be a string of Irish tenors going way back to County Clare, and a great-grandmother, Mary Kelly, nee Flannaghan, who legend has it, played the Irish harp like an angel but was sent to Tasmania as a convict for keeping a bawdy house. She is said to have earned her ticket of leave early by being regularly requested by Lady Jane Franklin, the wife of the governor, to be allowed to leave the Women's Prison to play the harp at her Friday-evening soirees at Government House in Hobart. So it was not unexpected that the Kelly and McKenzie combination made us a pretty musical bunch.

By island standards we were a small family, just four kids, with me the eldest, then Sue, followed by my twin brothers, Steve and Cory. Most of the fishermen bred like bunny rabbits with eight or nine kids just about the norm. Birth control, even among the Protestants, was unthinkable. Boys from the age of fourteen usually left school to work on the boats and the girls cleaned fish, mended nets and made craypots, the more kids the better being the prevailing philosophy.

'Thank Gawd for the mumps!' my mum would say after we'd visited one or another of our multitudinous relations or another fisherman's family. At the age of twenty-five Alf had contracted mumps, which, to the everlasting gratitude of my mother who'd conceived the four of us in slightly less than six years, caused him to become infertile. Furthermore, with him on a fishing boat most nights and suffering from brewer's droop of a Sunday and back on a trawler pre-dawn on Monday morning, she was seldom obliged to share the connubial bed. This was yet another reason why she'd come to believe there must be an understanding God in heaven, and at the age of forty she came to the conclusion He must be a Catholic. To everyone's surprise, she turned from a lukewarm 'Christenings and Christmas-morning communion Anglican' to a red-hot Catholic, to become one of Father Crosby's most devoted parishioners.

If it hadn't been for music we would have been pretty well anonymous, no different to any other fishing family. It was our expertise on the mouth organ that singularly separated us from the other interchangeable island family groups. The name McKenzie meant mouth-organ music and had done so for three generations. The mouth organ was cheap and melodious and could be carried in one's pocket, and so became a hugely popular instrument amongst the poor and in the bush. Many people on the island played it but, it seemed, the McKenzies had the sublime touch and could make a Hohner do things, hit notes it wasn't supposed to be capable of reaching. In his later years, playing a twenty-reed, ten-hole Hohner imported from Germany, my grandpa, leaving the island once a year for the championships on the big island, became Tasmanian champion two years running.

My dad often recalled how, in 1912 at the age of fourteen, his father presented him with the very latest mouth organ known as the 'Cobber', bought from the prize money he'd won at the last Tasmanian championships and subsequently placed on a horse that, for once, came good. It was Cliff McKenzie's way of saying that Alf was the one in the family who had 'the gift' and, in effect, passing on the musical baton to his youngest son.

Alf McKenzie didn't have much he could truly call his own, and the Cobber was to become his most treasured possession. The cabinet it rested in was crafted from specially selected Queensland maple and was proudly Australian-made. My grandpa Cliff made him learn 'The Cobber Song', an early version of an advertising jingle. In turn, as kids, Alf made us all memorise the words. When he was pleasantly oiled, say on a birthday or late on Christmas afternoons, the only occasions my mum allowed grog in the house, he'd take his Cobber out of its fancy maple box with its faded maroon velvet lining and we'd sing along while he played, extemporising an elaborate musical break of his own composition between each verse.

*My Cobber*
*Who cheers me up when I am sad,*
*And makes me feel supremely glad,*
*And quite a well-contented lad?*
*My Cobber.*

*Whose tones are so divinely sweet,*
*That when I play it in the street,*
*It soothes the bobbies on their beat?*
*My Cobber.*

*Who can produce the latest tunes,*
*The crazy rag, the song of coons?*
*O, greatest of all music boons.*
*My Cobber.*

*Who keeps me company all day,*
*When 'er I wander far away,*
*And 'Home Sweet Home' upon it play?*
*My Cobber.*

*Its fame is known from Cairns to Perth,*
*How can I estimate its worth?*
*The best mouth organ upon this earth.*
*My Cobber.*

Alf McKenzie followed in his father's footsteps and even went one better, winning the Tasmanian and Victorian championships three times in five years until, on the sixth, competing at the National Harmonica Championships held in the Colosseum at Ballarat, he was bitterly disappointed at the marks awarded him by one of the adjudicators, a certain Maestro Gustave Slapoffski. True to family tradition, Alf went out and buried his sorrows by getting pissed. Two hours later, filled to the brim with Dutch courage, he stormed back onto the stage to tell the audience what he thought of the two adjudicators, the second being a Mr Mansley Greer. He pointedly observed, not without wit for a man of no education, 'I can only say that one judge was "Mansley" enough to mark me better than average, but I'll bet London to a brick Mr "Fuckoffski" has a well-greased palm out to ensure some bloody sponsor's little darling gets the nod.' For this honest, if entirely specious appraisal, he received a lifetime ban from the championships and any future performances under the aegis of the Australian Harmonica Association. Alf's 'disgrace ban', as Gloria ever after termed it, ended the McKenzie family's brief flirtation with fame and we were back where we belonged, bumping our heads against the bottom rung of the ladder.

We all played the grand little instrument – Dad, Mum and the four kids, a sextet that could make a fair bit of ear-pleasing, foot-tapping noise when we put our minds to it. Alf's disgrace ban meant we were restricted to playing on the island, which didn't concern us overly much as we couldn't have afforded the money for the whole family to travel to the big island, let alone the mainland.

We'd scrub up pretty well, though. Mum with her curlers out, Sue wearing a green ribbon in her blazing copper-coloured hair. Alf and we boys, short back and sides with the parting arrow-straight to the left and the quiff in front held rigid by means of 'A little dab'll do ya', part of the jingle for Brylcreem, a universally popular hair grease where on the back of the jar it said it restored the life and shine that shampoos take out. I recall wondering what shampoo might do and why people would be stupid enough to use something on their hair that took away its life and shine. The label went on to say that it contained mineral oil and beeswax, which I assumed was what was meant to put life and shine back in. As we only used soap to wash our hair we obviously had no need for its shine-producing properties and used it only as a means to paste our hair down and to look snazzy.

*Brylcreem, a little dab'll do ya,*
*Use more, only if you dare.*
*Brylcreem, the gals'll all pursue ya,*
*Simply rub a little on your hair.*

I also noticed that not a single girl ever chased me when I was wearing it.

From the neck down, even if I say so myself, we were a bit of a sensation. We wore blindingly white starched shirts, pressed black pants with the centre crease sharp as a favourite kitchen knife and, to set everything off, Irish green bow ties, all made by my mum on her table-top Singer sewing machine. On the pocket of our shirts and blouses Mum and Sue had embroidered in green running writing the name of our family group, which, predictably enough, was The Cobbers. We wore black socks and our boots, only to be worn on special occasions, were so polished you could see your face in them. This sartorial elegance usually got applause from the audience even before we'd commenced to play, which pleased Gloria, my mum, no end, but really got up Alf's nose. My dad took himself seriously as a musician. With the audience applauding in anticipation you'd hear him mumble out of the corner of his mouth, 'The bludgers should judge us on our musicality, not our poncy clobber.'

We'd perform at most of the island events but were considered to be the star music turn at the Fish Co-op picnic and at the annual Masonic dance where, before the dance band came on (a bunch of badly rehearsed and not very talented island musicians assembled for the occasion), we'd play all the old favourites and some of the new hit tunes from the wireless.

I recall how one year at the Fish Co-op picnic, to Alf's total chagrin,

Gloria decided we'd blacken our faces and hands and perform what we'd bill as 'A Tribute to Al Jolson'.

We didn't know about greasepaint so we used Kiwi boot polish, which was our first big mistake.

'A man's gunna be the bloody laughing stock!' Alf protested vehemently.

Gloria had seen *The Jazz Singer*, the first talking movie starring Al Jolson, at the island's outdoor cinema in 1929 just before the New York stock exchange crashed and threw the world into the Great Depression. She was not to see another movie until 1936 and so Al Jolson singing on the celluloid was forever emblazoned onto her memory. While we had precious little of what you might call luxuries, we did have an old HMV wind-up gramophone she regarded as part of our professional equipment. We'd play records and then learn the music, translating it into a mouth-organ version for the sextet. In fact, the only birthday and Christmas presents any of us ever received were 78-rpm records suitable for adaptation to the harmonica – usually second-hand from an op shop Gloria corresponded with in Launceston and never of our own choosing.

We had all the Al Jolson hits, I can still recite them today. 'You Made Me Love You', 'My Mammy', 'Sonny Boy', 'Hallelujah I'm a Bum', we did a real good job of that one on the mouth organ, 'Go into Your Dance', 'Toot, Toot, Tootsie!', 'April Showers', and the crowd's all-time American favourite, 'Swanee'. I think they loved it especially because they could sing along to some of the Australian songs we played, 'Click Go the Shears', 'Waltzing Matilda' and 'The Road to Gundagai'.

So when Mum came up with her black-face idea there was no talking her out of it. 'What's good enough for Mr Jolson is good enough for us McKenzies,' she'd insisted, and Alf knew he was beaten beak and crop.

I must say I didn't like the idea much myself. A man felt a bit of a galah standing there in the hot sun on the makeshift boxing ring where later some of the likely lads, full of piss and vinegar, would pull on the dreaded twelve-ounce gloves and, with Father Crosby acting as referee, belt the tripe out of each other. I could see several of my schoolmates huddled together in the crowd pointing at us and pissing themselves. But, as it turned out, Mum was right, the island folk gave us a better-than-usual applause as we entered the ring. I don't know whether this was because they enjoyed the bit of extra theatre thrown in, or the fact that black boot polish combined with flaming red hair was not a real good look. All I know, at school the next Monday and for several weeks afterwards, we McKenzie kids copped a heap.

Anyway, one good thing happened out of the experience: halfway through one of the numbers Alf's black boot polish started to melt from his sweat and was running in streaks down his neck and staining his starched white shirt. When someone in the audience yelled, 'Alf, yer nigger paint's comin' orf!' that was finally it. Alf could take no more and he stopped playing mid-note and jumped down out of the ring. We all thought he was going to job the bloke who'd shouted out, but instead he headed straight for the pub. Gloria couldn't yell at him to come back as we were in the middle of a bracket and to stop would have been unprofessional. A crisis suddenly loomed, there was a solo bit coming next which my dad, as the lead mouth, always performed. Next thing I felt Mum give me a dig in the ribs, then with her eyes she indicated that I was to step forward for my solo debut.

I was the one in the family thought most likely to inherit 'the gift' and here was the unexpected confirmation. Feeling more than a bit of a fool I took two steps forward from the safety of the family line-up certain that my Kiwi-polished blackened face was streaked like a zebra's bum. Nevertheless, with knees trembling, I managed to grasp the moment and give it my best shot. To my surprise, the audience responded at the end of my solo with spontaneous applause.

Funny how these things work out. It was the first time in my life that I felt a bit more than dead ordinary. I'd managed to overcome my fear and do something on my own and it felt good. Even if as a family we weren't 'worth a pinch of the proverbial', I'd succeeded in front of my peers and I liked the feeling a lot. Perhaps I didn't have to be a fisherman after all? Perhaps I could be something else? I even had the temerity to hope, if I got a decent pass in my final exams, maybe I could be a trainee clerk in the bank. Though, as it turned out, this thought came to nothing. The following year, at the age of fourteen, I was yanked out of school and sent to work on a fishing boat.

My mum cried her heart out when this happened. She'd called me into the kitchen after school and made me a cup of tea with milk and three sugars, a special treat, then sat me down at the kitchen table. I knew there must be something wrong, because we boys were only allowed in the kitchen at mealtimes. At any other time the area embracing the sink, black wood stove and scrubbed pine table and the space covered by yellow and green patterned lino, the pattern long since worn through on the most stepped-on parts to show black patches, was secret women's business. While my sister Sue could come and go as she pleased, even Alf would ask politely to enter when he was home. Mum sat down in the chair beside mine and lit a cigarette, and then got up and fetched an ashtray, sat down again and sighed, then this big tear started to run down her cheek.

'Alf's crook,' she said at last.

'What's wrong with him?' I replied, thinking it was just some passing thing – sometimes he'd get the gout and have to stay home for two or three days with his leg resting on a chair. 'He got the gout again?'

She shook her head and then started to *really* cry. 'He's coughing real bad and Dr Light sent a blood sample to the big island and he's got cancer, they think it's of the lung!'

It had never occurred to me that Gloria loved Alf. He was just our dad and someone she had to put up with on Sunday mornings. Now I was surprised to see she cared greatly about him. 'What's gunna happen?' I asked, meaning what was going to happen to Alf. But that's not how she understood me.

'You're going to have to leave school, Jacko, go on the boats.'

I was stunned. I was good at school, with my memory I always topped the class. Mind you this wasn't hard and was largely because the rest of the kids only attended school because it was compulsory. Gloria had always insisted that I was going to be the one McKenzie who would complete high school, a glorious first among our numerous island relations. 'But Mum, you said . . .' I was choked and the lump in my throat wouldn't let me complete the sentence.

'I know, Jacko!' she wept. 'I know, I know!' I could see she was terribly distraught – I'd never before seen her blubbering like this. If Gloria did any crying it was in the privacy of her bedroom where we weren't supposed to hear her. 'I've let you down, mate,' she wailed, 'but I can't make up Alf's pay just with extra washing and ironing from the hospital!' She looked up at me and said in what began as almost a whisper and ended in a cry of despair, 'We need the money, son!' I was back in the proverbial, the stink of fish-wallop suddenly filling my nostrils.

In the year following my debut as a black-faced soloist I'd been increasingly called upon to do the solo parts in our performances as Alf had developed this persistent cough. We'd been embarrassed on several occasions when halfway through a solo he'd be overtaken with a fit of coughing and I'd have to cut in to complete as the mouth. This usually got applause as the audience liked the quick uptake I'd manage, sometimes even to catching the end of the note he hadn't completed so that some of them even thought it was a part of the act. We'd been worried, thinking Alf had the smoker's cough, which is not good if you play the mouth organ, and Mum said he had to cut down. It never occurred to us that because he'd smoked since the age of ten and was seldom to be found without a roll-yer-own dangling from his lips that it could be any more than this. In those days nobody told you smoking was dangerous. Eventually, against his protests, Gloria dragged him into Dr Light's surgery. Now here was the result: at the age of fourteen any future I may have imagined was dashed before it had begun.

I am ashamed to say that this was my reaction, rather than concern for my old man being on the way out. I can't think of an adequate excuse for thinking this way. It was just that Alf hadn't played a real big part in the lives of us kids. He'd be out to sea on a trawler all week and then he'd write off Saturday night and most of Sunday, so had very little time to get to know his children other than when we played the mouth organ together, always practising late on Sunday afternoons when his hangover was halfway settled down.

The sextet was Gloria's way of trying to keep us all together as a family. Unfortunately Alf, hangover notwithstanding, was a bit of a musical martinet and, with his head still hurting and him grouchy as a bear to boot, the practice sessions were seldom joyous occasions. When she was younger Sue was often reduced to tears and us three boys would try to remain stoic, but we'd secretly wish we could jack the whole thing in.

Gloria would let Alf carry on ranting and raving – I guess she thought it was really the only time he could assert any authority over us. After a while we came to understand that Alf McKenzie the music maker was the only thing that separated him from the other fishermen. It was something he was recognised and respected for among his peers, consequently his family group had to be perfect or we'd show him up, shame him in front of his mates and their wives. It made for a very good mouth-organ sextet but it didn't bring him any closer to us kids.

In his defence, we were no different from the other fishing families. The sea stole our fathers from us in more ways than one and, as I mentioned before, at least Alf didn't beat us up or have a go at creeping into his daughter's knickers. Those were hard times and you couldn't fault him as a provider, but whereas Mum was the centre of our lives, Alf was never a dad in the traditional sense, he simply did the best he could under the prevailing circumstances.

Getting through high school isn't a big deal these days, but at the time it was a major achievement. In fact, it became a social demarcation: pass your final high-school exams and you were a somebody; fail them, or fail to get to this point in your education, and you were regarded as a nobody forever onwards. My passing the last year at high school would have been seen as an educational milestone for a fisherman's family.

Now I was condemned to be just like every other McKenzie. Even at fourteen, having grown up with an illiterate father, I knew that without an education I was destined to be yet another of the long line of no-hopers and failures my family inherently produced. I hadn't the nous at the time to know, just by realising this, that I had sown the seeds of my emancipation. At least I could read, and so the gate was half open – I had somewhere for my mind to go.

From the age of eight I'd been an avid reader and much to the consternation of the other kids had inadvertently formed an association with the dreaded Miss Lenoir-Jourdan, justice of the peace, piano teacher and town librarian. I say inadvertently, because I felt myself dragooned, powerless to resist the authority that being a justice of the peace gave her. I also knew that she always had to be fierce and must never let her guard down, because being severe was what her job was all about.

Our association had begun when I was eight years old and in my third year of primary school. My sentence began when my class made its first excursion to the town library. Miss Lenoir-Jourdan made us sit cross-legged on the polished Tassie oak floor where, in turn, each one of us was required to shout out our names which, to our dismay, she entered in a big ledger-type book. We hadn't even done anything wrong and already we were being tagged and identified for future criminal reference. When it came my turn I called out, 'Jacko McKenzie, miss!'

Her head jerked up from the book and, removing her glasses slowly, she glared at me. 'Jacko? Jacko is not a name, boy!'

'Yes it is, miss. It's what I got being christened.'

'No, that's not correct. You are Jack, plain Jack. Now you will say your name again, this time correctly.'

'Jack McKenzie, miss,' I mumbled, my eyes fixed on my knees. It didn't sound right, it was as if suddenly I'd been transformed into someone else.

'So, I see we have a McKenzie,' she said. 'The seed that's widely and carelessly scattered on this godforsaken island.'

'No, miss,' I corrected her, 'we're not farmers, me dad's a fisherman.'

A hint of a smile appeared on her lips. 'My goodness! Could it be possible that we've spawned an intelligent McKenzie at long last?'

She was wrong again. Being from a fishing family I knew what the word 'spawned' meant, but I also knew that Mum had frequently and clearly stated our position on the island. 'No, miss, four generations of McKenzies and Kellys and we still haven't produced anyone worth a pinch of the proverbial!' I said, repeating Mum's oft-spoken words.

'The proverbial? I say, what a big word from a small boy!'

'It means *shit*, miss,' I explained.

All the kids laughed and Nicole Lenoir-Jourdan suddenly appeared to have sucked on a slice of very sour lemon. 'Silence!' she shouted. 'That's quite enough!' Then she added, 'Jack McKenzie, I shall be calling your teacher!'

Throughout the next day at school I waited in fear for the wrath to come. Here I was only eight and the justice of the peace already had me marked down for sentencing. When the final bell went, our teacher, Mrs Reilly, called as usual 'Class dismissed!' But then she added, 'Jacko, wait back a moment, please.' This was it, the beginning of the end. I wasn't sure what I'd done other than be forced to change into a different person, but whatever it was there was going to be no escape. 'Jacko, you have to report to the town library,' she instructed.

'When, miss?' I asked anxiously.

'Why right now on your way home, of course. Miss Lenoir-Jourdan is expecting you. I hope it's a nice surprise.'

*'Surprise, my arse!'* I thought. She's wrote all our names in that big book and I'm the first to be dealt with by the fierce justice of the peace. When I'd returned home from school the previous day I'd confirmed with my mother that my name really was Jack. If Miss Lenoir-Jourdan knew stuff about me I didn't know myself, then what else did she know?

'Ah, Jack McKenzie,' she said, looking up from her desk as I knocked on the open door to her office. 'You've come.'

'Yes, miss.'

'Sit!' she commanded, indicating the chair in front of her desk. I did as I was told, sitting with my head bowed grimly, clutching the arms of the chair. She continued writing but eventually looked up and removed her glasses, a gesture that looked real scary, like a judge about to pronounce sentence. 'Can you read?' she demanded.

'Yes, miss.'

'How well do you read, Jack?'

It was a dumb question. I ask you, how's a kid to know how well he reads? But I kept the thought to myself. Everyone knew she was probably the cleverest person on the island having read all them books in the library shelves and being the justice of the peace and also a piano teacher. 'I'm okay,' I mumbled, not looking up from my lap.

'Hmm, we'll soon see about that.' She replaced her glasses and out of the corner of my eye I saw her reach out for a book on the desk and place it down in front of her. She opened it and appeared to be scanning the contents, turning several pages after dabbing her forefinger onto the tip of her tongue. At last she came to the bit she must have been looking for. 'You'll read this aloud, *slowly*, pronouncing each word *clearly* and making sure to *pause* at the commas. You do know what a comma is, don't you, Jack?'

I didn't, but she'd just told me. 'It's where you pause, miss.'

'Quite right.'

The book was called *The Wind in the Willows*, the bit where Ratty and Mole go rowing on the river. Though this book was new to me and somewhat more difficult than the primers we'd been given to read at school, I read on and on, stumbling over a big word every once in a while but getting through to the end of the chapter at an increasingly confident pace.

'That will be sufficient for now,' Miss Lenoir-Jourdan announced at last, then she added, 'Your reading is monotonal, much too fast, you swallow your words and your accent is simply atrocious!' She leaned back in her chair and glared at me through the bottom of her glasses.

'However, Jack McKenzie, you're better clay to work with than most.' She reached over, closing and then lifting the book, and offered it to me. 'Now take this home and report back here after school on Friday, by which time you will have completed it.' She gave me a stern look. 'There will be a comprehensive test where questions will be asked. Now hop along, Jack McKenzie.'

When I reached home I went out into the back garden and did some weeding in the vegie patch, which Mum said to do, and then started to read the book. After a couple of pages, first making sure nobody was looking, I put the tip of my forefinger onto my tongue and then turned the page. It worked a treat with the page flipping back easy as anything but leaving a great dirty mark on the corner where my finger had been. So there it was, three pages into the new book and already I was in the shit, too late to wash my hands now. Later I tried to get rid of it with my school eraser but it seemed only to make it worse.

Thus began a long association with the librarian, the only person who ever called me Jack. Though I can't say the relationship ever developed into a warm one, Nicole Lenoir-Jourdan remained imperious, didactic and aloof in all things other than when discussing books. She had a long neck and a chin that seemed always to be raised at a forty-five-degree angle so that she was forced to look at you through the bottom of her glasses, an effect that made her appear as if she didn't much like what she saw. She would question me constantly, explaining concepts and ideas we might come across in the books she selected for me to read, sighing impatiently if I didn't catch on quickly enough for her liking. 'Snails are slow because they can't read,' she'd say, when I was stumped for an answer. I never quite knew what she meant by that, but never dared to ask.

She also spent a lot of her time correcting my spoken grammar and taught me what I came to think of as 'library talk'. It was still English, sort of, but not the kind of language you could use at school or at home when you were talking to real people. Also, she never fully trusted me to choose my own books from the shelves. 'You'll only read like a boy!'

she'd say disparagingly, whatever that was supposed to mean. But after a session, if she thought I'd answered her questions well, something that didn't happen very often, she would allow me to select a book of my own choice. She'd sniff dismissively when I showed her the title I'd selected, *Just William* by Richmal Crompton or some such book, the sniff sufficient to tell me once again I'd got it dead wrong and was reading rubbish.

When Mum was forced to take me out of school to work on the boats I trudged over to the library with a heavy heart and not a little trepidation. When I entered Miss Lenoir-Jourdan's office, after politely knocking and hearing the familiar command, 'Sit!', she continued, as she usually did, to work until finally looking up or rather down through the bottom of her glasses.

'I don't recall that we have an appointment, Jack?'

'No, miss. I need to see you, miss.'

'Oh? Pray tell?'

I proceeded to tell her that Mum said I had to go on the boats and wouldn't be able to attend any more of our reading discussions. It was the first time I'd ever seen emotion other than impatience from Nicole Lenoir-Jourdan.

'She's done what?' she shouted, leaping up from her chair then leaning forward, both her hands grasping the edge of the desk, her knuckles turning white. She glared at me. 'No!' she spat. Then shaking her head furiously, 'No! No! No!'

I was unprepared for her reaction and, shocked by her obvious fury, I forgot my 'library talk' completely. 'Me dad's real crook, he's got cancer, it's of the lung,' I blurted out.

'How dreadful, dreadful! How could your mother possibly do this to you!' she shouted.

'It's my father, miss. He's dying,' I repeated. 'We need the money.'

But she wasn't listening. 'You people! You ignorant people! How dare she!' She brought her hands up to her mouth, her eyes wide and panicky. 'The perfidious, stupid, stupid woman!' There were tears in her eyes and her long neck wobbled like a turkey hen's. Turning away from me suddenly she snatched at the pink cardigan hanging from the back of her chair and rushed from her office into the library beyond.

Now, completely taken aback, I didn't know how to react. 'It's not her fault, miss. Her washing don't pay enough!' I called after her, afraid to move.

After a while I plucked up sufficient courage and walked into the library proper. She was nowhere to be seen and after searching every corridor separating the bookshelves, I saw the back door was open. It led into a small dusty yard where the male and female toilets and the library dustbins stood. At first I hesitated, but then entered the yard. The door to the ladies' toilet was closed and then I heard the sobbing. The fiercest justice of the peace in the world was crying, crying over me, Jacko McKenzie, whose family's ignorance and stupidity, and therefore my own, she'd just confirmed for me.

It was only later in life that I was to realise how much Nicole Lenoir-Jourdan had come to care about the little boy whose mind and intellect she was training. How she suddenly saw all her efforts come to nothing. But the poor in those days didn't get a chance to choose. I was the eldest child and Alf was dying, there was nothing anyone could do. I would have liked to have explained this to the justice of the peace but, at fourteen, I simply lacked the courage to stand outside the door of the ladies' dunny and tell her how things were for us McKenzies. Anyway, what was the use, explaining wouldn't change things. So I turned and tiptoed back out of the library, then walked slowly home and didn't read another book for a year.

I admit to being bitter at the turn of events in my life. If I was condemned to be a fisherman then what was the point of filling my mind with stuff I didn't need? Books don't teach you how to catch fish. Besides, what right did I have to suppose I was better than anyone else? The justice of the peace was wrong. I should have known better than to have listened to her spouting on about using my mind and intellect to learn to think. Reading books and learning to think would only make working on a fishing boat worse – shit is shit and doesn't turn into chocolate pudding just because it's a similar colour. It was the pinch of the proverbial and nothing could ever change that.

My pay as a boy on a fishing boat wasn't much and couldn't compare with Alf's as a winch operator on the trawlers. I could have worked on a trawler and earned a little more but it meant being away from home all week and Gloria wouldn't hear of it. 'I want you home at night, Jacko. We can make some savings, as for the rest, we'll make ends meet somehow.' What she was saying was that the ten bob Alf spent at the pub of a Saturday would be saved as well as the couple of shillings for the shag he smoked and there'd be no more gramophone records for birthdays and Christmas.

The one advantage of going out daily in a fishing boat was I'd usually manage to bring home something for our tea. We had chooks that gave us eggs, a vegie garden and potato patch going in the backyard and Sue, preparing and yeasting the dough at night, baked our bread before she left for school. So, apart from Cory and Steve appearing a bit ragged and Sue's gym frock as well, with bits let into the waist and a few more inches added round the hem, things hardly changed for us.

When at eighteen I'd joined the military to catch the arse end of the Second World War, Sue was sixteen and doing her first-year nurse's training at the cottage hospital and both Steve and Cory, who'd also left school at fourteen, were on fishing boats, so we were doing okay. The army pay was slightly better than my wage on a fishing boat and I'd keep a bit back for toothpaste, boot polish and beer and then send the rest home by postal order. We were the same old failures going nowhere fast, though collectively doing enough to keep the wolf from the door and also to allow Mum to stop taking in washing except for Father Crosby's surplices and shirts. Sue told me she didn't do his vests or long johns because she didn't think, him being a priest, it would be right.

After the war I returned to the island but found it difficult to settle down. I'd seen a bit of the mainland, mostly Melbourne and the country area around Puckapunyal army base and, of course, New Guinea, and I knew I didn't want to go back to sea. I got several jobs, though none of them made me happy: driving a bulldozer on a road construction crew, working as a labourer on one of the new dairy farms, planting trees in the government experimental pine forest and working as a tally clerk at the new cheese factory. I was back to being a McKenzie and going nowhere as usual, but this time doing it ashore.

In the army I'd made the mistake of taking up reading again, and on my return to the island I rekindled my association with Nicole Lenoir-Jourdan. She'd retired as the librarian, justice of the peace and music teacher, and to everyone's surprise and the consternation of some, started the island's first newspaper, the *Queen Island Weekly Gazette*. There was much speculation about where she got the kind of money to buy a small second-hand letterpress printer from the Government Printing Works in Launceston, but nobody was game to ask her. She once confided in me that it was a legacy but explained no further. She had never in anyone's recall mentioned any kinfolk and while it was assumed, with her double-barrelled name and plummy accent, she came from England, she never confirmed this or ever spoke of her childhood.

She invited me to train to become her compositor but I turned her down. With my poor education I lacked the confidence in my spelling and grammar. Furthermore, while I enjoyed our now voluntary reading discussions, she was still the same old fire-eating dragon. The emotional breakdown in the dunny behind the library proved to be strictly a one-off; she hadn't grown any softer or less impatient, and while she was generous in rebuke she was a miser on praise. Working for her would begin the second half of the sentence that I'd commenced at the age of eight. So when the government had called for volunteers to go to Korea I'd jumped at the chance to get away from the island again.

Now I couldn't wait to get back. I knew we were managing pretty well and bringing Jimmy Oldcorn home wouldn't be a hassle for Gloria. There was now even shop-bought food on the table and a spare bed in the sleep-out and we'd long since graduated to proper bathroom towels and an indoor hot-water shower I'd built onto the back of the house when I'd returned from service in New Guinea.

As there had never been any Aborigines on the island, as long as anyone could remember, I doubt if Gloria had seen a black man in the flesh. I was confident this wouldn't make any difference to my mum. Despite our ignorance, as a family we weren't against anything, except authority. She would, I knew, accept Jimmy as somewhat of a curiosity, though nevertheless a welcome guest. She'd probably regard him as a status symbol and drag him around to all the rellos to show him off. When all was said and done, we were a pretty easygoing mob and Jimmy Oldcorn wasn't exactly coming to the Hilton in Paradise.

*Maybe*, I thought, *our lives being so different to what he'd told me about his own, time spent on the island would help Jimmy to scrub out the memory of his past*. Not just Korea but also the orphanage where the poor bugger had spent his early childhood. Or, for that matter, the Elmira Reformatory where he'd spent eighteen months and from which, at the age of eighteen, he'd been summarily ushered out of the front gates and onto the streets of the Bronx where he'd lived in an abandoned tenement as the leader of a gang of feral coloured kids known as the Red Socks.

At the age of twenty Jimmy had been charged and indicted for a stabbing using a flick-knife. The fight was with a rival Puerto Rican gang known as the San Cristos Boys. The Puerto Ricans were the newly arrived, the latest influx of migrants into New York, and the stoush was over a couple of hundred yards of Hunts Point sidewalk populated by mostly Polish Jews, earlier migrants who'd fled from the Nazis but hadn't yet fled from Hunts Point and Morrisania when the blacks and the Puerto Ricans, displaced by the slum-clearing in Manhattan, had moved in. It was a territory prized by both gangs where the shopkeepers, accustomed to stand-over tactics, shrugged philosophically and paid up for protection, but only to one gang, with the terms clearly established and not too onerous.

'Brother Fish, it was war!' Jimmy once explained. 'There ain't no respect on da street, man. Da cops dey ask you about something bad happen in da 'hood, you point out da deed done by a dirty Spic from da other gang an' if you see a Spic kid standing on da corner, if he look like he fourteen or more you look surprised, then you wide-eye da cop an' point, "Dat him, officer! Da Spic on da corner, he done da deed, he da gangster!"' Jimmy would throw back his head and laugh and mimic the Irish cop. '"You'd be sure now, Jimmy?" he asked me. "Sure, officer! I swear on my mama's grave!"' Jimmy grinned, recalling. 'Dem bad days, Brother Fish. You don't carry no blade you a dead man, dat for sure, you in a box wid no cross to mark yo' grave. Jesus ain't gonna find no nigger wid no cross to mark da spot.'

The judge had been generous, and had given Jimmy the option of enlisting in the US Army to fight in the Korean War or, alternatively, receiving three years for causing grievous bodily harm by using a flick-knife with a larger than three-inch blade.

'Dat judge he told me, "Jimmy, you join the army, we gonna tear up your juvenile record and drop all dem charges against you." The judge he say I could be a cleanskin if I vol-lun-teer me for the US of A Army to fight in some place he name Koo-ree-a! He don't tell me it da other side da fuckin' world, man!' Jimmy chuckled, shaking his head. 'Dat judge he's got me good, man. I already know from some of my buddies who left Elmira for a higher order of in-car-sir-ration what I can expect in Newark State Penitentiary. I has got myself a choice between a sore ass from bending over in da prison washroom at da pol-lite request of some big nigger who's da king, or havin' my black ass kicked by some big ol' drill sergeant while I is learning to take pride in da uniform of da United States of A-merica!'

I well recall his grin as he added with a shrug of his shoulders, 'Man, what can I say? I's protecting my virgin ass and so I put my des-tin-ee in da hands of Uncle Sam, who ab-sol-lu-telly guarantee, as a member of a coloured play-toon in the infantry, I'm gonna have me some self-esteem of which, at dat time, I had none whatsoever.' He'd paused as he slowly shook his head, 'Oh Brother Fish, I is sent to the 25th Infantry Division, 24th Reg-gee-ment. Dey call da "Deuce Four" and we's all niggers. Now dat ain't so bad, 'cept we got us a white officer! How's about dat? Dey telling us, ain't no coloured man can be a leader. 'Magine da e-ffect dat gonna have on us, man! Dat no way for a man to get no self-esteem! "Well fuck you, Uncle Sam!" I says. "Dat orphanage it ain't took my self-esteem, da reform-a-tory ain't took my self-esteem, da pol-ees dey ain't took my self-esteem, yo'all ain't gonna take it also, man!"'

As with me, success and the boardrooms of the world have greatly changed the way Jimmy Oldcorn speaks and today he's more likely to use the vernacular of a middle-class Australian or American, depending on where he is, though always with a Yank accent. As he's grown older, and, if he's to be believed, as a result of a pack and a half of cigarettes every day since the age of fifteen, his voice sounds as if he's mixing gravel and cement approximately halfway down his throat. It's the kind of voice to which men give their full attention, while women are seen to cling adoringly to his every word. He laughs when the latter are mentioned, and playfully changes his intonation and grammar back to when we were younger, 'I got me a preacher-quality voice, Brother Fish. Louis "Satchmo" Armstrong and me.' He shrugs, 'So what can I say, eh? Wimmen come to me for dey salvation and it's my born-again duty to oblige them any ways I can!'

It all seems so long ago when, at my suggestion, we'd made our way from Essendon Airport to take a quick look at Flinders Street and then straight to Webb Dock to catch the *Taroona* where we bought tickets to Launceston.

We'd arrived the following morning, docking at Beauty Point on the Tamar River, and made straight for the Anzac Hotel for no other reason than it happened to be the nearest one we could reach conveniently on our crutches. In a sentimental gesture that we both still take seriously we've met here, rain or shine, on the 9th of August every year to celebrate our release from POW camp. Two old mates who have spent much of their subsequent lives together, but who still come here on this one day of the year to celebrate their friendship over a quiet beer or two. Though I had only to fly the company helicopter the short hop across from Queen Island, Jimmy was coming overnight from Shanghai via Hong Kong.

The Anzac Hotel begs a short description, for it brilliantly illustrates the anodyne grog has always been for Australians from the time the first whimpering, rum-fortified convict was rowed onto the fatal shore. It is simply a place designed for drinking. A launching pad for child abuse, wife-beating and all the consequential horrors inherently brought home from the pub. In the crudest terms, it was and I expect still is a place where men go to get pissed, motherless, stonkered, loaded, blind, paralytic, legless or any of the other euphemistic expressions for being drunk or mean-spirited that abound in the Australian vernacular.

The Anzac is one of those unprepossessing red-brick pubs built immediately after the Great War, with rounded shoulders and small, dark, beady-eyed, leaded stained-glass windows that make no attempt to appear inviting. It butts belligerently up against the dockside where you take two wooden steps up from the planked boardwalk and arrive on a steel grid in place of a top step where the dark glint of the river water below can be seen through its bars. You are presented with a pair of scuffed swing doors fixed with dirty brass kick plates with the injunction 'Push' painted on the left-hand door. You push your way into a room about fifty feet in width and perhaps twenty-five in depth. The bar facing the door is fifteen or so paces from the entrance and stretches the entire fifty feet of the room except for two small openings at either end, one that leads to the 'males only' toilet and the other to the rear of the bar.

While age may have wearied the Anzac, it has done nothing to make it respectable. It has always been a bloodhouse, and to this day remains faithful to its roots. It comes as no surprise therefore when you notice the sign painted on the wall behind the bar which announces, 'Females should not feel they are welcome'. This is a fairly recent addition and its careful, almost polite phrasing is at odds with the remainder of the establishment. I can only assume it is designed to technically overcome the fairly recent anti-discrimination laws. In fact, the original sign 'No women allowed' in larger-than-necessary black lettering immediately to its left, has been so lightly overpainted that it can still be clearly read as a warning to any errant university student brave enough to assert her feminist rights.

The walls of the bar room are tiled to shoulder height in six-inch highly glazed bottle-green tiles, as is the facing wall of the bar with the exception of fifteen tiles halfway up, at its centre each containing a large glazed and raised yellow capital letter that collectively spell out:

'THE GALLIPOLI BAR'

The walls above the tiles and the ceiling, striped with fluorescent tubes, are painted a high-gloss enamel of pale green, while the floor is constructed of red building bricks with the three feet or so nearest the bar worn distinctly concave from the effect of eighty years of the dockside workers' hobnailed boots. The fact that the floor isn't covered in sawdust, as it was when Jimmy and I first came here in '53 and for a great many years thereafter, has nothing to do with adding ambience but may have something to do with today's health regulations.

However, despite all its obvious faults, the Gallipoli Bar at this early hour is spotless, with none of the smell of stale cigarettes and fermented hops so redolent of early-opening pubs. Whoever designed this room in those dark days after the end of the Great War did so with the singular purpose of making it easy to clean after a bunch of drunks had caroused, fallen about, thrown up into the sawdust and generally misbehaved until closing time. This process is clearly designed to employ the liberal use of a garden hose, as the tap to which it is attached can be seen to the left of the doorway with the brass handle temporarily removed in case some inebriant attempts to play silly buggers. The efficiency of the cleaning process is further aided by the absence of tables, chairs or bar stools. The Gallipoli Bar is standing room only, based on the premise that you stand up until you fall down whereupon you are dragged out onto the wharf by your mates. At closing time, the publican sweeps up the broken glass and hoses the human detritus out of the front door and down the guttering grille acting as a welcome mat, and into the harbour below.

But there is something about the Gallipoli Bar and the Anzac Hotel that could never have been anticipated by its misanthropic designer, a single touch of spontaneous humanity that changes everything.

Perhaps I may digress for a moment.

It has been my observation that men feel compelled to leave their mark wherever they go. By this I don't mean castles and ramparts, ruined buildings and ancient walls. Instead, I mean the small marks that individuals make to ensure that their passing has been noted. It may be a heart with the initials of a girlfriend carved into the smooth green bark of a gum tree, or a name scratched in the dark onto the wall of a solitary-confinement cell adding another mute presence and obdurate defiance to the hundreds of names and initials of those who had gone through the same humiliation. Today, young blokes leave their mark like dogs pissing on a post, their spray-can graffiti vandalising the outside of carriages of commuter trains or corrupting a vacant wall on a city building by turning it into a giant doodling pad containing a series of multicoloured angular and arcane names. Lacking even this talent to doodle with spray paint, some simply destroy an anonymous surface with a hurriedly swished obscenity in red or black. Names or announcements, 'Jack loves Jenny', are written under bridges or on the sides of overpasses, even chipped into the stone of great pyramids and temples, or they deface the walls containing cave paintings, themselves ancient graffiti that overpaint the marks made by the passing of a hundred generations.

And now here, in these anonymous tiled and sterile drinking premises, humans have once again wrested the initiative from the cynical brewer who, thinking his working-class patrons deserved no better, caused the Anzac Hotel to be designed to be little more than a pig swill. As a rite of passage, crudely carved along the full length of the dark polished surface of the wooden bar are the initials of every local lad and returning veteran who left the Launceston dockyards to fight a war. When a young bloke failed to return or a veteran passes on, a highly polished brass nail is hammered into the surface next to his initials, so that today the bar fair twinkles, a night sky of the dead. At the end of the bar stands a small box on the facing side of which is written in gold lettering, 'Lest We Forget'. Each morning and evening a fresh beer with a good, clean head is stood upon the box to remember fallen comrades who once stood, fresh-faced with elbows touching, at the Gallipoli Bar.

Ten years ago the story of our annual appointment in the Anzac Hotel on the same day each year became the subject of a newspaper article in the Launceston *Examiner*. The following year the proprietor approached us.

'You guys are veterans from the Korean War, aren't you?' We both nodded. 'Yeah, righto, we put it to the blokes, the regulars like . . . and they reckon after twenty-four years you're entitled.'

'Entitled?' Jimmy asked with mock surprise. 'Don't tell me we're getting a drink on the house!'

The barman gave him a sort of half-grin. 'No such luck, mate.' He produced a pocket knife with a well-worn blade, and placed it on the bar in front of us and indicated the surface of the bar. 'Go ahead, fellas, do us the honour. Carve your initials.'

I have been the recipient of a few honours in my life, not all of them deserved, but I count this one above most and, I confess, at the time I was hard put not to shed a tear. Jimmy would later confess that he felt much the same way. The publican then instructed us to leave the sum of one pound in our respective wills for the purpose of shouting drinks for the house when the time came, as he put it, 'to hammer in the nail'.

'One pound! That's two bucks, not much of a shout,' I said, amused.

He'd paused, unnecessarily wiping the surface of the mutilated bar, 'Yeah well, that's what it was way back in 1920 when we hammered in the first nail and we've never bothered to change it; the house shouts the rest.'

I'm now sitting directly in front of my carved initials lamenting the fact that I made a proper botch of them when I feel a hand the size of a soup bowl on my shoulder. Jimmy has arrived. 'Hiya, Brother Fish, how 'ya been, buddy,' he announces in his cement-mixer growl. 'Sorry I'm late, mate. Couldn't get a taxi from the airport, bunch of nuns commandeered the lot.' He grins. 'Extra! Extra! Giant black man slams nun to sidewalk and hijacks taxi!'

'Footpath, not sidewalk,' I correct him, grinning.

'Nah, footpath don't sound dangerous,' Jimmy laughs.

I have often wondered why other nationalities so easily pick up an American accent while Yanks, no matter how long they remain away from their birthplace, never lose theirs.

The barman, hearing Jimmy shout, appears a moment later from somewhere out back and pours him a draught beer, checks the level of my own, which I've barely touched, places an ashtray in front of Jimmy and returns from where he came.

'Cheers, Brother Fish,' Jimmy says.

'Here's to being mates, mate.' I sigh. 'The thirty-third time, the saddest of them all.'

That's about it. The formalities are over. It is the being here together on this day, the 9th of August, that matters, and we don't need any further ceremony or fanfare. Besides, there isn't anything to say that isn't already known between us. We remain silent for a while, easy in each other's company. I guess, like me, he is thinking back, gauging the distance travelled and the ups and downs that measure the sum of the lives we've led together.

He's been flying all night on the Qantas red-eye special from Hong Kong and he's failed to remove his coat – that's not like him. Jimmy, like me and most kids who grow up poor, is careful with his clobber, and accustomed to stepping off a plane after an all-night flight and walking straight into a board meeting. He produces a soft pack and a lighter, takes out a cigarette and places the rest on the bar. He lights up and takes a short, sharp drag, then places the fag into the lip of the glass ashtray and blows the smoke out through his nostrils. He turns to me and says, 'It's been a long journey, Brother Fish.'

'No longer than usual. I'm the one can't sleep on planes – you always look like you've just stepped out of Johnny Chang's tailor shop in Kowloon.'

'Nah, not da trip – da journey.' He picks up his glass. 'Our Countess,' he says, his voice low and gentle. 'Hell, man. I done love her so much.' Jimmy, his beer halfway raised to his mouth, is crying, softly, without a sound – just tears running down his 'high-yella' face.

# CHAPTER TWO

## *K Force*

Army training is much the same whatever war you are about to fight, and Puckapunyal is where it usually happens if you come from the bottom end of Australia. The major premise behind training a man to fight hasn't changed much since Alexander the Great and probably even predates that: do as you're told and never question a superior. In the history of warfare humans have achieved the most valiant as well as vainglorious outcomes by not being required to think for themselves. History is redolent with fools in command, field marshals, generals and brigadiers who have managed to send legions of men to their deaths on the principle that the greater force knows better than the individual soldier, and that dying needlessly is a peculiar privilege granted to the lower ranks.

It worked at Gallipoli when young Australians, untested in war, set out to prove their valour at a time in our history when fighting and dying for King and Empire was regarded by society as the highest possible ideal. In the Second World War Australians no longer felt the need to establish our fighting credentials, although this time Australia itself was threatened and it became necessary to defend our country against a possible invasion from the Japanese.

Korea was different – it was a conflict where the North, under a communist regime championed by Russia, and the South, ostensibly an elected democracy under the watchful eye of America, were separated by the 38th parallel with the United Nations acting as referee. When, in a deliberate act of aggression, the North invaded the South, the communist troops proved far too strong for the poorly equipped and under-trained South Korean Army. Within a week the South had lost almost half its effective fighting force. With the Americans and Russians already deeply committed to the Cold War, the Americans were not prepared to allow this to happen and called on the United Nations to intervene.

The UN Security Council met and decided that the time for a diplomatic solution was over and the North couldn't be allowed to ride roughshod over their southern brothers. They called for member nations to volunteer to send troops, the aim being to drive the communist army out of South Korea. Our government, an early and eager participant, sent in the RAAF 77 Squadron with their Mustangs as well as two naval ships, HMAS *Shoalhaven* and *Bataan*. After some little hesitation they decided to add an infantry battalion of around 1000 men to our contribution. At the time the 3rd Battalion, Royal Australian Regiment (3RAR) was stationed in Japan as part of the occupation force. The men in Japan were a mixture of World War II veterans holding most of the rank and pretty well-trained recent recruits to the Australian Regular Army, but the battalion was only at half strength. The war in Korea was going badly and men were urgently required at the front, and there simply wasn't sufficient time to train an additional 1000 recruits required to bring 3RAR up to full strength and provide a pool of reinforcements. The government hit on the idea of recruiting ex-army civilians, preferably with combat experience, who'd served in World War II and would only need a short refresher course to be combat ready. They called us 'K Force'. This, of course, meant that those of us who joined K Force were somewhat older than the Regular Army recruit.

When I arrived at Puckapunyal for the first time in late 1944 I was a bright-eyed and bushy-tailed eighteen-year-old anxiously waiting to turn nineteen so I could get into World War II before it ended. The huge military camp teemed with thousands of Australian and American troops with rows of ribbons on their chests that spoke for themselves. These were warriors, hardened in the furnace of war, while my ribbon-free chest testified to my status as a neophyte – the original virgin soldier.

At night the mess halls and canteens seemed to vibrate with light and raucous laughter as men threw back beers and competed with each other to talk of their experiences. I listened silently as they swapped stories of exotic places – Cairo, Palestine, Alexandria, London, Paris, Rome – or told of battles won – Tobruk, El Alamein and others less known. This huge military camp was definitely the most exciting place I'd ever been.

It was here that I attended my first evening at the theatre. It was a variety show billed as the 'All Sports Concert Party' and seemed impossibly glamorous to a kid from Queen Island whose previous theatrical experience had consisted of the open-air cinema where you reclined in a faded canvas deckchair if you were an adult or, if under thirteen, you sat up front, cross-legged in the 'sixpenny dirt'. Despite my usually good recall, I don't remember a great deal about the show, though there is a reason for this. But two things are forever emblazoned on my mind. The first, the moment when the red velvet curtain rose and the sweeping, swirling spotlights illuminated a row of motionless long-legged dancing girls smiling down at me. I had never seen such beautiful creatures in the flesh and they fair took my breath away. Then the music started and they danced and sang a song called 'Hello, Puckapunyal'. As I wrote in a letter home, 'I have never seen such grace combined with beautiful legs that moved as one.'

The second memory from that night was far more serious. She came on directly after the chorus line and is the cause of my lack of recall of the other performances. There was a drum roll and a clash of cymbals and a disembodied voice announced: 'Ladies and gentlemen, so young yet still Australia's leading torch singer, please welcome the very talented, the lovely, Miss Pat Brand!'

Raised up in front of me on the stage under a single spotlight stood the loveliest woman I had ever seen. She wore a white evening gown and red lipstick and the spotlight gave her hair a kind of a halo. This was the nearest I'd ever been to an angel in heaven and, I'm ashamed to say, I could feel an instant stirring in my army strides.

*'Fish gotta swim and birds gotta fly,*
*I gotta love one man till I die,*
*Can't help lovin' dat man o' mine.'*

I was in love, tumbling down the full vortex, head over heels in love, the full quiver of Cupid's bewitching arrows piercing my thumping heart. Fifty years later I'm not sure I've completely recovered.

*'Tell me he's lazy, tell me he's slow,*
*Tell me I'm crazy – maybe I know,*
*Can't help lovin' dat man o' mine.'*

The rest of the concert was a blur – even the return of the long-legged dancing girls did nothing for me. I was Pat Brand*ed* for life. The following morning, still in a zombie-like state, I waited near the entertainers' lines with the hope of catching a glimpse of my celestial object of desire. I was not the only one – several dozen soldiers, a number of Yanks among them, all trying to look nonchalant, were gathered for the same purpose. My heart filled with dismay – their faces wore the unmistakable lines of experience, both of war and women, their chests a veritable fruit salad, exploding with campaign ribbons. It was at once obvious to me that the kid from Queen Island didn't have a snowball's hope in hell. I stayed, head down, the toe of my boot kicking at the dirt.

When at last Pat Brand appeared, she gave us the briefest of smiles and got directly onto a bus, which moments later disappeared in a cloud of famous Puckapunyal dust. Later I would deconstruct her speedy departure, reassembling it to suit my fevered imagination. For months thereafter I would interpret her fleeting Mona Lisa smile as a message specially intended for me. Had she not looked directly at me? Straight into my eyes, in fact. It was obvious she couldn't give me the full twenty-four pearlies because she didn't want to hurt the feelings of the other men. My heart ached for her, the loneliness she must feel, her being a professional entertainer and me a man tragically going to war, with whom she couldn't allow herself to fall in love. I lived off that enigmatic smile for the remainder of the war.

Now, six years later, I was back in Puckapunyal, though this time I carried one pathetic little ribbon on my chest, more an embarrassment than anything, it was known in the vernacular as 'every-bugger's ribbon' because you got it if you served twenty-eight days or more in the army. Our incoming truckload of K Force volunteers drove past row upon row of empty huts. They seemed like the barracks of the dead, with windows cobwebbed and crusted with dust, old newspapers and twigs had gathered, blown against some of the doors, and once in a while a slab of corrugated iron had come loose from one of the walls allowing a dusty glimpse inside of a rusty bed or steel locker.

Feeling like intruders in a graveyard, we took up occupation in a small corner of the once-great military base grateful that we wouldn't be staying long – our instructors having been given the task of knocking the rust off us in the hope that some sound metal still lay underneath the corrosion caused by five years of indolent civilian life.

It was obvious the army was in a hurry, for we started training the following day with weapons and range practice. While it didn't do to show too much enthusiasm – after all, we were all supposed to be war-weary veterans – I loved the almost-forgotten feel of the rifle clamped into my shoulder. A .303 is a fairly heavy rifle and I'm a little bloke, but if handled properly, I could hold it as steady as anyone and fire just as accurately. Pulling the butt hard into the hollow of my shoulder while clamping the rifle steady with hands and arms, then seeing the foresight rising through the 'U' of the backsight, I'd hold my breath, taking the first trigger pressure. Then squeezing the right hand round the small of the butt until the pressure on the trigger fired. The kick of the recoil was like greeting an old and trusted friend after a long absence.

Notwithstanding the satisfaction of rifle, Bren gun and Owen gun range practice, the rest of our training was, to say the least, onerous. Sweating like a pig for hours on end, my lungs ached as we clambered over wooden walls, clung to ropes overhanging deep ditches meant to be rivers, and leopard-crawled, elbows hard into the ground, through obstacle courses. My feet burned and my shoulders were rubbed raw from carrying a heavy pack as we route-marched, sometimes for twenty miles, with only an occasional rest to use our water bottles.

At night we hobbled around our huts cursing and grumbling, nursing stiff, aching muscles we'd forgotten existed and treating our blistered feet with methylated spirits – although Rick Stackman, who'd been a prisoner of war under the Japanese, scoffed at the meths and used his own piss. He claimed it worked a damned sight better, although admitted the one disadvantage was that you couldn't drink it in an emergency.

As I recall, while we regarded ourselves as veterans and showed a fair degree of apathy for what we thought of as the same old senseless routines, like all recruits, we never stopped complaining. We saw ourselves as grown men and scorned the pedantic procedures, bellicose language and spit and polish so dear to the hearts of non-commissioned officers. As a consequence, both sides, the instructors and their whingeing charges, ended up with a fair amount of indifference towards each other.

We told ourselves we were anxious to be shipped to Japan where drafts of K Force were progressively joining up with 3RAR to make up a complete battalion to fight the communist noggies. We regarded much of the training as the usual army bullshit we could well do without.

While we were anxious to get going, the government wasn't holding back either. Prime Minister Bob Menzies had volunteered Australia to be the first nation, after America, to make a commitment to the UN forces. He was an avowed 'commie hater' and was always going on about the evils of world communism and was determined we would be early starters in the stoush against the reds.

As a result of this enthusiasm to see us at war again our training was only just sufficient to bring us back to, at best, an average World War II competency. We probably needed more training but told ourselves we'd done it all before and were battle-trained and experienced.

Time and history tend to bring with them respectability, but in truth the initial unit known as K Force was a bit of a mixed blessing – a place for misfits, malcontents and even petty criminals to hide, as well as some very competent and committed soldiers. This was hardly surprising – veterans who'd returned and had more or less adjusted to civilian life were unlikely to volunteer for a second helping of war. Every K Force volunteer had his own reason for returning to the army, we all had a personal agenda. Why else would a veteran so recently on active service, in some cases even a prisoner under the Japanese or Germans, volunteer to fight another war?

Traditionally, young lads volunteer to go to war believing they are bulletproof. Government propaganda relies on them responding to a combination of testosterone-driven madness, the promise of adventure and peer-group pressure. On the other hand, those of us who volunteered for K Force would have known better. We knew the proverbial bullet with your number on it when your time was up was fatalistic nonsense. Every soldier knows that every bullet, mortar or shell fired by the enemy is intended for you. By volunteering to go to war you deliberately put yourself in its path and are manipulating the odds in favour of being killed.

Many of the K Force volunteers had experienced mates dying in World War II and should have known the army for what it was – long stretches of boredom and short and infrequent periods of intense terror that pass for excitement after they are over. Having escaped unscathed the first time round, volunteering for a second helping seemed too big a price to pay for an occasional gratuitous rush of adrenaline. There had to be a reason, other than the early onset of dementia, for signing up for this further opportunity to prematurely end one's life.

The army wasn't into psychological profiling at the time, and K Force recruits were conveniently described in the newspapers as 'men who find it difficult to settle down in the aftermath of war'. This sounded respectable, almost heroic, and was preferable to the notion that anyone volunteering for K Force must, by reason of his actions, be in urgent need of psychiatric help.

I guess I was no different from the rest of the volunteers. I arrived in New Guinea a day after Japan surrendered. There I was, as useless as a hard-on in a bishop's trousers, a qualified master marksman destined never to fire a shot in anger. The only Jap I ever saw, dead or alive, was in a newsreel. When Korea came along with a request for volunteers I scratched around for a plausible excuse to volunteer and settled on the premise that I had a personal duty to uphold democracy in the Free World. The fact that Korea had never been in the Free World and had seen precious little democracy never occurred to me. The Cold War between Russia and America was hotting up and Uncle Sam and Australia were friends and, everyone knows, you don't let your mates down etc., etc., blah, blah, blah. Bob Menzies-type rhetoric was an ideal medium to conceal my real motives.

So that I would appear plausible I'd read somewhat on the two ideologies, communism versus capitalism. By the time I got to Puckapunyal I considered myself a bit of an expert on the subject. Compared with the men in my hut, my knowledge of the politics behind the conflict in Korea was positively encyclopedic. When we first arrived I'd rabbit on about the cornerstones of democracy, mankind's inalienable right to free speech and to make choices of our own. At first the blokes would listen more or less politely. But soon enough they lost patience with me. 'Ferchrissake, Jacko, put a sock in it, will ya!' someone would yell out. 'If yer gunna be a fuckin' blow-hard then do it on yer mouth organ and not through yer arse!' That's the trouble with being a little guy, everyone feels free to have a go at you.

Johnny Gordon, the Aboriginal cove, once asked me directly, 'Jacko, why did you join up?'

'International communism is a real threat to our way of life, Gordie, and I feel it is my duty as an able-bodied young man with military experience to stand up and be counted.'

'Yeah, sure, but what's the real reason?'

My throat suddenly tightened and my mouth went dry. 'That's about it,' I lied.

'Bullshit,' he said, losing respect and walking away.

He was right, of course. Watching him walking away I grew up a whole heap. Nobody joins the army to exercise their right to free speech, and you never get to make choices of your own. Moreover, just quietly, from what I'd read, communism seemed an okay idea to me and I couldn't see what all the fuss was about. Democracy hadn't done me any special favours and its offshoot, capitalism, had demonstrably eluded me.

So as well as being a smart-arse, I was also being a bit of a hypocrite. Of course, I was too chicken to say any of this. The Australian Government was running a campaign in an attempt to outlaw the Australian Communist Party, so it wasn't an altogether good idea to suggest that communism didn't seem such a bad system or to question why it was necessary to go to war to eliminate it. To my hut mates this would immediately turn me into a red-hot commo and I'd be equated with trade-union leaders and dockside workers who were always striking or downing tools and walking off the job. Everyone knew the commos were solely responsible for the nation's post-war industrial strife.

In truth, my volunteering had nothing to do with ideology. Like most Australians I was politically lukewarm and probably wouldn't have voted if it hadn't been compulsory. Like all the others at Puckapunyal, I was running away from something. As a matter of fact, in my case, a whole heap of things. From the island. From aimless, boring and mindless manual work. From becoming a professional fisherman. Perhaps, most of all, from the dreaded clutches of Nicole Lenoir-Jourdan and the likelihood that if I remained on the island she'd eventually succeed in prolonging my sentence by making me take up an apprenticeship as a compositor on her crummy newspaper. There was also something else. I'd been a soldier but had never been to war. Arriving in New Guinea too late meant that all I'd done was help clean up the mess. I guess, with my pathetic 'every-bugger's' medal I felt excluded from the club, and this only served to add to my abject sense of failure.

Korea was essentially my way of not facing up to my own inadequacy. I was supposed to be the first clever McKenzie and I was failing hand over fist. I'd convinced myself that when Alf died, forcing me to abandon my education, life had struck me a dastardly blow. I was the McKenzie who was destined to reach for the skies, yet even before taking to the air I'd nose-dived into the runway.

I assured myself it would have been better if Nicole Lenoir-Jourdan hadn't taught me to read in order to think. Which I now saw as a curse and not as the generous gift it truly was. I told myself I was a blue-singlet bloke with a white-collar mindset. I recall rather grandly conjuring up a picture in my mind of a deep chasm dividing two metaphorical landscapes, one in shadow and the other in sunlight. The dark side was where we McKenzies belonged, the pick-and-shovel side, using what we had from the neck down. The light side, the from-the-neck-up side, was the Lenoir-Jourdan landscape, where your hands stayed clean and your greatest asset was your head. In between the two sides was a gap too wide to jump and, through no fault of my own, I lacked the knowledge to build a bridge to cross over into the Elysian glades that lay beyond.

So I decided she, Nicole Lenoir-Jourdan, was largely to blame for my inadequacy. After all, if she hadn't trapped me in the library and blatantly interfered with my life I would never have aspired to becoming something more than the trawler man my father had been. She'd kidnapped my intelligence and put these high-falutin' ideas into my head. I hadn't asked for them, I wasn't a kid going around, intellectual cap in hand, seeking truth and knowledge. At the age of eight, like a prize butterfly specimen, I'd been pinned down to the library floor by the formidable and irresistible combination of justice of the peace, librarian and music teacher.

It was also partially Alf's fault for dying at the wrong time, though I'd try to cancel this thought whenever it surfaced – the poor bastard wasn't to know he was going to cark it early from smoking fags. I allowed that Gloria wasn't entirely innocent, either. She'd persistently told us we were 'the proverbial'. If you tell a child often enough that he's a heap of shit he eventually comes to believe it. Or so I justified my self-pity.

Sue, my sister, had by now completed her training and was a fully-fledged nurse and loving her vocation. Steve and Cory, my younger brothers, were fishermen and seemingly without a worry in the world. I was the misfit who had been socially and intellectually corrupted, neither fish nor fowl, no good to myself or anyone else. I was scared and resentful, more than a little conscious of my ignorance and feeling thoroughly sorry for myself. For a deadset ordinary bloke like me I'd got my head into a fair sort of mess.

All this self-loathing lay buried and squirming, hidden beneath my quasi-intellectual defence of democracy, which I gave as a reason to anyone who'd listen for signing on to go to Korea. Although Steve and Cory, not being veterans, appeared to be envious as hell of my good fortune, it must have been obvious to Gloria and probably Sue as well that I was attempting to run away from my responsibilities. Blind Freddy could have seen that my high-minded rhetoric was simply concealing the fact that I was handing my life over to the Australian Army. What a pathetic joke I'd become.

The big day arrived when, such as it was, our training was complete and, after the weekend I'd spent with Jason Matthews in Melbourne, we were ready to be shipped out to Japan to join 3RAR to receive a little additional integration training before being shipped to send the communists scuttling back across the 38th parallel to lick their wounds.

The joining of the two forces, 3RAR and K Force, was to prove a peculiar marriage. Many of the soldiers in 3RAR had their wives and children with them and were well settled, familiar with the Japanese environment and had happily become more like useful civil servants teaching Western ways to the Japanese than military personnel. Despite the order not to fraternise with the recent enemy, a fair number of the single soldiers were shacked up with Japanese girls. These women, some of them war widows, were compliant and willing mistresses. The military rations their Australian lovers obtained were vastly superior to what was available to the public in a post-war Japan severely short of food. A de facto relationship with a serviceman would enable them to feed their families as well as themselves. As the occupation forces lived pretty high on the hog it was a comfortable and secure life. Now they were being joined by a load of misfits, loners and larrikins. In combination it was to make for a strange mixture to take into a battlefield.

The first big surprise was upon leaving Puckapunyal. On the previous occasion I'd embarked for a war zone, I'd flown, equipped with a packet of stale cheese-and-tomato sandwiches, strapped into a canvas seat in the near-freezing interior of an RAAF Dakota bound for New Guinea. Now we were flying to Japan on a Qantas Douglas DC4. Talk about posh – there we were, sitting back like Jacky, clutching our bags of duty-free grog, the air hostesses bringing us beers and meals on a tray like a bunch of carefree holiday-makers on their first overseas trip.

Japan proved to be a bit of an eye-opener, just five years after Victory over Japan Day the people were doing it tough still trying to come to terms with the occupation forces and the concept of democracy. They seemed to be tentative in everything they did, as if afraid to make a mistake or to offend in any way. Even those who spoke a bit of English bowed and spoke softly in what appeared to us to be a servile manner. Australians become uncomfortable around too much bowing and scraping and so we had difficulty understanding the Japanese culture. The only other foreigners I'd met were the people of New Guinea – simple, mostly bare-topped village folk who laughed a lot and who were exactly the opposite of these socially rigid, overpolite and always acquiescent nips. The only good thing I could personally see about Japan was that most of the males were shorter than me.

In their formality the Japanese were almost exactly opposite in culture to the laid-back and easygoing Australians, and so naturally we concluded they must dislike us intensely. We decided that all this obsequious carry-on was their way of quietly sending us up. '*Yes, sir! No, sir! Three bags full, sir!*' '*Nobody carries on like that, do they?*' we told ourselves by way of confirmation. Under such circumstances it was easy to behave badly, and we didn't need any further encouragement. We told ourselves that if the nips didn't like us, tough luck – it was our turn now and Rick Stackman was there to remind us what the bastards had done to us in their death camps. Just as well we only had a couple of weeks in Japan, most of it spent training, or we may have got ourselves into a lot more trouble than we did.

For example, Rick, who'd been a prisoner under the Japanese on the Burma Railway, couldn't come to terms with the locals. I guess he had good reason to hate the Japs. After a few beers he became very difficult and we soon learned to split and leave him on his own. Rick was big enough and ugly enough to take care of himself and you wouldn't want to be around him when he turned nasty. He was a dark-haired, lantern-jawed kind of bloke who looked like he needed a shave only moments after he'd had one. Normally he was easygoing and pleasant though admittedly a bit of a loner, the sort of mate you'd want by your side if you found yourself in a dark alley in a strange city. Back home in Australia, after a bit of a piss-up he'd become a bit obstreperous, but he wasn't the only one and I can't say he ever went completely off the air. Now, in the land of Nippon, he'd become a maniac. He'd start fights at the drop of a hat, taking on three or four Japs at the one time, usually besting them. We'd speculate that one day he'd pick on a noggy who was an exponent of jujitsu who'd clean him up big time, but this never happened. Walking back to catch the bus after a night on the grog he'd deliberately shoulder the locals off the crowded pavements, often knocking several of them sprawling. Then, as some little Jap lay whimpering, bruised and bleeding in the gutter, he'd stab a great stubby finger at him and shout, 'That's for the Burma Railway, you little yellow bastard!' On three occasions the military police picked him up for creating a public nuisance and he'd been charged and placed in the guardhouse, and eventually he was confined to barracks where he seemed to go so quiet you could scarcely get a grunt out of him.

In later years I would have a great deal to do with the Japanese and when I could speak their language sufficiently well I got a better understanding of their highly structured and complex society, one which, it is my personal belief, the advent of democracy has done little to change. From the war we knew the Japanese had a capacity to be extraordinarily cruel, although this didn't show in their business dealings. Here they proved to be stubborn and patient negotiators, highly intelligent, hard-working, arrogant and, above all, suspicious. They invariably made decisions by consensus, or so it seemed, a process that seemed to take forever and initially greatly tried Jimmy's and my patience. Often, after endless days of negotiation, with every point covered a dozen times or more, we'd go to the airport with a business deal still unresolved. Then just as we were preparing to go through customs they'd nod and produce a contract or they'd try to wring a final concession out of us. But, as happened over the years to Jimmy and myself, many of them became our friends, and in this quite separate capacity they proved to be delightfully humorous, generous and loyal mates.

Jimmy and I found that in dealing with the Japanese, in business as well as at a more informal level, it was just as well to emulate their traditional ways of going about life. Although many of their social structures seem to contradict the very tenets of democracy and the freedom of the individual, they appear to be self-imposed. I guess any culture indoctrinated over hundreds of generations will always bend and twist a new ideology into an acceptable shape. Nothing has changed the notion that the hierarchical and formal structures, originally based on the samurai, are paramount in Japanese society. Democracy notwithstanding, they have only ever elected one party to their parliament. The Emperor, toppled from his celestial pinnacle at the insistence of the West, is no longer seen as divine, nevertheless, a great many Japanese have yet to be convinced, and all things still flow downwards from the throne. Japan is a bilateral society – you either make the rules or you obey them.

The chartered Qantas DC4 landed at Iwakuni where we took the train to the port of Kure, not far from Hiroshima where the Americans dropped the first atomic bomb. From Kure it was eight miles by truck to our barracks at Hiro. K Force arrived in dribs and drabs over the next two days, some even on scheduled Qantas flights. By the 11th of September 1950, 3RAR, previously at half strength, was now fully manned, though not quite ready for combat.

We'd been told that we could be called into action at any time and, while K Force had essentially taken it pretty easy at Puckapunyal, it began to dawn on some of us that we'd soon be fighting for our lives and that a bit of updated training might just come in handy. Added to this, the regular army blokes were a lot fitter than we were so when we headed off to the Hamamura training centre for Exercise Bolero we realised we would need to pull our fingers out if we didn't want to be seen as a complete shambles. The two weeks that followed soon sorted us out. The weather wasn't good. At times the rain came down in bucketsful and we were often up to our eyeballs in mud and slush. If only we'd known, with winter soon to be upon us in Korea, these training conditions were a Sunday-school picnic compared to what lay ahead.

On the 23rd of September, twelve days after we'd arrived in Japan, the call came to pack our gear for Korea. On the 27th we boarded the American transport ship *Aitken Victory* at Kure. We'd stowed our kit and the K Force blokes were leaning over the side of the ship watching the friends and families of the permanent army personnel crying and carrying on at the dockside. Then, John Lazarou yelled out from the opposite side of the deck, 'Crikey! Come take a squiz at this, fellas!'

By far the more interesting spectacle was on the opposite side of the ship. Across a short strip of water stood the Japanese girlfriends and de factos who'd shacked up with single blokes and had now lost their meal tickets. They were carrying on a treat, crying and clutching each other, some even throwing themselves down, grabbing at the feet of their friends. This was something we'd never seen before, the normally reserved Japanese emotionally overwrought to the point of hysteria. I guess they were not looking forward to returning to the harsh realities of post-war Japan and, I suppose, despite the clash of cultures, some of these relationships may have blossomed into genuine love affairs. Certainly several of the young permanent army coves standing with us seemed pretty miserable.

As we were watching all this carry-on, there was a sudden commotion among K Force and someone was pointing up to one of the dockside cranes. There, 150 feet into the sky, sat Rick Stackman at the very tip of the extended arm of a crane. How a big clumsy bloke like him ever got up there and then crawled on his hands and knees to the very end of the crane is a complete mystery. He'd gone practically mute on us in the final two days we were at the Hiro barracks and now he was perched like an angry gorilla at the end of the dockside crane.

Someone must have called the military police, as they soon arrived and tried to persuade Rick to come down. We all did the same, shouting up our pleas and reassurances for him to join us on deck. 'Bugger off!' he yelled down at them and then at us, 'I ain't goin', I've had a gutful!'

Johnny Gordon, the Aborigine from Condabri who'd fronted me over my reasons for joining up, eventually climbed onto the ship's rail and, taking a flying leap, landed spider-like onto the side of the crane and then clambered up to the beginning of its extended arm to try to persuade Rick to come back down. 'Come down, Rick, we're your mates, I'll look after you personal!' we heard him yelling. By this time Rick was sobbing and shaking his head like a small child who, punished by his parents, has climbed a tree and is too upset to come down.

The poor bastard had finally broken. He'd survived three and a half years of torture and starvation in the Japanese death camps and now, five years later, he could take no more. I guess his personal agenda for joining K Force must have been to get even with the enemy. But two weeks in Japan had brought all the memories back and cracked him wide open. We were eventually forced to sail without him. Later we heard he'd been flown back to Australia where he was court-martialled and given six months in the Military Corrective Establishment at Holsworthy before receiving a dishonourable discharge from the army.

In those days the military and the government still hadn't accepted the idea that war can damage men's minds and sometimes destroy them more permanently than any physical injury. Big Rick Stackman had a chest full of ribbons gained from honourable service to his country, but his record in Japan showed three arrests for being drunk and disorderly. All the army cared to see in him was a troublemaker who'd delayed the ship's departure by an hour and a half and had effectively deserted his post while on active duty. Today, of course, we know he was suffering from post-traumatic stress disorder and should have been declared TPI (Totally and Permanently Incapacitated) and given an honourable discharge and a disability pension. I've often wondered what happened to him, whether the army eventually relented and came good. He was a salt-of-the-earth type of bloke, the sort you come to think of as the backbone of the Australian army.

However, while Rick Stackman not coming with us had troubled us somewhat, we had another immediate anxiety to occupy our minds. On the 15th of September, a week before our date of departure for Korea had been announced, General MacArthur, the commander-in-chief of the UN forces, launched an amphibious landing at Inchon, halfway up the Korean peninsula where the 1st Marine Division immediately struck out for Seoul. By the 21st of September, while we were still training in the mud and slush, his troops were threatening the North Korean Army's lines of communication. The communists were caught between a rock and a hard place, and they didn't know whether to continue to attack the UN forces desperately defending the southern tip of the Korean peninsula, or to turn and fight the marines. In any event they left the decision to turn and fight too late and scores of thousands of the communist troops were trapped. Our greatest fear now was that by the time we arrived the war would be all over bar the shouting.

The *Aitken Victory* set sail for Korea at about eight at night, and during the crossing we heard a news broadcast by General MacArthur announcing the North Korean Army had been routed. The communists had retreated across the 38th parallel with the South Korean Army in hot pursuit, and the Americans were champing at the bit on the border waiting for the word from the UN to go after the Reds to finish them off.

However, it seems they need not have worried, for the communist army by now was a spent force, thirteen of their divisions having disintegrated in the panic that followed the American landing and many thousands having been taken prisoner. MacArthur, in an effort aimed to influence a hesitant United Nations General Assembly, announced to the world that, given the opportunity, his army would make short work of the demoralised North Koreans and quickly unify the country.

Which was all very well, except for the fact that we were in this war as well. It looked to me as if, for the second time, I would be going home without having fired a shot in anger. I still wouldn't qualify as a returned serviceman and I'd go home still wearing my meaningless medal. Of course, by now I'd quite forgotten my secretly professed sympathy for communism. MacArthur was jumping the gun and we didn't find this at all amusing, him hogging all the glory for the goddamn marines.

After all, we'd gone to a lot of trouble to volunteer and now this Yankee blow-hard was going it alone, soaking up the glory. This time he wouldn't have to say 'I shall return', as he did when the Japs kicked him out of the Philippines. Korea was turning out to be an anticlimax. It was all very well for MacArthur to be the surrogate Emperor of Japan, but, fair go, that didn't mean, with the help of the marines, he would again emerge as the all-conquering hero while we were still in Japan training, splashing around in the mud and the rain.

This wasn't entirely fair, of course. Throughout July, while coming to the aid of the South Korean forces, the Yanks had taken a fair old belting, notably at a town named Taejon on the mountainous Korean peninsula.

It seems the North Koreans hadn't yet understood that they ought to be afraid of America's might. Unfamiliar with the communist method of maintaining a strong frontal attack while, at the same time, by means of infiltration, initiating surprise attacks from the side and rear, the Americans had come off second best on their first encounters with the enemy.

The Australian papers at the time were full of the hiding the American occupation forces, rushed into battle with little preparation, were taking trying to expel the communist invaders. Even before the special K Force recruitment was announced, my interest in the new war must have been obvious to Gloria. She handed me a clipping from the newspaper, dated 22nd of July 1950. 'Before you go getting any ideas, Jacko, take a look what the communists are doing to the Americans.' It was the first of many clippings she was to cut out and paste into her 'war journal', which I've kept all these years.

## Young Americans, tired, shocked, straggle to safety

ADVANCED US HEADQUARTERS IN KOREA, Fri. – **Filthy young Americans with muscles crying for rest, and fear deep in their eyes and bellies, are straggling into this rear area today for what the Army calls 'regrouping', says the United Press correspondent, Gen. Symonds.**

They haven't eaten for hours. The only possessions they have are their powder-grimed rifles and carbines, clutched tight in their hands.

Hungry as they are, many of them don't have time to eat the rations waiting for them, but flop down in the dirt with a steel helmet for a pillow and fall into an uneasy sleep punctured by dreams of the 'nightmare alley' they had to travel to get here.

At first there was only a small group. Then, one by one, truck by truck, they began to come in. Unit sergeants try to make lists of their men, but for some the list is small. The sergeants look at the pitifully few names and mutter: 'Maybe they'll come in later.'

HOBART *MERCURY*, 22 JULY 1950

Taejon and the other skirmishes and battles the Americans had fought on behalf of the South were a case of too few men, mostly inexperienced, attempting to hold too large an area, with nobody to watch the flanks. This was to be an oft-repeated tale in Korea. Now, with the whole of the 1st Marine Division brought into the war, General MacArthur had every right to be pleased with the American recovery.

If only we'd cared to listen, there was a warning in all this that we might not be entirely ready for combat. While the present assault had been led by the crack 1st Marine Division, the initial tactic in Korea, driven by the urgency of the situation, consisted of dribbling weak detachments of American troops drawn from three divisions of the four doing duty as occupation forces in Japan. These were not battle-hardened fighting men but troops recruited since World War II, most without military experience except for the cushy conditions that prevailed in occupied post-war Japan.

Of course we saw it quite differently. We were, we argued, at least the equivalent of the highly trained, combat-fit American marines. We realised that while our soldiering skills were a bit rusty, they were still there – a skirmish or two would soon see them oiled and polished to their former brightness. Most of the blokes had been under fire at some time or another; we even had some 'thirty-niners' who'd been with the 2nd AIF from the start of World War II to the very end. You couldn't say they didn't know their stuff now, could you? Some, in fact most of us, had joined the war late but, with a few exceptions, me being one, had seen action in the Islands. Quite a few had held rank, which they'd relinquished in order to sign on for Korea, and there were some among our lot who'd been decorated. Rusty or not, we knew when the time came we would rise to the occasion.

As it turned out this wasn't exactly an accurate summation. For a start, some of the K Force blokes were getting on a bit and we'd all been corrupted by civilian life – you could see this in several of the blokes who hadn't yet managed to get rid of their beer gut and some still huffed and puffed a bit, stopping to hold their knees during a training run. It was a bit presumptuous at this stage to compare ourselves with the crack, super-fit up-to-the-minute marines. On the other hand, as older individuals and as soldiers with a fair bit of past experience, we were well ahead of your ordinary Yank grunt fighting on the peninsula at the time.

In our defence, we'd had next-to-bugger-all training as a battalion and later on when we'd been in a stoush or two and had got our shit together we were happy to compare ourselves with the marines and, for that matter, the crackerjack British permanent army units. Nevertheless, initially going in, it would be fair to say we were just a tad undercooked and overconfident.

Still, we were straining at the leash to have a go at the communist enemy and now the ref had gone and blown what seemed like the final whistle and we were going nowhere but home without having fired a shot at the enemy. I remember someone, I forget who, remarking that if only Rick Stackman hadn't got himself in the mess he was in, he'd be the only cove among us who'd be happy with MacArthur's victory.

We cheered ourselves up with the fact that we were on board the *Aitken Victory* on our way to Korea and we hadn't been ordered to turn back. At least we'd reach our intended destination and be able to claim we'd set foot on Korean soil.

We arrived at the port of Pusan the next morning and, somewhat to our surprise, were met by an American Army band playing 'If I Knew You Were Coming, I'd Have Baked a Cake' and a Korean Army band playing 'Waltzing Matilda' with a distinctly Asian flavour. Not to be outdone and pleased to have arrived, a group of blokes from our battalion returned the favour with a rendition of what had become a ditty much favoured by our company, D Company.

*'We're a pack of bastards, bastards are we,*
*We're from Aus-tra-lee-a,*
*The arsehole of the world and all the Universe.*
*We're a pack of bastards, bastards are we,*
*We'd rather fuck than fight for lib-er-tee!'*

At least the Yanks would know we'd arrived. It was fortunate that at the time of this patriotic choral rendition our commanding officer, Charlie Green, was out of earshot, being smothered in garlands of orchids by an official welcoming party of beautiful South Korean women. We assured ourselves, however, that he was a good bloke and would have privately enjoyed the joke.

The battalion was marched to the local station where we boarded an ancient train bound for Taegu where we were to be a part of the 27th Commonwealth Infantry Brigade. At Taegu we were joined by 1st Battalion, the Argyll and Southerland Highlanders and the 1st Battalion, the Middlesex Regiment.

Our first assignment was a behind-the-lines mopping-up operation in an area known as Plum Pudding Hills, which pretty well summed up our despair. A man would never be able to admit that he'd gone to Korea to fight the communists and had ended up doing what essentially amounted to military housework at, ferchrissake, an area named Plum Pudding Hills!

MacArthur, with his rapid victory, had done the dirty on us and we were far from happy little Vegemites.

# CHAPTER THREE

## *A Member of the Club*

Plum Pudding Hills was well named, being plumb in the middle of nothing much happening. Our job was supposed to be rounding up North Korean stragglers, which involved traipsing around aimlessly in the late-autumn sunshine – not bad if you like walking uphill all day carrying your haversack, rifle and full ammo. Maybe some of the other units caught one or two stragglers, but all we came across was a dead enemy soldier already pretty flyblown and high on the nose. We buried him and stuck a stick on his grave and placed one of his canvas boots on the stick. It was the best we could do – noggies aren't Christians so a cross wouldn't have made any sense, and at least the boot would tell anyone interested that a North Korean soldier lay under the little pile of windblown rock.

I guess we were pretty disillusioned – the morning radio was squawking the latest MacArthur pronouncement, and it was obvious that game, set and match wasn't far off. His 1st Cavalry Division was waiting on the border for UN permission to cross, where, if the broadcasts were to be believed, it would be all over in a matter of hours – well days, anyway. The bulletins told how the US Air Force was bombarding the hills on the far side of the 38th parallel where the enemy was in complete disarray.

We were sitting outside our tent attending to our blisters and generally feeling sorry for ourselves when Johnny Gordon suddenly up and said, 'This is bullshit, why don't we go AWL?'

We all looked up in amazement. 'What? Where? You got the urge to go walkabout, Johnny?' Ernie Stone joked.

'Go to the front, see some action. No good here,' Johnny replied.

'What, join the Yanks? Go missing, just like that? Yer mad?' I said.

Then Rex Wilson chimes in, 'Why not!' He turns to Johnny, 'Count me in, mate, bloody sight better than hangin' around this shithole.'

'Hey, whoa, wait on! That's desertion – we'd be court-martialled!' Lance Corporal John Lazarou says, trying to exert his ever-so-trivial rank.

'Yeah, that's if we were doin' a bunk like, you know, cowardice. But that ain't it now, is it? We'd be doin' the exact opposite. Who's ever heard of going AWL to get *into* a stoush with the enemy?' Ernie argued.

At the time Ernie's logic seemed totally compelling. We agreed we'd probably be docked a bit of pay and spend a few days in the guardhouse, but that was a small price to pay for being the first in the battalion – even the first diggers – to get a crack at the enemy.

'Let's do it for Rick Stackman,' Johnny Gordon now volunteered. This was nothing less than a stroke of genius and clinched the matter once and for all. There seemed to be little purpose in pointing out that Rick's problem was with the Japs and we would be fighting North Koreans. I guess, in our minds, we lumped all noggies together and, anyway, it was common knowledge that the Japanese had used Koreans as guards in the POW camps of World War II and that they'd been the cruellest bastards of all. We now had a purpose, you could say, in fact almost a duty to desert to the front. If the army was going to lock Rick up like a common criminal his mates were going to see to it that justice was done and that he was suitably avenged for what the Japs had done to him on the Burma Railway.

That night ten of us got our gear together, grabbed our rifles and slipped out of camp some time after midnight. It didn't take long to hit the main supply route from the port of Pusan to the front. I don't know about the others, but finding myself out on the road knowing I was AWL was a bit scary, but I kept telling myself that I was buggered if I was going to end up fighting in two wars in which I had never seen the enemy or fired a shot in anger. The army owed it to me to give me a chance to go into combat. If they weren't going to do the right thing then I had no option but to take the law into my own hands.

Vehicles of every description clogged the road. If the calibre of Yank soldiers at the time wasn't all that impressive their ordnance sure was: they had more firepower mounted on wheels or tracks than I'd ever seen in one long line. After a while it became apparent that the ten of us hitching a ride were too many in one group so we broke up into two threes and a four and I found myself with Johnny Gordon, Rex Wilson and Ernie Stone, all good blokes to have beside you. We walked for a couple of hours, often outpacing the slow-moving convoy. The dust was awful, almost choking us, clogging our mouths and ears and burning our eyes. We finally managed to get a ride in the back of a five-ton truck. We'd been out looking for stragglers the previous day and I guess the emotion of having gone AWL just after midnight plus the three hours on the road meant we were exhausted and soon fell asleep. Next thing the driver was tapping me on the shoulder to say he'd reached his destination.

'We at the front?' I asked, looking out at a hot dawn sky.

'No, buddy, fifty miles short.' He paused, 'What the hell you guys doing here, anyways?'

'Same as you,' I replied. 'We've come to fight.'

He laughed. 'You're kidding me?'

'Nah, we were getting impatient waiting behind the lines – thought we'd come forward a bit.'

'You guys AWOL?' I guessed he meant AWL.

'Well, yeah, sort of.' It was Rex Wilson who'd just woken and I noted that his face with yesterday's dust was almost as black as Johnny's, and mine must have been the same.

The driver pointed to my slouch hat. 'Regular cowboys, eh?' Then, 'Say, you wouldn't like to sell that hat?'

I was embarrassed, he'd given us a lift and seemed a nice enough guy. Then Rex Wilson chirped up, 'Mate, we're Australians. I'd gladly sell you my wife but not my slouch hat. A digger can't do that.'

'Sure. Well, good luck.' He shook his head, clucking to himself. 'Crazy. You guys are plumb crazy.'

We got our gear together and hopped out of the truck and, in turn, shook his hand and thanked him. 'Wait on,' he said suddenly, and went to the cabin of the truck to emerge moments later with four cartons of Lucky Strike and handed one to each of us.

On a sudden impulse I removed the pin and took the sunrise badge from my slouch hat. 'A keepsake,' I said, handing it to him.

'Crazy, man,' he said, pleased with the small gift. Then, not to be outdone, he removed the badge from his cap and handed it to me. 'Fair exchange – I'll wear yours with pride, buddy.'

'Me too,' I replied as we finally took our leave.

Quite soon after hitting the road we got a lift from another truck that dropped us twenty miles short of the 38th parallel. Here we found ourselves in a bit of a quandary. While there were plenty of trucks going to the brigade headquarters and even one or two going all the way to the forward battalions, reaching either destination and ending in a truck pool where questions would be asked wasn't all that smart. We were likely to run into an officer or even a senior non-commissioned officer who might not take too kindly to four soldiers appearing in their midst wearing the uniform of a foreign army.

'What you reckon we should do?' Johnny asked.

Rex didn't volunteer an opinion. I turned to Ernie, who merely shrugged his shoulders. 'Let's try to get as far up front as possible. They'll be reluctant to kick us out if we've made it all the way.' Then I added, 'The sharp end always needs men. We're four extra rifles, and they can't say no to that.'

There was a sudden roaring, clanking and squealing accompanied by a deep rumble that shook the ground under our feet. Moments later a tank hove into sight over a small rise. We nodded to each other, then removing our slouch hats we waved furiously. Like some great behemoth the tank came to a halt several yards ahead of us and turned its engines off. The commander, perched on the turret, grinned and shouted down at us, 'Last time I saw one o' them hats was in '45 in New Guinea. What can I do for you, boys?'

As all four of us had been in New Guinea we exchanged the usual where, what, how and when, after which we explained our problem. 'Climb aboard, I'm heading for the US 7th Cavalry Regiment and that's about as far forward as you can git without being right up a gook's arsehole.'

A couple of hours later we rumbled up a steep hill, passing US soldiers digging trenches who looked at us curiously. Some of them waved and shouted out but the tank made too much noise for us to hear what they were saying. The Yank troops were digging what looked like a company defensive position. Finally we rumbled to a halt and the commander indicated that we should stick around. 'Stay here, I need to find a way to introduce you guys,' he said, taking his leave.

A couple of GIs came up, 'Yo'all from the Texas Rangers?' one of them asked, pointing at our hats.

'Nah, Australians,' Johnny volunteered. 'Ow yer goin'?'

This started a fairly animated conversation, and others soon came up and joined in the questioning. Next thing the tank commander appeared along with a sergeant.

'Welcome aboard,' the American sergeant said in a friendly voice.

'Thank you, sergeant,' the four of us piped in unison. So far so good.

'Australians, eh?' He pronounced it 'Or-stralian'. He grinned. 'We sure as hell can use some replacements.' He reached out and took my rifle. 'This thing use our ammo?'

'No, sarge,' I replied, 'it takes .303 calibre.'

He handed back the rifle. 'We'll get you issued with M1s.' He gave me a quizzical look. 'Like to show us how you can shoot, soldier?'

'Jacko here can shoot the ticks off a bull's bum at 300 yards,' Rex chimed in.

I turned to him and said, 'Thanks a lot – you'll get yours, mate!'

'Sniper?' the sergeant asked.

'No, sarge, I only completed the sniper's course.' I was more than a bit embarrassed at being singled out and wasn't sure what to say after Rex had big-noted me. I tapped the side of my rifle. 'With this or one of yours?'

He smiled. 'I guess as you're seconded to the 1st Cavalry Regiment you might as well use one of ours.'

'Is that fair?' the tank commander asked.

'It's okay,' I said. In Japan we'd once fired American M1s at rifle practice.

He grinned. 'Spoken like a true marksman.' The sergeant turned to one of the grunts standing near. 'Soldier, bring your rifle over here.' The Yank private brought his rifle over and handed it to me.

'Is it calibrated?' I asked. He nodded. I turned to the sergeant. 'Can I have three shots to make sure, sarge?'

'Never trust another man's rifle, eh?'

My heart was pounding, and I confess I felt a bit of a galah. The sergeant called up a jeep and we drove to the makeshift rifle range, which was just over a small hill. We had to wait about fifteen minutes while a platoon finished using the 500-yard range, and by the time I got down to do the deed the news must have got out and a couple of hundred soldiers had gathered. Someone radioed the butts to put up a target and the sergeant said, 'In your own time, soldier.'

As the Yanks say, 'duck soup'. Given all the time in the world it's pretty hard to miss the red dot, and I squeezed off a shot and the butts signalled back a bullseye.

'Now three separate targets rapid fire,' the Yank sergeant suggested, and someone spoke to the butts again. The rifle felt okay and as the life-size targets came up in various parts of the range they lingered a bit so it wasn't too hard to smack them down.

The sergeant grinned. 'Say, not too bad! Not bad at all, soldier.'

'What about my three practice shots, sarge?' I said cheekily. I was a bit more confident now that I'd succeeded. Out of the corner of my eye I could see a number of American soldiers exchanging dollar notes – they must have been taking bets on me.

He laughed. 'Hell, soldier, we just gave you four!' He turned to my mates and said, 'You three do the same?'

Ernie laughed. 'Hell no, sarge. We're okay, but Jacko's *good*.'

'Nice to have you guys aboard,' the sergeant repeated. He indicated the tank commander and said, 'Orwell here tells me he saw you guys fighting in New Guinea and that you know your way around a battlefield.'

It was a nice compliment and besides, we were dead chuffed that he was going to let us stay. 'Thank you, sergeant, we'll do our best,' Rex replied.

'You'll come in right handy, son,' the American said.

He'd set me up, but I guess that's what sergeants do – otherwise he seemed a nice enough bloke. I thought to myself, *This wasn't exactly the Alamo*, and four extra rifles weren't going to make a scrap of difference, but he'd made us feel welcome, which was more than we could have expected if he'd decided to send us back. It was beginning to dawn on me that what we'd done was likely to get us into a lot more strife than a cursory rap on the knuckles. I turned to the tank commander who'd obviously smoothed the way for us. 'Thank you, sarge.'

'Good luck, boys,' he replied, smiling. 'Remember, the first gook you shoot is for Orwell J. Partridge and for the beautiful state of Idaho.'

We found ourselves adopted by what they referred to as an assault rifle squad, where we were made to dig a foxhole, what we'd call a weapon pit. After that we sat and waited for something to happen. For the next few days we watched the US Air Force putting on the full pyrotechnics as they bombed the hills across the border. One thing you've got to say for the Yanks, they don't do things by halves.

Then, just when it promised to hot up a bit, we got the bad news that the 27th Commonwealth Infantry Brigade had vacated Plum Pudding Hills and was now at Kimpo Airport near Seoul preparing for a move to the front. What's more, they were to be under the command of our adopted division. What this meant was that they'd be crossing the border together with the Americans and our silly shenanigans had been pointless. We were undecided about returning. I argued that it would all be over in a matter of days so, if we stuck it out with the Americans who weren't about to dob us in, by the end of the war, with a bit of luck we may have made enough of an impression for the generous-minded Yanks to put in a good word for us.

'What if we're killed?' Ernie asked.

Johnny grinned. 'Then we'd be heroes, mate. Crims alive, heroes dead, that's the army for yer.'

'We'd get a Yank combat medal – they couldn't exactly drum us out of the Australian Army then, could they?' Rex suggested.

'Don't worry, they'd find a way,' Johnny added ruefully.

'At least it would be another first: "Four dead AIF soldiers given Purple Heart and dishonourable Australian discharge,"' I quipped.

But, all jokes aside, we knew we were kidding ourselves. We were between a rock and a hard place and didn't know what we ought to do next.

However, the decision was made for us. Rex and Ernie were away drawing rations when they were sprung by an American war correspondent who noted their slouch hats and then checked their shoulder tabs and sleeve insignia. After hearing them out he informed them that what they had just given him was a scoop and in a day or two the story of our desertion to the front would be in newspapers around the world.

'We didn't tell them about you two or the others,' Rex said upon their return. 'Ernie and I reckoned if anyone was going to get into the shit it should be us two for getting sprung.'

How they expected to keep Johnny and myself and the rest of the deserters out of it I can't imagine. But, as it turned out, I was grateful for not being mentioned. The news appeared in *The Age* on the 9th of October, and Gloria duly cut it out for her scrapbook. She'd have had the full heart attack if she'd known her eldest son was included. Gloria liked things to be done properly, especially now that she'd turned Catholic and was accountable to a more particular God. It was bad enough me joining the army, but being a deserter, for whatever purpose, especially false heroics, just wasn't on.

## Two Australians hiked to war

TOKYO, OCT. 8.
A correspondent with the United Nations troops near the 38th parallel says that two grimy, stubble-bearded Australian soldiers dug into a foxhole on Saturday and vowed they would be the first foreign soldiers across the 38th parallel.

They are Privates Rex T. Wilson, of Adelaide, and Ernest S. Stone, of Melbourne, who arrived in Korea recently with the first detachment of Australian volunteer troops.

Wilson said: 'We joined up to fight, but when we arrived we found our unit too far from the front line, so we just took off and headed for the noise of the firing.'

Wilson and Stone trudged several miles along the dusty road to the north and then got a ride with the leading tank of a northbound convoy.

Stone said: 'We wanted to be the first Australians over the parallel. Now it looks as though we might even beat the Americans. Anyway, we are going to try.'

*THE AGE*, 9 OCTOBER 1950

We had no choice but to return to our battalion before the newspapers appeared with the story and our own mob came looking for us. It was not far to Kimpo and the Americans arranged for us to get a lift and wished us luck. The original sergeant who'd welcomed us, by the way his name was Crosby Jones Ovington Junior, shook our hands. 'Sorry we couldn't take you along with us, but it's real nice to know you'll be right there at our side. We enjoyed your company, boys.' He grinned, placing his hand on my shoulder. 'You're welcome back any time they let you out of jail.' He presented us each with a Zippo lighter with the 7th Cavalry emblem embossed on both sides. Johnny then presented him with his sunrise badge.

The American Army jeep dropped us on the outskirts of the airfield near Kimpo where our battalion was camped. We'd expected to be frog-marched from the guardhouse to the commanding officer but the battalion was preparing to move to Kaesong, a border town at the front. In the confusion we managed to walk in unnoticed until we got to D Company where we stumbled straight into the arms of Lieutenant Hamill, our platoon commander, who didn't look overpleased to see us.

'Where the bloody hell have you clowns been?' he roared.

We jumped to attention. 'To the front, skipper,' I said.

He seemed somewhat taken aback. 'The front?'

'Yes, skipper!' we chorused.

'Did I hear you correctly? You said you've been to the front?' he repeated slowly.

'US 7th Cavalry Regiment, sir,' Johnny volunteered.

Lieutenant Hamill was silent for a moment, glaring at us. 'Where'd you lose your cap badge, Private Gordon . . . you too, Private McKenzie, what's that thing you're wearing on your hat?'

'Keepsake, skipper,' I said, my voice only just above a whisper.

'Keepsake! A fucking keepsake!' That really sent him off, and what followed was a string of epithets any regimental sergeant major would have been proud to own. Finally he said, 'You're charged with leaving your post – I hardly need to tell you what that means. In the meantime, pack your gear – we're pulling out and moving to the . . .' He paused. 'But then you know where we're going, don't you?' he said with a sneer. 'Perhaps you'd like to show us the way, Private McKenzie.'

Over the next few hours the other six blokes returned, all with much the same story as ourselves. The following day we moved to Kaesong with the rest of the 27th Commonwealth Brigade. We were being referred to as 'the deserters', a thoroughly nasty term in army parlance. The seriousness of what we'd done was becoming increasingly apparent. Notwithstanding, it was a great joke among the blokes in our platoon, who even drew straws to see who would be chosen to man the firing squad. It would have been funny if it wasn't so bloody serious. By now the story had appeared in the morning newspapers around the world. It was a choice little filler – in a war which, up to this point, had been no laughing matter, it was something for people to grin about over their cornflakes.

That same day we were lined up outside company headquarters and had our belts and hats taken from us. Then we were marched in front of the commanding officer, Lieutenant Colonel Charlie Green DSO. We'd just come from a bollocking of the most extreme kind by a combination of the company sergeant major and the regimental sergeant major who, as they say, let their imagination run riot in an effort to find new ways to describe our miserable, worthless lives. In summary, we were a disgrace to our platoon, company, battalion, army and country. Now we stood ready for another verbal onslaught and final sentencing.

The adjutant read the charges, naming each of us, intoning the dreaded words ' . . . that he, whilst on active service on 30th September 1950, did unlawfully leave his post.'

'How do you plead?' said the old man.

We all replied, 'Guilty, sir!'

I got ready for the tirade I was expecting to follow. But instead, Charlie Green sat quietly looking at us fiddling with his fountain pen. After a few moments it became disquieting – any soldier is accustomed to a fair amount of verbal abuse, especially if you know you've got it coming to you. The commanding officer's silence was unnerving, to say the least. My imagination was taking over. *Wish the bugger would say something, anything*, I recall thinking. I could see myself standing in front of a firing squad. Worse still, I could visualise Mum cutting my death notice out of the newspaper and pasting it onto the last tear-splashed page of her war journal, the final pathetic chapter in my brilliant army career where I'd managed to get assassinated by my own side without ever pointing a rifle at the enemy.

When Charlie Green finally spoke he didn't raise his voice but looked directly at us, his tone of voice clearly registering disappointment. 'Well, you've made a right mess of things, haven't you?' he began.

Apart from looking up briefly when I heard his voice I was standing rigidly to attention with my eyes crossed looking straight down the ridge of my nose so that my boots were out of focus. I guess the others must have been doing the same because now he said, 'You'll oblige me by looking at me, please.' I brought my eyes up slowly and was shocked to see he was looking directly at me. 'Private McKenzie, you were in New Guinea weren't you?'

'Yes, sir.'

'So you've been in action?'

'No, sir. I arrived too late, sir.'

'And by absconding to the front you were making up for lost opportunities?'

'Yes, sir . . . er, no sir.'

'Well, I'm not sure I want a soldier like you in my battalion, Private McKenzie.'

He turned to Johnny Gordon. 'Private Gordon, your grandfather had a distinguished career in the Light Horse and was mentioned in dispatches in France. Do you think he'd be proud of you right now?'

'No, sir.'

'And your grandmother, how would she feel?'

'She'd be *real* cranky, sir.'

'Cranky?'

'Ashamed, sir.'

'We're all *ashamed*, private, you've brought my battalion into disrepute and that makes me very ashamed.' How the hell did the commanding officer know about Johnny Gordon's grandma?

He then did the same to every one of us, systematically reducing us all to a state of shocked contrition.

At this point a soldier entered and presented an envelope to the old man by placing it silently on the desk in front of him and then saluting as he left. I could read it upside down and printed in large letters on the outside it read 'URGENT MESSAGE', which is why I suppose the soldier interrupted the orderly room to deliver it.

Charlie Green reached down, picked up the envelope and opened it carefully. You could have heard a pin drop. I don't suppose it took too long to read but to me it seemed to be an eternity, even though I had no idea whether the message it contained had anything to do with us. But when he finally looked up I was left in no doubt.

'Headquarters in Japan have informed me that they are sending over a detachment of military police to escort you back to Hiroshima.' He paused and seemed to look at each of us in turn. 'I don't have to tell you what that means, do I?'

I thought I was going to piss my pants. Apart from being scared, I'd really fucked up this time. All my efforts to fight in a war were suddenly blown to smithereens and I could now expect a court martial and dishonourable discharge to boot. This time I couldn't blame the unfortunate circumstances of my life on Alf dying prematurely or Gloria convincing us we were the proverbial or even Nicole Lenoir-Jourdan exerting her imperious influence over me. I'd managed to be piss-weak and inadequate all on my own.

I barely heard the commanding officer say, 'I shall adjourn this hearing until the military police arrive. March out, regimental sergeant major.'

The regimental sergeant major then ordered us to left turn and quick march and I don't think I've ever felt more ashamed of myself. But, I knew, in the unlikely event that we got a reprieve, that I'd never let Charlie Green down again.

That night and the following day we truly shat ourselves. With the provosts arriving from Japan there could be only one outcome – we were going to face a court martial. We tried to comfort ourselves with the notion that Charlie Green would not have given us the big talking-to if he was simply going to send us off for court martial. But then someone said, 'The brass in Japan wouldn't give a rat's arse about that – they obviously want to make an example of you lot. No commanding officer's gunna go against them.'

I doubt if I slept a wink that night, and I was that nervous the next day that I threw up twice. I couldn't get it out of my mind that Gloria would add this to Alf's big disgrace – in fact, this would supersede the great harmonica judge incident and I'd be the next generation of McKenzie to prove that we were not worth a pinch of the proverbial.

The following boxed insert in a column about the ongoing war appeared in the *Sydney Morning Herald*, and tells the rest of the story.

## Fight to the death

The North Korean Premier, Kim Il-sung, called on the North Koreans today to fight to the death. Kim, who made no mention of the UN surrender demand, said on the Pyongyang radio that the country was facing a grave crisis. He said: 'We must learn from the beautiful example of the Soviet Union, which, after the October revolution, won its victory after a bitter struggle.'

The Communist Chinese Ministry of Foreign Affairs today announced that China 'could not sit idly by with regard to the serious situation created by the UN advance into North Korea.'

*SYDNEY MORNING HERALD*, 12 OCTOBER 1950

## 'Wanderers' forgiven

TOKYO, OCT. 11.
Several military policemen went from Tokyo to Korea to arrest ten Australians who had joined Americans to be the first over the 38th parallel. The commanding officer of the Australian troops, Lieut. Colonel C.H. Green, decided there would be no arrests. The police returned without their men.

*SYDNEY MORNING HERALD*, 12 OCTOBER 1950

I guess, in the end, we got off pretty lightly, thanks to a bloody decent commanding officer who gave us a severe reprimand and docked us two months' pay. Later a rumour spread that the old man had known about the arrival of the provosts from Japan all along. That the entry of the orderly with the message had been staged just so we'd *really* shit ourselves. If this was true, then the success of the ploy exceeded all expectations.

We'd escaped court martial but we were by no means forgiven. Besides the formal punishment we received it was decided that leaving the ten of us in the same platoon was only asking for more trouble. Johnny Gordon, Jason Matthews, John 'Lazy' Lazarou and myself ended up in 7 Platoon, C Company. This was probably the worst punishment of all, as most of the blokes with us were young regulars. Charlie Green had a way of doing things that were unexpected and this was perhaps only a small example, but he knew that bonding with your mates is part and parcel of the army experience; taking them away from you is a very severe punishment.

I'd heard a bit about Charlie Green from the Western Australian K Force blokes who'd served with him in New Guinea. Later I would read up on him. He'd joined the 2nd/2nd AIF at the beginning of World War II and went with them to Egypt where he fought at Bardia and Tobruk. His next theatre was Greece where he was part of the ill-fated expeditionary force, his brigade given the task of delaying the rapidly advancing Germans. He made his escape into the surrounding hills together with the survivors in his company. It was tough going and they were often without food and water as they escaped over the mountains and through insect-infested swamps. With the help of Greek villagers, they finally reached the coast where they managed to get hold of a boat. In a state of total exhaustion and near starvation, sailing by night and hiding in island tributaries by day, they eventually landed on the coast of neutral Turkey.

They had come ashore near a Turkish garrison and were taken into custody where they met the colonel in command. As it turned out, he had fought the Anzacs at Gallipoli where he had learned to greatly admire the bravery of the Australian diggers. Abandoning any pretence of neutrality, the garrison commander fed and cared for them until they'd recovered sufficiently, then issued them with clothes, rations, train tickets and boat passage back to Palestine to join what remained of their unit.

In 1945 Charlie Green was awarded the Distinguished Service Order while commanding a battalion in New Guinea. At twenty-five he was the youngest battalion commander in the 2nd AIF and he'd already been awarded a DSO whereas I, at twenty-four, had escaped being court-martialled by the skin of my teeth and definitely wasn't medal material. What a pathetic comparison.

We arrived in Kaesong where we were told that the UN had given the go-ahead for the Allies to cross the 38th parallel and to attack North Korea. The briefing that preceded the crossing was much too involved for the 'baggy arses', the ordinary soldiers, like me. Charlie Green was a leader who believed his men had a right to know what they were getting into, and I guess he overestimated our intelligence – as our sergeant major frequently pointed out, not a difficult thing to do. Anyway, what it essentially boiled down to was that we were under the ultimate command of the 1st Cavalry Division, a mob of about 16 000 troops. Along with two other divisions of similar strength we would be moving up the main routes leading directly to the North Korean capital Pyongyang some ninety miles north, then a further 120 miles to the Yalu River, North Korea's northern border. We'd either destroy the North Korean army on the way or force them to retreat into China.

We would be advancing up one side of the Korean peninsula, while a similar force moved up the other side. I was too ignorant to ask myself who would be advancing up the centre. As it turned out, this would have been a fair enough question. What the briefing failed to tell us was that a whacking great eighty-mile-wide mountain range ran up the middle of the peninsula like the knobs on a crocodile's back. If the invasion planners regarded the mountains as irrelevant to the combined advance they were about to be proved tragically mistaken.

3RAR set off in a convoy of trucks, our ultimate destination the capital of North Korea with, hopefully, a bit of real action on the way. On our previous journey to the Americans we'd been confounded by the dust, but now the late-autumn rains had turned it into deep mud. Our truck tyres often lost traction or sank into a quagmire, which meant we had to constantly dismount and push. Our boots stuck in the muck that often reached to our knees, whereas the remainder of our bodies became splattered with wheel spin, so by day's end we more closely resembled the mud men I'd encountered in New Guinea than soldiers.

We'd reached about halfway to the capital, Pyongyang, and were about four miles from the town of Sariwon when we heard firing, and soon afterwards learned that the Argylls, one of the British battalions, had engaged the North Koreans. Fierce fighting had broken out and we could hear the machine guns rattling away, then the louder crack of the nine-pounders from their Sherman tanks. The North Koreans appeared to be giving as much as they got, and their firepower seemed as competent and determined as our own. It certainly didn't sound as if the enemy was running away for dear life with its tail tucked between its legs. My earnest hope was that the Brits would call us in to help, but after quite a stoush the Argylls finally broke through the enemy lines and set up in the town. We moved through their position and in the late afternoon dug in five miles north of the town leaving our rear echelon in Sariwon to organise rations.

We were pretty exhausted, having seemingly pushed half the way to our destination, but we'd discovered that an additional punishment for desertion was to be given all the shit jobs around the place. Along with a couple of other miscreants I was sent some distance behind the battalion night defensive position to meet up with the battalion second-in-command. With soldiers from other companies, probably also being punished, we were to meet the resupply trucks coming in from Sariwon.

Our job was to unload them and get our rations and ammunition by jeep, if we were lucky, but as it turned out mostly on foot, back to our company position.

It was already dark when we reached the place where we were to meet and Major Nicholson gathered us around for a bit of a briefing. Then, instead of the sound of the grub vehicles, we heard the unmistakable sound of a great many marching feet.

'Hang on, what's this?' the major said, clearly as surprised as we were.

'Don't march like us or the Americans,' Johnny said. I suppose it was an Aboriginal thing because I couldn't tell if the marching was any different. 'Small men,' Johnny added, 'they's buggered, very tired, hardly lift their feet.'

The major turned on his jeep lights to reveal a battalion, probably more, of North Koreans marching towards us.

'Shit, what now?' I heard John Lazarou say beside me.

It's amazing how the mind focuses at a time such as this. I can clearly recall the surprised face of the North Korean officer as the lights hit him and when moments later he broke into an enormous smile. 'Russki! Russki!' he yelled, thinking we must be the Russians who'd come to their rescue. Bizarre as this incident may sound, it had been the Russians who had trained the North Korean army and who had encouraged them to invade the South. Now this poor, exhausted officer thought they'd put their money where their encouragement had previously been and had come galloping to their rescue.

Freddy Grimmond, another company guide, opened up with his Owen gun, which soon wiped the smile off the noggy officer's face. There was wild panic as the enemy broke ranks and scattered every which way.

Though surprise was on our side we were far from being in the clear. There were only a handful of us and several hundred North Koreans. The major was onto the radio frantically calling for help and was clearly becoming more and more agitated. 'Yes, North Koreans, at least a company!' he kept repeating.

Whoever was on the other end must not have believed him, which was reasonable. Technically speaking the enemy simply couldn't be where we were unless they'd found a way to become invisible when first the Argylls and then 3RAR had come through Sariwon earlier.

While all this was going on the North Koreans seemed as confused as we were and held their fire. The major's call for reinforcements must have finally sunk in because in a short while we could hear the comforting rumble of a tank.

'Wait on,' Major Nicholson said, 'I'm going to meet that tank.' He jumped from the jeep leaving the radio operator behind and telling one of our Korean interpreters to follow him. We watched as he disappeared into the night.

'Good one! What now? What happens if the noggies come for us?' John Lazarou said, his voice just a tad panicky.

'You're in control, Lazy,' Johnny said, smiling. 'You the lance corporal, mate.'

'No I fuckin' ain't!' Lazy protested, 'I lost me stripe when we deserted to the Yanks!'

'If they come at us now we can say our prayers – must be a thousand nogs,' I exaggerated, 'and only a handful of us blokes.' I knew it wouldn't be too long before the nogs caught on that there were very few of us. I wondered how many I might be able to take out with my rifle before I died, as I most certainly would. This wasn't in the script I'd written for my second army career. Even with the extra men the tank might bring, the situation would remain pretty hairy. The North Koreans couldn't retreat and were hell bent on joining up with their comrades – their only chance was to go straight through us and to keep moving north. They were desperate, and we'd been caught with our pants down. I was about to face my maker.

We waited a further five minutes and still the North Koreans hadn't come back at us, and then I witnessed one of the strangest incidents I was to experience in the war. The tank appeared rumbling out of the darkness, moving right past us towards the enemy, its nine-pounder cannon completely silent. On its turret stood Major Nicholson and the Korean interpreter who was yelling out in the local lingo using a loudhailer.

'What's going on?' I asked the radio operator, pointing to our second interpreter beside him.

'He says, the major's telling the nogs they're surrounded and is giving them two minutes to surrender.'

Johnny Gordon was standing listening beside me. I guess there wasn't too much that surprised him, but now he stood open-mouthed watching. 'Well, I'll be buggered,' he said slowly, which were my sentiments exactly.

Inside the required two minutes the North Koreans had surrendered. I'd underexaggerated the enemy force at 1000 men – there were in fact 2000! They turned out to be exhausted, short of food and ammunition and weary of being chased by swooping fighter jets. They'd become accustomed to being the aggressor and winning easy battles against their southern brothers and when they'd come against the initial contingent of Americans and had sent them packing, their egos had become inflated and they'd thought themselves invincible. Now they were taking a hiding and they weren't psychologically prepared for this reversal of fortune.

Major Nicholson received no award for this action, which was bloody pathetic. He should've got at least the Military Cross. Immediately after the surrender, he came over to Johnny Gordon and thanked him.

'Whaffor, boss?' Johnny asked, clearly surprised at being singled out.

'When you made the comment about their marching, saying they were dog-tired, when they revealed themselves as the enemy, that was when I got the idea they might be ready to throw in the towel.' Nicholson gave a short laugh and added, 'Mind you, if I'd known there were 2000 of the buggers I might have had second thoughts.'

It was all very dramatic and we got heaps of kudos for being there, but the fact remained that I hadn't yet fired a shot at the enemy. I was still the virgin soldier and it would be several days before I would finally lose my virginity.

It happened like this. We'd moved all the way to Pyongyang, which had been secured, and were due for rest, which wasn't to be. We were sent off to rescue the 187th Airborne Regiment who had landed twenty-five miles to our north, the idea being to cut off the North Koreans fleeing from Pyongyang. This regiment had been unsuccessful, the enemy having slipped through the net, and so they'd headed south to return to Pyongyang when one of their battalions hit the enemy at the town of Yongju. The fighting was fierce, and the Americans were taking a beating and called for help. The help was us, with the Middlesex battalion leading off the brigade advance. By late afternoon we'd reached Yongju and the Middlesex went into battle, and by the following morning they'd driven the enemy out of the town. As far as I was concerned it was another futile exercise with us sitting on our hands at the rear waiting for a chance to enter the battle. It looked as though the Poms were going to get all the glory.

However, what the Middlesex battalion had effectively done was to drive the enemy back hard against the 187th Airborne, who'd already had more than a gutful. Now the Americans found themselves under a renewed and even more frenzied attack. Again they called for help and our time had come, 3RAR was going into battle at last. What's more, it was our company's turn to lead the battalion. We advanced mounted on Sherman tanks and trucks. This was the real thing, and my mind tried to take in every detail. The road headed north along a valley floor divided into paddy fields, the usual Asian scene. The harvest had been completed and the fields were now covered with a yellow stubble with rice hay stooks dotted over them, some standing as high as a man. About a mile out of town a rounded spur line came sweeping down from the distant high ground and approached the road. The spur line was covered with apple trees. Funny that, rice paddies are Asian but apple trees are us – you don't think of apples being something Asians go for. Which is silly, of course, but that's what I was thinking when suddenly all hell broke loose from the direction of the apple orchard. We'd almost driven past it when they sprang the ambush. *Jesus, this is it!* I thought. *We're under attack!* I remember landing with a thump as I jumped from the tank, propelled forwards, almost losing my balance as my haversack jerked up to hit me behind the head. I took cover and started to return their fire. It took only a couple of shots for me to think, *This is it, mate! This is what's taken five, nearly six years to bring about*. I was much too excited to be afraid.

I could hear in the background our company commander yelling to Lieutenant Hamill, our platoon commander. Immediately after he began yelling orders to the section commanders. It seems we're going to take them on. It's a company attack with our mob, 7 Platoon, on the left and 8 Platoon on the right, with 9 Platoon pressing on up the road to protect our flank. I find myself thinking, *I'm in a platoon of young regulars, will they be up to what's ahead?* Which, in retrospect, was pretty arrogant – I should have been asking the same question of myself. We're in a heap of trouble as we have no supporting artillery or mortar fire because we're not sure where the 187th Airborne is exactly. Some smart-arse yells out, 'Why doesn't someone get on the radio and ask the Yanks their position?'

Back comes the answer, 'We bloody have, the buggers don't know!'

I'm comfortable enough, well concealed behind a paddy bund with a good sighting of the orchard, the familiar feel of my rifle butt hard into my shoulder giving me confidence. If I see any movement in the orchard he's mine, sharpshooter McKenzie is in his element at last.

But then the order comes to line up behind the paddy bund. 'Shake out, five yards apart!' our platoon sergeant yells and then unnecessarily, 'One up the spout!'

Then the order echoes along the line, 'Fix bayonets!'

There's a series of loud clicks as we comply. I look to the left and right. It's quite a sight, there's a line of us about 200 yards long, our long greatcoats flapping as we begin to walk steadily towards the enemy, our rifles held in front of us, bayonets pointing to the sky.

The nogs aren't stupid – they see what's coming and the mortar shells are starting to explode around us. Only a few moments and they'll adjust onto us and then the shit will *really* hit the fan. Then we're off. No matter how much you practise assaulting in line, nothing prepares you for the actual moment when you're out in the open moving towards the enemy. You're quite certain that you've just grown to the size of a truck, a can't-miss target for the waiting enemy. Funny, I'm not scared but I can feel my heart pumping overtime. Bullets are buzzing around us, *Just like bees in an apple orchard*, I think to myself. It's a feeble private joke. A bullet hits the dirt beside me and sends a splash of mud against my arm. I can see the nogs in the apple orchard jumping out of their weapon pits, which is an absolute no-no when repulsing an attack and can only mean they're green, inexperienced. They've become overexcited and feel trapped just sitting waiting for us. I can't believe our luck – now they're no better protected than we are. 'We're coming, you bastards!' I hear myself yelling. They're firing from the hip and any way they can instead of calmly lining us up and picking us off, one at a time.

'Charge!' The order comes. Now there's a screaming chorus of 'charge!' and a heap of other choice epithets as well and we're all running, not thinking. My .303 rifle feels about ten feet long with its bloody great steel bayonet catching the light. I see a nog jump out of a trench not far in front of me and I drop to the ground not even feeling the impact. I don't know if he's coming for me or is about to bolt. All the hours on the range are about to pay off. I line him up, the foresight drops neatly into the 'U' of the backsight, and I squeeze the trigger. The nog drops like a bunny rabbit. I'm up, feeling weightless, excited, yet in control. It's a combination I've never before experienced – frenzy and calm, a contradiction in terms that somehow works in this situation.

I leap to my feet. Everything seems effortless, almost as though I'm being carried along. A bunker appears immediately ahead and Johnny starts pouring Owen fire down it. *Rrrit-rrrit-rrrit-rrrit*! I pull the pin out of a grenade and lob it in and we go to ground. *Boom!* I hardly hear either sound as we jump to our feet and run on. My section leader is yelling, 'Give covering fire! Give covering fire!' I see him firing alone at two nogs in a trench who are firing back, bullets kicking up soil around him. We drop down and take the two North Koreans on and, with us coming at them from a different direction, the two nogs duck for cover just long enough for Jason Matthews and John Lazarou to charge in and take them out with their bayonets and move on sticking another three with the big blade.

The fire is becoming heavier now, coming from the enemy further up the hill. Bullets are smacking around us like a hailstorm and we're having trouble moving forward. Over to our right I see gunner Angus McGregor, who doesn't appear to give a stuff about the machine-gun fire. He's firing from the hip and charging into a pit where he digs out a couple of nogs on the point of his bayonet. As I watch, not yet game to follow, he heads for an apple-picker's hut and bursts through the door firing like you see in the movies, only this is for real. Angus is out there in front of us taking the enemy on by himself. His foolhardy courage is just what we need, and we're up and into them again. We fight on, pit by pit. The front lot of nogs may have been green, but further in they're seasoned fighters and we're facing strong resistance. Then suddenly, as sometimes happens in battle, there's enemy running everywhere. They've had enough, and it's every man for himself – the bayonets have panicked them big time.

We continue to fight our way to the top of the spur line against token resistance and just as we think the nogs are done for, the skipper hails into view shouting for us to regroup. On the road 9 Platoon is copping it from nogs concealed in the dry paddy fields below. The section commanders are calling us into line and we head down the hill. We hit the paddy fields and straighten our line. I recall I stepped into a still-muddy patch in the dry paddy and slipped, landing on my arse. I got up and lined up with the rest and thought no more about it. The enemy hidden behind the stooks must have seen our bayonets flashing in the sun and as we prepare to charge they panic, blow their cover and begin to run. We pick them off with rifle fire and soon they've got their hands up by the score and we begin to round them up.

Or more precisely, some of the other blokes do the rounding-up. I've suddenly gone flat, like someone has punched me hard in the gut, taken the wind out of me. I can't see too clearly and then I just sort of collapse, sink to my knees and throw up. Johnny comes over. 'You done good, Jacko,' he says, squatting down and placing his hand on my shoulder. 'Never mind about shittin' your pants, mate, it happens to all of us.' He's mistaken the wet patch where I'd slipped in the rice paddy for you know what. 'Anyway,' he says, 'welcome to the club.'

Then the skipper comes up, grinning. 'Well done, Jacko,' he says.

'It's not shit, skipper, it's mud . . . I slipped in the paddy field,' I protest gratuitously.

Now they're all laughing. 'That's what they all say,' John Lazarou says to further laughter. Needless to say I wasn't allowed to live it down, and henceforth the platoon's term for a visit to the latrines became 'Goin' for a slip in the paddy'.

Later we hear that Charlie Green had deployed three other companies as well as us and effectively blocked the North Korean retreat. One hundred and fifty of the enemy are dead and 239 captured. In turn, we've got seven men wounded, no dead and so, you can imagine, we feel pretty damned pleased with ourselves.

The only down side is that now our platoon will have to hear the never-ending saga of John Lazarou's successful bayonet charge 'Jab! Jab! Left then right! You should've heard them noggy bastards squealin'!' He's working up to the full Audie Murphy scenario where, after the first day's retelling he's already forgotten that Jason Matthews was at his side taking out three nogs to the two he managed to kill. Lazy didn't shut up about his warrior status till weeks later when it was announced that Private 'Gunner' Angus McGregor had been awarded the Military Medal. I obtained a copy of the citation which I read out to Lazy to the joy of the rest of the platoon who'd gathered around to watch him squirm.

*Yongu, 22 October 1950*

*Private McGregor was under heavy fire for two hours and displayed utter disregard for his personal safety. During the assault by his platoon he moved forward bayoneting and shooting a number of the enemy. Throughout the engagement his courage and determination were an inspiration to the younger, inexperienced men in his platoon.*

By the way, we finally made contact with the lost 187th Airborne Regiment who, while not far away, had played no part in the battle we'd just won in the bid to rescue them. Which was probably a good thing – they'd had a torrid time and compared to us seemed like sixteen-year-old kids, though I imagine they'd done a fair bit of growing up over the past forty-eight hours and deserved to sit this one out. When it came to growing up, I guess I'd done a bit myself in the final three hours of the six years it had taken me to finally fire my rifle at a bona fide enemy and so earn my membership of the club.

# CHAPTER FOUR

## *The First Winter*

The day following the Battle of the Apple Orchard the skipper told us – that is, the four deserters – that we were going back to D Company. 'They've copped a fair whack from the flu and are short of men, with no reinforcements coming through,' he explained. 'I'll miss you – you were good for the young blokes, a steadying element.'

When we arrived back at our old company our reception this time was different. It seemed they'd heard about our deeds at Apple Orchard, which in translation had become somewhat exaggerated, Angus McGregor's glory having rubbed off on us as well. Unfortunately, so had the story of me shitting in my pants and blaming it on a slip in the rice paddy. It was hopeless trying to deny it, as the expression 'Going for a slip in the paddy' had already been adopted, and I copped a fair bit of teasing. Still, with it came a new respect – the four of us had been in a big stoush and we'd covered ourselves in glory. Not quite mentioned in dispatches, but nevertheless pretty good and getting better with each telling.

I'm told that an adrenaline high settles down pretty quickly and your metabolism goes back to normal as soon as the stimulus is exhausted. All I can say is, it took two days for me to truly come down from the Battle of the Apple Orchard. One of the abnormal indications was that I was ravenous all the time, whereas, being a little bloke, my appetite has never been large. As a kid, Gloria would often comment that I ate like a bird. Unfortunately this craving for food coincided with a tucker crisis brought about, or so the skipper said, by our rapid advance towards the North Korea/China border where poor roads meant the supply system couldn't cope. This meant we were stuck with American B rations – tins of food designed to be cooked centrally and served hot to the troops. Which would have been okay if we'd been in one place long enough for the cooks to set up field kitchens. As it was, we had to eat our rations on the move.

Each of the oversized tins contained a single item: braised steak in one, carrots in another, potatoes in a third, peas in yet another so that, in the hands of an army cook, they could be turned into a meat, potatoes and two-veg dinner. But that's not what happened. The tins arrived at company headquarters, and each contained maybe five servings of something or other, but for some unknown reason they'd all lost their labels. At company headquarters they'd divide these anonymous tins into platoon lots, where they were again divided into section lots and then split and distributed, two tins to each weapon pit. So every two blokes would end up with ten servings in combination of something contained in two unlabelled cans. 'You'll just have to share what you get amongst the other blokes in your platoon,' our sergeant declared unhelpfully.

But hungry soldiers are selfish buggers and the tucker lucky dip didn't work quite like that. If you copped a tin of braised steak and another of potatoes you'd won the lottery and ate like a veritable prince, with blokes lining up to swap generous portions of whatever they had in return for a tiny serve of meat and spuds from your five-star weapon-pit restaurant. But should you end up with five servings of boiled carrots and five of pickled cucumber you faced potential starvation. Which is what happened to me. In my ravenous after-battle state when I could have eaten a horse, our weapon pit, John 'Lazy' Lazarou and myself, received a tin of beetroot and one of stewed tomatoes, both guaranteed to be non-negotiable items at any swap meet.

There never was a truer saying than 'An army marches on its stomach'. The two days after the battle were less than memorable and I became thoroughly miserable. Beetroot and stewed tomato is one of the less gratifying combinations in the lexicon of edible food. It was a good thing I'd drawn Lazy as my partner in the pit, as sensitivity wasn't one of his more noticeable characteristics – he didn't seem to notice my bad humour. Moreover, he relished the beetroot and tomato combination, piling his tin plate high and to the edges and often having a second helping. 'Makes you piss pink and shit red,' was his only comment.

However, on the third day on our way north the rations caught up with us and we were issued twenty-four-hour ration packs – one man's rations for a day and a vast improvement, I can tell you. But if the food improved, so did the enemy. The deeper we pushed into North Korea the better prepared they were. At Apple Orchard the enemy had been on the run, hungry, demoralised and lacking the determination needed for a sustained resistance. But now we met an entirely different opposition. These enemy nogs were well prepared for us. They'd marshalled more tanks and artillery and, more importantly, were determined to hold their ground. A man protecting his home and hearth is a far more determined foe than one fighting over neutral or impersonal territory. We, that is the Commonwealth Brigade, were leading the Allied army to the north with 3RAR in the very front and so could expect to take the full brunt of the enemy forces.

This proved to be the situation with our next encounter at the Battle of the Broken Bridge, my first experience of night fighting. This battle was for the high ground overlooking a vital crossing point on the Taeryong River. My platoon's part in the battle was to protect American engineers building a ford not far upstream from the crossing. I was at battalion headquarters waiting to guide signallers laying telephone cable to D Company headquarters. Across the river the battle was raging and they needed reinforcements. A group of us were hastily bundled in with a reserve platoon and sent across the river.

Fighting in the dark is an entirely different experience. Apart from the celestial pyrotechnics, their artillery and ours competing against a blistered night sky, I seemed to be firing at nothing substantial, at muzzle flashes, noises made by movement, the estimated source of the lines of a tracer bullet and shadowy figures that I half-suspected were imagined. But I need not have been concerned – by morning's light, when their attack was spent, around one hundred enemy dead lay outside our perimeter, though how many had been killed by small arms and how many by mortars and artillery was anyone's guess. Nevertheless, the North Koreans proved comprehensively that they were no pushover and we began to realise that MacArthur's easy path to victory was not to be taken for granted. These soldiers were not afraid to fight.

Broken Bridge was followed three days later by a battle at Chongju, a town some sixty miles from the Chinese border. The North Koreans were desperate to stop us and they'd dug their trenches deep with overhead cover. They'd also dug their tanks into the side of the hill, a good indication that they didn't intend to retreat any further and experience the humiliation of being forced to flee into China.

Charlie Green was proving to be a very effective battalion commander. There were several blokes in the company who'd fought in battles under diverse commanders, some going all the way back to the early part of the siege of Tobruk and the battle of El Alamein in World War II. They'd seen most of the leadership the army throws up and reckoned Charlie Green had 'the touch'. The general consensus was that Green was a rare bird indeed, a leader who thought his way through a battle, adapting to the conditions and unafraid to improvise. At Apple Orchard he'd quickly realised that speed was the way to win – quick, decisive action with bayonets to overwhelm an already demoralised enemy. At the Battle of the Broken Bridge he'd taken the initiative and risked sending two companies across the river during the night to grab the high ground overlooking the crossing, knowing that if the enemy got there first it would be twice the fight to get them down off the top. Now, at Chongju, Charlie Green realised that the nogs were going to make a stand and so he put in four hours of air strikes and a heavy barrage of artillery fire before sending us in with platoons of American tanks.

They say you grow up quickly in combat and you know you're a competent soldier when you finally realise that good leadership, air superiority and all the artillery cover you think you're going to need will not win a battle. The only element that finally counts is a line of infantry off their scones with a mixture of fear and the peculiar sustained excitement that comes with a natural injection of adrenaline pumping through your bloodstream.

In the end you're it. Muggins here has the job to dig the enemy out of their trenches with bullet and bayonet and you know that he's got cover and you haven't. You're out in the open coming towards him and he's tucked out of sight with his rifle or machine gun steadied and waiting. However clever the battle plan, and however well you're trained as a fighting unit, you know some of your mates are going to be killed or wounded and some are not going to be there in the end – and that you may be among the dead or casualties.

The veterans have a saying that has become a hoary old combat cliche, which nonetheless remains army lore: 'If the bullet has your name on it there's nothing you can do about it.' You can be reckless in a battle but you can't be careful. You can throw away your life by trying to be a hero but you can't preserve it by exercising extreme caution.

For all our cleverness and skill in the advance to the north, the battalion had so far suffered nine blokes killed and sixty-nine wounded. Going into the Chongju battle, with the enemy determined to make a stand, we knew the number of dead and wounded was likely to increase significantly. This proved to be the case – we lost several more men and suffered a lot more wounded before driving the enemy further north. By normal combat standards our casualties were light and, as a consequence, Charlie Green had yet another feather in his cap. A message of congratulations arrived for the battalion from the divisional commander: 'Congratulations on your sensational drive into enemy territory.' I guessed Green would soon add a second gong to his DSO.

Nice as this accolade was, we were battle-weary and happy enough to relinquish the lead to another battalion and grab a rest. Leading an advance is a pretty nerve-racking business. You're at the sharp end all the time and constantly concerned that, if things go wrong, you'll let down those that follow you. Nobody says it aloud, but it becomes a matter of pride – you don't want to be seen to have been caught with your pants down and be forced to radio for help. We told ourselves, perhaps foolishly, that Australians didn't do that sort of thing.

We may have lacked training at the beginning but there's nothing like a battle or two to knock the rust off and get down to the true mettle, if you'll pardon the pun. By now the Regular Army and K Force blokes were indistinguishable. Under Charlie Green we'd become combat-hardened and we were regarded by the other battalions as a crash-hot fighting unit. A battalion is formed of a group of disparate men, and Green had forged us into a bloody good team. A good commander gives a soldier a lot of confidence – he was definitely one of the best, and we loved him for it.

When you finally pull up for a rest and are no longer on high alert you realise for the first time how very weary you are. Putting it crudely, we were buggered. We dug in not far from Chongju, happy to put our feet up for a couple of days and let someone else take the responsibility.

But there's no rest for the wicked. Our new-found hero status soon disappeared, and we 'deserters' were still copping all the extra jobs around the place. Once the army has your number there's nothing private about being a private, there's simply no letting up. 'Private McKenzie, get up to headquarters and guide the sigs back to us,' our platoon sergeant, Ivan Freys, predictably known as 'Ivan the Terrible', instructed.

The battalion headquarters was tucked in safely behind a ridge line. I arrived to find the place a hive of activity – trenches being dug, tents erected and signal lines being laid. Even while resting, Charlie Green was a stickler for order and didn't like a slack-looking camp. I was in the process of briefing the signals sergeant when there was an explosion on the ridge directly above us, and I immediately hit the deck. The sergeant grinned down at me. 'Get up, soldier, you're safe enough here.' In what was considered more a nuisance than a real danger, the soldiers digging in on the ridge line above became an occasional target for an enemy tank or self-propelled gun. Every once in a while a shell would whistle high overhead or, as had just occurred, one would land on the forward slope. I stood up a little sheepishly, brushing the dirt from the front of my battle dress as I continued to brief him. 'Righto then, we'll attend to it shortly,' he said finally. I thanked him and turned to leave when another shell must have clipped the top of the ridge and diverted into a tree, sending bits of tree and shrapnel showering over headquarters below. There was momentary panic with soldiers everywhere hitting the deck, but it soon became apparent that nobody was hurt.

I looked up and grinned at the signals sergeant lying beside me wearing a mouthful of dirt. 'What was that bit about safety, sarge?'

'Don't be cheeky, son,' he said smiling, wiping the grit from his mouth.

Then we noticed several officers running towards Charlie Green's tent. A piece of shrapnel had ripped into his stomach. As they say in the army, Green was in the wrong place at the wrong time – the terrible irony being that for once in his life he was taking a rest. Our beloved commanding officer, the only casualty from the errant shell, was severely wounded and died two days later.

We were pretty choked up about his death and, when the news came that the Commonwealth Brigade was to step aside to allow the US 24th Division to pass through Chongju and head north for the border less than sixty miles away, we were mad as a cut snake. Battle fatigue notwithstanding, a couple of days' rest was all we reckoned we needed. We'd done all the hard yards, borne the full brunt of the advance, lost several dead including our beloved leader and suffered a lot more wounded, but we'd fought well and now the powers that be were going to let the Yanks take all the glory. Besides, we told ourselves we wanted to do it for Charlie Green. Now the Yanks would become the photo opportunity for the world's tabloids. It would be Iwo Jima all over again, with the marines beautifully posed and back-lit, raising the

Stars and Stripes on a cairn of carefully constructed rock, only this time on the China border. The world's photographers would be flown in to bear witness, with *Life* and *Look* magazines and the *Saturday Evening Post* along with the *New York Times* and United Press given the front positions with *The Age* and the *Sydney Morning Herald* on tiptoe at the back, their camera lenses peeping through a jostle of massed shoulders.

We were carrying on a treat about the Yanks grabbing the glory when it occurred to me that perhaps we weren't being entirely fair. 'Wait on,' I said, 'we've been made to fight bloody hard to get this far, the nogs are no pushover and the Yanks have still got sixty miles to go. Who says they won't do it tough?'

'You're not much of a map reader, are you, McKenzie?' It was Ivan the Terrible, our ever-loquacious platoon sergeant who specialised in putting people down. 'I'd have thought a bloody know-all like you would have the intelligence to consult a map before opening yer mouth.'

Several blokes rolled their eyes – the bastard couldn't help himself.

Now he removed a map from his map pocket and opened it up. 'Here, take a dekko at this.' His stubby finger ran across a short stretch of the map he held covering the distance to the border North Korea shared with China. 'See that? Nothing but flat land. There's nowhere for the nogs to put up any sort of defence – hardly a rise an ant could hide behind. It's an easy stroll to the border, then it's "lights, camera, action" – all the glory for the bloody Yanks.'

'Bloody typical! Uncle Sam stealing the show!' Ernie Stone remarked in disgust.

It wasn't the first time we'd been sidelined when it became time to call in the photographers. Our brigade had been in the lead during the advance to Pyongyang when we were sent on a mysterious detour while the 1st Cavalry Division did the victory march into the city. Gloria, as usual, cut the pictures out, happy with the thought that her son had been nowhere near the action leading up to the capture of the city.

It wasn't all doom and gloom – a couple of the blokes had family in Japan and you could see they were happy the war would soon be over, and didn't give a damn who got the kudos. 'Catflap' Buggins was also walking around grinning like he'd just won a chook raffle. Ever since we'd departed from Japan he'd had only one subject on his mind – an acrobatic little Japanese love-making machine from the Full Moon Bar in Kure. His previous nickname had been 'Stubby', which physically described him perfectly. But ever since Japan he'd regaled us endlessly with his various sexual exploits, and so Buggins' nickname had been changed to 'Catflap', in reference to those little two-way flaps built into the laundry or kitchen door to let the cat out, because the only subject ever to come out of his mouth was pussy.

'Lotus Blossom here I come!' he announced happily on hearing the news.

'Lotus Blossom?' several of us chorused.

'So? What's wrong with that?' Catflap asked defensively.

'Mate, that's only in musicals! Is that *really* her name?' Jason asked.

'Nah, that's what I call her.' He paused, looking pleased with himself. 'Wanna know why?'

We agreed we did. For once in his life Catflap wasn't talking in female anatomical terms but showing a genuine romantic streak, which I must say surprised us all.

'I done it because her little pink petals open up for me at night. Clever, eh?'

Catflap hadn't let us down.

But the army did. The 24th Division's dream of front-page fame, and Catflap's prospects of further sexual adventure with his little native of Japan, were to be dashed. The Americans were only halfway to the border when the order came to withdraw.

'Withdraw? Fuckin' withdraw?' John Lazarou shouted, when we were given the news. 'All I wanted was one more go at the bastards with me bayonet!' He still hadn't let up about his exploits at Apple Orchard, which by now included an entire nog platoon speared, kebab-like, on the end of his bayonet.

We'd made the usual infantryman's mistake: judging the state of the war by our own immediate experience of the enemy. We'd been successful in battle so had concluded the same must be true for all the other divisions. The skipper, Lieutenant Hamill, called us all together for a briefing. Charlie Green had always insisted that everyone must be kept informed – that is, see the big picture as well as the bit that's your responsibility – and the skipper was maintaining the tradition after Green's death.

'Okay, listen in!' he said. 'We're pulling back, and here's why.'

He'd made a model on the ground with piled dirt for hills, sticks for roads and signal wire for the rivers. 'You will recall about twenty-five miles back on the road to Chongju we crossed two rivers that flowed quite close together,' he began.

One of these crossings was in the general proximity of the Battle of the Broken Bridge and we didn't exactly have to remind ourselves where it was.

'Right then,' he continued, 'both these crossings are effectively the only point an army can cross at this time of the year. You will recall that with the recent rains both rivers are flowing swiftly, and that's the immediate problem. But more importantly, these crossings are a choke point, a classic bottleneck, which is a bloody nuisance for an advancing army but a disaster if we have to withdraw.'

He then explained that up to now these two choke points had been only of minor concern. 'We were winning the war and, at most, they somewhat inhibited our supply lines,' he said. Then he hit us with the bad news. 'That's no longer the case, lads. There have been some disturbing reversals on our right flank.'

He explained that some fifty miles to the east, the 6th Republic of Korea (ROK) Division, the South Koreans on our side, were in retreat, their soldiers abandoning their weapons and fleeing towards the two choke points. Furthermore, their 7th and 8th divisions were hanging on by the skin of their teeth twenty miles upstream from the crossings and about to make a run for it and were likely to collide with their 6th Division. But that wasn't all. A bit further to the north the 1st ROK Division, together with the US 1st Cavalry Division, while not yet retreating, were not making any headway and were beginning to look decidedly vulnerable. They too might soon be on the run. 'Put in simple terms, the crossings are under threat. Our lot and the US 24th Division are being withdrawn from the advance to protect these two vital choke points.'

It didn't take too much brain power to realise that if the enemy held these two points, anyone trying to cross would be decimated. Then Ivan the Terrible asked the question that was on everyone's mind except perhaps for John Lazarou's, because he didn't have one. 'Sir, we've managed to send the North Koreans packing on our front – how come they've suddenly grown such sharp teeth, winning on all the other fronts?' he asked.

His reply stunned us all. 'They haven't, sergeant. The Chinese have entered the war.'

This may not have meant a whole lot to the other blokes, except that now we faced a new enemy, and the likelihood of the war being over in a few more days was probably no longer the case. I knew a bit about China, thanks again to the redoubtable Nicole Lenoir-Jourdan who'd always been a bit of a China buff. She'd made me read a fair bit of Chinese history, starting way back with Marco Polo, then the Opium Wars against the British, where surprisingly she'd always taken the side of the Chinese. Then, as I grew a little older, she'd introduced me to current Chinese politics, the struggle between Chiang Kai-shek, who ruled most of China in the 1930s, and the communist upstart, Mao Zedong, who turned out to be one of Lenoir-Jourdan's favourites. I also learned that the ideological scrap between these two Chinese leaders was interrupted in 1937 when the Japanese, who had already annexed Manchuria, pushed south into China proper. In what was, to say the least, a curious alliance, the two factions joined forces to fight the invader.

Later, after I'd joined up and returned from New Guinea, Nicole Lenoir-Jourdan was back onto her favourite subject, which had now become the Long March by Mao Zedong. Thinking back, she was probably responsible for my initial sympathy for the communist cause.

I recalled how late in 1949 I'd been driving a DC8 bulldozer in a road construction crew, one of the many unsatisfactory jobs I'd had after the war. I was taking it back to the government works depot in Baldwin for a service, lumbering along and just about to enter the outskirts of the town, when I was confronted by my nemesis standing in the middle of the road. She was holding up the Hobart *Mercury* and shouting at me. Unable to hear what she was saying above the engine noise and, besides, I was about to flatten her, I ground the bulldozer to a halt and switched off the ignition.

'Look, Jack McKenzie! Look!' she shouted excitedly. The front page of the newspaper she held up read: 'COMMUNIST VICTORY IN CHINA!'

'We've won! Look, we've won!' Nicole Lenoir-Jourdan's pin-up boy had won the war and Chiang Kai-shek had fled to Formosa, which, of course, later became Taiwan.

Now, with China suddenly our enemy, I recalled the details of the People's Liberation Army. The Americans had backed Chiang Kai-shek, pouring hundreds of millions of US dollars into his cause all in the name of democracy, just as they were now doing in Korea. Despite America's support, Chiang's armies had been crushed, no match for the resourceful, hardened and enormously courageous communists. And then I remembered, at the end of the civil war Chairman Mao's army stood five million strong!

'Crikey, skipper!' I suddenly blurted out. 'The Chinese have an army of millions and they're still on a war footing, have been for twenty years. What now?'

Some of the blokes in our platoon looked around, probably thinking I was back to being a bloody know-all.

'In that case, Jacko, you'll be glad to know our intelligence estimates only about 20 000 Chinese volunteers are involved,' he replied.

This was small comfort. I knew that Chinese 'volunteering' wasn't the same as K Force. The number of fighting men who crossed the border to help their communist cousins in Korea would be entirely at the discretion of Chairman Mao. Who, quite apart from his opposition to capitalism, had every reason to dislike the Americans. It didn't take a whole heap of brains to realise that the Korean War had taken a turn for the worse.

We'd barely occupied our new position upstream from one of the crossings near the town of Pakchon when the Chinese swept in from the east. They headed for the gap between the Commonwealth Brigade and the unit on our right flank where they overran an American artillery position and took occupation of a hill overlooking the road. What they'd effectively achieved in one fell swoop was to cut off our withdrawal route and threaten the crossing. The call came for 3RAR to push them off the hill. We had no artillery support but called in the Mustangs from Australia's 77 Squadron who swooped in above the attacking troops, rocketing and strafing the hilltop held by the Chinese.

I won't go through the cut and thrust of battle – this was an attack similar to the Battle of the Apple Orchard and at Chongju. The Chinese were dug in snug as a bug in a rug on a bloody great hill and here we were, the mug infantry with rifle and bayonet going in against what were the most battle-hardened troops in the world. The call came and we were at them with our bayonets, which they didn't like a bit. They fought hard and didn't panic like the exhausted nogs at Apple Orchard, but in the end the dreaded pig-sticker did the job and we drove them off.

As they scampered back down the hill their retreat became my first true sighting of the Chinese hordes, the so-called yellow peril Australians were always being told about and which, at the coming of Federation in 1901, was the primary reason for our White Australia Policy. I watched as the sun set over the enemy our grandad had warned would one day come to get our abalone. True to my boyhood imagination, as the sky behind us bathed them in gold, they literally became the yellow peril. Though I must say it didn't seem to worry our blokes what colour peril they were taking on. This early success against the Chinese made me think that maybe you can read too much into these things.

We were soon to learn that Chairman Mao's boys didn't fight like their Korean cousins. That night a couple of thousand counterattacked, determined to knock us off the hill to get to the vital crossing. It was a moonless night and as we sat waiting in the dark I heard their bugle calls and whistle blasts as they marshalled their troops into position in the rice paddies below us. I must say, it was all a bit spooky. No commands shouted out, just the bugles and whistles. Then the attack commenced. A parachute flare sent up by mortar floated down, illuminating the scene. Line upon line of Chinese infantry were leaving the valley and invading the slope below us. I watched as the parachute dropped and their shadows lengthened, giving the appearance of huge dark insects crawling along the ground, coming for us. They wore these canvas rubber-soled boots, so the sound of their advance became a sort of muted thunder, like a storm heard at some distance.

It was a torrid fight made all the more difficult by the darkness, and could have swung their way on several occasions. By two a.m. they'd suddenly had enough. Bugles sounded and whistles blew and the chinks were gone.

The following morning at the debrief the skipper told us that the battalion had suffered a lot of casualties – sixteen killed and three times that number wounded. In war, news of the death of your comrades is inevitable but it doesn't make it any easier to take. You immediately think it could have been you or your best mate, and it's extra tough if you knew one of the blokes who copped his dose of eternity. But there was something to take out of the fight. The skipper pointed out that, what with the previous day and now the night, we were the first United Nations unit to give the Chinese a good kick in the arse.

'How many chinks we get?' someone asked.

'We, or the battalion?' the skipper queried.

'The battalion.'

The skipper seemed to be thinking. 'It's not that easy. We reckon a lot, a real lot. They sustained heavy losses, but quite how many we'll never know – they took almost all their dead and wounded with them.'

There was a general murmur among the platoon. You didn't need to be Einstein to know that these blokes were different. Like us they respected their dead and wounded, and that made them well and truly a cut above the other nogs who left their dead and dying on the battlefield.

As nothing seemed more certain than that the Chinese would attack again, we started patrolling immediately to try to find out what the enemy was up to. We'd witnessed their determination to achieve their objective and reckoned they weren't beyond having another crack at reaching the crossings. We moved forward cautiously, first setting up a battalion position then patrolling forward for a day or two before setting up again and moving further forward. The weather was getting increasingly cold, in fact colder than most of us had ever experienced. We began to realise that we were about to encounter an even more dangerous enemy than the Chinese – the Korean winter.

I'd had some previous experience of cold. On Queen Island in the winter with a gale-force westerly whipping up the seas, the cold seems to get right into your bones. If you are laying or emptying craypots in an open boat you certainly know what cold weather is all about. Now I thought of such conditions almost with affection – the cold that descended upon us at Pakchon was of a totally different order.

I don't know how one measures degrees of cold. 'Biting cold' is too mild a way to describe it; 'vicious, flesh-tearing, jaw-snapping cold' is getting a little closer. If you spilt a mug of steaming tea it would freeze the moment it hit the ground. If you needed a slash you didn't dare expose your penis to the elements more than to let a very small part peep out of your trousers, and that well protected with a thumb and forefinger wrapped in thick woolly gloves. The moment your piss hit the ground it froze. John Lazarou swore blind that his froze while still in the air, hitting the ground as a frozen arc before shattering into shards of pale-yellow ice.

You could wrap up most of your body but you could do nothing about your feet. Our boots inevitably got wet patrolling paddy fields and this became an ever-present danger. While you were walking about they retained their heat, but you wouldn't want to sit in them for too long. At night, when the temperature plummeted, wet boots and socks would be frozen stiff by morning. While you might find another pair of dry socks you only owned one pair of boots, and there was very little comfort in putting your feet into two casts of frozen leather and then hopping around in an attempt to soften them. We soon learned to keep our boots and socks within our sleeping bags, hugging them to the warmth of our stomachs. By morning they would still be somewhat damp, but thankfully not frozen.

The blokes in transport had the worst of it. In one of those oversights typical of the army there was no antifreeze available, so the jeep drivers had to take turns waking up every two hours to run the engines of all the vehicles for ten minutes to prevent the engine blocks from cracking and the water in the radiators from freezing.

The experience we all dreaded most was frostbite. It was something that could happen very easily if you failed to be careful. I recall how one evening five of us were sent out in bitter weather on a standing patrol. A standing patrol is literally what it suggests – you stay concealed in one spot. We took up our position on a particular hill behind which it was reckoned the enemy would be most likely to concentrate their troops in preparation for an attack. The idea was to give our side early warning if this should occur. Pretty soon Jason Matthews whispered to me, 'Jacko, are your feet getting numb?' I nodded; the tingly numb feeling had started about five minutes previously. 'Pass it on,' he whispered. Soon there were nods all round. 'Bugger it,' I said so they could all hear me, 'we have to move.'

'Mate, the chinks might hear us movin' about,' Jason protested.

'Fuck it, I'll take the chance. A man's losin' the feelin' in his feet,' Johnny Gordon retorted.

'As a once lance corporal I've got the seniority, I say we walk,' John Lazarou suddenly piped in.

'That's bullshit, Lazy, but I agree we walk.' It was Fitzy, another ginger-haired bloke, like me, from Broome, where his parents ran a greasy spoon famous for its hamburgers.

We had a unanimous decision, so we up and walked the circulation back into our feet, or so we thought. At first light we began to make our way back to the company position but after only a short distance Fitzy cried out in pain and soon it became agony for him to walk. We improvised a stretcher by cutting two poles from the scrubby bush and strapping Johnny's and my waterproof capes to them.

Back home we pulled off his boots and I was about to massage his feet when the company medic came running down from headquarters yelling, 'Ferchrissake, stop! Don't touch him!'

'His feet are frozen, corporal,' I said lamely.

'Never, never, never do that, you hear!' he said, his voice still on the rise.

He squatted beside Fitzy and gently pressed his swollen feet. The flesh was a stark, bloodless white, and where the medic touched him the indentation made by his finger remained. 'Did you go out with wet socks?' he asked.

'Didn't have time to change them,' Fitzy winced.

Johnny appeared with two steaming mugs of coffee and handed one of them to me. 'Here, give us those,' the medic corporal demanded. He took the mugs and placed them on the frozen ground beside him until the steam no longer rose, then he poured the warm coffee over Fitzy's feet and wrapped him in a blanket and we grabbed a stretcher and carried him up to RAP, the Regimental Aid Post. Well, that was the end of Fitzy's Korean adventure. They flew him back to Japan where they amputated four of his toes, three on one foot and his big toe on the other. Fitzy was a 3RAR career soldier and so, effectively, his army career was over. All because he'd been careless about changing his socks.

Fitzy's frostbite was a lesson to us all. We were learning that in extreme weather it's the little things you do that count. I mean, you'd quite naturally think that massaging frozen feet was the correct procedure to warm them up. That's fine if they're simply cold, but frozen means the cells of the skin have literally turned to ice.

When you place a bottle of beer in the freezer to cool it rapidly and then forget it's there, you discover later the bottle is broken. The beer has expanded beyond the capacity of the bottle to contain it. Well, that's pretty well what happens to frozen feet. The liquid freezing inside the skin cells expands and damages them, and rubbing the skin will exacerbate the damage – in a sense, your feet explode. The correct procedure to save the cells from further damage is to slowly melt the ice contained within them by systematically bathing the feet, or any other frozen part of the body, in warm water.

The army, in its usual bull-in-a-china-shop way, thought they'd solve the frostbite problem by creating waterproof rubber boots. They were rather cumbersome affairs as they needed to be sufficiently large to allow for two pairs of thick winter socks. Good thinking we all thought, until we started to walk in them. Rubber is an excellent conductor of heat and very soon our feet started to sweat and the sweat couldn't dissipate as it does with leather, and in minus thirteen degrees Fahrenheit, sweat turns to ice the moment you stop walking. Before you knew it your feet were encased in a thin layer of ice and you'd get that familiar numb feeling. If this happened you needed to keep walking until you could get to a source of warmth and were able to change your wet socks.

As the days grew shorter the cold increased in severity, and even the sweat under our armpits or on any other part of our bodies would routinely freeze. If you've ever seen monkeys scratching for fleas, that's how we were with ice. You'd feel a small sharp sting somewhere, in your crutch, under your arm or in the hollow of your neck – usually the first places to sweat – and your hand would dart inside your waterproof jacket or trousers to pick the tiny but sharp slivers of ice from your skin.

Sleeping warm was yet another difficulty. We were out in the field and except for those assigned to the battalion commander and a handful of the other brass, there were no conventional tents. We made a tent-like structure for two men by combining our waterproof capes, a shelter that became known as a 'hutchie'. A hutchie had both ends open and no way of closing them, so the wind would come whistling through. With a wind-chill factor even lower than the ambient temperature outside, a hutchie made for less than ideal sleeping quarters. The Americans had 'arctic' sleeping bags and they did the trick, but the Australian ones were hopeless and we were issued with two extra blankets. By wearing all the clothes you could find and two pairs of socks (a third pair wouldn't stretch over the bulk of the other two) you just about managed to survive a freezing night.

There was one incident it took me several years to talk about. I'm not sure why, perhaps because it showed how foolish I was and clearly demonstrated that in cold weather it is the little details that save you. One minus-twenty-degree night I was woken to take my turn at sentry duty. Still half asleep, I put on my socks, boots and fleecy-lined 'pile cap' and staggered over to the sentry's weapon pit. The Bren gun was set up at the entrance to the pit and as I stepped down into it, to steady myself, I grabbed hold of the barrel. My hand immediately froze to the metal and I was unable to pull it away. If I hadn't been so zonked I would have put on my gloves that were in the pocket of my battledress before leaving my hutchie. I can tell you I was fully awake in a moment and shouted out to the departing sentry to come back.

'Shit!' was all he said as he realised what had happened, and in a trice he'd pulled out his donger and pissed on my hand. The warm urine freed it from the Bren barrel but left a fair slice of my skin behind. Much to my chagrin, in a ceremony the following day, the platoon awarded him the DSO (Donger Service Order).

If the enemy had only known how completely ill prepared we were in the early-winter fighting conditions they could have strolled in and captured us without a shot being fired. For example, during the cautious move forward after the Battle of Pakchon, when we were all still a bit jumpy from the fighting, the sentry on duty thought he heard movement. Maybe it was the Chinese back for another go, he thought. He decided to wake us all, his decision based on the military principle that it is better to be safe than sorry. Staying alive even takes priority over a semi-warm sleeping bag and I slipped into my damp boots, this time making sure to wear gloves, grabbed my rifle and dropped into my weapon pit while calling for a sleepy John Lazarou to follow. I could hear the blokes all around me doing the same. As we began to routinely check our weapons, the muffled cursing began. Moisture had frozen the moving parts of our rifles and Owen guns, the ice virtually welding the rifle bolts and Owen cocking handles to the bodies of the weapons. If this hadn't been a false alarm and the Chinese had happened to attack at that moment they could have captured us using a pop-gun. In recruit training, soldiers are told to 'love your weapon'. From that time on we slept with them, keeping them warm, snuggled close to our bodies all night.

Life goes on, even in the cold, and a fortnight or so later the skipper called 12 Platoon together for a briefing. He told us that as a result of patrolling across the entire Korean front little contact had been made with the Chinese.

'They've scarpered,' he said.

'Why, skipper?' someone asked. 'They can't have lost that many men.'

'I can only hazard a guess,' Lieutenant Hamill replied. 'They've been at war with each other for damn near twenty years with Mao Zedong finally downing Chiang Kai-shek and with the Japs somewhere in the middle of all that. Perhaps they've had enough. The expeditionary force they sent against us did not go well for them and they've decided to hang up their boots. Who knows, the push to the Yalu is on again right across the front with the Allies meeting very little enemy opposition. If that's the case, as the top brass seem to think, this time General MacArthur may even be right.' He paused as we all laughed – MacArthur's broadcasts were a standing joke. Then he continued, 'I have a message passed on from company headquarters.'

He opened his field notebook. 'The supreme commander has said, and I quote: "I hope to have the boys home for Christmas."'

There were cheers all round and the blokes with families in Japan started to look happy again while Catflap Buggins was grinning fit to bust, no doubt thinking of resuming gymnastics with his little Japanese sheila.

That's the trouble with knowing a bit but not enough – it just didn't seem right to me. But what's a baggy arse to know or dare contradict, even in his mind, the opinion of the top brass, who now clearly indicated that they considered the Chinese army a spent force.

I guess I would have made a bad general, because the thought persisted that the Chinese wouldn't give up this easily. That night, taking a break on the reverse slope of our hill, a few of us sat around a forty-four-gallon drum we'd converted into a brazier by knocking holes in the side and lighting a fire within it. We were just rabbiting on when Ernie was foolish enough to ask my opinion of what the skipper had told us. 'The chinks fought pretty hard, those blokes weren't cowards by a long shot. Why would they suddenly up and disappear on us? What do you reckon, Jacko?'

Usually we'd sit around, and I'd wait until my hands were warm enough to remove my gloves, then I'd play the harmonica in what was known as 'Jacko's Musical Requests! Brought to the Australian forces in Korea by the one and only maestro of the golden harmonica, Lucky Lips and Paddy Slips McKenzie and his playful organ!' This introduction wasn't of my making, it was the work of 'poison lips' – Ivan the Terrible. Well, I started talking, not meaning to say much, but my previous thinking must have been backing up in my mind and now my thoughts just seemed to tumble out like a dam wall suddenly breached.

'Mao Zedong has only recently become what amounts to Emperor of China, though the term the communists use now that everyone is equal is "Chairman". He has just defeated a modern army bankrolled by the Yanks and is left with five million fighting men at his disposal. He has no reason to love the West, who have humiliated China more than once – the British, the Americans and the Germans, in particular.

The Chinese never forget an insult nor a humiliation, and they've built up a fair few whoppers over the last century or so.

'Now, put yourself in Chairman Mao's place. Here in neighbouring North Korea is yet another case of the West heading for the Chinese border. So what is he going to do? Here is the enemy, not just the Americans, but every Western nation who's ever humiliated you, with the exception of the Germans, gathered in one spot at your doorstep. Your troops are combat ready, hardened, the toughest in the world. Their morale is sky-high having wiped the floor with America's darling, Chiang Kai-shek. What's more, you have absolute control over them – if a million die fighting the West, who gives a shit? You don't need to answer to anyone. If two million die, that's acceptable odds given the circumstances, and your need to avenge the past. So you send 20 000 out to test the enemy, a mere toe in the water. They have a bit of a go, check us out then quickly withdraw.' I paused to catch my breath, afraid to look at the faces around me. 'Mao Zedong was only briefing himself with that offensive.' Then I foolishly added, 'I don't think, like the top brass said, he's sitting across the border licking his wounds. You'll see, he'll be back.'

'What utter bullshit!' John Lazarou shouted out. 'Home for Christmas, that's what the man said!'

'Yeah, mate, better stick to the mouth organ,' Jason Matthews advised, receiving a gratuitous laugh.

I could see they all thought I'd suddenly gone bonkers – stark, staring mad. So, to hide my acute embarrassment, I brought the harmonica to my lips and played through the whole of the 'Colonel Bogey March'. In the meanwhile thinking, *Why the fuck did Nicole Lenoir-Jourdan have to pick me out on the library floor all those years ago? 'My goodness! Could it be possible that we've spawned an intelligent McKenzie at long last?'* I wasn't even able to console myself with the knowledge that, when it came to world politics, the rest of the blokes sitting around the brazier were a pretty ignorant lot. Even so, the big brass wasn't, and I'd effectively told the blokes around me that the Allied high command were a bunch of wankers. I mean, c'mon, how arrogant is that? It was going to take a fair bit of time to live this one down – good thing we'd be home for Christmas.

Now that the Chinese, faced with a Western army, had shown their true colours, we could happily go ahead and win the war as quickly as possible. The 8th Army was to start its push for the Yalu River, the wide flowing stream that, together with the Tumen River, slices across the top of the Korean peninsula and divides China from North Korea.

The Allied advance got away with every division taking up more or less where they'd left off. The Commonwealth Brigade was sent into reserve and this time I don't think we were too indignant – the further north you went, the colder it got. Going into reserve meant moving to the outskirts of Pakchon and finding buildings to occupy where we would be warm and able to set up kitchens where hot food was served and, perhaps most glorious of all, where we would have access to hot water and bush showers. The blokes called it Operation Defrost, and I can still clearly recall the feeling of standing under a sprinkle of hot water and lathering myself with actual soap all over my body. The shower head was made from a jam tin with holes hammered in using a six-inch nail, but there never was a trickle from above more luxurious. Some enterprising photographer took a picture of me standing under the shower and also a close-up of the jam-tin shower head. Gloria was over the moon and the pic had pride of place in her by now burgeoning war journal. Fortunately she also pasted in the photo of the shower head. Many years later, when I built the big house on the island, I had it copied, using an IXL jam tin that I had chrome-plated and placed in the shower recess in my bathroom. Hardly a morning goes by when I don't look up, as the hot water splashes over my face, and remember.

The day after we went into reserve happened to be Thanksgiving Day and the Americans, always generous, saw to it that their allies had rations that featured turkey and ham, and Christmas pudding for good measure. They also included several truckloads of American beer. But the new Budweiser plant in Newark, New Jersey, hadn't calculated on the Korean winter, and a large part of the load arrived in frozen and broken bottles. Australians abhor in particular wasting the amber liquid and we soon found a way of gently removing the glass, which broke clean, to be left with a giant beer ice block. It was a very strange way to get pissed – nevertheless, a great many blokes managed to do so very effectively and the chilblains could be seen on our lips for several days afterwards.

We expected to be held in reserve for a week or so – you know, sit around an open fire, eat hot food, suck on a beer ice block or two, wake up in warm sleeping bags with dry boots and feel clean all over. All this while sitting on our arses doing next to bugger-all.

Alas, the Chinese had other ideas and we were up off our bums and reaching for our guns before we knew it.

# CHAPTER FIVE

## *Running Away*

So here we were again, gathered around one of Lieutenant Hamill's notorious three-dimensional maps. It was formed this time from clumps of packing sawdust for the hills, higher piles for the central mountain range, wire for the rivers, sticks for the bridges and ice-crusted lines drawn into the frozen dirt for roads and tracks. Scattered in various positions were beer bottles meant to indicate the positions of the various armies and divisions. He'd traced the Yalu River that forms the Chinese border with a piece of bright-blue electric tape.

'Righto, pay attention,' the skipper instructed. 'The blue tape, that's the Chinese border almost a hundred kilometres from where we stand – that's sixty miles in our measurements.' He then traced the routes of three 8th Army divisions that had passed through the choke point and were heading off towards the blue electric tape. Four more divisions in the form of bottles covered the remaining ground from the coast to the central mountain range so that the whole of the 8th Army front stretched for about sixty miles across. This was the final advance that was to take us to the Yalu River – what they were calling the 'Home-by-Christmas Offensive'.

Just as we'd grasped the plan the skipper stretched out his foot and kicked a bottle, sending it flying, and then let go at a second, which also took a tumble off the map. 'That's the two ROK divisions on our right flank. They're history – the Chinese have completely destroyed them.'

Normally we'd be somewhat taken aback by such a huge defeat – 20 000 men taken out of the battle plan is a loss few armies can afford. But we told ourselves they were South Korean divisions and not worth a pinch of the proverbial. They'd just turned up to make up the numbers, knowing they could hardly be bystanders while we were ostensibly fighting for their freedom. They'd been running away since day one, so what more could we expect?

Now the skipper put the sole of his boot on the top of the next bottle, wobbling it. 'The disintegration of the South Korean divisions has exposed the flank of the US 2nd Division, which is pulling back to avoid encirclement and to protect the 8th Army's right flank. The division next to it, the 25th, is also under pressure. And here's the really bad bit. The Chinese have the Turkish Brigade in trouble. The point is the Turkish Brigade was sitting quietly in reserve not far from Kunu-ri some sixty-five miles behind the forward troops.'

He looked around, his face serious. 'Men, the Chinese are threatening to crash through on the right flank and take not only the river crossings but also the vital road junction at Kunu-ri. As you all realise, that would trap a large portion of the 8th Army on the wrong side of the river crossings and lay it open to destruction.'

'Excuse me, skipper,' I said.

'Yes, Jacko, what is it?' he said, somewhat impatiently.

'Skipper, at our last briefing you said China had committed only 20 000 men to the war. Are you saying 20 000 Chinese have all but defeated four of our divisions?'

The skipper grinned a little sheepishly. 'Good question, Jacko. Well no, things have changed a fair bit – the Chinese numbers are now estimated at 200 000 and still counting.' He stopped talking and looked directly at me. 'I believe you delivered a bit of a lecture to the platoon after my last briefing. Something about the top brass being a bunch of wankers, wasn't it?' The group broke into sudden laughter and all eyes turned to me, and I wondered who among our platoon had the big mouth.

'Well no, sir, I didn't exactly say that. I said . . .'

'Well, whatever you said,' he interrupted, 'it seems you were right.' More laughter – the skipper was a good sport.

'The little general strikes again!' Ivan the Terrible quipped, encouraging still further hilarity.

It seemed pretty obvious Ivan the Terrible had told the skipper about my sounding off. No one else in the platoon would have done so. It was typical of him: his way of maintaining discipline was to put you down. He had a big mouth and an acerbic tongue and if he could say something unpleasant it seemed to come far more naturally to him than a compliment. He was always kicking someone's arse whether they deserved it or not, and the blokes regarded him as a bit of a bastard. Catflap and John Lazarou were his favourite marks and bore the major brunt. When he was out of earshot Lazy often threatened to put a bullet through his head, accidentally on purpose, the next time we went into battle. And Catflap frequently used a particularly uncomplimentary name for his favourite part of the female anatomy to describe him.

Despite Ivan the Terrible's attempt to send me up, I was stoked that I'd been vindicated. Just as I'd predicted, Chairman Mao's little soldiers had been given the message that they were volunteers and had been pouring across the border like army ants. I now thought to ask Lieutenant Hamill how 200 000 Chinese had managed to slip across the border and travel over sixty miles into Korea and through the United Nations Command front-line without being detected, but then I thought better of it – coming so soon after I'd been vindicated, it might have been seen as an attempt to bung it on a bit. I couldn't help turning to look at Lazy, hoping he had the decency to look contrite about the way he'd poured shit on me after I'd doubted that the Chinese had exited the war and returned home licking their wounds. But, of course, Lazy had long since forgotten the incident.

Now he reached over and touched me lightly on the shoulder and mumbled under his breath, 'Good one, Jacko. You should've been a bloody general.' I decided, for the umpteenth time, that there simply wasn't any point in taking offence. John Lazarou was an unredeemable idiot.

After the Battle of Chongju I recalled the US 24th Division passing through the town to take over the lead. The Yanks don't believe in doing things by halves. They had the usual 10 000 men, but it was their ordnance and vehicles that boggled the mind. I didn't see the whole convoy but even in the few hours I watched, hundreds of trucks packed with troops passed me. There were literally scores of armoured vehicles, artillery pieces being towed by enormous gun tractors, trucks packed with artillery shells, engineer vehicles with bridging equipment and barbed wire, stores trucks galore, and jeeps, jeeps, jeeps everywhere you looked, hundreds of them. And of course the petrol tankers needed to keep this giant snake moving forward. Already many tankers, having fed the beast, were returning to the rear to refill. One of the Yanks told me there were over 2000 vehicles carrying the combat elements of the division. 'And there's a whole lot more way back carrying the resupply.' It'd take twenty-four hours for the whole lot to pass through if all went well, he said.

The point being that this great convoy of vehicles now had to go back through the choke point of the river crossings. And it was not just the 24th Division; convoys of two other divisions had to pass through too. It was hard to imagine the traffic jam: vehicle convoys stretching back many miles converging on the narrow crossing points, confusion as the traffic merged, delays as trucks broke down or skidded and crashed on the frozen roads. It wouldn't take hours for them to cross to safety – it would take at least a couple of days. And all the time the enemy pressing their attack on the right flank to capture the crossing points and cut the road further south at Kunu-ri. If the Chinese succeeded, those divisions would be cut off from supply and reinforcement and, with the Chinese numerical superiority, would soon be destroyed. Only the US 2nd Infantry Division, precariously holding off the marauding masses of enemy infantry, stood in the way of military disaster. The question was whether or not the 2nd Division could hold off the enemy for those vital two days.

'Well, that's the situation, boys,' the skipper concluded. 'The good news is that we are being sent to the rescue. Pack your woollies – we're leaving for Kunu-ri.'

We set off for Kunu-ri on an ice-rutted poor excuse for a road jammed bumper to bumper with trucks, jeeps, petrol tankers and gun tractors, and choked with refugees.

I had never witnessed a mass exodus of civilians before. Men carrying enormous loads on wooden A-frames strapped to their backs, loads so heavy they could only move a hundred yards or so before stopping to rest. Women carried babies strapped to their breasts and pushed handcarts packed with the family belongings – pots and pans that banged together and created a cacophony you could hear for miles in the clear, cold air. Children led oxen and pigs while old people sat hunched over on donkeys that often stumbled, falling into the freezing mud up to their hocks and knee joints so that their legs were caked with mud and blood. It was difficult to imagine how this continuous stream of humans would survive the deep-freeze nights and bitter days, much less the long journey on foot to the South.

There is a saying in the army, 'Greatcoats on, greatcoats off'. This is when orders are issued then changed, then changed again. It's not only a wearisome business to your average digger, but also of some concern because it usually indicates the top brass are confused. Soon after arriving at Kunu-ri the order came for us to move back north. Then we were told we would be moving north but not until the following morning because it would be impossible to move against the flow of the traffic scrambling south at night. Morning came and the order was cancelled and we were told to move south to a place called Chasan. But then there was a delay – they said they were trying to organise transport. Finally the word came that the Yanks had no spare trucks, so some of us would have to march to our destination.

B and D companies and a couple of companies of the Argylls set off on foot. At first we were accompanied by a confusion of traffic and a mass of refugees, but as we marched into the night, the last of the retreating traffic using this road passed through us and disappeared south. The refugees disappeared, too. Curiously, wartime refugees seem to have a sixth sense for when an attack is about to take place. On the other hand, on this occasion they may simply have gone off to seek refuge from the freezing night temperatures.

In normal circumstances I would have enjoyed the solitude of a night where the moonlight reflected on the frozen paddy fields. But on this occasion I was afraid some Chinese might have been not far behind. I wondered if we were marching fast enough to outpace them, and there was no thought of enjoying the quiet. On a long march you can get right inside yourself in a kind of self-hypnosis. It seemed to grow colder as the night wore on and my face and ears stung in the frosty atmosphere. Except for the crunch of our boots on the frozen ground and the distant wail of the bagpipes from a lone Argyll piper in the company ahead of us, the night, defeated by the cold, had completely closed down. The sound of our boots seemed an intrusion into the total stillness, but strangely the sad wail of the bagpipes seemed appropriate to the frozen world around us.

I was suddenly snapped out of this reverie and reminded of the horror of war. At the side of the road, sitting upright on a small heap of frozen mud, was a dead baby with one hand held out as if its tiny fingers were waving at us.

Funny how you can kill a man, run right up to him and put a bayonet into him and come out of it feeling okay – pretty upset, but okay. But the effect the frozen baby had on me, and the men immediately surrounding me, was devastating. John Lazarou, beside me, gasped. 'Oh, Jesus!' he said. Shortly afterwards, I heard him sobbing. Several blokes around me were the same, and the lump in my throat wouldn't go away until we'd marched a good few miles away from the poor little bastard. We always seem to forget that war isn't only about combat, soldiers fighting each other for whatever reason – it's also about civilians having their lives destroyed and their babies left to die on a heap of frozen mud.

As we marched towards Chasan I noted the road was often flanked by high ground ideal for an ambush. But the Americans appeared to be in such a hurry that they were neglecting to clear and secure it. It made me nervous and I kept glancing up, half expecting to fall victim to some enterprising Chinamen who had managed to get ahead of us.

To be ambushed is a soldier's worst nightmare. It means you have been caught by surprise in a killing zone that has been chosen by the enemy for its potential effectiveness. Suddenly your column is hit from the flank by withering and carefully aimed machine-gun fire. Bullets whine about you claiming your mates, and the wounded are screaming, begging for help, but if you move to get to one you reveal your position and you're dead meat before you reach them. Making a run for it is usually terminal – the enemy is prepared for this, waiting to cut you down the moment you reveal yourself. Your best chance is to lie still, to play possum. Returning fire is pointless – the enemy is concealed and well protected and your chances of killing him are negligible. Conversely, your gunfire gives away your position and he'll pick you off with a burst from a machine gun. You pray that with any luck they'll withdraw without coming in to look for spoils – that is, assaulting into the ambush.

I was relieved when, at three-fifteen a.m., we arrived unscathed, and dug in to protect a road junction and ferry crossing. A day or so later the US 2nd Division, following the same route we'd marched, began its own withdrawal. We saw the first lot come through. They seemed to be making a fairly good job of it, but then a little later the troop convoy heading south started to dry up and we observed ambulance after ambulance heading in the opposite direction.

'Something's happened to those guys,' I said to Jason Matthews, who was on sentry duty with me. 'Why all the ambulances?' Then a couple of hours later the ambulances started returning, whole convoys, more than I'd ever seen at one time. We'd come to the end of sentry duty and I made an excuse to stroll up to company headquarters where I knew Ian Ferrier was the wireless operator. I'd known Ian from way back – we'd been in New Guinea together at the tail end of the last war, where both of us were pretty upset that we'd missed out on the fighting. In Korea we'd renewed our friendship.

Some wireless operators are pretty uptight and don't let you in on anything. They want you to believe that they know stuff that might blow your tiny mind if it was revealed. Ian wasn't like that – he was a knob twiddler, always on the search for something juicy. 'Freq-goss' was what he called it. If anyone would know what was happening to the Yanks, he'd be the one.

I could hear the crackle and squeak of his wireless gear from fifty feet away. I entered his tent to see him bent over his equipment, earphones on, listening intently, fingertips delicately twiddling knobs to tap into the frequencies of the other networks. Strictly speaking this was forbidden, but it had never occurred to Ian to take any notice of the rules – he was a frequency junkie, a stickybeak addicted to radio gossip. I touched him on the shoulder and he tweaked a moment longer, then stopped and removed his earphones.

'Oh g'day, Jacko, what can I do you for?' he asked in his usual flippant way.

'Mate, what's going on with the US 2nd? Judging from the ambulances, they've been copping heaps.'

'You're not wrong,' he answered. 'There's been one bloody great fuck-up – they've been ambushed by what they reckon is an entire division of Chinese dug in along the ten-mile stretch of high ground overlooking the road. The chinks waited until the Yanks were well into their trap and then let them have it. They were sitting ducks, mate, it's the full turkey shoot!' he said, mixing his metaphors.

Ian was talking about that high ground I'd worried about during our march only a day before. It made my skin prickle.

'It's this way,' said Ian. 'The US 2nd Division managed to hold off the chinks just long enough for the rest of the 8th Army to get to safety. Quite an effort, really. But that was about a day too long for them to save themselves. In that time the chinks had been able to find their way round the flanks of 2nd Division's defence and get thousands of men dug in on their withdrawal route. In a way, the 2nd Division was sacrificed to save the rest of us.'

'That makes sense,' I said, 'but maybe the sacrifice wouldn't have been half so great if they'd got out of their bloody trucks and tried to clear the high ground instead of haring down the road and hoping for the best.'

'Mate, what can you expect – they're Yanks,' replied Ian, as if this explained everything.

That was the beginning of a withdrawal that drove us back deep inside South Korea in a very short time. The first 250 miles were completed in two frantic weeks.

We joined the Americans going south and while we maintained a tidy convoy, theirs seemed to be in chaos. The going was pretty rough – their trucks lost traction in the icy conditions and slipped off the road, where they were simply abandoned. The same happened to us on three occasions and it was everybody out and push until we got going again. When this happened the Yanks would yell at us, 'Ferchrissakes, leave it buddy, get moving, the gooks are burning our ass!'

After a while you can smell fear in warfare, and as the days wore on there was the distinct whiff of it in the bitterly cold air. The signs of an army in chaos were beginning to accumulate. For instance, there seemed to be no traffic control. Vehicles wanting to join the traffic flow had to bully their way into the queue as best they could. Despite the examples of the US 2nd Division ambush and the occasional burned-out, bullet-riddled hulk of a truck standing by the roadside, the Yanks failed to clear and secure the high ground overlooking the road.

American failure to observe normal military procedure was a constant worry. No one said as much but I know we couldn't help thinking that the Chinese might catch up with us and the Americans would be in such disarray they'd be more a hindrance than a help. Sandwiched into the middle of a jittery American convoy of conscript soldiers wasn't a whole heap of fun. It would have been a lot more comforting had they been the US Marines and not the frightened schoolboys they were, who wondered why they were in Korea in the first place and now found themselves constantly running for their lives.

In the parlance of the military we were all withdrawing, which suggests a high degree of order and planning. In effect, we were running away as fast as our transport could carry us. The roadside was strewn with American trucks of all types that had skidded off the track and been abandoned. We'd picked up a Yank truck driver who'd abandoned his vehicle when it had left the road. 'What's going on with you guys?' I asked him.

'It's the big bug out!' he replied.

The Yanks certainly know how to fashion a succinct phrase – 'the big bug out' explained everything going on. We picked it up and used it for just about anything that seemed like a cop-out by our leaders or anyone avoiding doing a specific job. In the great Australian tradition of shortening everything, this soon led to the phrase 'bugging out', which, even today, you hear in use often enough.

If you're withdrawing properly, you're making the enemy pay for every inch of territory he's gaining. You pull out through another unit behind you who are ready to engage and delay the enemy, then they do the same, and so on. But there was none of this – the enemy had a free run. They must have thought all their Christmases had come at once. We'd had only one small skirmish with the chinks during the withdrawal and that was in the first few days. This 'bugging out' was getting us down and we longed for a decent stoush with the Chinese. But as we galloped south as hard as we could go we barely glanced backwards, let alone waited to take them on.

I am beginning to sound as if we were in perfect control and everywhere you looked the Yanks were falling over themselves in their haste to flee the enemy. Sure, we'd given the Chinese a good hiding at Pakchon but it must be remembered that, unlike the American units who had borne the brunt of the recent Chinese offensive, we had not yet come across the Chinese in such overwhelming numbers. Defeat is infectious, and we were afraid that we might just find ourselves running scared even before we came up against the enemy. I recall that at the time what we most wanted was to be rid of the American convoys and the chaos of their withdrawal. It was becoming increasingly difficult to stay calm in the atmosphere of panic around us.

Still back-pedalling frantically, one late afternoon we arrived at Pyongyang, the North Korean capital. On the previous occasion we'd entered Pyongyang the mood had been one of supreme optimism – the North Koreans were in total disarray and the Korean War would soon be a distant memory with very few of us carrying scars.

Now the capital was possessed by a sense of impending disaster. At the side of the road leading out of the city were great stacks of clothing being prepared for destruction, along with vehicles being put to the torch. When we came across a Yank sergeant who was about to torch hundreds of boxes of B rations, we banged on the roof of the cabin of our truck for the driver to stop.

'Hang on, mate!' Jason Matthews yelled at the American. 'We could use some of those!'

'Help yourself, take what you like – you've got five minutes, buddy, then the lot goes up in smoke,' the sergeant shouted back.

Cold as we were, we jumped out of that truck like jack rabbits and in five minutes the blokes had damn nearly filled the available space in the back of the truck with boxes. While the others were piling in the rations I noticed a second pile of US Army winter clothing a few yards down the road. I called to Johnny Gordon and we hot-footed over.

'Yiz gunna burn this also?' Johnny asked.

'Right on, buddy,' the Yank in charge replied.

With a toss of the head I indicated the pile, 'Mind if we, you know . . . ?'

'Help yourselves, ain't gonna do nothing but torch 'em,' he generously replied.

We each grabbed a dozen or so standard-issue US Army fleecy-lined parkas that were greatly superior to our own.

Johnny then yelled, 'Gloves – find the bloody Yank gloves!'

The American laughed, pointing to a truck. 'They're back in yonder truck, buddy.' We'd all lusted after the gloves the Americans wore and we grabbed two boxes, each containing a dozen pairs of leather gloves. Thanking the American we staggered away, each under a load of parkas with a box of gloves on top of them, and returned to our truck just as the Yank sergeant put the torch to the remaining B rations. We watched as sufficient food to just about feed an army went up in smoke. You couldn't help but feel that handing it over to the refugees may have been a better, though perhaps less practical, way to dispose of the rations, although that's not how retreating armies traditionally behave.

'You beauty!' several yelled. 'Giddonya, Jacko, Gordie!' We became instant heroes as we handed a parka and a pair of gloves to each of the blokes in the truck. We kept four coats for ourselves, one that fitted and one that was oversize, big enough to fit over the one that fitted. Both Johnny and I, being small blokes, had no problems getting an S and XOS to fit over each other. For the first time ever in Korea I felt warm.

We drove into the night, leaving the panic of Pyongyang and joining the madness of the road south. Up to this point the Commonwealth Brigade had been pretty successful in the war, even if we Australians hadn't yet come up against the full force of the Chinese. An *esprit de corps* had grown up between the various men in the Commonwealth countries, among whom heaping shit on the Yanks was the most common subject of discussion. We'd shake our heads and laugh. 'Bloody Yanks wouldn't know how to fight their way out of a wet paper bag,' we'd say, with evident satisfaction.

Of course, we had yet to experience the humiliation that comes with total defeat and were, to say the least, bloody arrogant enough, or perhaps the word is foolish, to think that given the same circumstances we would do better than the Americans.

The deepening winter had only one advantage – the bridges were clear of fleeing civilians, who had chosen to use the frozen rivers as the roadway south. This, of course, begged the obvious question: what was to stop the Chinese from doing the same thing?

How quickly things can change in combat. We were passing landmarks we'd come across in our advance and now we were seeing them from the opposite direction. Late in the afternoon we passed the hill where we'd dug in with the US 7th Cavalry Regiment when, anxious to see action, we'd deserted to the front. I wondered what had happened to the tank commander Orwell J. Partridge, who'd given us a lift in the dust and heat of the time and to whom I'd given the badge from my slouch hat, and to Sergeant Crosby Jones Ovington Junior who'd welcomed us into the 7th Cavalry. *Were they still alive?* So much had happened since then. I sighed inwardly to think that at that time I thought I'd miss the war and have to go back home a virgin soldier for the second time.

On the way north the 1st Cavalry had erected a sign that read: 'You are entering North Korea by courtesy of the 1st Cavalry Division.' Now heading south, some disillusioned Yank had erected a sign in its place that read: 'You are now entering South Korea by courtesy of the Chinese People's Army.' The irony was not lost on us.

We arrived at Uijongbu, hacked weapon pits out of the snow-covered, frozen ground and patrolled forward looking for the Chinese. But then it became apparent that we were victims of just about the biggest intelligence fuck-up since Napoleon's advance into Russia. Interrogation of the Chinese prisoners of war had put together an amazing story.

You will recall that when I explained the nature of the Korean peninsula I mentioned the mountains that run like a crocodile's back through the centre – peaks that are impassable so that, even in an overcrowded country, the Koreans, with the exception of a few small villages situated on the lower slopes, were unable to settle within them. It was obvious to the Allies that the war must take place on either side of this towering and inhospitable spine. While it was accepted that small marauding guerilla units might try to exist within the protection of the mountains, the Yank brass, on the premise that 'If we can't go there then nobody can', believed the mountain range too rugged and precipitous to shelter any significant number of the enemy.

However, the nobody-who-could turned out to be the Chinese. Around 300 000 Chinese had used the mountains to infiltrate over sixty miles inside Korea without anyone knowing. They'd travelled on foot, donkey and horse at night and at first light, before our planes could get into the air, they'd camouflaged themselves carefully. What few villages they'd encountered they'd contained, so that no word of their infiltration leaked out onto the plains below.

When we were being briefed on the advance to the Yalu, I'd noticed there were no 8th Army troops in the mountains. Someone had asked the skipper – okay, I admit it was me – 'Skipper, are the Americans sending patrols up into the mountains?' The skipper was usually careful not to be critical of the Americans, or, for that matter, any of our allies, so his reply had been all the more surprising. 'The Americans don't like going off the roads – if they can't reach their objective by tank or truck they tend to avoid it.' Without tanks or trucks, the Chinese had moved deeper and deeper into Korea until they were well behind the advancing 8th Army. Meanwhile we'd decided the Chinese had taken one look at us and shat their pants running back across the border. Everyone had been optimistic about reaching the Yalu River and concluding the war in time to be home for Christmas.

As the 8th Army had headed for the Yalu, the Chinese had swept down out of the mountains decimating two South Korean divisions, hitting the exposed flank of the US 2nd Division, threatening the choke point, and overrunning the Turkish Brigade that waited in reserve near Kunu-ri and sending us all scuttling back into South Korea.

Effectively, the Chinese had done in reverse what MacArthur's earlier Inchon landing had achieved when he'd sent the North Koreans racing backwards. But there was a small difference: the Chinese had achieved the same result without the benefit of aeroplanes, tanks, trucks and artillery. This did not go unnoticed – we were fighting warriors whose only weapons were the burp gun, machine gun and some mortars and they were beating us with one hand tied behind their backs.

Nicole Lenoir-Jourdan had been very big on how the West, in

particular the British, Germans, French and Americans, had exploited China's technological backwardness for over a century with what she termed 'gunboat diplomacy'.

'The Chinese have very long memories and great patience,' she'd explained. 'You must understand that one hundred years is a very short time for them, Jack. You may be sure that one day they will avenge this greedy and arrogant rape of the Celestial Empire by the foreign devils who came from over the sea.'

It had sounded rather problematic to me, even at the age of nine. At the time Mao Zedong was still on his Long March. Together with about 40 000 followers he had established a modest communist soviet in Shaanxi Province, and it was inconceivable that his little slant-eyed, bandy-legged soldiers could avenge themselves against the might of Britain and America. As I mentioned previously, since childhood I'd been led to believe that the yellow hordes were poised to attack Australia at any moment in order to get to our abalone. But in my mind we'd tell them to go ahead and help themselves as the bloody stuff was inedible anyway. Then we'd stand by and watch as half of them drowned in the attempt. Who'd ever heard of a Chinaman who could swim? They wouldn't know that abalone is only to be found in the deepest and narrowest underwater gullies. Ha ha ha, so much for the so-called yellow hordes.

Now here I was fighting alongside two of the most mighty of the gunboat diplomacy nations and clearly we were receiving a hiding at the hands of the Chinese. Perhaps we *would* indeed be home by Christmas, though by courtesy of the Celestial Empire who would sweep us into the sea, the full kaboodle, planes, tanks, trucks and all the foreign devils diving over the cliff tops and into the waves. This time it would be our turn to swim for our lives.

Despite the reality of our situation, some of the blokes remained optimistic. I was putting up my hutchie next to Catflap Buggins and John Lazarou when Catflap said to Lazy, 'Hey mate, what you gonna do when you get 'ome for Chrissie?'

Lazy then said to him, 'Don't be bloody stupid, we ain't gonna be home for Christmas no more – the fuckin' chinks have got us by the fuckin' short and curlies.'

'That's just bloody it, mate. They'll be saying to themselves, "Whacko! At this rate we'll be home for Chinese New Year, these fuckers can't fight,"' Catflap replied.

'Not all of us can't fight,' Lazy said indignantly. 'We can fight, and the Poms are doing okay. It's just the noggies and the Yanks.'

'Yeah, but there's more of them can't fight than there's us who can, so it goes without sayin' the chinks are gonna win and we'll be 'ome for Christmas and them for their New Year firecracker night.'

There was silence as Lazy thought about this for a moment. Then he said, 'How much? What'll you give me?'

'Odds? Yeah, okay, three to one the chinks smack our arse and I'm back with Lotus Blossom in Japan.'

'Righto, you're on. A month's pay, okay?'

You had to hand it to Lazy – he was loyal, all right. Although the way things were going for us, Catflap must have been pretty confident. Later I said to Lazy, 'Mate, the bet you made, you and Catflap, a month's pay, that's a lot of bread.'

'Nah, I won't never have to pay the bugger,' Lazy answered confidently.

'Why – you think we'll win, do you?'

'Don't matter if we don't win,' Lazy grinned. 'I reckon I'll be dead, so I won't have to pay him anyway!'

Three weeks passed at Uijongbu without a sign of the Chinese. Christmas came and went and New Year arrived and was duly celebrated with a good ration of beer and several cases of rum the company storeman had somehow got his hands on, claiming he'd liberated them on the way to the officer's mess. The next morning, suffering from a combination of rum with beer chasers, we learned that the Chinese had finally caught up and attacked the 6th ROK Division who, with the US 24th Division, were to our front. Once again the bloody South Koreans had let us down. This time they should have done better though – they'd had plenty of time to dig in and prepare and we'd thought they'd be okay. But as usual they'd broken and run almost the moment the Chinese launched the attack.

We were sent forward to secure the Tokchon road junction, through which the withdrawing troops were to pass. Already the South Korean troops were fleeing down the road in panic as fast as their short legs could carry them. Most of them had jettisoned their equipment and anything else they thought might encumber their escape. You couldn't help feeling contempt for them until you saw the look of terror in their faces. It was obvious that they greatly feared the Chinese.

With the South Koreans not even putting up token resistance, the Chinese troops advanced so fast they were able to put in a road block between us and Tokchon. Then, with the help of American tanks, we managed to send them packing and secured the road junction. But the place was swarming with Chinese and we soon got the order to withdraw and head back down the road, feeling that the Chinese were on both of our flanks. Sure enough, with the South Koreans disappearing, two small groups of Chinese decided to have a go at us. A platoon from A Company took on one lot and an American tank took care of the other. It wasn't what you'd call a major attack but it was good just taking them on face to face, so to speak, to remind ourselves that they were human and prepared to withdraw when things hotted up a bit.

But these triumphant skirmishes did nothing to stem the sheer panic of so much of the Allied withdrawal. So chaotic had most of the remainder of the withdrawal become that we imagined the Chinese must be laughing at the forces ranged against them.

The Commonwealth Brigade continued to withdraw in an orderly fashion, pulling back through the South Korean capital, Seoul, then another hundred miles to a defensive line simply referred to as Line D where we waited for the Chinese. Some of the American units arrived in reasonable order and others were a complete shambles, with a great many vehicles and much ordnance missing.

We braced ourselves for another Chinese attack, but several weeks of patrolling found no sign of them. The skipper told us air reconnaissance hadn't detected any sign of a build-up, either. It seemed as though they might finally have outrun their capacity to get supplied. If ever there was an army that could exist off the land it was this one, and I have no doubt had it not been winter they would have kept coming at us. Put into their shoes, I know we'd have run out of supplies months ago. They seemed to be able to exist on the smell of an oily rag.

With the Chinese temporarily out of action the 8th Army started to advance again, but without the gung-ho previously shown by the American commanders. The long, fast and utterly humiliating retreat seemed to have shocked some sense into them, into all of us. The Chinese had taught us a little respect and the previously arrogant top brass had begun to realise that technical superiority and unlimited ordnance weren't a guarantee of victory. That warfare was still the business of men with rifles sitting in foxholes with commanders like Charlie Green who were prepared to think outside the square.

Over the next few months we advanced very slowly. This time we included our previous nemesis, the central mountain range. It meant getting back to basics, leaving the trucks behind and heading off into the high country with scores of Korean porters bringing up the supplies and taking out the wounded. We were beginning to fight the Chinese their way, moving along ill-defined goat tracks and fighting along ridge lines and up steep, narrow spur lines. February turned into March and winter gave way to the spring rains, torrential downpours that turned the steep slopes and goat tracks into quagmire. It was familiar territory for those of us who had been to New Guinea, but that didn't make it any easier.

By mid-April we'd advanced about sixty miles, pushing the Chinese back in pretty much continuous fighting. They were retreating the way we ought to have done, making us pay for every mile gained. I reckon we'd earned a bit of respect from them the hard way by winning against a skilled and determined enemy and taking a fair deal of punishment in the process. We'd learned that these Chinese gave as good as they got and we'd lost a number of mates killed or wounded. I'm sure, like me, most of the blokes wondered when the bullet would arrive with their name on it.

# CHAPTER SIX

## *Hill 504*

We'd largely lost our enthusiasm for a big showdown with the Chinese. We'd fought them often enough and long enough and we all felt it was about time we went home. Besides, moving forward, even without fighting, was bloody hard work. Putting it mildly, we were near exhausted when the word came through that we were to move back into Corps reserve. This meant we would be able to relax, forget for a while about mud, slush, slipping, slopes, spur lines, shrapnel and that bullet with your name inscribed on it. We'd be on easy street for a couple of weeks of good food and glorious rest. Anzac Day was coming up and we were all happy that we'd be out of action and into the grog ration when it came along. I don't know, somehow dying on Anzac Day seemed a bit show-off, almost un-Australian, if you know what I mean.

The rain stopped for a few days as we retired to the rear and made our camp in a lovely wooded area. The trees, bright with new leaf, made the whole world seem young again. The camp was near the town of Kapyong, situated in the Kapyong Valley. Twenty-five miles up the valley to the north was the front-line. Not that we cared – we were well away from the business end of the war with no patrols or calls to stand-to, fresh food cooked for us, the ultimate luxury of a shower, clean clothes and, best of all, Anzac Day on the horizon. As luck would have it the Turkish Brigade was camped not that far from us and our commanding officer sent a delegation inviting them to celebrate the big day with us. Imagine celebrating Gallipoli with the enemy – I reckoned it couldn't get much better than that.

We had an American with us as our artillery forward observer, a nice bloke. One evening after dinner he asked me, 'ANZAC? What's that stand for, Jacko?'

'Australian and New Zealand Army Corps,' I explained. He seemed none the wiser, so I continued, 'Along with the New Zealanders we stormed the beach at Gallipoli in 1915.'

'So, is that your . . .' he paused to think, 'Battle of Iwo Jima?'

'Well, I suppose. It was the first time that Australia and New Zealand fought as independent nations – were like, you know, blooded.'

'Oh, I see – first time out and a big victory.'

'Well no, we endured eight months of fierce fighting against the Turks and lost 11 000 men between us.'

'But in the end a great victory?' he repeated.

I laughed and shook my head. 'Nah, we lost.'

'Lost!' The American looked decidedly puzzled. 'You celebrate the defeat?'

'No, the blooding. We reckoned it was a draw. It was the first time we fought under our own flag and we did okay. The Turks lost 65 000 men at Gallipoli, though, of course, not all of them to us. We celebrate the spirit. The spirit of Anzac.'

'Hmm . . .' He thought for a moment, then said, 'Okay, I can pay that.' Then he asked, 'If the New Zealanders are your buddies, you know, your brothers in arms, how come when we passed through the gun position of the New Zealand 16th Field Artillery they shouted abuse at you? Calling you a bunch of convicts and you yelling back with a rude reference to their sexual activity with sheep?'

'Yeah, well, that's what brothers do, isn't it?'

'And you've invited the Turks, *your enemy*, to celebrate your Anzac Day?'

'We honour them as great warriors,' I replied, but I could see he didn't understand. 'It's the spirit of Anzac,' I said, trying once more to explain. 'Respect for your enemy. Know what I mean?' But I don't think he did, nor for that matter, could he imagine the prospect of inviting a bunch of Chinese communists to commemorate the Korean War after this particular stoush was over.

However, the spirit of Anzac was about to be terminated and we never did get a chance to share a beer with the Turks. The Chinese mounted a massive attack on the front-line and that was the end of the holiday – the Commonwealth Brigade was called in to occupy a blocking position astride the valley in case of a Chinese breakthrough at the front.

At first we hadn't taken it too seriously – it seemed to be pretty much routine procedure. Anyway, recently the whole front seemed to have been pretty well holding up. We reckoned we'd soon be back in our holiday camp munching goodies with an extra beer ration for Anzac Day. We were positioned on Hill 504, where I'd been separated from my platoon and relegated to company headquarters to be a runner. Somewhat reluctantly I dug a weapon pit in the still half-frozen ground. The front was miles away and I reckoned any breakthrough would be stopped long before it reached us. From my weapon pit the view was magnificent. I looked out across paddy fields and in the distance I could see a road snaking its way through the Kapyong Valley towards us. It cut right through the battalion position a good distance below. As usual, it was packed with refugees.

I recall looking down at 12 Platoon, who were digging in a couple of hundred yards further down the hill at the forward edge of the company position. I must admit I would have preferred to be with my mates, but Ivan the Terrible had told me to get my arse into gear and report to company headquarters for runner duty. Communications in the mountains can get a bit dicey at times and breakdowns were not uncommon, so a company runner was pretty normal. Nevertheless, a soldier is never happy to be away from his platoon, from his mates. I'd consoled myself with the thought that things could be worse – I'd be with my old mate from New Guinea, Ian Ferrier. Being habitually curious, in the unlikely event of a battle, at least I'd have some idea of what was happening up front.

'Welcome aboard, Jacko. How'd you cop the runner's job?' Ian asked.

'Ivan,' I replied, as if this explained everything. '"Give you a chance to be the little general," he said. Sarcastic bastard! He knows nothing will happen and I'll get bugger-all sleep.'

'Never know your luck,' Ian replied.

'Nah, it's a good twenty miles to the front. We'll be sitting here like a shag on a rock.'

'Oh yeah?' he handed me his binoculars. 'Take a dekko.'

I focused on the road below. It was filled with the usual refugees going south. 'Refugees, so what's new?'

'Take a closer look, mate.'

'Jesus! Not again!' I now made out the fleeing South Korean soldiers among the refugees. 'What outfit?'

He'd stopped rolling a cigarette, '6th ROK Division.'

'Why don't we just tell them to pack up and go home? They're bloody useless, anyway.'

Ian grinned. 'I'd dig that weapon pit a bit deeper if I was you, mate.'

At dusk, with the light failing and having dug my weapon pit, I took a last look at the road. 'The road's full of the bastards!' Below me the South Koreans were thick as flies, some in the back of trucks although most on foot, running for their lives. Circumstances had definitely changed and we may just have been in for a long and uncomfortable night.

Describing the positions of the various units in battle can be difficult – you have to get a picture in your mind. But here goes. Imagine Hill 504 rising 1300 feet out of the valley below. It was a big feature and completely dominated the area surrounding it. From it, a spur line ran for a mile or so down to the road that snaked through the valley. By the way, a spur line is a narrow ridge projecting from a mountain, a bit like an above-ground root extending from a large Moreton Bay fig tree. D Company was positioned on Hill 504. We were on the right flank. A Company occupied the spur line and was at the centre. Across the road on our left flank was B Company, situated on a much smaller hill rising no more than 300 feet up from the valley. These three companies, each of about a hundred men, were stretched across the main route down the Kapyong Valley. Not far behind this forward line was C Company, held in reserve. If the proverbial hit the fan and any of the companies were overrun it was their job to come to the rescue. Finally, a little over a mile further back was battalion headquarters with our mortars and support personnel. That's the best 'the little general' can do; hopefully you get the idea.

It may have been early spring but it was still bloody cold. Ian was busy on the radio and I was feeling lonely away from my platoon, sitting on my arse in my weapon pit with bugger-all to do. Night fell not long before nine p.m. and soon after a pale, near-full moon rose over the valley. It was an ideal night for an attack and, of course, the Chinese were aware of this. Half an hour later the first shots rang out.

'There ya go, mate, the chinks are coming,' Ian shouted from the radio pit. 'Keep your head down, Jacko!'

You always hear the echo of the first shots, but after that your ears tune to the trajectory of an incoming shell or the direction from which the small-arms fire is coming. I could hear these first shots being directed at some tanks to the front of B Company because, in reply to the fast *rrr-rrrt* of the Chinese burp guns there followed the pedantic, heavier sound of the thirty and fifty calibre machine guns fired from the tanks. Shots rang out to our rear, in the direction of battalion headquarters. They appeared intermittent and didn't sound too determined. What was getting really hairy was less than half a mile down the spur line towards the road, where the Chinese were beginning to mount an attack against A Company.

I don't know why, but the Chinese preparation for battle is somehow different to any other enemy's. On the one hand the sound of their bugles is like something out of *Boys' Own Annual*, but on the other, it's scary as shit when it's combined with their various whistles signalling the start of an assault. First the bugles then the whistles, followed by silence. We knew what that meant – they were moving forward up the steep slope in the dark, heading for the A Company blokes on the spur line below us.

I could hear my heart pumping as I waited for the next set of bugle calls. They sounded suddenly, indicating the enemy had reached the correct distance from our defences to hurl their stick grenades. These now showed out of the semi-darkness as a sudden burst of fireworks, and then the screaming began. Their sound when they attack, I guess, is the equivalent of the yelling we do when we mount a bayonet charge. But, of course, when this occurs you only hear your own voice belting out the courage to rush into the jaws of possible death. It's quite a different sound when you're on the receiving end. It's frightening, yet you can sense the fear of the attackers, their muscles pumped with adrenaline, their voices attempting to silence their fiercely beating hearts.

The Chinese infantry were coming in to kill or to be killed. The vociferant charge was immediately mixed with the brash, clattering sound of our machine guns attempting to halt them in their tracks. Barrels that would soon be too hot to touch were spitting bullets determined to mow them down, to obliterate the advancing human horde, to silence it forever. The last thing they would see would be a flash of malice from the barrel of a machine gun, the last thing they would smell would be the acrid stench of cordite. Looking down I could see the red-and-yellow bursts of light as the grenades exploded and the lines of red tracers from our machine guns criss-crossing the battlefield as the killing commenced.

This was fighting at the closest possible quarters, the Chinese bursting out of the darkness only five or six yards in front of 1 Platoon, who took the brunt of the charge. Our blokes were holding their nerve, careful not to fire into the darkness, waiting until they could squeeze off a killing shot. A careless shot that missed could cost you your life. The Chinese would be dropping like flies but some would be getting through, their burp guns ablaze, and they'd have to be dealt with by bullet or bayonet from the next line of defence. The pressure was relentless – as the first wave was cut down the second appeared screaming out of the darkness, jumping over their dead and wounded comrades. By the time the third wave came at us it would be a flurry of recharging magazines and, God forbid, dealing with weapon stoppages. Regardless of loss of life the Chinese would keep coming, until you believed they couldn't be beaten. With all this going on we knew enough about the enemy to know that, in addition, their patrols would be probing to see what troops were defending Hill 504. We were going to be the next to die, nothing was more certain.

Our company commander motioned over to Ian to call battalion headquarters. 'Comms ain't good, boss,' Ian said, then repeated his call sign, twiddling knobs and yelling into the handset. Finally, he passed it to the boss.

'Where the hell is the artillery?' The company commander shouted, without first introducing himself. It was then that I realised I hadn't heard the familiar *crump, crump, crump* of artillery shell and mortar bombs. It is a sound that always brings hope to the soldier in his weapon pit and now it was missing. Below me the boys in A Company were fighting the chinks without artillery support. In military terms this is a bit like fighting with one hand tied behind your back. The company commander appeared to be listening for a few moments then, shaking his head in disbelief, he handed the set back to Ian in disgust. 'Get through to A Company and bring me up to date,' he snapped, not explaining the absence of artillery.

The firing from A Company seemed to have diminished somewhat, but we didn't know if they'd been overrun and the Chinese were heading our way or they'd seen the enemy off. After some time Ian looked up from the handset. 'They've sent 'em packing, boss, but they're sure they'll be back. They report the Chinese are in big numbers and appear even more fired up than usual.'

'That's understandable,' the boss, still annoyed, replied. 'We are the only thing stopping the bloody Chinese from a headlong rush to Seoul.'

So much for being a back-up battalion: the bastards had turned us into the front-line. Down below us A Company would be attending to their dead and wounded, carrying them to a position in the rear while some of the blokes in the second line of weapon pits would be filling the vacancies in the front stalls.

The boss departed and Ian got off the radio to take a break, getting out the makings to roll a smoke. 'Here, mate.' I struck a match, shielding its light in my pile cap, lit a fag I'd previously rolled and offered it to him. 'Where the bloody hell's our fire support?' I asked, not really expecting him to know.

He took a slow drag, careful to shield the glow, then exhaled. 'Just about to tell you. The New Zealanders, with the Middlesex Battalion alongside them, were way up the valley supporting the no-hopers in the South Korean division. Now they've come back, retreating among the rabble clogging the roads. The Poms are supposed to occupy a position on our left flank but they're somewhere way to our rear now.' He paused and took another drag of his fag. 'Christ knows where the guns are. If you ask me, it's an unholy fuck-up – a wide-open left flank and bugger-all artillery support.' Forgetting himself he waved his fag in the air. 'Christ help us if the chinks come at us now.'

What he was saying was that there were less than 400 of us blocking the enemy's way to Seoul and the Chinese intended to go through us like a dose of salts and get to the capital pronto. With no artillery support and an unprotected left flank we'd have Buckley's – or as Ian put it in his colourful way, 'We're going to hell in a hand basket!' He went back to the radio, twiddled a few knobs then listened, and moments later looked up. 'Fuck me dead! The cunning bastards!'

'What? What's happening?' I asked anxiously.

'Some of the Chinese must've infiltrated to our rear by placing themselves among the fleeing South Koreans, and now they're having a go at battalion headquarters!' he explained. 'HQ are saying we can't expect mortar support – they've got their hands full and can't fire 'em.' He jumped up from his weapon pit and walked over to the boss, and I heard him giving the company commander the bad news.

When he returned I asked, 'What about the Yank crew? Their heavy mortars are supposed to be there to support us!'

'Can't raise the bludgers. They must have caught bug-out fever and headed for the hills,' Ian replied.

'Jesus, mate, we're up shit creek!'

I'd hardly completed this remark when we heard the Chinese bugles, followed by the whistles, then the dreaded waiting in silence, broken at last by the exploding grenades, their screaming and the burp guns banging away like cracker night. Our answering fire came almost immediately. Below me was a confusion of thousands of muzzle flashes criss-crossed by red tracer fire from our Vickers machine guns. Exploding grenades, like camera flashes, momentarily illuminated the grim battle.

Three hours passed with the sound of bugles and whistles continually in my ears, the pale moonlight not sufficient to see the battle. A thousand or so Chinese had attacked 1 Platoon and Ian informed me they were down to thirteen men from the original strength of thirty. Christ only knows what the chink casualties must have been, but later we were told the dead were piled high on the perimeter. Anyway, thirteen men were not enough to hold out any more attacks so 1 Platoon withdrew back up the spur line to company headquarters, and now the chinks occupied their position. That was the first link in our chain of defence broken. Things were looking decidedly crook.

The company commander was back trying to make contact on the handset, though without much success. Finally he handed it back to Ian.

'What happens if A Company can't survive the night?' I asked him. It wasn't my place to ask such a question. And I didn't really expect an answer. Besides, I almost knew what would be going through his head: *No artillery or mortar support, no barbed wire or anti-personnel mine defences. Let's say, maybe fifty men alive and still able to fight, only machine guns, rifles, bayonets, grenades and courage against an inexhaustible number of fired-up Chinese soldiers.* He sighed, then to my surprise, answered, 'If they can hold out 'til morning, the Chinese won't have such freedom to move and we'll have a chance to maybe find out what's happened to the bloody artillery. Might even get some air support.' The way he said it made it painfully obvious that, short of a miracle, A Company was doomed. What this meant was that D Company would be next onto the starting blocks. But then he added, 'Yeah, well, with A Company gone the Chinese will get behind us, then we're surrounded.' It was his way of saying we wouldn't be able to withdraw and would almost certainly share the fate of A Company.

Baggy-arsed diggers didn't see much of the company commander, he being somewhat out of our realm up there with God directing operations. Now I was to have the doubtful pleasure of dying alongside him on a lonely hill that didn't even rejoice in a name and was simply known as number 504 on a military ordnance map.

We waited for the inevitable attack from the chinks who now occupied 1 Platoon's position, but it didn't come. Not much happened for a while then, close to two a.m., the Chinese sent a barrage of mortars, including incendiaries, into A Company. The incendiaries set alight the low brush and started fires racing through their positions. *This is it!* I thought. With the fires raging I was able to see more clearly for the first time and could now make out a few of our blokes moving about and the Chinese dead lying right up against our weapon pits. Only the Kiwi artillery coming back on line could save them now. But to my surprise the Chinese attacked in far fewer numbers and with a great deal less shouting and enthusiasm when next they came at us. Maybe they'd taken too many casualties and were looking for a softer target for their main effort. The boys in A Company had put up such fierce resistance that the chinks may have been unaware of how close they'd come to breaking through again. I recall thinking, *Please God, don't let them wake up to the situation and mount an all-out attack while it is still dark*. In the meantime, A Company wasn't answering our calls.

Dawn came and A Company was still holding out, and with daylight the hope was that as the Chinese preferred to fight at night they would withdraw. Ian managed to get A Company back on the radio and was told they were down to less than fifty men and had been trying to raise our own battalion headquarters without success. They'd finally managed to get through on the radio to the headquarters of an American outfit. Ian first told the boss and when he returned, told me the story, the way he'd heard it from his A Company counterpart:

'Hello one, hello one, how do you hear me, how do you hear me? Over.'

This, he claimed, was repeated several times with no response, then an American voice came on.

'One, this is Red Dog three, send, over.'

'One for Red Dog three, we are out of comms with our headquarters. We are under Chinese attack and need artillery support and relief. Can you help? Over.'

'This is Red Dog three, send your unit name and location in clear, over.'

'One for Red Dog three, A Company, 3rd Battalion, Royal Australian Regiment with the British Commonwealth Brigade, location five miles north of Kapyong 487356.'

There is a pause. 'Red Dog three, say again your unit, over.'

'One, we are bloody A Company 3RAR. You bastards deaf or something, over!'

Silence. Then, 'Red Dog three, our information is firm, these units were overrun and destroyed last night. Whoever you are, leave the net immediately, out.'

I'm not sure how much of this dialogue was Ian Ferrier's sense of drama at play, but what was obvious was that the Yanks had written us off and the only hope of help – 'rescue' is probably a better word – was to get through to someone at our own battalion headquarters. The fighting appeared to have stopped, with only an occasional mortar bomb going off. With daylight, the chinks would be expecting an air attack and artillery and I wondered how long it would take for them to realise that neither of these was going to eventuate. The Americans were convinced we had been wiped out, the Kiwis hadn't yet been located and we couldn't talk to battalion headquarters. With no help coming the question was were we in for it or would the Chinese melt away until nightfall?

We hadn't long to wait for the answer. The need to break through and go on to capture Seoul was imperative because no sooner had Ian told me the radio communication story than I heard some small-arms fire coming from the direction of 12 Platoon. I listened in dismay as my platoon defended the forward edge of the company position, aware that I should've been with them copping the flak.

You don't like to be standing by while your mates are in the firing line, and when the boss arrived a short while later I requested permission to join my platoon. 'Yeah, righto, now it's daytime we can do without you. On yer bike, son.'

As I arrived, the medics were taking out Ray Davis, who appeared to have a shattered arm. Ivan the Terrible yelled out for me to take his place beside Ted Shearer, Ray's partner. I slipped into the weapon pit. 'G'day,' I said to Ted. 'What happened to Ray?'

'Bloody machine gun, his wrist, welcome back to 12 Platoon,' he replied, all in the one rapid sentence. He and Ray were real good mates and with the battle at hand he clearly didn't want to dwell on the matter.

'What's going on?' I asked.

'At first light, most of 8 Section went out on a routine clearing patrol down the spur line,' he explained. 'About 400 yards down they came across some Chinese setting up a machine gun on the high ground to the left.' He pointed to our left front. 'Across yonder gully, on the high ground, chink machine gun.'

I looked to where he'd pointed and could see that the enemy machine gunner was well sited to give us a heap of trouble. The odd burst of automatic fire was already shredding some of the scrub not far from us.

'Ken can't get to the bugger,' Ted said. I looked across to where Ken Carter, the section's Bren light machine gunner, was trying to identify exactly where the chink fire was coming from. Then he opened fire and the Chinese machine-gun position suddenly went quiet. Hopefully he'd got the bastard.

To our direct front a narrow ridge line fell away. A couple of hundred yards down, it descended steeply and disappeared from view. The ten of us in 8 Section were positioned nicely to cover any enemy coming up the ridge towards us. There was not a lot of cover for an attacking force and what's more, the ridge was only wide enough for a four- or five-man frontage. Attacking uphill is hard, slow work, so if they came this way there were going to be a lot of dead Chinese. This thought was immediately followed by the chilling knowledge that ratios didn't matter to them – twenty of their men killed for every one of ours were acceptable odds. They seemed prepared to sacrifice whatever was required to win.

I heard the distinctive 'pop' of a mortar fired in the distance and wondered if it was heading for us. The bomb soared high into the air, losing speed as it climbed, then turned and plummeted to earth. I listened for the sound of its downward path, like stones rattling in a tin can, the rattle growing louder and louder, meaning that it was headed in our direction. We ducked into our weapon pits as the bomb landed about a hundred yards away with an ear-splitting *whamphar!* followed by the sound of shrapnel slicing through the low scrub and zinging off the rocky outcrops. There was a pause then six more bombs followed, landing much closer. The chinks had got our range.

The mortar barrage ceased at last and we put our heads up and, through the dust and smoke, Ted pointed to the Chinese troops about a hundred yards down the ridge advancing towards us. They could only fit five up front on the narrow ridge and those five were copping all the fire from our section. But as we dropped them, we could see those behind taking their place, rank after rank extending back as far as we could see. I wasn't sure whether I'd rather fight at night when you couldn't see what was coming at you, or during the day, when you became aware of the seemingly inexhaustible depth of the enemy.

We were throwing everything we had at them without making too much impression. There was something missing. I heard our section commander, Bob Roland, yelling orders, and Ken Carter then turned his Bren machine gun onto the ridge line to create havoc. *That's better!* But this freed the chink machine gun on the hill and his bullets were kicking up the dust around our pits, making it bloody hard to concentrate on the enemy coming up the ridge. Ken swung back to have another go at the machine gunner, but of course this in turn took pressure off the assaulting Chinese, who surged forward, firing at us as they came. It scared the shit out of me as I realised how remorseless and competent they were – the bastards had done this before and *really* knew their business.

Every shot we squeezed off had to count. Missing even one shot increased the odds. Deadly accuracy was the only way we were going to contain this mob. We were so busy killing them that there was no time to be in awe of the bravery and determination of the enemy. You dropped one in his tracks yet the bloke behind him didn't even slow down, kept coming at you. It was like watching a steam train coming down the track towards you and being unable to move. Some of the enemy were soon close enough to throw stick grenades. If they landed nearby you had to duck into your pit till they exploded. And if you were a bit slow at re-emerging, it gave any chink close enough a chance to charge forward and take you out.

Shortly after we'd commenced the battle, one of these stick grenades landed near me. I ducked for cover and it exploded. Maybe I was a bit slow to pop my head up again – a Chinese soldier was no more than three yards from me with his burp gun spitting bullets that kicked up the soil three feet in front of me. Ted took him out.

'Thanks mate, I owe you one,' I shouted hastily, aiming at another line of chinks heading towards us. Even in the heat of battle, after a while it starts to sink in that you're not going to be able to kill them all, that they're getting closer and closer despite their fearful casualties. I was beginning to accept that being overrun was inevitable and I was almost certainly going to die.

The point was that the act of killing a man was no longer a thing of blood, shattered bone and viscera, but a grim process of defeating a team opposed to you. But it was a team who had a supply of fresh players they kept bringing onto the field and you'd long since used up all your reserves.

This must sound pretty crass, but there were so many men dying in front of us that we couldn't grasp the meaning of death. Defending our right to stay alive, to win against the odds, was the only thing on our minds.

Then there were some mighty explosions. Dust, debris and smoke filled the air. For a moment I thought the end was finally here – we were gone for all money. But when the air cleared I was still alive and there were dead and wounded chinks lying everywhere along the ridge line. The Kiwis had been found and their artillery, as usual, was dead on target. But the Chinese seemed undeterred and came running up from the rear, rifles and burp guns ablaze, and the attack gathered momentum again. Down came another salvo, and I swore if I lived I'd never say anything nasty about the All Blacks again. Some of the shells landed harmlessly in the deep gullies on each side of the ridge line and one landed uselessly, well behind the action. But once again the rest were bang on target and several shells landed slap-bang in the middle of our attackers. Through the smoke I saw several bodies thrown high into the air like rag dolls thrown upwards by a child at play.

Suddenly everything stopped. The referee had blown his whistle in the form of a dozen or so twenty-five-pounder artillery shells. While the Chinese were able to press their attack despite the casualties we inflicted with rifles, Owens and even our Bren machine gun, there was no way they could withstand the decimation caused by the accurate artillery of our beautiful cousins across the Tasman. The chinks halted the attack and dragged their dead and wounded down the ridge line out of sight.

'Well, I'll be buggered. I think we've seen them off,' I said to Ted, then I realised I was almost too tired to stand.

No reply came and I glanced over to where he sat with his chin on his chest and his arms folded, his right hand holding his wrist. It was as if he'd just fallen asleep during a boring lecture, so I touched him lightly on the shoulder. 'Ted?' I asked. Then, concealed by his arm, I saw the blood. A piece of shrapnel had torn through his chest and I could see a part of his heart, which was a bloody mess. With the cessation of fighting, death became real again.

I called over to the medical orderly, 'Chunky' Dunbar, who took Ted away. Chunky had copped some shrapnel in the head himself but was simply carrying on regardless. I began to feel a terrible remorse and it was difficult not to cry. I hadn't even seen it happen to Ted. Surely he would have said something, cried out, or given me a final message I might have passed on to someone he loved. I'd let him down – Ted, who had saved my life not long before, had died, so to speak, in front of my eyes, and I hadn't even noticed.

Shortly afterwards, to my surprise, John Lazarou slipped into the weapon pit beside me. 'Come to join yiz, mate.'

His sudden presence put a stop to my introspection. 'G'day, Lazy, who are you with?' I asked, still somewhat dazed, meaning, who was his partner in what would normally be his weapon pit.

'Catflap, wounded in the hand. Bullet. Pinkie took clean off.'

'That's all? Lucky bastard.'

Lazy grinned. 'Yeah, he said it was lucky it wasn't his pussy finger or Lotus Flower would be real cranky.'

'Hadn't you better get back? Chinks'll probably be returning any minute.'

'Nah, I'm staying put. If I'm gonna be killed in this fuckin' shithole, I want to cark it next to me mate.'

I laughed. I don't know why. After the shock of Ted I should have been more sensitive, but I just laughed and said, 'Well, mate, you've made an excellent choice. The odds are you'll achieve your objective, this pit is attracting more than its fair share of attention.'

I waited for the usual ingenuous reaction from Lazy. I could almost paraphrase him. It would come in slow motion, something like: '*Shit . . . I didn't think of that . . . yeah, right, Jacko, good one.*' But instead he slammed a round into the breach of his rifle and replied, 'Them's acceptable odds, Jacko. We done things together before.'

'Yeah, but not yet died together,' I quipped. Lazy didn't see the joke.

'That's okay by me, Jacko,' he said in all seriousness.

I could see Ken Carter disengage from his ongoing duel with the

Chinese machine gunner and swing around to the right to engage the ridge line. The Chinese were back. Mortars exploded around us with that deafening *whampar!* and we ducked for our lives. As the mortars lifted we raised our heads for a look. Here they came again, rank upon rank of them advancing into our small-arms fire. The enemy machine gun on the hill was giving us a bit of curry and Ken was swinging left and right like a yo-yo going sideways, taking them both on. A salvo of artillery fire exploded in front of us and as the smoke cleared I saw that the narrow ridge line hadn't been hit and the Chinese were coming in fast. Thank Christ it was uphill for them, although they appeared to be pretty fit. 'Storming in' wouldn't be entirely the wrong expression to use.

The clatter of small-arms fire seemed deafening but I could still hear Bob Roland, our section commander, shouting an order and we responded by throwing hand grenades that rolled down the hill and exploded among the leading attackers. We kept hurling them, taking cover as they exploded and then going again. We were stopping a fair few but the rest kept coming. Now quite a few chink soldiers were close enough to throw their own grenades – the fighting was getting close and desperate. Then I heard another salvo screaming towards us and at least one twenty-five-pounder round hit the ridge and the silver fern had done its magic again and saved our Aussie arses.

'Shit, yer was right about this fuckin' pit,' Lazy chuckled, reaching for his water bottle.

The Kiwi artillery were never given the accolades due to them in the Korean War. Putting it mildly, they were remarkable and saved a great many Australian lives. I know we were proud to think of them as our brothers. Like close family, we knew they'd always be there if they possibly could. However, it was not just the big guns saving the day. Bob Roland kept the section together, coordinating our defences even though wounded. Blood was streaming down the side of his face and he kept wiping it out of his eyes using his sleeve. Ken Carter was still firing, the barrel of his Bren red hot. He too was wounded, the back of his khaki shirt dark from wet blood. Chunky Dunbar and his off-sider, Harry Robertson, were ignoring the bee-swarm of bullets to get to the wounded. Ivan the Terrible, reluctant as I am to admit, was everywhere at once, dragging a box of ammunition and resupplying anyone running short. It seemed such a pity a great team like this was almost certainly going to die.

The Chinese attacks seemed never-ending. We'd repulse one and no sooner had we evacuated our casualties and refilled our magazines than they'd be back again. Maybe they couldn't quite get their heads around the fact that a handful of blokes with only small arms and grenades with some artillery support could withstand their most determined attacks and repulse limitless manpower. After all, they'd just sent a whole South Korean division fleeing before them in terror.

We somehow held them off for six terrifying, exhausting hours, then there was a lull. It seemed unlikely that they'd run out of men and I could only conclude that they'd temporarily withdrawn and were in the act of devising new tactics. The enemy was now familiar with our battleground, and with the casualties we'd suffered we wondered how much longer we could hold out. The word was that the boss was worried too, especially about how we might fare in a night attack, and he pulled us back closer to the rest of the company on Hill 504. We started to dig in and this time I was thankful that our platoon wasn't the first in line to meet the enemy.

Ten Platoon was situated adjacent to the summit and we were not far below them, and as we dug our weapon pits two American Corsair ground-attack aircraft appeared in the distance.

'You bloody beauty! It's the Yanks!' Lazy called out.

We all stopped digging to look. Their timing was perfect – they'd catch the Chinese below and out in the open and give them heaps, knock the living daylights out of them. I could see several blokes up ahead of me looking up and waving encouragement. Then the spotter plane dived and fired a yellow smoke marker spigot into the heart of 10 Platoon's position.

What happened next was too bizarre for words. One of the Corsair fighters came in low and fast and released a napalm canister from under its wing. It smashed into the ground near the yellow smoke marker and broke open to release the flaming jellied petrol over a good part of the 10 Platoon position. I couldn't believe my eyes. The iridescent pink-and-yellow marker panels that identified us, situated as they were at the very summit, must have been easy to see from the air. The spotter plane would have needed to be blind not to identify them as ours. Later, the most charitable excuse was that the Yanks concluded the Chinese had captured us and left the identification up to deceive attacking aircraft. But that's not how we saw it then – or ever after, for that matter.

The second Corsair made its run just as one of our blokes grabbed the identification panel and waved it at the spotter plane. At the last second it pulled out and roared away. I was running as hard as I could to get to 10 Platoon. The sight that met me when I arrived still sometimes wakes me in a cold sweat in the middle of the night. Lazy headed for one bloke who was burning and I went towards another one in flames. Wherever I looked there were horribly burned diggers scattered around with their mates trying to kill the flames that simply wouldn't go out. Napalm sticks, then penetrates and burns from the inside of the flesh outwards. The victims were screaming in pain and terror while fires raged through the scrub, setting off boxes of ammunition. Near me was the redoubtable Chunky Dunbar, our stretcher bearer, who came running as well. We were both heading for a bloke who was enveloped in flames, but as Chunky got close, a grenade lined up on the edge of the weapon pit the burning bloke was in went off in the heat and blew Chunky down the hill. I dropped, expecting another grenade to pop. Bluey Walsh of 10 Platoon crossed my path and dropped in a flaming heap next to me. I started to empty my water bottle onto his burns. Suddenly he raised his head and in a surprised voice said, 'Oh shit!' and died. I ran over to the original bloke sitting in his weapon pit. His body was as black as tar and the flesh hung from his face and arms. Then I saw Chunky approaching, limping badly, his trouser leg torn to the knee, and there was a lot of blood and gore. 'Better get back, Jacko, the chinks are coming again,' he said calmly. 'Leave this one to me.' The poor bastard dying in front of me recognised Chunky and saw the bloody mess his leg was in and amazingly said, 'Jesus, Chunky, you're having a rough day, ain't ya.'

The Chinese attack was finally repulsed by 11 Platoon. But, disconcertingly, this time the chinks approached from our unprotected right flank. This meant it wouldn't be too long before they worked their way to our rear and cut us off. I continued helping with the wounded even during the attack as our platoon wasn't involved. Now on my way back to my weapon pit I passed Ian Ferrier, as usual with his ear glued to the radio. I tapped him on the shoulder and he paused and removed the headphone and greeted me.

'Why are we still here, Ian? The bloody chinks are close to surrounding us!' I shouted.

'Never fear, Jacko, a Yank regiment is . . .' he corrected himself, '*was* supposed to arrive this arvo.'

I didn't like the two words 'was' and 'supposed'. 'And?' I asked trenchantly.

'And they're not.' He shrugged. 'That's the bad news.'

'And the good?'

He smiled. 'Message just came through, the battalion has permission to withdraw.'

'Mate, we've waited too long!' I protested. I was playing the little general again, although it wasn't a difficult conclusion. We'd outstayed our welcome on the mountain and even the chinks knew it was only a matter of time before we were completely encircled.

'I know – let's just hope, eh?' Ian, ever the optimist, replied. He was the perfect radio operator, hearing all the good and the bad news and taking both in his stride. His job was both to gather information and to convey it, and he did so calmly without getting emotionally involved. But, because he was an inveterate knob twiddler, he always seemed to know more than anyone else. The boss was lucky to have him, because he had the benefit of Ian's ability to gather scraps of seemingly irrelevant information from various sources and then to draw them together into a proper conclusion.

At the time I was having this conversation with Ian I didn't know that when the napalm struck the fire had swept through company headquarters, and Ian had dived through the flames in the nick of time to save the company radio set. It didn't bear thinking what might have happened if we hadn't been able to maintain radio contact.

Later, as we withdrew while under heavy attack, Ian played a key part in communicating fire orders to the Kiwis during the final phase of the thinning-out process. Without this artillery support, we almost certainly would have been overwhelmed by the Chinese. Ian remained behind to the last and I'm delighted to say he was mentioned in despatches for the Battle of Kapyong.

The Chinese, while retired from a direct onslaught, were still harassing us with mortars and machine guns, so Lieutenant Hamill couldn't gather us around for one of his famous stick-and-sand talks. Instead he briefed the section commanders and they hopped into the various weapon pits and gave us the salient points. What it boiled down to was simple enough – there weren't too many options, in fact, none. The Chinese were in charge of the main road to the South so the only possible way for the whole battalion to withdraw was through our position on Hill 504. From there, it was down a two-and-a-half mile long wooded spur line descending gradually to finally come to a ford across the Kapyong River not far from where the Middlesex Battalion was dug in waiting for us to arrive.

At four p.m. a great barrage of high explosives and smoke was laid down to cover the withdrawal of the companies from the front-line. From our position higher up we could see them approaching us, snaking along with a cloud of thick smoke behind them. Our biggest concern was that the Chinese would cotton on to the fact that we were getting out and would move to intercept them. There was a palpable sense of relief as each company made it safely up to our position on the hill and then to the rear down the spur line to the ford. This left D

Company, that is, us, the last to withdraw. I confess I was really packing it – the chinks had to wake up to what was happening.

As the last company passed through our position the Chinese twigged. Determined not to be robbed of a victory, they came at us with even greater ferocity than we'd hitherto witnessed. Nicole Lenoir-Jourdan's warning of celestial revenge on the British Empire was about to manifest itself and, what's more, her star pupil, Jack McKenzie, was going to cop the lot. This time the chinks wouldn't be thwarted. Lazy and I were flat out trying to keep our end up when I heard Ian Ferrier's voice behind me. *Christ, what's he doing here?* I thought. We were at the very front of the action – company headquarters was supposed to be well back from us.

Then I heard the boss's voice. 'Drop 100, two rounds gunfire, over!' he shouted into the radio handset.

Moments later the Kiwi shells came over our heads with their peculiar paper-tearing sound and landed fifty yards to our front, the shells exploding right in amongst the advancing chinks. Dust and smoke billowed upwards and body parts flew everywhere. A foot, sliced through above the ankle with its canvas boot still attached, landed no more than five yards from where we were, tumbled a few feet backwards and came to rest against a small outcrop of rock directly in front of me.

'Repeat, over,' the boss barked down the receiver.

Despite the carnage in front of us the Chinese kept coming, while the artillery continued mowing them down with a little help from our rifles and machine guns. I confess I have never seen men as brave. Or, in our terms, as bloody foolhardy. They seemed to have no regard for their own lives and it was obvious they expected to die. Muslims believe that when they die in battle they will be immediately transported to paradise, and we've got some sort of idea about going to heaven. For these blokes there was no special redemption or reward for the warrior after death. One couldn't help wondering how they could meet it so calmly, becoming utterly heedless of risks, palpably discounting their own lives and, as a result, becoming a ferocious and almost unstoppable force.

At last a lull occurred in the fighting and we received the immediate order to withdraw and head down the spur line. The Chinese were soon enough at us again and the only way I can find to describe the way the battalion withdrew, D Company in particular, is to say that this was no bug out. Sure we were back-pedalling fit to bust, but with our fists flailing. It was ten p.m. when we crossed the river and joined the waiting Middlesex troops. I was too tired to feel anything, much less elation. We'd been fighting for fifteen hours, I'd had little or no sleep the night before and I was completely buggered.

Thank God the Chinese hadn't followed us across the ford. Instead, they'd turned on the 2nd Battalion, Princess Patricia's Canadian Light Infantry, on the opposite side of the valley. Frustrated at allowing us to escape, they attacked them as fiercely as at any time against us. The Princess Patricias fought all night until dawn in a heroic encounter where they lost many of their men but managed to hold on until the enemy finally ran out of steam and melted into the early-morning landscape.

The following day the brigadier came around to congratulate us. You don't see too many blokes with red bands around their caps turning up at the company level. He told us our thin, isolated line had almost certainly prevented the taking of Seoul by the Chinese and therefore the capture of thousands of United Nations support troops stationed there. But it wasn't without a price, the ultimate one for many of our mates – 3RAR had lost thirty-two killed and fifty-nine wounded with three of our number missing in action.

I guess we'd done our bit and, for the next few months anyway, we were covered in glory. In June it was announced that 3RAR had been awarded the US Presidential Citation for our stand at Kapyong. No higher foreign compliment exists for an Allied unit. The Princess Patricia's Canadian Light Infantry got one as well, as did the American Company A, 72nd Heavy Tank Battalion.

We were all pretty stoked at the announcement, but there was one big omission. If ever a unit deserved this same honour it was the Kiwi artillery, and they'd missed out. The citation concerning 3RAR reads in part: '. . . displayed such gallantry, determination and *esprit de corps* as to set them apart and above the other units participating in the campaign'. Furthermore, our section didn't go unrecognised. Bob Roland was awarded the Distinguished Conduct Medal, Chunky Dunbar got the Military Medal and a bloke named Snowy Tyler, who had fought with a bullet in his shoulder, also got one. Finally, Harry Robertson, who was killed while evacuating the wounded, was mentioned, posthumously, in dispatches.

I guess we'd been vindicated. The rag-tag K Force volunteers, with their mostly piss-poor excuses for joining up when the real reason was that they'd failed at civilian life after World War II, had redeemed themselves. We were soldiers of whom it could be said were '*Set apart and above other units*', which was something a man could take pride in and hold onto.

Several months went by, through a hot dusty summer and into the autumn with the air a little sharper on the nostrils each morning. The war was changing – now we stayed in one place for longer stretches and built more substantial defences as we learnt how to effectively fight the Chinese. But mostly we patrolled in dangerous territory, which kept our wits about us.

In October we slogged our way into the Maryang San complex of mountains where D Company, that's us, fought fiercely in a protracted battle with the Chinese to take a series of fortified knolls leading to the heavily defended Hill 317. This time we got a taste of what it was like to fight against a well-dug-in and determined enemy, and it wasn't a very nice experience even though the battalion finally managed to get them off the hill. After this it was more foot-slogging, more patrolling, more boring bloody war.

I had only three weeks to go before returning to Australia, to Queen Island. This time, though, I would be returning with a few more ribbons on my chest, including the citation from the American president. I was no longer a virgin soldier and had fired many – too many – shots I had seen hit my enemy. So much so that killing men had caused in me a deepening sadness that I hoped would go away in time. If the Chinese didn't seem to care if they lived or died then I found I was beginning to care on their behalf. It was time to go home – this sort of warfare was at too close quarters. I kept seeing the foot with the dirty canvas boot attached to it landing near me, tumbling end over end and then settling, wedged between two small sharp rocks, the bloody stump still oozing blood. Man is a notoriously superficial animal and I would be lying if I didn't admit that the best thing of all was that I would escape another Korean winter. I would be returning to late spring on the island, always a wonderful time to be home.

In the meantime my platoon was setting out on yet another of our bloody endless patrols. We were to see if there were any enemy on a hill called 258 on the map, and on the way check out a deserted Korean village. More boot leather used, more muscle fatigue at the end of another thoroughly nerve-racking day. Ian Ferrier, listening to the weather report, called out to me that some early snow was expected and I decided, despite its additional weight, to take one of my American parkas along. It was to be one of the best decisions I ever made.

# CHAPTER SEVEN

## *The Milk Chocolate Initiative*

A bright, near-full moon, with a ring of haze surrounding it, gave the village and the surrounding landscape the look of a monochrome negative held up to the light. We could see patches of early snow clinging precariously to the thatch of the wattle-and-daub huts. While the village appeared to be deserted, we approached slowly. Even in the winter, when natural sounds close down, you can usually hear the odd squawk of a chicken or the peremptory grunt of a sow. But there was nothing here – the villagers had long since joined the crowds of refugees heading south. There is a sense of melancholy about an abandoned village in an old and crowded country. This simple place must have existed for a hundred harvest seasons and then, for reasons its small community didn't understand and in the name of causes meaningless to them, the village had become the detritus of war.

We moved through the perimeter of the village, the bright moonlight casting strong shadows ahead of us. Despite the quietness, I began to feel jittery. They say the moon affects the psyche and that people in the loony bin go right off their scones during full moon. There must be something to this – Gloria would cluck her tongue as she watched Alf trot off to the pub on a big-moon Saturday night, and she'd say,

'Lookit the moon. Bad night comin' up.' She was seldom wrong. On the occasions Saturday coincided with a full moon, or a day or two on either side of it, the pub would be strangely aggro and Alf would come home even more battered than usual.

My ears continued to strain for the slightest sound. The Korean peasants burned charcoal for their cooking fires and as they grew older they developed bronchial problems, so there was always the sound of someone snoring in a hut or coughing in their sleep. Silence was never quite total. Stillness wasn't emptiness. But the only sound for now came from our boots crunching down on the patches of fresh snow that mottled the compound.

I was following Johnny Gordon, who was about fifteen yards ahead of me, my mind momentarily distracted by the fact that, even on the crunchy patina of snow, he managed to put his feet down with less sound than the rest of us. If that sounds patronising, well it ain't – Johnny was the best scout in the group and usually led us into new territory. There were things he would note and a quietness in his step none of us could duplicate.

Fifteen yards behind me the remaining eight blokes in my section were quietly moving into an arrowhead formation, and further back came the platoon headquarters followed by the remaining two sections in file, ready to deploy if it became necessary. I looked back to see our section commander signalling for Johnny and me to move forward cautiously. I passed the hand signal on to Johnny. It seems stupid now, but my eyes were still on Johnny's heels when the burp gun opened up. His left heel suddenly kicked backwards and flew up into the air and a moment later, with a surprised grunt, he crashed to earth.

I hit the ground hard, yelling, 'Contact front!' I'd seen the muzzle flash of the burp gun about thirty yards to my left front and was already firing off shots as fast as I could. Catflap Buggins charged up from behind and belly-slid into a patch of snow, bringing his Bren gun into action. Moments later chunks of wattle and mud were flying everywhere, one hut torn to bits by our rifle and machine-gun fire. No return fire followed the initial burst aimed at Johnny and I yelled at Catflap to cease firing.

In the sudden silence that followed I called out, 'Just a lone sentry!' It was an incautious judgement and one too hastily made, conditioned by my need to rush to Johnny's aid. I told myself the chink who had opened fire was probably dead. If not, he'd be well on his way back to the main enemy position, likely to be well back from us.

'I'm going forward to get Johnny,' I called out, and ran the fifteen yards between us and dropped beside him. Johnny lay on his back and was jerking as if in a fit. I could see several gunshot wounds across the front of his body. 'You okay, mate?' I asked, but he didn't answer, his eyes turned upwards into his head. I glanced around at the scattering of village huts and my soldier's good sense returned and I knew we were in real danger. There was no time to waste, so I grabbed him by the ankles and stood up to drag him back.

Then all hell broke loose. Bullets cracked around my head and kicked up the snow at my feet. I was still holding onto Johnny's ankles, back-pedalling furiously, his shoulders on the ground, head bumping, when something hit me like a steam train and I flew into the air and landed on my backside three or four feet behind where Johnny lay. He was quivering now, his arms flung out, one of his dark hands resting in a small patch of moonlit snow.

I had to get out of the enemy line of fire fast. Leopard-crawl away, elbows hitting the ground, knees propelling me forward. I instinctively knew the drill, only problem was I couldn't move. My elbows dug into the cold dirt ready to go, digging furiously, but the back half, my hips, wouldn't cooperate. I became aware I couldn't feel anything below the waist. *Shit, I'm hit!* was all I could think. *I'm hit and I can't move. Shit, shit, shit!* I tried once more, elbows digging in, chin thrust forward, frantically willing myself to move, but my legs refused to budge. I was up shit creek with a broken paddle. 'I'm hit!' I yelled out, 'can't bloody move!'

I could see some chinks coming in from the left flank, moving tactically, some on the ground firing, others moving forward, lots of them, their shadows like dark capes dragging behind them. Someone called out that they were also coming at us from the right flank. Johnny and I were sandwiched between the enemy and our own blokes. So that our section could retrieve the two of us, the skipper was yelling orders to the section commanders, deploying them forward to take on the Chinese attacking from the flanks. I could hear the artillery forward observer through the clatter of gunfire as he called on his radio, 'Hello two-three for two-zero, battery target over!' Funny that, his voice should have been drowned in the furious gunfire but I heard it clear as a bell. The other voices were coming through as well, telling the skipper we were in danger of being overrun. The sections taking on the enemy were meeting stiff resistance, these Chinese weren't here to hit and run. 'Can't get to 'em, skipper!' was the next thing I heard. Ivan the Terrible's voice now came through. 'Stan, move back now!' he was yelling. 'Back, get back!'

I could feel my heart thumping and an overwhelming panic made it difficult to breathe. *Jesus! They're going to leave us. The bastards are going to desert us, leave us to die!*

'YOU BASTARDS!' I screamed, but they were already on their way out. Johnny gave a final convulsive jerk and died. I lay there listening to the distinctive chatter of our Bren guns and the *rrrt rrrt rrrt* of the Owens mixed with the sound of the Chinese burp guns becoming fainter and fainter. The Chinese had gone after them, ignoring the two of us. *What now?* I thought to myself. *No way I can get away from here*. In my confused state I now thought it was Ivan the Terrible's idea to withdraw, to desert me – the bastard had finally got me. 'BASTARD!' I screamed.

The adrenaline in my system started to diminish and my pulse began to normalise, causing the pain to surface. *If I'm hurt real bad they'll finish me off*, I thought. I didn't quite know how I felt about this. Johnny's life was over, no more racism for him. He'd given his life for his country and he'd be forgotten in a minute by that fuckwit town in Queensland.

And me? *Well, what about me?* Gloria, Sue and the boys, they'd grieve some, but how about Queen Island? Not a sausage. They'd all be at the memorial service, of course, where that ageing old fart Daintree, the vicar of St Stephen's, if he could still stand up, would dredge up something to say that was complimentary to me or the family. Gloria would put on a bit of a wake, but the grog would soon run out because she wouldn't be able to afford to quench their all-powerful thirsts and the fishermen would all retire to the pub – I'd be their 'any excuse to get pissed'.

With Alf's death there'd been a hundred stories and a million laughs, whereas I'd just be the McKenzie kid, the solo harmonica player who'd taken over when Alf ran out of puff from the cancer. The young bloke who thought he was too fuckin' good to go on the boats, always had his nose in a book, too many high-falutin' ideas that come from him hangin' round that snotty-nose, Nicole Lenoir-Jourdan. 'Broke his mum's heart goin' off to the war and gettin' hisself killed. Useless bastard. Family don't play the mouth organ no more, it's because of him pissin' off like that.'

Gloria had disbanded the Cobbers awaiting my return. She, like Alf, was a perfectionist and reckoned neither Cory nor Steve had the gift, and she had too much pride to go off with a half-cocked quartet. Dying wouldn't be too bad – as a matter of fact, it might solve a whole heap of problems. But this was only a momentary thought, immediately overpowered by the urgent need to live. By now I was beginning to hurt a lot and it was getting bloody cold.

Then a familiar sound set me panicking again. There was a screaming locomotive heading my way, the noise made by artillery shells tearing through the cold air as they suddenly descended. They landed a hundred yards to my left, shaking the earth beneath me. Another salvo landed the same distance to my right and then a third to my front. They'd been laid on to help get Johnny and me out. 'Bit fucking late!' I shouted into the mayhem going on around me.

Almost two years later I would hear the full story. The skipper had hoped to make a clean break, hit the chinks with artillery fire and cause them to retreat, whereupon they'd return for the two of us. But these were not the North Koreans. The Chinese were in a fighting mood and knew they outnumbered us. They came in for the kill and our platoon was flat out trying to make their getaway. In retrospect it was the correct thing to do – the enemy was the superior force and any further attempt at rescuing us would have caused more casualties.

The artillery ceased at last, and miraculously I was still alive. I couldn't fault the Kiwi forward observer on his map references. Several of the huts were ablaze and others torn to shreds, but he'd left a safe island for Johnny and me. I waited in the silence, though not for long. Soon enough I heard the softer trudge of rubber-soled canvas boots, and shortly after a group of Chinese soldiers arrived. One of them stood immediately behind me, his rifle pointed at my back. Another approached my lifeless feet, kicking away my weapon and prodding me in the side with the barrel of his rifle – fortunately not the side where the bullet had smashed into my upper leg. I winced and he laughed, the others grinning like a group of chimps who have just caught a small monkey they intend to rip apart and eat. Then, satisfied I was harmless, he slung his rifle and grabbed the foot of my wounded leg and started to drag me. It was as though I'd been struck by lightning – the pain seemed to electrify my entire body. I screamed, and he dropped my leg in surprise. Then the pain overwhelmed me and I lost consciousness, though the last thing I remember was hysterical laughter.

I awoke to a sea of oriental faces surrounding me. They must have taken me into a partially demolished hut because a large hole in the thatch revealed the moon with its frosty aura, a great searchlight beaming down at me, bathing the hut in moonlight. I looked around to where several of the soldiers were examining my rifle and Johnny's Owen, one of them removing the magazine and ejecting the round in the breech, then cocking the rifle and pointing it at my head. 'Bam!' he said, as he pulled the trigger. More laughter. *These coves amuse real easily*, I thought, in an attempt to ignore the terrible pain in my leg.

My eyes explored the rest of the hut and saw that they'd made it into a temporary first-aid station. Several wounded Chinese, no doubt the result of the artillery barrage, lay on stretchers to the right of me. The bloke nearest me had his arm ripped off and I could see the tourniquet tied a couple of inches above his ragged flesh. This wound would have been caused in the same way as Charlie Green's death – a decent-sized piece of red-hot shrapnel scooping out the contents of the commanding officer's stomach and, in this case, slicing through the chink's upper arm, severing it, bone and all. The tourniquet was so high up that it couldn't adequately stop the bleeding, and blood dripped slowly from his severed arm like a slow-leaking tap.

Three Chinese soldiers were going through my combat pack and soon enough found the small bar of chocolate we carried as a quick sugar fix in the field. The incident I've noted previously took place, which ended in the unfortunate chocolate eater snatching up his rifle and smashing the butt into the side of my jaw, breaking several teeth. I would never again eat a chocolate without thinking of this moment. It was also a lesson in understanding different cultures. Whoever would have thought chocolate could be repulsive to anyone? But it was a lesson well learned – I would never again take anything for granted when dealing with someone from another culture. Assume nothing. I was to use this lesson time and time again in the years to come and would refer to it as 'the chocolate-bar factor'. Little did I know, when the butt of the Chinese rifle smashed into my jaw, that as a result of this single retaliatory blow I would end up making millions of dollars.

But right then I needed morphine urgently. 'Morphine!' I said through my swollen mouth. They looked on blankly. I opened my forefinger and largest finger slightly and pushed my thumb forward in the action of a syringe. 'Morphine?' I repeated. We'd been told that the North Koreans knew the name of the painkiller and I assumed this was true of the chinks as well.

They still looked unknowingly at me and I repeated the action, saying the word a third time.

One of the soldiers shook his head. 'Morp,' he said. I took this to mean they had no morphine. I should have worked it out for myself – the Chinese wounded, particularly the bloke with the severed arm, were in obvious pain and plainly hadn't received any morphine. They were not just holding out on me – they had none, even for their own.

My next request, for a smoke, was more successful, and one of them handed me the cigarette he'd just lit for himself. The right side of my jaw was swollen from the hit to my mouth and I tasted blood, but I managed to push the smoke into the left side of my jaw. The cigarette seemed to consist largely of saltpetre, and it flared every few seconds with the smoke drawn hot into my chest as I inhaled.

I decided, while I was still conscious and semi-focused, to try to do something about my broken leg. The ends of the bones were scraping against each other and I concluded that if I could get the chinks to fix some sort of splint to straighten my leg I'd be much better off. I reached for a length of straw among a small heap that had fallen when the roof had partially collapsed. First, pointing to my broken leg, I snapped the straw. They all nodded. Good, at least they knew I had a broken leg. Now for the splint. But all my miming was to no avail, they didn't seem to cotton on to my request. Then, in part due to my befuddled mind, I did something incredibly stupid. My .303 stood against the wall and I reached out and grabbed it, intending to show them that they could use it as a splint. But that's not the message I transmitted. Chinks dived from everywhere, wrenching the rifle from my grasp. I then felt the butt of a Chinese rifle land across my mouth, this time harder than the first, knocking several more teeth out in the process. Another chink butt-stroked me across the back of the head and knocked me out.

When I eventually came to, I was on a stretcher and on the move. The moon was much lower on the horizon and the night darker. The chinks were vacating the village, assuming a larger force would soon be arriving, and as it grew light, they knew a spotter plane would be circling overhead and seeking a target for an air strike.

We followed a very poor mountain track of rocky, uneven ground, and with every jolt the jagged ends of the broken bone in my leg scraped together causing me to cry out. On several occasions the stretcher bearers stumbled, tipping me out, and I screamed out in agony as I landed. I became conscious that my captors might decide my screaming was putting them at risk and simply shoot me and dump me for the pigs and crows to eat. I was also aware that my fellow wounded remained quietly stoic – occasionally a soft moan came from their stretchers, though never a scream. I promised myself, should I be dropped again, somehow I would remain mute. But I was dropped and couldn't keep from crying out. The pain totally possessed me and my screams were entirely involuntary.

We walked steadily, climbing into the hills, and then took cover at dawn in a large cave where I was lifted onto a platform with ten wounded Chinese soldiers. By sheer coincidence the soldier lying beside me was the bloke with his arm severed up near his shoulder and now, surprisingly, he smiled at me. I tried to return the smile but my swollen mouth began to quiver and I could feel hot tears running down my face. *Shit, what a fucking wimp!*

Without the constant bumping of the stretcher to distract me, instead of the pain lessening, it now seemed to grow worse. I kept moaning as the spasms of pain hit me, yet I can remember being ashamed of myself. I was surrounded by the uncomplaining Chinese wounded and the particularly poor bastard with the severed arm who'd been steadily losing blood and yet was capable of a sympathetic smile. It was the all-conquering white man who was doing the wailing. I was failing to keep up my end, unable to show the same courage as my enemy.

It isn't true that the Chinese don't feel pain the way we do: they had a discipline born of years of guerilla fighting that allowed them to stay stoic under the most onerous conditions. I once read somewhere that in convict times an inmate might receive a hundred lashes with the cat-o'-nine-tails, the flesh of his back exposing his rib cage, yet he'd not cry out. The article went on to say that the same treatment today would most likely kill a man. Humans can learn to endure incredible pain but it is something we acquire gradually, our pain threshold built up over long periods of hardship. Twenty years at war and the effects of the Long March had inured these Chinese against hardship where pain was a constant part of their daily lives. If these blokes were representative of their kind, then the enemy opposing us was tough, formidable and dangerous – one who might, in the end, prove too much for the soft Caucasian soldier to handle.

The one-armed soldier, observing my involuntary tears, had somehow managed to roll and light a cigarette and now placed it between my lips. Using the back of my hands I wiped my eyes and smiled my thanks and he returned my smile. Then I watched as, one-handed, he rolled a cigarette for himself and lit it and we smoked silently together. Quite suddenly he gave a soft sigh and his chin dropped and he jerked forward, his mouth open, and with the cigarette still glued to his bottom lip, he died.

I left Korea with some harsh memories that would haunt my sleep for the next fifty years, but this was one of the most poignant. On Anzac Day, and if I happen to be in a RSL Club at sundown and the lights are dimmed and 'For the Fallen' is read:

*At the going down of the sun*
*And in the morning . . .*
*We will remember them.*

I remember Johnny Gordon, his dark hand lying in a patch of pristine snow. Then I see the little chink smiling and placing a cigarette between my lips and it is to him that I finish with the words, 'Lest we forget'.

Years later I would tell this story to a physician and question why the Chinese soldier died so suddenly. 'Trauma and the loss of blood, although fairly slow, say ten hours, would finally shut down his kidneys, in fact shut down everything, and this would cause him to have a massive heart attack,' is how he'd explained the soldier's death. Then he'd added, 'He must have been extraordinarily tough to have lasted that long.'

I spent the day in and out of consciousness and that night we were on the move again, but this time without my Chinese escorts, who were leaving to go back, I imagined, to their battalion. They handed us over to a squad of North Korean guards. To my surprise I felt real regret at the departure of my Chinese captors. Apart from the chocolate incident, and their response to my rather stupid decision to reach for my rifle, they'd treated me exactly the same as their own wounded and shared their rations equally. It would have been much easier for them to put a bullet through my brain or simply leave me to die, but they'd carried me all night over very hilly and difficult terrain and never once complained. As they were leaving, each of them filed past me and touched me lightly on the shoulder. What else can I say, they were good blokes.

As for the North Korean soldiers they'd left in charge, I was about to learn a lesson in contrasts. Only minutes after the Chinese had left, one of the Koreans approached me and yanked at the boot on my broken leg, twisting it from side to side until it was finally released from my foot. The pain this caused was indescribable but, surprisingly, I didn't pass out. My screaming seemed to amuse them all and the soldier then pulled the boot from my good leg. Then, to the general hilarity of the others, he removed his own and forced them onto my feet. Thank God I was a little bloke and they fitted – without boots I would have had little chance of avoiding frostbite. He then pulled on my boots and commenced to stomp around the cave, swinging his arms in an exaggerated march and laughing at their weight.

A North Korean officer then approached me. 'Soldier take boots.' He pointed at the soldier's canvas boots now on my feet. 'You soldier boot.'

I couldn't believe my luck. 'You speak English?' I asked. He nodded. 'Please can you find a stick to splint my leg?' I asked very slowly, demonstrating the action of tying a splint to my broken leg.

He grinned, shaking his head. 'Not allow,' he said. 'We go now.'

'Where are we going?' I asked.

'To be educated . . . to learn truth.' He turned and walked away and said something to one of the soldiers, who immediately came over and removed the canvas boots and, at the same time, my socks. I knew I was history – without my boots my chances of survival were zilch.

As the Koreans mustered to depart I realised that this large cave was a collection point and that we'd been joined by other prisoners, mostly South Koreans but among them Dave McCombe. Dave was also K Force, and while not in my company we'd heard of his capture several days ago. I'd also met him once in the pub at Puckapunyal.

He walked up to me. 'G'day! Jacko, isn't it? Jacko McKenzie?'

I was surprised that he remembered me – we couldn't have shared more than a couple of beers together and that was more than a year ago. 'Jesus, Dave, it's good to see you,' I answered. Later he'd tell me he'd been equally surprised that I'd remembered his name.

He grinned down at me. 'Mate, we'll be seeing a fair bit of each other – I'm on one end of your stretcher.'

We travelled for hours that night, all of it over mountain tracks, with Dave at the top end of my stretcher and two nogs at the other. While the two guards at my feet were changed on a regular basis, Dave was made to remain on the other end. He was a big raw-boned man not unlike Rick Stackman, maybe six foot and then a bit, but the task must have taxed him mightily, though he didn't falter, even once. 'Dave, I'm sorry,' I said on several occasions during the night.

'No worries, mate,' he'd always reply, though the first time he added with a bit of a laugh, 'Yiz only a little bloke, thank gawd.'

Then an hour or so before dawn, with my bare feet exposed to below-zero night air, we stopped to rest. For the past couple of hours I'd felt the familiar signs of impending frostbite. Dave was leaning over me. 'How ya goin', Jacko?' he asked as he did every rest.

'Mate, it's me feet. They're stinging and aching a bit.'

I didn't have to say any more, Dave knew what I was saying and he knelt down beside me and unbuttoned his battledress jacket. Then, ever so gently, he lifted my broken leg and, along with the good one, tucked them under his armpits, pulling the jacket around them for additional warmth. After ten minutes or so the guards approached, indicating that it was time to move on.

'How they feeling?' Dave asked me. I hesitated. 'Not good, eh?' he suggested. I nodded. 'Then we stay put,' he said firmly.

'Better get going,' I said. 'The bastards are likely to get cranky.'

Dave laughed. 'Fuck 'em, Jacko, they won't harm me – it would mean two o' them would have to take my end.'

The guards continued shouting, becoming very agitated, but they never laid a finger on him. Finally the circulation returned to my feet and we set off again. Without Dave McCombe I could have lost both my feet to frostbite.

After another difficult night made bearable for me by Dave's quiet and reassuring voice, we arrived at a transit camp of several well-constructed huts. Here I was carried into a room and put into a cage roughly ten feet square, its roof no more than three feet above the ground. Dave was pushed in after me. 'Bit snug, eh?' was all he said, sitting with his knees up near his chin.

The cage had been designed so that its occupants would be unable to stand or walk around, which didn't concern me, as I could do neither. Three South Korean prisoners already occupied the premises and they didn't look too pleased to see us. The remnants of their uniforms hung in tatters from their emaciated bodies and it appeared they'd been there for some time. Now, with five people occupying the cage, Dave taking up almost the space required for two, and with me forced to lie down, movement of any kind was restricted. The nog next to me would scratch frantically at his hair and a shower of lice would fall onto my body so that I was soon to share his condition and learn to live with lice as with everything else. Curiously, while the louse-ridden nog had bitten most of his nails to the quick, he had allowed the nails on the two longest fingers of his right hand to grow to at least an inch and a half, each curved into a bow shape, and in the process creating the perfect vermin-scratching instrument.

Pretty soon we were approached by two English-speaking North

Koreans who began asking me questions, ignoring Dave, perhaps thinking that in my wounded state I'd offer less resistance.

'My leg is broken. Please, I need a splint,' I pleaded.

'First you answer question, then we fix,' came the reply.

In the fifteen minutes or so that followed came a barrage of questions, some relevant, some not. For instance they wanted information about our patrol objective, its strength and duration, while other questions appeared to be totally pointless. While I didn't know it at the time, it was the silly questions that mattered to them. They would return later and repeat these irrelevant questions and if they found inconsistencies they'd know my answers to the relevant ones were not to be trusted. It was a curious way of going about an interrogation – rather than first seeking to establish the truth they began by probing for lies.

But this was early times and in answer to each question I would simply repeat the prisoner's mantra: my number, rank and name. This displeased them mightily. 'No medical treatments!' they'd shout. 'You answer questions, you have!'

Then the process would begin all over again. 'What your unit?' 'Why your patrol go to village?' 'Where else you go patrol?' 'Where you go holiday?' 'Where you live before come to Korea?' 'What your mother maidens name?' 'How old you are?' 'Where you go school?' 'Your wife name before marry?'

'I can only give you my number, rank and name,' I'd insist. They'd finally leave, only to return the following day to repeat the procedure. We'd nicknamed them Bib and Bub because they had the habit of each asking the same questions but taking it in turns to be first. 'Where you go school?' Bib would ask, whereupon in a much more strident tone Bub would say, 'WHERE YOU GO SCHOOL?' Then they'd reverse the order and the tonal roles for the next question.

Each morning a small bucket of rice swill, not sufficient to give any of us even half a decent feed, was placed in the cage. The ragged South Koreans, yabbering like monkeys, would grab at the bucket, the three of them too much for even Dave to handle. He'd struggle to shoulder them out of the way in order to get just a handful of rice for himself and then another to feed me.

'Open yer mouth wide, Jacko,' he'd shout above the yabbering. Then he'd lunge at the nogs, knocking one out of the way sufficiently to get his hand into the dish and scoop up a handful of rice swill, swing it up and slap it directly into my open mouth, holding his hand across my mouth so that I got as much as possible. Then he'd do the same for himself. I can't remember the contents of the dish ever lasting long enough for a second go.

Soon enough interrogation by the North Koreans was directed at Dave as well as me, and the nogs found another way to get to me: sleep deprivation. I was in a fair bit of pain, not only from my leg but also because of my mouth, where my broken teeth were giving me hell, but sheer exhaustion would finally take over and put me to sleep. The bastards soon observed this and a guard would shout out as soon as he noticed me nodding off and Bib and Bub would come running, pad and pen in hand, and prod me through the bars with a length of bamboo, whereupon they'd commence questioning me again.

'You answer question we give morphine.' This was the carrot always dangled in front of me, pronounced 'morfin'.

In desperation I decided to answer all their questions with lies. Unbeknownst to me this too was pretty routine and meant I'd reached the second stage of interrogation. They appeared quite elated at my lies and when they came forward with a little morphine I was convinced I'd tricked them and felt pretty pleased with myself. As their captive I had won very few rounds, and Dave's quiet congratulation, 'Giddonya, Jacko', when the first syringe of morphine arrived, boosted my ego no end.

Of course, several days later they'd ask the same questions and check them against the meticulous notes they'd made of my previous answers. When they didn't match they were infuriated, even though they were probably expecting this to occur. They'd jump up and down with their dark eyes bulging and in duplicate yell, 'No medicine! No morfin! You lie me!'

But after two weeks, one morning I'd had enough. I was in the kind of pain where I didn't much care if I died, just so I didn't have to put up with this shit any longer. I turned to Dave. 'Mate, I've had enough, I ain't gunna answer any more Bib and Bub questions.'

Dave nodded his head, 'Suits me, Jacko. Righto then, let's give the bastards a serve. We might as well go out telling the buggers what we think of them, their wives, their kin, their ancestors and their fuckin' noggie nation.'

This we commenced to do, calling them every combination of name and adjective we could think of, including several deeply offensive though imaginative monologues involving their offspring, wives, mothers and their poxy nation.

At first this infuriated them. But then they grew accustomed to our outbursts and seemed to be genuinely perplexed at our behaviour. They must have finally decided we'd gone round the twist, because one morning they came to fetch me and placed me in a nearby cave, disastrously separating me from Dave McCombe, whom I was never to see again. I recall his last words, called out to me as they carried me away, 'Jacko, don't die, don't let the fuckers win!'

The cave was in permanent twilight – at its entrance they'd built a crude wooden stockade that blocked most of the light – and towards the back it was almost totally dark. Even by the standards of the previous caves and the cage we'd been in for two weeks, the stink of rotting gangrenous flesh and human faeces was overwhelming. At night rats brazenly attacked the open wounds of the cave's twenty or so prisoners. Thank God it was so cold that our nostrils were all but anaesthetised, making the fetid air slightly more bearable. All about me men lay moaning, lying in their own excrement. Stink and shit notwithstanding, the only way we could prevent freezing to death was by lying huddled against each other. A few rice sacks had been thrown into the cave and those wounded men strong enough to fight quarrelled like mongrel dogs over them, pulling hair, biting, kicking and punching to secure one. I saw one prisoner with his hands around another's throat throttling him until he released his grip on a sack.

On my first morning one of the inmates crawled towards me, a bearded American with a dirty bandage around his forehead from which a crop of dark matted hair protruded straight up to a height of about twelve inches. What remained of his uniform was crusted with filth and one of his eyes was closed or missing – pus oozed from the corner suppurating wetly down his jowl and into his beard. He crawled past me to the prisoner who lay beside me asleep and stole his portion of rice swill. I looked at him and he returned the look. 'He's dead meat, buddy,' he said with a slight shrug.

I was too spent to react, to feel indignation, in fact to feel anything, anger or pity. Constant pain and hunger and the separation from my mate Dave McCombe had turned me inwards, all my energy absorbed in my own self-pity. The shock of losing Dave had been enormous and I realised that he had been the real factor in keeping me alive. Now I was alone in this living hell. I was among wild animals and knew I wasn't up to the task required to survive.

The bearded Yank sat on his haunches, about to eat the swill he'd stolen, when suddenly a dark hand reached over the sleeping soldier beside me and grabbed his wrist. The American gave a cry of anguish as the grip tightened. 'Put it back, soldier!' a deep voice demanded. I followed the arm and saw it was attached to a very large man lying one body over and parallel to me. Whimpering in fright, the bearded American put the sleeping man's portion back and the large hand released its grip, allowing him to slink away into the darker interior of the cave.

'Giddonya, mate,' I managed to say. Was it possible there was someone here who wasn't reduced to an animal state? I was astonished at the effect this had on me.

I heard a grunt of acknowledgement and then the single word, 'Sonofabitch!'

I lay quiet for a while then asked, 'What's your name, mate?'

'Jimmy . . . Jimmy Oldcorn.' He said the name slowly and it came out like organ music, real deep.

'G'day, Jimmy. Jacko McKenzie. 'Ow ya goin'?'

A fair silence followed, then, 'Where yoh from, man, yoh talk funny.'

'Australia.'

'Aus-tray-lee-ah.' He pronounced each syllable. 'Man, dat da other side da fuckin' world!'

'Yeah, you're not wrong,' I replied. 'They don't call it Down-under for nothing.'

'What yoh got, Jacko?'

I wasn't sure what he meant by this question. 'What do you mean, Jimmy?'

'Yoh sick? Wounded? Able-bodied?'

'Broken leg, bullet, bone shattered.'

'Me also – I got me a broken leg.' He said it with a chuckle, as if it was an amazing coincidence. 'Dis nigger ain't gonna do no 'scapin', dat for sure.'

I was growing increasingly weary, the conversation taxing the little strength remaining in me, but I wanted him to continue if only for the comfort of his voice. 'You did good stopping that bloke,' I said.

'Goddamn muth'fucker!' he replied. 'No-good sonofabitch!'

Despite my need for him to continue I could no longer concentrate, and dropped into an exhausted sleep. When I woke, the bloke next to me whose food had been stolen then salvaged was no longer there. Now Jimmy Oldcorn lay next to me, the biggest goddamn black man I had ever seen in my life.

'How yoh doing?' he asked.

'Could be better,' I replied.

'Or worse.' He indicated the spot where he now lay. 'Dis poor guy, he gone died on us, man.' He seemed to be suggesting that I ought to feel fortunate to be alive.

I felt slightly ashamed. 'I just need a bit of a stick to make a splint,' I said, trying to explain. 'That'd help a fair bit to stop the pain.'

'Yeah, I can see dat,' he said sympathetically, and just the tone of his voice was remarkable. In this hellhole there was no room for sympathy, each of us totally preoccupied with our own misery, so the big black bloke's apparent concern came as a surprise.

I recalled a rather ponderous saying Gloria had when someone showed a callous disregard for the misfortune of another: 'Sympathy was a stranger knocking on a firmly bolted door'. Jimmy had a crude splint down the lower part of his left leg and would have been in much the same sort of pain as me, yet he still found the strength to be concerned about someone else.

Nevertheless, in a voice filled with sickening self-pity, I found myself saying, 'You wouldn't think it would be that bloody hard for the bastards to find a bit of wood.'

'Dat a natural part of being da enemy – dey ain't suppose to show no concern, man.'

We talked for a while and it was obvious he'd been through much the same experience I'd endured, the only difference being his spirit remained dominant and unbroken while mine was just about spent. But all the time I was too preoccupied and sorry for myself, convinced that I was about to die, to benefit from his obvious courage.

'I guess this is the end,' I sighed.

Jimmy Oldcorn didn't reply at first, then he said quietly, 'We cain't make it on our own, Jacko.'

'You can say that in spades!' I replied.

'We gotta work together, brother.'

I fell silent, trying to think what we could possibly do that would make the slightest difference. Together or on our own, we were powerless. 'Mate, we're stuffed,' I said at last. 'Rooted.'

'Rooted?' he questioned.

'It means we're fucked, up shit creek . . . it's Australian.'

'Rooted! Hey, dat's good, man! I'm rooted.' Pronounced in his mellifluous voice it sounded round and substantial.

'No, that's not the same thing,' I said. 'When you say "*I'm* rooted" it means you're tired. "*We're* rooted" means we're stuffed, finished, washed up.' I laughed, continuing. '"Get rooted" means piss off, beat it, scram. "I've been rooted" means I've been cheated or badly done by. "I rooted her" means I had sex with a woman.'

'Whoa, man, dat Aus-tray-lee-an a mighty strange language for sure!' A sudden silence followed until eventually he said quietly, 'Don't do nothin', ain't nothin' gonna happen – den we surely be rooted, man.'

'What do you propose then, mate?' I said with just a touch of sarcasm.

'Pro-pose?' Again, his voice gave the word a kind of energy of its own. 'I pro-pose yoh and me begin a move-a-ment.'

'Movement?' I tried to laugh. 'Neither of us can walk.'

He didn't appear to hear me, or if he did he missed or ignored the play on words. Now he spread his hand to take in the dark cave and its miserable occupants. 'Ain't nobody here but us got the strength, Brother Jacko.'

Strength! Me? What a joke! *The bastard must be mad!* I thought to myself. 'Look, mate, I'm a private, I do what I'm told and don't ask questions.'

'Dat good, man, me too.' He paused, then announced, 'Private James Pentecost Oldcorn, 24th Infantry Nigger Regiment, US 25th Infantry Division.'

'So, Jimmy, you're all black blokes, the whole flamin' regiment?' I asked, surprised.

'Negro,' he corrected. Even though he'd used the word 'nigger' against himself, he was letting me know the correct form of address for someone of colour.

'Negro,' I said, accepting his correction. Then, wishing to change the subject, I asked, 'This *movement*, what will you call it?'

He thought for a while and again I wondered to myself if he was, you know, a bit simple. 'Operation Get Offa Yo' Arse,' he said finally, chuckling as he said the words.

I thought for a moment, then to humour him said, 'Ogoya.'

'Huh? What yoh say? O-go-a?'

'It's an acronym,' I explained. 'Like you take the first letter of each word and they add up to something you can pronounce, a kind of shorthand for the whole title: O – operation, G – get, O – off, Y – your, A – arse, Ogoya!' It was a word trick Nicole Lenoir-Jourdan had once taught me.

'Ogoya,' he pronounced, trying out the sound for himself. 'Dat good!' he chuckled. 'Dat a fine acro-name. We got here a move-a-ment, name of Ogoya.'

'We've got only one problem, Jimmy.'

'What problem? What problem we got?'

'We've both got broken legs so we can't get off our arse.' It was another feeble attempt at roughly the same joke I'd tried with the word 'movement'.

'Dat our first problem,' Jimmy replied confidently. 'Dat da first problem Ogoya got isself.'

And that's how it all began.

Jimmy left my side a few minutes later. Using his arms, and kicking with his one good leg in a sort of modified half-arsed spider crawl, he disappeared towards the front of the cave. When he returned several hours later, despite the freezing interior, beads of sweat showed on his forehead. Then I noticed protruding about ten inches out of the back of the collar of his jacket were two flat wooden planks about three inches wide. He was plainly exhausted as he dragged himself into place beside me.

'What have you been up to, Jimmy?' I asked, 'You look buggered, mate.'

'Ogoya,' he gasped. 'We got our splints, Brother Jack. We in business, my good man!' He turned slightly, his back to me so that the two lengths of wood showed sticking up out of the back of his collar. 'Pull,' he instructed.

'Jesus, Jimmy, where'd you get these?' I asked, pulling at one of the planks.

Jimmy held up one arm and tapped his left wrist. 'Watch.'

'What, in exchange? You gave one of the nogs your watch?'

'Nogs?'

'Gooks to you, nogs to us,' I said, pulling at the second plank.

'I took dem offa da stockade up front. I gave da gook guard my watch so he be inclined to agree there ain't nothin' happening to dat stockade. Tomorrow we get us walking sticks,' he announced triumphantly. Turning back to face me he smiled. 'We offa our ass, Brother Jack, the move-a-ment has begun.'

The first time he'd used the appellation 'brother' I'd ignored it, thinking it was like us saying 'mate'. Now I accepted it for what it was – a name for one's partner in crime. The way he said it sounded good, as if I was a somebody. 'Walking sticks, eh? Don't like your chances, mate – bloody gook won't come good with the walking sticks now he's got your flamin' watch.'

Jimmy put his hand inside his flak jacket and withdrew a gold watchband. 'He get da rest when he brings dem walkin' sticks.'

I removed my watch. 'Here . . . it's yours,' I said, offering it to Jimmy. I lifted one of the precious splints. 'Thanks for these, mate.'

Jimmy laughed. 'Keep it, Brother Jack, we is gonna need it sometime for somethin' else, dat for sure. No big deal, man. Dat watch I give to da gook, it a Timex, two lousy bucks from da pawnbroker.' He held up the metal band. 'Solid eighteen-carat gold, two dollars – and the salesman ain't done me no special price, neither.' He chuckled, his finger tapping the inside of the gold band. 'Yoh know what it says here? It says "Made in China". Now ain't that somethin'. Yoh got something else we can trade, Brother Jack?'

I dug into my American parka and produced my harmonica, holding it up. 'This, I guess.'

'Well, I be goddamned. Yoh play? Yoh play da harmonica?'

'Sure.'

'What yoh play? Jazz? Blues?'

I put the little instrument to my mouth and proceeded to play the World War II hit, Glenn Miller's 'In the Mood', which sounds so great on the harmonica. To my astonishment after the first few bars the cave grew completely quiet. I played through the tune to where, towards the end, a couple of bars are repeated four times, each quieter than the one before, until it suddenly bursts up into a climax. For a moment the complete silence continued and then the cave erupted, not only cheers and claps but I could see a number of the soldiers were sobbing. I waited only a moment before swinging into 'Chattanoogie Shoe Shine Boy' . . .

*Have you ever passed the corner of Fourth and Grand,*
*Where a little ball of rhythm has a shoe shine stand?*
*People gather 'round and they clap their hands,*
*He's a great big bundle of joy.*
*He pops the boogie woogie rag*
*The Chattanoogie shoe shine boy.*

It only took the opening bars for the clapping to start and you could feel that the atmosphere in the cave had been transformed. The young blokes, who'd been grim-faced and moribund, were smiling or weeping. I followed 'Chattanoogie Shoe Shine Boy' with 'Sunny Side of the Street.'

*Grab your coat and get your hat,*
*Leave your worries on the doorstep,*
*Just direct your feet*
*To the sunny side of the street . . .*

I guess 'Sunny Side' wasn't exactly appropriate to our situation, but it worked – the soldiers were smiling, the mood had changed.

Jimmy was ecstatic, beaming at me. 'Now we truly got us a move-a-ment, Brother Jacko. Dat harmonica ain't for no trading, man, dat da call to arms, dat da reveille, dat da war cry, dat da way to get da muth'fuckers offa der ass!'

We strapped the two palings Jimmy had pried from the stockade to my leg using our belts and an extra belt Jimmy produced seemingly from nowhere. He noted my look of surprise when it appeared. 'Dat dude next to us who dead now, he ain't gonna need no belt no more,' he explained. The splints he'd procured for me were much longer than his own, but he hadn't thought to exchange them, even though, being a much bigger man, it would have been a reasonable thing to do and, moreover, I would have been no less grateful to him for his generosity. It was obvious that he'd planned to help me even before he'd declared his 'move-a-ment' and made me the inaugural member of Ogoya.

I was to learn that Jimmy Oldcorn was usually well ahead of the game and would arrive at a conclusion long before any of us. Like taking the dead bloke's webbing belt – he'd removed it even before he'd gone looking for splints, before we'd even properly established a relationship – now I came to think of it, before even he'd asked me what was wrong with me. He must have examined my broken leg while I was asleep.

But he had one further surprise in store for me. After he'd fixed my splint he produced the dead man's boots. 'Yoh ain't got no boots, Brother Jacko. When we get dem sticks we's gonna be walking, man. Ain't no point wastin' a nice pair of Uncle Sam's boots dat has hardly seen no action. We's got walkin' to do, man . . . on da sunny side o' da street!'

# CHAPTER EIGHT

## *Frau Kraus and the Gobbling Spider*

Over the days that followed, Jimmy began to tell me his story. He had no father and a mother who, lacking the means to care for him, delivered him directly to the doorstep of the Colored Orphan Asylum. This institution was started in 1836 by two Quaker women who found two small coloured children abandoned in the doorway of a Lower East Side building, and consequently discovered that no orphanage would accept coloured children.

In the grand tradition of the original foundlings, Jimmy – a gooey-eyed, mewling package wrapped in newspaper and still covered in vernix – was scooped up from the doorstep by Matron Mary Pentecost directly after early-morning prayers. She took him into the dispensary and unwrapped him to discover that his umbilical cord had been crudely severed, probably by his mother's teeth, then tied too long so that the knot at the end of the greasy twist lay between his chubby little knees. She fetched a sharp pair of scissors, retied and cut the cord expertly and treated it with a dab of iodine. As she bathed him she was not to know that within two hours the New York Stock Exchange would collapse to trigger the Great Depression. Jimmy's birth was recorded as having occurred on Black Tuesday,

29th of October 1929, the day the world held its head in its hands and yesterday's rich men fell to their doom.

That morning's bible study reading had been from the New Testament book of St James. As was the custom at the orphanage, Matron Mary Pentecost had the right to give Jimmy any Christian name she chose, so she called him Pentecost, after herself. She was a practical woman, and must have realised that Pentecost might prove too burdensome a name for a small boy to lug around, so she added James, from the morning's reading. As James Pentecost, the infant now had an identity but was yet to gain a family name. As the bible was a poor source of Protestant surnames, Jimmy's last name was arrived at by way of the phone directory. Matron Mary Pentecost simply opened this at random and stabbed the point of a pencil down onto the facing page. A pause or a slight slip of the point in the 1929 Riverdale telephone directory and he may well have ended up as Jimmy Oldchekowitz.

Jimmy would sometimes repeat his real names to himself with a certain satisfaction. 'Dat my lucky day, Brother Fish, lotsa rich men who got money in dat stock exchange dey jump out da skyscraper window – but I got me a good name an' my life begin.' He paused, and smiled. 'James Pentecost Oldcorn – dat a real nice name, a gentle-man's name. Yessir! It got a good, good sound.'

The orphanage was run entirely by white women and along strict Protestant lines where Jesus was constantly invoked as a source of tenderness, love and compassion, but the rules employed to bring up the children were in direct contradiction to this pious ethos. The Old Testament God of wrath ruled their everyday lives, and fear and punishment were the primary means of control. 'We soon learn dat da lovin' Jesus for da white folk – da Lord we s'pose to love don't care 'bout da black chillen in dat place,' was how Jimmy once put it.

In its then almost hundred-year existence the Colored Orphan Asylum hadn't changed much in its attitude to the raising of children in its care. Like all coloured folk of the day, they were predestined to belong to the lowest social order and were prepared for life accordingly. The children lived in cottages in the expansive grounds, and were locked in at night under the charge of a house mother. Godliness and cleanliness were the two paramount concerns of the women who ran the institution. Jimmy's earliest memory was of being on his knees with a bucket and soapy rag. Cleanliness was achieved by means of elbow grease and the scrubbing brush, while godliness was taught by rote, bible verses repeated until they were indelibly stamped onto a small child's consciousness. The majority of the texts chosen announced in various ways that the wages of sin are death and eternal hellfire and the act of being born again, and thereby receiving Jesus into your life, the only means of redemption.

Any of the children who, upon examination, stumbled and hesitated over the lines of a bible passage previously taught were given three separate chances to correct their mistakes. If they failed on the fourth occasion, they were sent to 'the lock-up'. This was a locked cupboard deep in the basement of the main institution building where, according to Jimmy, the records of all children who had died in the orphanage over the past hundred years were kept in ancient wooden filing cabinets, each of which was secured by a door as well as drawers.

But in the frightened imagination of the orphans, the basement had been transmuted into the place they'd put all the dead children. The 150 wooden cabinets standing in rows were clearly coffins. Why else would the handles be removed from the cabinet doors and the doors nailed shut? In the children's imagination this was certain evidence that they contained the skeletons of dead children.

The lock-up was a cabinet identical to the others with the drawers pulled out and two holes 'the size of a quarter' drilled in the top and again in the door one third up from the floor to allow the air to enter. The cupboard was only large enough for a small child to sit cross-legged or to stand with their arms held to their sides. To a chastened and frightened child, being sent to the lock-up meant being placed in a coffin beside the rows of dead children who had undoubtedly been left to perish because they too failed to correctly recite their bible verses. To add to the misery of the dark cupboard, the lights in the basement of the old stone building were extinguished so that a child couldn't look through the breathing holes for the small reassurance of a beam of pale electric light.

A terrified child would sit in the cramped cupboard and listen to the gurgling and knocking of the ancient plumbing and the moaning of the furnace flue. They would soon become convinced these were the cries of the ghosts of the dead children. In the stygian darkness the numerous rats in the basement squeaking and scratching could only mean that the hungry rodents were coming to get them.

'Dem rats deys scratchin' and chewin' dat cupboard – dey get inside dey gonna eat you, man!' When I grinned at this notion Jimmy pulled his head back and said, 'It true, Brother Fish. I seen dem rats, dey same size a pussy cat. Ain't no cat gonna fight one dem mothers! Dey get inside when you in dat box dey gonna eat you, man!' It was plain to see the frightened little boy that still lived within him was entirely convinced.

On another occasion he'd explained to me, 'Some kids when dey got to ree-cite dem bible verses on der own, dey stutter – 'cos dey nervous, man! "Ha!" da matron, she shout, "Dat's da devil talking inside you, child! Dat's Satan spoiling God's precious word!" Den dey take him down and he gonna go sit in the lock-up till da devil come out o' him.'

'How'd they know when the devil was gone?' I asked.

'Dat easy, man. Da matron come down every two hours an' ask you to ree-cite yo' bible verses. If you can do it den da devil he gone, if you stutter some more da devil still der inside.'

'That's ridiculous, Jimmy,' I protested. 'What if a kid has a permanent stutter or he can't control his nerves?'

Jimmy shook his head sadly. 'Nah, it don't work like dat. A chile put in dat cupboard, he gonna get hysterical in 'bout four hours. He gonna think dem rats dey's gonna eat him. He gonna hear da dead children moanin' and der bones rattlin' in da coffin and da ghosts callin' out, he gonna soon be screamin' and shakin' and moanin' hisself. "Ha!" da matron say. "Praise da Lord! Now da devil is comin' out! Hallelujah! Hear da devil comin' out o' Jesus' precious child. Hear him moanin' an' cryin' out inside dat poor child. Hear him hissin' and roarin' and wrestlin' wid da Lord Jesus. Praise His precious name!"' Jimmy paused, his eyes sad. 'When dat chile he can't scream no more an' he sit huggin' his knees shakin' an' shiverin' an' sobbin', den dey take him out an' carry him to his cottage an' put him in his bed an' da house mother she give him hot choco-late an' she tell him how Jesus loves him, savin' him from da devil in da nick o' time.'

It wasn't too hard to guess that Jimmy had been through this experience, perhaps more than once. He'd never dwell too long on the orphanage, telling me disconnected bits and pieces, such as the devil-evicting episode. Perhaps his memories of the orphanage were too deeply buried to surface in other than episodic snatches of conversation, pushing momentarily to the surface and then retreating before too much anger and sadness became attached to them.

I was left with the impression of a place where godliness and cleanliness took the place of love and compassion, a place of icy showers and chilblained skin rubbed raw by the hard, unforgiving edges of crude blocks of blue carbolic soap. Of small children on their knees muttering earnest and confused prayers to a Jesus they were told to love but grew to fear. Where small children lived in permanent terror that they might offend, often not understanding why they were being punished, and finally coming to accept that punishment was arbitrary. The naturally timid became submissive, overanxious in all things and sycophantic, while others, such as Jimmy, grew to be deeply resentful, which, in turn, eventually led them astray.

What was also apparent was that no serious attempt was made to develope their intellect. The education they received was rudimentary, the three Rs of reading, writing and arithmetic taught to a point of basic competency. The boys worked in the vegetable gardens and the grounds or the carpentry shop; the girls worked in the kitchen, did sewing or quilting or simply completed the domestic chores around the orphanage. From the age of eight to twelve they worked in the laundry, which took in washing and ironing from the nearby monastery and the College of Mount St Vincent.

In the minds of many they were the biblical children of Ham and destined to become maids and labourers. Accordingly they were being trained as good Christian coloured folk competent in those tasks for which it was thought they were intellectually capable. The white women who held the future of these black children in their hands firmly believed they were doing the Lord's work. The idea of a black orphan aspiring to rise above his or her predestined station in life simply never occurred to them. Children such as Jimmy who were demonstrably bright were regarded as potentially dangerous. They would only become frustrated in later life and, as a consequence, turn to crime. It was better to subdue them while they were young so that they didn't aspire to achieve a status in society they would not be allowed to sustain. This was referred to as becoming 'too big for their boots'. Jimmy was one of the few children who remained unbroken and thus confirmed this hypothesis when he eventually ended up at Elmira Reformatory, a tough institution for boys.

The white women gave thanks to a bountiful God when, at the age of twelve, the orphans were required to leave the Colored Orphan Asylum. The girls were indentured as maids in good homes and the young boys were taken on as gardeners on the estates of the rich or as rural workers. The women never failed to pray for the souls of those of their boys and girls who had strayed from the Lord and subsequently found themselves in Elmira or the Hanavah Lavenburg Home for Working Girls.

The good Protestant ladies took great pride in the fact that they had a permanent waiting list of white folk who wanted their twelve-year-old orphans. It never seemed to have occurred to them that this was hardly surprising – even at the tender age of twelve the children were skilled, passive and submissive domestic servants, and capable and obedient gardeners and farm labourers. They could be snapped up for the cost of the food they ate and the second-hand clothes they wore, and could be regarded as free labour until they grew old enough to leave for salaried employment or, as more often happened with the boys, decided to run away to the city.

However, singing was one area where the women who ran the institution allowed the children to excel. They accepted that the Lord had especially gifted coloured folk with a talent for music and song, and the Colored Orphan Asylum Children's Choir had become a famous New York institution that earned the orphanage a great deal of public approbation. The choir often appeared at functions within the white community. They were popular additions to private weddings and funerals and performed publicly at events such as mayoral receptions, gala occasions and the like.

On several occasions, when a choir in a particular year had been exceptional, they'd appear at the Metropolitan. On the 4th of July it had become a cherished annual tradition for the choir to assemble between the two great Piccirilli lions on the steps of the New York State Library. Here they would sing the national anthem at the raising of the flag, and thereafter entertain the crowd with a medley of patriotic songs.

In return for these private and civic appearances the orphanage never asked for recompense; instead, a donation to the American Missionary Society's work in Africa was considered an appropriate response. From the time of Dr David Livingstone, the orphanage choir had helped to fund the work of the society in darkest Africa and this had further helped to boost its reputation as a praiseworthy Christian institution.

'Dat da big joke – we singin' all dem songs an' people, dey clappin', an' we's gettin' money dey gonna send to Africa so da black brothers over der dey gonna have Jesus in der souls. Once I ask da house mother, "Ma'am, we's black so why's dey don't pay us money so's we can have da Lord Jesus in our souls?" She reply we American blacks, we don't need to get no money to have Jesus – we got Him for nothing. It only da African blacks dat get da money we send so as dey gonna convert!' Jimmy laughed. 'Dem black cats in Africa – dey know somthin' we don't know, man! Dey done make Christianity a fine-payin' prop-o-sition.'

In his own way Jimmy was right – it seemed never to have struck any of the Quakers as an irony that these were the voices of orphans descended from slaves who may very well have been captured 200 or more years previously from the very tribes being urged to repent their sins and to accept the Lord Jesus into their lives. Or perhaps it did, and they simply marvelled at the mysterious ways of the Lord.

The choir had become the acceptable – if not celebrated – public face of the Colored Orphan Asylum so that when, from time to time, rumours of the way the orphanage was run surfaced and questions were raised about the uncommonly high number of deaths among its children, they were quietly ignored by city welfare officials. Without exception the politicians of the day regarded people of colour as inferior and a constant drain on the city's resources. They would have seen an inquiry into conditions at the orphanage as a blatant misuse of public funds.

When the orphanage was closed in 1946, public examination of its often mouldy but extensive and carefully kept basement records showed that several hundred children had died in its care, with the term 'accidental death' on death certificates too common a thread through the files not to have caused major concern had the orphanage housed any other than coloured children. Instead, the Negro and American Indian orphans who 'Passed away in the arms of Jesus' were buried quietly and forgotten in unmarked graves in the Bronx and Westchester cemeteries.

In fairness, the existence of the Colored Orphan Asylum spanned 110 years during which time standards of hygiene and basic medical care changed enormously, with most of the childhood diseases that commonly led to death eradicated over time. While the conditions in which the children were housed and the way they were cared for might today seem reprehensible, they would not have been atypical of the domestic accommodation and health facilities available to working-class communities at the time. Moreover, they would have been considerably better than those existing in the slums of Manhattan the year Jimmy was born.

When I'd asked Jimmy to come to the island with me I'd naturally assumed his life in an orphanage in New York and time spent in Elmira Reformatory were about as far removed from mine on the island as it was possible to get. I promised him long, lazy days diving for crays, surfing (I'd teach him how to ride a surfboard), fishing or simply lazing about on the beach. It would be, I told myself, a wonderful new experience, something someone with his background would have difficulty comprehending at first. Or so I fondly imagined.

In fact, children are by nature tough, irrepressible and optimistic souls and make the best of such means as are put at their disposal. A bank of the Hudson River formed part of the orphanage boundary, and in Jimmy's time the river had not yet become polluted by industrial effluent. It was clear and clean and often referred to as 'the blue Hudson'. I recall on one occasion talking enthusiastically about catching the large island crabs that Sue, the family expert, would cook on an open wood fire on the beach and serve with her secret Chinaman's sauce. I'd made it sound quite idyllic and expected Jimmy to express his bewilderment. Instead he volunteered, 'Yeah man, dat sound good. Catchin' dem crabs to cook an' fishin' and swimmin', we done dat in da Hudson River. It good fun and den we take tomatoes and onion and potato from da garden and we make us a fire down by da river and cook a dee-lish-us fish stew in some ole boilin' pot we find on a garbage heap.'

It was a rare glimpse into a universal childhood I'd not allowed Jimmy Oldcorn to experience. Instead I'd created my own mind-pictures of his time in the orphanage, and they hadn't allowed that even the most underprivileged children have fun. By inviting him to the island I was to be his benefactor, allowing him the catch-up experiences denied him in childhood. Now that I think of it, it was both patronising and presumptuous. He told of climbing the stone wall surrounding the Mount St Vincent monastery and stealing apples, cherries and strawberries from the monks' garden. Of visits to Coney Island, sponsored by Mayor Fiorello La Guardia, and once a year a visit to Radio City Music Hall sponsored by a Jewish businessmen's charity in the Bronx. Also, of the pig-outs that would occur after the choir performed at the various receptions, where they were allowed to eat all they could stuff into their hungry stomachs but forbidden to take anything away with them. Jimmy laughingly recalled how the boys concealed cakes in their shirt fronts while the girls did the same in their knickers. 'One girl, we called her Cup Cake Connie, when her knickers full put two o' dem cup cakes where her boobies, what she ain't got none, suppose to be!'

As his twelfth birthday approached and the time for his indenture drew closer, Jimmy, who hitherto had conducted a fairly casual relationship with God, now took to getting down on his knees and praying to Jesus in earnest. He was asking for a reprieve from being sent away to become a farm labourer somewhere unfamiliar and lonely. He was big for his age, naturally intelligent and not afraid to assert himself. He was also popular with the other children, who saw him as their leader. As a consequence he was regarded as somewhat of a troublemaker, and he knew the orphanage would be anxious to see the last of him. But he was also an exceptionally good boy soprano, and while he retained his childhood voice he knew he was safe. The choir needed him. He was a charismatic performer with a smile that made an audience grin. His solo during Handel's *Messiah* had been commented on by the resident music critic of the *New York Times*, who lamented the fact that he had not been discovered earlier in his life and better use made of his exceptional voice. And so Jimmy prayed to the supposedly loving Jesus that the onset of puberty would be delayed.

When Jimmy talked about the past he seemed to return to it physically as well as in his mind. His face and mannerisms took on the concerns of the orphan child he'd once been, and his voice seemed to rise an octave. He was, and still is, a consummate actor and could turn a simple explanation into a compelling performance, which made it almost impossible to refuse him anything he desired. He'd never quite forgiven the Lord Jesus for being able to resist his considerable powers of persuasion. 'Brother Fish, dat last year I pray every night to da Lord Jesus – I ask him to keep mah voice so it not broke. "Lord, let me sing yo' praise," I says to him. "I done good in dat choir singin' for you, Jesus. Maybe yo' read what da man say in da *New York Times*? I worth keepin', Lord. I done mah best singin' da gospel. Now I needs a small favour. Jus' one more year, please Lord? Jus' one more year to be a boy soprano – after dat I ain't gonna ask no more favours no more. Please Jesus, let me keep mah chile voice. Praise yo' precious name, Amen."'

When a month before his twelfth birthday his voice broke and his name appeared on the dreaded orphans' indenture list, his days as a praying man were over. Jimmy had a forgiving nature, particularly if he thought a genuine mistake had been made. On the other hand, if a deliberate effort to bring him undone was attempted or he became aware of malice towards himself or a friend, he became an implacable enemy. He was also no respecter of persons and the Lord was no longer his friend and saviour. As far as he was concerned the Lord had deliberately let him down, and in his book that meant they had nothing more to say to each other.

'Brother Fish, I'm outta der an' goin' who-know-where, man! It Jesus's fault. I'm twelve years old an' croakin' like a big ole frog. All dat prayin' to Him ain't done me no good what-so-ever. He don't have no time to do no lis-nin' to no orphan nigger! I wore out da knees o' mah britches prayin', man!' He looked up, appealing to me. 'Whaffor I done that? I ain't never got mah voice back neither!' He saw me grinning. 'Ain't no joke, Brother Fish. Frank Sinatra done got his voice back. Bing Crosby he got his voice back. Sure, dey white folk, natcherly Jesus love dem. Satchmo, he bin raspin' an' croakin', he don't get no voice back! He black, Jesus don't love him. Ray Charles he got his voice back but da Lord He done take his eyes away. He blind now, dat da payment for his voice.'

As far as I knew Ray Charles had always been blind, but I refrained from saying so. 'What about Nat King Cole?' I asked.

'Ha! Dat mah point! Dat mah exact point!' He sang a few bars of 'Mona Lisa' in what wasn't a bad imitation of the butter-smooth crooner. 'Dat not a voice for a black guy, man! Dat a cockamamie white-man voice, dat a voice to shame a black man! Dat a faggot voice. Jesus done punish him *special*.'

I'd learned that there wasn't much point in arguing with Jimmy. Anyway, most of the time he was secretly laughing at himself.

The orphanage placed Jimmy with a tomato farmer in New Jersey, a Lutheran family named Kraus who'd migrated from Germany in 1920. The Kraus family were so stereotypically German that they were almost comic-book material. The father, Otto, parted his hair in the centre and wore a waxed moustache turned up at the ends. His twin sons, Fritz and Henrik, were tall, blue-eyed and alarmingly blond with all the predictable mannerisms inherited from their Aryan forefathers. Had they been born in the Fatherland, Adolf Hitler would have rejoiced in their racial perfection. They were respectful, polite, stood to attention in front of their elders, and were obedient and unimaginative, while being neither clever nor excessively dull.

Father and sons worked hard and kept a model fifty-acre farm with the fields planted in perfect rows. The beech trees lining the evenly gravelled and raked driveway leading to the well-kept farmhouse were equally distanced and perfectly aligned, all of them the same size and shape. If an errant bough should disrupt their symmetry it would be quickly lopped to conform. The Kraus farm was a consistent winner in the New York State 4-H competition for working farms on fifty acres or less, and had made the national finals on two separate occasions. Their tomatoes had earned a host of blue ribbons at various agricultural shows and these ribbons hung in line along one wall of the packing shed spaced precisely three inches apart, the red, the blue and the green each in their own section.

The two barns and packing shed were freshly painted, the roof tomato red with 'KRAUS TOMATOES' painted in large white letters that could be seen by motorists travelling along the nearby highway and by the aeroplanes flying out of Newark Airfield. The walls were the colour of freshly churned butter. The outlines of each of the farm tools were painted on one of the inside walls of the main barn, and each piece of equipment was hung accordingly. The John Deere tractor was hosed down, refuelled and checked after each day's work and parked, always in precisely the same location between two white painted lines on the barn floor. The ploughs and harrows were freshly painted at the end of each summer. The packing shed was in perfect order, the conveyor belts oiled and running at their optimum efficiency and the soft pine timber for the tomato cases stacked and sorted according to size.

The twenty per cent aerated soil in the seedling trays resting on wire racks in the hothouses was correctly formulated. The ambient temperature and precise water-misting routine were designed to maintain the humidity and to produce seedlings of an even size. The young tomato plants stood at rigid attention, never yellowed or mysteriously wilted, and seemed to know that they were destined to produce future American Beauty tomatoes of the correct shape, preferred size and absolutely top quality.

Otto's sons, while thoroughly trained by their male parent in the way of their Teutonic forebears, were nevertheless proudly American and fanatical New York Yankee fans. Both had been offered baseball scholarships to Columbia but Otto Kraus, who wanted his boys to remain on the farm, had forbidden them to take the scholarships. In his opinion a college education wouldn't make them grow better tomatoes. He had recently purchased a further hundred acres adjoining his own and, when the time came for the two boys to marry, a home would be built for each that carried its own separate title for fifty acres. In Otto's mind there was no room for discussion – the future for his sons was settled, and it had never occurred to them to resist his will.

But storm clouds were beginning to gather. In 1940 they'd been required to register as aliens, meaning German-born American citizens. With the increasing likelihood of America entering the war, the American-born offspring of German, Italian and Japanese migrants were preparing to face the prospect of their parents being interned as enemy aliens. Furthermore, at the age of twenty, the twins would almost certainly be conscripted, which was another reason why Otto wasn't preparing the newly acquired acres. He had hatched a plan whereby the twins would volunteer for the armed forces in an attempt to prove, with two sons fighting for America, that he was a loyal American citizen, and so he might escape internment. If this failed he conceded that they would be forced to cease the production of tomatoes for the duration of the war, putting the farm into mothballs and leaving Frau Kraus to take care of things until they returned.

Frau Kraus was a solidly built woman of peasant stock. She had small, sharp blue eyes set into a face as expressionless as a scrubbed potato. Her cheeks were blushed with tiny surface veins and her top lip carried the suggestion of an errant moustache. The pinpoint brightness of her eyes in so plain a visage suggested a natural shrewdness, but if this was true she had little opportunity to exercise it because Otto made all the purchases and important farm and household decisions. She seldom smiled or spoke unless personally addressed, and the expression she assumed for everyday use was one of disapproval. Her mouth was turned downwards even in repose, as if she'd decided that her life had little chance of being enjoyable and was simply to be endured in silent protest. There seemed not to be the slightest suggestion of frivolity in her make-up. She spoke functional English in a heavy Bavarian accent, though she hadn't mastered the language to the point where she could understand the jokes on the radio or in the Sunday comic papers.

She was referred to as Frau Kraus by both her husband Otto and her twin sons. Moreover, because her Christian name was unpronounceable to the American families who attended the Lutheran church, they too called her 'Fraukraus', joining the two words into a single Christian name. When required to adopt a more formal approach they referred to her as Mrs Otto.

Adding to Frau Kraus's peculiar plainness was the manner in which she wore her hair. It was a deep chestnut, with distinct white stripes running through it approximately the width of a pencil and evenly dispersed every four inches or so. The chestnut carried not a single white strand and the white not a wisp of chestnut. In effect, she had naturally striped hair. She wore it pulled back and up from her face and tied into a tight bun on top of her head. The evenly spaced stripes emanating from the centre of the bun wound around its burnished perimeter to disappear into its underside and then remerge as legs. This gave the appearance of a very large and dangerous looking spider clamped to the top of her head. Small children, seeing her for the first time, would often cry out or draw back clutching at their mother's skirt.

Six days a week Frau Kraus wore shapeless floral dresses of the same design with the hemline down to her ankles, then an identical all-black version for Sunday church services. Her Sabbath attire was set off by a small straw hat, also black, which covered her spider bun and was decorated with two artificial cherries with two additional stems sticking up where cherries had once been attached. The small hat made the spider-like effect even more pronounced – the hat now became the giant insect's body with the two cherries acting as its protruding eyes and the empty stems as antennae. She always wore men's boots, a good pair for church and a not-so-good pair for work. Her black church boots were carefully polished and when not in use stored in muslin bags, while her heavy industrial steel-capped work boots were kept at the kitchen door and forbidden entry to the house. While indoors, she wore two sheepskin pads about twelve inches in diameter, woolly side to the floor and with two elastic bands sewn into the flip side of the pads into which she would fit her rather large flat feet. With a feather duster in hand she would then move about the house much as a figure skater might do on a winter pond, the polishing footwear designed to keep the wooden floors throughout the house gleaming, and the duster to swipe at any speck of dust that might be seen on the furniture. If Otto was indoors she would put the first movement of a Wagner symphony, his favourite, on the gramophone to conceal her heavy panting as she worked up a sweat at polishing. She would polish as if her life depended on it and would only rest when her legs couldn't continue and she was forced to catch her breath by bending over with her hands on her knees.

At home Frau Kraus wore a heavily starched white cotton apron that crackled when she bent over. She couldn't tolerate the presence of even the tiniest speck of dirt and would change her apron the moment a small spot appeared on its snowy surface. At any given time two large iron buckets in the washhouse adjacent to her kitchen carried a dozen discarded aprons soaking in bleach ready to be consigned to the belly of her Maytag. All that she found good in America (which admittedly wasn't much) was summed up by this wonderful washing machine prepared to work around the clock to indulge her obsession with cleanliness. While the remainder of her family's washing was strung out on an extensive three-strand washing line every Monday morning, on the remaining days of the week, with the exception of the Sabbath, the line was crowded with aprons.

It would never have occurred to Frau Kraus to ask herself if she was happy. Her work precluded such an unnecessary state of being. Cleaning was her happiness, America her cross to bear. Her house with its heavy Germanic furniture was immaculate. Work was what life was composed of and there wasn't much she could do about it. She prepared four meals three times each day, kept a well-stocked kitchen garden going, a dozen chickens for eggs, a neat pond for an equal number of ducks and geese fattened for Christmas sale to German families who'd place their orders in January, as well as a turkey run that supplied three dozen plump birds of a specific weight to a Lower Manhattan restaurant for Thanksgiving. Finally, she had a small orchid house where she raised a dozen or so orchids ready for sale to a Brooklyn florist. She deliberately kept her farmyard endeavour small, knowing that if she expanded with more ducks, turkeys, eggs and orchids, Otto would demand the rewards. The money she made went on brooms, buckets and mops and every manner of cleaning aid that soaked, scrubbed, wiped, polished, waxed, brushed or bleached.

All her livestock was contained within a small, neat field adjacent to the house, which was ploughed in early spring and sown with rye grass and clover. It contained a small barn that acted as a milking shed, hayloft and winter shelter for the resident Jersey cow she milked daily for household milk and to make freshly churned butter, and a nanny goat she kept for cheese. Neither the cow nor the goat enjoyed a name and if a child should ask, Frau Kraus would point to one and then the other and pronounce, 'This ist Cow; this ist Goat.' Her work routine entailed at least a dozen changes of apron during the day and a final change just moments before she sat down to supper.

Washed and wearing a fresh shirt, denim overalls and slippers, Otto, at the head of the dining-room table, and the boys, seated on either side, sat waiting silently for Frau Kraus to join them. The food – meat, potatoes and vegetables from her garden piled high on their plates – would have been placed on the table moments before they entered the dining room and Frau Kraus would have returned to the kitchen. A stein of lager beer sat to the side of each plate. The men would wait until she emerged again from the kitchen when Otto, together with the boys, would look up and raise their beer steins as she reached her chair at the opposite end of the table, and Otto would say, '*Danke, meine saubere Frau.*'

It was a toast that contained not the slightest element of gratitude, nor, for that matter, did it seem intended as a compliment. 'Thank you, my clean wife' were simply the words that, over the years, had come to mean the evening meal was about to commence. Frau Kraus would answer with an impatient grunt all but lost in the crackling sound of her starched apron as, stiff-backed, she seated herself at the opposite end of the table. Otto, having taken a sip from his stein and placed it down with a loud smack of his lips, now proceeded to deliver a mumbling thanks to God in his native tongue for what they were about to receive.

The meal would be consumed almost entirely in silence, with perhaps an occasional remark about the market price of tomatoes or some incident that had occurred on the farm. The boys never inquired after their mother's welfare, and the first part of the proceedings would ritually be brought to an end when Otto, having completed his meal, placed his used knife and fork on the tablecloth, and reaching for a slice of bread used it to mop up what gravy remained on his plate. As in all things he was thorough, using the bread to polish the plate until not the tiniest smear of gravy remained. The twins, who had completed their dinner first, waited for the moment when Otto placed the last of the gravy-soaked bread in his mouth, licked his fat fingers and reached for his napkin to wipe his moustache. Without looking at their mother they would recite, '*Danke, Frau Kraus.*'

'*Bitte,*' Frau Kraus would reply tonelessly, not glancing up. The boys' cursory 'thank you' for the meal was intended simply as her cue to fetch the strudel and cream, a dessert that never varied and that was already waiting in plates resting on a tray on the kitchen table. Clearing their dinner plates, including her own, regardless of whether she'd completed her meal, she'd leave and return with the dessert, her starched apron now replaced by a small pinafore embroidered with pink roses. If any of the men ever noticed this small ceremonial apron change they saw no reason to comment. Several years back she had delivered the strudel wearing a pinafore onto which she had embroidered 'Today is my birthday', which had gone unnoticed.

With dessert completed Otto would wipe his waxed moustache, which was the signal for Frau Kraus to rise and fetch her husband's pipe and tobacco. After this she'd remove two Dresden china cups and saucers and a matching sugar bowl from the sideboard and place them down at her end of the table, then return to the kitchen to retrieve the enamel coffee pot from where it sat brewing at the back of the stove.

Seated once again, she'd pour thick black coffee into one delicate porcelain cup, add three teaspoons of sugar and stir, somehow managing to avoid touching the sides of the cup. She'd then pour the second cup, this time not adding sugar. Leaving the first cup where it was, she'd rise from the table and take up the unsugared coffee and walk towards the kitchen door, where she'd pause momentarily and say what would often be the only consecutive words spoken by her during the entire meal: 'That coffee will kill you, Otto. You should not drink it.' Otto, holding his pipe in his mouth, would grunt his lack of concern and at the same time nod to the twins, granting them permission to leave the table. Frau Kraus then moved through to the kitchen and poured the cup of coffee she held down the sink, rinsed the cup thoroughly and switched off the light. Seated in the dark at the kitchen table, she waited.

This small act of defiance, repeated every night over twenty years, was her single show of resistance. She'd long since ceased to feel any affection for the three men in her life. She hated their loud masticating noises; the careless and frenetic clatter of knife and fork stabbing at food on her willow-patterned plates; Otto's crude and deliberate burp as he finished his beer; the way they all gnawed off the gluey nubs at the end of veal chops; Otto's disgusting habit of polishing his plate clean with a slice of bread, then leaning back and patting his large belly before emitting a second satisfied burp; the cursory, pig-like grunts as she placed the strudel down beside each of them; and the fact that they invariably spilled custard or cream on her spotless tablecloth, not to mention the frequent gravy spots. Above all, she hated her husband's smelly pipe, the tobacco crumbs he left on the tablecloth, the clouds of foul smoke that polluted the air as he stoked up and repeatedly lit it, and the dead matches thrown into his dessert plate.

All of this deeply offended her sense of order. Why, she repeatedly asked herself, when they kept their farm so perfectly ordered, did they feel they could desecrate her home with their filthy habits? Her world of starched aprons and clean surfaces was as important to her as their neat rows of tomatoes and painted barns were to them. The twins were as bad as their father. It was he, Otto, who had taken her sons from her and by simply allowing them to emulate his behaviour had taught them to show no respect for their mother and to behave like pigs. It was of some consolation to her that they would eventually find wives and leave, but Otto was here to stay – she would have to endure him until he died.

She was aware that in Otto's mind his coffee cup left standing at her end of the table had become an all-but-meaningless protest. She would listen, waiting until she heard his chair scrape back, then imagine him standing, stretching, scratching his fat gut with the stem of his pipe, leaving a nicotine stain on his freshly laundered dungarees. She'd wait to hear the creak of a floorboard as his heavy footfall advanced towards the cup of coffee, which, every night over the past six months, she'd laced with a tiny dose of arsenic. Just sufficient to add to the slow build-up of poison in his system.

The farm would be left to her. It was all settled. The twins were each to get fifty acres next door. She'd sell it for a good price – after all, it was a prize-winning farm. Then she'd return to her beloved Bavaria after the war, where Herr Hitler was doing so well, sending the enemy running for their lives across Europe like a pack of mongrel dogs and the British scuttling back across the Channel where the glorious Luftwaffe was bombing London in a blitzkrieg. As an all-conquering hero, Herr Hitler would return from his conquests to make the Fatherland into a paradise free of Jews and gypsies. She, who had accepted American citizenship only because Otto had demanded it, would be going home to a master race who had conquered the world. She would buy a farm in Bavaria and live happily ever after.

She told herself it wouldn't be murder. How could it be? She'd never offered him the coffee, never actually lifted it from the table and placed it in front of him. She'd clearly and repeatedly warned him against drinking it. He'd retrieved it in an act of self-will despite her urging him against doing so. Surely this was the gesture of a loving wife caring about the welfare of her husband. How could it be seen as otherwise? The twins would corroborate her concern for his heart, the coffee warning repeated in their presence every night since they'd been children. A slow smile would appear across the plain, scrubbed face as she waited in the kitchen. She had taken almost twenty years to gain the courage to put her plan into action. But she was right to do it. She'd suffered enough. She'd taken her time, thought a great deal about it, worked it all out, given him every chance. Even if they did a post-mortem, the arsenic could easily have been absorbed when he mixed it with bread, moulding the soft, dough-like substance with his fingers into pellets to attract rats and mice. Again, her sons could substantiate this.

This then was the family with whom Jimmy would begin his working life.

If I appear to know a great deal about the Kraus family, it is because Jimmy is a man who observes things very closely and has the ability to encapsulate any incident in his past into a complete and colourful story. In turn, I seem to have the capacity to recall seemingly disconnected incidents over the years and to piece them together to make a whole. Jimmy, in his usual way, will bring up an incident in his past and, like some sort of mental bowerbird, I will snatch it up to see where it fits in the overall narrative of his life prior to our friendship. With a bit of luck, eventually an entire episode, such as the one above, evolves into a cohesive whole. His ability to observe the smallest details and my skill in piecing them together were to make us a formidable combination in our business dealings with the Chinese.

Otto Kraus was not a man to leave anything to chance, and he prepared for the likelihood of America entering the war as carefully as if he were planting a row of tomato plants. Completely devoid of imagination, he dealt with things as they were. He knew tomatoes would not be necessary for the war effort – moreover, the boys would be conscripted and he might be interned as an enemy alien. The farm could be shut down easily enough but would require a fair amount of everyday maintenance, which Frau Kraus would have to attend to. Over several weeks he kept an eye on her daily activities, and finally ended up with a list of the precise time she would spend doing the required chores.

*Washing, Cleaning, Aprons . . . 4 hrs*
*Cooking . . . 1 hr*
*Vegetables . . . 2 hrs*
*Orchids . . . 1 hr*
*Cow & stable . . . 1 hr*
*Goat . . . nein*
*Poultry . . . 1 hr*
*Farm machinery oiling etc. . . . 1 hr*
*Trip to town to sell produce . . . 4 hrs (average ¾ hr per day)*
*Recreation . . . 15 mins*
*Total per day . . . 12 hrs*
*Sunday: Church . . . 4 hrs*
*Various chores . . . 8 hrs.*

Of course, the list was written in German and so it had the absolute ring of precise instructions to be followed to the letter. By his calculations her obsessive preoccupation with cleaning and laundering her aprons took up nearly half a day, calculated on the basis of a twelve-hour day. This could be spent more profitably tending to her poultry, slaughtering and dressing ducks and turkeys, stuffing down pillows and grading eggs for the market. She would decrease her time spent in the vegetable garden and increase the number of ducks, turkeys and chickens, using the extra money she made from the sale of meat and eggs to live on, buy winter hay for the cow and do the necessary farm maintenance, painting, oiling machinery, etc. He calculated that the field containing the cow and goat would only need to be ploughed and sown with rye and clover every two years if she got rid of the goat, which ate a disproportionate amount of the available grazing. In addition the hothouse used to raise his tomato seedlings would be turned over to orchids, which she would propagate and sell. He would arrange for his bank account to be frozen for the duration of his internment but tell her this would undoubtedly be done by the authorities, and so she must learn to be entirely self-sufficient as there would be no additional money to hire help. None of this was discussed with Frau Kraus. Otto had never thought to ask her opinion and considered it best to have everything worked out before he revealed his plans for her.

It was around this time that a church elder alerted him to the possibility of obtaining an indentured orphan from the Colored Orphan Asylum. The idea that he could obtain a servant virtually for the cost of their food appealed to Otto greatly. He loved a bargain, and free labour until the coloured boy or girl was eighteen years old was not to be sneered at. The elder explained that the coloured children were already accustomed to work, and Otto felt that he'd soon enough train them in his particular ways. Wearing their Sunday best and armed with a letter of introduction from the Lutheran minister as well as half a dozen cases of tomatoes as a gift to the institution, Otto and the twins piled into the Dodge truck and turned up at Riverdale on visitor's day.

At first they thought a girl might be suitable to help Frau Kraus, but then Otto, in a rare moment of sensitivity, realised that she would not allow a *Schwarze* into her spotless home. There were also the twins to contend with – putting unnecessary temptation in their path wasn't a sensible idea. Besides, they needed an outdoor nigger – which suggested a boy. Otto saw Jimmy, who, at eleven, was the size of a fifteen-year-old and seemed strong enough to be trained to do a great many of the maintenance tasks around the farm. Otto regarded the *Schwarze* boy as an intelligent addition to the livestock, so he figured no special accommodation would be needed – Jimmy would sleep in the animal barn, the cow and goat in the bottom and Jimmy in the hayloft.

Jimmy recalled the day that the Kraus men arrived at Riverdale early in 1941. '"*Komm*, boy!" Mr Otto he say to me. "Stand! I look you." Den he feel mah muscles. "Strong boy," he says. "*Ja, gut.*" Den he say, "Teeths!" I don't unnerstand what he say. "Open za teeths!" he say again.

'"Why he don't speak no proper English?" I ask dem boys.

'"He's German," one o' dem says. "He wants you to open your mouth." I open mah mouth and he gone stick his finger inside and pull dis way den dat way. He is lookin' in like I is a fuckin' horse.

'"*Ja, gut, gut!*" he says again. I can taste da tobacco on his finger and his breath don't smell good. "*Gut,*" he say one more time, den he take out his finger and wipe it on da back o' his britches. "*Komm*, boy!" he say, and he walk away, den he stop and says, "You come, *schnell.*"

'"What yoh say please, sir?" I ask dat Germ-man real polite.

'"He wants you to follow him," one of his boys says. I follow him an' he take me to a bush, like a hedge, an' he say I should stand behind it. Den he point to mah britches.

'"Open za button!" he says. I ain't gonna do it. No way, man. I shake mah head.

'"Nossir, I ain't," I says. He turns and says somethin' to one o' his boys.

'"He wants to know if you've got any hair around your cock." Dey's laughin', dey think it funny, man. I want to cry, but I ain't gonna let da muth'fuckers get no satisfaction.

'"I jus' eleven year old, man!" I say. "Mah voice it jus' done broke!"

'"*Nein*," one da boys says to dat Germ-man, "*Nein*, *Papa*."

'"*Gut*," dat Germ-man say, and den he say somethin' in da language an' dem boys dey nods der heads. Den dey tell da matron I der man, dey gonna give me a "*gut*" home!'

Shortly after his twelfth birthday the Kraus farm became Jimmy's new home.

With the Japanese attack on Pearl Harbor on Sunday, 7th of December 1941, a surprised and angry America was kick-started into the war. Allowed to make up its own timetable to enter the war in Europe its treatment of aliens may have been different, but now an enraged American public wasn't willing to listen to pleas of loyalty or even dispassionately examine the integrity of their Japanese-, German- and Italian-born citizens. President Roosevelt immediately reactivated the Alien Enemy Act of 1798 and issued two proclamations that together branded all German, Italian and Japanese nationals as enemy aliens and authorised their internment, travel restrictions and, if necessary, the confiscation of their assets and property.

By the end of the first day the FBI had arrested several hundred German aliens after raids on their homes, detaining them even before war was declared on Germany. This rush for revenge did not include Otto and Frau Kraus, though Otto, by nature a pessimist, began to make frantic preparations. Five weeks later, all enemy aliens over the age of fourteen – that is, foreign-born Germans, Italians and Japanese – had to apply to re-register their domicile in America and be issued with certificates of identification, which had the effect of restricting their movement and their ability to sell their property.

Otto and Frau Kraus were among the 300 000 German-born aliens to register, which meant they were restricted to the tomato farm and only allowed to attend church services if they were escorted by two American-born members of the congregation.

Hysteria gripped the population, and the newspapers and radio warned of 'the enemy in our midst' so that soon people suspected anyone who spoke with the slightest accent to be potential aliens. Folk who'd been friends and neighbours with German, Italian and Japanese or, for that matter, any foreign-born couples, now fell over themselves to report them to the FBI. A German-born male looking for his cat by torchlight in his own garden in Newark was reported by his neighbour of thirty years, arrested for spying and jailed without trial.

Church congregations turned on their foreign-born parishioners by refusing to supply an escort for them to attend Sunday worship. This sudden alienation by the pious included the local Lutheran church, whose members were essentially made up of the descendants of German and Swedish migrants and three foreign-born families, including the family of Otto and Frau Kraus. The legislation had been cleverly contrived to isolate the so-called enemy aliens without the congregation having to suffer the embarrassment of appearing to deliberately avoid people they had known, some all their lives. Frau Kraus felt secretly vindicated – she'd long since decided that Americans were fair-weather friends and, at best, a superficial people, while Otto, who liked to give the impression of a bluff and hearty regular guy, grew flustered and confused, flying into sudden rages and pointing out that he'd paid his tithe to the church for twenty years only to be rebuffed when he most needed its support.

The minister, Pastor Karl Stennholz, a second-generation German American, visited Otto at home and suggested that if he paid his tithes to the church, ten per cent of his anticipated annual income, three years in advance, he felt sure the church would be able to intercede on behalf of him and Frau Kraus should the time come. He pointed out that the FBI had interviewed a number of ministers of religion concerning their foreign-born parishioners, sometimes with good results. Otto agreed, but insisted on a receipt and the return of his money if the war didn't last the full three years. The minister silently registered this as a lack of good faith and immediately felt less inclined to defend Otto, telling himself that the bible clearly stated that the meek shall inherit the earth and perhaps he would do better when the FBI arrived to concentrate his efforts in the defence of Frau Kraus.

With the proclamation of aliens issued almost weekly, Otto realised that he was running out of time. While his internment might be stayed, it also might not. It was time to outline his plans for the running of the farm in his absence, and after the evening meal that night, as his wife got up to get his pipe and tobacco, he bid her remain seated. Frau Kraus listened in silence, and when he'd completed his monologue, making sure she understood that there was no money in the bank she would be able to count on, he watched as she nodded then rose from her chair to fetch his pipe and tobacco and prepare his coffee, as usual.

Ottto Kraus hadn't expected any resistance, and so he was satisfied that his plans would be faithfully undertaken. He'd give his wife the money for additional turkey chicks, ducklings and day-old chicks, and agree to finance the purchase of a hundred young orchid plants, growing mixture and pots. All this was completed in the weeks immediately after the attack on Pearl Harbor, and by the time the FBI arrived to interview him he'd done all he could to keep the home fires burning in his absence. He also told himself that he'd trained the *Schwarze* well enough and that he was sufficiently cowed to be a diligent and obsequious servant to Frau Kraus.

Jimmy's life on the farm was a hard existence of strictly followed orders. Herr Otto, as Jimmy was required to call him, didn't believe that black people had sufficient brains to be allowed to use their initiative – the only way to teach them was to beat them. The twins would take great delight in showing Jimmy procedures that were incorrect to then watch as Otto took to him with a sulky whip he kept for the purpose. As patience was not one of Otto's virtues, Jimmy was also frequently beaten for being unable to follow instructions delivered in a mixture of German and truncated English.

Furthermore, Jimmy was regarded as outside help, in the same way a dog might be restricted to the farmyard, and wasn't allowed to enter the house – though Frau Kraus, who never spoke to him, fed him the same food as she did her husband and the twins and Jimmy found himself eating better than he'd ever done. It was small compensation for a difficult existence. His meals were served piled together in a large enamel dish that, at dinner time, included the strudel mixed in with meat and veg. He wasn't given a knife, fork or spoon and had no way of obtaining one, and so was forced to eat using his hands, licking the gravy from the surface of his plate. He'd take his meals in the washhouse with ice clinging to the edges of the windowpanes, and frequently had to shovel the snowdrifts from outside the door before entering. Once inside he'd sit with his back against the laundry hot-water tank, wrapped in an old blanket, with his feet propped against the heated pipe leading from the tank to Frau Kraus's mighty Maytag. He became convinced he would never be warm again.

Jimmy was a sad, lost and lonely boy going through the agony of early puberty, when young men begin the slow and confusing task of emerging from the agitated body of a child into adulthood. He masturbated at every opportunity, and his inability to muster the self-discipline to stop abusing his tortured penis, rubbed raw by his urgent needs, left him miserable and disgusted with himself. His life had been dominated by women, and he'd had little or no experience of adult men or how he was supposed to behave. He simply didn't understand what was happening; nor could he explain his depression or suddenly changing moods. He felt as if he must be going mad.

He watched the twins before they volunteered for the army, but they gave him very few useful clues into adulthood, teasing, shouting, playfully insulting and slapping at each other – no different to the way he'd handled himself with the boys in the orphanage. He watched carefully to see if they'd sneak away to masturbate at every opportunity as he did, becoming even more confused when they appeared not to have this necessity.

Maybe it was just a nigger thing, or maybe he was sick? Then one of the boys caught him at it behind the tractor and shouted gleefully to his twin, 'Hey, Jimmy's pulling his putz!' This had caused a great deal of merriment among the three men, with the twins continuing to tease him mercilessly until they'd finally left for boot camp. Despite their teasing, Jimmy found he had taken something positive out of the experience. Firstly, he now knew it was called, 'pulling yo' putz', which on the face of it didn't seem too harmful and, secondly, the fact that he wasn't beaten meant it must not be considered either a sin or a sickness.

He often thought of escaping, but he didn't know how to go about such an endeavour. He'd been institutionalised from birth and was not streetwise, and had no idea how to survive on his own. Besides, he worked from sun-up until sunset and often beyond and was too weary at night to do anything other than fall into his rickety bed, often lacking even the energy to cry himself to sleep.

He became deeply depressed and, with the departure of the twins, seldom spoke to or saw anyone except the 'Germ-man' and occasionally, when delivering a message, a grim-faced Frau Kraus whom he now called the 'spider woman' to himself. Frau Kraus would curl her top lip when she saw Jimmy approaching and once, in the presence of her husband, she'd spat at her feet as he drew closer. He only spoke when he was addressed, and then with his eyes averted.

Jimmy, unable to communicate, became a silent observer, watching the Kraus household, seeing it for the cold and loveless place it was. When the weather grew warmer he'd gulp down his dinner and move around to the side of the house where, through a crack in the curtains, he'd spy on the family as they took their evening meal. In his childhood he'd often imagined having a mother, someone who cared for and loved him. Having no other mother-and-son relationship with which to make a comparison, Jimmy, observing Frau Kraus and the twins at the dining-room table and on other occasions, decided that he'd been fortunate to avoid this additional calamity in his life. He knew enough about women to stay well clear of this ugly, sharp-eyed one who spat at niggers.

Despite the misery and the back-breaking labour, Jimmy was a quick learner. With the twins gone he helped Otto to harvest and pack the final tomato crop and to close the farm down, leaving only the Frau Kraus content to be maintained. He was competent with both a harrow and a plough behind the John Deere tractor, and by necessity had learned to drive the Dodge truck. Otto, along with all the enemy aliens, was restricted from entering any area designated as a military zone, and the town of Somerville, New Jersey, where they shopped and shipped their tomatoes and poultry, was designated as such a zone. With Otto and Frau Kraus, who couldn't drive, restricted to the farm, Jimmy was required to deliver the produce and do the shopping. At thirteen he was tall enough to be taken as sixteen and, by means of a heavy bribe to the local sheriff, Otto obtained a truck licence for him.

So that, by the 12th of January 1943, when the FBI arrived at the farm to interview the German couple, Jimmy had become a capable farm assistant while still being treated by his master with contempt. Otto had never once complimented him on a task well done, and in his arrogance simply congratulated himself for so completely whipping the boy into shape that Jimmy was now some sort of alter ego when it came to farm duties. By this time Otto was leaving more and more to the *Schwarze*, complaining of frequent and severe stomach cramps. He now spent two or three days each week in bed, refusing to allow Frau Kraus to call the doctor, one of the many members of the Lutheran congregation who had snubbed them. Ever dutiful and concerned for her sick husband, Frau Kraus would wring the neck of one of her beloved chickens and prepare a broth that she forced him to drink and that he churlishly complained had a distinctly bitter taste.

Otto and Frau Kraus became caught up in the second great series of enemy-alien arrests when, at last, the building of internment camps, located at Crystal City and Seagoville in Texas and Fort Lincoln, North Dakota, was completed. The two FBI agents who now called at the farm to question them had previously paid a visit to Pastor Stennholz, the Lutheran minister.

It was one of the days Otto had taken to his bed and Frau Kraus, wearing her polishing pads, had put the first movement of her husband's favourite Wagner symphony on the gramophone and was skating hell for leather across the polished floors, so she didn't hear the knock at the door. The two FBI agents, their persistent knocking ignored and hearing the strident music coming from the interior of the farmhouse, moved over to a window to witness a large woman wearing a floral dress with white apron, who appeared to be skating haphazardly across a large expanse of wooden floor wearing what looked like two large platters on her feet and a gigantic spider on her head.

The interview with the Lutheran minister had prepared them somewhat for the confrontation. In the course of the interview he'd dutifully pointed out that Otto Kraus and his wife were loyal, hardworking citizens who paid their taxes and always contributed to the welfare of the church and, besides, their twin boys were in the American armed forces. On being questioned more closely he admitted that the Kraus family had kept to themselves and hadn't as a rule joined in church activities, though, he was quick to point out, they'd never missed a Sunday service and contributed two cases of tomatoes to the annual church fete. Asked if they'd made any close friends with members of the congregation, the answer was again negative. Was there any particular reason for this? The minister hesitated, scratching his head. Finally he ventured, 'Her, that is, Mrs Otto, she . . . well, she isn't easy to approach, doesn't have much to say for herself and they don't encourage visitors to their farm.'

'Would you say she's secretive?' one of the men asked.

The minister laughed. 'No, not in the way you may mean it. Silent. Nothing to say. Beaten down by life. She seems to be . . .' he searched for a word, '. . . crushed.'

'Not all there?' one of the FBI men suggested. 'You know . . . ?' He brought his forefinger up to the side of his head and wiggled it.

The minister of religion hesitated before replying, 'Yes . . . perhaps, but I'd prefer to say harmless. Yes, that's more the case, completely harmless.'

Pastor Stennholz then told them that while he well understood the need for vigilance and was aware that national security was of primary importance, he felt that the Kraus family were above reproach, and while Otto might be a little domineering this was to be expected from a Prussian.

'Prussian!' both officers chorused, suddenly alerted.

'Prussian' and now 'domineering' were both key words. When asked if he could illustrate Otto Kraus's domineering nature, the minister made example of his refusal to allow his sons to take up a baseball scholarship to attend college. The case against Otto Kraus was suddenly mounting. Denying his twin sons the opportunity to go to college was positively un-American behaviour, particularly as they'd excelled at baseball, the most American of sports.

'I often think that the poor woman could do with a little relief away from him,' the Lutheran minister now said lightly. 'The boys too – the army will do them the world of good.'

'Has he ever expressed any political opinions?' they asked Pastor Stennholz.

'No, never. Well, not to me, anyways.' He appeared to be thinking, then added, 'Which is strange, as he was a sergeant in the Great War – on the other side, of course. He certainly takes pride in his Prussian background, and still wears his waxed military moustache.'

'Pride in his Prussian background, on *their* side, domineering, waxed military moustache, un-American denial of college and baseball scholarship, don't encourage visitors.' It was all the FBI officers needed to hear, and shortly afterwards they concluded the interview with the Lutheran minister.

Approaching the farm they saw the words 'KRAUS TOMATOES' painted in large letters on the barn roof. They immediately concluded that, as the farm fell directly under the flight path of aircraft leaving Teterboro Airport, this blatant identification of the property was clearly intended for invading enemy aircraft. The noose about Otto's neck was about to choke him.

The interview with Otto and Frau Kraus went badly from the start. Otto had risen from his bed and insisted on standing to rigid attention behind his chair while the two FBI officers questioning him sat at the dining-room table. Otto's great gut had burst through the two lower buttons on his pyjama jacket and his fly gaped slightly to reveal a very small, uncircumcised appendage resting in a nest of greying pubic hair. Frau Kraus was either too terrified or too embarrassed in the presence of the two officers to bring his visibly nesting penis to her husband's attention. With every question asked, Otto would stiffen further to attention and shout, '*Ja*, sir!' before proceeding to answer. When a question was directed at Frau Kraus he would immediately answer for her, spitting out the answer as if he was a sergeant in the army being questioned by two superior officers. Every once in a while he'd suddenly grip his stomach and double over. With his teeth clamped together, hissing with the pain of the cramps, he refused to complain or explain. When the spasm finally passed he immediately resumed his rigid position.

The FBI men took this display of courage in the face of pain to be an attempt to seek their sympathy. Frau Kraus had previously brought coffee without asking and the two cups she'd placed silently beside them now grew cold and remained untouched. The FBI had a policy of not accepting gestures of hospitality from enemy aliens as they were clearly intended by the perpetrator as an attempt to lessen the tension generated by the interview. Ignoring Otto's stomach cramps was yet another demonstration of their professionalism. When, during one of the cramps, they finally managed to address Frau Kraus on her own they asked, 'The music you were playing, Mrs Kraus . . . it's German, isn't it?'

Frau Kraus, looking confused, answered in her customary 'This ist Cow. This ist Goat' manner, delivering her reply in three distinct statements. 'I polish. Herr Wagner. Myn husbant like zis music.'

The FBI men looked at each other in surprise. The Lutheran minister had failed to tell them Frau Kraus was Polish. 'You Polish?' one of them asked.

Frau Kraus nodded. 'I polish.'

This put an entirely different complexion on things. Germany had invaded Poland and crushed it mercilessly, just as Otto had crushed his unfortunate Polish wife, humiliating her by forcing the poor, unfortunate woman to race about the room with his triumphant, all-conquering German music blaring at her from the gramophone.

Otto was arrested, handcuffed and taken to the police station at Somerville where the same sheriff he'd bribed in order to get Jimmy a driver's licence booked him on suspicion, fingerprinted him and drove him out to the county jail where he was incarcerated. He would be held in a cell prior to passage being arranged on a prison train to the new camp for enemy aliens at Crystal City, Texas. But Otto never made it to Crystal City. He died at approximately two a.m. of a severe stomach haemorrhage while handcuffed to a bunk in the hospital carriage on the prison train somewhere between Little Rock and Texarkana.

A hurried and carelessly conducted post mortem showed the presence of arsenic in Otto's stomach, the coroner's finding being that Otto Wilhelm Kraus, suspected of being a German spy recruited in America, having been apprehended by the FBI and incarcerated, committed suicide by the self-administration of a poison identified as arsenic.

By peacetime standards this wouldn't be regarded as a very plausible explanation, but in the prevailing climate of enemy-alien hysteria it was readily accepted and made for excellent propaganda. Otto's face appeared in newspapers all over the US, where his waxed moustache turned up at the corners and centre parting showing two little winglets of hair resting on the crown of his balding head gave him every appearance of a comic-book German general in the previous war. Americans seemed oblivious to the parody his image represented, and the Department of Justice couldn't have hoped for a better story and more precise profile of 'the enemy in our midst'. In the end, the prize-winning tomato farmer, ex-sergeant in the Kaiser's army, was inadvertently to prove of great patriotic service to his adopted country.

Many of the members of Pastor Stennholz's congregation were quick to point out that they'd suspected Otto all along. That he'd given himself away in a hundred small ways, always trying to ingratiate himself. Apart from a good deal of self-congratulation for their sagacity, they also pointed to the fact that the FBI had acted with great probity and even some bureaucratic sensitivity. Realising that Frau Kraus was the innocent victim of a cruel and despotic Nazi spy, they had allowed the dear, sweet, hardworking Christian woman to remain in her American home and to enjoy the life of an American woman safe in the land of the free. All in all, the outcome was a fine example of justice tempered with mercy.

Frau Kraus attended Otto's funeral with only Pastor Stennholz and Jimmy at her side. Jimmy, in fact, not quite literally at her side. He'd driven her in the Dodge truck to the cemetery and now stood in the freezing cold outside the gates while the minister and Frau Kraus, wearing a black woollen coat and scarf, black gloves and her polished Sunday boots and on her head her extra-terrible spider's-body hat with protruding cherry eyes and antennae, got through the funeral proceedings dry-eyed. Fresh flowers at this inclement time of the year were prohibitively expensive so Frau Kraus had fashioned a black paper rose with a picture-wire stem wrapped around with green crinkle paper. As she placed it on the coffin Pastor Stennholz thought he saw her smile and distinctly say, '*Danke, meine saubere Frau.*'

The following Sunday, after attending church worship, several of the women in the congregation came up to Frau Kraus to wish her well and were surprised and delighted when they were rewarded with the first smile they'd ever witnessed coming from her scrubbed-potato face.

Jimmy had been in the Kraus family employ just over a year, during which time he'd received no wages, although he'd been the beneficiary of two pairs of worn denim dungarees and an old woollen overcoat that had belonged to one of the twins. Otto had also been forced to buy him a pair of work boots for the winter, as his feet were already too large for a pair discarded by the family.

Alone now with the hated Frau Kraus, Jimmy at last summoned up sufficient courage to run away at the earliest opportunity, though he sensibly told himself it was winter and he'd have to wait until the warmer weather arrived. On the night following the funeral it was bitterly cold when he entered the washhouse for his evening meal only to find Frau Kraus waiting for him. She carried a worn towel and a bar of soap. Jimmy hesitated, starting to back out when she pointed to the washtub and commanded, '*Wasche*!'

Jimmy took the soap and towel and approached the wash tub to find that it contained several inches of hot water. His mind was in total confusion as he watched the steam rising up to the windowpanes to be converted to droplets that immediately froze, turning to translucent pimples stuck to the inside of the window. As he scooped water onto his bewildered face, he went through a multitude of what, why, how and what-for transitions.

Having washed and dried his face and hands, he waited. '*Komm*!' Frau Kraus demanded and, turning on her heels, opened the door to a short passageway that led to the kitchen. Jimmy, afraid he'd heard incorrectly, hesitated. Then, to his surprise, Frau Kraus turned and smiled and with a friendly nod of the head beckoned him to follow her. He hesitated again at the closed door at the far end of the passageway, reluctant to go any further. 'Take off za coat, also za boots,' Frau Kraus instructed, pointing to several coat hooks on the wall immediately outside the kitchen door.

Jimmy's overcoat was somewhat the worse for wear and very dirty, as he was forced to wear it while at work. Under it, directly against his skin, he wore a filthy chocolate-brown cardigan he'd found wrapped around a tractor part in the barn. It was full of holes but had been knitted by hand in heavy cable stitch from coarse wool, and he greatly treasured it for its warmth.

Jimmy first removed his boots and placed them against the wall, then his coat, which he hung on one of the hooks. His socks, with the toes and heels worn through, had come from the orphanage, and he now felt cold from the cement floor rising up through the wool on his feet. Shivering, he clasped his arms across his chest against the cold.

Frau Kraus opened the kitchen door and Jimmy was met with a blast of warm air. '*Komm*,' she beckoned again, and he entered a large kitchen with a fire blazing in a hearth at one end, the recipient of the wood he'd chopped and stacked behind the house during the summer. Frau Kraus closed the door behind him and, sensing Jimmy's acute embarrassment at finding himself alone with her inside the house, she smiled and pointed to the scrubbed pine table that he now saw was set for two. 'Sit!' she commanded, indicating one of the places.

Jimmy had yet to say a word, but now he cleared his throat. 'I cain't, ma'am. I ain't allowed.'

'*Ja, ja,* sit!' Frau Kraus called impatiently, as she moved to the refrigerator behind him.

Jimmy sat down slowly, his eyes fixed on the cutlery laid out on the table in front of him. He hadn't used a knife and fork in a year and he felt a slight panic at the idea of taking them up again. His knees trembled under the table and he realised that his hands were shaking. He heard a soft clunk as the handle of the refrigerator door locked into place and shortly afterwards Frau Kraus appeared holding a stein of beer, which she proceeded to place in front of him. Then, speaking in German she said, '*Danke, meine saubere Frau.*' To Jimmy's surprise she proceeded to giggle, which soon turned to laughter and then to convulsive, hysterical mirth until she was forced to sit on the bench beside Jimmy holding onto the side of the table, her huge frame shaking, jowls wobbling, tears running down her fat cheeks, her laughter seemingly completely beyond her control.

Jimmy sat rigid with fear, unable to decide what to do next. Frau Kraus had obviously gone mad. He thought about making a run for it, but by the time he'd put his boots and coat back on she'd be onto him. Carrying them out into the snow with him was the next option, but then what? Mixed with her laughter he could hear the wind howling in the kitchen chimney as the snowstorm outside gathered momentum. Then, as suddenly as her laughter had begun it stopped, and Frau Kraus rose from the table. Bringing the edge of her apron up to her face she wiped away the tears and moved towards the stove. Jimmy watched fearfully as she took up a pair of oven mittens and, opening the oven door, removed two plates piled with meat, roast potatoes, boiled cabbage and onion. She moved back to the table and placed the plates down, one in front of Jimmy and the other at the second place setting. She returned to the stove and brought back a large jug of gravy and, without asking him, poured a generous amount over his food. While she may have been plumb crazy, Frau Kraus still knew how to feed a growing boy.

Jimmy, who'd been working hard all day, always looked forward to his dinner. Now, despite his present predicament and anxiety, he began to eat ravenously, expecting at any moment to be told to leave. 'You drink now za beer,' Frau Kraus said at one stage. Jimmy had never before tasted beer and he took a tentative mouthful and reacted immediately, the foul-tasting liquid hardly in his mouth before he sent it spraying over the table. Jimmy was mortified and jumped up, ready to run for his life. 'Sorry, ma'am, I ain't meant it!' he cried, distressed. But Frau Kraus was laughing. 'You like milk?' Rising, she wiped the beer-splashed table clean with her napkin, removed the stein and commanded Jimmy to sit, whereupon she fetched him a glass of milk.

The meal was followed by strudel and cream, and Jimmy accepted a second helping, still not quite believing what was happening and expecting the worst to occur at any moment. Despite the warmth of the kitchen, the splendid meal and, except for the laughter, an otherwise benign Frau Kraus, Jimmy couldn't wait to make his escape into the howling snowstorm outside. He couldn't possibly explain Frau Kraus's complete change of attitude towards him, and could only think she must have gone mad – that the death of Herr Otto had been too much for her senses. While she seemed happy enough, calmly smiling at him as he ate, this only served to confirm Jimmy's suspicion that something had gone terribly wrong in her head. This was the same spider woman who'd spat at his approach. The meal drew to a conclusion and his heart started to pound as Frau Kraus rose from the table and stretched out her hand to him, again smiling, inviting him to take it.

Jimmy, suddenly panic-stricken at this unexpected gesture, jumped up fearfully, kicking at the bench behind him, tripping and falling, then propelling himself backwards on all fours until he bumped against the wall, and finally scrambling frantically to his feet. He found himself standing between the stove and the refrigerator with the large shape of Frau Kraus, hand still outstretched, advancing inexorably towards him, a benign smile on her plain German face.

'*Komm, Liebling,*' she said gently, reaching him and taking his dark, almost paralysed hand in her own and leading him from the kitchen. Frau Kraus led Jimmy through the house, down a hallway and through a door at the end, which turned out to be a large bathroom. It contained a spacious shower recess and no bath, and Jimmy guessed it was probably the bathroom the twins had customarily used.

Frau Kraus locked the door behind her and, instructing Jimmy to stand on the bathroom mat, she commenced to undress him. Jimmy stood mesmerised, reduced to being a small boy again when his house mother at the orphanage would make him stand naked in the shower room while she examined him for bed-bug bites, scabies and lice. The bathroom was cold and he began to shiver, and when she pulled his dungarees down he quickly covered his genitals and closed his eyes tightly while she removed his brown cardigan. Then he felt her exerting pressure on his right ankle. 'Up' she said, as she raised his foot and removed what remained of his filthy orphanage socks, then she did the same to the left foot. With his eyes still tightly shut Jimmy now stood naked. He heard the sudden hiss as the shower was turned on and after a few moments he felt her hand in the small of his back and the words, '*Komm, Liebling*, we *wasche* now,' as he was pushed gently under the shower rose.

Jimmy immediately opened his eyes to locate the taps in the wall and turned to face them, his back to the opening of the recess, in this way hiding his abused private parts from Frau Kraus's scrutiny. Despite his anxiety, the hot water tumbling over him felt glorious and he simply stood, eyes tightly shut again, relishing the hundreds of warm spikes from the shower rose beating against his skin.

He felt a hand begin to travel across his back, tenderly soaping him, caressing him. Jimmy couldn't remember another human hand touching him, though it must have happened at some time when he'd been a child. The hand slipped down to his waist, the bar of soap within it sensuous as it glided smoothly across the surface of his skin. Now it slipped in between his buttocks. He stiffened, waiting for it to grasp at his genitals, but it glided away, returning to soap his buttocks and slipping down the back of his legs right down to his calves and ankles and then he felt the fingers working the lather between his toes. Jimmy was afraid to open his eyes, afraid of what he might see. So he kept them shut.

Now the hand grasped his elbow and pulled him slightly backwards so that the shower beat against the front of his thighs and, as suddenly, he felt himself being turned. His hands clutched at his privates, concealing them from view. The shower fell against his back and the hand, which seemed to possess a will of its own, started to soap and caress his stomach in the area immediately above his cupped hands.

Almost immediately Jimmy felt his penis begin to stiffen under his protective grasp. The remorseless soapy hand kept moving in slow circles, the fingers dancing across his stomach moving ever closer to his own hands until he felt his fingers being slowly, almost casually, prised apart. He seemed unable to resist, and the soapy hand now contained its rigid prize and began to work up and down its length, stopping just as Jimmy, gasping, thought he could contain himself no longer. The hand now pushed him gently backwards so that the shower splashed down his chest and stomach rinsing the suds from his crotch and erection. Jimmy gasped as he felt himself once again encompassed, though this time it was different, soft and urgent, not unlike the soapy hand that had preceded it, but even more sensuous. He could contain himself no longer and climaxed, shuddering, the joy of it far in excess of his own attempts at masturbation. He opened his eyes at last to see he was being engorged by what appeared to be an enormous spider, its hairy striped body glistening, its long white legs only just visible as they disappeared into the steam-clouded atmosphere of the shower recess.

Thus began Jimmy's halcyon days in the care of Frau Kraus, who made no other demands on his body than the pleasure she obtained from performing fellatio. This always occurred in the shower recess, where her hands created movements that became agonisingly sensual. Frau Kraus was the grand mistress of touch, and her oral seduction became a performance with its own developed rituals involving elaborate sequences of soaping that brought Jimmy slowly to the point when she would take him in her mouth, the gobbling spider becoming the gift of pleasure she generously brought him as she found someone she was permitted to love at last.

Jimmy took up residence in the room the twins had shared even as adults and wore freshly laundered clothes each day, selected from the combined wardrobes of the dead Otto and the twins away fighting the Japs in the Pacific. He ate at the dining-room table, freshly showered and changed, his feet encased in a pair of red leather slippers that had belonged to Otto and now had the heel uppers cut out and neatly stitched so as to accommodate his larger foot. He would enter the dining room ravenously hungry to find a stein of foaming lager, which he'd grown to enjoy, placed to the side of a steaming plate piled high with a delicious dinner.

Frau Kraus and Jimmy formed a good working partnership and the farm began to prosper under their combined care. At night, seated happily at the dinner table, she would discuss the day's work with him and her English improved out of sight, although her Bavarian accent spiked with Jimmy's peculiar vernacular required an accustomed ear. To her great delight he never failed to admire the pretty embroidery contained in each of the ceremonial pinafores she carefully selected to present her strudel.

He even rose and kissed her tenderly on the cheek when one evening she wore the pinny with the embroidered words, 'Today is my birthday'. It was the first time Jimmy had kissed a female person, even in such a circumspect way. It was also the first time since the twins were born that Frau Kraus had received a kiss from an adult male. In that instance it had been Otto, who, overcome with the news of twin boys, had planted a wet, hairy kiss on her cheek. For she no longer regarded Jimmy as a child. He did a man's work and stood nearly six feet, with more than sufficient tackle between his legs to qualify him as an adult male.

For Jimmy's fourteenth birthday she presented him with a Timex watch complete with a gold band and with his name inscribed on the back – the same watch he bartered with the North Korean guard for the two planks that were to form my splints. Only, of course, that's not what he'd told me at the time, claiming he'd bought it from a pawnbroker and that it meant little or nothing to him, which was quite untrue. It was the first gift he had ever received, and he must have greatly treasured it.

There was only one small ritual between the two of them that left him somewhat bemused. At the commencement of every evening meal as she entered the dining room from the kitchen Frau Kraus required him to lift his stein and say, '*Danke, meine saubere Frau.*' When Jimmy eventually learned the meaning of the phrase he laughingly pointed out that she was not his wife.

'It a salute – you have to say it, uzzerwise yo' beer it gonna turn sour, man,' she replied, laughing.

'Brother Fish, I ain't to know it dat time, but mah beer it gonna turn sour soon 'nough and dis nigger he 'bout to fall upon hard, hard times,' Jimmy said to me in the prison camp on the day he concluded the story of Frau Kraus and the gobbling spider.

# CHAPTER NINE

## *The Fish Man*

As I recall, I left off to talk about the early stages of Jimmy's life at the point when he swapped the Timex watch Frau Kraus had given him for two planks to be used as a splint for my leg, torn from the stockade fence at the entrance of the cave. Shortly after the gruel of rice and millet arrived, Jimmy took his leave. 'I gotta do da busi-ness, Brother Jacko,' he said. 'Ogoya busi-ness.'

With my broken leg now in a splint, I tried all morning to get to my feet, and finally managed to do so by around noon. While not yet game to attempt to hobble a few steps around the crowded cave, it felt glorious to be vertical again. Viewing the world from a horizontal position, as I had done for two weeks, somehow made everything seem hopeless – now I felt the beginnings of hope returning.

As soon as I stood, the shouts began. 'Give us "In the Mood", buddy.' I had no idea how they'd picked me out from the crowd – after all, on the previous occasion I'd played lying on my back and I'm not exactly a big bloke. But they knew who I was and wanted more of the same, though I can't say I was in much of a performance mood. The pain in my broken leg was pretty bad, and my jaw was still swollen with several teeth cracked or broken from the blow I had taken on the two separate occasions I'd copped the end of a nog rifle butt. Still and all, I'd certainly been in worse shape in the past few days and there were others here a lot worse off than me. I took out the harmonica and played the Glenn Miller classic, and followed this with 'Harbor Lights' . . .

*I saw the harbor lights,*
*They only told me we were parting . . .*

All these years later I forget the lyrics . . . something, something, something . . . oh yes . . .

*. . . I long to hold you near and kiss you just once more,*
*But you were on the ship and I was on the shore.*

I continued with 'We'll Meet Again', 'I'm in the Mood for Love', 'Stardust' and, for the southerners, 'Stars Fell on Alabama'. Then, because Jimmy wasn't there to roll his eyes, I concluded with his all-time big hate singer, Nat King Cole, and his saccharine-sweet melody, 'Too Young' . . .

*They try to tell us we're too young,*
*Too young to really be in love.*

In my mind I could hear Jimmy raving, '*Dat not a voice for a black guy, man! Dat a cockamamie white-man voice, dat a voice to shame a black man! Dat a faggot voice. Jesus done punish him special.*' Nevertheless it went down a treat, and throughout the various numbers there had been several dozen voices joining in, supplying the lyrics.

But after about twenty minutes I had to stop. I was completely buggered, with the blood running from the corners of my mouth. The effect of the harmonica on the prisoners was the same as the previous time I'd played, with some openly weeping. It should be remembered these were just kids, some of them not yet twenty, and the tunes that brought with them memories of a happier time and place had been too much for them. But, all in all, the general mood in the cave seemed to have lifted a good deal and there was quite a lot of clapping and whistling. 'What's your name?' someone shouted. Then another added, 'Where you from?'

'Jacko McKenzie, Queen Island,' I said, not thinking.

'Queen Island?' someone close by said. 'What state is that in?'

'No, no, I'm Australian,' I corrected. I was wearing my Yank parka, which approached my knees, and the boots Jimmy had saved for me, and they must have taken me for a Yank.

Just then Jimmy arrived back. He must have been listening somewhere near the front of the cave and heard the questions, though he didn't mention the Nat King Cole number at the end of the bracket. He came limping along, upright this time, walking with the aid of two sticks, using them to balance as he swung his broken leg forward. 'Listen up!' he said in his big voice. 'Dis Brother Jacko from Down-under – dat da other side da fuckin' world, man! It named Or-stralia. 'Case you cats don't hear o' dat place, it like da Wild West, only it bigger den Texas, almost bigger den da whole United States o' America, man! It truly awesome! Yoh drive three, four days yoh don't see nothin', just dem kangaroos and dem wild men Aborigines, dey's chasin' yoh wid der deadly didgeridoo, dey catch yoh dey point da bone, dey ain't touched yoh and yo' a dead man.'

In the process of giving Jimmy some of the facts about Australia I'd talked about the outback and the size of Australia. He'd interrupted me and asked if it was bigger than Texas and I'd replied, in land mass, it's almost bigger than America, but with a predominance of desert. I told him about the Aborigines and the fact that they could kill a man by pointing the bone, and somewhere I must also have mentioned that they played the digeridoo. Now I was hearing his interpretation, although the Wild West analogy was entirely of his own invention.

Jimmy continued, 'The gooks, they done broke Brother Jacko's jaw and his teeth. His leg, it broke real bad from a machine-gun bull-let, but he still done played dat harmonica for yoh'all.' He paused. 'Dis man we gotta pay a little respec', you hear?'

'Ferchrissake, Jimmy, take it easy, will ya?' I pleaded, mortified at his outburst.

Jimmy grinned and turned to look at me, and must then have seen the blood at the corners of my mouth. 'No shit! Da blood it runnin' from his mouth from playin' dat fine music.' He waited for his statement to sink in before adding in a melodramatic voice, 'Brother Jacko he da man.' He paused again, 'Hey, yoh guys, what yoh say, eh? Put yo' hands together for Brother Jacko!'

Then followed a whole heap more applause and whistles, which only served to add to my acute embarrassment.

Later I turned to him. 'Mate, what was that all about? All that crap you went on about, there are blokes in here far worse off than me, than the both of us! My jaw ain't broke, neither.' He'd humiliated me in front of the wounded men in the cave and I wasn't happy. All I'd done was give them a bit of a cheer-up session on the mouth organ and he'd turned it into a big deal, like I was a hero or something. 'A man won't be able to raise his head around here after what you said!' I was hurting a fair bit from standing too long, and I guess I was pretty aggro because I turned on him again: 'By the way, you ignorant bastard, a didgeridoo is a musical instrument, not a bloody weapon, and the Aboriginal people are not wild men.'

Jimmy looked at me ingenuously, eyes wide. 'Did-geri-doo, it *do* sound dangerous, Brother Jacko.' Then, quick as lightning, he added, 'But dat mah point exact! Yoh harmonica, dat ain't no musical ins-strament, dat *our* deadly weapon, dat our didgeridoo, man. I tol' yoh, it what gonna get dem cats offa der ass!' Jimmy, not in the least contrite, grinned and handed me one of the walking sticks. 'Now *you* offa yoh ass, Brother Jacko.'

What was the use? Getting cranky with a cove like Jimmy was pointless – once he got an idea into his head you couldn't remove it with a meat cleaver. I accepted the walking stick reluctantly. I'd observed him coming towards me, moving steadily. It was something you could only do with two sticks, using them as short crutches. With one stick only, his means of locomotion had to be tackled differently – a method by no means as efficient.

'You need both, Jimmy,' I protested. 'I saw you approaching, you were goin' real good using both them sticks.'

He gave me an indignant look, as if I'd insulted him. 'Nah, one for me, one for yoh – we partners, man! Dat jes mah way o' carryin' yo' stick.'

Within a few days, Jimmy had begun to sort the cave out. The morning after he'd big-noted me I did a bit of a concert where quite a lot of those who were not severely wounded joined in. Jimmy stopped me in between brackets, and whispered, 'Deys four grunts here dat could be a quartet. You call dem out, Brother Jacko.'

'Shit no, Jimmy, you do it – they won't take no notice of me, mate.'

'Dat not true. Yoh da man!'

I asked him to point the four men out and swallowed hard, then cleared my throat, pointing to the Yank nearest to us. 'Excuse me, mate,' I called.

'Who, me, buddy?' he asked.

'Yeah, you sing real good, could you come over here please?' I pointed to the other three and asked them to do the same.

'Ever sung in a quartet?' I asked. One of them said he had. 'Choir?' Two more had. 'Harmonise?' Again two. 'Giddonya, I think we've got ourselves a barbershop quartet. Can we see you after?' I looked at Jimmy, who nodded. 'Perhaps we could have a bit of a private session?' The men looked at each other, a bit querulous. 'See how we go, eh?' I said quickly, to prevent any of them from objecting. I then continued playing, with the newly found would-be quartet standing beside me soon catching on to the harmonies. Jimmy's ear must have been pretty good because their voices blended well. By the end of the session I think they were quite pleased with themselves.

In the next few days we formed a choir, just a very few volunteers at first but over the following week others joined in until it included almost all the men who weren't too sick to participate. Jimmy became choirmaster and it was apparent that his training in the Colored Orphan Asylum choir hadn't been wasted.

'Now we got da basis, Brother Jacko. Now we got dem grunts offa der ass, now we gonna fix dis place, or we all gonna die.'

He was referring to the fact that the smell inside the cave was overwhelming – a lot of it coming from the wounded, who couldn't move and lay in their own excreta. It wouldn't be too long before we were all down with dysentery, roundworm and all the other diseases that thrive in unsanitary conditions. Perhaps the only good thing about the freezing conditions was that the customary diseases would take longer to spread among us. Until I'd been given the splints I too had been guilty of shitting where I lay, though only the once, and I'd tried to scrape a bit of a hole in the thin layer of soil covering the cave floor to bury the mess I'd made. There were no facilities for washing, which meant the men were eating with their hands covered in their own excreta.

Now Jimmy and I set about changing things. I only include myself because as a foreigner among the Yanks and the so-called 'hero', Jimmy insisted they listen to me. He was the boss and I pretty well did as I was told. It was also the first time I'd heard the expression 'Talk soft and carry a big stick', which was Jimmy's advice to me. His sheer bulk and the walking stick he carried seemed to give him all the authority he needed and he never seemed to raise his voice.

Only once did someone challenge him, and judging from his accent it was a southerner objecting to taking instructions from a black man. Jimmy had asked him to help move one of the wounded men and take him to the latrine, situated in a narrow offshoot at the back of the cave. 'Hey, you tellin' me what I gotta do, nigger?' he asked. He wore a crew cut and was a mean-looking bugger. The men close by, including myself, waited. The southerner was a big bloke with a bandaged head but otherwise able-bodied, and it was for this reason Jimmy had asked him to help take one of the badly wounded to the latrine.

'Whoa! What da matter, man? You cain't help dis sick man?' Jimmy pointed to his bandaged head. 'Yo' head – it's bad, eh?'

The southerner rose to his feet. 'What did you say to me, nigger?' He stood a good six feet and was broad across the shoulders. Jimmy was still the bigger man but, if it came to a fight, with one leg broken he clearly wouldn't be a match for the southerner.

Jimmy stood about a foot from the cave wall, and now he backed up slowly until he was hard against it. 'I said, yo' head – you sick bad? It a question, man!'

'Fuck – what's it to you, nigger?' He suddenly lashed out, kicking Jimmy's broken leg just below the knee. There was a gasp from those of us watching, and Jimmy's face creased with excruciating pain. How he remained standing, I'll never know. If it had happened to me I would have been on my back in the dirt writhing at the southerner's feet. But then we saw that Jimmy held the other man by the throat – he must have anticipated the kick, and his arm had shot out to grab his assailant's throat as his boot went into Jimmy's knee. Jimmy's eyes were still screwed tight as he grappled with the pain, but his fingers seemed to have entered the flesh of the other man's neck as they tightened. The southerner, eyes rolling, sunk to his knees with both his hands tearing helplessly at Jimmy's grip. Jimmy's arm was fully extended, holding the other man sufficiently far from his body so that he couldn't grab at his legs and pull him down. But the southerner hadn't even thought to do this – he'd panicked, and all his strength was concentrated on getting Jimmy's hand away from his throat. Finally Jimmy opened his eyes. The sudden pain seemed to have burst the blood vessels and his eyes looked like two burning coals. His face was completely blank and he stared straight ahead, as if he was unaware of the man on his knees in front of him. He simply squeezed until the southerner's tongue protruded and his eyes began to pop. The white bloke was a strong man but he made absolutely no impression on Jimmy's grip, although his nails had torn several scarlet furrows along the back of Jimmy's hand.

'Leave him, Jimmy! Let him go, you'll kill him!' I screamed. Either the pain or something even more primal within him had closed his senses down, and he continued to squeeze, grunting softly from the effort, unable to hear me. 'Jimmy, stop!' I yelled again, and at the same time I lashed out with my walking stick, striking at the huge hand that held the white guy's throat. Jimmy must have felt the blow because he suddenly came to his senses and let go of the southerner, who collapsed unconscious on the floor like a rag doll.

Jimmy stood with his back to the wall, chin raised, eyes looking upwards, panting, saying nothing. Then he looked down at the bloody hand I'd struck. He hadn't even wrung it to ease the pain. He slowly worked his fingers until he reached his thumb, flicking it. 'Well, dat one thing good – it don't look purdy, but I ain't broke no fingers,' he said, still panting. The unconscious man at his feet was starting to come around, a sort of wheezing, hissing, coughing sound coming from his bruised throat. 'Dat another thing good – I gone shut his big honky mouth.' He looked up from the man on the ground and into my eyes and I could see he was back to being Jimmy again. 'Thank you, Brother Jacko,' he said quietly. He reached out to touch me and I could see his wounded hand was already beginning to balloon from where I'd struck him.

Jimmy's technique to get things going was simple enough – he never demanded help, he simply asked politely, and while sometimes the person requested to help would simply turn and shuffle away, slowly the idea of taking responsibility for our living conditions caught on. Using my watch and three others and several Zippo lighters offered to him for the purpose of bribing the guards, he swapped them for the two halves of a cut-down petrol drum, some fencing wire, a six-foot length and two three-foot lengths of timber prised from the stockade, several pieces of rag and two whisk brooms we would use for cleaning and sweeping the cave. Using the wire to fashion handles for the drums, we hung one from the centre of the six-foot timber pole, and with a man taking either end we would gather loads of snow from outside and bring them into the cave to melt. The water was then used by the more or less able-bodied among us to do our ablutions and clean our wounds. Although the cave was designated a hospital by the enemy, there were no medics, no medicine and no attempt at treatment. It was left up to us, and we attended to the totally incapacitated the best we could, using strips from the shirts of the dead as bandages. We had no painkillers or even aspirin, so a more or less clean bandage was the best we could do. Finally we washed the filth from the walls and swept the cave floor every day.

Dysentery was inevitable under the prevailing conditions and a lot of the men suffered from it, but it was roundworm we feared the most. Several of the prisoners who'd been captured much earlier than me had been infected. The worms could grow to be two or three inches long and about the diameter of a pencil. They were passed in the faeces, which was painful though bearable. But a part of the roundworm's life cycle is spent in the bloodstream, during which time it penetrates the lungs, where it grows to maturity to be constantly coughed up by the prisoner – an excruciatingly painful process.

The second half of the drum was used as a latrine, the two three-foot planks placed parallel across the top, ten inches separating them, to act as a crude toilet seat. Every morning the latrine drum would be taken out and the contents disposed of by emptying them into a hole made in the snow, where they would instantly freeze. The guards permitted the able-bodied wounded to go outside the cave to defecate provided they first removed their boots and socks and could be observed at all times. Watching a man trying to go to the toilet in the snow while at the same time hopping from one foot to the other caused the guards no end of mirth and became a daily comedy routine for them, not to be missed. Eventually it became too cold to expose our private parts to the elements, and everyone used the cut-down drum latrine within the cave. The prisoners taking turns to empty the contents every morning continued to supply the daily quota of mirth for the North Korean guards.

There was also a more serious reason for having to venture outside, which was to dispose of the dead. Burial would be the wrong word – at best we'd manage a shallow ditch scraped out of the snow with the body hastily dumped into it. In conditions such as this the ritual of death went almost unobserved. Apart from a short prayer before the body was removed from the cave, the cold dictated everything, and the dead soldier became a macabre asset. His parka, boots, socks and belt, as well as his warm undershirt, were removed – the boots for bribes to the guards and the rest for use by the living.

Jimmy also attempted to create a rice-bag blanket redistribution. At the very beginning the less sick and those men with the ability to defend themselves had grabbed the rice bags, while the badly wounded and immobile had been left to freeze. When I first arrived in the cave, most mornings the guards would move around to see who had died during the night and order them removed. These were invariably the badly wounded who lacked the physical strength to beat the cold and had simply frozen to death. Attempting a fairer distribution wasn't easy. Survival is a strong instinct and those among us who possessed bags were not interested in the argument that redistribution was for the greater good. Altruism is not commonly observed in a POW camp.

Jimmy counted the rice bags and discovered there were twenty-seven supplied for forty men. Twenty-seven prisoners would need to be persuaded to part with an object they believed would save their lives. Frankly, I thought he had Buckley's. But then one of the prisoners talked to him about convection heat and how it worked. What it amounted to was this: if he could get all the rice-bag blankets and make them into one large blanket and then use it to trap the heat generated from all the bodies placed under it, the sum of the heat retained would be greater for each individual body than the heat generated by a single rice bag that covered less than half an individual's body. Jimmy then got him to work out the total area of the twenty-seven rice bags joined together. If we all slept cheek by jowl, the single sheet created would be sufficient to cover everyone.

I think I pointed out earlier that Jimmy could persuade anyone to do anything, but getting the owners of the rice bags to part with them was, as far as I was concerned, a new benchmark in the art of persuasion. Over fifty years I've seen Jimmy pull off some remarkable deals, but I still rate Operation Rice Bag as the best of them. All but six prisoners agreed to contribute to the community blanket – not unexpectedly, those in protest were all southerners, and among the dissenters was Ward Brady Buckworth Junior, the bloke Jimmy had damn near throttled to death. I hasten to say that the soldiers from the South were not all uncooperative – there was a fair number among us, and most of them had joined in to create better communal conditions.

Jimmy traded another Zippo lighter with a guard for an awl, whereupon the stitching was carefully unpicked from the top and bottom edges of the rice bags and the thread used to sew the twenty-one bags together. It worked a treat, not that we ended up exactly cosy, but the mass body heat generated and trapped under one large rice-bag blanket worked a lot better to maintain warmth than a single rice bag. Nor did it take too long to bring the six renegade southern rice bags in from the cold, though only after Ward Brady Buckworth Junior (who'd not yet recovered his voice beyond a sort of wheezing sound) and his cohorts made Jimmy agree to have the choir drop 'The Battle Hymn of the Republic' from its repertoire. Jimmy very nearly baulked at this as it was the anthem of the Unionists during the American Civil War, and their primary reason for going to war had been to free the Negro slaves in the South.

When we'd learned the words, Jimmy had told us how they sang the 'Battle Hymn' in the orphanage choir not because it was a Unionist song, but because it was originally sung as a tribute to John Brown, who had been hanged in 1859 for leading an attempted slave insurrection at a place known as Harper's Ferry. 'We learned dat story 'bout John Brown an' we sing da words dey use dat time when dey hanged him. Da words we sing here, dey da words of Julia Ward Howe – she done make dem new ones for da Civil War. But when I hear dat song I think o' John Brown, he my hero, man!'

Jimmy finally agreed to eliminate the hymn on the basis that the greater good was involved, but he added, 'It don't rightly matter, Brother Jacko. Da slaves, dey's gonna get der revenge. Iffen we get out o' dis pree-dick-kay-ment I's gonna whup dat bastid Brady Buckworth one time real good!'

But I must say I liked the words Julia Ward Howe had written – the version we sang in the cave. I memorised them, determined that if ever I got home again we'd add it to our harmonica repertoire.

**Battle Hymn of the Republic**

*Mine eyes have seen the glory of the coming of the Lord:*
*He is trampling out the vintage where the grapes of wrath are stored;*
*He hath loosed the fateful lightning of his terrible swift sword:*
*His truth is marching on.*

*Glory! Glory! Hallelujah!*
*Glory! Glory! Hallelujah!*
*Glory! Glory! Hallelujah!*
*His truth is marching on.*

*I have seen Him in the watch-fires of a hundred circling camps;*
*They have builded Him an altar in the evening dews and damps;*
*I can read His righteous sentence by the dim and flaring lamps:*
*His day is marching on.*

*Glory! Glory! Hallelujah! . . .*

*I have read a fiery gospel, writ in burnished rows of steel:*
*'As ye deal with my contemners, so with you my grace shall deal;*
*Let the Hero, born of woman, crush the serpent with his heel,*
*Since God is marching on.'*

*Glory! Glory! Hallelujah! . . .*

*He has sounded forth the trumpet that shall never call retreat;*
*He is sifting out the hearts of men before His judgment-seat:*
*O, be swift, my soul, to answer Him! be jubilant, my feet!*
*Our God is marching on.*

*Glory! Glory! Hallelujah! . . .*

*In the beauty of the lilies Christ was born across the sea,*
*With a glory in His bosom that transfigures you and me:*
*As He died to make men holy, let us die to make men free.*
*While God is marching on.*

*Glory! Glory! Hallelujah! . . .*

I don't want to exaggerate Jimmy's Ogoya activity – it's not as if it suddenly transformed us into a model POW group. While conditions were infinitely improved and the men were working more or less as a team, without medication wounds continued to fester and men still died. But there was a new ray of hope, and soldiers weren't dying of despair or trying to survive on their own.

During this time something happened that, at the time, seemed of little or no consequence. Of an afternoon I'd try to get to the mouth of the cave to look at the world outside. It was freezing but the cave inside was almost as cold, and just watching the clean white landscape stretching to the mountains on the horizon seemed to give me hope that there was life going on beyond the misery of the cave. On one such occasion a guard, protected from the icy wind by the wooden stockade fence and seated beside a brazier, a contraption constructed from a petrol drum with holes knocked in the side in which charcoal was burning, was singing a song. The way noggies sing is different to us but his voice was strong and steady and the melody, obviously a folksong, had a longing, haunting sound that was pleasant even to my untrained occidental ear. I listened for a while then reached into the pocket of my parka for my mouth organ, and soon enough picked up the tune. He seemed delighted with my accompaniment, and after a while he stopped singing and turned to me and then sang a new verse of what appeared to be quite a long song, then he repeated it to my accompaniment. I don't have too many natural gifts, but Gloria always used to say, 'Hum anything once and Jacko'll have it down pat.'

His first name turned out to be Kim, though it was only later that I learned his other name. Kim and I got to doing the song on a regular basis until I'd learned the lyrics phonetically. Over a period of two weeks I taught it to the choir, with Jimmy doing a solo part we'd devised, the barbershop quartet coming in for some beautiful four-part harmony for some of the lyrics and the choir swelling for the chorus. It was very much a Western arrangement, and quite different to the way it might have been sung in Kim's village, but because of the very strong melody it seemed to work.

When we reckoned we had it down pat Jimmy went to see the officer in charge of the guards, who had a few words of English, and invited them to hear us. They, of course, knew something was going on because of the rehearsals, but they all turned up, even the off-duty men. I invited Kim to join us, but he declined. I guess it would have amounted to consorting with the enemy in his eyes, and those of his comrades. Anyway, they clapped and cheered when we'd completed the folksong and made us repeat it three times. It seemed we had a hit on our hands. Only the lieutenant remained poker-faced, playing the mandatory role of the inscrutable Oriental.

'Brother Jacko, yo' da man,' Jimmy said, congratulating me afterwards. 'Dem gook cats, dey ain't gonna forget dis – dey gonna tell der gran-chillen what happen tonight.'

But he couldn't have been more wrong. The following morning the guards, led by the lieutenant of the inscrutable face, took Jimmy away. He was returned three days later when the guards carried him into the cave and dropped him unconscious beside me. His face and body were badly swollen, blood running from the corner of his mouth, and his splints had been removed. He'd obviously taken an unmerciful beating.

The lieutenant pointed to Jimmy's unconscious form. 'No cop-perate! Song insul Norse Korea pipple!' Then he turned to look at the prisoners who'd gathered around, and with a sweep of his hand indicated the entire cave. 'You die dis caves!'

Jimmy had been made to pay for my dumb idea to do Kim's song. The North Koreans, or their lieutenant anyway, had seen the gesture as an insult. I was consumed by the remorse I felt for what had happened and insisted that two of the blokes who worked as medics remove my splints and strap them to Jimmy's leg. It wasn't a big deal – despite the splints, my leg had started to bother me in a different way and I was finding it increasingly hard to get around. As long as someone could pull me up to a vertical position so I could still stand for a while I could play for the choir.

Jimmy, of course, received the best care we were capable of giving him, which wasn't much, but it wasn't going to be easy to kill him, and in a week or so he'd recovered sufficiently to be back with us. But by this time my leg was troubling me a great deal – the swelling had increased, and it felt as though it was going to burst. Infection had set in, and the pain was accompanied by a high fever that on occasions made me delirious. Jimmy, himself not yet fully recovered, never left my side, but I knew I was on the way out. In my rational moments all I could think was that I hoped when my time came it would be quick. I envied the way Johnny Gordon had died – a hail of Chinese bullets and a few moments later, the end.

Then one morning, during one of my now-infrequent periods of lucidity, 'Inscrutable', the North Korean officer who'd done for Jimmy, arrived accompanied by a Chinese officer and six soldiers. The North Korean pointed to me and the Chinese officer stooped and threw off the rice sack covering my leg and examined it, then turned and jabbered something to two Chinese soldiers.

'Don't let the bastards take me, Jimmy!' I pleaded. 'Let me die here.'

Jimmy moved towards me and the Chinese officer put his arm out, restraining him. 'He go hospital,' he said.

'Yoh gonna be okay,' Jimmy said softly, 'they gonna take yoh to hospital.'

'No! Don't let them take me, Jimmy!' I cried again. Of course, there was nothing Jimmy could have done to stop them.

'He don't want to go, sir,' he said to the officer.

'He go – leg velly bad,' the officer said, not unkindly. 'Hospital, we fix – he no die.'

'Let me come with him, sir,' Jimmy pleaded. He pointed to his splint. 'I got me a broken leg also.'

'No, dis one only,' the officer insisted.

Then the two Chinese soldiers bent and lifted me, one under my armpits and the other round my buttocks allowing my broken leg to hang loose. The pain was so intense I screamed, then passed out.

It was dark when I became conscious again, the sky clear. A near-full moon shone down, its glow reflecting from the snow to light the surrounding countryside and dim the stars. It was almost an exact replica of the night I'd been captured, though deeper into winter. I was lying on straw in the back of a bullock cart. The track we were taking was extremely rough and it was bitterly cold, although they'd thrown a blanket over me. Two Chinese with their backs to me were seated each on a box at the front of the cart; a third holding his rifle was seated beside me. I turned to look at him and thought I must be hallucinating – the man beside me wasn't Chinese, it was Kim, the singer of songs.

'G'day, Kim,' I murmured weakly. It was the way I'd greeted him on each occasion when we'd met at the entrance of the cave, and now hearing my greeting again he smiled. I must have still been half out of it because then I attempted to sing the first line of the folksong and one of the Chinese turned around and cracked me across the face with the back of his hand. Kim clasped his hand over my mouth and placed his forefinger to his mouth to tell me to shut up.

The track got worse and worse and with each pothole we hit,

despite myself, I yelled out. The Chinese would immediately turn around and crack me one until my nose streamed blood and had probably been broken again. Each time Kim would shout at them and they'd shout back at him, though I'm not sure they were speaking the same language. Eventually Kim sat on my chest facing the front so that when I screamed out the Chinese guards couldn't get to me. The Koreans are meant to be the cruellest people on earth, and certainly I'd met some terrible bastards among them, but Kim wasn't one of them. He was a good bloke, and a mate is a mate in any language.

The nightmare ride continued until dawn, and thankfully I spent a reasonable part of it unconscious. We stopped at what appeared to be a farmhouse, and Kim took his leave. Pointing to his chest he repeated several times, 'Kim Sun'.

That's how I finally learned his name. I was pretty out of it by then but managed the words, 'Kim Sun, you're a good bloke, mate,' and stretched out and touched him on the arm, and then I must have passed out again.

When I came to I was lying on a large raised platform together with several wounded Korean and Chinese soldiers. The bloke next to me was sitting up as if he was frozen into position, with his hands clasped about his knees. He was a blackish-brown colour, the skin on his body so completely burned that only his eyes moved. Only napalm does that. It was only months ago that I'd held Bluey Walsh in my arms, ineffectually emptying a water bottle over his scorched body as he died. I recoiled inwardly at the horror of it happening to any human being. Despite my own condition, I felt deep sorrow for the poor bastard. I looked into his eyes but was forced to turn away – I could see the hatred for me in them. I felt ashamed and appalled that my side could do this to a fellow human being. He would have killed me, choked the life out of me, if only he could have unclasped his blackened arms. Korea has left me with several recurring nightmares. Those accusing brown eyes watching me, never leaving me, is one that still causes me to wake up sobbing. I recall thinking how glad I would be if only those terrible arms would reach out and do the deed. I didn't want to live, I reckoned I'd had enough. The next day I watched the poor bastard die without even crying out. I guess his vocal cords had been crisped.

Night came again and I suppose it must have been fairly early the next morning when they came to fetch me, because I recall a rooster crowing in the farmyard. I was carried into an adjoining room with roughly cut pole rafters and a thatched roof. Down its centre ran a narrow table made of wooden slats and above it hung a hissing pressure lamp, its bluish-white glow throwing a wide circle of light over the centre of the table and spilling onto the earthen floor. I guessed correctly that this was the operating theatre. I was placed on the table and an orderly cut away what remained of my tattered army pants and pulled my parka up to my chest so that I lay naked from the chest down. He then swabbed me from the waist halfway down my hugely swollen broken leg with what I took from the smell to be surgery alcohol, and then turned me on my side. A Chinese doctor entered the room jabbering away, seemingly at no one in particular, and gave me a spinal injection.

I couldn't believe the relief as the area below my torso became anaesthetised. It was the first time in a couple of months that I'd been relatively free of pain and I remember starting to cry from the relief. The doctor, still jabbering away, made me half sit up so that I was leaning back on my elbows. I think he was talking to me in Chinese but he made no eye contact so it was impossible to tell. He cut a six-inch incision to release the pus and blood that had caused the swelling, and this took quite a while to drain. Meanwhile, he poked and prodded, locating pieces of my shattered femur, which he removed with tweezers. I was beginning to panic as the anaesthetic was starting to wear off when he began to stitch me up. By the time it was completed I was biting down on my lip to prevent myself from crying out. As they lifted me onto a stretcher, one of the attendants lost his grip and my leg fell loose, the movement causing the stitches to unravel. I screamed out in pain – the idea of going through the process of restitching the wound without an anaesthetic filled me with dread. The doctor, still muttering and apparently unconcerned, simply sprinkled my wound with sulphanilamide from an American first-aid pack and the attendants carried me through to an adjacent room, which in retrospect I refer to as the torture room.

They placed me onto a device not unlike one of those ancient torture racks you see in cartoons, my leg strapped to the uppermost bar, composed of two facing wooden strips with a ratchet attached to the end. One of two female nurses in the room worked the ratchet, which pulled the topmost bar to which my broken leg was attached towards her until my leg could stretch no further and felt as if it was about to part from my body. Needless to say, I screamed and sobbed. Throughout this torture the expression on the faces of the two nurses remained impassive. They performed the task as if the leg was detached and not a part of my body. With the rack completed they applied plaster that made a cast that covered my entire leg from the ankle to my waist.

I was in dreadful pain, and to add to it something happened that I have never been able to explain. Completely out of the blue, without any thought on my part, I had a full-blown erection. This caused the two nurses to giggle, holding their hands up to their mouths, unable to restrain their mirth. I'd heard of dead men having an erection, and I wondered if this was a precursor to my own death. Then a diminutive Chinese cameraman appeared and began to set up a tripod onto which he placed an old-fashioned portrait camera complete with bellows. I wasn't sure that I wasn't hallucinating, what with the two nurses giggling and the dwarf camera operator fussing around, completely oblivious to my erection. It seemed more like something out of a pornographic version of a Charlie Chaplin comedy. The tiny cameraman poured flash powder into a holder, repeatedly baring his teeth in the manner of a chimpanzee, which he quite closely resembled. I think he was trying to tell me to smile. Then he held it aloft and disappeared beneath the black cloth behind the camera. He triggered the flash powder, which exploded in a great whoosh of smoke and set the roof thatch alight. Thankfully, it also caused my erection to subside.

People came running from everywhere and the fire was somehow doused, though I was too preoccupied with my pain to take note quite how this was done. I guess the photograph, originally intended for the *Daily Worker* as propaganda to show how well UN prisoners were being treated, would have become a collector's item, and there are probably faded prints of my '*election*' still doing the rounds among junior medical staff somewhere in China.

I was taken back to the room with the platform and left with the other wounded soldiers. The pain seemed to steady somewhat – by that, I mean it didn't increase. Pain on a consistent level is bearable: even if severe, the mind somehow accommodates it so that it becomes possible to think of other things as well. None of my fellow patients spoke English and I felt terribly alone. The cave had been gruesome, but at least I'd been with people who spoke my language. The unfortunate erection was also preoccupying my thoughts. Sex is not a factor when men are starving and sick, and I hadn't had the slightest inclination or even indication in the weeks I'd been a prisoner of war. Nor, for that matter, did I immediately after the photographic incident. But it must have triggered something because now my mind was longing for a woman's arms to be around me. I'd had a few girlfriends on the island and tried to imagine them holding me, but I couldn't quite visualise the process I so longed for. It was not a sexual thing – the arms I needed would be more a comfort and a reassurance, and they'd all been too young to meet this need. Then, ridiculously, my mind's eye settled on the strongest female image it had ever encountered – Miss Pat Brand, the torch singer who had performed at Puckapunyal. My head filled with the lyrics and the tune she'd sung to us that night when I had fallen head over heels in love. I found my harmonica in the pocket of my parka and began to play.

*Fish gotta swim and birds gotta fly,*
*I gotta love one man till I die,*
*Can't help lovin' dat man of mine.*

All I could manage was one verse before I started to weep, pain and loneliness overwhelming me so that I howled like a small child. I became aware of someone close by and through my ridiculous tears saw it was one of the Chinese wounded. He sat beside me as I tried to gain control, to get a hold of myself, but the tears wouldn't stop and I continued to sob. Then I felt the soldier beside me reach out and take me in his arms and cradle my head against his breast. Then in perfect English, with an American accent, he began to sing.

*'I looked over Jordan, and what did I see?*
*Comin' for to carry me home.*
*A band of angels comin' after me,*
*Comin' for to carry me home.*

*Swing low, sweet chariot,*
*Comin' for to carry me home.*
*Swing low, sweet chariot,*
*Comin' for to carry me home.*

*If you get there before I do,*
*Comin' for to carry me home,*
*Tell all my friends I'm comin' too,*
*Comin' for to carry me home.*

*Swing low, sweet chariot . . .*

*I'm sometimes up and sometimes down,*
*Comin' for to carry me home,*
*But still my soul feels heavenly bound,*
*Comin' for to carry me home.*

*Swing low, sweet chariot . . .*

*The brightest day that I can say,*
*Comin' for to carry me home,*
*When Jesus washed my sins away,*
*Comin' for to carry me home.*

*Swing low, sweet chariot . . .'*

Apart from these perfectly accented lyrics he only had one other word in English – '*Missionary*'. He must have learned the words of the hymn by rote as a child from an American missionary. I sometimes play this beautiful Negro spiritual and it never fails to reduce me to tears as I recall the little bloke. He too had been wounded, but he'd reached out to me and held me in his arms, comforting me with the words in a song, the meaning of which he probably didn't understand, but with a sense of compassion that transcended language and culture.

Later I would reflect on the Chinese. First there had been the soldier who had slowly bled to death, who had rolled a cigarette and placed it in my mouth and then, rolling one for himself, died in front of my eyes, the half-smoked fag stuck to his bottom lip. Then this second wounded soldier, comforting me with his song. We would have our moments with the Chinese, but as far as I was concerned, these two soldiers went a long way to earning my admiration for a strangely complex and contradictory race of people.

Despite the incident with the singing soldier that first night after my operation and long-hoped-for plaster cast, I was pretty bloody miserable. I felt sure that the medical attention I'd finally received was too little, too late, and I was almost certainly going to die. But by early morning I felt a little better and managed to fall asleep, and finally woke up in the late afternoon to find Jimmy lying beside me.

'Jesus!' was all I could manage to say.

'No sir! Jesus, he got other eggs to fry! Dis James Pentecost Oldcorn at yo' service, Brother Fish.'

I let the 'Brother Fish' pass, thinking Jimmy had simply made a mistake. Then he explained that the Chinese officer who'd picked me out to have my leg set had returned the following day and demanded to hear the choir sing the North Korean folksong. Jimmy had called them together and they'd duly performed it for him. In contrast to 'Inscrutable', his North Korean cousin, he seemed delighted. The Chinese officer spoke halting but reasonable English. He explained that he knew the song, which, as it turned out, was in a dialect used by the people who lived on the Yalu River and was used by both nations, the river being the common border where the villagers on either side had mixed for countless generations.

The song, he explained, was about a fisherman who had sailed too far down the river and found himself blown into the Gulf, where he was caught in a terrible storm and became lost at sea. After many days without sighting land, when he was about to perish from thirst, he heard a fish calling his mother's name in the voice of his younger brother, who had drowned at sea as a young man. The fish drew alongside the boat and told him to hoist sail and follow it. It guided him back to the shore and up the river to his own village, where his mother lay dying of grief because she had only two sons and both had been lost to the merciless sea. The last two happy verses were about a great feast to celebrate his return and his mother's recovery.

'Dat gook officer, he say we all gonna go to a hospital, dey gonna fix mah leg, we all gonna get good treatment. He say when we sing dat fish song in der language it like a com-plee-ment to da Chinese People's Revolution.' He shrugged, 'So yoh see, it a e-stab-lish fact – we owe our lives to you, Brother Fish.'

'That's complete bullshit,' I replied. 'And what's going on? That's the second time you've called me Brother *Fish*!'

Jimmy laughed, 'Dat yo' name now, man! You da fish man!'

Like I said before, when Jimmy got a notion into his head it would take more than a tempest at sea to remove it. 'Dat Chinee song, it da brother who become da fish dat show him da way home – it like a re-in-carn-nation, man! It da brother fish dat done da deed and save his life.' He shook his head, obviously impressed at this remarkable juxtaposition of the word 'brother'. 'It simple, man, you dat brother fish.' In Jimmy's mind that was as good as a message from on high, and ever afterwards he referred to me as Brother Fish, a name I've now held for just on fifty years.

Jimmy's leg had originally been broken midway between his left ankle and knee. He'd been fortunate and there had been no complications such as the festering, swelling and high fever I'd copped, though, of course, he had to endure the torture of the rack when they straightened his leg to plaster it. Within a couple of days, with the help of a pair of Chinese crutches, which were much too small for him so that he appeared to move as if doubled up, he was hopping about. Whereas I was still much too weak to get to my feet.

I was to learn that the Chinese have very little sense of privacy and they don't feel shame over the same things as we do. There was no such thing as a bedpan in this hospital. With a plaster cast from ankle to waist, too weak to make my own way to the outside latrine, I was carried over to a four-gallon kerosene can with the top sawn off to perform my morning bowel and bladder movements. They hadn't replaced my tattered army trousers and apart from the plaster cast I was bollocky naked from the waist down. It was normally okay, as my precious Yank parka covered my private parts, but in order to do my business this was lifted high above my waist to reveal my tackle.

Latrine time became the signal for all 'n' sundry to come running. My round blue eyes and red hair had already drawn a lot of attention, and the platform for the wounded never had as many visitors. People came from far and near to gawk at me and also the huge shape of Jimmy, who, while not much darker than some of the Chinese, differed in ethnic type in every other conceivable way. To the Chinese both of us were remarkable exhibits, and visiting the platform of wounded men must have been their equivalent of seeing two newly acquired, rare species at the zoo.

But latrine time was the special show. Both men and women would jostle to get a good position beside the kerosene can, where they could reach in and pull at my bright-red pubic hair to see if it was real. They'd take a tug and everyone would let out a gasp as it stayed put. Quite why they imagined it might be fake or why I would want artificial pubic hair I can't say. Under the circumstances it was hardly surprising that I was finding it difficult to have a bowel movement. The crowd would watch as I strained and some, in an effort to encourage me, would screw up their eyes, stretch their lips into a grimace and emit straining sounds on my behalf, while all showed genuine concern for my lack of action. Finally, on the fourth day their patience was rewarded. I expelled, with surprising force, a dozen or so small dry pellets that ricocheted and pinged around the can to prolonged applause. Several onlookers were so moved that they reached out to pat me on the shoulder.

While Jimmy would ever after insist that my learning the folksong from Kim Sun and its subsequent performance in front of Ho Ling, the Chinese officer who transferred us to the farm hospital, was what saved the lives of the men in the North Korean cave, this was probably untrue. But, just as I like to believe that Kim Sun had cadged a lift on the bullock cart so that he could take care of me, so Jimmy is entitled to his fish story. And anyway, true or false, it made no difference – I was landed with the Brother Fish nickname for the duration.

Much more likely to be the reason we were given medical treatment was that cease-fire talks had recommenced at around this time and the question of prisoner exchange had been placed on the agenda. Prisoners of war were now a valuable commodity, a bargaining tool, where the more you had the more persuasive you were likely to be. It suddenly became imperative to keep as many prisoners of war alive as possible, and the plaster casts Jimmy and I had received were strictly for cosmetic purposes and had nothing to do with duty of care, compassion or even folksongs.

A week after I'd arrived at the farmhouse hospital, and only a day after I managed to get around on my Chinese crutches, we were declared fit to leave. As far as the Chinese farmhouse hospital system was concerned, provided you weren't flat on your back you were ready to move. Convalescence wasn't built into their system, which was true for their own men as well as for us.

Late the following day, with darkness already settling over the landscape, a five-ton truck arrived and we were hastily loaded aboard to join a truckful of Chinese soldiers who shuffled to make sufficient room for us to sit. We hadn't gone more than a couple of miles before we joined a convoy of about fifty trucks, tucking in close to the front. Upon our departure we'd been issued with a blanket, which did very little to keep out the biting cold, and I can remember grumbling to Jimmy that it wasn't our wounds we needed to worry about because we'd eventually perish from the bloody cold. In fact, I should have been grateful – later we would learn that the previous winter several columns of UN Command prisoners had marched this same route for hundreds of miles with those unable to keep up shot on the spot. With our broken legs we'd have been shot before they lifted the starting gate.

It was slow going over bad roads and there was little chance of sleep. Hours passed, and sometime in the early morning we heard warning shots from Chinese lookouts situated high on the surrounding hills. Shortly afterwards came the sound of aeroplane engines. The convoy stopped and we could hear whistles blowing as the soldiers in the remainder of the convoy and those in our truck hastily evacuated to take cover and we were left, sitting ducks, not sufficiently mobile to leave the truck on our own.

'How 'bout dat?' Jimmy sighed grimly. 'We gonna get our ass kicked by da fuckin' US Air Force.'

Next thing the surrounding landscape was illuminated by parachute flares and the attack began. My mind went back to Bluey Walsh and the Chinese soldier who'd been burned by napalm and I'm still surprised I didn't shit the kapok-quilted cotton trousers they'd given me in the hospital. I had been frightened, very frightened, before this, but now I was absolutely terrified. The vision of Bluey Walsh taking his last breath and the Chinese soldier sitting with his arms welded around his knees, his entire body crisped by napalm, filled my panicked mind. I prayed that whatever hit me was for keeps and that it wasn't napalm. We could hear each plane as it came in low, its roar drowning everything out, the truck rattling on its chassis. They started at the back of the convoy, working methodically as a team. It was rockets, not napalm, destroying one vehicle after the other. It was precision work and in military terms good shooting and no doubt the pilots were experiencing a buzz, not aware that the only kill they would make in this early-morning raid was on their side. Then just three trucks from where we stood in the convoy they stopped and left, presumably because they'd run out of rockets.

My body was filled with an overwhelming joy such as I'd never before experienced, and complete calm replaced the terror of a few moments before. 'Well, I'll be fucked!' I remember saying, smiling at Jimmy, knowing we'd emerged unscathed.

Jimmy hadn't seen my reaction of a few moments before – the truck was still in half-darkness and I guess he had been pretty preoccupied with his own final thoughts. Hearing my calm voice and the familiar Australian expletive for surprise and wonder, he reached out and shook my hand. 'Brother Fish, yoh da coolest cat dat I ever did know. Yoh still da man.'

'I was shitting myself, Jimmy,' I replied truthfully. But I could see he didn't believe me.

It was fast getting light when we moved off again. The bulk of the Chinese soldiers, now without trucks, marched behind us, and we soon turned onto a narrow track mostly hidden by snow to reach a complex of caves where we disembarked. I guess this wasn't our intended destination and more like a transit station. The attack had delayed us nearly two hours as the soldiers had had to push the wrecks off the road before we finally got away. It was now daylight, and the Chinese did not run their convoys during the day lest they be even more exposed to being spotted and attacked from the air. The remaining trucks were driven into several of the bigger caves and we were taken into a smaller one occupied by fifteen wounded Chinese and North Korean soldiers. A Chinese officer spoke to the wounded men, presumably telling them not to harm us, because they moved over, leaving two straw pallets in the far corner for Jimmy and me to occupy. This surprised us, as the back of the cave, furthermost from the opening, was always the least cold. The officer had obviously elevated us in the pecking order.

The men in the cave ignored our presence except for one little cove, who appeared to be suffering shell shock and seemed to be trying to tell us his name, jabbering away thirteen to the dozen and gesticulating madly, to the amusement of his wounded comrades. His name sounded like Hok, or something similar, but he spoke it so fast it could have been anything – Og, Sok, Nok, Tok – so we finally settled for Hok and left it at that. This seemed to please him and Hok became our mate. Then Jimmy, obviously impressed by my expletive immediately following the air attack, taught him to say, 'Well, I'll be fucked', and once he'd mastered the expression Hok would rattle off something in Chinese and then end whatever it was he was saying with, 'Well, I'll be fucked!'

Those of the Chinese and Korean wounded who could walk were permitted to leave the cave whereas we were not, and Hok would disappear and later return and go and sit on our pallet and pull a blanket over his knees pretending to be cold. We soon learned that he was concealing food, in the form of hard, almost-tasteless biscuits, and an occasional cigarette under our blankets. We presumed he must have stolen these from somewhere by the care he took to conceal them. We'd touch him on the shoulder and thank him and he'd always reply, 'Well, I'll be fucked!' Which, I'm ashamed to say given our miserable circumstances, was good for a bit of a laugh. Hok, mad as a March hare, was proving to be a good friend when we most needed one.

We'd been in the cave for three days when, late in the afternoon of the third day, two North Korean officers entered and walked over to where we were sitting on our pallets. One of them pulled a Luger pistol from his holster and held it against Jimmy's temple.

'Whoa, man!' Jimmy said, not moving.

'He's just trying to scare you, mate,' I said unconvincingly.

'He done succeeded, man,' Jimmy said, his eyes grown wide and fearful.

The next moment the second officer drew his pistol and I felt the end of its cold metal barrel on the centre of my forehead. All I could think was, *What a bloody stupid way to die*. Then they must have glanced at each other, because they pulled the triggers simultaneously. I don't suppose you can have such a thing as a thunderous click but that's what it sounded like to me. Despite the cold, I'd broken into a sweat.

The two Koreans chortled, highly amused, slapping each other on the back, immensely pleased at this neat trick. Then the one with the Luger cleared his throat and, with the laughter gone from his eyes, reached into his quilted jacket pocket and took out a fully loaded magazine and slipped it into the pistol. Then he turned to look menacingly at us. *Jesus! The first time was to put the wind up us. This time it's for real!* I thought. At that moment Hok arrived and launched himself at the two officers, his hands flapping every which way while he shouted furious abuse at them. The North Koreans turned and retreated hastily with Hok shooing them out of the cave as though they were a couple of trespassing chickens. With the two officers gone he turned to face us, his hands on his hips. 'Well, I'll be fucked!' he said, with exactly the right intonation.

A convoy with new trucks arrived at the caves around midnight on the fourth day and loaded up the Chinese soldiers and the two of us, and we left leaving a plainly distressed Hok behind. After the second day in the cave cracks had appeared in my plaster cast, and now as the truck bumped along the road, flickers of pain shot down my leg. My only hope was that it wasn't the start of another infection and simply the effects of slow healing.

Towards dawn we halted in what appeared to be a village, in the centre of which was a large shed about thirty foot long and ten foot wide. It had possibly once been a communal shed but was now converted into another farmhouse hospital, with the usual thatched roof and dirt floor. At the end furthermost from the door a small charcoal stove struggled unsuccessfully to heat the hut against the deepening winter. Against the wall on either side of it were the usual raised platforms running all the way along two-thirds of the hut and containing thirteen UN Command wounded and sick. This was a hospital not as big as the other, with no modern equipment and few, if any, drugs beyond the barest necessities, but with its own doctor.

The wounded and sick, all of them American Caucasians, were in a pretty bad way. One had a leg missing, another's kneecap had been sheared off by shrapnel, several, like us, wore plaster casts and two had arms missing. But it was the general condition they were in that was horrendous – wounds openly oozed pus, the plaster casts festered from within and gas gangrene was quietly rotting the stump of the soldier with the amputated leg. All of this emitting an odour that only those inured to living with it could endure. The Chinese doctor and the orderlies wore masks, but even they couldn't tolerate staying in our presence too long. Both Jimmy and I vomited the first time we entered the hut, and a voice from one of the wounded men rang out, 'Welcome to the stink pit, comrades!'

Like the previous hospital, the hut was regarded as a human zoo, an irresistible attraction for the soldiers who occupied the village. They'd congregate outside until apparently someone gave them permission to enter, when they'd barge in, shouldering each other out of the way in their anxiety to be the first to gawk at us. Despite the condition of the wounded men it was deeply humiliating and unwelcome, but there was nothing we could do about it. Shouting at them didn't work and was simply regarded as part of the performance. The intrusions would occur a dozen times a day and they made our lives even more miserable than they already were.

After the second day Jimmy had had enough. 'It Ogoya time, Brother Fish. Da gooks – dey gettin' on mah nerves, man.'

Jimmy's counterattack was simple enough. As the Chinese soldiers barged through the door we would all lift and flap our blankets and the odour would greatly intensify, wafting directly into the faces of the oncoming soldiers. We had learned that Chinese foot soldiers have pretty strong stomachs, but this odoriferous welcome was to prove their nemesis. Expectant faces would suddenly contort into grimaces as their hands shot up to cover their noses and mouths. Those in the front would turn in an effort to get away, often knocking down the others coming in. The hut soon emptied and we'd hear our unwelcome visitors retching and vomiting outside. Even in these most miserable of circumstances this got a laugh from the men in the hut and Jimmy, in an attempt to emulate my accent, would exclaim, 'Well, I'll be fucked.' He was once again in control.

As with the previous situation in the North Korean cave, these were men who'd basically lost the plot – they were disillusioned and reduced to the status of animals, and most had given up hope of staying alive. Somehow Jimmy got them going again with the help of the harmonica. Don't let anyone ever tell you that music isn't a powerful medium – it's perhaps the most powerful. When the human voice can no longer reach a man, a ballad or a tune from when his life was good can touch him and make him respond. If Jimmy was wrong about 'The Fish Song', he was dead right about the mouth organ and its latent power to change men's attitudes.

Staying clean was, of course, impossible, though an orderly would deliver a medium-sized enamel basin containing hot water to the hut every morning. It was first come, first served, with the fittest men always getting to use it and the sick almost never. After the first three people had used it the water was dirty and possibly even dangerous to use, as their infected parts had been cleansed in it. By the time it got to the last patient the bowl was almost empty, the remaining water black and foul. Jimmy organised that a different bloke got first go every morning so that each of us got to get a proper wash every two weeks or so. It may not sound like a big thing, but it was everything. Just knowing that your turn would eventually come around kept a man going. You'd feel the hot water splashing on your face and arms and know it was about as close to heaven as you could get under the circumstances.

The weeks crawled by. Wade Fernance, the amputee, died, and Gary Reilly, in civilian life an Olympic horseman, lost his leg to gas gangrene, which had also been the ultimate cause of Wade's death. Though we'd cleaned up the best we could, we all suffered from dysentery, and the latrine bucket in the corner added to the foul surroundings. This was also where the lice I talked about earlier established themselves under my plaster cast and behind my left knee – there seemed to be hundreds of them and they were driving me half-crazy with itch. I'd pull a thin twig from the thatched roof and push it down the back of my plaster in an attempt to scratch the bastards until the blood ran out at my ankle, but the irritation never seemed to stop and the scratching seemed only to stir them up further. But there wasn't any point whingeing and there were lots worse off than me. This was also when Chuck Ward, the American B29 tail gunner I mentioned before, who'd walked for hours with frostbite after his plane was shot down, was brought in across the frozen landscape and where we heard his screaming coming at us from way out. Despite the best efforts of the Chinese doctor to save his feet, they were finally amputated. Another Yank died of blood poisoning and it seemed, even when the Chinese were trying, desperately short of medical supplies, they couldn't keep us alive.

Apart from the lice, the pain in my leg gradually ceased and Jimmy and I began to practise walking, him on his modified 'Captain Hook' crutch and me on the bamboo pair the Chinese had given me at the previous farmhouse hospital. The weeks turned into months, winter into summer and with it unbearable heat. After winter I thought I'd never find a summer too hot for me, but I was wrong. Dirt, sweat, suppurating wounds and open sores were a lousy combination and attracted flies in such numbers that their buzzing made it hard to hear what your neighbour was saying – not to mention the irritation they caused and the maggots from where they laid their eggs in your open flesh.

The passing of time also brought healing, and prisoners seen to be mobile and not running a fever were considered by the Chinese to be healed. We knew our time was close when my plaster was finally removed and the bizarre scene with the lice escaping took place. The day to leave finally arrived and, with a warning to go easy on our newly healed legs and still needing the support of our crutches, we were lifted into a truck to make the journey to a POW camp. So far so good – Jimmy and I had survived. With the UN prisoner-exchange negotiations with the Chinese well under way we even began to feel a tad optimistic. I guess hope springs eternal in the human breast, but then, if something can go wrong it usually does. As things turned out we were far from being out of the woods.

# CHAPTER TEN

## *Learning Good How to be Bad*

Victory over Japan was declared and, while all of America rejoiced, a dark cloud appeared in the hitherto clear blue skies of the relationship Jimmy and Frau Kraus enjoyed. While they said nothing to each other, each concerned with their own private fears, they knew it wouldn't be long before the Kraus twins would be returning from the Pacific. In the two and a half years Jimmy and Frau Kraus had been left on the farm on their own they'd become a prosperous working partnership while, at the same time, becoming firm and loving friends.

Their newfound prosperity had nothing to do with the didactic farm-maintenance plan laid out for Frau Kraus by her dead and long-forgotten husband. This had proved to be unworkable on every front with the exception of her vegetable garden, though that had never been his concern anyway. The Thanksgiving turkeys made barely enough to pay for the feed required for the poultry. Frau Kraus's dressed-duck business all but disappeared when most of her ethnic German customers were sent to an internment camp. The eggs from her chickens brought in scarcely enough to buy bread and salt – with eight million men away in the armed forces the consumption of eggs had fallen and so had the price, while the price of grain to feed poultry and livestock had skyrocketed. Finally, the orchid market proved to require a horticultural expertise they had yet to perfect and the flower market much harder to enter than Otto Kraus had anticipated.

Otto Kraus's will, in the end, left nothing to his wife other than a caveat that required their twin sons, who inherited everything, including a surprisingly sizeable bank account, to provide for Frau Kraus until her death. Initially it had been hard to make ends meet, and the newly found wartime partnership was forced to rely on vegetables from the garden and eggs from the ducks with an occasional scrawny chicken killed when it stopped laying. Finally, in desperation, Frau Kraus and Jimmy had turned back to tomatoes, a decision that came about in a most fortuitous way.

One of the great pleasures of their relationship was Jimmy reading the weekly newspaper to Frau Kraus after dinner at night. While Jimmy's limited education meant he wasn't a fluent reader, his slow and measured pace ideally suited her even slower comprehension of the English language. Each night of the week they would read most of the newspaper, and in particular the farm page, which contained snippets of interest to local farmers, orchardists and market gardeners. On one such occasion Jimmy read about M. Charles Byers, who ran a truck-repair business in West Virginia and, as a hobby, propagated tomatoes. He'd come up with what the newspaper described as a new variety of the traditional beefsteak tomato, not overpulpy and with a surprisingly sweet taste, weighing two and a half pounds and, better still, maturing in seventy-nine days. He'd named the cultivar 'Radiator Charlie's Mortgage Lifter', and in the article offered to sell a packet of seed for one dollar plus ten cents postage to anyone in the United States.

'Ma'am, we gotta get dis bif-steak tomato,' Jimmy declared, ''cos da orchids dey ain't doin' no damn good. Folks gonna buy a tomato plant dat grow a two-and-a-half-pound tomato dat juicy an' sweet, dat for sure,' Jimmy declared.

Frau Kraus needed no persuasion – in tomatoes, she trusted. '*Ja*, Jimmy – we send Mister Charlie Radiator *schnell* zat money!' she exclaimed excitedly.

Pretty soon the hothouse was filled with tomato plants in papier-mâché pots made by Frau Kraus from the newspaper off-cuts collected by Jimmy from the *Messenger-Gazette* in Somerset. The plants were raised to eight inches and attached to each pot using bright-red twine was a ticket that carried the words 'Each Famous Mortgage Lifter Tomato Ways 2lbs'. Twice weekly the plants were taken in the Dodge truck to Somerville, where Jimmy despatched them by freight car on the Central Railroad of New Jersey to their agent, Solly Shakenovsky, at the New York markets. There they soon became the latest fad in suburban backyards and apartment balconies. A two-and-a-half-pound tomato grown by a housewife or her husband was something to boast about in any neighbourhood.

Radiator Charlie's Mortgage Lifter proved to be a robust plant that delivered the goods with a minimum of fuss. The label claimed a two-pound tomato but the half-dozen or so tomatoes the plant produced usually exceeded this claim, giving the domestic gardener additional pride in the fact that they'd personally exceeded the grower's claim. Apart from seeing the potential of Radiator Charlie's Mortgage Lifter as an individually sold plant for domestic gardens, this simple understatement of weight on the misspelled label was yet another indication of Jimmy's instinctive ability to think outside the square.

Purchased for the exorbitant amount of one dollar per pot, the beefsteak tomato brought in a clear profit of seventy-five cents per plant and it wasn't long before they were earning several dozen times more than all Frau Kraus's barnyard enterprises put together. As a further indication of Jimmy's instinctive marketing nous, he was insistent that the plants be priced high to make them seem exotic and worthy of possessing. 'Ma'am, when everybody got somethin' it ain't got no value to nobody.' He laughed. 'We done no damn good wid dem orchids cos dem other growers dey got da market first, but dem bif-steak tomatoes dey gonna be da orchids o' da tomato fam-bly an' dis time we gonna get dem first.' Frau Kraus, even if she hadn't understood Jimmy's logic, agreed and it worked – the high price made the buyers see them as exotic and rare and they were often given as gifts.

With the poultry no longer the source of the odd couple's livelihood, the hens and ducks multiplied. As Thanksgiving approached, the turkeys didn't have to look anxiously over their shoulders, Frau Kraus being much too busy making pots for her beefsteak tomatoes to find time to pluck and dress the turkey meat for her New York customers.

For his birthday, Jimmy received a pair of hand-stitched western riding boots, a fine Stetson hat, a tooled leather belt with a fancy buckle that sported two large turquoise stones set into the silver surround, new blue jeans and a long-sleeved tartan wool shirt, all ordered by Frau Kraus from the Sears Roebuck catalogue. In addition she knitted him two pairs of bright-red woollen socks. These were the first new clothes Jimmy had ever owned, and he wore them when he drove Frau Kraus to church on Sunday. He'd wait under a large oak tree outside the Lutheran church and raise his Stetson to the members of the congregation, thinking himself the best-dressed dude in Somerset County. After the white folk had filed into church Jimmy would remove his Stetson and, along with the other coloured folk, enter and sit in the very last pew with the hat on his lap, his work-calloused thumb constantly running along the nap of its brim.

Sundays were special – other than feeding the poultry and checking the heating in the hothouse in the winter, they observed the Lord's Day by not working. They'd eat their main meal after returning from church. Frau Kraus would cook a chicken or a duck with vegetables and roast potatoes from the garden, leaving it to slow-roast in the oven while they attended the church service. At this weekly feast she'd wear her special 'Thank you, Charlie' apron, which featured a life-size embroidery of Radiator Charlie's Mortgage Lifter and, emblazoned under it, '*Danke*, Charlie'. In the afternoon Frau Kraus would take a nap and Jimmy would retire to his room to practise his reading. As the only book in the house was the bible in the German language he used the Somerset *Messenger-Gazette* for this purpose, practising the more difficult words so when he read it a second time to Frau Kraus over the following week he would sound less hesitant.

As they say in the classics, 'All good things must eventually come to an end.' The partnership consummated in the bathroom came to an abrupt end in Frau Kraus's kitchen. With the surrender of Japan and the end of the war in the Pacific, the Kraus twins were among the first Pacific war troops to steam up New York Harbor at dawn on the 17th of October 1945. They were on board the light carrier USS *Bataan*, a part of the advance armada of nine ships, the greatest among them being the giant USS *Enterprise*, queen of the Nimitz navy.

Naturally enough they hadn't bothered to inform their mother of their homecoming. The Greyhound bus had dropped them at the farm gate the following morning at six-thirty a.m. and they'd walked down the neatly pruned elm-lined driveway and, as they'd always done, walked to the back of the house to enter through the laundry and into the kitchen. Their return home was to bring an abrupt end to the happiest days of Frau Kraus's life in America.

She was fixing ham and eggs in the kitchen when she heard the commotion at the laundry door. Thinking it was Jimmy coming in early from the hothouse for breakfast, she called out, '*Guten Morgen, meine Liebling!*' Then, sensing something amiss, she glanced back at the door to be confronted by her twin sons. She screamed and dropped the cast-iron skillet, spilling ham and eggs over the scrubbed kitchen floor. Then she sank to her knees and began to howl.

Not having any idea of how to pacify their mother, the twins left her where she knelt weeping and went through to their bedroom to drop their kit. Here they discovered Frau Kraus had a boarder who owned a pair of highly polished western riding boots, a carefully brushed white Stetson, a neatly ironed tartan shirt and a pair of freshly laundered blue jeans. They returned to the kitchen to find her now lying prostrate, sobbing into her folded arms.

'Who's the cowboy staying in our room?' Fritz demanded.

Frau Kraus clutched Fritz around his ankles. 'Jimmy *gut* boy!' she pleaded.

'Jesus Christ! She's let the nigger stay in our room!' Henrik exclaimed. 'The dirty black bastard is staying in *our* room!'

'The old bitch is probably shagging him,' Fritz declared contemptuously. 'You sleeping with the nigger, Frau Kraus?'

Frau Kraus was too overcome to answer, other than to repeat, 'Jimmy *gut* boy!' and then commence to sob afresh, repeating the three words over and over.

'Why, you dirty old bitch!' Henrik shouted down at her. 'Where is he?'

This only caused Frau Kraus to sob with greater gusto.

Jimmy was in the tomato hothouse cleaning and scrubbing the large structure. Cleaning and making potting mix, as well as preparing the seed trays they would plant in mid-January, took from mid-October until the early part of January. It was cold and dirty work, and Jimmy was looking forward to his breakfast when he heard footsteps outside the hothouse and looked up to see two uniformed soldiers enter, each armed with a baseball bat.

Jimmy recognised the Kraus twins immediately. 'You done come home!' Jimmy called, walking towards them, wiping his hand on his overalls before extending it to greet them.

'You've been fucking Frau Kraus, nigger!' Then, not waiting for a reply, Fritz swung the baseball bat at Jimmy's head.

Jimmy lifted his right arm to avoid the blow that struck him hard on the hand.

The twins beat Jimmy to a pulp and then loaded his unconscious body onto the back of the Dodge truck. They drove him well past Somerville and eventually headed along the Kinderkamack Road, which runs beside the Hackensack River in Bergen County. They may well have thought about throwing him in the river but elected instead to dump him on the outskirts of the borough of River Edge, for all intents and purposes making it look like a hit-and-run accident.

It was here that the highway patrol discovered Jimmy after responding to a call from a member of the public claiming a dead Negro lay at the side of the road about two miles out near the Erie

Railroad track. The police officers concluded that he'd been the victim of a hit-and-run accident and radioed for an ambulance. Jimmy, still unconscious, was wrapped in a blanket and taken to Holy Name Hospital on the outskirts of River Edge, where he was admitted to the emergency room. Medical staff checked his blood pressure and vital signs, and put him on a drip.

Jimmy regained consciousness several hours later and was asked where he hurt. He could neither speak nor use his dislocated arm or broken hand to indicate and, in any case, had been so thoroughly beaten he wouldn't have known where to begin. He was taken into theatre and examined. The X-rays showed he'd broken his hand and his nose, and six of his ribs. His jaw was badly swollen but did not appear to be broken, and his shoulder was dislocated. In the care of the Holy Name medical staff, his shoulder was realigned, his hand set and plastered and his ribs strapped. In addition, a laceration on the left side of his face required twenty-seven stitches.

Five days later Jimmy, now black and blue from multiple bruising, the swelling in his jaw somewhat subsided, was sufficiently recovered to be interviewed. The sister in charge of the ward asked him if he'd seen the vehicle that hit him, as the police were anxious to interview him. Jimmy then proceeded to tell the nun the story of his beating. She immediately reported what she'd heard to her Mother General, Agatha Black, the hospital superintendent, who then called Somerville County Courthouse where she was put through to the sheriff.

Sheriff Daimon T. Waterman, a bear of a man who weighed close to 280 pounds and was locally known as Diamond T., the make of a large road-haulage truck common at the time, decided to personally take charge of the case. He arrived at the hospital that same afternoon, ostensibly to conduct an interview and take a statement from Jimmy.

'Dat sheriff, he da man who done give me mah special drivin' licence,' Jimmy explained. 'He da man who arrest Herr Kraus dat one time dey take him away. He know me, man. He know I's a good nigger!' Jimmy sighed. 'But now suddenly he don't want to know me no more.

'"Jimmy, you're in big trouble," he say to me straight off. "Big, big, trouble."

'"Why so, sheriff, sir?" I ask, "I ain't done nothing wrong!"

'He thinks some, den he say, "You put your black dick in a white woman's pussy, Jimmy."

'"I ain't, Sheriff! I swear I ain't put no dick in dat place! Frau Kraus she mah friend, you can ask her yohself."

'"Hmm," the sheriff say, den he think some more an' he rub his chin. "Jimmy, the boys, the Kraus twins, they're war heroes who fought at Guadalcanal, Iwo Jima and Okinawa. They've survived the Japanese to come home to find the black help is fornicating with their mama. Naturally, they're mighty upset."

'I don't know what dis forn-catin' is, but I can tell from what he say it ain't good. "Sheriff, I tol' you I ain't done dat. I ain't done no forn-catin' wid der mama, wid Frau Kraus. God's truth, I swear it!"

'He don't say nothin', he jes look at me, den he open his briefcase and take out a piece of paper and he hold it up so, in da air in front mah face. "Jimmy, I have here a signed statement from the Kraus twins. It states that they arrived home at six-thirty a.m on the 18th of October to find you in the act of having intercourse with their mother."

'"What dis intercourse?" I ask him. I also don't know dat time what means dis word. 'I always in da tomato hothouse dat time, sheriff. I's mixin' pottin' an' scubbin' an' cleaning. I always start early, five-thirty o'clock. At seven o'clock Frau Kraus she always fixin' mah breakfast. I in da hothouse dat time Mr Fritz and Mr Henrik say I done do what dey say I done to Frau Kraus."

'He shake his head. "Jimmy, it's your word against theirs. A black kid from an institution, against the word of two war heroes defending their mother's honour. Who do you think the judge will believe, eh?"

'"I don't know, sheriff, but I ain't lying – I ain't done nothin' bad," I say to him.

'He sit and I can see he thinking, then he say, "Jimmy, can I give you some advice?"

'"Yessir, sheriff."

'"Well now, let's see, you are in big trouble, boy. Big, big trouble." He smile. "But boys will be boys, sowing their wild oats, eh?"

'I don't ask him what mean sowin' wild oats. I already got all dem other things he say I done, which I ain't. Tomatoes I done sow plenty, but I ain't never sowed no wild oats, dat another thing I ain't done.

'"I don't want you to say anything to anyone, you hear boy?" he asks. "I'm not going to take down your statement – not today, anyhow. I want you to think about what I've said, then you can talk to me again. You *only* talk to me and I talk to the judge and I tell him you're a good, hardworking boy and that you've never been in trouble before. We can settle this thing if you do as I say." He stop and he look at me and shake his head. "If you don't the judge will send you to Elmira. You heard of Elmira, Jimmy?"

'I tell him I don't know dis place. He explain Elmira a Re-form-a-tory for boys in New York.

'"If I hear you've been talking to anyone else, you're in big trouble, Jimmy. Do you understand?" he asks, and he point his finger at me.

'"Yessir, sheriff," I say to him. I scared, man. I's fifteen years old and I don't want to go to no Elmira Re-form-a-tory. I ain't done dem things he say – forn-catin', intercourse and sowin' dem wild oats, but I's a nigger – nobody gonna believe me. Maybe da sheriff he's gonna find out about da gobblin' spider, maybe dat just as bad as dem other things I ain't done.' Jimmy laughed. 'And gobblin' spider, dat somethin' I def-fin-nately done and den maybe I in big, big trouble, man!

'"Jimmy, I've got an idea," da sheriff now say. "You're a man now – do you think you can look after yourself?"

'"Yessir, sheriff."

'"Then listen to me, boy. It's much better that you *vamoose*. You know what I mean? Get lost. Go to New York, stay there, maybe change your name."

'"Why I gonna do dat, sheriff?" I ask him. "You jes say you gonna speak to the judge, tell him I'm a good nigger?"

'Da sheriff, he nod his head and smile. "Certainly I can do that, and it might work. But your case is to be heard at the County Courthouse in Hackensack and not in Somerset County – that's not my jurisdiction, I won't be able to help you that much." He think some den he say, "You want my honest opinion, Jimmy?"

'I nods mah head.

'"You are fifteen years old and a dependent child, also a foster child, and there is strong evidence that you've been having sexual relations with your foster mother." He look at me. "That's called carnal knowledge – the judge ain't going to like that, and he's very likely to sentence you to Elmira Reformatory."

'"But I tol' you, I ain't done nothin', sheriff!"

'He sigh, den he say, "It's your word against the Kraus twins, the war heroes. I don't think the judge will take the word of a Negro boy against theirs."

'"Sheriff, sir," I say, "I ain't got no clothes, I ain't got no money! How's I gonna get me the bus to New York?"

'"Have you got clothes at the farm? With Frau Kraus?" he ask.

'"I got mah Sunday best for drivin' Frau Kraus to church," I tell him.

'Before he leave he take out two bills an' make to shake my hand an' now I'm holdin' da money. Den he say real quiet, "Jimmy, you're doing the right thing, you hear? This way you save everyone a lot of trouble, but mostly yourself. I'll tell the judge your jaw was too swollen to talk, to make a statement, then later when I returned you'd run away. If you want to stay out of the reformatory, you'll catch that bus. You hear, boy? Catch the bus. I don't want to see you in Somerville ever again."

'When the sheriff gone, in come da Mother General who don't know what jus' happen with Sheriff Diamond T. "Jimmy, don't worry, I've spoken to the bishop and we're going to make sure you get justice," she says to me.

'"Yes, ma'am, thank you." I say to her. Now I really scared, man! She wrong one hundred per cent! A boy like me ain't gonna get no justice. The sheriff, he right – da judge he gonna put me in dat Elmira Re-form-a-tory, dat for sure! Ain't no bish-op gonna help me get no justice, man.

'Den da Mother General, she say, "Jimmy, the doctor says you can leave the hospital in four days and as you cannot return to your foster home you revert to being a dependent child, a ward of the court. We applied to the court to release you into the care of the church and the bishop has agreed to make a place for you in a Catholic boys' home. But the court has decided that you should go to a local institution, just down the street from the courthouse, and you will be going to the Bergen County Children's Home in Hackensack." She smiled. "I'm sorry you can't experience the Catholic influence, but you'll be in safe enough hands where you're going."

'Now I got me some more big trouble, man. I don't want to go to no children's home. I's a man now, I done me a man's work foh three years. I don't want to be treated like no chile no more. Frau Kraus she treat me good, like a man. Next day someone leave a hessian sack at the hospital for me. It tied at da top wid red twine the same as we use for tying labels to dem bif-steak tomato plants. Inside is my Stetson, boots, mah belt wid' a solid silver buckle an' dem tore-quoi stones, tar-tan shirt, jeans an' mah two pair special knitted Frau Kraus red birthday socks. In da shirt pocket is a note, '*Jimmy, danke meine Liebling, Frau Kraus*'. Also in da pocket she put fifty dollars. I's rich, man! I got me two ten-dollar bills from da sheriff and now I got seventy dollars. It time to kick da dust. I'm outta dere pronto, I'm gonna find me a life in da big wide worl.'

'What about the court case?' I asked him. 'What happened?'

'Nah, man, I too scared da judge gonna send me to dat Elmira Re-form-a-tory.'

'But you were innocent!' I protested.

Jimmy shrugged. 'Nigger ain't never innocent, dat for sure, Brother Fish. I never done find out what happened. Four o'clock next mornin' da ward sister she asleep, she snorin' like she cuttin' logs. I get me up and dress in mah Frau Kraus birthday clothes and I carry mah boots 'til I outside dat place. Den I escape myself away from dat hospital an' da bishop an' me gettin' no justice I ain't gonna get an' da boys home an' da judge who gonna send me to Elmira Re-form-a-tory. I gone, man! I sad 'bout only one thing – I ain't never gonna see Frau Kraus no more. She bin kind to me. She always treat me like her own son. I love her big time, man!'

At the time Jimmy told me the story I confess I was disappointed. In my imagination I had him winning the case, with the twins receiving a lengthy jail sentence. I guess everyone likes a happy ending.

But, of course, life doesn't work like that. In particular, it doesn't for a fifteen-year-old Negro boy without anyone to guide him. It wasn't hard to understand why he'd run away. The sheriff had convinced him he was in big trouble. Despite not having done any of the things the Kraus twins had accused him of he'd nevertheless participated in frequent gobbling-spider episodes. If the judge were to discover these he'd be a dead cert for Elmira. Even if he didn't find out, the sheriff had already warned him that the judge wouldn't take his word against two war heroes. He'd be found guilty of intercourse, 'forn-cation', sowing wild oats and, possibly, spider-gobbling.

Furthermore, there was the highly undesirable prospect of being placed in the care of the Bergen County Children's Home. Jimmy would be returning to an institution with all its rules and restrictions after having been treated like the man of the house by Frau Kraus. He'd proved he could run the farm as well as Otto Kraus. In fact, the bank manager at Somerville's First National, Mr Simon Lean, told Frau Kraus she was making more money from her pots of beefsteak tomato plants than her husband had ever banked in a season from his entire tomato crop.

The untimely death of Otto Kraus was yet another thing on Jimmy's overburdened mind. In the urge to confess what humans so often feel when they've got something on their conscience, Frau Kraus had told

Jimmy about the arsenic she'd put into her husband's after-dinner coffee. She'd emphasised that she'd diligently warned her husband on every single occasion *not* to drink the coffee, adding that she'd also never personally placed it in front of him.

Jimmy, who had observed how Otto Kraus treated his wife, accepted her revenge as rough and simple justice. The fact that she'd warned him not to drink it and hadn't placed it in front of him, in his mind, made her practically innocent. He didn't see it as an act perpetrated by someone who might not be entirely sane. He accepted that Frau Kraus was a strange woman but lacked the experience to judge her actions against those of any other woman in similar circumstances. The only women he'd known previously were the ones at the orphanage, who, even without husbands, had been pretty strange, while none of them had shown him the loving-kindness and generosity Frau Kraus had lavished on him. She'd treated him like the mother he'd never had and while the occasional gobbling-spider episode was something that happened between them, it had never led to anything else. In fact, with the arrogance typical of the young male, he'd come to regard the little incidents in the shower as a service he rendered to Frau Kraus with the added bonus of mutual pleasure. Nevertheless Jimmy knew enough to know her poisoning of Otto Kraus was a secret that must never be revealed. He felt sure that the judge might force this knowledge out of him by some devious and trick questioning. Everyone knew judges were the cleverest people in the world and could get you to confess everything you'd ever done, and more. He'd be responsible for Frau Kraus going to prison, or even being sentenced to the electric chair.

Come to think of it, if I had found myself in the same circumstances at Jimmy's age, and with nobody to reassure or advise me, I'm pretty certain I would have come to the same decision as he had and done a runner to New York. He was simply carrying too much emotional weight for a fifteen-year-old.

When Jimmy told me his side of the story in prison camp, I'd always wanted to know what happened after he'd taken his unauthorised leave of absence from Holy Name Hospital. In particular, I was anxious to know how Frau Kraus had ended up.

Some twenty years after the Korean War, I was in New York negotiating to buy a fishing trawler. Finding myself with a day to spare I hired an Avis car and drove the short distance to Somerville. To my surprise Somerset County was still a rural community growing apples, peaches and blueberries, as well as mixed farming. I saw a soya-bean crop, potatoes and corn and several fields where jersey cows grazed. The town must have grown a little since Jimmy's time as there seemed to be some recent new buildings, but it had missed the post-war development I observed in Teaneck and Hackensack in neighbouring Bergen County. I called in at the offices of the Somerset *Messenger-Gazette* and made inquiries. The editor knew nothing about the Kraus case and told me they only kept files for fifteen years, except for exceptional events, and he suggested that a court case such as the one I'd mentioned was unlikely to fall into this category. 'We'll ask Bessie,' he volunteered. 'She's been in our cutting service for thirty-five years – she may remember a case like that.'

Bessie not only remembered the case, but also recalled the name of the lawyer who'd defended the Kraus twins, a man named Abe Stennholz. She produced a cutting that had appeared in the *Messenger-Gazette* two years previously that noted his retirement and the fact that he'd recently lost his wife. It went on to say he intended remaining in the family home they'd occupied for the entire forty years of their marriage. In the obliging way of most Americans, Bessie offered to look him up for me in the local telephone directory. She found his name, dialled his number and then handed me the receiver.

Abe Stennholz answered the telephone himself. I explained why I wanted to meet him and at first he sounded reluctant, that is, until I told him I'd come all the way from Australia, something I've found works a treat with Americans. He agreed to talk to me, setting a time of three o'clock the following afternoon. I was disappointed that he wouldn't see me that afternoon, but as my next appointment in New York was mid-morning the following day it didn't really matter. I drove back to my hotel in Manhattan and left for Somerville again after lunch the next day.

At the time Bessie mentioned the lawyer's name it had seemed vaguely familiar. But I couldn't quite place it until, during our interview the following afternoon, Abe Stennholz happened to mention that his brother, also retired, had been the local Lutheran minister and very close to the Kraus family. He was, of course, the same bloke the FBI had interviewed prior to Otto Kraus's internment. He'd also presided at the grave site where Frau Kraus, as the solitary mourner, had placed a black homemade crinkle-paper rose on Otto's grave. Later, she'd laughingly confessed to Jimmy that her final words to her husband had been, '*Danke, meine saubere Frau*', whereupon she'd been unable to stop laughing.

The lawyer's home was on a quiet street lined with beautiful old maple trees just beginning to show their autumn colour, and from the look of the houses on either side it was an older part of the town. Abe Stennholz was a tall, slightly overweight man with the smooth facial complexion of someone who is a teetotaller and has spent most of his life indoors. Perhaps his most striking features were an abundance of carefully combed snowy-white hair and the palest blue eyes, seen through square-cut frameless spectacles. He greeted me with a firm grip and without smiling, then suggested we sit on the porch, where he claimed the afternoon sunshine was pleasant at that time of the year.

Almost immediately a maid appeared and he asked her to bring out a jug of lemonade. We sat on the porch drinking the homemade lemonade, passing the usual pleasantries, prior to commencing with the reason why I'd come. He told me he was a widower of two years. Smiling and patting his stomach he declared that Martha, who hailed from Louisiana, took good care of him. I took it that Martha was the maid who'd brought the lemonade. Then quite suddenly he said, 'Before we begin, Mr McKenzie, I ask that you understand that times have changed and attitudes towards coloured folk were very different at the time the Kraus twins asked me to represent them.'

'Changed for the better, I imagine?'

'Certainly. Today a case such as this one may well have turned out differently.'

'Differently – how?' I asked.

'Well, quite clearly the Negro boy, Jimmy Oldcorn, wasn't guilty of any crime.'

Given his carefully qualified opening remarks, I was surprised at this admission. 'I guess it all happened a long time ago, sir. I'd really appreciate it if you'd tell it just the way it was at the time. What the circumstances were that caused the Kraus twins to come to you.'

He seemed reassured. 'Well, they initially called in to see the sheriff around noon on the day they arrived home. They told him that Jimmy Oldcorn had run away when they'd appeared unexpectedly at the farm that morning. This, they claimed, had caused Frau Kraus . . .' he stopped to explain that this was how she was always referred to in the community '. . . to become very distraught. They wished to report the incident, as Jimmy Oldcorn was a minor and under the foster care of their family.'

'And that's all they claimed happened?'

'Initially, yes. But unbeknownst to them, the sheriff had received an earlier call from a near-hysterical Frau Kraus who claimed that her two sons had returned home and had taken to Jimmy Oldcorn with baseball bats and then thrown his lifeless body into the truck and driven away.'

'In effect, she thought she was reporting a murder?'

'Yes. She'd entered the hothouse to see a fair amount of blood and thought they'd killed the boy.'

'Didn't the sheriff find it rather strange that a mother would report her sons? I mean, they'd only just returned from active service that very morning.'

'Well, of course. He'd driven directly to the farm to discover a distraught Frau Kraus, who'd led him to the tomato hothouse where he observed the blood on the floor. They then returned to the kitchen where she handed him the two baseball bats she claimed she'd found in the hothouse. The sheriff explained that she should have left them at the scene and not handled them. Frau Kraus told the sheriff she had washed the baseball bats. She was a fanatic about cleanliness,' Abe Stennholz explained. 'She would wear up to a dozen different freshly starched aprons every day. Now she had unwittingly destroyed perhaps the most important evidence in a prosecution that might be brought against the Kraus twins.'

'How did the sheriff react to this?'

'You mean about her destroying the evidence?' Abe shrugged. 'It was well known that Frau Kraus was . . . er, a little strange. I guess he accepted that, *if* the baseball bats had contained traces of blood, she'd acted in good faith. Especially when she seemed determined that the twins should be charged for Jimmy's presumed murder.'

'Did he send out a police alert to find them?'

'There wasn't any need. Shortly after the sheriff returned from the farm they turned up at his office in East Main Street, unaware, of course, that Frau Kraus had called him and that he'd been out to the farm. Sheriff Waterman took down their statement and then asked if they'd told him *everything*, at the same time cautioning them to be careful how they answered. He then asked them if they'd personally harmed the boy. The twins, perhaps realising the sheriff knew something in addition to what they'd just told him, admitted to . . . let me think of the exact phrase, that's right . . . to teaching him a lesson by giving him a bloody nose.'

'So he arrested them?'

'Not so fast, Mr McKenzie,' the lawyer chided me. 'There was no proof that they'd killed the boy – the sheriff only had Frau Kraus's word for it.

'What about the blood in the hothouse?'

'Hardly definitive proof. After all, they'd admitted to giving him a bloody nose. The blood on the floor could well have been from that incident.'

'But they'd beaten him severely with the baseball bats!' I protested.

Abe Stennholz bristled visibly. 'Oh, you know this for certain do you, Mr McKenzie? The sheriff only had Frau Kraus's word that she'd found the baseball bats in the hothouse, and even if true, she hadn't witnessed them used on the boy – and furthermore, they apparently contained no trace of blood.'

I realised that I was getting a little ahead of myself. I would need to be careful with this man. I apologised to him, silently hoping I hadn't blown the interview.

Abe Stennholz looked sternly at me, and then said, 'Perhaps a little background might be useful, Mr McKenzie. At the time all this happened Somerville was a tight-knit community where the Kraus twins were well known and popular. They'd been the local high-school baseball and football heroes and Diamond T. – that is, Sheriff Waterman – had been their football coach. Both of them had won sport scholarships to college that Otto Kraus, their father, hadn't allowed them to accept. The community, Sheriff Waterman among them, had consequently regarded the twins as the victims of a stubborn and selfish father. At the time America was not far from entering the war and Otto Kraus was a German and a foreigner who'd denied his two sons a baseball scholarship, the dream of every American boy.' Abe paused. 'Putting it as politely as possible, there were not a great many tears shed in the community when Otto Kraus was interned and subsequently died. The newspapers at the time suggested he may have been a spy and that he'd committed suicide by taking poison. To add to the status the Kraus twins held in the town they'd enlisted and fought with honour in the Pacific, having participated in the battle of Iwo Jima. This was their first day home from the war and the sheriff clearly saw that he would need to be very sure of his facts before he arrested them as murder suspects.'

'But what about Frau Kraus saying she'd seen them dump Jimmy's body in the back of the Dodge truck?'

'Yes, of course, I hadn't forgotten about that. Given the known nature of the person, this may well have been the ranting of an hysterical woman. It was at this point that Sheriff Waterman advised the Kraus twins of their rights. He then confronted them with their mother's testimony that they'd thrown Jimmy's lifeless body into the back of the truck. They strenuously denied this, but admitted to the boy resisting them and so between them they'd lifted him into the truck.'

'Don't you suppose that if Jimmy had been relatively unhurt he would have jumped from the truck?' I asked.

'Ah, good question – that's precisely what they claimed happened. They explained that they'd intended driving him out of the county and sending him on his way somewhere in Bergen County, but instead he'd escaped by jumping from the back of the truck somewhere along the Kinderkamack Road. The sheriff then advised them to see a lawyer. As I'd represented the family in several other matters in the past, they came to me.'

'Did Sheriff Waterman put out a state-wide alert for Jimmy?

'An APB? Certainly.' I took this to mean an All Points Bulletin, or something similar.

'Then why didn't the highway patrol who found Jimmy report back to the Somerville sheriff's office? As I understand, the Mother General of Holy Name Hospital called Sheriff Waterman five days later?'

'I can see you're well briefed, Mr McKenzie. The same point was made during the trial. In fact, the answer was simple enough. The APB described the victim as a fifteen-year-old Negro boy and the two patrolmen later testified that the victim of the hit-and-run was, in their opinion, a male in his early twenties. Jimmy Oldcorn at fifteen was six foot tall and well muscled. His face was badly swollen and cut and this probably concealed the fact that he was only a teenager. In fact, the highway patrol report stated that they'd picked up an *adult* Negro male and, furthermore, the ambulance report described the accident victim as a Negro male of about twenty. As Jimmy wasn't capable of talking until five days later, it took that long to identify him.'

'And, of course, with Jimmy alive, circumstances changed.'

'Well, not quite everything changed. But you're correct in as much as we no longer had murder suspects on our hands.'

'You said not quite everything changed?'

'Yes, Frau Kraus stubbornly refused to withdraw her evidence.'

'Which was that Jimmy was attacked with two baseball bats and beaten unconscious, or, as she claimed, murdered?'

Abe Stennholz smiled. 'Yes, but as I previously mentioned, my clients strenuously denied this account, saying they'd merely taken the baseball bats they found in their bedroom in order to scare the boy. But, in fact, one of them had punched him in the face, which had caused his nose to bleed. At no time had the bats been used. They pointed out that they were both big men and quite capable of handling a teenage boy without having to beat him senseless with baseball bats.'

'And this explained the lack of blood on the bats?'

'Yes, of course.'

'So you suggested Frau Kraus lied about washing the bats?'

'Well, it's not unreasonable to suggest that nobody in their right mind would do such an absurd thing.'

'So, she was either crazy or she was lying?'

Abe smiled. 'Don't you think if either was the case she would have to be considered . . .' he seemed to be struggling for a word, and finally said, 'unreliable?'

'You mean she'd be lying not to *protect* her sons but in order to *harm* them?'

'Quite right. Not the actions of a mother or someone of sound mind.'

'Unless of course she *was* telling the truth and truly wanted justice for Jimmy Oldcorn. You said yourself she was obsessed with cleaning. Given this fact, wiping the bats clean was stupid but at least a plausible action, don't you think?'

Abe Stennholz smiled. 'Mr McKenzie, I was working for the defence, not the prosecution. Now let me ask *you* a question. What if there had been a more compelling reason for doubting the true state of her mind?'

'What could this possibly be?'

'Well, for instance, if the Kraus twins had arrived to find the boy in bed with Frau Kraus.'

This, of course, was the claim the sheriff had used to confront Jimmy in hospital, but I didn't let on that I knew about it. 'But that didn't happen,' I ventured instead.

'Well, as a matter of fact, when Frau Kraus seemed determined to implicate them, the Kraus twins were finally forced to submit that it did. In an attempt to protect their mother, they'd not revealed the true facts, which were that, upon their arrival home, they'd found her in bed with the Negro boy.'

'But she would deny this, and so would Jimmy.'

'There wasn't any Jimmy,' the lawyer reminded me. 'He'd effectively disappeared.'

At this point, I'm ashamed to say, I lost it again. 'Disappeared! Is that what you call it? The sheriff frightened the life out of him in hospital, then gave him twenty dollars and instructions to catch the bus to New York or he'd be in serious trouble with the law!' I cried.

Abe Stennholz leaned forward, a look of surprise and annoyance on his face. 'Oh? That's news to me, Mr McKenzie! Just where did this information come from?'

'Are you saying that isn't what happened?'

'Of course I am! There has never been the slightest suggestion that the sheriff did any such thing. The hospital report showed that Jimmy Oldcorn left the premises sometime in the early hours of the morning, and of his own accord.'

I gave him a lopsided grin and shook my head, forced to give him the benefit of the doubt. Perhaps the sheriff hadn't informed Abe Stennholz of this essential little detail.

'The law can only deal with the prevailing facts, Mr McKenzie,' Abe Stennholz now claimed self-righteously.

'Which left your case very simple. That Frau Kraus was discovered in bed with Jimmy Oldcorn by her sons returning from the war. Acting to protect her honour, they'd "helped" Jimmy on his way. If she denied this is what happened it *could* be taken as yet another instance of her disturbed state of mind. After all, no mother "in her right mind" would protect herself at the cost of her children. But here was a woman who was *prepared* to see her children accused of murder, rather than risk being indicted for corrupting a minor. Is that it?'

'Well, yes, that seems correct. The court would need to accept her testimony or that of the twins.'

'And you felt certain her word could be proved to be unreliable? That she had a motive, albeit a misguided one, for seeing that the twins were found guilty?'

Abe Stennholz shrugged. 'As the defence laywer I was obliged to make the best possible case for my clients. However, I sincerely believed what they told me. It hardly seemed plausible that they'd see the Negro boy off the property simply because Frau Kraus had allowed him to occupy their bedroom. Finding him in bed with her was a much more compelling reason for such an action.'

'So, in these changed circumstances, chasing Jimmy from the property and sending him away with a bloody nose was a very understandable reaction and could hardly be regarded as a major assault?'

'That was my contention, Mr McKenzie. I feel no need to apologise for it,' Abe Stennholz said, looking steadfast.

'What about the Mother General at the Holy Name Hospital? Wasn't she prepared to bear witness that she believed Jimmy had been beaten into a state of unconsciousness? How did you handle that?'

'Handle what? I had nothing to do with it! Are you suggesting I conspired to . . .'

About to get the lawyer badly off side, I quickly interjected. 'No, of course not, sir. I meant, what happened with the hospital testimony? Wasn't the Mother General going to testify?'

Abe Stennholz seemed only slightly mollified, but thankfully continued with the interview. 'In fact, she never appeared in court. As I was told, the doctor who attended to Jimmy when they'd brought him in, as well as the doctors who subsequently looked after him during his stay in hospital, were not prepared to swear that his injuries had been caused by a severe beating. At the time, the police had appealed for anyone witnessing the hit-and-run to come forward, and until Jimmy was able to talk, the medical staff were quite prepared on the evidence presented by his condition to accept that he'd been the victim of a hit-and-run accident. With no reliable eyewitness able to claim the boy had been beaten it was an understandable conclusion. I understood at the time that the public prosecutor decided against using Mother General Black's testimony.'

'So the case became Kraus versus Kraus? No witnesses, no victim present and no official statement from Jimmy.'

'Yes, that is correct.'

'So if you could prove Frau Kraus was an unreliable witness, you were home and hosed?'

'Home and hosed? I don't understand?'

'Ah, it's an Australian racing expression – it means it's all over, bar the shouting.'

Abe Stennholz was silent for a few moments, then said softly, 'We thought, under the circumstances, it was best that Frau Kraus wasn't put through the public humiliation of a trial.'

'I beg your pardon? I'm not sure I understand.'

Abe Stennholz looked directly at me. 'Mr McKenzie, I was a lawyer for the defence and was giving my clients the only possible legal advice I could. I also believed I could spare their mother a great deal of public humiliation if she didn't testify at the trial.'

I wasn't sure what he was getting at. 'Just what advice could you give them that would prevent Frau Kraus giving testimony and at the same time spare her public humiliation?'

'I advised them to have Frau Kraus examined by a psychiatrist.'

'Ah, I see. Naturally they accepted your advice?'

'Yes. As I guessed might be the case, the psychiatrist found that she suffered from delusions and acute paranoia.'

'These delusions, what were they? The blood on the baseball bats?'

'No, no. She was clearly disorientated and kept claiming she'd murdered her husband and that she'd also murdered the Negro boy. That his death was her fault for letting him stay in the house.'

'And the paranoia?'

'When the psychiatrist told her that Jimmy was alive, she refused to believe him and demanded to see him for herself.'

'Which, under the circumstances, wasn't unreasonable.'

'But impossible. The psychiatrist suggested she should be placed in a clinic and, in his opinion, her testimony would not have been reliable. We submitted his findings to the court, where the judge ordered a second opinion. The court appointed a psychiatrist from the State Mental Institution at Greystone Park Psychiatric Hospital, Morris Plains.'

'Let me guess – he agreed with his colleague in private practice?'

'Yes, but not until he'd closely examined her past behaviour and all the circumstances leading up to the Negro boy being chased from the Kraus farm. Then there was the fact that Frau Kraus still persisted with claiming she'd murdered her husband and was responsible for the boy's death. Abe Stennholz paused and then asked me, 'Do you know the circumstances of Otto Kraus's death?'

'Only that he died on the way to the internment camp,' I lied, again not wishing to reveal to him that I knew the complete story.

'Yes, well, he'd been incarcerated in the county jail for some time before the train journey to the internment camp. In the confusion at the time, what with war having been declared, there wasn't an official post mortem or coroner's inquiry into his death. But the military doctor who examined him came to the conclusion that he'd committed suicide, as a blood analysis after he died showed traces of arsenic poisoning in his system. The point being that Frau Kraus quite obviously had nothing to do with his death. She also confessed to an intense dislike of her sons, supporting their own evidence of her complete and early rejection of them in childhood. Finally, the Lutheran minister who attended the . . .'

'Your brother, wasn't it?' I interjected.

Abe Stennholz didn't miss a beat, completely ignoring my remark. '. . . funeral of her husband, Otto Kraus, told how she'd placed a crude black paper rose on his grave, whereupon she'd spat onto the casket and announced, '*Danke, meine saubere Frau*,' after which she'd laughed hysterically, so that he was forced to slap her to calm her down. This, taken along with the further evidence from several members of her church congregation of her strange or erratic behaviour in their presence, all added up to a profile of someone who was mentally disturbed.'

'So Frau Kraus wasn't present at the trial. I take it the twins agreed to have her committed to a clinic for treatment.'

'No, she was admitted to Greystone Park.'

'Why not a clinic?' I asked.

'The Kraus twins had her examined a third time by a forensic psychiatrist who told them there was no possibility that she'd recover, even with electric-shock treatment. Greystone Park was the logical recommendation.'

'Putting her away for keeps.'

Abe Stennholz didn't reply.

I've subsequently done a little research on Greystone Park Hospital, one of the very few mental institutions in New Jersey at the time. In 1945, the year Frau Kraus entered this notorious place, the inmate population exceeded 5000! Frau Kraus would simply have disappeared into this bedlam, never to surface again.

'With nobody to testify for the prosecution, did any trial eventuate?' I asked.

Abe Stennholz gave me an indignant look. 'Of course – my clients had wilfully attacked a minor, there was no getting away from that.'

'And the judge's verdict?'

'You think it was a conspiracy, don't you, Mr McKenzie?'

'Well, sir, you have to admit, everything seems to have fallen very neatly into place for the Kraus twins.'

'You could say so, but there was additional evidence to suggest they were telling the truth.'

'Oh?'

'Sheriff Waterman sent the two baseball bats in for forensic examination. Blood, as you may know, is very difficult to eliminate and they did find a very small trace.'

'Ah! They then tested it against Jimmy's blood group? The hospital would have known what that was.'

'Of course. The blood trace they found was well into the grain of one of the bats, high up on the grip, and it didn't match the Negro boy's. In fact, it turned out to belong to Fritz Kraus. At some time in the past he must have received a crack on the hand from a baseball that had caused him to bleed.'

'What about the back of the truck? If, as you say, blood is difficult to eliminate, would there not have been traces of blood there as well?'

'Unfortunately, the truck had been steam cleaned. This was easily enough explained. As any nurseryman will tell you, tomato plants need to be transported in a very clean environment so as not to pick up diseases. But they did find a trace of blood that matched the Negro boy's blood group. This was put down to him having suffered a haemorrhage from the nose, explained by the nosebleed the twins had admitted giving him.'

'And that was the final conclusive evidence?'

'That, and the report of the two psychiatrists, and the fact that the Negro boy had disappeared without making a statement.'

Any further questioning seemed pointless. Abe Stennholz had all the answers.

'You have a remarkable memory, sir,' I said. 'After all, this took place over twenty years ago.'

'Thank you, Mr McKenzie, but that's not entirely true. The reason I wouldn't see you yesterday was so that I could read through the case file and acquaint myself with the precise facts.'

'Which leaves me only three further things to ask you. What verdict did the judge come to?'

'The judge accepted that my clients had acted unlawfully. They were found guilty and fined fifty dollars each and placed on a good-behaviour bond.'

'And so a violent and unprovoked racial crime, perpetrated against an innocent juvenile, was reduced to a confrontation that involved giving a minor a bloody nose and driving him out of the county, where, due to no fault of the perpetrators, he met with an unfortunate road accident. The net result being a hundred-dollar rap on the knuckles for the Kraus twins and an admonishment not to do it again, not to mention Frau Kraus's permanent loss of freedom!' Abe Stennholz chose to ignore this outburst. 'What happened to the twins?' I then asked.

'Fritz never recovered from the war and became an alcoholic. He was eventually killed in an automobile accident. Henrik took up politics and still serves in the New Jersey legislature. He sold the farm and later took up real estate and has made a considerable fortune.'

'Are you likely to see him at any time?'

'Not deliberately, but he's not hard to contact.'

'I wonder if you would be kind enough to give him a message?' I asked.

'That would depend entirely on the message,' Abe Stennholz said cautiously.

'Can you tell him Jimmy hasn't forgotten the beating and he'll be around to see him one of these days.'

'I don't believe I will give him that message, sir!' the lawyer said sharply. Then he added, 'You had a third question?'

'Do you feel justice was served, sir?'

Abe Stennholz's blue eyes showed a momentary flash of anger and he rose from his chair. 'I think it's time you left, Mr McKenzie.' Then, almost as quickly, he recovered, pointing at the sky. 'It's getting dark, and Martha will be fixing my supper,' he announced.

'And you feel no remorse?' I asked, standing up and preparing to leave.

I fully expected him to dismiss me angrily. But I told myself what the hell, I had nothing to lose. Instead, Abe Stennholz looked at me steadily and then said, 'Mr McKenzie, as a born-again Christian and also a lawyer, the secular and the spiritual worlds are not always compatible. While I have no doubt whatsoever that Frau Kraus was mentally disturbed, she was harmless enough. I truly regret that this normally quiet and in many ways competent woman was forced, due to the prevailing circumstances, to spend the remainder of her life in a state mental institution.'

'Do you know if she is still alive?'

'I believe she passed away about a year ago.'

'And Jimmy Oldcorn? No regrets?'

He seemed genuinely surprised at my question. 'Regrets? None! I never knew the boy.'

'Would you like to know what happened to him?' I asked.

'No, sir, I would not!' he said firmly. 'I must go in now, Martha will be waiting to serve my dinner.'

I extended my hand. 'Thank you, Mr Stennholz, I appreciate the time you've given me.'

He took my hand, his grip no longer firm as he shook it in an uninterested manner, looking over my head. 'You're welcome,' he said, then, turning, walked through the door into the darkness beyond.

Jimmy, with a nose now permanently flattened by way of a baseball bat and wearing an ugly scar down the left side of his face, looked a great deal older and meaner than his fifteen years. Which was a good thing – taken along with his size, these are the sort of looks that street kids take seriously.

Jimmy managed to live on his seventy dollars for sufficient time to see his bruises all but disappear and to get the plaster from his hand removed and his fingers working again. But this was not until the plaster had served him well, so that he was almost reluctant to see it go.

After a month of wandering around, sleeping in a disused shed behind a mechanic's workshop until he was moved on by the cops, he finally found a room on the first floor of a condemned tenement. The major feature of the disused and dirty room was that it contained a fireplace. It was now the beginning of December, with the days closing in and the nights bitterly cold. On the first night Jimmy managed to gather sufficient wood from bits of old discarded furniture for a fire, although when it died down in the early hours of the morning he nearly froze to death.

The following day he came across a pile of old blankets in the basement of the same building and helped himself to four of them. Late that same afternoon a gang of black kids burst into his room, accusing him of stealing their blankets. The leader, a boy nearly Jimmy's size, confronted him with the theft and, without warning, punched Jimmy on the jaw, knocking him to the ground.

'Dat time I ain't no fightin' man, Brother Fish. Dis dude he hit me where mah jaw still sore an' I git up, I mad as hell an' I hit him back wid da hand got da plaster. I don't think about it got plaster – it mah right hand an' I hit dat dude natural, 'cos I right-handed. He go straight down like he pole-axed an' he lay der, his eyes dey rolled back in his head, he ain't done no movin'. I sup-prised – I also scared, man! Der's eight dem mothers standin' der.'

'"Fuck, one punch!" one dem says, and he pull a switchblade on me.

'"Hey man, you wanna be next?" I say to him, like as if I ain't scared. But o' course inside I shittin' mah birthday jeans. But dis little dude wid da switchblade, his name it turn out is Marty, he make me a prop-po-sition. He say maybe I can join Da Brotherhood? Dat what der name is, der motto, he tell me, it "one for all, all for one". Well, I ain't got no better idea for survivin' and mah money it jus' about all gone. So I bullshit an' I tell him I think about it, 'cos I got me one or two offers from some da other gangs in da borough and I ain't made up my mind yet. "Come back in two days, but meantime I keep dem blankets," I say to him. Two days later dey come back an' I tell dem, okay, I der man. Dat when I start to learn good how to be bad.'

I guess a gang of homeless kids doesn't change much over the years, requiring two essential characteristics – sufficient members to defend themselves and their territory, and yet to be small enough to supply their collective needs. It was here that Jimmy first began to show his talent for organisation. While the gang had borrowed the motto from *The Three Musketeers* – 'All for one, one for all' – they had little idea of how to make it work. This was well illustrated by the fact that they hadn't rushed to overpower Jimmy when he'd knocked their leader down with his plastered hand. Now they looked to him for leadership, unaware that he'd never done any street fighting and had little or no experience in the business of staying alive on the streets of New York.

It was most fortunate for Jimmy that, with the exception of the recipient of his lucky plaster punch, the gang he now led were all younger and smaller than him. As it turned out, the guy he'd king-hit was a bully and a coward, and constantly made a mockery of their motto by ruling the rest of the gang by violence and intimidation. When he'd finally regained consciousness, to Jimmy's relief, he hadn't been game to take the matter any further. Instead, he'd skulked away, leaving the room and calling out to the others to follow him. They'd left reluctantly, with Marty, the kid who'd pulled the switchblade, the last to go. Pausing momentarily at the door, he said, 'Hey, Joe Louis, one fuckin' punch, eh!'

Two days later they returned and Jimmy agreed to be part of the Brotherhood. They then introduced themselves, prefacing each of their names with the word 'brother', a habit Jimmy brought with him to Korea when he pronounced me first Brother Jacko and then later Brother Fish.

Somewhat to Jimmy's surprise the Brotherhood immediately elected him as their leader, with Brother Marty second in command. The bloke Jimmy had knocked out moved on, no longer able to command the gang's respect. Jimmy found himself leading the youngest street gang in the borough. With fourteen-year-old Brother Marty as his offsider, he was about to learn the value of leadership qualities on the streets of the Bronx under extreme combat conditions.

It was a credit to Jimmy's leadership that the gang avoided trouble with the police for nine months, but eventually they were caught breaking into a warehouse and Jimmy was sent to Elmira Reformatory. He learned a lot at Elmira, but not what the strict military routine and intense Christian indoctrination had intended. Like the orphanage, Elmira's agenda had been to make him a God-fearing nigger with the 'right' attitude, subservient enough for the humblest of work.

After eighteen months, at the age of eighteen, Jimmy's time was up and he was on the streets again. To survive, he found himself another gang, which lived by 'protecting' a row of shops for a moderate but accepted sum from shopkeepers. But conflict erupted when another gang moved in on the territory, and resulted in Jimmy being charged with grievous bodily harm. Jimmy ended up in the US Army as an alternative to jail.

Of course, Jimmy wasn't to know then that what he would learn running a New York street gang would one day serve him brilliantly as a prisoner of war in Korea. I haven't the slightest doubt that Jimmy's qualities of leadership saved my life, as well as the lives of many other prisoners of war – men who would otherwise have given up out of a sense of hopelessness and despair. It only ever takes one man to stand up and spit in the face of extreme adversity to save the clan. Jimmy Oldcorn was our man.

# CHAPTER ELEVEN

## *A Place Where the Guards Wear Horace Horse Boots*

We joined a truckload of prisoners heading north, and the two-and-a-half-day journey, with the end of summer approaching but the flies not yet gone, was miserable but uneventful. We finally arrived at the POW camp somewhere on the border of China just after dawn, though quite where the camp was situated along the border was anybody's guess. We'd travelled by night to avoid observation by enemy aircraft, this time successfully. Though all the way I kept thinking that if our aircraft found us and dropped flares prior to destroying our convoy, this time Jimmy and I would be able to leave the truck and seek safety rather than be sitting ducks, alone in a truck, anchored by our plastered legs.

The POW camp was huge and seemed to contain members of just about every army fighting for the United Nations, though, understandably, the predominance of prisoners were the Americans, of which there were around a thousand.

A great deal has been written about the collapse of morale and the unpatriotic behaviour of American prisoners under the Chinese in the Korean War. It has become one of those dark chapters in American military history, and as a consequence the Korean War is given less historical attention than many of the other conflicts in which America has been engaged. Many believe that in the Korean War, American soldiers taken as prisoners of war failed the expectations of the American people.

However, while I have been somewhat critical of the way some of the young, poorly trained US soldiers fought in Korea, I would say that based on my own experience in a POW camp, to come down exclusively on the Yank behaviour in captivity is unfair. In truth, few of us came out of the experience untainted. This was due, in part, to the way the Chinese operated, and not necessarily caused by a lack of courage under extreme hardship and privation.

I've touched on the subject before: war and extreme challenge are things for which men need to be prepared. We are not natural predators – the warrior has to be trained into us. In the face of fight or flight, the latter is the much more powerful instinct. Early man soon discovered that to escape a dangerous opponent was almost always the better option. If you want a man to stand and fight, or to endure physical and emotional hardship and aggression, you have to prepare him slowly. Good citizens without training make lousy soldiers. The warrior you can rely on to do his duty is not born out of a few weeks of yelling and square-bashing in boot camp. It takes a long period of hard training during which soldiers overcome hardships together to forge the bonds, loyalty, confidence and mateship that help to withstand the stresses of the battlefield and those experienced in captivity.

Among the men fighting in the United Nations forces, a far greater proportion of Americans were conscripts. They were young, callow, soft and vastly under-trained with no physical and psychological preparation for what they found waiting for them in Korea. Most of the earlier troops in Korea had come from the occupation forces in Japan. Those that hadn't been conscripts were boys playing at being men, lured to Japan by promises of a good time. They were virgin soldiers in every possible meaning of the term, and should never have been allowed near the business end of a rifle. Now, as prisoners of war, they found themselves living in appalling conditions, lacking even the most basic medical treatment. Depending on the time of the year, they were either bitterly cold or dying of dehydration caused by dysentery and the heat. They were starving, lice-ridden, dirty and sick with beri-beri, roundworm or any of the other little destroyers that come from living in sub-human conditions without antibiotics. They also lacked the maturity and leadership that held the professionally trained soldiers from the other nations more or less together. The thirty-eight per cent death rate amongst the US prisoners was nearly three times higher than for any other nation and the American rate of collaboration with the enemy was later to cause anxiety and a Senate inquiry at home. All this suggested a lack of physical and mental preparation for the exigencies of war.

The undoing of many of these young American prisoners was something known as the Chinese Lenient Policy. The policy's underlying promise was that living conditions within the prison camp would be greatly improved in return for cooperation from prisoners with their captors. Coming to accept 'the truth' meant more food, warm clothing and some rudimentary medical care. At the time, many prisoners believed cooperating with the enemy would save their lives. In some instances they may have been correct. Declaring that they'd seen the error of their ways and publicly admitting to the shortcomings of the capitalist system was to become yet another survival technique.

Under these prevailing conditions it wasn't all that difficult to compromise one's principles. Especially if, in the first instance, these principles weren't all that well grounded in past experience. It wasn't as if collaboration with the Chinese was going to affect the outcome of the war. No lives would be lost as a consequence of non-military information given to the enemy. Nothing you could say would seriously compromise America. Collaboration could be rationalised by a starving soldier as a purely pyrrhic victory for the communists – no more than propaganda and of no real or permanent consequence.

Every prisoner of war has to decide just how far he will cooperate with his captors. The legal minimum is, of course, to provide number, rank and name, but this was never going to be enough for the Chinese.

To refuse to answer all other questions was to invite punishment often so severe it led to death. For instance, one Australian prisoner, Private Madden, captured at the Battle of Kapyong, resisted all attempts to make him collaborate and died of malnutrition and sickness. Madden must have been quite a guy, because he was said to have shared his starvation rations with those of his mates who were, in his opinion, worse off than him. I'm happy to know that he was awarded the George Cross posthumously. While I'd like to think I might have behaved in the same way, a small voice within tells me that I probably would have failed in the extreme bravery stakes.

In the cave where I had first met Jimmy we'd witnessed the combined effects of malnutrition, bitter cold, mistreatment and sickness, and how it affected the morale of a soldier. In combination these conditions often promoted self-survival and selfish behaviour. But we were not prepared for the extent this had occurred in the POW camp. Here, 'I'm all right, Jack' – the Australian euphemism for putting your own needs ahead of the greater good – had gained an entirely new dimension.

While I was not the only Australian prisoner of war in Korea, I was only one of two in this particular camp, where, incidentally, the Chinese separated the American Negro prisoners from the Caucasians. Jimmy twigged to this soon after we arrived and told a Chinese officer that I was an Aboriginal albino and should therefore stay with him. I confirmed the story and the confused officer consulted his superior. I later learned the request went all the way along the line to the camp commandant, who reasoned my story must be true, otherwise why on earth would I, a white-skinned person, want to live with blacks. Anyway, they swallowed it and this was how I ended up among the Americans instead of the British Commonwealth group.

The Americans had been in the camp longest and many had endured two winters in captivity. Even worse, they'd initially been under the control of the North Koreans, whose brutality far exceeded the Chinese and who were totally indifferent to human suffering. In that first fiercely cold winter the prisoners had even been denied wood for heating. They were in terrible shape, and those confined to the so-called hospital hut were pitiful in the extreme. They lay in their own excrement, unwashed, uncared for, with maggots crawling over their suppurating sores and open wounds.

'Holy shit, Brother Fish, what we got here?' Jimmy said, rubbing his beard.

'A bloody sight more than we can handle between us, mate,' I answered.

'We gotta try – dese men, dey got no more respect. Dey gonna die 'cos dey cain't find no reason to live.' He turned and looked at me. 'We gotta find dat reason an' give it back to dem cats.'

'Mate, these blokes are past it. We'd be wasting our time,' I protested.

'Ain't got nothin' better to do wid our time, Brother Fish.'

*Here we bloody go again.* 'Jimmy, you can't save the whole fucking world!' I protested.

Jimmy turned and looked down at me. 'Brother Fish, if we don't try we gonna die in dis place. Trying, dat what gonna keep you an' me a-live.'

The morale of the Americans had long since hit rock bottom. Discipline had broken down completely, and compassion for the sick and wounded was non-existent. Officer and sergeant prisoners had been segregated in their own compounds and there didn't seem to be any organised attempts to help each other within their group. Everyone was living in a cocoon known as 'selfish survival behaviour' – a contradictory condition, because it invariably shortens the survival factor and eventually leads to death or complete mental collapse.

'We gotta find "da man", Brother Fish,' Jimmy said.

'The man? What man?'

'Der always one, maybe two. Dey rule, dey bad – dey "da man".'

'Mate, how do you know there's one?' I asked him.

'Dis a prison, ain't it? In prison dere always "da man". You'll see, it da same here.'

It didn't take us long. His name was Corporal Steve O'Rourke, a white American from Little Rock, Arkansas – the standover man and resident psychopath. We learned that during the previous winter he'd tossed two men, both gravely weakened by dysentery, out of the barracks, where they'd frozen to death. The stink caused by their condition apparently offended him. Such was the impoverished moral condition in the camp that there had been no recrimination, no protest – O'Rourke had literally been allowed to get away with murder. Now, together with a bunch of fellow thugs, he ruled the American camp by means of fear and intimidation, and frustrated any attempts to restore order. His power lay in anarchy.

'How are you going to get at him, mate?' I asked Jimmy. 'He's got a dozen enforcers with him, and there's only the two of us.'

'We wait – he come to us. Den maybe da rumble happen,' Jimmy replied, then added the single word 'Ogoya'.

I had absolutely no idea what he meant by this – why would Operation Get Off Your Arse be a reason for Corporal Steve O'Rourke to confront us? I had forgotten the example of the hospital cave where the creation of a collective had frustrated the selfish aspirations of the individual and brought about the challenge of the big southerner, Ward Brady Buckworth Junior.

It had been less than a week since our plaster had been removed and we were still on crutches – me with my standard Chinese bamboo pair and Jimmy on his Captain Hook. We were certainly in no condition to fight anyone, even supposing I was a handy man to have at your side in a fight – which I wasn't. I hadn't inherited my old man Alf's ability with his fists. In my poor condition I wasn't much looking forward to the confrontation with O'Rourke that Jimmy seemed to think was inevitable.

It was difficult enough coping with the conditions in the camp – particularly for me in a hut comprised entirely of Negro soldiers. I found myself the single white guy, and also the smallest amongst us. If it hadn't been for Jimmy's large, facially scarred presence, I don't think I would have lasted very long. The prisoners in our barracks were completely demoralised and for the first two days very few words were spoken to us. Men with blank eyes would stare through us as if we weren't there. They'd ignore our questions or answer with a mumbled monosyllable. Moreover, I was to discover that while my ear had become attuned to Jimmy's 'dis and dat' dialect, his mode of expression was by no means universal among his kind. Coloured Americans, even in the 1950s, didn't all sound the same. There were several regional and ghetto dialects and expressions among the prisoners in our barracks, and most of them were initially incomprehensible to me until I began to understand the different argot. There were also one or two who spoke what Jimmy referred to as 'turkey talk', though even the way the white blokes spoke often showed vast syntactical and cultural differences. In Australia, while the odd expression may differ, we all sound pretty much the same. It hadn't occurred to me that America's population was so large that the different states could be likened to different countries and cultures.

The day we arrived, those of us who'd travelled together in the truck were lined up on parade in front of a dais where the camp commandant began by delivering what might be described as a 'spit-flecked' address, shouting at us angrily, though in surprisingly good English. 'You are war criminals!' he accused, pointing his finger down at us. 'You have fought in an illegal and unjust war of aggression against the peace-loving people of Korea! Under the precedents set by the Nuremberg war crimes trials, we have the right to execute every one of you!'

'Here come da judge,' Jimmy said, out of the corner of his mouth. 'First come da bad news, den come da good news.'

I had become accustomed to Jimmy's perspicacity, and sure enough, after a bit more invective, the commandant's demeanour suddenly changed and his verbal outrage screamed to a sudden and quite unexpected halt, like a truck forced to stop suddenly on a dirt road. He shifted down two gears into what might be described as the 'benevolent uncle' tone of voice.

'But we are not like you,' he continued, slowly and calmly. 'We regard you as *misguided*. You do not know you are criminals! You have been duped by your capitalist masters, but do not know this. It is not your fault.' He smiled sadly as if sympathising with us. 'So the Chinese People's Volunteers extend to you their Lenient Policy.' He paused and then smiled down at us benignly. 'The Lenient Policy means that we will not extract our rightful blood debt. It also means something else just as important.' He smiled again and spread his hands. 'We are going to give you the opportunity to learn *the truth*.'

'And da truth shall set yoh free . . . dat from da bible,' Jimmy whispered to me.

The commandant changed gear once again and assumed a semi-menacing manner. 'But the Lenient Policy has its limits! Those who *refuse* to learn *the truth* will put themselves outside its mercy and benefits.'

Eventually, with a bit more hot'n'cold rhetoric, he completed his address, and we were commanded to salute before being marched away.

This was quite unlike any prison camp I'd imagined or seen in newsreels or movies. There were no towers, searchlights or high barbed-wire fences. In every direction were thatched mud-and-wattle houses and an occasional slightly bigger building with a corrugated-iron roof. They were the kind of structures you'd expect to find in any large Korean village, which the camp may well have once been. This, of course, made it difficult to distinguish it as a prison camp from the air. But this need for camouflage opened the way for prisoners to escape as there couldn't possibly be sufficient guards to watch the whole perimeter of this vast camp, and the few we saw didn't look too concerned. Perhaps they correctly surmised that we were in the middle of the boondocks and that there wasn't an easy and safe destination to escape to.

The mud houses that were referred to as barracks were for the prisoners, and the tin-roofed buildings housed the Chinese soldiers and staff. The guard escorting us to our accommodation rather proudly ran a commentary for us in broken English, and pointed to a set of distant buildings somewhat separated from the rest of the camp. 'No want go that place,' he said. 'Velly bad.'

Our group was divided between two mud houses while Jimmy and I were told to stand aside. After all the others had been allocated their quarters we were taken a few rows further down where the Negro compound stood. 'You not black foreign devil. Why I ordered you stay here?' the guard said, obviously surprised that I was to be placed among the American Negroes and apologising for what he thought must be an administrative bungle he was nevertheless forced to obey.

'Ho!' Jimmy said later. 'Da Chinese too – dey got dis-crim-in-nation, Brother Fish.' In the years to come we would learn that the Chinese people were possibly the most racist people on earth and that, to them, to be black-skinned placed a person on the very bottom rung of the human evolutionary ladder. Although, I must say, the Chinese guards in the POW camp, while separating black from white, did not appear to discriminate and the black soldiers fared no worse than the white.

Jimmy and I were ushered into a room about eight feet square and a Negro prisoner pointed to a spot against the wall. 'Y'all take Ed and Charlie's place,' he said.

We placed our gear down where he'd indicated. 'What happened to them?' I asked.

The soldier looked at me and then at Jimmy, and then asked, 'Who dis punk?'

Jimmy looked suddenly angry. 'Don't call him no punk, yoh hear? He mah friend, dude. Now answer da man's question. What happen to dem two?'

'One, he got beri-beri, he in hospital. D'other he jus' back from Kennel Club – he also in hospital.'

'Kennel Club?' Jimmy asked.

'Punishment box, five feet long, four feet high.' The soldier separated his hands about two feet. 'This wide, an' yoh lie on your back. They don't let yoh outta der – only for latrine or so they can beat you, and yoh got no blanket at night.'

The effort it took to give this explanation seemed to have been too much for him and he suddenly sat down against the wall hugging his knees, head thrown back, eyes closed. I remembered my own stay in the cage with Dave McCombe and shuddered. I noticed the cracks around his mouth, indicating he was malnourished. We all had these cracks, but somehow I'd hoped the grub at the POW camp might be a little better than the various field hospitals we'd been in. Fat hope.

'What happen when dem cats get back?' Jimmy asked.

'Ain't comin' back,' the man said, then closed down again, this time resting his chin on his chest, his knees obscuring his mouth as if to indicate that he'd terminated the conversation. We were to learn that going to hospital was an almost certain death sentence.

On the way to our compound I'd seen a hand-printed sign that read 'Royal Ulster Rifles'. As most Australians have more than a dash of Irish in them, I made my way over to make their acquaintance. I confess I'd been with Americans too long and looked forward to a slightly different viewpoint. In my experience, the Irish and Australians have a good deal in common. Approaching on crutches, I observed a scrawny, red-headed bloke sitting outside a mud house sewing a button onto his tunic.

'G'day,' I said.

He looked up and smiled. 'You'd be Australian, then?' he said right off.

I nodded. 'Know if there are any others around?' I was hoping I might find Dave McCombe.

'Was one, if I remember rightly. Moved on.'

'Moved on? What, died?'

'No, I'd be thinking they moved him on to another camp.'

'You wouldn't remember his name?'

'Now, I'd by lying if I said I did. To be honest, I didn't know him meself,' he replied.

'By the way, I'm Jacko McKenzie,' I offered.

'Doug Waterman.' He extended his hand. 'Pleased t'meetcha, Jacko. Just come in, have you?'

'Yeah, early this morning.'

'I see. When and where were you captured?'

'November. Wounded on patrol north of the Imjin River practically on the border.'

'We've been hearin' you fellas gave the boogers a bit of a belting at Kapyong.'

'Well, I don't know about that, mate. We certainly brought a good few of 'em to a screaming, if temporary, halt.'

He looked at his watch and bit the end off the cotton, the button on his tunic once again secure. 'Well, we'd better be down to the company kitchen for a feed – for what it's worth.' Then he corrected himself. 'The food's pretty bloody awful – it smells and tastes like shit, and it might well be exactly that and all, but you'll be taking my advice, Jacko; eat it and eat it all – there's that many dying of malnutrition, it's no joke.'

'I'm not with you blokes.' I pointed to the American compound.

'How come? You should be with the Commonwealth lot, with us.'

I explained about Jimmy and his albino ploy and the Irishman laughed. 'If you're going to lie to this lot, be extravagant and remember what you said – it's the simple explanations they suspect. Come along, anyway, you'll not be taking anyone else's food. You'll be getting no more than the smell of an oily rag, and there's no seconds.'

On the way he explained the camp system to me. There were three rooms to every mud house with a squad of a dozen or more in each room to make up a platoon. The houses were in a cluster roughly sufficient to house a company of soldiers and the cluster was known as a compound. 'Except for your lot,' he laughed. 'You're known as the ghetto.' He went on to explain that the officer and sergeant prisoners had their own compounds where the men had very little contact with them.

At the company cookhouse we were given a bowl of boiled millet and a spoon. I had grown to detest the vile stuff, but I took Doug Waterman's advice and ate every grain. It later became apparent that, in the grub stakes, the Chinese didn't discriminate – the food in our cookhouse was every bit as bad as the stuff I'd shared with the Ulsterman.

When I got back to our compound the company was assembling and we were marched to a parade ground in the centre of the camp. We arrived to find more than a thousand men already standing at ease, and I could see a lot more prisoners and their guards streaming in from every direction. A public-address system in front of a better-looking building than most had been set up on a raised platform flanked by wooden steps. These buildings were apparently the camp headquarters.

After the last of the prisoners had arrived, a Chinese officer rose to the platform. He cleared his throat in front of the mike and hawked the result in an arch over the platform to the feet of the front row of men standing below him. The effect had been magnified by the microphone and drew a titter from the crowd. The Chinese did this all the time and it didn't necessarily indicate contempt. We'd got accustomed to the practice, though I'd never before heard the disgusting habit dramatised over a loudspeaker.

'Four prisoners try to escape!' he yelled, holding his hand above his head with four fingers extended. 'They have rejected the generosity of the Lenient Policy and are war criminals! They can now be legitimately shot!' The commandant paused, and looked around at the assembly. 'But we are not capitalist warmongers and have given them the chance to repent and embrace *the truth*.' He turned to look towards the wooden steps where a tall, gaunt man looking much the worse for wear was being escorted by a guard to the microphone. The prisoner began to speak, hesitatingly at first, the microphone positioned too low for us to catch his voice except for small snatches that made little sense. A Chinese soldier rushed up carrying a set of mud bricks under his chin then, lowering himself to his knees, he unloaded the bricks and built them into a platform, placing the microphone stand upon it. Evidently

Chinese microphones were not built to extend any further than roughly the height of the officer who'd just addressed us.

'I shall begin again,' the gaunt man said, in a pronounced English accent. 'I have been wrong to try to escape and I am only now beginning to understand that the warmongers of Wall Street have had me in their greedy grasp. They have befuddled my mind. Their lies have been a blindfold so secure that even though I have received the kindness of the Chinese People's Volunteers I have previously been unable to see the light. But now they have shown me the *true* path, lighting my way in what was previously the darkness of my mind.' His voice then seemed close to tears as he announced, 'I want to apologise for abusing the hospitality of the Chinese People's Volunteers.

'I want to warn you all of the folly of trying to escape. I want to remind you of the generosity of our Chinese hosts, who feed us. I want to tell you food is very difficult to find beyond this camp. Here the Chinese People's Volunteers' kitchens cook our food; out there how can you cook what little food you come across? Why suffer sore feet following the rough mountain track north, why wade through three dangerous rivers and risk getting lost, when you can enjoy the comfort of the housing of the Chinese People's Volunteers? I want to apologise to the Chinese People's Volunteers at the checkpoints along the bridges and roads for causing them unnecessary trouble. But most of all, I am forever grateful to the small boy from the village close to the confluence of the two rivers who saw me and reported me to the authorities. It is through him I was brought back here where I can have the blindfold lifted that has prevented me from seeing the truth.'

The camp commandant and the officers with him on the platform were beaming from ear to ear and, to my enormous surprise, a large number of the prisoners were cheering.

'Jesus, Jimmy, what's goin' on? These blokes are bloody cheering?'

'Brother Fish, I been most of mah life in places like this. What dat soldier sayin' he ain't saying – he sayin' somethin' contrariwise and opposite.'

'Huh? Whaddyamean?'

'Well, the way's I heard it like so. He done told us iffen we escape we gotta take food and somethin' to cook it. He say make sure yo' boots is in good re-pair, follow da mountain track north, cross three rivers and watch for da guards – dey stationed at da bridges and roads. He say to take some navigation e-quip-ment wid you and, above all, stay clear dem North Korean chillen near where two rivers meet.'

Doug Waterman later gave me a more or less identical interpretation. He explained that the gaunt bloke was the British forces escape organiser. What Jimmy knew instinctively, I had yet to learn. But I did learn something from the episode without Jimmy's assistance. I'd guessed correctly the reason the Chinese were not concerned about the camp's lack of perimeter security was that they considered it near impossible for anyone to last long outside. The British soldier had said it all – rugged terrain, a population hostile to the prisoners and Chinese soldiers patrolling the roads and bridges. Add to that our weakened state and the distance to the front-line and I could see why they would sacrifice perimeter security for camouflage from the air.

However, learning of a quite different kind was in store for us. The following day the twenty new arrivals were assembled for our first talk by the company political officer. It seemed every company was allotted one of these coves whose job it was to indoctrinate us. Our bloke, Lieutenant Dinh, spoke passable English and informed us that the day's topic would be 'The South's Aggression Against the North'.

The rave was pretty predictable stuff. The South attacked the innocent, peace-loving and prosperous North when the American running-dog president Syngman Rhee decided he wanted all of Korea for the purpose of capitalist exploitation by his few millionaire cronies in the South, who had grown rich by keeping the masses poverty-stricken and enslaved. The criminal, Syngman Rhee, could not allow the remainder of the world to see how the people of the North prospered under communism while the South suffered great hardship under capitalism, so he'd decided to invade with the help of the Wall

Street profiteers who stood to make untold fortunes from supplying him with weapons.

However, determined to defend their gains under communism, the shocked and peace-loving North bravely repelled the criminal attack. When, armed with a righteous cause, they'd beaten back the *invading* army from the South, lo and behold, the Americans had arrived to save their South Korean lackeys from humiliation and defeat, blah, blah, blah. This, of course, is an encapsulated version of Dinh's talk, which continued for more than two immensely dreary hours.

Once Dinh had finished speaking, he invited discussion and questions. Silence followed, and when he insisted I have a go I spoke my mind, which, in retrospect, was bloody stupid. 'I have seen North Korea. I have been in the capital, Pyongyang, and in many of the villages, and there is no prosperity – and it is easy to see there has never been any. Am I to tell my eyes that they are lying, Lieutenant Dinh?' I then asked what was to be my killer question. 'Why didn't I see any refugees streaming North?'

I could sense Jimmy's discomfort beside me, and at one point he cleared his throat noisily as a warning not to continue. But in my Little General mode I wasn't going to waste all that good stuff I'd learned as my so-called excuse for joining K Force, so I let Dinh have the lot – the whole catastrophe, chapter and verse.

Lieutenant Dinh made no attempt to answer me. 'So,' he said, 'we have a *reactionary* amongst us.' He looked at me disdainfully. 'You may try to prevent your fellow war criminals learning the truth, but you will not succeed. You must please understand that a hostile attitude will put you outside the Lenient Policy. I will give you one more chance.'

And then Dinh began to talk again. Blah, blah, bloody blah, going on forever about Wall Street warmongers and profiteers bought by the blood of the proletariat. Before he finally stopped this seemingly endless monologue, he frequently paused to ask if we understood him, without waiting for any confirmation before continuing. At the conclusion of his talk he started to quiz us on what he'd said. This took another hour.

It was late, and finally the time for our afternoon meal came and went, but still he continued. When he'd finally finished we hot-footed it to the company cookhouse where we were waved away, the food all long since gone. To add insult to injury, Jimmy and I were told to stay back to wash a whole pile of enamel dishes. There wasn't a hope of finding any leftovers on them as the plates had been licked clean.

It wasn't difficult to tell that everyone knew that because of my stupid carry-on we were being deliberately punished. Even being chosen for the dishwashing chore wasn't exactly a coincidence.

'What a shit act of Dinh!' I exclaimed to Jimmy in an effort to shift the blame.

'Brother Fish, da new arrivals here dey ain't happy, man. Yoh fucked us real good! No chow, dat da punishment we got.'

'Yeah, I know,' I finally admitted, thoroughly ashamed of myself.

'In America,' Jimmy replied, 'iffen a white man he tell a Negro somethin', it da God's truth. It ain't da truth because it make good sense, it ain't da truth because it based on a fact or der lotsa ev-e-dence. It da truth because he a white man and you a nigger.' He paused, and sighed. 'In dis camp we all niggers, Brother Fish.' It was the closest Jimmy had ever come to reprimanding me.

'Mate, I've been a real prick. What can I do to make it up to the blokes?'

'Somethin' will come up – never yoh mind 'bout dat, Brother Fish,' Jimmy said calmly.

The next day the whole company was assembled and we were marched once again to the company lecture area to endure another two-hour lecture.

'Brother Fish, you listen up good,' Jimmy said to me.

'Don't worry, mate, I'm not going to open my big trap,' I replied, still chastened from the previous day's verbal diarrhoea.

'Nah, it ain't dat – jus' listen up *real* good,' he suggested again.

To our surprise, Lieutenant Dinh started by saying that the cookhouse had reported that a tin plate had gone missing and although he knew we were not responsible, as we'd missed the afternoon meal, this was a typical capitalist act and against the spirit of the Lenient Policy. I wanted to ask why this was so. One tin plate missing among hundreds was hardly a misdemeanour worth mentioning, but of course, after the previous day, I wasn't going to open my mouth. He carried on about the tin plate for ages, pointing out that the smallest dishonesty was no less harmful to the proletariat than the largest possible crime. Somehow he managed to weave the goddamn tin plate into the day's lecture theme, which was 'The Inevitable March of World History Towards Communism'.

We were allowed to sit on the ground during this long preface, followed by a much longer and extremely tedious lecture. I noted how most of the blokes around me had nodded off. At the end of the verbal marathon we returned to our compound where we were instructed to run a discussion. To my surprise, Jimmy led me over to the white American compound where the new arrivals who'd been present at the previous day's lecture lived. To ensure the discussion took place the Chinese gave us a list of written questions, and we were required to produce written responses. But upon arrival at the two white American houses most of the blokes promptly fell asleep, and one or two small groups started a desultory game of cards.

'Hey, what about the written answers?' I asked Jimmy.

'Dat somethin' I mention be sure to come up – well, it jus' come up, Brother Fish,' Jimmy said, grinning.

My punishment had arrived. I was required to be scribe for the next five lectures before we finally returned to our own compound. Jimmy had established yet another gesture of leadership, this time at my expense. Though I couldn't really complain – I'd had it coming to me. One of the men was allocated to stand watch so that if a political officer should approach to make sure the discussion they'd ordered was taking place, we would know well in advance. If he called out that Dinh was approaching everyone would gather around and I'd start verbalising, with the others pretending to be totally absorbed, nodding their heads and clapping and saying, 'Yeah, man!' or 'Ain't that the truth!' when I made a particularly salient point.

However, after I'd served my sentence and we were back in the Negro compound, my prowess as a scribe hadn't gone unnoticed, and I was called upon to do the daily listening and to answer the questions for every subsequent lecture. Jimmy explained that this made me an integral and indispensable part of the group. 'Ogoya, Brother Fish,' was all he'd said by way of explanation when I'd accused him of dobbing me in for the 'ears'n'pencil' job. But the truth was, in the eyes of our compound, being the ears as well as the scribe was the one thing, except, of course, for the harmonica, that made me trustworthy and accepted. I was small, talked with a funny accent and they had no reason to trust someone with white skin, but to compensate, I'd become a useful and vital part of the daily procedure.

As a result of my after-lecture discussion reports, our Chinese captors singled us out for meritorious endeavour in the cause of universal communism. Lieutenant Dinh reported that I had seen the error of my ways and it was clear, by the high standard of my reports, I had embraced the teachings of communism with enthusiasm. He also noted that he had come in on several lively discussions and it was obvious our compound was clearly seeing the light of 'the truth' beaming from the hilltop. As a reward, under the Lenient Policy, we were granted extra food rations, which was, I suspect, the real reason why I was finally accepted in the Negro compound.

But I soon realised that yet another agenda was under way, and was probably the truly *real* reason that we started to get slightly preferential treatment. Lieutenant Dinh was obviously interested in converting the Negroes. He would stress at every session that the American Negro logically belonged on the side of the communist cause: 'After nearly 300 years you are still the slaves of the white American imperialists. The capitalists use you as cannon fodder in this war,' he'd say, as an example of his approach, then he'd add, 'This is what we will discuss today.' He'd continue in this vein, bringing up a specific instance of

Negro oppression in the United States every session. Often it was difficult to refute his logic and I could see many of the men nodding and often afterwards there would be a real lively discussion, although Jimmy would never be a participant. Later he'd say to me, 'It clever but I ain't fooled – only people gonna save mah people are mah people demself.'

Of course, as official scribe I'd have to take notes of the discussions and, as a result, I can still remember just about the whole communist discourse. My wife often accuses me of spouting it in my sleep, with phrases such as '*Wall Street warmongers*' and '*Profits bought with the blood of the Negro people*', or as an alternative, '*the blood of the proletariat*'. All this liberally interspersed with my snoring.

However, as in the cave and the farm hospital, the harmonica was to prove the key to progress in our part of the POW camp. It was also to cause the rumpus Jimmy had warned would happen with 'da man'.

Operation Harmonica had begun slowly, with me knocking out a few tunes – mostly blues – in our room. At first there was the nodding of a few heads, coloured folk seemingly unable to remain motionless when music is about. Then, someone from another room would appear at the door and then more and more would arrive, and then a little humming, and finally, two or three days on, one of the men started singing along, followed shortly by others. Soon enough there was a bit of a concert going on in the compound after the afternoon's lecture or parade.

It didn't take too long before Jimmy had another choir going, with the inevitable result that morale among the prisoners picked up. Cleanliness and cooperation between the men in the compound began to follow, all of which was carefully orchestrated by Jimmy. Pretty soon the Negro compound had regained a sense of self-respect – the blokes were washing their clothes and cleaning their rooms, and the sick among us were being cared for within the compound so as to avoid the hospital death sentence.

One afternoon after a parade I invited Doug Waterman from the Royal Ulster Rifles to come round. 'Mind if I bring a few mates, Jacko?' he asked.

Pretty soon we had an audience, not only from the Commonwealth forces but also some of the Americans, and this was what finally caused Corporal Steve O'Rourke – 'da man' – to surface. With a dozen or so of his henchmen he appeared at one of the afternoon concerts and, walking up to Jimmy, who was busy conducting the choir, he demanded the singing cease and the harmonica be handed over to him.

O'Rourke wasn't a small man, but by Jimmy's standards he appeared so. Jimmy stopped the choir and waited, saying nothing.

'What's your name, nigger?' O'Rourke asked.

Jimmy smiled. 'What's yours, punk?' he retaliated.

'You know mine,' O'Rourke said belligerently.

'Yeah? White trash, ain't it?' Jimmy offered.

'What you say, nigger? Did I hear you call me punk and white trash? Now I don't like that none,' O'Rourke said, a nasty little smile playing over his face.

'Well, I ain't too partial to nigger, neither, punk.' Jimmy smiled back at him seemingly unafraid and then gave a casual little shrug. 'It jus' ain't nice, man.'

O'Rourke's men gathered around him, pushing closer. 'We're closin' you down, nigger. You want trouble? You can have it any time you want. Now, hand over that harmonica,' O'Rourke said.

Jimmy didn't reply for some moments. Instead he cocked his head slightly and looked at O'Rourke, a querulous expression on his face. Finally he asked, 'Hey man, yoh want to join da choir? We needs us a soprano voice bad.'

Up to that moment the crowd, including the choir, had listened in dead silence. Now there was a gasp, and then a spontaneous roar of laughter. O'Rourke's face turned crimson. I don't suppose, with his hoons standing around him, too many of them saw the shiv come out of his trouser pocket. I caught the glint of the homemade blade as it sunk into Jimmy's gut. 'Fuck!' I shouted, lunging towards O'Rourke. I was propped up on my crutches because I'd been playing the harmonica and needed both hands to do so, and as I rushed forward the crutches fell to the ground. But it was all over before I got to where the white corporal was standing. There was an audible tin-like snap and the blade dropped from O'Rourke's fingers. The look of surprise on his face lasted only a moment before Jimmy grabbed the front of his tunic and, with his free hand, did the same to one of O'Rourke's henchmen standing beside him. With a sudden vicious jerk, he brought their heads together so hard that those of us in the front row of the choir could hear the crack as their skulls collided. Both men sank to the ground at Jimmy's feet, unconscious. A thin trickle of blood started running down O'Rourke's jowl.

Jimmy turned to the hoon standing nearest to him. 'Take dem away!' he commanded. 'We got us some choir singin' to do, an' dis a private session wid no white trash allowed.'

Someone started to clap and then everyone did – not just our company, but Doug Waterman's mob from the Royal Ulster Rifles and the white Americans present. A cheer rose from the crowd. Nobody quite knew what had happened – all they could see was O'Rourke and one of his men lying unconscious at Jimmy's feet. Then Jimmy stooped down and picked up two broken pieces of blade, examined them cursorily and then threw them aside with a grunt. There was a sudden sigh from the crowd as they realised Jimmy had been attacked before he'd grabbed hold of the two men now lying unconscious at his feet.

I simply couldn't imagine what had happened. I'd seen the shiv enter, I was sure of it. What's more I was quite certain it had entered well above Jimmy's belt, so that it couldn't have protected him or caused the blade to snap in two. 'Jesus, what happened?' I asked Jimmy.

'Later,' he growled softly. 'Now we play – "St James".'

I returned to the choir, not stopping to pick up my crutches, and blew the opening chords of 'St James Infirmary Blues'. We watched as four of O'Rourke's men carried their leader and his offsider away.

I wondered if Jimmy had killed them, because neither of them showed any signs of coming around. With the first bars of the music the choir began to hum and the crowd had grown quiet. If the humiliation of O'Rourke meant that Jimmy was now 'da man' then things around the POW camp were in for a big change.

Later in our room I asked Jimmy again what had happened, exclaiming at the same time, 'Mate, I bloody saw the knife go into your gut with me own eyes!'

'Nah, that don't happen, Brother Fish, I done pro-tek myself.' He unbuttoned his tunic and pulled out a tin plate, one of the plates our food was served on at the cookhouse. Now I knew where Lieutenant Dinh's missing 'downfall of capitalism' plate had gone – Jimmy had lifted it when we'd been doing the washing-up after we'd missed our afternoon meal. I felt a whole heap better.

It was also typical of Jimmy not to remove the plate from his tunic in front of the crowd. By doing so he would have gained a second gratuitous laugh and cheer from the crowd. Later one of my fellow inmates in the house explained to me, 'Jimmy – he a real cool dude, man!'

Jimmy told me his tin-plate protection was something he'd learned at Elmira Reformatory. Evidently he'd been wearing it in anticipation from the second day we'd arrived. He'd not known when O'Rourke would come for him, but was convinced that sooner or later he must.

In the way these things happen the rumour got about that the blade O'Rourke had used had snapped on Jimmy's abs, and that Jimmy hadn't even flinched when the knife entered his gut. As far as the American compound was concerned, Jimmy was 'the man'. Shortly after the incident at choir practice the Chinese found a reason to put O'Rourke in the camp prison – the group of huts on the perimeter of the camp that the guard had pointed out to us with the caution, 'No want go that place.' We didn't hear any more about him for some time, but it was a universal hope that he would be the recipient of some of the more painful tortures the Chinese were capable of administering while still keeping a prisoner alive. Although, in his case, keeping the bloke alive wasn't of great concern.

The tedium in the camp continued. It was by now getting pretty cold and the endless lectures were made even harder to bear by the inclement weather, the bad food and sickness everywhere. For me, the only good thing was that the time I'd lunged towards O'Rourke, leaving my crutches to fall to the ground, was the last time I ever used them. Two days later Jimmy discarded Captain Hook.

We could hardly be described as fit, but being no longer dependent on our crutches made us feel invincible. Moreover, news came through that peace talks were making good progress and it was now only a matter of hanging on. Furthermore, it was in the interest of the enemy to keep us alive for negotiating reasons. The blokes who reckoned they'd nearly frozen last winter were relieved to be allowed to collect a little more wood, and rations increased just sufficiently to stop men dying of starvation and some medication was also made available. The death rate of around ten men a day fell to half that number.

In Doug Waterman's words, 'It's what you'd be calling a balancing act. The boogers want to keep us alive, if that's what you'd call our present condition, but not so alive that we'll be after resisting indoctrination and not taking advantage of the Lenient Policy in return for our confessing to be dupes of our capitalist oppressors. By Jesus, if I get out of this, I'm going to buy me a ticket to America and I'm going to go to Wall Street and tell them warmongering boogers they owe me a pension for life for the abuse I've taken in defence of their sodding name!'

As the war progressed we became more and more disillusioned, and it was increasingly difficult to justify the South Korean regime as the bulwark of democracy in Asia – the reason we were fighting in the first place. Doug told of how the Royal Ulster Rifles were placed in reserve in Seoul during the big bug out of winter 1950–51. It was Christmas, and the snow was up to their knees as the South Koreans prepared for the evacuation of the city. The first thing the South Korean police did was round up a large number of women and children and herd them into the streets, where they shot them. 'We had to stand by and watch the slaughter of innocent women and children, unable to do anything on what was their sovereign territory,' Doug said, plainly still upset from the memory. 'Well, we're Irishmen, see, and we'll not put up with that – our own mothers and bairns safely at home, and theirs being shot down in the streets in front of our very eyes – it's not to be put up with, whatever the reason. So we fixed bayonets and ordered the police to stop, half hoping they'd defy us so we could clean the bastards up good and proper once and for all. The boogers stopped all right, but who knows what happened when our backs were turned. It makes you bloody wonder what we're fighting for, don't it? I mean, when the Chinese go on about Syngman Rhee exploiting his people it's hard not to agree with them now, isn't it?'

This brought us to our favourite subject of the Republic of Korea and the bloody hopeless South Korean forces who'd proved themselves cowards and no-hopers time and time again, costing the lives of the rest of us who'd come to help them keep their country safe from communism. Although, after Doug's story of the massacre of women and children, I suppose the forces of South Korea could hardly be blamed for their lack of enthusiasm for the war. Doug then told us what subsequently happened to the Royal Ulster Rifles.

They were given the job of preparing a fall-back position for the 1st ROK Division, who were the front-line troops some twelve miles to the north of Seoul. 'We'd created trenches, bunkers, telephone lines – the whole box'n'dice. Lovely job, if I say so myself,' Doug began. 'The Chinese hit on New Year's Day and the ROK were supposed to take the initial shock, hold for a while, then withdraw to the fall-back position. But almost from the first enemy mortar the cowards broke and ran for their lives. They passed through our lines like a dose of salts and we were forced to man the fall-back position designed for three times our number. We held the chinks a good bit but the boogers were everywhere, crawling over us like ants. The front had crumbled so quickly we didn't stand a chance.'

'Same here,' I said. 'The bloody ROK did it to us at Uijongbu and Kapyong. Is that how you were personally captured and brought here?' I asked.

'I'd be happy to tell you, Jacko, but it's a long story. Are you sure now you'd want to be hearing it?'

I laughed. 'Mate, I'm so busy pickin' my nose I've hardly got time to scratch my arse.'

Doug grinned. 'You'd make a good Irishman, Jacko. The Chinese finally overwhelmed us and we became isolated. Most fought their way out but quite a few of us got taken prisoner.' Doug shook his head slowly. 'How I'm sittin' here talkin' to you is a fookin' miracle. We were lumped together with a large number of other prisoners and started to march north. We marched through the freezing winter nights and holed up anywhere we could during the day – caves, ditches and abandoned villages. I was never warm. The chinks had taken our warm boots and given us their canvas shoes to wear. There was precious little food, and no medicine. The wounded died mercifully early on in the march, which grew harder as we grew weaker and the weather turned even colder. We'd huddle together for warmth during the day and often, when night came and it was time to continue, there were dead lying among us. Often men could go no further, suffering from frostbite and exhaustion. The guards would try to get them going with kicks and blows from their rifle butts, but to no avail. Near me were two brothers, one unable to carry on and the other too weak to carry him, so they both stayed behind to die. There comes a time when a man gives up his life willingly just to be left behind in the snow. Some even pleaded to be shot. The march took us two months, and by the time we arrived here we'd lost three quarters of our column.' He looked up at me. 'We're not out of it yet, Jacko, but if I was a Catholic I'd be saying a hundred "Hail Marys" every day for getting me through that particular nightmare. No matter how hard it is in here, I thank God for a straw mat, a louse-ridden blanket and the handful of vile food we get.'

Later, I told Jimmy Doug's story. 'Jesus, makes our journey seem like a Saturday-night pub crawl,' I concluded.

'Pub crawl?' he asked, moved by Doug's story.

'Getting drunk by moving from one bar to another on a Saturday night,' I explained. It was as close as I could come to the meaning of a peripatetic piss-up. It had never occurred to me to be grateful for being alive and in a Chinese POW camp.

As the peace talks grew more intense, so did the afternoon lectures and indoctrination sessions. The Chinese seemed determined that we'd leave them as communists, proselytes ready to spread our new-found political dogma back in our own countries. More importantly, they wanted to persuade more of us to write statements denouncing the 'American war of aggression' and accusing the US Army of bombing hospitals and of other atrocities. Not that we'd seen any of these events, but they encouraged us to take their word for it. As far as the conversions were concerned, they did have some success. Twenty-one Americans and one British soldier refused repatriation after the war and went to live in China. A few others returned home embracing the communist doctrine.

Quite suddenly, the discussions became more relaxed – almost casual, and seemingly without the usual end motive to convert us. We were asked for our thoughts on the running of the camp and encouraged to discuss our lives before the war and our hopes for the future. One afternoon Lieutenant Dinh participated in the group by telling us about his own earlier life before the Long March, which he'd joined at the age of ten and where he had been selected to be educated and trained as an English translator. He told us about his fishing village named Jieshi in Guangdong Province, and at one stage seemed to really relax and wax nostalgic about the fisherfolk in his region, whom he boasted were the best in China. I invited him to hear 'The Fish Song', which we'd taught the new choir, and he willingly accepted. Jimmy wasn't all that pleased, but we had the choir perform it for him and Dinh seemed delighted and clapped furiously at the conclusion, claiming later that our entire compound was now well within the Lenient Policy.

Things seemed to be looking up. Certainly the quality and quantity of the food improved marginally. I joined in the discussions without first being asked a question, and always Jimmy would caution me. 'Things ain't right, Brother Fish,' he'd say.

'Mate, it's only a discussion – no harm in that. I ain't gunna turn into a commo overnight.'

'I been in dis kind o'discussion be-fore – all ain't what it seems, we still in da jailhouse,' Jimmy warned.

I must admit, there were times when he really got on my goat – the way he always seemed to see something ominous in every situation. He'd spent too much time in institutions and found it impossible to trust anyone in authority. Jimmy always looked for the motive behind people's actions and couldn't understand that sometimes there wasn't one. We all knew the peace talks were under way and that the Chinese were attempting to make things look better than they were. So, I guess to show my independence, I kept on joining in the conversations that, as far as I was concerned, made the meetings a bloody sight less boring. Dinh even seemed to enjoy a bit of banter where I (cleverly, I thought) subtly criticised the Chinese People's Volunteers.

Then came the big announcement. There was a special parade called with the commandant addressing us, but this time his opening patter had changed somewhat. 'We, the Chinese people, love democracy!' he began. There was a ripple of amusement among the assembled prisoners. 'Not capitalism, where the Wall Street warmongers exploit the proletariat, but *true* democracy of the people!' He went on a bit in this manner before announcing, 'We will soon have Daily Life Committees in every company. You will have your opinions heard and, if they are sound, we will act on them. You will be able to tell the world how the Chinese People's Volunteers have set you free.'

Now I understood the softening of their attitude over the past few weeks – it had been orchestrated to lead up to the so-called 'democracy' to be introduced into camp procedure. The question now was, why?

'Ha! Brother Fish, somebody come to visit us,' Jimmy said knowingly.

As part of the new democratic system, Jimmy was elected as a squad leader in our compound and I was the monitor. In our case nothing much had changed – the ghetto had long since got its act together under Jimmy's leadership, and as usual I was his dogsbody. Of course, he was right about the visit. No sooner had the Daily Life Committees been established, the hospital cleaned up and the chow improved, than the Chinese authorities announced World Press Day. This turned out to be a visit by photographers and journalists from the English communist newspaper *The Daily Worker* and the French Communist Party paper *L'Humanité* as well as newspapers from most of the communist and many neutral countries. They took photographs of the assembled committees, of food we'd never before received and interviewed a carefully selected group of prisoners – the converts to communism and prisoners known as 'progressives', men who had responded to indoctrination and the Lenient Policy with a willingness to denounce the Americans as 'warmongers'. Altogether it was a carefully staged propaganda coup intended to strengthen the Chinese hand in the peace negotiations.

Nevertheless, we welcomed the better conditions. With marginally bigger portions and slightly better food our strength improved a little. Now off our crutches, Jimmy and I were selected for various work parties unloading bags of rice or corn. Jimmy called it 'nigger work', as we seemed to do more of it than the other compounds. If we were lucky, we'd be sent to gather wood outside the camp. On one such wood-collecting expedition, one of the blokes in the ghetto found some bush tobacco growing. How a guy from Kentucky knew what Chinese bush tobacco looked like I'm buggered if I know, but he turned out to be right – the stuff was smokeable. Well, smokeable under the prevailing circumstances, anyway, where anything vaguely resembling tobacco was prized above rubies.

We cured the bush tobacco leaves by hanging them above the barrack room fire, but our next problem was that we possessed no paper for making fags. My notes made after the various discussions were written on three pieces of paper issued to me after every lecture. These had to be filled in and handed back at the next day's session. As the Muslims say, '*God is great*' – the tobacco had hardly been properly cured when, after an indoctrination session, Lieutenant Dinh gave me a copy of *The Daily Worker*. It was the copy that showed the photographs of the visit by the 'World Press' and, naturally, reported in glowing terms the findings of one of the visiting journalists, a bloke called Wilfred Burchett, who I later discovered was an Australian and a long-term communist sympathiser and friend of the Chinese. I was instructed by Dinh to read the feature article at the after-lecture squad meeting and to conduct the usual discussion and deliver my notes on it to him afterwards. I recall the front page showed a beaming commandant sitting in the centre of the newly elected Central Committee. *Hoo-bloody-ray!* I thought to myself – *have faith and God will provide, my son*. We'd got our cigarette paper, with maybe enough over to distribute a strip to everyone in the barracks to have one glorious arse-wiping crap!

As it turned out, it was just about the stupidest thing I could have done. Two days later Lieutenant Dinh asked for the return of the newspaper, and when I couldn't produce it I made up a story that I'd passed it on to some GIs passing the compound and I couldn't remember who they were. The guards searched our houses and found several tiny scraps of the paper and two hoarded bush tobacco cigarettes wrapped in it. I was marched away to the dreaded row of buildings on the edge of the camp.

The camp prison was a row of small rooms with tiny windows placed high in three of the walls. Entry was through a small grilled door. I was forced to sit at attention from four-thirty in the morning until eleven p.m. at night. My wounded leg ached unmercifully, but if I moved and a guard observed me he would open the grille and kick me and knock my torso to the ground with his rifle butt. They would routinely pull me out and beat me with long bamboo sticks. A favourite trick was to push a small bamboo rod through the grille so that it protruded on both sides, whereupon I was required to kneel and take my end of the stick between my teeth, which had been loosened by malnutrition with several broken off at the stumps from copping the rifle butt to the side of my jaw on the night of the chocolate incident when I'd first been captured. From time to time the guard would hit the stick as he passed, slamming my end of the stick to the side of my mouth – or worse, down my throat, forcing me to swallow the blood, which in turn brought on a raging thirst I was unable to quench with the meagre ration of water I was given. Finally, I was never allowed to sleep for any sustained period. As I lay without a blanket on the floor, the guard would frequently wake me up by prodding me through the grille until I sat up. This would happen perhaps twenty times each night. What I didn't know at the time was that this was only the beginning – the softening-up process – before my serious interrogation began.

Every afternoon I was hauled out of my cell for interrogation, each day more exhausted and confused. I was accused of 'destroying the people's property' – a very serious charge, they insisted, and one that might lead to me being shot. After a few days of this, and when I refused to give them the names of all the men who had benefited from the illicit tobacco and subsequent destruction of the newspaper, they moved me to a second cell. This one was no different from the one I'd been in except for a solid beam that ran across the ceiling.

Now my interrogation turned to my personal attitude – my hostile attitude to 'the truth'. The interrogators read out screeds of notes made by Lieutenant Dinh that detailed the conversations we'd had in the discussion groups, and emphasised my replies. Jimmy had been right – the more relaxed attitude Dinh had adopted was designed to flush out the hardliners. They accused me of being an unrepentant war criminal, and therefore outside the Lenient Policy.

Then one afternoon, out of the blue, they accused me of aiding in the escape of one of the prisoners in our house, a man named Joe Bellows. I was the monitor and was accused of not reporting his absence from the compound. In the ghetto we'd looked after our own sick, but when the conditions improved in the hospital and some sulphur drugs were being used we'd grabbed the chance and taken him to the camp hospital. I'd forgotten to report his absence from the compound. As it eventually turned out, Joe, in a state of delirium, had staggered out of the hospital and was eventually found dead just outside the perimeter of the camp. I was accused of aiding in his escape, and the real torture began.

My hands were tied behind my back using a long rope that was then swung over the ceiling beam and pulled up until my arms were fully stretched and felt as if they were about to be torn from my shoulder sockets, and my toes only just touched the floor. Seemingly in minutes the pain began. If I relaxed my legs by lifting my toes from the floor my arms attempted to pop out of their sockets; if I maintained the position where my toes balanced my body keeping it steady, the pain in my legs, particularly the one that had been broken, became excruciating. I was kept like this for hours at a time, and when I was eventually taken down I would be given a severe beating.

They accused me of being on the escape committee and demanded to know the names of the other men on it. I admitted to forgetting to report Joe Bellows' absence, but vehemently denied the rest. In fact, I knew the name of one of the men involved, as Jimmy had been asked by Doug Waterman to join the committee but had refused. At the time it became another one of his decisions I was hard put to understand. They'd loosen the rope and say, 'You give names now!' I'd shake my head and deny I knew anything, upon which they'd yank the rope tight leaving me dangling and screaming in agony. This would go on for two or three hours at a time. After a week, when I frequently begged them to kill me, I was interrogated one last time, this time by Dinh himself, and then dragged back to the ghetto by two guards with Dinh accompanying us. I was made to stand in front of our compound, which had been assembled for the purpose of hearing me confess to wantonly destroying the people's property.

I did so, stuttering like a gibbering fool, unable to control my mouth, or the tears that ran down my cheeks, or the shaking as if I was experiencing a high fever.

When I'd finished Dinh held up his hand and then dismissed the prison guards and started to talk. 'The prisoner has seen the error of his ways and you have heard him confess to destroying the people's property.' He paused, then continued. 'We are not a vengeful people, and I tell you all that the prisoner is now back inside the Lenient Policy.'

There was a sudden murmur from the crowd and Dinh must have taken this as approval for this act of forgiveness, because he was smiling. But the sudden sound had come from Jimmy, pushing his way through the mob. He emerged in front of Dinh and walked directly up to him, halting so close to the little Chinaman that Dinh was forced to take a step backwards. 'Muth'fucker!' he said. Dinh reached for his revolver but then hesitated – Jimmy was too close, and would have killed him before he'd got the weapon halfway out of its holster. Jimmy turned and walked up to me and picked me up, allowing Dinh plenty of time to shoot him. Then he turned back towards the officer, now carrying me cradled in his arms. 'Shoot, you muth'fucker!' he repeated. I could hear him softly weeping. The crowd surged forward and Dinh, realising he was about to be mobbed, put his hand up and the crowd hesitated momentarily. 'This is a very brave man,' he shouted to the crowd. 'It is also a fortunate man who has such a friend – he will not be punished!' Dinh must have been a brave man himself, and also a resourceful one, because he had just averted his own death by keeping his cool.

Jimmy put me straight to bed and nursed me, spending every moment he was allowed at my side. I was black and blue and couldn't use my arms, so he had to feed me my morning bowl of millet. My mouth had become infected and I couldn't talk or eat properly. On the third day I felt a little better and was able to rise from my pallet and make the confession that had plagued my mind since leaving the prison.

'Jimmy, I have something to say,' I began.

'Brother Fish, yoh rest now. Talk later.'

I shook my head. 'No, I have something I have to tell you.'

'Okay, fire,' he said, trying to sound cheerful.

I explained that I'd tried to hold out and I'd never given them Doug's name. They still wouldn't let up even though, in the end, I think they believed that I had nothing to do with the escape committee and didn't know who they were. Eventually the pain got so bad I thought I was going to die. Then, when they realised I didn't care, they made a deal – no more torture if I turned informer. I started to weep. 'I agreed,' I stammered.

Jimmy grinned. 'It don't matter, Brother Fish, yoh safe now,' he said, attempting to comfort me.

I shook my head vigorously. 'No, no! You don't understand, mate. I couldn't go through that again. From time to time they're gunna haul me up and grill me for information and they'll threaten to take me back to the torture cell, and I can't trust myself not to tell them all I know!'

'Well, we lost our jobs, man! I's no longer squad leader and yoh no longer mon-it-or, so we know nothin' – no way, eh, Brother Fish?'

But this wasn't good enough to comfort me. 'Jimmy, you've got to promise to tell me *nothing* and pass the word to the other blokes, they mustn't tell me *anything*!'

He nodded quietly. 'I got it.'

Jimmy and I were not the only ones to lose our positions – almost all the squad officers and Daily Life Committee members were being carted off for interrogation, where they were made to confess their unsuitability for the job and dismissed. Doug Waterman reported the same was true for the Ulster mob. They'd returned, having been dismissed from their previous positions. Soon enough a pattern formed – for a couple of weeks the political officers at the indoctrination sessions raved on about the 'reactionaries', heaping more and more scorn on us, while at the same time they spoke of the good sense of the 'progressives'. Pretty soon all the committee members, squad leaders and monitors were progressives who started having separate meetings where they were given extra rations.

Jimmy laughed. 'I hope dem progressive cats don't think dat chow gonna be for free,' he said.

It didn't take long before the Central Committee started producing documents criticising American aggression. Nor were the Brits spared – I recall one such document was headed 'Britain: Running Dog of the American Imperialists', which got a big mention in *The Daily Worker* of my previous downfall. But the big news item that consistently appeared in the newspaper was the Chinese insistence, backed by dozens of affidavits from converts and progressives, that as the committee was democratically elected it spoke for all the prisoners. There are always people who are prepared to believe this kind of propaganda, and there was no one who could refute this blatant codswallop by telling the outside world things were not quite the way they appeared in the columns of the pro-communist newspaper.

Things began to hot up, but it was the 'Petition for the Cessation of Hostilities' that really caused the proverbial to hit the fan. It accused the United States of making unreasonable demands at the peace talks and unnecessarily prolonging the war. The Chinese were running out of time and they needed us to sign. The political officers emphasised at each indoctrination meeting that failure to sign was tantamount to the betrayal of true democracy and deserved no leniency. Attempts to argue with prisoners who refused to sign ceased, and they were labelled reactionaries and severely punished. This reached the stage where it was pointless not to sign. So some bright spark – I wish it had been me – signed his name and then added 'Mickey Mouse' beside it. This sparked a process where the document was filled with names such as the Lone Ranger, Donald Duck, Goofy, Horace Horse, Snow White, Uncle Sam, Abraham Lincoln, Joe Louis, Superman and the like, which rendered it useless for propaganda purposes. It became a small win for the side of the reactionaries.

But it was to be the only bright spot in my life for some time to come. Shortly after the abortive document, we were required to attend another gathering on the main parade ground. This time I arrived alone, as Jimmy had been in one work party and I in another. It was obvious the Chinese regarded this parade as important as the commandant was present, perched on the stage directly below the big picture of Chairman Mao, which was fixed in a wooden frame to the main administration building. We waited for him to front the microphone and begin one of his diatribes. Then I noticed the bricks in place under the microphone that made it much too high for the tiny commandant. He remained seated then finally turned in the direction of the wooden step leading up to the platform and nodded. To my absolute astonishment, moments later Jimmy appeared and walked, unescorted, to the microphone. *Jesus, what's going on?* I thought to myself.

Jimmy paused and looked around, and for a moment I thought he'd picked me out in the crowd, but then his eyes swept on. 'My Negro brothers,' he began, 'we must all unite to defeat American imperialism. Those of you who are reactionaries must look into your past. What has America given you? Let me tell you. It brought you in as slaves, and we are *still* slaves. The American Bill of Rights does not apply to you – you have been duped! Your brothers are in the prisons, your wives have become whores to feed your starving children! The American Negro does not have freedom, no Lenient Policy applies to us . . .'

I was too shocked to quite register what was happening. My heart was thumping in my chest and I thought I was going to throw up – my best mate, the bloke I loved the best in the world and trusted with my life, was collaborating with the enemy. Jimmy's speech went on and on but I heard none of it after the opening few words. My entire world had been shattered, smashed to smithereens. The parade finally came to an end and I hardly know how I got back to the ghetto. But when I arrived one of the blokes said Jimmy had checked out and had asked me not to look for him. As long as I stayed a reactionary we could no longer be friends.

'Where'd he go to?' I asked.

'Special compound. He's been elected to the Central Committee,' came the answer.

I had never felt so alone, and the following morning I was told that I was to leave the ghetto and be housed with the Commonwealth prisoners. I tried to pick up the pieces and see if they made sense. My febrile imagination soon took over and I saw all sorts of signs I hadn't noticed before. *Jimmy had been planning to betray me all along*. It was obvious he'd danced with the devil. Why, I asked myself, hadn't Lieutenant Dinh shot him when he'd broken ranks and called him a 'muth'fucker'? Not once, but twice. The second time Dinh could easily have plugged him. The Chinaman had lost enormous face, and it was unimaginable that he wouldn't repay the insult with death. There was only one reason: it had all been a set-up between Dinh and Jimmy. *The fucking nigger was always gunna betray you!* my mind screamed, forgetting all we'd been through together and the fact that I owed my very life to him. I had never had a racist thought in my life, and now the silent use of the word 'nigger' to describe Jimmy caused an inward pain that seemed unbearable. I thought of John Lazarou and how I'd always dismissed him as a boofhead and often sent him up. How he'd stuck with me and how he'd slipped into the weapon pit at Kapyong, sacrificing a much safer position in the rear, prepared to die alongside me simply because I was his mate. *Some bloody mate!* I was ashamed and mortified at my careless behaviour towards such a good bloke, and didn't know if I really wanted to continue living. Now I was getting my comeuppance. I walked around like a zombie for days, and then I was hit with yet another terrible blow.

There was another reason the Chinese were not too concerned about having no perimeter fence and watchtowers – their network of undercover progressives. Doug Waterman had been informed on and accused of being on the escape committee and they'd dragged him off to the cells. I confess I had been so distressed and preoccupied with Jimmy's betrayal that I hadn't paid sufficient attention to this second catastrophe. When he returned ten days later I could barely recognise him. I had returned from the cells in pretty bad shape, but he was ten times worse. I sat beside his pallet where he lay motionless for three days, taking turns with his many friends to give him a little water. Finally on the fourth day he managed to talk, and he told me he could take no more.

'You can do it, Dougie, we're almost there – the peace talks are progressing. Hang in, mate, we need you!' I begged.

'Jacko, I've agreed to be an informer,' he whispered.

'Me too!' I protested. 'You don't have to inform, the beatings aren't too severe.' But my heart skipped a beat. My situation had been different. I genuinely didn't know anyone on the escape committee. I hadn't even been absolutely sure that Doug was a member. But he probably knew everyone on it and if the Chinese hadn't got their names from him they eventually would – nothing was more certain.

Doug lay on his bed and looked at the wall and said not a word more. We tried everything, even force-feeding him, but the food just came up again. Finally he refused water, and his eyes remained mostly closed for the next three days. He had survived the death march. He had survived near-starvation, the brutality of the earlier camp and the harsh punishments that killed so many of his mates. But he couldn't survive the shame of being an informer. The thought of the further torture to come if he didn't inform was too much, and his spirit had finally been broken. A week after he came back from the cells I was seated beside his bed and he whispered through cracked lips that he wanted water. My heart surged, and I reached for the tin mug on the floor beside him and poured a few drops into his mouth. He opened his eyes and looked up at me. 'I'm so ashamed,' he said, and then he died.

We buried him the following day, and while I wept I was conscious that I was also weeping for myself. I had lost a mate who refused to betray his friends and one who had willingly done so. The day of

Doug's funeral was without any doubt the most miserable of my life. I confess that on more than one occasion during the days that followed I determined to join Doug Waterman. But I guess I didn't have the guts to kill myself, and decided I would have to leave it to the Chinese to do it for me. I vowed that I would remain a reactionary with whatever defiance remained in me until they did the job and I was put out of my misery.

If I appear to be wallowing in self-pity then I apologise. Being an informer, I found myself utterly alone. I couldn't talk to anyone, or they to me. Most things concerning the human soul are healed by talk, and I lived and breathed among a thousand men yet I was completely isolated. While things were hotting up, and the interrogation sessions getting more and more intense, even Dinh seemed to give up on me. This had the effect of isolating me even further – even my intellectual enemy had withdrawn from me. He would send me off to be beaten without explaining the reason. I seemed to have become impervious to pain. 'More,' I'd say to them. 'Kill me now, you bastards!' Looking back it was too bloody pathetic for words, and I still feel ashamed thinking about it.

Despite the hard work the Chinese were putting in with their boots, the long cane and their various tortures, they were not having it all their own way. Their precious progressives, who had become the foot soldiers of our oppression, were copping a heap. Though I can't speak for myself, as I was too numbed and isolated to be a part of anything, quite suddenly there was resistance coming from the prisoners. This was sparked off when the Chinese proudly paraded Corporal O'Rourke and announced that he'd seen 'the truth' and was henceforth a progressive. He was attacked and cut about and discovered bleeding behind the latrines one night, and then several of the more odious progressives received the same treatment. Some of the progressives reported the attackers, who were badly beaten by the Chinese. But then posters began to appear with the headline 'Traitors and Spies', followed by the names of the better known progressives and others who had been secretly informing on their mates. I lived in dread that my name might appear, even though I hadn't given the chinks any information and continued to take my weekly beatings. The posters promised never to forget the treachery and ended with the words, 'You cannot kill us all, and the last man standing will carry your names to justice. We will never forget your treachery!!'

Perhaps the most effective morale booster came when the poster of Chairman Mao on the wall of the camp headquarters was defaced one night with the slogan, 'Running Dog of the Russian Imperialists!' And another of Joe Stalin, only recently displayed, was altered to read 'Emperor of China'. In retrospect these captions may not seem like very courageous initiatives, but in the context of the time they were enormously brave – the perpetrators risked their lives in the process. In the eyes of the Chinese, the disfigurement of the posters was a crime that merited the death sentence.

The peace talks seemed to have slowed down and *The Daily Worker*, our only source of information, mirroring the line of the petition we had been forced to sign, accused America of stalling the negotiations so that the greedy Wall Street capitalists could continue to enjoy the profits of war. Tucked away in the same issue was a small piece that suggested that part of the continuing negotiations might involve each side exchanging prisoners. You couldn't believe anything you read in *The Daily Worker*, but for a moment my heart soared. Though almost as quickly my common sense told me not to be fooled by what I'd read. But what this did mean was that in some small part of me hope remained.

The weeks passed with working parties unloading rice and more of the same daily routines, but with the disruptions continuing. Nobody seemed to know who was responsible, and while the guards became more active and vigilant the incidents didn't stop. Whoever was behind this continued defiance must have controlled a pretty tight-lipped mob because no one had yet broken ranks. Perhaps most of the reactionary prisoners *did* know who was behind the continued fracas, but morale had lifted to such an extent that even the wimps became bold and the secret was kept.

I longed to be a part of this covert revolution but I was outside the loop. It was like being a ghost, aware that you are present among people but that they appear unable to see you. As a child, one of the most onerous punishments at primary school was known as 'being sent to purgatory'. This was when the other kids were instructed not to talk to you. I can remember how even after a couple of hours of this treatment a small child would be reduced to copious tears. Now, with Doug Waterman gone and Jimmy out of my life, I found myself in a continual state of purgatory.

I had also come to realise how very much I had depended on Jimmy's presence in my life. His peculiar syntax and grammar had added colour and humour to even the darkest hours, and his sanguine outlook had never failed to lift me out of my despair. After I recovered sufficiently from the initial shock of his betrayal, what puzzled me was that his 'betrayal speech' had been delivered in almost perfect English. It drove me crazy thinking why this might be, or even how he'd achieved the change in the way he spoke. I'd not, even once, heard him speak this way – even as a send-up or while telling a joke. I was unaware he could speak in any other manner than in his 'dis'n'dat' vernacular. Was he trying to get some sort of message to me? If so, what was it? Was he telling me not to take what he was doing seriously? If so, it hadn't worked. I was unable to convince myself that this was the reason.

I mean, the whole way he'd gone about it was totally alien to his personality. If Jimmy had decided to convert to communism he would have thought it out carefully and talked about it to me. There were no secrets between us. Besides, Jimmy never did anything spontaneously. He was a natural-born thinker. He would have argued, debated, persuaded, turned every aspect upside down and the right way up again. That was his way. He was the most persuasive person I had ever known and could talk the hind leg off a donkey, but he always made sense. He'd often talked about the situation of Negroes in America and the injustice meted out to coloured folk. He'd remarked bitterly about the disparities in misdemeanour sentencing and the disproportionate numbers of Negro prisoners within the US prison system. But he'd always seen it as an ongoing struggle against racism, and was completely aware that America wasn't unique in this respect. We had also discovered that the Chinese were racist, particularly against blacks, and that a dogma such as communism wasn't going to be the answer for the American Negro.

He'd once remarked, 'It done start in da bible, Brother Fish. It say we da chillen of Ham – we gotta hew wood and draw water forevah, man. Amen! But dat time der ain't no Christians. So, how come it da Christian folk dat hate da Negro? Dey all Jews dat time, and da Christians dey *also* hate da Jews? Dat don't make no sense. Da Jews, dey don't hate da Negro – no way, man. King Solomon, he done marry dat Queen o' Sheba – she black da ace of spades. He da wisest man in da world at dat time, and he gone marry dat beautiful queen.' It was one of Jimmy's more playful theories but it clearly indicated that he didn't simply blame America for the troubles of his human tribe.

So, why had he remained silent? Despite the fact that I'd warned him not to give me any pertinent information, I told myself surely this was different. Spilling the beans to my Chinese interrogators by telling them he'd decided to be a progressive wouldn't be informing or spying. Just the opposite, I would be bringing them glad tidings, and the news would have been accepted as another coup in the cause of communism. *Why, why, why?* It damn near drove me crazy.

The Chinese announced another parade in front of headquarters, this time to listen to some visiting expert pronouncing 'the truth'. His truth was titled 'Russia, the Workers' Paradise'. I confess I was beyond listening, simply too mentally exhausted to take in any more communist claptrap. I could hear words and phrases such as 'capitalist oppression', 'working class no longer shackled', 'production lifted by 300 per cent', blah, blah, blah, when I felt a sudden tugging at my sleeve.

'Don't turn 'round, Brother Fish,' Jimmy's voice said. My heart started to pound fiercely but I managed to nod my head. 'We meet two nights' time, one o'clock, da millet storehouse behind da latrines. Trust me.' I nodded again, suddenly feeling quite dizzy. Then he added, 'Bring yo' parka an' dress warm.'

The speaker raved on and on for an hour or so but I didn't hear another word. My mind filled with possibilities, not all of them good. Perhaps Jimmy was trying to compromise me – there'd be guards waiting when I arrived at the storehouse and I'd be placed back in the cells for attempting to escape. His advice to dress warm and to wear my parka could have been so that the chinks would be further convinced that I'd planned to escape. I'm ashamed of this and other such thoughts now, but at the time my confusion, disappointment and distrust were so great, anything seemed plausible.

Moving very far from your compound unobserved after curfew, or at any time, wasn't easy. The camp comprised a large number of staff, and every one of them saw it as their duty to report even the slightest suspicious movement. The staff lived in the tin-roofed accommodation scattered throughout the camp, which meant there were always eyes on the lookout for aberrant behaviour. The Chinese people, if nothing else, were ever-conscientious in their duties towards the State.

However, both the staff and the guards were accustomed to seeing prisoners going to the latrines at any time during the day and night. Dysentery was so common among the men that the guards took no notice of someone shambling towards this building, which had been built on the outskirts of the compound, supposedly to prevent the smell from reaching their own accommodation. Though why they'd put a millet storehouse close to the latrines was difficult to fathom – it was yet another example of Chinese inscrutability, and the joke, of course, was that this was one of the reasons why the food tasted like shit.

Next day I checked my sandshoes and made sure the laces were strong. Those of us still wearing our boots on arrival at the camp had soon lost them on the grounds that they might help us to escape. It wasn't long before they'd appeared on the feet of the guards. As the

Chinese are a small race it was amusing to see a pair of size-eleven boots on the feet of a diminutive guard. These became known as 'Horace boots' after the cartoon character Horace Horse. I also had a small store of food that I'd pilfered, one handful at a time, while unloading rice on working parties, when inevitably a sack would be dropped on a carefully positioned sharp-edged rock so that it broke open. We took turns getting beaten for this 'accident'.

On the afternoon of the second day I left the political discussion group on three occasions saying I had a touch of dysentery, and watched as Lieutenant Dinh noted my various departures down in his notebook. Nobody would suspect me for doing a runner, though on the other hand, if all this was a set-up, it would be further evidence of my intention to escape. I wore all my clothes to bed and at a quarter to one that morning, wrapped in my blanket (the usual way to go to the latrines in the cold) I left my room in the barracks. Jimmy was waiting for me, and without saying a word we hid as a strolling sentry passed, then headed south into the hills.

We walked until dawn, Jimmy doing most of the speaking. It was early spring, and a misty vapour rose from our mouths as we started to climb. 'There gonna be eight of us cats,' he said. 'Dey all da bad guys.'

'You mean the blokes that caused the attacks on the progressives and wrote the captions on the Mao and Stalin posters?'

'Yoh got it, Brother Fish. Da Chinese, dey done jus' about work out who we is and it be time to vamoose!'

'Thanks for including me,' I said.

Jimmy smiled, and then to save me any mawkish sentimentality he said, 'Yoh part da plan, Brother Fish. It ain't gonna work yoh not der, man.' He went on to explain the escape plan to me. They had the combined knowledge of several previous escape attempts to help them, and at first they decided to head south in an attempt to get to the front-line. But on the latest reports they would not get there till they had traversed 200 miles of the rugged central mountain range. 'Maybe it too far an' we ain't got enough food to get der, which is what we suspek,' Jimmy said. 'Even if we make it der, we gotta creep our way through miles o' da Chinese army before we get to ours. So we change da plan. We head south foh a couple o' days, den west foh 'bout fifty miles till we reach da coast. We steal us a fishing boat an' go out to sea an' hope one of our planes or ships come.' He paused. 'Ain't none of us know nothin' 'bout sailing no fishin' boat – yoh da man, Brother Fish.'

There was no way of evaluating whether this was a sound plan or not, but the sea sounded a much safer place to be than on land and the Chinese would not be expecting it. We continued walking for a while and at one stage, after a steady climb, we drew to a halt and rested. That was when Jimmy said, 'I guess I got me some explaining to do, Brother Fish.'

'Yeah, just a tad, you black bastard,' I replied.

Jimmy grinned. 'Do dat mean I ain't comin' to yo' island? Ain't gonna get none o' yo' mama's cray stew?' Jimmy had long since come to understand the different meanings of the pejorative 'bastard' in the Australian lingo.

'I'm thinking real hard about withdrawing the invitation,' I said, trying not to laugh.

He went on to explain that all along it had been obvious to him that the Chinese regarded the coloured prisoners in the camp as a soft target. 'So I listen up some and soon 'nuff Dinh, he bring up da subject foh general discussion. Dis mah chance. "Boss, we should be comrades," I say to him, 'cos dis the right jar-gon. He done light up like a Christmas tree. "We must fight the American imperialist together," he say. "Your people and mine." Because he heard 'bout me do dat busi-ness with O'Rourke an' how everything clean an' orderly 'round here, he reckon he done caught himself a big fish – da biggest in da black sea.' Jimmy laughed at his own pun. 'He say I should come to headquarters straight off. Dem Chinese cats dey parade me 'front da commandant and I tell dem my story – da orphanage, how da Kraus twins done beat me up, Elmira Reformatory.' Jimmy laughed suddenly. 'I tell dem stuff I don't even know happened. Time I finish da commandant, he shake mah hand. "You is a true believer," he says to me. All dem other officials, dey smilin' an' shakin' mah hand, an' I think pretty soon Lieutenant Dinh he gonna be Captain Dinh. Dey say from now on I gonna work at da camp headquarters, man!'

'So it was you who leaked the traitors and the spies list?' I asked.

Jimmy nodded, and then added, 'I get to see da notes dem undercover progressives dey write. It ain't good, man – dem muth'fuckers dey reporting on what da other prisoners dey bin talkin' 'bout. So I makes me a list. But who I gonna trust wid dat list? Well, Brother Fish, dat easy, man. Dey send me roun' to talk at indoctrination an' give me da names of da bad guys so as I can target dem, try to convert dem. Well, I target dem all right. I pass da lists o' dem undercover progressives to dem an' den we start talkin' 'bout makin' us an escape team.'

'There were six of them on the escape committee?'

'Nah, only three. I tell dem bring a companion dey trust wid der life who ain't sick or got hisself dysentery. Iffen we gonna make it we gonna need eight men for sentry duty, an' to steal da crew an' boat.' He explained that we were to rendezvous with the others at a river junction the following morning.

'Well, mate, I've got to admit – you fooled me. I was convinced you'd betrayed me.'

Jimmy looked surprised. 'Brother Fish, I give you dat signal.'

'What bloody signal?'

'Mah speech, when I stan' up by da microphone. I done speak like I some white turkey. Dat means yoh know it ain't me, man! Dat da signal!'

'Well, I want you to know it was a bloody piss-poor signal because I didn't get it.' I paused, and then asked, 'Where did you learn to speak like that, anyway?'

'Da Somerset *Messenger-Gazette* newspaper, when I read to Frau Kraus. It easy, man – think like a turkey, talk like a turkey.'

'Well, I'll be buggered,' was all I could think to say. As always, Jimmy had managed to surprise me. I had to make up my mind on the spot whether to remain shitty with him or to forgive him. The bastard had put me through hell, but it was damn near impossible to resent him for too long. He'd come back and he'd included me in the escape plan, so it served no purpose to remain angry with him.

We continued on our way, and every once in a while we'd stop and Jimmy would check his crude homemade compass. At last he pointed to what appeared to be a small cave – not really a cave, more like an overhanging rock. 'We stop here foh a while – chow time,' he said. We gathered a few twigs, made a fire and cooked a little rice, and Jimmy produced a nearly full bottle of fish sauce and added a dash to the rice. Rice was a luxury in itself, but with the fish sauce added it became sheer ambrosia.

We walked all that day to within striking distance of the rendezvous point, and slept in a hollow between two rocks in order to avoid the icy wind. Christ help anyone trying to escape in winter. Next morning we headed off at daylight, hoping to come across a road Jimmy said ought to be there if our navigation was right. He'd handed me the compass along with the written directions. Navigation was something I'd learned very early in life, but I have to say I was bloody glad when we hit the road at just about the spot we ought to have come upon it. Staying well concealed within the surrounding bush, we walked parallel to the road for some distance, then veered off down a gully until we reached the river junction.

'According to your notes we must be just about there – it says to look for a group of big rocks just downriver from the junction,' I said.

Jimmy gave a soft whistle and I was surprised to hear a reply. 'Da compass, it works – yoh da man, Brother Fish,' he said, congratulating me.

Four other prisoners were waiting, concealed within the rocks. I was introduced to everyone and Jimmy to the two mates the escape committee had brought along. We lit a fire and cooked the last of the rice and Jimmy added more of the precious fish sauce. From now on it would be millet and whatever we could scrounge off the land – or steal. Pretty soon a seventh bloke arrived, whom Jimmy addressed as Don Bradman. I couldn't help smiling, which the bloke noticed.

'Aye, and I'm not even Australian,' he volunteered, grinning wearily. 'North Yorkshire. Me dah was the village cricket umpire.'

I guess he'd accepted his name as the particular cross he was forced to bear in life. Jimmy handed him his portion of the rice and he devoured it hungrily.

'Where yo' partner?' Jimmy asked, when he'd completed eating.

'Sick, mon. He didna want to come – said he'd be holdin' us up,' Don Bradman replied.

Jimmy's face drained and went the grey colour folk of his race turn when they're deeply shocked, but there was nothing he could say or do about it. My only hope was that the bloke was genuinely sick.

We moved straight off, following the river and making good time. Then, late in the afternoon, when we'd almost decided to settle in for the night, we rounded a bend in the river and were suddenly surrounded by North Korean security police.

Jimmy, who was standing beside me, shrugged and turned to Don Bradman. 'Hey, dat one informer yoh don't know about, comrade.'

Don Bradman blushed furiously. 'Sorry, Jimmy, we coom from the same village – Sheriff Hutton. We went t'same fooking school.'

'These are gooks, mate,' I said quietly to Jimmy, as the North Koreans, yabbering excitedly, surrounded us. 'Let's hope to Christ they take us back to the chink camp and don't handle this themselves.' The likelihood of coming out alive after the North Koreans had manifested their charming little ways to make us talk was close to zero.

Fortunately they took us back to our previous captors and I found myself back in the cells, where the Chinese frequently bashed us and subjected us to endless interrogation. Dinh, in particular, was furious, as I guess he'd lost enormous face. In fact, he had recently been promoted to captain but the second day back we noted that he'd been stripped of his promotion and was back to lieutenant, which did nothing to improve his mood.

The bashing and interrogation continued for several weeks, with Jimmy copping far the worst of it. In the cells they gave us no covering against the still cold nights. Then before the morning sun could warm us, they thrashed our bodies while we were still shivering, which, of course, was much more painful. I deeply dreaded that the rafter treatment might follow and that I'd be put in the Kennel Club. But to our surprise we were released and, of course, each of us was required to deliver a public confession. Which, by the way, we'd done with a degree of mock repentance that completely escaped the Chinese but set the congregated prisoners to clapping. The applause was again misunderstood by our captors, who took it for a general show of approval for our deeply soulful repentance.

As it subsequently turned out, the reason why we'd escaped the truly horrific torture was because the parties at the peace talks had exchanged lists of the names of all the prisoners held and their current physical condition – which, according to the Chinese, in our case was excellent. At the same time they were accusing the Americans of mistreating the Chinese and North Koreans held in United Nations POW camps. I guess they couldn't afford to risk any further deaths such as Doug Waterman's. Of course, we were unaware that the peace talks were so advanced – otherwise, perhaps Jimmy may have taken the chance of being discovered and may not have escaped.

There followed several months of waiting, with our spirits rising on rumours that a cease-fire was close and falling on news of new disagreements emerging.

The 27th of July 1953 began as just another day – same lousy bowl of millet, same morning routine – but by mid-morning there was a buzz around the camp, although no one seemed to know quite why. Then, to our surprise, Lieutenant Dinh approached Jimmy and told him the Korean Armistice had been signed. He shook his hand, and then mine. 'I'm glad you make it to the end,' he said to our surprise, then added, 'You good men, good soldier.'

'Yeah, mate, thanks for not shooting us,' I said, grinning. Talk about the inscrutable Chinese! Who would have thought this final gesture was possible from such a determined enemy. We talked a little further and he told us he was leaving the army after nineteen years and was returning to his fishing village in Guangdong Province. I told him we were doing the same, and he laughed. Jimmy then said, 'Yoh catch communist fish, we gonna catch us some capitalist fish!'

If the war wasn't technically over, and the armistice was simply a way of everyone saving face, it was over for us. We'd made it through to the end and were going home – that is, I was, and Jimmy was hopefully accompanying me. The almost two years in captivity had steeled us into accepting constantly bad outcomes, so when a good one came along we simply couldn't quite grasp it. There was excitement in the camp, certainly, but we hadn't the energy to rush around whooping for joy like schoolboys. We were weary and sick beyond celebration, and hope had to be rekindled in our spirits. Some of us even thought news of the armistice may have been another Chinese trick to further reduce our resistance. But Jimmy and I felt we could trust Lieutenant Dinh, who, despite everything, was a man of some honour.

'You know what I's gonna do first thing, Brother Fish?' Jimmy asked.

'What, mate?'

'Straw-berry malted.' He parted his hands to indicate about twelve inches. 'This fuckin' big!'

I'd dreamed of chocolate and Jimmy of a strawberry milkshake, and I was reminded that freedom is about the little things. We were free at last to do the little things. It was a glorious feeling.

One of the first things I was going to do was write to Gloria, my mum. We'd been allowed to write home every month, but I hadn't heard from her since I'd been taken prisoner. I didn't even know if the Chinese had posted my letters. Not sending letters was one of the threats used on reactionaries, and conversely, a promise to send them was a bribe to become a progressive. Until the prisoner list came out, Gloria may well have assumed I was dead.

We travelled by truck, train and finally by foot to a holding camp at Kaesong. What an irony – Kaesong was where 3RAR had waited eagerly to start the pursuit north. I had been a virgin soldier at the time and couldn't wait to be blooded, to go into battle, to prove I was worthy of the rifle slung across my shoulder and the ribbons not yet on my chest. I recalled the rhyme we'd chanted with such glee at school.

*Ching Chong Chinaman, born in a bath,*
*Christened in a teacup . . . ha, ha, ha!*
*Ching Chong Chinaman went to war,*
*First-class Dutchman shot him in the jaw.*
*'Oh,' said chinky, 'that's not fair!'*
*'Oh,' said the Dutchman, 'I don't care!'*

I would never take the Chinese for granted again. I am certain that, in the end, they would have beaten us. They could have hung on indefinitely while we were clinging on for dear life. They were good soldiers and fought with courage and enormous tenacity, and while some of us fought valiantly and some did not, we'd all lost our taste for war. In the end we knew we were fighting for something pretty meaningless to us, something called 'the Cold War', where one great power was huffing and puffing at another great power in a global game of one-upmanship. I'd seen all I ever wanted to see of war and killing and was anxious to get to the handing-over point at Panmunjom and from there to be shipped out of Korea forever.

I decided I never wanted to return to any part of the world where people's eyes were shaped differently from my own. The South Koreans clearly didn't want democracy enough to fight for it. The North Koreans were already committed communists, with their Chinese allies prepared to fight alongside them and to die defending what they believed to be a superior system, so it was bloody difficult to believe in what we were doing and why we were there in the first place.

Yet I have remained intrigued by the two great Cold War ideologies, democracy and communism. Years after my experience in Korea I read a haunting quote by Mao Zedong.

> *If the US monopoly capitalist groups persist in pushing their policies of aggression and war, the day is bound to come when they will be hanged by the people of the whole world. The same fate awaits the accomplices of the United States.*

Back in the early 1950s I would have accepted Mao's statement as Chinese posturing – merely communist propaganda. As prisoners of war Jimmy and I, and many other good men, had suffered greatly to defend our belief system. I guess I still believe in democracy – and besides, we are unashamedly capitalist. God knows, both the ideology and the mercantile system have been very good to us. Nevertheless, after Australia's involvement with the Americans in Vietnam, Mao's quote has an uncomfortable ring to it. While alliances are important, the right to question them is also essential. Asking why rather than following blindly isn't being disloyal, it is simply being intelligent. America is not always the most convincing ideological friend to have beside you in your weapon pit.

# BOOK TWO

# CHAPTER TWELVE

## *The Homecoming*

After we'd had a deep-cleansing ale at the Anzac Hotel I phoned the airport, only to be told that the Douglas DC3 was in for servicing and there wouldn't be any flights to the island for three days. This meant staying in Launceston or taking the bus the 100 miles or so to Stanley, then catching the *Queen Islander* to Livingston. If I'd known the Douglas DC3 was on the blink we'd have caught the old tub from Melbourne in the first place. We made our way to the post office and I sent a telegram to Gloria telling her we'd be coming in by boat, and would therefore be a few days late. Jimmy didn't seem to mind – he couldn't get over the weather. 'It December, man! It ain't cold. I never seen dat before, Brother Fish!'

Just before we were due to catch the bus I asked Jimmy if he'd brought along a supply of frenchies. I'd written to him in Japan and told him to stock up at his PX where they were issued to the American troops free. He shook his head. 'I ain't done like yoh said, Brother Fish – ain't right.'

I looked at him, astonished. 'Jimmy, do you have any idea of the effect you're going to have on the sheilas when we get to the island?'

He shook his head again. 'T'ain't right – I's a coloured person, Brother Fish.'

'So?'

He shrugged. 'T'ain't right,' he repeated, suddenly looking miserable.

'What do you mean? Coloured blokes don't screw girls? It's against their religion?'

'Nah, it da other way – white girls, dey don't like to do it wid Negro men.'

I couldn't believe what I was hearing. 'Jimmy, mate, on the island they're going to be scratching and kicking and elbowing each other out of the way to be the first to get to your body!'

Jimmy looked generally surprised, and even a little frightened, and I realised that he may never have been in a situation – amorous or otherwise – where he'd been in the presence of a white woman other than Frau Kraus and, of course, the Lutheran Church congregation, where the Negro worshippers sat at the back of the church. 'What about . . . Frau Kraus?' I asked, somewhat mischievously.

'Dat different, dat ain't da same. Gobblin' Spider don't need no rubbers, man,' he protested.

Of course we'd talked about sex in the past – all men do, no matter what the circumstances. In the POW camp, with all of us starving and sick, if you'd presented Carmen Miranda to us with the platter of fruit on her head for a hat, our libidos were so shot we couldn't have raised the necessary equipment and we would have opted for the fruit. But we still talked, and some of the more experienced coves in the camp even bragged about doing *it*. I'd personally done very little of *it*. In fact, the sum total of my sexual life was a going-away-to-the-Korean-War present from Angela Kelly, the wife of my cousin Percy, while he was away for the night at sea on a cray boat, and a visit to a St Kilda brothel the weekend I'd been to Melbourne with Jason Matthews.

On both occasions *it* had happened in the dark, so that while I could claim to have entered *it* I'd never seen *it* face to face, so to speak. Women, and the various methods of stimulating their interesting parts, were still a complete mystery to me, and when coves talked details I was all ears, hoping to learn enough so that at my next encounter (if that should ever happen) I would seem experienced.

By my mid-twenties I should have had a heap of experience, but I'd somehow missed out. When I got back home after New Guinea I still had the *chanteuse* Pat Brand on my mind as the only one for me, and I told myself the island girls simply couldn't compete and that I wasn't prepared to settle for anything less – which was a whole heap of crap, of course. I would have happily dropped my daks at a moment's notice had any young female offered to make love to me – I simply lacked the courage to proposition any of the island girls. Moreover, I'd not much enjoyed going to the brothel in St Kilda, and besides, there wasn't one on the island. I couldn't get my precious little head around bonking anyone who was doing it for money. My head was full of stuff like this, and I decided the island girls wouldn't have understood me – that I desired more than just an occasional quick naughty to get the water off my chest. In other words, I was a thoroughgoing prick, if that isn't the wrong name to use in this context. I remained a virgin until Angela Kelly put the hard word on me at my farewell party.

I'd asked Jimmy several anatomical questions about women, and he'd answered them with a vagueness not typical of him. I knew he wasn't inexperienced, as he'd told me one or two stories about life on the streets of New York, which he always referred to as 'When I been gettin' myself street-poisoned'. He'd explained how it was every black street kid's dream to grow up to be a flash pimp with a stable of girls, a purple Cadillac with whitewall Firestone tyres, a big flashy pad with a bar and a barman serving anything you wanted, and the constant coming and going of honey-sweet pussy for hire to the chump johns.

Then one day he'd passed a shoeshine stand with a rheumy-eyed old man calling out for customers, his hand too gnarled and his arm too frail to pop his shoeshine rag. 'One dem whores standin' der, she say to me, "See dat old man, Jimmy, dat Sugar John Cassidy – he once da king of all da pimps, he got da biggest pussy stable in New York. He done offer dem chump johns every trick in da book so long dey got da bread. Now he can't hardly make 'nough dough for a bottle o'whisky to cool down his hot sorrows." Den she say, "Don't go der, Jimmy – old whores, dat bad, but old pimps, dat da end da whole worl'."'

From all this I gathered that Jimmy knew a fair bit about sex, but I now realised that, improbable as it seemed, he may have thought white women were somehow different from black ones. It had never occurred to me that Jimmy may never have slept with a white woman, or that he might be afraid of being rejected simply on the basis of skin colour.

On one occasion I'd told him the story of the loss of my virginity to Angela Kelly, who'd attended the bit of a party Gloria had thrown as my send-off. Angela had cornered me in the back garden where I'd gone out for a quick slash, as the outside dunny was occupied and I was busting for a leak. I'd barely done up my fly when out of the dark I heard her say, 'Come for dinner termorra night, Jacko.' Then she added, 'Percy Pig is out on the big cray boat all night.' She giggled. 'Bit of a soldier's farewell present, eh?' My heart started to thump thirteen to the dozen. Angela Kelly was a real good-looking sort with lovely breasts, and from Wagga Wagga on the mainland. Everyone wondered how a no-hoper like Percy Kelly could have scored her, as she hadn't even been up the duff when they'd married.

'Percy Pig' was what we'd all called him from childhood, though I was surprised to see that Angela did so as well. Percy's father, Les – Gloria's brother – was a drunk who beat up his kids, and Percy had been bashed on the nose so many times as a child that it was almost flat against his face and he'd sniff and snuffle all the time because his sinuses were blocked. He also looked a lot like a prime porker, with small, pointy ears and tiny, mean, pink-rimmed eyes that never looked directly at you. He couldn't dive for cray because of his sinuses, so he worked as a deckhand. Normally you'd feel sorry for a bloke like him but he was a liar and a cheat, as well as following in his father's footsteps as a dedicated piss-pot. He was also a strong argument, this time on Gloria's side, to add to our combined family not being worth a pinch of the proverbial. Him and Angela didn't have any kids and

Gloria kept saying it couldn't last – the marriage, that is – but it was going nigh on three years they'd been together. 'Miracles will never cease,' was how Mum described their improbable marriage, then she'd add, 'she must have committed a murder or something and only Percy Pig knows she done it, or else a pretty girl like her would have scarpered long ago.'

When I got back into the house I glanced over at Angela, who was sitting on the old chesterfield with the broken springs and the holes in the upholstery that Gloria refused to throw out when I bought her a new one, but maintained it wasn't worth the cost of re-covering. Angela looked up, and directly at me, but her expression gave nothing away – except I could see she'd probably had one too many sherries from the Orlando flagon Gloria had turned on for the ladies.

The whole of the next day I kept panicking. Thinking that when she woke up she'd be sober and change her mind, or she might have a hangover and would have forgotten and I'd turn up all bright-eyed and bushytailed to find myself rejected or severely mocked. I panicked again for the umpteenth time during the day at the thought that even if we ended up doing *it*, she might find out I was a virgin and didn't know how. I bought a box of Cadbury's Roses and blushed when Mrs Dunne at the local shop asked who the lucky girl was. I mumbled something about 'Me mum', then, realising the stupid old stickybeak would mention it to Gloria the next time she saw her – '*What a nice boy to buy his mum chocolates . . .*' – I hastily added, 'Er . . . for a friend of hers.'

I turned up at Angela Kelly's house with the chocolates concealed within my shirt just in case she gave me the bum's rush while I was standing at the door holding them. But she was all smiles and I could see she was pleased to see me, and she asked me in and sat me down at the kitchen table and opened a bottle of beer. She was frying onions, so I said, 'Something smells good.'

'Sausages and mash with onions'n'gravy,' she said.

'Hey! How'd you know that's my favourite?' I said, trying to sound sort of casual and worldly.

She looked at me from under her eyelashes and smiled and said in a real sexy sort of throaty voice, 'Me too – nothing beats a good firm sausage.'

I immediately panicked. I wasn't worried about the firm bit – my tentpole under the table had already risen just from looking at her bent over the stove – but it was the way she said it, as if she expected a good firm sausage to be *big* as well. I mean, you wouldn't describe a small sausage as a 'good firm sausage', would you? Some small blokes end up with big dicks – but mine was about average, even a bit on the small side, and definitely not in the 'good firm sausage' category if you were a good sort like Angela Kelly who was probably pretty experienced, coming from the mainland and all. Then I recalled from school that Percy Pig had an enormous dick, and my tentpole wavered for a moment as I plunged into yet another panic.

I remembered the chocolates and thought that a bit of gallantry might make up for my lack of size in Angela's eyes, so I started to undo my shirt, my fingers trembling in the process. At that very moment Angela turned around from the stove and caught me. She laughed, 'Now, now, Jacko – I had that in mind for dessert,' she said, again in that throaty voice. I thought, *Bloody hell, she must have X-ray eyes that know the box of Cadbury's Roses is concealed in my shirt*. I produced the box, and held it out.

'For me?' she asked, surprised. I nodded dumbly. She came right up to me and took the box of chocolates and placed it on the table, then she bent down over me and the top of her dress sort of scalloped and I could see her beautiful breasts straining in her brassiere, firm as anything. 'Better eat first before you get dessert, Jacko,' she said, her voice all throaty again. Then she kissed me, her tongue going straight into my mouth and halfway down my throat. She slipped her hand into my open shirt and stroked my chest. There was the smell of burning and it wasn't my tentpole about to shoot the buttons on my fly up into the bottom of the kitchen table, it was the onions. 'Jesus, the fuckin' onions!' she cried, and straightened up and hurried over to the stove.

We ate the sausages and the slightly burned onions, which she immersed in a pool of brown gravy made in the top of a volcano of mashed potatoes. There were also tinned peas, if I remember correctly. Though, to tell you the truth, I don't remember tasting anything, or even if the sausages were firm. I hardly touched the glass of beer she'd given me and it had gone almost flat. She poured one for herself. 'Hair of the dog,' she said, picking it up and throwing back her head so her glorious breasts pointed straight at me as she swallowed almost half the beer in one gulp.

With her breasts in my face like that, my latest panic became how to undo her bra. I'd heard older blokes say how you had to do it with one hand so she didn't even notice, until you just casually slid or sort of pulled it away, and there were the naked breasts ready for action. Then you sort of tested the nipples with your thumb, and if they were real stiff then you knew she was ready for *it*. I gathered from their talk that stiffened nipples were like a sheila version of our erection, and you wouldn't get *any* until they were hard. I also knew from these conversations that removing the brassiere was a matter of practice, lots of practice. Because you had to do it by feel, sort of backwards, while kissing her at the same time. There were these hooks that slid into pockets in the strap at the back and if you didn't get the angle dead right they wouldn't come out, and then she'd know you were trying to get her bra off and she might go stone cold on you.

Alone in the house on one occasion I'd tried doing it on one of Sue's brassieres I'd found in the wash basket she'd brought in from the line before going off to her morning shift at the cottage hospital. I slipped two lemons from the tree in the backyard into the cups, and strapped the bra around the middle of the inside back of a chair so the hooks were facing the kitchen wall. Then I sat on the chair facing its back and brought my arms around and kissed the top of the back of the chair while trying to undo the bra purely by feel. But nothing budged, and after about twenty minutes I gave up because one of the hooks had torn the pocket it was lodged in. Besides, the lemons kept falling out and rolling across the lino floor. I decided not to take the exercise any further in case Gloria returned and saw me in her kitchen without permission – not to mention in such a compromising position with the chair, the bra and the lemons. Now I was confronted with the real thing, and so it wasn't any wonder that I couldn't taste the sausages and the burned onions that slipped down my dry throat like tasteless worms.

But I needn't have worried. Angela Kelly stood up from the table and in a matter-of-fact voice said, 'Stand up, Jacko.' I confess I'd dreaded this moment, because I could feel there was a patch of preliminary wet on the front of my light-coloured trousers. But she didn't seem to notice, and led me gently by the hand into her bedroom, which contained a big brass double bed. Then she undressed me so that I stood starkers, my old fellow in full ceremonial salute. 'Nice one, Jacko,' she said, her throaty voice almost purring. 'Just the size I like.' I will always love her for that single reassuring remark. Then she took me in her hand.

*Oh, Jesus! Please God, don't let her squeeze!* I pleaded silently. She reached out and switched off the light. 'Lie on your back,' she commanded, still leading me by the tentpole and with her free hand pushing me gently onto the bed. I did as I was told, but I confess I was confused. *Wasn't she the one supposed to lie on her back?* But I wasn't game to move. The moon was up and moonlight came through the window just enough so I could see her in silhouette as she pulled off her dress, undid her bra easy as anything and stepped out of her panties. I couldn't see any of the vital details, just her general shape, which, I can tell you, was very, very sexy. Then she moved over to the window and drew the curtains and I caught a flash of moonlight on her breasts before we were in the pitch dark. I heard her breathing coming towards me and then the springs on the bed creaked as she climbed onto it. Then her whole body was over me, one leg on either side of me. Her mouth came down on mine and her tongue filled me. *Shit, what now?* I thought desperately. *Do I pull her over onto her back and climb aboard? If I do, how do I find it?* But then her hand found me, and the next thing

I knew I was in paradise. A creamy smoothness surrounded me that was indescribable and wonderful, unlike anything I'd ever imagined, even in the shower. Angela was sitting on me. 'Buck, you bastard!' she said, gasping as she started to rise and fall on top of me.

Jimmy had laughed heartily when I'd described my first sexual encounter. 'Me too, Brother Fish, it a co-in-see-dence. I got dat same bucking ex-pere-ee-ence. I jus' sixteen an' dis pretty lady who I know is a whore and who stand on da street corner, she done proposition me. "You wanna good time, baby?" she say to me. Now, I ain't had no gobblin' spider for near nine months and I need it bad, man! "Yoh look like yo' a frisky young stallion," she say to me.

'"I ain't got no bread, ma'am," I say to her, real cool.

'"Ten bucks," she say. "It a special matinee price – I's a twenty-five-buck whore, but it a slow afternoon, sugar baby." She put her head one side an' she look at me from da top to da bottom. "Yoh some fast young stud who need his big mama bad or I ain't no sassy whore," she says to me.

'She right in dat department, an' I got me ten bucks from sellin' some contraban' me an' da gang done find in a shed we broke open. Fifteen bran' new carburettors, dey still packed in der General Motors boxes. Da shed, it ain't even a service station – some dude, he stole dem somewheres foh sure. Now we's stealing dem back. So I got me ten bucks that's my share, compliments General Motors. Dat greaser who think he got hisself some nice little profit in his shed, safe behin' his big ole Yale lock, in foh a big surprise, man. So I says, "Okay, lead me away, pretty lady."

'I get me laid real good, twenty-five bucks for ten greenbacks, but den she say dat what she like is a young stallion permanent dat ain't broke in yet, 'cos he still willin' to buck good when she ride him. Iffen I jus' lie on mah back it don't cost me another cent. Dat was real nice, man! She tell me I's a strong young stud and I can come back any time and it ain't gonna cost me a dime, always pro-vide-ding I stay on mah back as her bucking horse. Soon I's a young stallion dat bucking her regular, so I's broke in real good and to her ulti-mate satisfaction.'

Jimmy grinned, enjoying the play on words. 'But den her pimp he fine out 'bout da young stallion who bucking her and who ain't earning her no income to pass on his share of the bucking rights. Two punks come to visit me one night an' dey beat me up real bad.' Jimmy laughed. 'Dat da sad end of my career in da US of A Cavalry.'

Standing at the bus stop in Launceston and remembering the story he'd told me, I said, 'Well, mate, you'd better brush up on your bucking – the island's women have never seen a big black stallion before and they're bound to want to ride him.' I wondered briefly what Angela Kelly would make of Jimmy – that is, if she was still with Percy Pig.

I looked down the street and saw there was a chemist shop directly opposite the bus stop. 'Hang on,' I said to Jimmy, 'I'll be back in a mo. Don't let the bus go without us.' I crossed the street going hell for leather, the metal tips of my crutches going clickety-clack on the hard surface of the road. As luck would have it the chemist was at the back of the shop with his female assistant at the cash register near the front. I hopped past her. 'G'day,' I said to her, without really looking, and made for the chemist at the back. He looked up as I approached, and I saw he was mixing something with a mortar and pestle.

'G'day. I'm in a bit of a hurry, sir,' I said a little breathlessly.

'Not too many soldiers drop in here, and even fewer on crutches,' he said, smiling.

'Can I have two dozen crutches . . . er, I mean, contraceptives please?' I corrected. I'd intended to sound real casual, like it was a request I made all the time, but now I'd messed it all up.

He nodded, not changing expression. 'Certainly, son,' he said. 'In a hurry, and two dozen?'

I nodded dumbly, failing to see the joke. He turned and went into a small room at the back of the shop, and returned a few moments later holding a brown paper bag.

'How much?' I blurted out, when I'd intended saying, 'What do I owe you, please?'

'Wendy, there's no charge for the soldier,' he called over to the girl at the front. Then he said quietly, pointing down to my chest, 'I recognise the ribbons. You see, my son was killed in a napalm attack at the Battle of Kapyong.' He paused, then said, 'Perhaps you knew him? Harry Walsh?' He handed me the bag and added, 'Enjoy – life is much too short.'

I was stunned and panicked all at the same time. 'Bluey Walsh! 10 Platoon, the Yank planes, I was there!' I said in astonishment.

I knew I should stay and talk to him, but the bus to Stanley was due any minute. Then I heard Jimmy yelling out from across the road that the bus had arrived.

'Better get going, son,' the chemist said, smiling.

'I'll come and see you next time I'm in town, Mr Walsh,' I said lamely.

'I'd like that very much,' he replied.

I was halfway back across the street when I realised I hadn't even offered my condolences. *What a piss-weak bastard you are, McKenzie!* I almost decided to turn back and talk to him about Bluey, but the bus was waiting and Jimmy called out again, 'Get yo' ass ovah here, Brother Fish!' I could hear the passengers in the bus laughing at Jimmy's hollering out to me. So, of course, as usual, I lacked the character to do the right thing. It wouldn't have killed us to stay a couple more days in Launceston to speak to Mr Walsh about his son – I would've liked someone to take the time with Gloria if I'd died in battle. Arriving a few days late on the island wouldn't have been a big deal, and after I explained the circumstances to Gloria she'd have understood. But I did no such thing – I got on the bus and said nothing to Jimmy until we were fifty miles or so down the road to Stanley. He didn't say much, just nodded his head. 'Dat too bad,' he said slowly, but I knew he was thinking we should have stayed to talk to Bluey's dad.

We arrived at Stanley around two o'clock to find the boat was waiting for the bus, which meant we'd be docking in Livingston Harbour around midnight. During the entire trip Jimmy was still in uniform and attracting a lot of local attention everywhere we went. The idea had been to buy him some clobber in Melbourne, but he couldn't find a pair of trousers his size off the rack at Myer and there wasn't a tailor handy who could make him a pair in the time available. A Yank the size of Jimmy in uniform and on crutches was an eye-popper anywhere we went, and so to save him embarrassment I'd decided to wear my uniform as well.

We must have looked pretty weird with my slouch hat not rising all that far above Jimmy's waist, and both of us on our double sticks. This time at least my chest sported four ribbons. There was the original one I'd got for turning up to World War II too late to fight. This had been issued soon after the war ended. There was another issued for much the same reason later, and which caught up with me in hospital in Japan. Now there were the two campaign ribbons for Korea. The first, the Korea Medal sanctioned by the King of England, who had died before it was struck so it bore the uncrowned head of Elizabeth II. The second, the United Nations Korea Medal, which everyone called the 'Butcher's Apron', because the ribbon was blue and white similar to a butcher's apron. And then there was the emblem of the US Presidential Citation, a blue rectangle bordered in gold and worn above the right breast pocket. Jimmy had four ribbons – the Purple Heart that Americans get for being wounded in battle, the Korean Service Medal, which was the American campaign medal, the Butcher's Apron the same as me, and something called the National Defence Service medal. He also wore a combat infantryman's badge. I'd be lying if I didn't admit that these extra ribbons on my chest made a big difference to how I felt about myself. I reckoned they'd been hard earned, even though no civilian would have a clue what they were for and probably couldn't have cared less.

Bass Strait behaved itself for a change and we had a calm and uneventful trip, with the sun going down over the horizon around eight o'clock – a spectacular sunset falling against fast-rising cumulus cloud to bring on a moonless night. At about eleven-thirty, standing on deck, I pointed out the lighthouse winking away on the steep rise above Livingston Harbour. 'Hope we can get a lift, mate – the harbour's a good couple of miles from town.'

'We catch us a yellow cab,' Jimmy replied simply.

I laughed, then explained, 'Mate, there's only one taxi on the island – Arthur Cooper's 1932 Morris Major – but old Arthur is usually pissed by six o'clock. Even if he met the boat, which is highly improbable, we haven't come all this way to die on the final stretch at the hands of a drunken taxi driver.' Then it occurred to me that with the Douglas DC3 on the blink the skipper would have brought the mail and maybe Busta Gut would meet the boat with the post-office van. In this second unlikely event, we could get a lift into town with him.

'Busta Gut – dat his name for real?' Jimmy asked.

'Nah, it's Buster Gutherie, big idle bastard. His mum, Ma Gutherie, is the postmistress, which is just as well for Busta Gut or he'd be unemployable. His idea of delivering an urgent telegram is sometime in the next couple of days if he happens to find himself in the vicinity of your street. He's probably still got the one I sent to Gloria from Launceston in the bottom of his mailbag.'

The harbour was in darkness as we approached – not even the fish co-op lights were on, or the big blue light that usually lit up the dockside. Stranger still, all the fishing boats were in, which was weird – at this time of the year the boats would be out all night cray fishing or shark longlining. *Someone's mucked around with the lights*, I thought, *surely they must know the boat comes in at midnight*. The skipper gave a blast of the ship's horn as he started to bring the bow around in order to dock. Suddenly all the co-op lights went on, and the lights from several parked trucks flashed on in the dark, then the big dockside light flared up washing the area in pale-blue light. Truck horns started to blast out and a great cheer rose from the shore.

'*Jesus!*' I exclaimed.

'Look like yoh got yourself a welcome committee, Brother Fish,' Jimmy said, laughing. Now we could see a crowd of about 200 people on the dockside outside the co-op.

'The whole bloody island's turned up! Shit, what do we do now?' It was the last thing on earth I would have expected. A banner strung across the front of the co-op read, 'Welcome Home Jacko!' then, hastily added, was, '& Jimmy!' They must have rigged up a loudspeaker because on a small platform standing at the very forefront stood Gloria, Sue and the twins, Cory and Steve, with a bit of a brass band arranged around them. Moments later it struck up, with the four harmonicas to the fore belting out 'When Johnny Comes Marching Home'. Gloria was the lead mouth, and she was good, but she didn't *quite* have the authority a lead needs. I guess there was still a place for me in the family group.

By the time we'd drawn alongside people were cheering their heads off, throwing streamers, whistling and carrying on a treat. 'Giddonya Jacko!', 'Bloody beauty, mate!', 'Well done, son!' individual voices in the crowd yelled. One female voice cried out, 'Thanks for bringing me a Yank, Jacko!' It was Dora Kelly, one of my numerous cousins on Gloria's side. I was surprised – she'd turned into a real good-looking sort in the time I'd been away. It was a grand welcome home and everywhere people were opening bottles of beer and filling paper cups from a flagon of sherry and passing them to the ladies present. Then the band struck up 'For They are Jolly Good Fellows', with everyone singing at the top of their voices.

'Three cheers for Jacko and his Yank mate!' Father Crosby yelled, and the crowd responded. When the gangplank went down and Jimmy and I came down on our crutches the crowd hushed, then someone in the band started a drum roll and the clapping began, and the cheering started all over again with all the women crying. Gloria and Sue came rushing up, both of them bawling their eyes out as they hugged me. Then they turned to Jimmy and did the same, welcoming him to the island. I'd forgotten to mention to Gloria in my letter from Korea that Jimmy was a Negro, and the island kids who'd been allowed to stay up to meet the boat stood gaping, their mouths around their kneecaps. It wasn't just the kids – I doubt if one in twenty of the islanders had ever seen a black bloke before, and I'll guarantee none had seen a six-foot-nine American Negro in full military dress uniform.

After Gloria had stopped blubbering, she kept saying, 'You're skin and bone, Jacko! What did those mongrels do to you?' Sue just cried and hugged me and cried some more, sniffing and bursting into tears, and then drawing back and looking at me, and then doing it all over again with me patting her on the back and 'there-there-ing' her each time. Finally, between gulps, she managed to say, 'Jacko, you look bloody awful!' Then off she'd go again. Some nurse, eh?

A little girl of about five with a pink ribbon in her blonde hair and wearing a matching pink kewpie-doll dress, who should have been asleep hours earlier, came forward with a large bunch of gladioli that almost obscured her. She hastily presented it to Jimmy, then dashed back and grabbed her mum by the skirt and stuck her thumb in her mouth.

It was then that Nicole Lenoir-Jourdan stepped out of the crowd. I was leaning on my crutches with a bottle of beer someone had thrust at me in one hand, grinning like an ape, completely overwhelmed, trying to introduce Jimmy to everyone, being hugged by the women and patted on the back or grabbed by my free hand by the blokes. When Nicole Lenoir-Jourdan came forward the babble of voices around me seemed to go silent and I was alone, a little boy sitting cross-legged staring nervously down at the library floor. *Oh Christ, what now?* I could feel the panic rising in my stomach. *What'll I do if she kisses me? Oh, Jesus, I've got this bottle of beer in my hand!*

I forced myself back to the present and smiled as she drew closer. 'Welcome home, Jack,' she said in her stentorian headmistress-style voice. The mob started to crowd in. She took the bottle of beer from my hand and handed it to Cory, who was standing beside me, then reached out and hugged me. She smelled of some sort of perfume, roses maybe or something else, some flower anyway, quite nice. 'Congratulations – you're a hero, Jack,' she said. There was more clapping, and she shook Jimmy by the hand. 'My goodness, you are a big boy! Welcome to the island,' she said warmly.

Jimmy smiled, recognising her from my numerous references over the months. 'Thank yoh, ma'am, I done bring Brother Fish back safe an' soun'.'

'Brother Fish? Oh. I see, you mean Jack! Thank you – I can't say how much we've missed him.' Then she turned to the crowd and held her hand up for silence. She may not have been the librarian any longer but she was still the justice of the peace and the owner of the *Queen Island Weekly Gazette*, and seemed to command as much respect as ever – even Father Crosby shut up, prepared to share the limelight in her case.

'Ladies and gentlemen,' she began, 'at precisely eight this evening, news came through on the Australian Associated Press wire service to the *Gazette* office from Canberra.' She paused to let the importance of this statement sink in. It wasn't very often anything came from Canberra to the island, and when it did it was usually bad news. Then she started to read from a slip of paper. 'The Minister for the Army has announced that Private Jack McKenzie has been awarded the Military Medal for outstanding bravery while serving with 12 Platoon, D Company, 3rd Battalion, Royal Australian Regiment, in the Battle of Kapyong in Korea.' She looked at me, beaming. 'Congratulations, Jack!' she said.

Well, you should have heard the carry-on. If I'd won the Victoria Cross they couldn't have cheered any louder. As for me, I was completely gobsmacked. There were lots who'd fought better than me in that battle – brave warriors deserving recognition long before I did. The first night of the battle I'd sat on my arse in a weapon pit next to Ian Ferrier, our company radio operator, watching the fighting take place below me. I even wondered momentarily if they'd got the wrong McKenzie, but as I was the only one of that name in our battalion and they'd nominated the right company and platoon I guessed it had to be me they were referring to.

Jimmy grabbed me by the hand and I thought he might tear it off at the wrist, he was that pleased for me. 'Brother Fish, yo' da best! Da bravest and da best!'

Gloria once again burst into tears, and so did Sue. Cory and Steve kept walking around and shaking their heads and exclaiming, 'Shit, eh?', 'You beauty!' and words to that effect.

For the moment, anyway, I was a far cry from the little bloke who'd slunk off to war with his tail between his legs and his head full of ideological bullshit and jargon about fighting to defend the free world from communism. I wondered briefly if the medal might mean that the McKenzies were no longer worth only a pinch of the proverbial in Gloria's eyes, or if Alf's disgrace ban would finally be lifted. Gloria was a hard woman and it might take more than a tin medal from the queen to lift the curse and cancel out the ban. Besides, bravery never got us anywhere. Alf had been the bravest little bugger you could ever meet and would've taken on a wounded buffalo with his bare hands if it meant defending Gloria. All it got him was a regular thumping down at the pub of a Saturday night. Then I thought of the chemist in Launceston. *You're the same gutless wonder you always were, McKenzie. The medal ain't gunna change that, mate.*

A welcoming party had always been planned at the dockside. Later I learned that the pub had donated four wooden kegs of Boag's Draught as well as three flagons of McWilliams' Sweet Sherry for the ladies, but now the party really got going and it was dawn before people started to go home – dawn being only a coincidence and the empty kegs being the real reason for departure. I don't think I've ever seen half the island, including Father Crosby, motherless all at the same time. People piled onto the backs of trucks laughing and shouting to the drivers, who were just as pissed as they were. In one instance I saw a kid who couldn't have been a day over twelve years old, his little sister beside him in the cabin, driving a four-ton truck, the two kids the only sober ones among the couple of dozen adults piled giggling in the back. In the island tradition you could be quite sure more than one future islander would be born out of wedlock nine months after my and Jimmy's arrival on the island.

When – after much drunken back-slapping and sloppy-kissing – we were finally ready to leave, Busta Gut staggered up to me. 'Jeezus, Jacko, I nearly forgot, mate!' He waved his arm unsteadily above his head, and I saw that it contained a mangled envelope. 'Telegram f'yiz!' He handed the envelope to me.

'Can't be for me, mate,' I replied. 'Must be the one I sent Mum from Launceston.'

'Nah, me mum said that was about yiz comin' 'ome in the boat. She sent me right off to deliver it urgent.' He pointed to the crumpled envelope in my hand. 'It's f'yizorrite.'

I was too tired to open it, and so I stuffed it into my pocket just as Steve drove up in the fish co-op truck. When there was any driving to be done Steve was always at the wheel, because he was the mechanical whiz in the family and could fix anything – as well as drive in just about any state of inebriation. They'd placed a bench against the back of the driver's cabin so that Jimmy and I could sit with our plaster casts straight out in front of us. Fixed to the radiator were crossed flags – the Stars and Stripes and ours. Trailing on one side of the back of the truck were streamers of red, white and blue crinkle paper and on the other, green and gold. I'm sure the truck had been scrubbed and hosed down thoroughly, but it still smelled vaguely of fish.

Jimmy and I were hoisted up onto the bench in the back of the truck, and those still standing climbed in – and one or two who weren't were hoisted into the back. Even before we pulled away Gloria, who sat in the front holding Jimmy's bunch of gladdies clutched to her breast, was fast asleep with her nose buried in the orange and pink flowers. Off we went in low gear, doing a full fifteen miles an hour up the hill from the harbour.

Along the way we had to stop to pick up Father Crosby, who'd fallen off his bicycle and was snoring at the side of the road. We dropped him off at the presbytery in time for mass. I thought about waking Mum, who never missed early-morning mass, but then decided to let her sleep and to cop the flak when she woke. Later she would explain that Father Crosby had arranged a special dispensation from God and had cancelled six o'clock mass in anticipation of the grand welcoming event. 'We'll transfer mass to the evening,' Father Crosby had promised. 'God won't mind a twelve-hour delay.'

I think it was Mum's proudest moment, even more so than the announcement of the medal, when he'd come up to her the previous morning after mass and said, 'My dear, the Good Lord has brought Jacko home safely and as a hero, which is the next best thing to being a saint. I have thanked the Lord for your son's safe return and I clearly understood Him to say that, as his humble servant on earth, I should drink a cup or two of kindness in the lad's honour. Now, I couldn't be doing His will and taking early mass tomorrow morning, could I?'

Old Mrs Scobie, who hadn't missed early-morning mass in thirty years, came up to Gloria and told her it was iniquitous and that she'd be punished by God. Gloria replied, 'Agnes, it's such a pity you'll be too pissed to attend evening mass. God will not be happy, my dear.'

Every once in a while someone would bang on the truck's cabin roof as we reached one or another home on the way. I reckoned most of Livingston would be closed until pretty late in the morning, as this mob was certainly in no shape to go to work. Several people had passed out and were still on the truck when we reached home, so Steve drove it under the big old fig tree so they'd have shade, as the sun was already well up by the time we arrived. Then Cory, pissed as a newt himself, carried over a bucket of water and a tin mug, spilling half of it over his head as he lifted it onto the back of the truck. When the drunks finally woke up they'd be spitting cotton.

By the time we got home I felt like an ageing labrador at the end of a duck shoot. My leg hurt like hell – and the grog mixed with the antibiotics we were still taking wasn't doing my head a favour, either. We'd been up around twenty-three hours, but I don't think I've been happier in my life – happy for myself and happy for my mate, whom the island had well and truly taken to their hearts. Sue wanted to cook us breakfast but Jimmy and I were too buggered to stay up any longer, and we staggered to the back of the house where I'd built the indoor shower and extension bedroom when I came back from New Guinea.

As he pulled off his boots, Jimmy said to me, 'Brother Fish, yoh got good folks and lotsa fine love, an' yoh done share dem both with me. I thank yoh from da bottom of mah heart.' To my astonishment he turned away quickly, though not before I saw the tears well up in his eyes. Like me he was pretty pissed, but I knew he meant it. I guess Jimmy's life had been way short on love, and it was a safe bet he'd never been presented with a bunch of pink and orange gladioli before.

'G'night, mate. We'll go out tomorrow with Cory and Steve and get us some crays for . . .' but I don't remember completing the sentence before I was asleep.

The following morning Sue demanded our clothes for laundering, and a few minutes later returned with the crumpled envelope Busta Gut had given me at the welcome-home party. 'It's a telegram. You haven't opened it yet!' she said accusingly. I explained how Busta Gut had handed it to me as we were about to depart. 'Probably been in his bag for days,' Sue said. 'Open it – it could be important,' she demanded. Telegrams were not often received in our family and when we did get one, it was never good news. I could see the anxious look on Sue's face. 'At least it can't be about you being dead or wounded like the last one we got that said you were missing in action,' she said. I smoothed out the window envelope, removed the telegram and quickly read it, then began to laugh. 'What's so funny?' Sue asked, relieved.

'It arrived three days ago!' I began to read it to her.

CANBERRA ACT
PRIVATE J. MCKENZIE
4 DECEMBER 1953

DESIRE TO CONVEY CONGRATULATIONS THAT YOUR SERVICE HAS BEEN RECOGNISED BY BEING DECORATED WITH THE MILITARY MEDAL SIGNED JOSHUA FISHER MINISTER FOR THE ARMY.

As I said to Sue, the date the telegram had been sent was three days prior. Obviously Ma Gutherie hadn't thought it worth a gee-up for Busta Gut, whereas the news of my arrival home on the boat had got urgent priority. In fact, the telegram from Canberra must have arrived at least a day before the one I'd sent to Gloria. Nothing much had changed on the island.

Jimmy was a big hit and we had cousins and distant relations turning up at all hours to visit, bringing eggs or a couple of bottles of beer to show they hadn't come empty-handed. I reckon every single sheila on the island dropped by in the first week, ostensibly to welcome me back. I'd been at school with several of them. They all left having given Jimmy their address and extracted a firm promise from him to call by soon.

Clothes – well, trousers anyway – were a big problem for Jimmy, and in the end Gloria cut a pattern and made two pairs of long pants from some good blue cotton she'd ordered from McKinlay's in Launceston. They also sent some grey flannel, sufficient for a couple of pairs of good trousers, and Gloria wasn't game to just run them up like the blue cotton ones so she unpicked a pair from his dress uniform, cut a pattern from them and then sewed them back together again. Then she made the two flannel pairs, all on her trusty table-model Singer sewing machine. Jimmy was still skinny from the POW camp, so shirts were no problem, and nobody wore a jacket on the island in summer anyway.

Christmas came and Jimmy flew Gloria and Sue over to Launceston to stock up on supplies, and paid for all the goodies we'd never before had at Christmas-day lunch – including the first turkey the family, excluding myself, had ever tasted. He also paid for all the grog. This was no mean gesture, as just about every rello on the island turned up after lunch, ostensibly to wish us Merry Christmas, but really so that the various Kelly and McKenzie single girls could have another go at persuading Jimmy to call around some time.

The first month back home went by quickly and the time came for us to have our plaster removed, so we took the Douglas DC3 over to Launceston with Sue accompanying us. At Launceston General Hospital they got rid of the plasters and X-rayed our legs, and the young quack showed us how the bones that had been rebroken and properly pinned when we'd come out of the POW camp had this time grown straight. He said they'd done a good job. I then asked him about the limp both Jimmy and I had been left with after the Chinese had removed our plaster the first time. He said that provided we walked up to our waists in the surf every morning for an hour for the next month to strengthen our leg muscles, he saw no reason why the limp would return. Afterwards, Sue and Jimmy went to the museum while I visited Mr Walsh at the chemist shop.

I was in a bit of a quandary as I couldn't tell Bluey Walsh's old man that the last words his son had muttered before he died were 'Oh shit!', but I couldn't think of any words he might have said that would comfort his old man. If I told him Bluey had said nothing he'd be disappointed, because as a soldier you're always supposed to have last words when you're about to die. I couldn't just say Bluey had died in my arms saying, 'Mum, Dad, I love you,' because he may have sisters and brothers and he wouldn't have left them out, would he? Besides, if he'd said those words as he died I should have told his Dad when we'd first met despite my hurry at the time to catch the bus.

Jimmy and I had once had a conversation about last words. According to Jimmy, most American soldiers cried out for their mother. I guess ours did as well, although I hadn't witnessed this. Ted Shearer, for instance, had died in the weapon pit in the Battle of Kapyong without me even knowing, and Johnny Gordon, in the village where we'd been ambushed, hadn't uttered a word. If Ted had had any last words I wouldn't have heard them in the clatter of machine guns, mortars landing and rifle fire. When Jimmy told me about blokes calling out for their mum he'd speculated, not knowing his mother, that he wouldn't know what to say when he bit the dust. He'd laughed. 'Hey, maybe I gonna say, "So long, Gobblin' Spider!" because it don't sound right foh me to say, "I love you, Frau Kraus!"'

As for me, I guess I'd have to send my love to the whole family, not just Gloria. If I didn't she'd maybe add me to the disgrace ban for not including Sue, Cory and Steve in my last thoughts. Anyway, it seemed only natural that you'd include the whole family if you had enough breath left.

I arrived at the chemist shop still not sure what my words of comfort and Bluey Walsh's last words should be. Mr Walsh recognised me immediately. 'No more crutches, hey! That's good, son.'

I grinned. 'G'day, Mr Walsh, it feels strange walking more or less normally again.' I noticed for the first time that he had hair the same colour as my own but turning sort of salt-and-cayenne-peppery, which accounted for Bluey. I'm normally pretty observant, but I'd been that anxious to get the condoms in a hurry last time that I hadn't noticed very much about him.

'Come in for more supplies, have you?' he asked.

'No, sir, I came in to see you – as I promised.'

He looked relieved. 'I was hoping you wouldn't forget – the family is very excited.'

*Shit, I didn't even phone ahead to say I was coming. He's obviously told his family about my last visit and how I rushed out, and here it is a month later! What if I'd chickened out?* 'I'm sorry I didn't come in sooner, Mr Walsh.' I wanted to make some plausible excuse but couldn't think of one – you can't exactly say you were too busy to see a bloke about his son's death.

'Would you mind if we nipped home?' he asked. 'My wife would like to be with us, and Harry's brother and sister could be there in a few minutes as well. Is that okay?'

I felt the familiar panic rise within me – they'd want more than a couple of words I might invent as Bluey's – Harry's – last words. On my first visit to the chemist I'd been in such a rush I'd barely glanced at the shop assistant, but now I could see she was an absolute stunner. She gave me a big smile and then said to Mr Walsh, 'You've got Mrs Dougherty's medicine to get ready – she'll be here in ten minutes. She's always on the dot, and she'll be furious if you're not here.'

Mr Walsh gave an impatient jerk of his head and clucked his tongue in annoyance, then looked at me. 'Would you mind, Mr McKenzie?'

I then realised that we hadn't been formally introduced and looked at him, surprised. 'You know my name?'

'On the radio. It was on the local radio when you won the Military Medal. We were all proud of you.'

'I apologise, sir. I should have introduced myself before.'

He grinned. 'I think you had other things on your mind at the time.'

He turned to the shop assistant. 'And this is Wendy,' he said, smiling again.

'G'day, Wendy,' I said, sticking out my hand, then unnecessarily saying, 'Jacko McKenzie, Queen Island.'

'The war hero?' she asked right off.

I blushed. 'Nah, lucky – they must've tossed a coin. There were heaps more deserved a medal before me.'

'And modest, too!' she exclaimed.

'You're Wendy, er . . .'

'Kalbfell,' she said.

Wendy Kalbfell wasn't any taller than me – in fact, she was maybe an inch or so shorter. She had brown hair, mousey-brown I suppose, but she had these green eyes you couldn't believe and was *really* pretty, with a knockout smile. She was wearing a chemist smock like Mr Walsh, so I asked, 'Are you a chemist?' In those days they weren't known as pharmacists.

She laughed, shaking her head. 'No. Mr Walsh insists it looks professional.'

'It does,' I said. 'Very.'

'That's good,' she said.

The conversation wasn't exactly progressing, then she said, 'You knew Bluey Walsh, didn't you?'

'Yeah, great bloke. He died in my arms.' Suddenly, I saw Bluey Walsh in flames falling at my feet with me uselessly emptying my water bottle over him and him looking up at me in surprise and saying, 'Oh shit!', then dying right in front of my eyes. In my nervous state I started to talk, telling Wendy Kalbfell about the two American planes and the yellow smoke flare the spotter plane had dropped and then our astonishment and horror as the first plane had come in low dropping napalm. I told her about pouring my water bottle over Bluey and trying to beat out the flames. 'Then he looked at me, and said, "Bloody good life, Jacko, but I'm gunna miss my wonderful family."' It was a lie, but it had come out that way without me even thinking about it. Then I realised that Mr Walsh was standing next to me and had heard the whole or part of it.

Wendy was crying, and I could see Mr Walsh was pretty choked. 'Could you tell it again when we get home, Jacko, the way you just did?'

I nodded dumbly. *I'd fucked up again!* I'd been trying to impress Wendy Kalbfell and it had all come out in a rush with a lie at the end. There are things soldiers see they shouldn't talk about to civilians, and I'd just broken the cardinal rule. The sheer horror of warfare is something you don't talk about with anyone, especially women. I realised that the napalm incident and Bluey's death were all there under the surface, waiting to come out without me knowing. So when it was triggered it just spurted out like vomit. At least I'd managed to say something in the end that wasn't true but would be of some comfort to them. Later I told myself that it was exactly what I would have said with my last breath, which was probably crap.

Just then Mrs Dougherty came in, all fuss and bother like a broody pouter pigeon entering the pigeon loft. 'How are you today, Mrs Dougherty?' Mr Walsh asked.

'Don't ask! Worst day of my life!' she said, then walked right past us with her huge bosom sticking out and halted at the dispensary at the back of the shop, waiting for Mr Walsh to follow.

'Your medicine isn't doing a thing!' she said accusingly, as Mr Walsh reached onto the dispensary counter and handed her a paper bag. 'Might as well take a Bex for all the good it's doing me.'

'Have you seen Dr Kalbfell lately? Maybe he needs to prescribe something else?' Mr Walsh offered.

The pouter pigeon turned slightly to look at Wendy, then turned back and let out a 'Hmmph!'

Wendy sniffed back her tears and tried to smile. 'Silly old cow!' she whispered. 'She says exactly the same thing every week: "Don't ask! Worst day of my life!"'

'I wouldn't take too many Bex if I were you,' I heard Mr Walsh caution the pouter pigeon.

'Hmmph!' Mrs Dougherty replied again, clearly indicating that she wasn't interested in his advice. She turned and looked over at Wendy. 'On my account, girl – and why are you sniffing? Have you got a cold? If you have you shouldn't be here spreading it – kindly don't come near me!'

'Certainly, Mrs Dougherty,' Wendy replied sweetly, as the old bag – breast thrust out like the prow of a sailing ship, nose in the air – left the chemist shop without waiting for Wendy to explain her sniffs.

I knew that you could fall in love instantly because I'd done so with Miss Pat Brand at the concert at Puckapunyal all those years back, when I'd first enlisted to be trained before being sent to New Guinea.

*Fish gotta swim and birds gotta fly,*
*I gotta love one man till I die,*
*Can't help lovin' dat man o' mine.*

The lyrics had become my mantra, and when I was especially lonely I'd play the tune on the harmonica and it would bring me close to tears. Now it was the same thing all over again – I was bowled over by Wendy Kalbfell. She was Pat Brand in spades.

'We should be going,' Mr Walsh said. 'Wendy, you shut up shop while I go for the car.'

I was curious as to why Wendy was coming home with us instead of staying to look after the shop. Then Mr Walsh, perhaps seeing my surprise, said, 'Wendy was Harry's fiancée.'

I couldn't believe my ears. I should have twigged something was up when she'd started to cry. But then sheilas cry all the time – how was I to know this wasn't just a free cry for Bluey Walsh, whom she'd probably known. *Oh, Jesus! Bluey didn't say he loved her when he died!* I thought in dismay. My last-words lie hadn't included her as any decent last words like that would naturally have done. She must have felt devastated that her fiancé hadn't had the decency to die with her name on his lips.

Wendy wrote a 'Back after lunch' note and pinned it to the door before she locked up. 'Come on, Jacko,' she said, as a brand-new 1953 black Humber Super Snipe pulled up. To my delight she took my hand as we walked over to the car. *Perhaps she's decided to forgive me*, I thought, which was bloody silly, of course, because she didn't know I'd been lying about Bluey's last words in the first instance.

'I'll sit in the back,' Wendy volunteered. I'd have done anything to join her but, of course, it was necessary to sit in the front seat with Mr Walsh.

All the way to the Walsh family home I could feel the effect of her hand in mine – sort of soft and loving, as if she already belonged to me. She hadn't held it for more than three or four steps, but it seemed as though a lifetime of anticipation had run up my arm and into my heart. But, of course, she didn't belong to me and couldn't even if she wanted to, because she was mourning for Bluey Walsh. But on the other hand, I told myself, Kapyong had been just over two and a half years ago and maybe she was coming out of it and I'd have a bit of a chance if I played my hand carefully and didn't rush things now that I'd found the girl of my life.

I repeated the story of Bluey's death to the Walsh family, but without the gruesome details. I thought desperately of inventing something Bluey may have previously told me about his gorgeous fiancée that I could sort of throw in before we got to his last words – something to comfort Wendy and reassure her that he truly loved her. But I couldn't think of anything, and I'd always been a lousy liar anyway. So I simply repeated Bluey's 'made-up' last words, by which time all three women were weeping – Mrs Walsh and Bluey's sister, Anne, and Wendy, who was doing it all over again.

Bluey's younger brother, Phillip, reached out and shook me by the hand. 'Thanks, Jacko – thanks for telling us the whole story.' I could see he was pretty choked up as well.

Then Wendy stood and came over to me and hugged me. 'Thank you for telling me about Harry, Jacko. You're a lovely man. A brave and truly lovely bloke.' The way she smiled at me, I could see she meant it. At that moment I would have done anything in the world to go back to the meeting in the chemist shop with me knowing about her being Bluey's fiancée and including her name in Bluey's last words to make her happy. I knew then and there that I'd do anything and everything in my power to make this incredible woman happy if ever I got the chance. Despite her grief she'd called me a 'truly lovely bloke'. How good is that? I'd never had a girl, a proper woman, say anything as nice to me – not even a compliment that was close. The best before what Wendy had just said was when Angela Kelly had said in the dark, 'Buck, you bastard!'

When we arrived back at the chemist shop Phillip Walsh came as well. He sat next to Mr Walsh in the front, so I sat next to Wendy in the back. After about two minutes I thought I'd have a go at holding her by the hand. But very lightly, so if she didn't like it she could draw her hand away and no one would notice. At the same time she'd be able to give me the dreaded 'no trespassing' message if she wanted to. I reached out and touched her hand with the tips of my fingers, ready to pull back instantly if nothing happened. But she took my hand and squeezed and smiled and I was totally stoked. If anyone had asked me the next day how to get to town from Mr Walsh's house no way could I have told them, as I'd just climbed the stairway to heaven.

Sue and Jimmy were waiting when we got back to the chemist shop. They'd been to the museum and when they arrived at the chemist they'd seen the 'Back after lunch' sign, so Jimmy had bought Sue lunch at a nearby cafe. I introduced them to Mr Walsh and Wendy and Phillip, and then it was time to leave because the Douglas DC3 left at a quarter to three and we had to catch the bus to the airport.

'We'd better be going,' Sue said, 'the bus leaves for the airport in five minutes.'

'Oh, Phillip's taking you in the Humber Super Snipe,' Mr Walsh said, pronouncing each word. You could see he was pretty proud of the big black car shining at the kerb in the bright afternoon sunlight.

Meanwhile, Wendy had walked into the shop to serve a customer who'd arrived while we were chatting on the footpath. I walked in just as the customer emerged. 'We've got to go, Wendy. It's been—' but then I couldn't bear the thought of completing the sentence.

'Jacko, if you come to Launceston again I'd love to see you,' Wendy said right off, saving me the embarrassment of having to ask her and chancing a knock-back. Her smile seemed to come from somewhere near her toes, because it included her whole being.

'Can I come back next week?'

She put her head to one side and looked at me. 'Sooner, if you like.'

'I'll bring you a couple of cray – they're moulting, but they're real nice,' I volunteered, not thinking how stupid this must sound.

'Yum, I'd love that,' she said, smiling again. Then she came from behind the counter and kissed me, her green eyes closed. Not a big tongue job like Angela Kelly's, but soft and nice and perfect as anything I might have expected from Miss Pat Brand. 'See you soon, brave and lovely bloke,' she said, drawing away again.

Back on the island, walking in the surf every morning at sun-up was a perfect way to start the day. We borrowed a couple of masks and snorkels from Cory and Steve, and Steve's flippers for me. Jimmy's feet were miles too big for Cory's flippers. I remembered that Busta Gut, who was a big bloke at around six feet, had had enormous feet even when he'd been at school, and had to wear a size-twelve boot in the winter when he was fourteen. Everyone on the island dived, so I reckoned he might have a pair he wanted to sell. 'What's your offer? Ain't got no time f'divin' no more, Jacko. Me mum makes me work like a friggin' blackfella.'

'Not the best choice of words around here, mate,' I cautioned him.

'What I say?' he asked, confused.

'Mate, Jimmy's a Negro,' I replied.

'Yeah, I know. Is that the same as a blackfella?' he asked ingenuously. What could you say?

'I'll give you five bob for your flippers, sight unseen,' I said, changing the subject.

'What's that mean?'

'It means they might not be in good shape but I'll take them anyway.'

'Ain't nothing wrong with them, Jacko,' he protested. 'Just a small tear in one.'

'There you go,' I said. 'Three bob, not a penny more.'

'Righto,' he said.

Jimmy didn't know a lot about diving but to my surprise he was a strong swimmer. He explained that the Colored Orphan Asylum had been situated on the banks of the Hudson River, where they'd spent many a long summer's day swimming. It didn't take long to teach him the technique of finding a crayfish, and after a couple of weeks he was so adept at it that he was bringing more to the surface than I was. September to October is when crayfish moult and the shells are soft. Soft-shelled crayfish were not caught commercially, but it was okay to take a few, always provided that we left the females while they carried their eggs externally and that the males we took measured ten inches or more overall.

Jimmy and I soon exhausted the immediate family's need for crays – plus the needs of cousins and assorted visitors – with the gifts we caught exercising our leg muscles. Crayfish are not such a big deal on the island. You had to cook and eat them right off, or get ice from the co-op for the ice box to keep them for a couple of days even when you'd cooked them. So the gift of a brace of decent-sized crayfish had its limitations.

We ordered a couple of spear guns from the fishing-gear shop in

Launceston, and soon enough we were bringing home enough fish to feed the entire neighbourhood – yet another underwhelming gift. In the minds of the islanders, a bucketful of plump young trumpeter equated roughly to a pound of pretty ordinary sirloin steak. We'd all been brought up poor, and as kids had grown to hate the seemingly endless diet of fish. But all this had changed for me. After watery bowls of millet for more than a year, I simply couldn't eat enough fish. And Jimmy loved fish – especially cray stew – so Gloria had no problem feeding us and we ate like proverbial kings.

Needless to say, Jimmy was a big hit with everyone on the island, male and female, and I'd been right about the sheilas – they flocked around him like gulls when the sardines, or sprats, are running. And not just the single ones, either. The frenchies ran out after only a month, and I think Jimmy was happy enough to take a rest for a while. 'Brother Fish, when I pays my com-plee-ments to one dem girls den da other one she want to know what wrong wid her, so I got to do da same wid her. I exhausted, man!'

As for me, I was using my accumulated leave money on the Douglas DC3. Two years' salary accumulated while I was a prisoner of war meant I could hop over to Launceston of a Saturday, leaving Jimmy to have his wicked way with one or another of the island girls.

Worse luck, Wendy lived with her parents. Her dad was the doctor Mr Walsh had mentioned to the pouter pigeon, and her family was very proper and rather posh and certainly what passed for 'society' in Launceston. Fortunately, Gloria had this piece she'd cut out of the *Women's Weekly* when we were kids that instructed people on correct table manners. She'd pasted it into her recipe book and drilled us mercilessly at every meal, and in every detail. When we ate with our cousins we tried to eat badly so they wouldn't mock us. Now I was glad of my earlier training.

However, I confess I got caught out once. I'd been invited by Wendy's mum to come to Sunday-morning breakfast and there was this half grapefruit on the plate in front of me and beside it a little knife with a serrated edge for cutting round the rim, only the one I'd got was badly bent. So I picked it up and took it under the table so no one would be embarrassed that they'd given me a bent knife, and straightened it out. Then I saw Wendy using hers and realised the knife was meant to be like that so you could cut neatly around the edges of the grapefruit and scoop the flesh out and away from the skin. So I let my straightened knife drop on the carpet under the table and told Mrs Kalbfell I wasn't partial to grapefruit. When I told Wendy later she laughed and said our affair was definitely off – but on the other hand, if I'd do it again the next time I came to breakfast in front of her mum so she could witness her expression, she'd forgive me.

I stayed in a boarding house of a Saturday night and went back to the island on the last flight in the Douglas DC3 of a Sunday afternoon, usually with a severe dose of lover's balls. When we'd hit an air pocket flying over the Strait I'd practically scream out in pain, whereupon I'd swear to myself that the next time I'd book a hotel room where Wendy and I could go so I didn't have to continue the torture.

I discovered that Wendy had been Miss Launceston and then Miss Tasmania in the Miss Australia contest, and everyone knew who she was. What's more, she was considered the best catch in town – the blokes had all been waiting until her grieving for Bluey Walsh was over before they came swarming like bees around a honey pot. Everywhere we went there'd be young blokes ogling her, their tongues practically hanging out down to their knees. I'd happened along and for reasons I'll never understand, she'd decided Jacko McKenzie was going to be the bloke she chose. So no hotel ploy for yours truly. I loved her that much. Anyway, I'd have waited as long as it took – despite the aching gonad flight home of a Sunday afternoon.

It wasn't as though Wendy was a prude. She'd confessed she wasn't a virgin, that Bluey and she had been lovers. It seems the Walsh family had a fishing shack on the Tamar she and Bluey would use. They'd go down on their bicycles and spend the weekend together. I couldn't even invite her home to the island, as now that Gloria was a Catholic she wouldn't tolerate any hanky-panky in the house. We might have been a pinch of the proverbial but, as far as Gloria was concerned, this didn't extend to our morals or our table manners.

One Saturday I was in the chemist shop waiting for Wendy. Saturday was a half-day in business, and she was just balancing the cash register when Mr Walsh called me over from the dispensary. 'Got a moment, Jacko? I'd like to talk to you. Mind if we go out the back?' he asked. I wondered what could be so private – we'd become pretty good mates and talked freely about things.

I walked around the dispensary counter and into the little storeroom out the back that contained floor-to-ceiling shelves packed with boxes and bottles of chemist stuff. 'It's about . . . Wendy,' he began hesitantly. I waited for him to continue. 'How do you feel about her, son?'

'I love her, Mr Walsh.' I couldn't think of any other way to put it.

'To the exclusion of all the other women in your life?'

For a moment I wasn't sure I'd heard him correctly. 'What other women?' I asked, puzzled.

He looked down at me sternly. 'Jacko, understand – I love Wendy like a daughter. Almost as much as Anne, my own daughter. We've known her family all our married lives. Wendy grew up with our children. Anne went to school with her. I can tell you, she's a very special young lady.'

'You don't have to tell me, Mr Walsh,' I burst out. 'I'd do anything for her.'

'Even give up your womanising?'

'My what?' I exclaimed, shocked.

'Son, you're free to live your life any way you choose. God knows, after what you've been through you deserve a good time. But Wendy is precious to all of us, a very special person and . . .' He seemed stuck for words to continue.

'And what?' I asked, suddenly angry. I knew he was going to tell me a McKenzie wasn't good enough for her – that I'd better rack off and find a girl suitable for someone of my own class. 'What are you trying to say, Mr Walsh? That I'm not good enough for her?'

It was his turn to look shocked. 'No, by no means, Jacko! I, that is, Mrs Walsh and I admire you greatly. I'm sure Dr and Mrs Kalbfell feel the same way about you. All things being equal, you'd make an ideal couple.'

'But all things are not equal. That's what you're trying to say, isn't it?'

'Jacko, it's the contraceptives. Two dozen! Nobody buys two dozen at a time unless he has frequent use for them. Now I know you're a single bloke, but Wendy tells me she's your first girlfriend since you got back from Korea. How can I believe that? I ask you, if that's true then why would you want two dozen contraceptives?'

I was grinning before he'd completed the last sentence. 'I wish what you'd just said was true, Mr Walsh. No, I take that back. I'll wait for Wendy for as long as it takes. I bought them for Jimmy.'

'He sent *you* in to buy them?' he asked, plainly puzzled and also somewhat alarmed.

'No, of course not. It was my idea. He didn't want a bar of it, but I know our island and the effect a six-foot-nine American Negro would have on the island girls.' I grinned. 'Or the Launceston ones, for that matter. I knew Jimmy wouldn't be able to knock them back with a pick-axe handle in both hands – they'd be falling over each other to get to him! So, instead of multiple pregnancies in around nine months' time, I did what I thought was necessary for the mutual benefit of all parties concerned.'

Mr Walsh laughed heartily. 'Very sensible, too. I'm truly sorry, Jacko. I like you immensely but I thought you must be some sort of gigolo.'

'Me?' I cried, astonished, then hastily added, 'Mr Walsh, I wouldn't swap Wendy for every skirt in Ali Baba's harem.' *Just quietly, not even for Pat Brand*, I thought to myself. Then I added, 'I'll wait as long as Wendy wants me to.'

He grinned. 'That's great, Jacko. I apologise again for the misunderstanding.'

I laughed. 'In a way it was sort of a compliment, sir.' I considered asking him if there was any cure for lover's balls, but thought better of it.

'Good! It's good we've cleared things up,' he repeated. He reached into his trouser pocket and produced a small bunch of keys. 'They're for the fishing shack – the small one is for the shed out the back, where you'll find all the fishing gear. It's only ten miles downriver. Wendy knows where it is and we have an extra bicycle you can use.' Then he reached onto a shelf and gave me a brown-paper package. 'Have a good time, son.'

# CHAPTER THIRTEEN

## *'Johnny, I Hardly Knew Ye'*

The letter from the Governor of Tasmania arrived and I guess old Ma Gutherie gave Busta Gut the hurry-up because it had the Government House imprint on the back of the envelope and 'OHMS' on the front. Gloria went to the letterbox when she heard his whistle only to find the world's laziest postie waiting, the letter in his hand. 'Letter for Jacko, Mrs McKenzie,' Busta Gut said, handing it to her. Gloria thanked him, took the letter and turned to go when she heard him say, 'Looks important.'

'Tell your mum I'm sure she'll find out soon enough if it is,' Gloria said, dismissing him.

'Don't get too many letters from Government House,' Busta Gut said, completely missing her sarcasm. 'See, on the back it says "Government House" – and Jacko's already received that telegram I brung him from Canberra.'

Gloria flipped the envelope. 'So?' she said, trying to sound casual. 'Tell your mother the governor is going to make me a dame.'

Busta Gut looked puzzled. 'A dame? But you *are* a dame, Mrs McKenzie. I'm a *bloke* and you're a *dame*,' he explained carefully.

Gloria, who was a devoted reader of the *Women's Weekly* and up on British aristocracy, replied, 'It's like being made a sir, only it's for ladies. I'm gunna be a dame of the British Empire.'

'A what?' Busta Gut exclaimed, mystified.

Gloria finally lost patience with him. 'Tell your mum to mind her own business!' she said abruptly, turning away and walking up the garden path to the house.

'I was only askin',' Busta Gut whined. 'Anyway, letters *is* her business.'

'Cheeky bugger,' Gloria said, walking through the front door. 'Letter from Government House, Jacko,' she said, trying to conceal her excitement.

'G'arn – you open it, Mum,' I said, wanting her to enjoy the moment. Her fingers trembled as she carefully tore the envelope open. 'Read it to me, Mum.'

She unfolded the single-page letter. 'Me glasses, where are me glasses?' she called out, panic-stricken. 'On the shelf above the stove! Quick, Jacko.'

Gloria's glasses were always in the same place as she always read in the kitchen, using them for reading recipes, the *Queen Island Weekly Gazette* and anything else she could lay her hands on, provided it was a magazine or a newspaper. I'd never seen her read a book. 'All them big words for nothing,' she'd say, dismissing any book I suggested she'd enjoy. 'If them words are so important why don't they use them in the *Women's Weekly*, eh?' It was a good question, but not one I was willing to put to Nicole Lenoir-Jourdan.

I crossed into the kitchen for her glasses and for the millionth time promised myself that come next Christmas time I'd give her new lino. Christmas had just passed and, as usual, it hadn't happened. Instead, Jimmy and I had clubbed together to buy her a washing machine. She'd always done the washing in the copper in the shed out the back. When she'd completed her first wash on the new machine she'd taken out every single piece of washing and examined it minutely, sniffing each piece, in particular Cory and Steve's work clothes for the smell of fish. 'I dunno, son,' she said doubtfully, 'I didn't hear it boiling and I reckon that tumblin' business that goes on in there don't do what the mangle does and it's going to harm the clothes.' But, after one or two goes, she was convinced enough to admit that it had changed her life.

I returned with her glasses and told myself she needed a new pair, as these were held together with sticking plaster and the lenses were badly scratched. I reckon she must have had them since she'd been a young bride. There was only one problem – you had to go to Launceston to have your eyes examined, and there was no way Gloria was going to fly in the Douglas DC3. What's more, the last time she'd been over on the boat the Strait had played up 'something terrible' and she'd been sick as a dog all the way there and all the way back. She swore 'never again' and, as a consequence, had been island-bound for the past fifteen years.

Adjusting her glasses and clearing her throat, she began to read the letter aloud.

*Government House*
*Hobart*

*5th January, 1954*

*Dear Private McKenzie,*
*I am writing to inform you that His Excellency the Governor has received the Military Medal, which Her Majesty the Queen is graciously pleased to award to you.*

*I would be grateful if you would let me know whether you would prefer to receive this medal at the next Vice-Regal Ceremony at Government House or whether you would prefer it to be forwarded to you now by registered post.*

*Would you also be good enough to advise me of any*

*change to your address. At the same time would you confirm your rank as shown in this letter is correct.*

*Yours faithfully,*
*T.M. Mathews*
*Official Secretary to the Governor of Tasmania*

'That's good,' I said, 'they can post it to us.'

Gloria held the top edge of the letter to her lips, her eyes closed. Now they shot open as a look of horror crossed her face. 'They can *what*? *What* did you say?' she exclaimed.

'Mum, I wouldn't want to go without you,' I explained.

'Without me? Nobody's going nowhere *without* me.'

'The boat or the plane, you'll be sick or afraid to fly. How are we going to get you there?'

Gloria sighed. 'Some things are worth it. Can't you see that your medal cancels out Alf's disgrace ban?'

This was a huge gesture but I thought I might as well have a go at pushing the envelope a bit further. 'What about our being a pinch of the proverbial?' I asked, cheekily.

Gloria seemed to be thinking, then she smiled slowly. 'When you went to Korea I kept this scrapbook. Sue got a five-shilling-a-week rise when she got her second nursing certificate and she ordered *The Examiner* for me. It came from Launceston every day on the aeroplane. I'd cut out bits about the war and paste them into the scrapbook I called my "War Journal", though I never wrote nothing in it – but all your letters are there, and other bits'n'pieces, and the terrible telegram telling us you were wounded and missing in action. Then when month after month went by and we didn't hear from you, I thought you must be dead.' I could see Gloria's eyes were teary as she recalled the incident, and now she wiped them on her sleeve. '"Well," I said to Sue and the twins, "Jacko was the only one could've got this family out of being a pinch of the proverbial and now it's too late." Sue would get real cranky at me, and she'd always say, "You don't know he's dead, Mum! We haven't got another telegram, have we?"' Gloria smiled. 'Yeah, mate, I reckon you've done it – no more pinch of the proverbial for this family.' She smiled, and put her hand on my shoulder. 'You've done us proud, Jacko. We're all gunna go to the governor's house to get yer medal, even if it kills me.'

'By boat or plane?' I asked.

'By boat! Sick's better than dead,' Gloria said quickly.

I wrote back to say we would attend the ceremony when it happened and a reply came back a few weeks later. Fortunately I got to it first as Gloria was out somewhere and everyone else was at work, and Jimmy had gone to see Nicole Lenoir-Jourdan.

*Government House*
*Hobart*

*25th January, 1954*

*Dear Sir,*
*His Excellency the Governor will hold an investiture at Government House, Hobart, at 11 a.m. on 25th of February 1954, and I am, therefore, desired by His Excellency to invite you to be present on this occasion to receive the Military Medal awarded to you.*

*If you so desire, you may be accompanied by two relatives, or friends, and it would be appreciated . . .*

Shocked out of my tiny mind at this news, I read no further before panicking. *Two relatives, or friends. No, no, no!* How could that possibly be? Gloria and Sue had already cut out the material from the patterns they'd chosen for their outfits. I'd asked Wendy to come and she was terribly excited, and said it was going to be much better than being crowned Miss Tasmania. Then there was Jimmy – it was unthinkable that he wouldn't be with us. I'd never live it down if I didn't invite Nicole Lenoir-Jourdan, who was the closest thing we had on the island to posh people and who was bound to know her way around a ceremony like this, pointing things out to us. Finally the twins – they might just understand, and would say they were glad because they wouldn't have to dress up in a jacket and tie, but secretly they'd be pretty narked. Our disgrace ban and our pinch-of-the-proverbial curse were being lifted at one fell swoop and all I was allowed to invite was two members of my family, or Gloria and Wendy. *Oh, Jesus, not Wendy, not without Sue, how was I going to tell them!*

I read the rest of the letter with my heart pounding and with a deep sense of despair. For once I'd got something right, and now it was all smashed to smithereens. Gloria certainly wouldn't go without the family, and going with Wendy and Jimmy alone just wouldn't be right.

> *. . . if you and your party could arrive at Government House not later than 10.30 a.m.*
>
> *If you are unable to be present, would you kindly state whether you desire to have the decoration forwarded to you by registered post? If so, please indicate the full address to which it should be sent.*
>
> *Yours faithfully,*
> *T.M. Mathews*
> *Official Secretary to the Governor of Tasmania*

*There you go!* I said to myself. They said that bit about posting it in the last letter – that's how the bastards get out of it. They don't really want you there, so they trick you like this. I bet if I'd been some high-ranking officer, a major or a colonel, they'd invite my family – probably include cousins, and the whole bloody neighbourhood. 'Would you kindly let us know, for catering purposes, how many people will be attending?' That's what would be in *their* letter, for sure. Of course, this was immature and indicative of the chip on my shoulder. But I was still a soldier with all the usual enlisted man's paranoia. I was also confused and resentful and found myself in a predicament I couldn't solve without hurting a number of people I loved. It just wasn't bloody fair.

I sat there for at least an hour feeling miserable and sorry for myself. Finally I decided to say nothing to anyone about receiving the second letter and take the bull by the horns and write to the governor and ask him for clemency. I'd read about people doing that, though it was usually for murder and such like crimes.

I got out the blue Croxley pad from the kitchen drawer and uncapped my fountain pen, and then I hit my first problem. *How the hell do you address a governor?* I examined the letter I'd just received and then went and got the first letter, which Gloria had had framed and which now stood alongside her other precious possessions on the shelf above the stove. I thought there must be titles and phrasing that were common to both letters; protocol I would need to use. I also thought of consulting Nicole Lenoir-Jourdan. But then, of course, I would have let the cat out of the bag. So finally I just sat down at the kitchen table and wrote.

*His Excellency the Governor*
*Government House*
*Hobart*

*28th January, 1954*

*Dear Your Excellency,*
*I am writing to you to beg for your clemency as I find myself in a terrible predicament.*

*Recently I was awarded the MM, although this was a big surprise as there were lots braver soldiers than me who deserved the honour much more than I did.*

*Your secretary wrote inviting me to receive the medal from your own hands and I replied saying I'd be honoured on behalf of my family.*

*Now, here comes the predicament.*

*The most recent letter I received restricts me to two guests. But that's not how it works with my family – with us it's one in, all in. Mum, Sue and the twins, Cory and Steve.*

*But there's worse to come, Your Excellency. I've already invited my girlfriend, Wendy Kalbfell, who was Miss Tasmania in 1951, and Jimmy Oldcorn, an American who saved my life as a prisoner of war in Korea more than once, and who is visiting our family on the island while recovering from his wounds the same as I am. Finally, there is Miss Nicole Lenoir-Jourdan, who you may know, as she is the justice of the peace on the island, the ex-librarian and now runs the* Queen Island Weekly Gazette. *She taught me everything I know.*

*My mother and Sue, my sister, have already cut out the material they ordered from McKinlay's in Launceston for their dresses, and they've layby'd their gloves and high-heel shoes.*

*Please, sir, even if we all stand at the gate and you come out and give me my medal that would be okay, or if you like, we won't drink any tea or eat any cake if there's not enough to go around and we won't hobnob with anyone.*

*I beg your indulgence.*

*Yours sincerely,*
*Private Jacko McKenzie*

I admit there are bits in there I could have written differently at the time – or, if you like, in a more sophisticated vein. Even then I was less ingenuous than the letter is made to sound, though how much less I can't really say. But, if this makes me a phoney, then I don't apologise. You only get one chance in these things, and if only two guests could accompany me to the investiture then none of us was going. I knew Gloria too well to know she wouldn't compromise. I could almost hear her saying, '*Jacko, if that's all they care about our family they might as well shove your medal in the mail or up their bums as far as I'm concerned. We're staying put, love.*' I confess I felt exactly the same, only along with my family I included Jimmy and Wendy. And, because I had come to realise how much I owed Nicole Lenoir-Jourdan, her as well.

Every soldier knows the Military Medal is not the biggest deal in the army. But it wasn't me wanting all the kerfuffle – the folk at Government House were the ones making all the fuss. If it wasn't for Gloria I'd have preferred the bloody medal to come in the mail. When I said others had deserved to get it more than me, it was the truth. The more the island people shook my hand to congratulate me, the more isolated from them I felt. No McKenzie had ever been special in the eyes of his peers, and it constantly embarrassed me to be singled out for attention. But if we were going to go through with the whole business then I wanted my family at my side, and I was savvy enough to know that writing a strictly formal letter to the governor wasn't going to help achieve this end.

Anyway, I told myself we were yobbos from way back and I couldn't help it if I'd received a bit of gratuitous education in correct grammar and punctuation from Nicole Lenoir-Jourdan and should probably not have worked the ingenuous angle in the letter. She, for one, would have been appalled at what she'd refer to as 'theatrics'. But I reckon if anyone else in the family had written the letter, they'd have put it just about the way I'd written it. Only, of course, with Steve and Cory there would have been heaps of spelling mistakes. I confess I even thought of throwing a few in for good measure, but decided that I'd be laying it on a bit too thick and the governor might smell a rat.

I was sweating on the reply because Gloria kept saying, 'When are the bludgers goin' to tell us when it is?' Her and Sue's dresses were completed and were hanging on her best satin-covered padded hangers behind her bedroom door. I knew she needed a firm date so that she could pluck up sufficient courage for the boat trip across Bass Strait to Stanley. Gloria worked up to things – 'slowly, slowly, catchy monkey' was practically her motto.

I mentioned earlier that Jimmy was in the clutches of the dreaded Nicole Lenoir-Jourdan, who, early on in our stay on the island, had asked if she could interview him for the *Gazette*. She referred to him as James from the beginning, in the same formal way she'd done with me as a small boy seated cross-legged on the library floor. Jimmy, despite my warning not to fall into her clutches, agreed to an interview. When he arrived she said in her typically forthright manner, 'James, I'm afraid there is a problem.'

'Problem, ma'am – what problem yoh got?'

'With your grammar and syntax. If I write down the words exactly as you say them my readers may find the article distinctly peculiar.'

'It only peculiar iffen I tells you somethin' dat's peculiar, ma'am,' Jimmy said, laughing. He was well prepared for Nicole Lenoir-Jourdan. 'Foh instance, dat word "peculiar" it also mean "belonging ex-clu-sive-ly" and dat how I talk – ex-clu-sive-ly like *me*, ma'am. Now what yoh want is I should talk like some honky turkey.'

'Goodness gracious, a turkey! No, no, no! One should *never* gobble one's words,' she replied hastily.

Jimmy laughed. '"Talk like a turkey", dat mean talk like white folk, ma'am. I can do dat.' Whereupon he did as he'd done in the POW camp when he'd tried to tell me not to worry about him going over to the Chinese side. He answered all Nicole Lenoir-Jourdan's questions using the correct grammar and pronunciation, which put her nicely in her place and impressed the pants off her at the same time. I'd learned as a prisoner of war that Jimmy had a wonderful ear and a real gift when it came to learning languages. He'd impressed the Chinese in the POW camp with the way he picked up words and phrases, and towards the end could make himself understood in Cantonese, which was another reason they'd embraced him so willingly when he'd pretended to become a progressive. In later years he would become fluent in Mandarin as well, and also spoke Japanese as fluently as a Westerner possibly could. With my ear for music I wasn't all that bad myself, but I could never compete with him.

Nicole Lenoir-Jourdan wasn't the first to make the mistake of thinking Jimmy's way of talking meant he was – well, to put it bluntly – a bit ignorant. But now she became absolutely intrigued by his intelligence and, as usual, wanted to take over. Jimmy went along with her in as much as he accepted the books she recommended and found time, between his various liaisons, to read them. Then he discussed them in depth with her. It was like the old days, except that, unlike myself, who'd been young, callow and intimidated by her formidable presence, Jimmy argued back and often won, though mostly when he pointed out that the life described in the literature he was reading and his own observations were two entirely different experiences. 'To draw con-clu-sions from dat fiction narration, ma'am, dat a most dangerous exer-cise. Yoh too refine, ma'am,' he'd often say to her in 'Jimmy talk'. 'Yoh ain't been street-poisoned.'

For her part, Nicole Lenoir-Jourdan loved him for his ability to convince her that he was right because he could back his arguments with logic or explain how it was different in his own experience. She'd even asked him to stop calling her ma'am and to call her Nicole. Jimmy thought for a few moments, then said aloud, 'Nicole, baby', as if he was testing it on his tongue. He shook his head. 'No, ma'am – it ain't gonna work none,' he said, and then addressed her ever after as 'Nicole ma'am', adding 'ma'am' to her name in the same way he did with Gloria's name, when she had made a smiliar request.

Jimmy was working his magic on Nicole Lenoir-Jourdan and she simply loved it. She found him sanguine and open-minded but far from stupid, with a willingness to learn that amounted almost to a hunger. With him she also abandoned her bossy-boots attitude and became less didactic and pedantic. 'You've got a good mind, James,' she'd sigh. 'Such a pity I couldn't cultivate it sooner.'

'I ain't goin' nowhere, Nicole ma'am – help yo'self. We got plenty time to plant all dem in-tee-lec-to-al vegie-tables in mah mind.'

Jimmy had talked to me about returning to the island after he was discharged from the forces. In two weeks he was due to fly to Japan, where he would attend his final parade and receive his honourable discharge from the United States Army. From there he'd head straight back to the island. We'd discussed the future together and decided to give fishing a go. How I'd hated the idea of being a fisherman before I'd left for Korea! But now I found myself feeling differently about the prospect of earning a living from the sea. Jimmy loved fishing and went out on a boat with the professional fishermen whenever he could. To coin an obvious phrase, he took to the life like a fish to water.

This was despite my initial warning to him that the life of a fisherman working for wages was far from a pleasant or even a prosperous experience. 'It's mostly sheer bloody drudgery, mate. What's more, Bass Strait is a real bitch – unpredictable and treacherous. A lot of what you do takes place in bloody terrible weather. A nor'westerly will blow up out of a clear blue sky, and a full-scale gale can hit you in half an hour. Ask Cory and Steve – they'll tell you how much fun they're having making a crust.'

But, as usual, Jimmy saw it differently. He said nothing until he'd gone out with one or another of the boats in most weather conditions, and he always returned grinning. 'We ain't workin' for some cocksucka foh no wages, Brother Fish. We gonna work foh ourself, man. Der lotsa fish in da sea and some o' dem belong to us, same as dey belong to dem fish bosses. I reckon we gonna special-lise in crayfishes.'

'It's not that easy, mate,' I warned him. In the POW camp I'd once told him about Alf's venture into cray fishing, pointing out what a bitch of a way it was of making a living.

In 1939 Alf had decided he'd had enough of working for a bigger boat and being paid barely enough to keep his family eating regularly. So he resolved to branch into crayfish on his own, and managed to borrow fifty pounds from the bank by putting the house up for security. He bought a twelve-foot second-hand dinghy, none too seaworthy, caulked, repaired and painted it the best he could and then fitted it with a new set of sails. He powered the little dinghy with a two-and-a-half-horsepower BSA motorcycle engine from a motorbike our Uncle Les, Percy Pig's father, pranged fifty yards down the lane from us when coming home drunk from the pub one night. We heard the bike go past the house, then the bang that followed as he hit one of the new telegraph poles. We came running only to hear a series of oaths and cusses that would have burned your ears off if you'd been a little closer. Alf told me to wait and went off to see if the driver was okay. It turned out to be Uncle Les, who was all scrapes and bleeding – but nothing seemed to be broken, and he staggered off into the night still cussing. Alf returned and told me to go home and bring the hurricane lamp and the wheelbarrow and his set of spanners from the shed. I was thirteen at the time and when I returned I held the lantern while Alf salvaged the engine from the wrecked motorbike.

When Les came looking for his bike the next day he found it bent beyond repair from the initial smash, but mysteriously without its engine. He couldn't remember a thing and had even forgotten that Alf had been on the spot to see if he was okay. Alf would laugh, and say, 'Next time I was in the pub I waited until he was pissed and skint and starting to bludge drinks, and I bought him a beer and asked him what he was going to do with the smashed BSA.'

'Can't do nothin', mate – some dirty bastard stole the fuckin' engine!' he'd replied.

'Nah, mate, I removed it,' Alf admitted. 'Wouldn't want someone to nick it, would ya?'

'*You've* got it? Well I'll be buggered!' Les said, a little unsteady on his feet. He pointed a finger at Alf, having to take a step back to keep his balance and squinting at him through one eye. 'Me sister, she was always too bloody good fer ya, Alf McKenzie.' Les then turned to address the other members at the bar. 'Lissshin to thish – me fuckin' brother-in-law nicked me beeza motorbike engine!'

Alf cleared his throat, preparing for his pitch. 'Les, mate, the flamin' BSA's a write-off! How fast were ya goin' when ya hit that telegraph pole?'

'Bloody mongrel shouldn't have been there. Weren't there last month, were it?' Les said accusingly.

'Modern progress, mate. We're gunna have street lights an' all – you'll be able to see where yer goin' next time!' This caused general laughter.

'Where's me fuckin' beeza engine?' Les said drunkenly.

'Les, yer not thinking of repairing it, are ya?'

'I might,' Les replied. 'Bloody good mo . . . bike, that.'

'Not any more it ain't,' Alf retaliated. 'Flamin' frame's bent real bad, both wheels gorn – ya couldn't hope to straighten 'em – handlebars are history, light's ratshit, the tyres were smooth as a baby's backside, thread showin' through the rubber an' all.' Alf paused to let all this sink in, then he made his offer. 'I tell ya what, Les, I'll buy ya another beer and give ya five bob for the engine, which ain't in such good shape neither. Whatcha say, mate?'

'Five bob! Yer mad, ya bastard! S'worth two quid *attheverylease*.'

'Okay, me last offer. Two beers and seven'n'sixpence, take it or leave it – no further negotiations will be entered into.'

'Go t'buggery!' Les Kelly said, and turned to Greg Woon, the barman, and asked if he could chalk up a beer.

Greg pointed to the slate at the back of the bar, and shook his head. 'Sorry, mate – you've already chalked up five bob, and you know that's the house limit. Anyway, you've had a skinful.'

Les turned to Alf. 'Two beers and eight bob? No nego . . . shins will be . . .' he said, losing track of the sentence.

Alf shook his head. 'Sorry, mate – seven'n'six, that's me best offer.' Alf took the money out of his pocket and slapped five shillings on the counter in front of Greg Woon. 'That's to wipe Les's slate clean, mate.' He put down an extra shilling. 'That's for two beers for Les.' Then he gave Les one and sixpence, enough for three beers.

Les sniffed and accepted the money, grumbling that he'd been rooked by his own brother-in-law.

'I've gotta go, mate,' Alf said. 'Plenty to do.'

'What? Yiz not gunna buy us a beer after I let ya have th'fuckin' engine?' Les accused.

Alf grinned, recalling the story. 'I just did when I come in,' he'd pointed out. 'Greggie says ya had enough.'

'Yeah, but ya got th' fuckin' beeza engine cheap!' Les protested.

Les was right – tradition dictated that Alf buy him a beer to consummate the deal. Greg would have poured him another beer under the circumstances. It was the right thing to do.

'I was dead broke,' Alf explained. 'I'd hoped to get the BSA engine for five bob and the extra two'n'six was for a packet of shag and goin' to the pub on Saturday night. It was gunna be a long week, I can tell ya. I said to him, "Sorry, mate, buy ya a beer next time. Ya cleaned me out. Tell ya what, though, you've got a clean slate and one'n'six in yer pocket. Why don't ya buy me one?"

'"Get fucked!" Les shouted. "I ain't buyin' no fuckin' beer fer no mongrel wants them street lights jus' so's I can break me fuckin' neck on one them fuckin' poles so's he can nick me fuckin' beeza engine!"'

Alf would laugh as he told the story – though, of course, when he told it to the family, he left out Uncle Les's worst expletives. I only heard them replaced where they belonged when he was telling the story to a group of men on the beach while repairing craypots and didn't know I'd come up behind him. I recall how Uncle Les's reason for not buying Alf a beer got a big laugh from the men listening. They all knew Les Kelly for what he was, but also would have reckoned Alf had taken advantage of him while he was drunk and so deserved the opprobrious dismissal. Alf knew it too, although, in truth, Les Kelly was always either drunk or had a bad hangover so he was never really in a position to think straight.

The little BSA engine was cooled by a fan that Alf fitted so it didn't overheat when pulling a much bigger load than it was originally designed for. Alf claimed it almost never let him down, and never in a crisis.

He begged and borrowed some disused craypots and bought some new cane and tea-tree. Sue and I would repair the craypots with the cane and tea-tree after school and on the weekend. By this time Alf's borrowed capital was about used up. He'd load the boat with craypots and a coff, which is a square box made from wooden slats an inch wide and spaced an inch apart, with a hinged lid at the top. It's roughly six feet long and wide, and four feet high, and is weighted down in sufficient water to cover it even when the tide goes out. A coff could hold up to 1000 crays, fed every day with mutton-fish – that is, abalone – so that they maintained their prime condition.

Alf would go out for up to a week at a time, camping on shore at night, and set up his craypots behind offshore reefs in protected lagoons of smooth water. He'd bait crayfish in a dead simple but nevertheless ingenious way. On the island no jam tin ever had its lid opened more than three quarters, because once it was empty it could be used as a 'bait saver'. You'd knock a few holes in the bottom of the tin, then place your bait inside and push down the lid to close it sufficiently to keep the bait inside and anything else out. With the tin placed inside a craypot the cray would smell the bait through the holes in the tin and enter the pot and be caught. Cray after cray would be attracted to the bait without it ever being used up.

Alf would harvest the full pots every day and put them into the coff, where the crays could enjoy a good feed of mutton-fish. At the end of the trip he'd empty them all into wet hessian spud bags and head for home.

It was bloody hard work, and Alf said he'd boil the billy and have a brew first thing in the morning and by sundown he'd be that starving he could have eaten a baby's bum through a wicker chair! On his first trip, Gloria had packed him a feast fit for a king – a roast leg of mutton, corned beef, sausages, flour for damper, lard for frying, a jar of jam for his sweet tooth, spuds and a hessian sack full of vegies from the garden. He'd trapped sufficient crays to cover his expenses and pay back his first fortnightly instalment to the bank, but it soon became obvious that he couldn't afford to keep eating like a king. So he'd set off with the basic essentials and take the old .22 rifle. Alf used to amuse us, particularly Cory and Steve, by telling how he got by on the tucker front.

'When the food is gone, ya have to look out for yourself,' he'd said to them. 'I'd take the gun just in case I got attacked by a killer kangaroo. *Pow!* I'd fire in self-defence – and just in time, too, or the monster would've ripped me to pieces, took out me guts with its big claws!' The twins' eyes were wide as they imagined the scene. 'After this narrow escape,' Alf said, ' . . . well, you couldn't leave a perfectly good killer kangaroo there to rot, could ya?'

'No!' the twins would chorus. 'Serves the killer kangaroo right!'

'Too right!' Alf agreed. 'It was him or me, and this time I won. Can't waste fresh meat, though, can you?'

'Was the killer kangaroo tough?' Cory asked.

'How do you mean? Tough like being a killer, or to eat?'

'To eat,' came the reply.

'Nah, this particular roo was good eating, 'cept for his heart.'

'What was wrong with his heart?' Steve asked, falling into the trap.

'Mate, he was a real hard-hearted kangaroo!' Alf laughed.

He'd tell them how in the season he'd known mutton-birds to mysteriously commit harakiri by flying into the boat and breaking their necks as they plopped straight into a sizzling frying pan. How the odd swan would have a nasty accident by swimming into the boat in the dark and die of fright thinking it must be a killer whale or something.

'What about the feathers?' Steve, ever the practical twin, asked.

'What feathers?' Alf replied.

'If them mutton-birds plopped into the frying pan they'd have feathers on them,' Steve correctly pointed out.

'Oh, *those* feathers! I see what you mean,' Alf said, scratching his head at a momentary loss for an explanation, but soon recovering. 'Have you heard of people being frightened out of their skin?' The twins nodded their heads. 'Well, with mutton-birds it's the same – they're frightened out of their skin, only with them it's their feathers because they've only got feathers for skin. Well, with the terrible fright they get, all them feathers fly into the air and they're blown away in the wind and there they are ready for frying, lying on their backs with their toes in the air, lard sizzling in the ole frying pan.'

'Oh yeah? So what about the guts?' Steve asked.

'Delicious! When you're hungry, mate, that's all part of the meal.'

'Even the poop bag?' Steve persisted, while Cory giggled.

'Delicious! It's filled with these little prawns and baby crabs all mashed up somethin' beautiful – fried in the lard pan, you couldn't eat better,' Alf said, licking his chops in an exaggerated manner.

'Yuk!' the twins would chorus joyfully.

But cray fishing in a small boat was anything but fun. Alf would be out for a week, with no radio on board to tell anyone where he was. Bass Strait is treacherous water, and it was hell on the family. Often a sudden gale would blow up, the wind howling over the island and the rain hitting the corrugated-iron roof like lead sinkers striking down. If you put your ear to the bedroom door you'd hear Gloria sobbing, not knowing if she'd ever see Alf again.

But this venture didn't last long – the dinghy was too small, and Alf couldn't place sufficient pots to bring in the catch and make a decent living. There was no mother ship to unload his catch onto on a daily basis, so he had to keep the crays in the coff all week and bring them all in at the same time so they got to the co-op still alive.

In just over a year Alf had paid the bank all but ten pounds of the original loan, but after the fortnightly repayments there was precious little left and we were worse off than when he'd worked on one of the big boats. Alf had his pride, and even during the Great Depression he'd been a good provider and wasn't someone who gave up. He probably secretly knew it couldn't last, but couldn't bear to be seen to fail. Just bringing in enough cray to survive was a credit to his seamanship and skill as a fisherman. The dinghy was in reality no more than something you'd use for a bit of weekend cray fishing and couldn't hope to cope with a week or more out at sea or to bring in enough to support a family and repay the bank.

Then Alf only just survived a bad storm and had to walk two days through the bush to get home. The dinghy ended up on the rocks badly damaged, and he lost most of his pots and fixed-gear flag line, so Gloria finally put her foot down. No more cray fishing, or she was taking the kids and moving out. It wasn't just that she was having difficulty making ends meet – she'd have washed more sheets and scrubbed floors until she dropped if she could've fitted more hours into the day – but she was scared she was going to lose Alf. She was afraid that he'd become just another memorial plaque on the wall of the Anglican church. Although, even though Alf was Anglican, she would probably have opted for the Catholic church, which had its fair share of plaques as well, because Father Crosby would have done a better oration than the Reverend John Daintree. The Anglican minister was known as 'His slowly dying, never retiring misery', and even then was older than Methuselah.

Reverend Daintree had taken to rambling disconnected sermons and had long since lost the plot, so that only the old people who were profoundly deaf turned up of a Sunday morning. Sometimes you'd hear the church bell going on a Tuesday or a Friday morning. If you were foolish enough not to know any better and, thinking something might have happened, went around to have a look, what you'd see would be the silly old bugger delivering his rambling, confused sermon to an empty church, having mistaken the day for a Sunday.

Nobody complained, as he could still do a passable christening and funeral, though he'd usually forget somewhere along the line who he was burying, even to the point of changing the gender of the deceased. Both christenings and funerals often attracted a bigger crowd than they might normally, there to see how he would manage to screw things up. For instance, when he buried old Murtle Barnes, who'd been one of his parishioners for fifty years, halfway through the funeral service he turned her into a turtle that had died in a barn. He assured everyone present that God loved all creatures great and small as much as He loved all of us – that he felt privileged to be burying one of His slower-moving creations, as he was having trouble getting about himself. He then admonished everyone for keeping turtles in barns when it was as plain as the nose on your face that the order Chelonia had webbed feet and belonged in ponds, where the dear creature wasn't slow-moving at all. Then he commended Murtle, the supposed turtle, to the grave: 'Dust to dust, ashes to ashes and turtles to water.'

With the dinghy wrecked, Alf had the opportunity to quit with honour and take back his old job on one of the bigger boats. It took him another three months to pay the last instalment to the bank, which charged him interest because he was six weeks late with the final three payments.

Of course things were a bit different now that Jimmy and I were contemplating going into the cray business. All the boats had transceivers, which were usually army-disposal radios from World War II and weren't all that crash hot, although a damn sight better than nothing at all. The fishermen complained bitterly when radios were made compulsory – the fact that a two-way radio on board might save their life meant very little against the notion that the Tasmanian Fisheries Department had imposed a survey fee for a radio network.

Jimmy, as usual, did as much homework as possible, and looked into the business of crayfish and the possibility of doing our training on one of the bigger commercial cray boats and eventually working for ourselves. He even came up with the idea of flying crayfish from Flinders Island to the mainland and from there to the States. I told him it was a crazy idea – who'd be mad enough to go into such a venture? Jimmy thought for a moment. 'Plenty pilots left from da war and Korea. We buy us a C47 war surplus – you calls dem Dakotas – and we in da busi-ness, Brother Fish.'

'You're mad, ya bugger!' I told him. Not only were we thinking of becoming cray fishermen off our own bat, a big enough leap in the dark, but now we were also into aircraft! It was too big a step for my imagination to embrace. There had never been a McKenzie who was self-employed except for Alf's short and ultimately doomed cray experience, and possibly my grandfather – who, when you think about it, never really worked at all, except as a failed gold prospector, ne'er-do-well gambler, sometime professional harmonica player, small-time con man and lover and spinner of tall yarns. The rest of us, on both the Kelly and the McKenzie sides, had always ended up with some boss calling the shots and deciding how our lives would be led. Now Jimmy was proposing to send crayfish halfway round the world in our own aircraft.

With the exception of having to work for someone in order to learn the ropes, I vowed I'd never work for anyone else again. Jimmy felt the same way. Apart from nearly three years becoming street-poisoned he'd been in institutions almost all his life, the only respite being the short spell with Frau Kraus. When you added the army and the prisoner-of-war experience, we knew we were both through obeying orders and taking any more crap from some bastard whose job you could do better than he could. Making enough to get by was just about the extent of my ambition, but Jimmy was beginning to see things differently.

At one of their discussions, Jimmy mentioned to Nicole Lenoir-Jourdan that he'd be returning to the island after he had taken his discharge from the army. She'd acquired a little grey Ford Prefect, and that night she called around and asked if I'd accompany her on a drive as she had something she needed to discuss with me. We drove down to the headlands, where she parked. She chatted all the way about this and that, though mostly concerning the woes of running a weekly newspaper with what she referred to as a bunch of 'dunderheads' for staff. Once we stopped she was silent for a while. It was a near-full moon and the great orb ran a silver path across the sea, seemingly all the way to South America. Finally, she said, 'James tells me he's thinking of returning permanently to the island.'

'Yeah, that's right. He likes it here a lot,' I replied, then added, 'There's nothing for him to look forward to when he gets back to America.'

'That doesn't surprise me,' she said. 'He doesn't talk about it much, but every once in a while he says something in a discussion that makes you wonder about his past.' It was then that she hit me with a bombshell. 'What about the White Australia Policy, Jack?'

'The what?' I asked.

'Australia won't accept James as a migrant – he's Negro.'

'Surely that can't be possible!' I said, laughing. 'We fought together in the same war – they can't ignore that!'

Nicole Lenoir-Jourdan remained silent again for quite a while, and the longer she remained silent the more I started to panic. 'Let's hope you're right,' she finally sighed, then turned to look directly at me. 'Jack, we need to know the extra facts. Would you mind if I sourced the actual statute from Canberra?'

'No, of course not.'

'If we're going to fight for James we need to be thoroughly acquainted with the law,' she said in her typically firm way. 'We have to know it chapter and verse.'

I wasn't listening, my mind elsewhere, thinking about what I owed Jimmy. 'But, but . . . if it hadn't have been for Jimmy I'm certain I'd have died more than once – doesn't that count for something?' I bleated lamely. 'Besides, Mr Menzies is dead against communism, and Jimmy fought against communism. Surely that counts for something?'

'Perhaps, Jack.' She could see how confused I was. 'That's the very point – we need to know a lot more. I'll get straight onto the wire service tomorrow.'

'What shall I say to Jimmy?' I asked, feeling a hopelessness beginning to take hold of me. After all I'd said to him, after all we'd been through together. In those frequent times when I hadn't thought we were going to make it, Jimmy had always been there for me. '*Brother Fish, we's gonna make it! I'm gonna have me some yo' mama's cray stew. Ain't nothin' gonna stop dis nigger!*' How could I tell him he was unwelcome in Australia – that we had a law, a special law, that effectively branded him as inferior to us?

I thought of Johnny Gordon, who had been even more one of us than we were ourselves, who'd died beside me in the deserted Korean village, and the story of his grandmother, who only became 'white' once a year on Anzac Day. Of Johnny himself, who'd ultimately given his life for his country yet hadn't been allowed in the RSL Club when he returned from the Second World War, his chest blazing with campaign ribbons. My heart sank. If there were people around who could do that to Johnny and his grandma, then the politicians in Canberra could ban Jimmy. I'd already made up my mind to go and see Johnny's grandma and tell her what a great bloke he was.

However, deep inside I kept telling myself, *Jimmy's different, he's an American! They wouldn't do it to an American*. But then I recalled Jimmy's frequent references to racism in the army – in fact, almost everywhere in America. It seemed most Americans would understand and accept our White Australia Policy.

Nicole Lenoir-Jourdan reached for the starter button. 'I suggest we say nothing to James at the moment – let's first see what we're up against, Jack.' I can't recall any conversation between us on the return trip except for a single sentence: 'Nothing in life is immutable – eventually the walls of Babylon fall down.' There must have been something else said but I was too shocked to remember anything but this single sentence. She dropped me at the door. 'Remember, say nothing, Jack,' she advised. 'It's much too early to start jumping to conclusions.' Then she drove off.

Steve walked out onto the verandah. 'Her tappets need looking at,' he said.

But, of course, I'd long since jumped to conclusions and barely heard Steve's remark. I didn't sleep a great deal that night and every once in a while when Jimmy cried out in his sleep I'd feel the anxiety rise in my stomach.

The very next day a letter arrived with my name and our address handwritten on a Government House envelope. I opened the single sheet of paper to see, apart from the embossed type at the top of the page, that it too was written in a strong, clear hand.

*Rt. Hon., Sir Ronald Cross, Bt, KCVO*
*Government House*
*Hobart*

*2nd February, 1954*

*Dear Private McKenzie,*
*It would give my wife and me a great deal of pleasure to welcome your immediate family plus your three friends to Government House on the 25th of February. I look forward especially to meeting your American comrade-in-arms.*

*Please rest assured that the gates will be thrown open for you to enter and we will have sufficient tea and cake for the occasion. Furthermore, I look forward to hobnobbing with you all.*

*Yours sincerely,*
*Ronald Cross*
*Governor of Tasmania*

The following day a letter from the personal secretary of Ronald Cross, Mr Mathews, arrived with invitations inscribed with each of our names, plus a free travel voucher for eight people. Gloria was overjoyed, but immediately smelled a rat when I showed her the letter from the governor. 'Why has the governor written that last bit?' she asked suspiciously.

'What last bit?' I replied, acting innocent.

'About the gates being thrown open and having enough tea and cake to go around, and the hobnobbing business. You read us your reply when we got the letter and it didn't say anything about who was coming and tea and cake or the gates and hobnobbing,' she said accusingly. 'What's going on?'

There was no point in lying – Gloria was too tinny and the news was good, anyway. So I produced the letter I'd written to the governor asking for clemency. 'Otherwise,' I concluded, 'I for one wasn't going to turn up for the ceremony without my family.'

'Quite right, too – they could stick their ceremony up their backsides!' Gloria suggested, as I'd predicted she would. 'Ronnie Cross, the governor, seems like a good bloke,' Gloria admitted. 'Perhaps he'd like us to play for him?'

'I don't think so, Mum – they'll probably have a quartet,' I said, my heart taking a sudden jolt.

'Well, we can do better than that – there's five of us!'

'Classical music, Mum.'

'We can play classical music,' Gloria persisted. '"Ave Maria", "Danny Boy", "O Sole Mio".'

'Probably Mozart,' I replied, trying to settle the question quickly.

'Oh, him! Well, I *beg* your pardon!' Gloria sniffed.

I thought that was the end of it – Mozart was pretty formidable competition for a harmonica group. The next day Gloria went up to Mrs Dunne's shop and bought a photographic frame and framed 'Ronnie's letter', as the governor's letter became known overnight, and added it to the mantelpiece above the stove. At tea that night she said, 'I've been thinking.'

We all stopped eating, except for Jimmy – but when he saw the look on my face and my fork poised halfway to my mouth, he stopped too. Whenever Gloria used the dreaded 'I've been thinking' words, there was usually trouble of one sort or another on the way for all of us.

'We'll take them anyway. You never know, do you?' she said.

Twenty-four hours had passed since the Mozart quartet conversation. 'We'll take *what*?' Sue asked.

'Our harmonicas, of course!'

There was a howl of protest around the kitchen table. 'Mum, it's a vice-regal occasion – there'll be all sorts of people there!' By this she knew I meant posh people, not our sort of folk.

'It's not the first time, you know,' Gloria pointed out. 'We've played there before.' Then she added tartly, 'Well, at least the *Kelly* side of the family has.'

'What are you talking about, Mum?' Cory asked, thoroughly confused as usual.

'Government House. Mary Kelly played the harp for Lady Jane Franklin – not just once, lotsa times. They were called *soirées* them times.'

'Mum, Mary Kelly was a *convict*!' Sue protested.

'So? Does that make her a bad musician?'

'No, but it's not exactly the same, is it?' Sue persisted. 'We're guests.'

'Can't see why it's different. She was a *guest* of the British Government. They used to send a soldier to fetch her – Jacko's a soldier.'

The logic escaped us all. 'Mum, she was invited to play. *We are not!*' Sue said emphatically.

'I didn't say we were going to play. Just to take our harmonicas. We haven't performed off the island since Alf's disgrace ban. We're bound to find somewhere to play, and it will be the first time Jacko has performed publicly with us since he went to Korea.'

There was a palpable sigh of relief and we all began to eat again. There was always somewhere to play – a pub on the way to Hobart or somewhere else. We were a professional enough group to know we'd be welcome in almost any place where ordinary people congregated. Besides, I think we all quite liked the idea of taking our music off the island again. To do so was symbolic, a part of the act of lifting the disgrace ban. I could sense that we were all happy we'd reached a compromise we could live with.

'Well, at least we won't have to paint our faces and arms black with Kiwi boot polish like the time we did for your Al Jolson concert,' Sue said, remembering the disastrous experience.

Gloria chuckled. 'I'll never forget your father escaping to the pub halfway through the concert, running for dear life, melting Kiwi polish streaking down his dear little face and neck.'

Alf's face hadn't been big, but for its size it was pretty mashed up. Gloria must have really loved him heaps to refer to it in this way. Then she'd glanced over to me. 'You ought to be grateful, Jacko. That's when you got your chance to be the lead mouth for the first time.' She then turned to Jimmy and explained the Al Jolson performance at length to him.

'Hey, man, I always knew dat der a bit o' da black brotherhood in yoh, Brother Fish.' Jimmy looked over to Gloria. 'Anyways, we owe our lives to dat harmonica. Brother Fish done save us wid his music more den one time, dat foh sure, Gloria ma'am.'

'There you go!' Gloria said happily. 'We'll take them along and see what happens. Never know your luck in the big city.'

'Mum, *not Government House*! We'll be humiliated, that's what will happen in the big city!' Sue protested.

Gloria, all innocent, looked around the table. 'Did I say anything about Government House?'

There was silence. It was stupid of Sue to come in like that now things were more or less resolved. But she knew, as we all did, that with Gloria things were never that easily sorted out. The Al Jolson concert was only one of dozens of humiliating experiences with the harmonica we'd endured at her hands.

Then Jimmy broke the silence and said right out of the blue, 'Maybe we can do same as yoh done at da welcome-home party, "When Johnny Comes Marching Home". Dat classical, dat more den one hundred years old. I can sing dat an' yoh can play it. Den we a sextet.'

'Oh Jesus, not *you* on her side!' I protested, bringing my hands up to my head.

'We'll do our first practice after dinner,' Gloria declared, obviously dead chuffed with the whole idea now she could blame it all on Jimmy. 'Who's ready for bread'n'butter pudding? Sue, get the cream, will you love?'

'Mum, promise me it's only a "perhaps" and not a "definite" – that you're not going to force the issue with the governor on the day,' I begged.

Sue had risen to serve dessert but now stopped midway to the stove, nodding furiously to add emphasis to my plea. 'Please, Mum, promise on your word of honour!' she said, like we used to do as kids.

'Of course, love, no "When Johnny Comes Marching Home"!' Gloria said smoothly, looking at us. 'Like you said, it's a vice-regal occasion. These things are organised to the last detail. How could I possibly force anything to happen?'

I wasn't the only family member at the table who looked doubtful at these words. We'd all seen that look in her eyes before. 'Just remember you said that, Mum,' I said, attempting to drive the final nail into the coffin of what we all hoped was now a dead idea. The medal ceremony was meant to lift Alf's disgrace ban, and if we didn't make Gloria promise not to play at Government House, no sooner would it be lifted than we'd bring another crashing down on our heads. After all I'd managed to do to get us all into the ceremony, being humiliated – 'disgraced' might be a better word, the laughing stock of Hobart another way of putting it – would have been just too much to bear. I wondered if maybe we couldn't help ourselves, whether it was genetically bred into the McKenzie family to screw things up, and the Kellys too – Alf and Gloria's marriage a lethal combination, because this time the disgrace ban would be brought about by Gloria.

In the days leading up to our departure I became more and more disconsolate about Jimmy's prospects of staying. I hadn't heard any more from Nicole Lenoir-Jourdan, other than the news that Canberra was taking an inordinate amount of time to reply and appeared to be stalling her request for information. I wondered how long I would be able to keep from telling him the terrible news, as he had about two months to go before his convalescent leave was up.

I'm ashamed to say I even thought of saying nothing, letting Jimmy go off and then having him find out later when he tried to immigrate. Then when he informed me, I could play dumb and yell and scream and mentally throw myself around, huffing'n'puffing and making vainglorious promises that I'd get to the bottom of things, come what may. Then I'd suggest I come over and join him on some American island where people fished for a living and we could start up there.

But I knew I couldn't run away again, not this time. Jimmy was my mate. More than this, he'd saved my life and given me hope when I'd despaired for my very existence. There could be no duplicity between us, no hiding behind this legislation with a fatalistic shrug and a self-righteous curse at a government prepared to maintain such a heinous racial policy. We simply had to stand and fight. I wanted him to stay more than anything else I could have wished for. My dream was to have Jimmy as my business partner and mate and Wendy as my wife. Wasn't I supposed to be the one getting the medal for bravery? Shit, what a joke! It was my turn now. This time I was 'Jimmy in the North Korean cave'. I wondered if I had the strength, the guts, to go through with it, whether my resolve would crack if Nicole Lenoir-Jourdan wasn't with me – someone who could say and really mean, '*Nothing in life is immutable – eventually the walls of Babylon fall down.*'

The great day for the medal ceremony at Government House approached, and Jimmy and the family left the island on the morning boat to Stanley two days before the grand event. The idea was that I would take the Douglas DC3 to Launceston to meet Wendy. She had managed to borrow a Volkswagen Kombi from the Red Cross Blood Bank that could seat eight people, and we planned to drive to Stanley, meet the boat and then drive down to Hobart, arriving the night before the ceremony.

I was learning that Wendy was one of those women who could do things and who wasn't afraid of being beautiful. 'People will do things for you when you're pretty,' she'd say, laughing. 'It won't last forever – might as well make use of it while I can.' But she was putting herself down unnecessarily. She never took advantage of her looks, and always gave back as much as she received. As Miss Tasmania she appeared in several newspaper advertisements for Volkswagen free of charge. She worked as a volunteer for the Red Cross on Fridays, her day off from the chemist shop. She'd drive the Kombi to bring people from the surrounding district to give blood. 'As long as we're back by Friday we have the loan of the Kombi,' she said to me.

'Won't they need it in the meantime?' I asked, amazed at such generosity.

'I've made other arrangements, Jacko,' she said, then added by way of explanation, 'when I became Miss Tasmania I managed to get the Kombi donated by the Volkswagen people to the Red Cross, so I don't feel embarrassed asking for it. It isn't the only vehicle they've got, and borrowing it won't greatly inconvenience them. There's a blood bank pick-up on Wednesdays, but I've organised that with some of my mum and dad's friends who'll use their own cars.'

So there we were in the white Kombi van with the big red crosses painted on either side, off to meet the boat in Stanley. Nicole Lenoir-Jourdan had managed, through the *Gazette*, to book us into a boarding house in Stanley that night, and in another one when we arrived in Hobart. 'I'm told the one in Hobart is very reasonable and spotless – what's more, they serve a good breakfast,' she'd announced, looking fondly at Jimmy. She'd booked four double rooms in both places. Her and Wendy, Sue and Gloria, Jimmy and me, and the twins, so there was no chance of Wendy and me getting together for a bit of a cuddle. It would have been nice, but we now had the key to the Walsh fishing shack on the Tamar, which we could use for two weekends each month – although Wendy's parents, the good Dr Kalbfell and his wife, Joan, didn't seem too pleased about this arrangement. But more about that later.

Our group excursion to Hobart wasn't the first time Wendy had met the family. She'd visited the island on three occasions and met Jimmy and the others, and they'd all fallen instantly in love with her. When Cory and Steve first saw her I thought their eyes were going to pop out of their sockets. I admit, it was nice showing Wendy off. You could almost hear the people on the island thinking, *How'd a bloke like Jacko McKenzie score a flamin' beauty like her?* Mind you, this wasn't surprising – I don't think even a McKenzie thought a McKenzie could manage to end up with a good sort like Wendy.

Wendy and I arrived at the wharf in Stanley just as the *Queen Islander* was docking. The family were almost first off the boat, with

Steve and Cory at the lead, each lugging a huge suitcase Gloria had brought. She'd also sewn two long bags out of muslin, each designed to carry 'the frocks' without creasing them, one of her special padded satin hangers in each bag with the handle poking out the top. These were entrusted to Jimmy on the basis that he was sufficiently tall to hold them up without the bottom of the bags trailing on the ground, as would have been the case if a McKenzie had been given the job.

At dinner each night leading up to our departure we had been given a blow-by-blow description of the two dresses being made. Gloria called them 'à la coronation'. If you recall, 1953 was coronation year and Gloria had departed from her usual source of everything female, the *Women's Weekly*, and had consulted two magazines, *Vanity Fair* and *Simplicity Magazine*, the latter specialising in actual patterns. She'd read *Vanity Fair* to us at the kitchen table on the subject of style.

*'The fashion story of coronation year is a colour story. Out with the greys, the beiges and the other indefinite, muted tones so popular in the post-war years! Brilliant bursts of glorious colour is in! Guardsmen red, crown emerald, sovereign yellow, cavalry tan and two lovely blues often worn by the Queen Mother, garter blue and royal herald. Black, in either contrasting stripes or black accessories, is the smart woman's answer to all her fashion problems.'*

'What do you think about crown emerald for you, darl?' Gloria asked Sue. 'Look lovely with your hair.'

Sue nodded. Green was a colour that always looked great on her. 'Not too fussed with the black – I'd rather have white gloves and shoes, Mum.'

'You won't be in fashion!' Gloria cautioned.

Sue didn't reply, except to say, 'What about you, Mum?'

'I think the garter blue. They've done colour swatches here.' She passed the magazine to Sue, who studied it for a few moments. 'What do you think, love?' Gloria now asked again.

Sue moved her head to one side. 'Sovereign yellow's pretty.'

'Nah, I'm too old for that. It's blue, the Queen Mum's choice. That'll do me nicely. You'll have to go into McKinlay's to match the material, and get the shoes and gloves at the same time.'

'Mum, Jimmy and I would like to contribute. You know, pay for the material and the shoes and gloves and everything,' I offered.

'You don't have to do that, Jacko. I've got a bit put away,' Gloria said primly.

'Be mah pleasure, Gloria ma'am,' Jimmy insisted.

Sue thanked us both, then said, 'I still think I'd prefer white shoes and gloves.'

'Oh, well – I don't suppose we have to be slaves to fashion, do we?' Gloria said, though with a tinge of disappointment.

'It's just that black's for funerals,' Sue replied firmly.

'Only if it's all over, love,' Gloria corrected, having the last word. 'Oh, my God! What about our hats?' Gloria yelled suddenly, the mention of funerals reminding her. She shot up from the table like a rocket and returned shortly with a copy of the *Australian Home Journal*. 'Hats, hats, hats,' she said absently, thumbing through the pages. 'Ah, here we go. *Hats*.' She started to read.

*'In England, masses of tiny hats all made of flowers. In Paris, pillboxes in black and brown worn afternoon and evening, and for the day, floral half-hats. In Italy, washed straw cloth worn with earrings made with a combination of brightly coloured china and straw.'*

'What's a half-hat? Cory asked.

Gloria thought for a moment. 'It wouldn't be floppy brimmed, unless they cut out the top of the crown,' she declared, not really knowing the answer. Then she turned to Sue. 'Don't fancy the straw, not for Government House. Definitely not right.'

'Me neither. And the pillbox – look stupid perched on top of our heads.'

'It's the flowers then.' Gloria tapped the magazine. 'There's pictures in here. They don't look too hard to make.'

Sue and Jimmy had gone on a shopping excursion to Launceston, the second since they'd gone together to do the Christmas shopping. Sue had returned with two dress lengths of stuff called silk shantung in blue and green that seemed more or less the same as the colours shown in the magazine. She bought black gloves that went right up to Gloria's elbows and small white ones for herself, and a pair of white court shoes. Gloria had decided to stick with her good church shoes because they were black and sufficiently worn to accommodate her bunions. Sue had also bought a pair of nylon stockings for them both. The dresses, when Gloria had finished making them, had this sheen to them and seemed to change colour when they moved. They looked expensive, and Gloria commented that the material must have cost us an arm and a leg.

Jimmy was also delegated to carry the ironing board under his other arm. Gloria insisted on carrying the electric iron herself, as she didn't trust anyone else with it. She'd read that the irons in places you stay can't be trusted and left marks on your clothes if you were not careful, and that ironing boards in boarding houses were 'a disgrace to behold'. The article went on to recommend that you take a box of steel wool with you when you travel to scour out the black patch on the surface of the iron. Gloria's iron was her one big indulgence. She had the latest General Electric with five different settings. 'It's not just for us and the shantung,' she explained. 'I want the twins to look properly groomed for once in their lives, and you and Jimmy's uniforms must be perfect. This is a vice-regal occasion and we're all gunna look regal if it kills me!'

There was no way possible the twins would look properly groomed. They were grown men but they were fishermen, which meant they were just naturally untidy. A clean shirt wouldn't last more than a few minutes on either of them – especially Steve, who had an irresistible compulsion to approach and tinker with anything with a grease-covered surface.

On the trip to Hobart, Steve drove and checked everything was hunky-dory with the Kombi engine every time we stopped for more than five minutes. Like, for instance, on one occasion he decided to check the carburettor, even though the Kombi was practically brand-new. 'Never know with engines, and this one's German and in the back,' he muttered darkly. 'Don't want to be caught short in the middle of nowhere.' 'Nowhere' was this dirty great road right down the centre of Tasmania with cars and trucks passing every few minutes. I'm not sure why he mentioned the engine being German and in the back. Maybe, because we'd fought Germany in World War II, he felt the engine might be sabotaged and blow up – a payback by the Germans for us winning the war. Before we'd take off to continue our journey you could count on him having a grease mark somewhere, usually right down the front of a clean white shirt. Gloria would go apeshit, but she shouldn't have wasted the energy to remonstrate with him – nothing helped, and Cory wasn't a lot better. Both of them seemed to be experts on basic untidiness, and specialists in accumulating dirt. Gloria would constantly complain that she spent a fortune on bleach.

I guess I was the same until the army got a hold of me, whereas Jimmy, having been brought up in institutions, was always tidy. Before he went to sleep, he'd ball his socks and place one within each boot so it fitted precisely round the top, preventing any creepy-crawly from entering. I often wondered what kind of dangerous creepy-crawlies might exist in New York City besides cockroaches, which were dirty but basically harmless. Then one day he explained that in Elmira Reformatory a favourite trick among fellow inmates was to put bootmaker's tacks in your boots when you were asleep.

'But they could still do that,' I'd argued. 'They'd simply take the sock out, put the tacks in and stuff the sock back into the boot.'

'I always push dem socks one inch from da top, a-range mah boots toe to toe in one line. Iffen dey not perfek like dat in da mornin', den I know somebody been der wid dem bootmaker tacks.'

'Why didn't you just turn the boot upside down and shake it before you put it on?' I insisted pedantically.

'Sure,' he replied. 'It six o'clock, it a freezin' cold mornin', yoh lie in yo' bed to da last poss-bill minute. Den da second bell go an' yoh got to get yo' ass down to mornin' parade. Yoh ain't got no time to do no shakin' boots, Brother Fish. 'Fore you know you got dem tacks through da sole yo' foot, man.'

They all came down the gangplank, ladies first, Gloria carrying her precious GE electric iron perched on top of a big wicker basket we occasionally used for picnics on the beach. No doubt it contained food for the journey, together with a billy and teapot. Gloria was deeply suspicious of cafes. 'I'm not paying good money for food you can't eat and tea they have the hide to charge a pound a pot. It's simply iniquitous! Always lukewarm, and tastes like regurgitated dishwater!' Nobody ever pointed out to her that you didn't drink dishwater – this was just one of Gloria's sayings.

Nicole Lenoir-Jourdan followed Gloria, carrying a small alligator-skin suitcase and matching hatbox. Even then, in the 1950s, that kind of luggage was a bit old-fashioned and owned only by the very wealthy. Watching her I wondered fleetingly, for the umpteenth time, about her past. Nobody had ever heard her talk about it. She'd simply arrived on the island by boat as a young woman one morning in 1933, and stayed. Sue walked behind her carrying a hatbox and Jimmy's and my dress uniforms in another muslin bag Gloria had run up on her Singer. The twins were the last to disembark. It was late afternoon when we finally reached the boarding house on the outskirts of Stanley.

The journey the following day to Hobart was uneventful. Despite Steve's reservations, the Kombi's high-revving engine whined along with typical German efficiency. With Nicole Lenoir-Jourdan in charge of the AA map of Hobart we had little difficulty finding the boarding house she'd booked, which wasn't far from the Botanical Gardens and Government House.

It was quite a posh place, with floral carpets and big leather couches in the lounge, the carpet on the stairs held down by those brass runners. Gloria said the lace curtains were good quality. The bathroom for the men was just down the hall, and everyone got their own proper big towel that wasn't worn one bit. That night we all walked to the wharf and had fish and chips, then the ladies went back to the boarding house and the four of us blokes had a couple of beers at a pub. It was all pretty nice, and if I hadn't had the problem of Jimmy not being able to stay in Australia almost constantly on my mind it would have been just about perfect. My leg was better, my family were all with me, except of course for Alf, the girl I loved was on my arm and Jimmy, my best mate, was there to share the occasion. Even having Nicole Lenoir-Jourdan with us gave me a great deal of pleasure. She'd claimed she'd been 'terribly touched' when I invited her to come along.

By half-past nine the next morning we were ready, the girls dressed to the hilt. Wendy wore a very pretty pink dress she'd worn as one of her outfits for Miss Tasmania, with a pink pillbox hat and white shoes and gloves. She had this wide belt of the same material as her dress and her waist looked as if I could have put my hands around it and still a bit more. Nicole Lenoir-Jourdan wore what Gloria later said was 'a beautifully tailored suit' with a coffee-brown blouse Wendy said was made from guipure lace. She had these brown, pushed-up gloves to her elbows, and a brown straw hat with a pheasant feather sticking out the side. All the ladies looked beaut and seemed very happy with their outfits, which I've discovered is very important as this decides whether they're going to have a good time or not. We were about to go when Gloria started digging in her new bag, a big black leather handbag we'd not seen before, which she said she'd sent away for after seeing it in a catalogue in Mrs Dunne's shop. 'A spare hanky, I need a spare handkerchief!' she exclaimed. 'Won't be a mo, back in a tick.'

There'd been no mention of the harmonicas and I'd given the word to Sue, Cory and Steve to leave theirs behind as I'd done myself, just so Gloria couldn't decide to do the dirty on us. In fact, she seemed to be too busy to even think about it. She'd knocked on our door when we were getting ready and asked if we were decent. When she came in she'd sergeant-majored us by inspecting our uniforms to make sure they were spotless. She'd done the same with Cory and Steve and told us they'd complained about wearing ties and jackets. She'd threatened Steve with his life if he touched anything mechanical besides the steering wheel of the Kombi. 'Give me your room keys,' she'd demanded of Steve and Cory. 'You're bound to lose them and they'll be safe in my new handbag,' she'd instructed. Then she'd demanded our key, which was attached to a six-inch-by-two-inch plank with the room number on it. 'Don't want it showing in the pocket of your uniform, Jacko,' she'd reasoned.

Gloria returned from her hanky expedition. 'I expect I'll have a good howl,' she said, waving a hanky in the air before stuffing it into her handbag. I should have been suspicious then, her waving the hanky like that – Gloria wasn't given to superfluous gestures. But we were running late and I was anxious to get going, for the letter had said to be on time.

But we needn't have worried. Our destination was less than ten minutes away, and soon enough we turned into the road that led to Government House, though only to be brought to an abrupt halt. Everyone had arrived at the same time and there was a long queue of cars and taxis, so we took our place at the end to wait. Suddenly a cop on a motorcycle came up and told Steve to follow him at once, then moved off with his siren blaring. 'What did I do wrong?' Steve asked. 'I drove real careful!' We got out of line and followed the cop, passing all the cars as they moved over to the edge of the road to let us get by. *We haven't even got there and already we're in trouble!* My stomach started to play up as I felt the familiar panic sensation. We arrived at the gates of Government House where two soldiers ran out to swing them open and the motorcycle cop roared in, signalling us to follow. We stopped at a side door of this big sandy-greyish house – 'palace' would be a better word. The cop did a U-turn, saluted us and roared off.

We looked at each other, totally confused. 'What now?' asked Gloria.

Wendy started to giggle and I looked at her, surprised. 'They think this is an ambulance and it's an emergency and we're delivering blood,' she said. 'It happens in Launceston all the time!'

'Oh, shit,' I cried. 'What do we do now?'

'We act as if nothing unusual has happened and we mind our language, Jack,' Nicole Lenoir-Jourdan said primly.

'Hey, Nicole ma'am, dat right. When in doubt, bluff it out. Smile, dat's da style.'

Sue and the twins started to laugh and then Gloria joined in, but I didn't think it was funny. 'This is a vice-regal occasion!' I reminded everyone. 'And already we've stuffed it up!'

But my anger didn't help. Wendy tried to restrain her laughter but couldn't, and burst out full throttle, and everyone – even Nicole Lenoir-Jourdan – broke up.

Suddenly a soldier's face appeared at the window. 'Is there an emergency, sir?' he asked.

I slid the Kombi door back and climbed out. Thank God he was a private, like me. 'There's been a mistake, mate, we borrowed the Red Cross bus.'

'What, nicked it?' he asked, concerned.

'Nah, it's legit,' I said.

He thought for a moment. 'Bloody clever – beat the queue. Parking's round the back.' He paused. 'You're Jacko McKenzie, ain't ya?'

'Yeah,' I replied.

He extended his hand. 'Put it there, mate. Bloody beauty!'

We were among the first to park, and waited on the lawn admiring the gardens. Nicole Lenoir-Jourdan informed us that the governor's house was a fine example of an early-Victorian country house in neo-Gothic style. She pointed to the individually carved sandstone chimney pots and what she called the bas-relief sculptures. 'The scale detail and the finish of the entrance hall, grand corridor and state rooms as well as their furniture are unequalled in Australia,' she said, as if she was reading it out of a tourist leaflet.

'Have you been here before?' Cory asked.

'No, I read up on it before coming. I do so look forward to seeing the ballroom – I believe it's quite magnificent, with its vaulted ceiling, chandeliers and mirrors, and the floors, of course, are of Huon pine.'

'Like a palace, eh?' Steve said.

'Well, not exactly. Rather smaller, I'd say, but nothing we need to be ashamed of – quite splendid, really.' Everywhere she pointed Jimmy upped with the fancy camera he'd bought in Japan and took a snapshot.

We were glad we didn't need to be ashamed of the governor's house, because I for one had never been in a place as posh as this. A naval bloke in white dress uniform and gold aiguillettes appeared on the steps. You pronounce it 'eglets' – the gold cords that decorate his shoulder are reserved for aides-de-camp of governors and generals. I'd never seen them face to face before but I knew they were called 'scrambled egg' in the army. This naval officer, a lieutenant, came out to greet us, touched his cap and smiled.

'Good morning, ladies,' he said, then turned to Jimmy and me who stood at attention saluting. He returned the salute. 'At ease, men. Caps off when you enter Government House, and keep them off. You refer to the governor as "Your Excellency" if he addresses you.' He turned to me. 'When they announce your name, Private McKenzie, you walk up to His Excellency and come to attention and you give him a nod, like this.' He sort of dropped his chin quickly and then pulled it up again. 'Got that?' I nodded, demonstrating. 'Good,' he looked around. 'It's time to go in, please.' Then he saw Jimmy's camera. 'No photographs of the ceremony – the official photographer will take a record of it for you,' he said crisply, then turned smartly, saluted the ladies and walked over to another group standing close by. I'd previously noticed that the people who were standing around were in groups of three, some only two, husband and wife. I now realised that the governor had truly made an exception for us. Gloria was right – Ronnie Cross *was* a good bloke.

I turned to Jimmy as we moved towards the entrance, and

whispered, 'Mate, caps off. You don't salute any officers once we're indoors.' I wasn't sure whether this was true of the US Army. Jimmy nodded. 'Dat make a nice change, Brother Fish.'

I've got to admit, Nicole Lenoir-Jourdan had been right – the ballroom was a knockout. Huge crystal chandeliers blazed with light and gave the floor a sort of soft-butter shade that kicked back the reflections, so that all the chairs lined up seemed to half-disappear in a shimmer of light. Two huge mirrors up one end on the stage or podium, or whatever it's called, reflected the room back at us to make it look like it went on for yonks.

The dignitaries entered, then others like us followed, and the chairs were soon filled with people chatting quietly. Wendy was sitting next to me not too far from the front and she squeezed my hand and I squeezed back. 'Are you nervous?' she whispered. I nodded my head. 'This is where I was crowned Miss Tasmania,' she said. I looked at her, amazed. She'd not said a word to any of us about being there before.

'Did he, you know, the governor, do it?' Wendy shook her head and was about to explain when the ballroom suddenly went silent.

A bloke in striped pants and tails entered from a door on the stage and stood for a moment until the room was completely silent. He cleared his throat. 'Good morning, ladies and gentlemen, welcome to Government House. My name is Thomas Mathews, and I'm the official secretary to the governor. May I ask you please to be upstanding when His Excellency enters the room and remain standing for the national anthem.'

Gloria nudged me, and whispered, 'That's the one who signed the letters.'

The secretary then announced, 'Ladies and gentlemen, His Excellency, the Governor of Tasmania!' The governor walked onto the stage and stood at the centre and the band struck up 'God Save the Queen'. When it was all over he sat on this big chair, and then his secretary said, 'Please be seated.' Talk about scrambled egg! This bloke was covered with the stuff, from his chest to down the sides of his cut-away coat, which went almost to the floor. It was tassles and gold embroidery everywhere you looked, and must have weighed a ton!

Everyone who was anyone was there, dressed to the nines. On the official side there was the Premier of Tasmania, Sir Robert Cosgrove. I only knew this because Nicole Lenoir-Jourdan had pointed him out when we entered the ballroom. There were also lots of politicians, several mayors with their gold chains draped around their necks, judges in wigs, high-ranking army, air force and navy officers with enough fruit salad on their chests to cover an army blanket, and civilians galore wearing medals on the lapels of their suits and war medals on their chests. It was altogether a dead-serious occasion, and I wondered how we'd ever got there in the first place. This was definitely *not* McKenzie country. But here we were anyway, everyone looking beaut, Gloria and Sue changing colour in their shantung dresses every time they moved and the disgrace ban and pinch-of-the-proverbial curse both about to be lifted forever.

The secretary would call out a name, mostly an old bloke, and he would go up to get his Officer of the Order of the British Empire or Member of the Order of the British Empire. The governor's secretary would then read out why each candidate had been honoured. Then the governor would say a few words to them and pin on their medal. After each presentation, everyone clapped.

At last the secretary announced, 'Your Excellency, may I introduce Private Jack McKenzie, who has been decorated with the Military Medal.' Wendy squeezed my hand on one side and Gloria on the other, and glancing at Gloria I could see she'd got her hanky out, her eyes already watery.

I walked to the stage, climbed the three steps, stood to attention in front of the governor and bowed my head, which was like a sort of official nod instead of a salute I suppose.

'Ah, Private McKenzie. I have been looking forward to meeting you,' the governor said. He hadn't said this to any of the others, and I wasn't sure how to reply – or even if I should.

'Thank you, sir . . . er, Your Excellency. Me too,' I replied, panicking. There was a bit of a titter from the front row, but the governor cleared his throat and there was dead silence again. The secretary had been reading out the blurb for each of the recipients, but now the governor reached out and accepted the citation and read it himself.

*'The 3rd Battalion, Royal Australian Regiment, was defending an area north of Kapyong on the 23rd and the 24th of April 1951. D Company had been assigned the role of right-flank protection on the feature 504 and the ridge line to the north-east. Twelve Platoon was the company's forward platoon, and 8 Section the left-forward section of this forward platoon. On the morning of the 24th of April 1951, the enemy in strength maintained continuous attacks against this section's position for a period of five to six hours. Private McKenzie's own position took much of the enemy assault each time they attacked, and on each occasion the enemy was repulsed with heavy casualties.*

*'Private McKenzie showed outstanding courage of a very high order and was an inspiration to the remainder of the hard-pressed section.*

*'Later in the day, Private McKenzie was near 10 Platoon when they were mistakenly bombed with napalm. He disregarded the danger of exploding grenades and other ammunition set off by the flames racing through the position to go to the aid of the casualties.*

*'Private McKenzie showed by his actions a devotion to duty that was an inspiration to the entire company.'*

It didn't sound a bit like it was, and it didn't feel like me he was talking about.

Just when I thought he'd finished, the governor looked up at the crowd and added, 'I have since discovered that in November 1951, Private McKenzie was wounded in a patrol action against a superior Chinese force and taken prisoner of war.' He handed the citation back to the secretary, who handed him the medal, which he pinned to my chest. 'Well done, soldier,' he said, so that everyone could hear. 'The Battle of

Kapyong will go down in history as one of Australia's great military feats. Furthermore, your endurance and fortitude as a prisoner of war was a great personal achievement, where despite torture and extreme hardship you maintained your integrity. Our nation is justly proud of you.' He paused, and smiled. 'I am informed that Private McKenzie has brought a friend with him today, Private James Pentecost Oldcorn of the American infantry, whom he credits with saving his life as a prisoner of war on more than one occasion. I extend my country's good wishes to you, Private Oldcorn, and hope your stay with us will be a pleasant one.'

To my amazement, people started to clap. The governor waited until the applause subsided and then shook me by the hand. I pulled myself to stiff attention and bowed my head in that sort of a nod again. 'Perhaps we can have a chat a little later. I'd like to meet your American friend,' he said softly.

When I got back to my seat Wendy was crying in the arms of an equally tearful Gloria, Sue was sniffing, and Nicole Lenoir-Jourdan was dabbing her eyes furiously with a lace handkerchief. I put my arms around Wendy and held her to my chest. There was nothing I could possibly say – she was with me but grieving for Bluey Walsh, and that was okay by me. She was perhaps lucky Bluey hadn't lived. In my mind's eye I could see the little Chinese soldier sitting beside me in the field hospital, his body blackened, only his eyes moving, accusing me, the rest of him welded in a seated position, knees up to his chest, arms permanently fused to his kneecaps by napalm. It was good she could cry for the memory of a laughing, happy young bloke beside her on his bicycle going down to the fishing shack on the Tamar.

The ceremony went on a bit longer and several firemen and a bloke from the Forestry Commission got awards, and then we were told to be upstanding. The governor took his leave and we all traipsed out into the reception rooms for refreshments. Strangers were coming up and congratulating me, and then the premier came up and shook Gloria's hand and congratulated her over raising me. I thought she was going to faint on the spot. But that was nothing compared to when the governor entered. He'd changed his gear and was now in a grey suit, and was accompanied by his wife. He went over to the premier, shook his hand and then shook the hands of several of the other big nobs – judges, and people like that. Then he looked around and saw Jimmy, who wasn't hard to miss as he stood about a foot higher than most of the people in the room. He excused himself, and turned and walked towards us. Thank God there was a table close by to rest our teacups and cake on before he came up. 'I think I'm gunna faint,' Gloria said, bringing her fingers up to her mouth. 'Oh, dear, I've been cryin' – my make-up!' she choked.

'It's fine, Mum,' Sue reassured her, but I could see she was pretty nervous herself, rubbing her gloved hands down the sides of her waist. Wendy had this smile on her face that would melt an iceberg. She knows it camouflages any nervousness she may have. Nicole Lenoir-Jourdan, on the other hand, was perfectly composed, though you could never tell what was going on inside.

Behind me I heard Steve say to Cory, 'Shit, what now?'

Jimmy seemed okay. 'Here come da governor!' he announced, which made us relax and Wendy giggle.

Jimmy and I jumped to attention as he came up. The governor smiled. 'Take it easy, chaps,' he said, and turned to Gloria. 'And you must be Mrs McKenzie?' Gloria nodded dumbly – for once in her life she was lost for words. 'How do you do?' he asked, and extended his hand.

Gloria clasped his hand in hers and curtsied. 'Good, thanks, Your Excellency. Thanks for the invite,' she said, regaining her composure.

The governor turned to me. 'Perhaps you'd like to introduce me to your family and friends, Private McKenzie?'

I did as he asked, introducing each of us in the order of age, leaving Jimmy for last so that I could single him out. But when we got to Wendy, who wore her break-your-heart smile, he said, 'How very nice to meet you, Miss Kalbfell. May I offer my sincere condolences to you on the death of Private Harry Walsh, who, I am assured, was a brave soldier and fine man.'

Well, I can tell ya, we were gobsmacked. What a bonzer sort of a human being he turned out to be, doing his homework on Wendy like that. Wendy lost her composure for a moment, her bottom lip quivering, but then immediately regained it and smiled – although her eyes glistened and she reached out and took my hand. 'Thank you, Your Excellency, you're very kind,' she said quietly.

I introduced the twins, who kept their eyes on their boots when they shook his hand, and then I turned at last to Jimmy. 'And this is my great friend, Jimmy Oldcorn, Your Excellency.'

Jimmy drew to attention and took the governor's extended hand. 'I is honoured, Yo' Excellency. Dis a great day foh Brother Fish an' I thank yoh foh invitin' me.'

The governor smiled. 'It's a pleasure to have you. How is your leg coming along?'

'It fine, Yo' Excellency, jus' fine. I done me a complete re-coo-per-ration in dis fine country. Brother Fish an' his family, dey been real good to me.'

'Brother Fish?' the governor asked, suddenly confused.

Jimmy pointed towards me. 'Dat Jacko. He called dat because o' da "Fish Song" and his harmonica when we prisoners of war,' Jimmy explained, no doubt leaving the governor even further confused.

The governor turned to me. 'You play the harmonica? I've always been rather fond of the little instrument but could never get past "Daisy, Daisy". It looks so easy, but it's dammed difficult to master.'

'He da master!' Jimmy chuckled. 'He da best. Brother Fish done save our lives with da "Fish Song" and his harmonica.'

'I don't suppose you have your harmonica with you?' the governor asked me.

'No, Your Excellency,' I said, vastly relieved.

'Yes we do!' Gloria said, holding up her big black bag.

*Oh Jesus! Bloody Gloria's tricked us!* I was suddenly overcome with embarrassment. That's why she'd demanded the keys to our rooms in the boarding house – her excuse to get an extra handkerchief had been to nick our harmonicas. I should have bloody known.

'Would it be too much to ask you to play this "Fish Song" for us?' the governor asked quietly.

'What – here, now?' I said, too surprised to remember to add 'Your Excellency'.

'Of course! If you'd rather not, I completely understand. However, it could just add a little bit to the proceedings. I do get so very tired of that damned quartet playing Mozart and Brahms. Never was too fond of Jerry music.'

'Jimmy can sing it, Jacko'll take the lead and we'll be the backing,' Gloria volunteered, bold as brass and back in charge, bossing us around as usual.

'Oh, you all sing?' the governor asked.

'No, we play the harmonica – modern and classical,' Gloria said proudly, dead chuffed with the outcome. Then she remembered and added, 'Your Excellency.'

The governor laughed. 'That's excellent!' He seemed genuinely pleased, and motioned for his aide-de-camp, the lieutenant in the white uniform, to come closer.

So there we were up on this little stage, previously occupied by the quartet, who'd taken their instruments through to the kitchen and were now munching cake and holding cups of tea and looking, I thought, a bit superior as we got ourselves organised in a half-circle around the microphone.

People had started to crowd closer, sensing something was about to happen – all the dignitaries and big nobs, as well as the folk like us. The governor stepped up and addressed the crowd from the microphone. 'I have just heard the beginnings of what I think may turn out to be a remarkable story,' he announced. 'The McKenzie family, along with Private Jimmy Oldcorn, will honour us with a performance of what is known as "The Fish Song". He paused momentarily, and turned to Jimmy. 'Perhaps, Private Oldcorn, you would introduce the song and give us the background before the performance begins?'

We all knew Jimmy was good – a raconteur not easily equalled –

but now he excelled himself, telling the story of the North Korean hospital cave and giving me much too much of the glory when it really belonged to him.

'Ladies and gennelmen, and o' course Yo' Excellency,' he began. 'Iffen my fren Jack McKenzie he got dis medal from yo' queen for bravery at Kapyong, it ain't nothin' compared to da bravery he done show when we prisoner o' war. I gonna try mah best to be respectful o' da occasion here and da del-lee-cate feelin's o' da ladies present, but iffen I gonna tell o' true bravery it ain't no purty story.'

The large room grew completely silent as Jimmy described the hospital cave – the freezing temperatures, the stench of illness, the lack of food, the cruelty of the North Korean guards and the sense of hopelessness and despair among prisoners. He then turned and pointed to me. 'Dat how it be, da day dat da Aus-tra-lian he come. He got his leg broke bad an' he ain't got no splint. Da side his jaw, it swollen bad where dey hit him wid da rifle butt. He wounded real bad and he cain't walk. I am in dat cave and he lie next to me and I think he gonna surely die.' Jimmy proceeded to leave out all the details, which, of course, was how he'd had to convince me to be a part of trying to change the morale in the cave, how with great pain and suffering he'd secured a splint for my leg and boots for my naked feet, how it was his idea that I play the harmonica.

'Den he take out his harmonica an' he begin to play sweet an' low. In dat hell he done bring dat beautiful music. We all American dat time, so he play da Glenn Miller classic "In the Mood" an' follow wid "Chattanoogie Shoe Shine Boy". He play so good, so sweet, we done weep, but now from da music we also got hope and we got us some spirit.' Jimmy smiled. 'Dis good man, Jack, he ain't a real big dude, but man, he got a heart it da size a trolley bus.'

By this stage I was completely mortified. People were looking at me and smiling, eyes glistening. I could see they admired me greatly and my face burned with the terrible embarrassment of it all. Jimmy then told them how, with the power of music, the cave had been reorganised and the morale improved.

He then went on to tell the story of how one day I had heard a guard singing and had learned to play the tune on the harmonica, then patiently over several days sat in the freezing cold and learned the Chinese words so that we could teach them to the choir. How this had changed the attitudes of the guards towards us and we'd eventually been transferred to a field hospital where our broken legs had been placed in casts. How we'd learned the meaning of the lyrics from a Chinese officer who spoke English, so that Jimmy had dubbed me Brother Fish, in honour of saving so many American lives, including his own.

I wanted to rush forward and tell the story of the real hero, but it would have disrupted everything and spoiled the proceedings. The place was a mess – women were openly weeping and by the time he'd finished, even the governor's wife was sobbing into her handkerchief.

We then performed the song, me leading in with the haunting introduction, and then Jimmy coming in, singing the words in the Chinese dialect with the other harmonicas sweet and clean in the background. I came in solo in several parts, building up the storm at sea with the backing carrying the effects of the roaring wind and waves. Then came the calm after the storm as the great fish guided the fisherman back to his village, and then the joy of the villagers as they gave a feast for the fisherman's return and in honour of the great fish. Finally the beautiful opening melody repeated, but softer this time as the fisherman's mother gave thanks and prayers to the goddess for returning her son. When the song came to an end you could have heard a pin drop, and then the applause started and continued and continued. And just when I thought it was all over, Gloria stepped up to the microphone, held up her hand and brought the mob to silence.

'Your Excellency, premier, chief justice, members of parliament, ladies and gentlemen,' she began. *Where'd she get all that from? The sneaky bugger's been practising this all along!* 'Almost one hundred years ago my great-grandmother was a convict in the Female Factory here in Hobart. Her name was Mary Kelly, and she played the harp beautifully. Lady Jane Franklin would often send a redcoat to fetch her so she could play to the ladies at one of her *soirées* . . .' Gloria stopped, and gave the crowd a smile, '. . . I think that's how you pronounce it, anyway,' she said, then added ingenuously, 'it's French.' There was a bit of a titter and then laughter among the crowd, and then she continued. 'Among other tunes, she played a particular melody from her childhood in Ireland that became a great favourite with Lady Jane and her ladies.' Gloria paused and smiled and then, with just the right touch of humility, said, 'I . . . er, just thought you might like to have us play it for you today?'

There were cheers and claps, some of the ladies still dabbing their eyes from 'The Fish Song'. Gloria looked over at the governor, who nodded his head. I admit I was a bit confused – we'd discussed 'When Johnny Comes Marching Home'. What was she on about, bringing Mary Kelly into it?

Gloria stepped up to me. 'I'll take the lead, Jacko,' she said quietly. I nodded, still confused, and stepped back with the others. 'It's called "Johnny, I Hardly Knew Ye",' she announced. She turned to face Jimmy. 'Jimmy will sing the lyrics – though, except for the first few lines, it's really a women's song.' Sue and the twins looked at me, mystified, our harmonicas at the ready. 'I'll solo the first verse and Jimmy will come in on the reprise,' she announced to us. The crowd fell silent and Gloria led us in and we realised immediately that with very little rearrangement the melody was identical to 'When Johnny Comes Marching Home'. I glanced over to Sue and the twins and could see their relief. Gloria was a sly one, but what about Jimmy? He would have had to learn the lyrics – *the buggers had planned this behind our backs all along!*

Gloria played the opening verse and then did a reprise to let Jimmy come in. Jimmy had a deep baritone, but it was pure and clean and you could hear every word, sharp as a piano note. Incredibly, he sang it with an Irish brogue. Later he would tell me he'd got the inflections from Doug Waterman, the brave Irishman from the Royal Ulster Rifles who'd died of shame in the POW camp.

*'While goin' the road to sweet Athy, hurroo, hurroo,*
*While goin' the road to sweet Athy, hurroo, hurroo.*
*While goin' the road to sweet Athy,*
*A stick in me hand and a drop in me eye,*
*A doleful damsel I heard cry,*
*Johnny, I hardly knew ye.*

*With your drums and guns and guns and drums, hurroo, hurroo,*
*With your drums and guns and guns and drums, hurroo, hurroo.*
*With your drums and guns and guns and drums,*
*The enemy nearly slew ye,*
*Oh my darling dear, ye look so queer,*
*Johnny, I hardly knew ye.*

*Where are your eyes that were so mild, hurroo, hurroo,*
*Where are your eyes that were so mild, hurroo, hurroo.*
*Where are your eyes that were so mild,*
*When my heart you so beguiled?*
*Why did ye run from me and the child?*
*Oh Johnny, I hardly knew ye.*

*With your drums and guns and guns and drums, hurroo, hurroo . . .*

*Where are your legs that used to run, hurroo, hurroo,*
*Where are your legs that used to run, hurroo, hurroo.*
*Where are your legs that used to run,*
*When you went for to carry a gun?*
*Indeed your dancin' days are done,*
*Oh Johnny, I hardly knew ye.*

*With your drums and guns and guns and drums, hurroo, hurroo . . .*

*Ye haven't an arm, ye haven't a leg, hurroo, hurroo,*
*Ye haven't an arm, ye haven't a leg, hurroo, hurroo.*
*Ye haven't an arm, ye haven't a leg,*
*Ye're an armless, boneless, chickenless egg,*
*Ye'll have to be put with a bowl out to beg,*
*Oh Johnny, I hardly knew ye.*

*With your drums and guns and guns and drums, hurroo, hurroo . . .*

*They're rolling out the guns again, hurroo, hurroo,*
*They're rolling out the guns again, hurroo, hurroo.*
*They're rolling out the guns again,*
*But they never will take our sons again,*
*No they never will take our sons again,*
*Johnny, I'm swearing to ye!*

*With your drums and guns and guns and drums, hurroo, hurroo . . .'*

Well, you wouldn't believe the cheering and the weeping. The governor and the premier came over and stood with us, together with Wendy and Nicole Lenoir-Jourdan, while the aide-de-camp used Jimmy's camera to take a photograph. Then the two dignitaries stood with Jimmy and me and he took another. There was also a press photographer snapping away for all he was worth, like we were really important.

What a day it turned out to be. Gloria not only saw me get the medal; she'd come full circle. It had taken a hundred years to return to Government House and to openly sing a song her great-grandmother had played on the harp as a protest against the English killings in Ireland. Every disgrace ban that ever was had been lifted, and as for a pinch of the proverbial – that too had been blown to smithereens. It would have been perfect except for two things: Jimmy not being allowed to stay, but I comforted myself that that wasn't over yet, and darling Wendy being put through the agony of Bluey Walsh's death. Oh God, I loved her so much!

# CHAPTER FOURTEEN

## *Admission Impossible*

Jimmy gave Wendy the film he'd taken at Government House to be developed at the chemist shop. She visited the island the following weekend and brought the photos with her. Jimmy selected several to be blown up as keepsakes for the family and unbeknownst to us asked Wendy to have each of these framed as his farewell gifts to us before leaving to demob in Japan.

Wendy packed them with enormous care in tissue paper and several layers of protective cardboard, then sent them via Douglas DC3 air freight. She was not prepared to trust the Busta Gut delivery system and its casual approach to parcels, known to be even more unreliable and careless than in the case of letters or telegrams. A precious parcel was likely to lie in his van at the bottom of a pile of heavy objects for days so that the originally posted version seldom resembled the one he eventually delivered. Busta Gut would hand over a badly mangled parcel with the words, 'Me mum's very sorry. She says *they* must'a damaged it in the post.' It never occurred to him that he was the *they*. He'd shrug philosophically and announce, ''Fraid yiz'll have to blame the queen,' which was his much-loved private joke, delivered with a serious face. Once you'd turned to go back indoors the cretinous bugger would snigger behind his hand, enjoying his joke for the hundredth time. For this reason he was also referred to on the island as 'The Royal Saboteur', because he seemed to do everything possible to sabotage the Royal Australian Postal Service.

In addition to the photographs Jimmy had taken and had framed, he organised for Nicole Lenoir-Jourdan to get the three official press photographs – one of the group of us standing with the governor and Sir Robert Cosgrove, the Tasmanian Premier; one with Jimmy, me and the two bigwigs; and the official photograph of me receiving my medal. He sent these to Wendy to be framed in solid-silver frames. With the addition of the new framed photographs Gloria's cluttered kitchen mantelpiece was finally stretched to capacity, with various objects teetering on the edges. When the three splendid silver frames arrived it meant removing treasures from the back of the shelf that hadn't been seen since my childhood.

We watched as Gloria picked up a small, faded, orange-coloured cardboard box, scuffed at the corners and generally much the worse for wear, and hugged it to her chest. 'Your father brought these for me the first time he came calling,' she said, suddenly all misty-eyed. I couldn't help wondering if Alf had bought the small box of MacRobertson's 'Old Gold' chocolates with the same lascivious thought I'd entertained the night I'd called on Percy Pig's wife, Angela. Gloria opened the battered box to reveal the little dark-brown serrated paper cups that had once held the soft- and hard-centred chocolates. 'I can't possibly part with this,' she said, and placed it back on the shelf. She proceeded to do the same with every object in residence, including an abalone shell onto which Alf had scratched the first verse of 'Summertime' from the George Gershwin opera, *Porgy and Bess*. It had been a favourite of Gloria's at the time and she now told us Alf would play it to her on his harmonica last thing at night – a romantic touch none of us would have suspected. Alf's spelling wasn't all that crash-hot, but then he was no worse than most of the blokes on the island.

*Summer time and the livin is eazy*
*Fish are jumpin and the coton is high*
*Yer daddys rich and yer mamas good lookin*
*So hush little baby, don't ya cry*

*Happy Birthday*
*Love Alf 8/6/1936*

When Gloria reached the abalone shell she started to sob quietly, again clutching it to her breast. 'It was the tail end of the Great Depression, Alf hadn't worked on the boats for a year and was thinking of rolling his swag and heading for the big island to try to find work. We didn't have a brass razoo between us and I honestly didn't know where our next meal was coming from.' She turned to me. 'You were just nine years old and your clothes were made from sugar bags. I remember how terribly ashamed we were because we owed the shop two pounds for groceries. It was my birthday and Alf went out and dived for this shell and cleaned it up and then wrote the words of "Summertime" on the mother of pearl, scratched them in with his penknife. He could've given me a diamond ring and I wouldn't have valued it more.'

Placed in chronological order, the pictures, 'objects' and paraphernalia on the kitchen mantelpiece represented her entire life. Gloria was a collector and a compulsive hoarder. Her kitchen drawers bulged with bits of uninteresting everything – scraps of ribbon, bits of string, carefully folded tissue paper, ancient coupons from packets of Bushells tea where she hadn't collected the required number to send off for the set of EPNS teaspoons, bottle tops and lids, corks and bottle stoppers of various sizes that might some day fit something, and, of course, recipes. These were yellowed and crackly with age and had never been attempted – they were the 'maybe somedays' of Gloria's cuisine. Her tried-and-true recipes were cut and pasted into an old, used leather-bound accounts ledger she'd found somewhere as a young girl. Its pages were covered with descriptions of various plumbing fittings, and neatly ruled columns showed amounts ordered and monies due, debits in faded red ink and credits in blue, all wrought in a beautiful copperplate hand over which she'd neatly stuck her favourite recipes using paste made out of flour.

The mantelpiece problem was eventually solved when Steve and Cory arrived home with a wheelbarrow full of bricks they'd taken turns to push two miles from the government depot on the edge of town. Steve's mate, who was a builder's apprentice in the workshop, had tossed them over the depot fence in return for a couple of fresh crays for his girlfriend's aunty. Steve extended the mantelpiece shelf by two feet on either side so that it took up the entire rear wall of the kitchen. Pride of place in the centre was given to the three press photographs in their posh silver frames, together with the Government House letter and a little porcelain thimble holder with pink rosebuds on the lid that was perhaps Gloria's most precious possession.

The thimble holder, complete with a tiny battered tin thimble too small for any contemporary woman's finger, had been Gloria's only inheritance from her convict great-grandmother, Mary Kelly, of the now-famous 'Johnny, I Hardly Knew Ye' song.

Gloria's immense pride in her convict ancestor was in contradiction to the times. In the 1950s it was simply not done to admit to a ticket-of-leave convict in the family. Such family secrets were kept well hidden, even to the point of erasing them from the family bible or visiting the museum in Hobart, looking up the appropriate convict record and surreptitiously tearing the offending portion of the page from the book. The wife of the mayor of a small town in the Huon Valley was sprung by a museum guard in the act of tearing a section of a page from the dreaded record. When he'd tried to recover the torn strip of paper she'd placed it in her mouth, chewed hastily and swallowed. These records had been referred to by the convicts as 'the black book', as every convict upon arriving in Van Diemen's Land, later named Tasmania, had his or her details entered in one of these black-covered books. The governor's secretary would be seated at a table on the wharf, and as each convict stepped ashore from the rowing boat that brought them in from the convict ship they would stand with head bowed while their name, crime and length of sentence were recorded – which may have been how the expression 'You're in his black books' came about.

But Gloria wasn't one of these clandestine expungers of past family felons. She didn't require the family slate to be wiped clean – on the contrary, she referred to it at every opportunity. She was inordinately proud of Mary Kelly and the musical patronage of Lady Jane Franklin. As far as Gloria was concerned, her liaison with the governor's wife clearly indicated that Mary was a respectable woman, despite the overwhelming evidence to the contrary.

Nations, too, have a way of drawing curtains on the past, often seeing an unsavoury incident in history for what it wasn't. If not constantly reminded, the public memory of a shameful occurrence soon fades and past inglorious events are either forgotten completely or arranged into a satisfactory explanation a hundred years on. It is no different with families, where rogues become 'interesting characters' or even heroes, while thieves and harlots are seen as the unfortunate victims of circumstance. In Gloria's eyes, Mary Kelly had been an Irish patriot sentenced by a bibulous English judge to be transported for prostitution and unruly behaviour and described at the time by the judge as 'an incorrigible termagant'.

Back in Ireland, Mary Kelly had been a maid in a big house situated close to the village of Kildoon in County Kildare. As a twelve-year-old maidservant she had been seen to have a pretty voice, and her mistress had allowed her to sing as an accompaniment to the harp. One thing led to another and Mary Kelly became a talented harpist as well as having what eventually matured into a lovely voice – but being of a bold and extroverted nature, she lacked the demure personality usually associated with a player of that celestial instrument.

By the age of eighteen she had risen to the position of lady's maid, and upon her mistress's absence on a visit to Dublin, she borrowed one of her bonnets and a fancy gown to attend a wedding in the village. She proceeded to get drunk and into a fight over a footman from another manor house, and her mistress's pretty gown was torn and her bonnet trampled in the mud. As a consequence, on her ladyship's return Mary Kelly was dismissed without a reference. Those were hard times in Ireland, and without a suitable reference she had no hope of finding another position as a maid. So Mary was effectively thrown onto the street.

To cut a long and sad story short, she'd somehow made her way to Dublin, where her pretty voice allowed her to join up with a group of street musicians who played in ale houses and at middle-class weddings and the like. Mary Kelly soon discovered that the incident at the wedding hadn't been aberrant behaviour and she had a distinct weakness both for grog and the opposite sex. Soon enough she was neglecting the group and using her charms to make the latter pay for the former. While she could sing like a lark she could also scrap like an alley cat, and because of her temper and increasing unreliability she was eventually given the push by her fellow musicians. She took to singing solo on the streets of Dublin, where she quickly learned there was a more profitable way to earn a living by standing on a street corner. Fighting, drunkenness and prostitution saw her frequently in front of the beak, until finally the magistrate declared her incorrigible and sentenced her to a trip in a leaky boat to the Fatal Shore.

All of this had been transmogrified by Gloria to where Mary Kelly had been an Irish patriot who had taken to the streets to sing protest songs of a seditious nature, of which 'Johnny, I Hardly Knew Ye' had been but one small example. This, in turn, had caused the Crown, in the form of a vindictive English judge, to transport her to Van Diemen's Land.

Mary Kelly's subsequent post-convict behaviour was rather more difficult for Gloria to explain. On being granted her ticket-of-leave she'd found herself on an island where men outnumbered women roughly four to one. Had she been vaguely respectable she would have attracted dozens of eager suitors falling to their knees begging for her hand in marriage. Seven ragged, under-nourished, snotty-nosed street urchins all named Kelly, conceived to seven different fathers in ten years, did little to underpin her respectability. The English judge had been quite correct – Mary Kelly was undoubtedly a confirmed termagant with a fondness for the bottle who lifted her petticoats frequently, and not only to jump puddles.

But once again Gloria had seen her way around this by declaring this minor blemish in Mary's character was due to a shortage at the time of Irish Catholic ticket-of-leavers, as most were condemned to serve longer sentences than their English counterparts for similar crimes. Mary Kelly, Gloria claimed, had deliberately chosen bastardry for her precious children rather than submit herself to the vile clutches of a Protestant husband – forgetting of course that Alf was a Protestant, and we were the results of just such vile clutches.

Gloria approached Mary Kelly's reputation as a respectable woman with the zealotry of a converted Catholic. Or, as she insisted, a *reverted* one. She maintained that her own recent return to the 'true faith' was meant to be in order that her convict great-grandmother might receive justice in the eyes of God. She frequently pointed out that all her immediate relations were living in mortal sin, as the Kelly family had only become Anglicans because of a spiritually weak-minded grandfather.

Charlie Kelly, Gloria's father, had been born a Catholic, and her mother, his second wife, was a strong-willed Protestant woman who'd lost her first husband in a drowning accident on the Tamar. She'd subsequently hitched up with Charlie, mistakenly thinking at the time that, compared with spinsterhood, it was the lesser of two evils. Despite being married to Charlie she'd insisted on being called 'Mrs Wilson', her first husband's surname. She justified this by maintaining that Captain Wilson, the captain of the first steam dredger on the Tamar River, had been a 'somebody'. This, in turn, implied that Charlie was a 'nobody', which was by no means an inaccurate assessment.

Charlie's sole contribution to this ill-conceived partnership was his virility, and he gave the previously barren woman five sons and a daughter, Gloria. Mrs Wilson asserted that her children had a chance of being a 'somebody' if they were raised Protestant, but were likely to take after their father should they be raised Catholic. As it turned out, choice of religion played no part in her children's future social status. Mrs Wilson had vastly underestimated the power of the otiose Kelly blood that coursed through their veins. Gloria eventually defected to her father's faith, while her five brothers remained Protestant. But, she maintained, as they collectively didn't amount to a pinch of the proverbial, the Catholic faith could count itself fortunate not to have been saddled with them.

Gloria's five brothers, of whom Les Kelly was not an untypical example, had dutifully inherited their great-grandmother's powerful thirst, and drank as fast as their elbows would allow them. They also passed on the profound apathy they held towards religion of whichever persuasion to the thirty children they collectively spawned. To Gloria's almost certain knowledge the Kelly brats had only entered St Stephens to be christened by the Reverend Daintree. They would undoubtedly do so again to be married, and all would visit on a third doleful occasion when they were carried to the altar in a wooden box fitted with the funeral parlour's rented and retrievable silver ceremonial handles, with a bunch of gladdies perched on the top.

While Gloria didn't want Mary Kelly removed from the black book, she nevertheless shared with Mrs Wilson a desperate need for respectability. She dearly wanted her convict ancestor to take what she regarded as her rightful place in Australian history, which was as a musician who kept company with what at the time passed for high society. If she couldn't achieve this in a statutory manner she hoped to do so in an ecclesiastical one. So she'd taken the problem of Mary's criminal status and her numerous conceived-out-of-wedlock children to Father Crosby.

He listened to her with great sympathy, frequently nodding his head while clucking his tongue. When Gloria finally came to the end of Mary Kelly's sad tale the redoubtable Father Crosby couldn't see a way clear for the Church to grant Mary Kelly absolution. The evidence against her, even told in Gloria's justificatory way, was simply too condemning.

Fornication outside of wedlock is a sin in the eyes of the Church, whatever way you look at it. But Father Crosby wasn't one who liked to disappoint his parishioners, and believed in a just and merciful God.

'Now let me see, Gloria,' he said, after having thought for quite a while. 'This woman named after the Blessed Virgin was an Irish convict who had seven children out of wedlock but was blessed with a wonderful talent to play the instrument of heaven. Is that correct, my dear?'

'Father, she played the harp like an angel and was a good mother.'

'Aye, to be sure. She was an Irish mother and there are none better,' he reassured her.

So Mary was given points for motherhood, and as a skilled player of the most heavenly instrument – no mention was made of grog. But this still wasn't sufficient to grant her forgiveness in the eyes of God or Father Crosby. That is, until he brilliantly brought up the subject of purgatory.

'Have you prayed for her soul?' he asked.

'Every day since I've been converted back to the true faith, Father,' Gloria assured him.

'And others, have they prayed?'

Gloria was forced to admit that, as the good father was already aware, her immediate generation had been raised as Protestants, and she doubted very much if any of the numerous Big Island and mainland Catholic Kelly cousins, aunts and uncles had done any praying for Mary Kelly's immortal soul. Gloria had no illusions about her extended family. The men were invariably unreliable, confirmed drunks and notorious layabouts, and the woman were, with herself perhaps the single exception, shrill, fat and frumpish. As far as she knew there had been no single male Kelly ever born who had risen above the indolence that typified the clan and, furthermore, to her almost certain knowledge they were all lapsed Catholics.

Father Crosby continued his peroration. 'That poor woman has remained in purgatory for nigh on one hundred years without a prayer uttered until recently!' he declared, his voice deeply sympathetic. 'Can you imagine that, my dear?' Gloria agreed that this was too sad and too long. 'Taking into consideration that the dear woman has had an entire century to contemplate her mortal sins, I feel sure the Lord – who is a just and merciful God – will allow us to speed up the process of Mary Kelly's elevation to heaven. You will pray for her forgiveness for some time in the future.'

'How long will it be?' Gloria asked anxiously.

'Ah, my dear, the Lord works in mysterious ways. We will know when the time has come. Shall we begin by praying for Mary Kelly's immortal soul?'

'Thank you, Father. I shall pray for her three times every day,' Gloria promised gratefully.

Father Crosby smiled, his eyes cast upwards to the nave where a vivid plaster-cast statue of the Blessed Virgin clutched her divine child to her breast. With a deep sigh, and in suitably pontifical tones, he pronounced, 'Let us pray.' Gloria sank to her knees, and the slow redemption of Mary Kelly commenced. 'Mary Kelly, you have paid dearly for your sins on this mortal coil, and in the name of the Father, the Son and the Holy Ghost I ask that you be forgiven your transgressions and that in God's chosen time you will be granted absolution, when you will take your place beside the saints in heaven. *Requiescat in pace*, amen.'

Father Crosby looked down at Gloria at his knees, then smiling again, with his hands outstretched, palms turned upwards, he made a small lifting motion as if to nudge the long-neglected soul of Mary Kelly just a fraction of the way to glory. 'May the saints applaud when Mary Kelly is finally granted forgiveness and leaves purgatory and rises up into heaven where, for all eternity, she will play her harp in the company of angels,' he said to a tearfully grateful Gloria.

Later that day, when we all gathered around the kitchen table for supper, Gloria gave us a 'blow by blow' delivery of her session with Father Crosby. The retelling went on a bit and she seemed to have entirely forgotten about our dinner. So we were all pretty hungry by the time she got to the part where Father Crosby, wearing a smug smile on his bog-Irish face, with his eyes cast upwards at the Virgin and child, was about to begin the protracted process of raising Mary Kelly from purgatory. Gloria stopped at the beginning of this eventually-to-come soul-departing moment and looked around the kitchen table, her blue eyes blazing with her faith, her voice tremulous. 'His Irish eyes were smiling when he prayed to send Mary to heaven,' she said softly.

This time she'd gone too far! We all simultaneously reached for our harmonicas and commenced to render 'When Irish Eyes are Smiling'. Gloria's eyes popped wide open, a shocked expression on her face. The frumpish, shrill-voiced Kelly in her came rushing to the fore. 'Bloody heathen! Protestant scum! God will punish you for this! You're goin' straight to hell, the lot of you!' she screamed. We continued playing, until she finally said, 'Stop it! Or ya'll get no bloody dinner!'

In Gloria's eyes Mary Kelly, who'd been well prayed into heaven even before I left for the Korean War, had been elevated to the position of principal harpist in God's foremost heavenly choir, and Gloria claimed Mary was largely responsible for our family's musical talent. While it was as plain as the nose on your face that we'd inherited it from both sides of the family – perhaps more so from the McKenzies than the Kellys – Mary-bloody-Kelly was always credited with passing her 'amazing gift' to ensuing generations. She'd done that all right, but it had been her propensity for the whisky bottle and not the harp.

I think, in telling all this, I'm trying to make a salient point – though perhaps not very well. My point is, with us coming from nothing and amounting to nothing – and there were lots like us – I simply couldn't reconcile how, as a nation, we could unilaterally dismiss black or yellow people as inferior.

My experience of the Chinese and our time in Japan certainly contradicted this notion and you would have had to go a long way to find a better type of bloke than Johnny Gordon, who didn't even have the vote when he died for his country. And, of course, there was Jimmy. Sure, there were drunks among the Aboriginal people, but fair go – my own family testified to the fact that these were greatly outnumbered by drunks of my own race. The white male population remained more or less pissed for the first hundred years in Australia. Moreover, the second century of white occupation isn't proving to be a hell of an improvement.

I'd once read about the arrival of the Chinese in New South Wales in a history book given to me by Nicole Lenoir-Jourdan when, as a young bloke, I was still in her dreaded clutches. 'Know your history, Jack, and that way you won't repeat it,' she'd cautioned me darkly as she'd handed me a large, dull-looking tome. In the book there was the story of the Chinese who came to New South Wales in the 1860s to take part in the gold rush. Rather than stake original claims, which they mostly couldn't afford and if they could would alienate them further from the white miners, they would take over the abandoned claims where the easy pickings were no longer to be gained and sheer hard work was required to extract whatever ore remained. The Chinese recovered significant amounts of gold from these supposedly worked-out diggings and were greatly resented by the white miners for their success. Race riots followed against 'the celestials', as the Chinese miners were known at the time, and several Chinese miners were killed. Nevertheless, the thrifty celestials prospered and, when the gold at Lambing Flat was finally exhausted, they moved on to Sydney and opened shops, cheap eating houses and commercial vegetable gardens. As a consequence, they were deeply despised by the large influx to Sydney of ne'er-do-wells left over from the gold rush who'd squandered the money they made at the diggings and had lost the taste for hard work.

This resentment of the Chinese who stayed behind after the gold rush caused the politicians of the day to focus on the fact that the celestials had opened opium dens in Sydney, largely for use by their own kind. They asserted that these devilishly wicked opium dens were a conspiracy by the celestials to reduce the young female population of the city to dependence on the poppy. In doing so, their sweet maidenhood was supposedly rendered into the lascivious clutches of the Chinese, who, having used them to satisfy their own carnal appetites, would then employ these hapless innocents as prostitutes for their own gain. This accusation was based on the fact that many young Sydney prostitutes smoked opium, just as today many of the same profession use heroin.

As Nicole Lenoir-Jourdan had pointed out later when we discussed the book, 'Double standards are a prerequisite in the business of politics, Jack. Outcomes are seldom brought about for the good of the people, but invariably for the benefit of enhancing a political career or maintaining a political party in power. When the two ideas coincide, this is considered a fortunate accident. When a political leader arrives among his people who doesn't put his own self-interest or that of his party above those he represents, then we think of him as a great man and raise a statue in the park to his memory. Those very same politicians who called for the return of the Chinese to their homeland wouldn't have dreamed of standing up in parliament and calling for the closure of Sydney's notorious sly grog shops or the banning of opium-based cough mixture or children's soothing syrup. For them to do so would have quickly terminated their careers. Politicians may be vainglorious and self-serving, but they all have a well-developed sense of survival.'

The politicians at the time had vociferously demanded that the celestials be sent packing by being forced to return to China. It was here that the idea of the White Australia Policy had been born. It would take another generation before, at the time of Federation, the policy was written into law. Fifty years on it remained unaltered and immovable, tenaciously clinging to the layers of prejudice carefully constructed in the emotional education of most Australians.

Nicole Lenoir-Jourdan called our campaign to allow Jimmy to stay 'Admission Impossible'. 'We might as well know what we're up against, Jack,' she announced. 'If we accept that the most obdurate position will be taken by the forces of evil then we will not become disillusioned. When the fight gets hard and we keep on butting our heads against an adamantine wall of government intransigence, we must never let them see us emotionally affected and must remain strong and resolute at all times.' It was her way of saying that, come what may, we should keep our cool and never give up.

We started with a small piece of luck when we discovered that Jimmy didn't have to go back to Japan to be demobbed – he could take his discharge from the army at the US consulate in Melbourne. In the meantime, posing as a journalist, which I suppose she was, being the owner of the *Gazette*, Nicole Lenoir-Jourdan began gathering background information. We discovered that after the scare of the fall of Singapore in World War II and the possibility at the time of a Japanese invasion, Australia's population of seven million had been seen as dangerously inadequate. The nation embarked on a strong, almost desperate push to increase its population. Migrants were coming in from far and wide under the 'populate or perish' incentive initiated by the immigration minister, Arthur Calwell, in 1945. While we hadn't seen any of the effects of this on the island it seemed just about anyone could come in, so we were terrifically encouraged that things might have changed. The next piece of good news was that ever since the war, US ex-servicemen were to be considered one of the categories the government was anxious to encourage to immigrate.

'Whacko!' I exclaimed, when Nicole Lenoir-Jourdan told me this.

'Don't get your hopes up too far, Jack. We'll just have to wait and see,' she cautioned.

But it seemed her caution was misplaced. When she rang the Commonwealth immigration officer in Hobart he checked that Jimmy had a visitor's visa, and when she told him that Jimmy was an American and a Korean War veteran and wanted to remain in Australia – immigrate, that is – he sounded quite encouraging. 'He's Category A, shouldn't be too much trouble. You'll need to come into the office to complete the forms and we'll have to do a check on his background.'

'We only have one worry,' I said to Nicole Lenoir-Jourdan when she told me what the immigration official had said. 'Jimmy's past life has not been without the odd incident. On the other hand, the judge said if he went to Korea they'd wipe his reform-school history and later street-gang convictions from the records and he'd be a cleanskin.'

'Let's hope for his sake the judge kept his word,' she answered, adding, 'though I can't imagine James doing anything truly disgraceful.'

Buoyed by the news of American ex-servicemen being in a priority immigration category, we still hadn't told Jimmy about the White Australia Policy. 'No point in jumping the gun. Hopefully, he'll never have to know,' I said to Nicole Lenoir-Jourdan.

We took the Douglas DC3 to Launceston then the bus to Hobart, staying at the same boarding house we'd been at for my medal ceremony. Nothing is very far from anything else in Hobart, so the following morning the three of us walked to the immigration office on the ground floor of the Colonial Mutual Life Assurance Society at 97 Macquarie Street. Jimmy and I were dressed in our army uniforms, me hoping the ribbons on our chests would impress the immigration officer. Blokes like him might just know what they meant. Nicole Lenoir-Jourdan wore the same summer suit she'd worn at the medal ceremony, only she wore short white gloves and was without her straw hat with the pheasant feather. She saw me glance at her silvery-blonde hair as we left the boarding house. 'Women don't wear hats when they mean business,' she said quietly to me, out of Jimmy's hearing. I was pretty confident that our visit would be a good one, and so was surprised at the note of caution in her voice.

The office turned out to be small and crowded and seemed pretty busy with clerks coming and going, calling out names from the reception desk. The receptionist, a thin woman in her fifties, wore heavy-rimmed tortoiseshell glasses with her dyed black hair pulled back into a severe bun on the top of her head. I glanced at Jimmy. 'Gobblin' spider,' I teased, grinning.

Jimmy grinned back. 'Spider got dem big googly eyes but ain't got no legs,' he said, out of the corner of his mouth.

I approached the desk and the receptionist looked up at me without interest. 'Yes?' she said.

'We have an appointment with Mr Cuffe.' Then I added gratuitously, 'It's about my friend here, migrating. My name is Jack McKenzie – I'm the sponsor.'

She removed her glasses and, moving her head to one side so she could see past me, looked over at Jimmy and Nicole Lenoir-Jourdan. 'The soldier or the lady?' she asked.

I grinned. 'The soldier.'

'Are you sure?' she then asked.

'Yes, of course. We phoned Mr Cuffe from Queen Island.' *This bird's real strange*, I thought to myself.

She looked down at her appointment book. 'Mr Oldcorn? Mr James Pentecost Oldcorn?'

'Yes, that's right.'

She bent with her mouth close to a small intercom on her desk and, pressing the button, announced, 'Mr Oldcorn and his sponsor have arrived, Mr Cuffe.'

'Sponsor*s*,' I said quickly. She glanced up, sighed, and pressed the button again. 'Sponsor*s*,' she added in an impatient voice.

A crackly male voice came back. 'Send them in, please.'

The receptionist didn't rise, but instead pointed to a door to the side of the desk. 'You may go in.'

I opened the door, allowing Nicole Lenoir-Jourdan to enter first, then Jimmy. The bloke behind the desk facing us was busy writing and I could see he had a bald spot on the top of his head that resembled a monk's tonsure. He was big – or rather he was fat – sitting in his shirt sleeves, and had those elasticised metal bands halfway up his arm keeping his cuffs clear. When he glanced up I saw the bushiest eyebrows I'd ever seen, even bushier than Bob Menzies, the prime minister. He started to smile at Nicole Lenoir-Jourdan as he rose ponderously from the desk to greet her. Then he saw Jimmy enter the room, and his smile abruptly disappeared. His mouth formed a distinct 'Oh', although he remained silent. *Oh shit! What now?* I thought.

Cuffe's manner became formal and official as he indicated the three chairs in front of his desk. 'Please, be seated.' He returned to his seat without shaking hands and began to shuffle a pile of papers, finally bringing one to the top.

'Lovely day,' Nicole Lenoir-Jourdan ventured. 'You have a nice glimpse of the water.'

Cuffe looked surprised, and glanced in the direction of the office window. 'Never look at it,' he said abruptly. I could tell right from the start things were not going to go well. He cleared his throat and addressed Jimmy directly. 'Mr Oldcorn, I was just wondering, what is your ancestry?'

Jimmy looked surprised. 'My ancestry?'

Cuffe cut in quickly. 'I notice that your, er, skin is a honey colour, and I was just wondering what proportion of you is European and what proportion is, well, other?'

'Dat a hard question, sir. I's an orphan, born and bred.'

'It is African, isn't it?' Cuffe persisted.

'I suppose,' Jimmy said, bemused. He glanced at us. 'Most American Negro, dey come from Africa long time back.'

'I see,' said Cuffe, now coldly correct. 'I must ask you to do a dictation test.'

Jimmy smiled, obviously relieved. 'Sure, I guess that's pretty normal under the circumstances,' he said, his grammar and enunciation correct so that I was forced to smile.

'In English?' Nicole Lenoir-Jourdan asked, frowning.

'In the language of our choosing,' the immigration official replied, and spoke into the intercom. 'Send in Helmut, please.'

Helmut entered the room and greeted us with a pronounced European accent. Mr Cuffe handed Helmut a folder and pushed a notepad and a freshly sharpened pencil in front of Jimmy. 'Would you please write down what you hear, Mr Oldcorn.'

'Sure,' Jimmy said, sounding confident as usual. He picked up the pencil and waited as Helmut began to read slowly.

*'Das Urteil*
*Es war an einem Sonntagvormittag im schönsten Früjahr. Georg Bendemann, ein junger Kaufmann, saß in seinem Privatzimmer im ersten Stock eines der niedrigen, leichtgebauten Häuser, die entlang des Flusses in einer langen Reihe, fast nur in der Höhe und Färbung unterschieden, sich hinzogen . . .'*

Helmut looked up at last, just as Nicole Lenoir-Jourdan said, '*Er hatte gerade einen Brief an einen sich im Ausland befindenden Jugendfreund beendet* . . . That's terribly unfair, Mr Cuffe. That passage is German – Franz Kafka's opening paragraph to *The Judgement*.'

Cuffe looked surprised, but quickly recovered. 'I was not aware that you were taking the dictation,' he said officiously, and then looked over at Jimmy who lifted his pencil from the paper in front of him.

'Hey, man – yoh guys really do yo' homework, sir. How yoh know I live wid dem German folk?' He handed his paper to Helmut.

Cuffe looked concerned and then confused as Helmut handed him Jimmy's dictation with a nod. As for me, I sat there dumbfounded.

'How'd I go?' Jimmy asked. 'I might have missed one or two o' dem dots, but I think da rest's okay.'

'You seem to understand German,' Cuffe said, giving Jimmy a mirthless smile. 'But I'm afraid we require you to take another dictation test.'

'This is iniquitous!' Nicole Lenoir-Jourdan exclaimed. I could see she was close to losing her cool. 'Then there'll be a third, until . . .' her angry voice broke off.

Cuffe shrugged. 'It's the law, madam,' he said.

'You mean the White Australia Policy, don't you?'

'There is no such thing – only the dictation test,' Cuffe said evenly. Then, handing the pad and pencil back to Jimmy, he nodded to Helmut, who began reading.

*'Le Colonel Chabert*
*Allons! encore notre vieux carrick—'*

'Those are the opening words to Balzac's *Colonel Chabert*,' Nicole Lenoir-Jourdan interrupted with more than a hint of sarcasm. 'Perhaps, Mr Cuffe, you'd like James to do Cantonese next. Perhaps the Chinese *Communist Manifesto*?'

*Jimmy could probably do Cantonese*, I thought to myself. But Helmut continued to read the passage from Balzac, the French words coming from his mouth sounding like complete gibberish to me, but then so had the German. Later, Nicole Lenoir-Jourdan would tell us that while Helmut spoke good German, his French pronunciation was so bad that any Frenchman listening would have had difficulty understanding him.

Jimmy placed the pencil down on the blank pad. 'I don't speak no French language, sir.' He glanced at Nicole Lenoir-Jourdan and smiled. 'Hey! Maybe Cantonese I can do.'

Cuffe actually had the temerity to look relieved. 'I'm afraid you have failed the dictation test, Mr Oldcorn, and, in accordance with the law, you are ineligible to remain in Australia when your visa expires. Should you remain in Australia after that you will be a "prohibited immigrant" and liable for deportation.'

'You bastard!' I shouted, jumping to my feet and grabbing him by the front of the shirt and pulling him halfway across the desk, his fat stomach jammed against the far edge so I couldn't pull him any further. 'I fought for shitbags like you!'

Cuffe looked terrified, though I wasn't near his size. But then I felt Jimmy's hand on my arm. 'Dat okay, Brother Fish. Take it easy, man.'

I released Cuffe, who pulled back, smoothing the front of his shirt. 'I'm only following instructions, Mr McKenzie,' he whined.

Nicole Lenoir-Jourdan rose, her voice icy-cold. 'You ought to follow your conscience, sir. That's exactly what the SS officers said at Belsen and Treblinka. "I was only following instructions." Ha! You perfidious and shameless excuse for a man!'

But by this time Cuffe, realising he wasn't going to be physically attacked further, had regained his composure. 'I'm a busy man, madam. Please leave my office,' he said, with a peremptory wave of the back of his hand, not bothering to rise from his desk.

But it wasn't over yet. Jimmy, still standing and towering above Cuffe, now bent over and placed his huge hands on Cuffe's desk, leaning over the bureaucrat. The immigration official pulled back hastily, the back of his chair banging into the wall behind him.

'Dese folk, dey been lovin' and kind to me, sir. Dey done show me more love den I evah done have before in mah life. Yoh and yo' kind cain't take dat away from dis yella nigger – not now, not evah!' Cuffe shuffled in his chair, and in the process scattered the papers from his desk all over the carpet. Jimmy turned away with a grim smile. 'Come, we leave now. Dis honky, he need to change his britches.'

So much for remaining strong and resolute. What was it again? Something like '*We must never let them see us emotionally affected and must remain strong and resolute at all times*.' Or my pathetic version – come what may, we must keep our cool and never give up. *What a joke!* We'd failed at the very first hurdle and Jimmy was the only one among us who'd kept his temper and remained calm.

With both of us fuming on the footpath outside, Jimmy said quietly, 'Brother Fish, maybe we got to make ourselves some dif-ferent plans.'

'Whaddyamean?' I yelled. 'Mate, it's not over yet!' I pointed up at the window of the insurance building. 'That fat fuckwit's not gunna get the better of us!' For once Nicole Lenoir-Jourdan didn't pull me up for my language.

Jimmy shook his head sadly. 'I had me a good, good time on yo' island, Brother Fish. It time now to go home.'

'James, you're sounding mawkish,' Nicole Lenoir-Jourdan said sharply. 'Jack and I disgraced ourselves in there. We let you down, I'm afraid. I apologise, and promise it won't happen again. So both of you pull yourselves together, please.' Then she smiled, her tone of voice changing. 'Come along, you two – we have a morning tea to go to, and there's no time to lose.'

We looked at each other. 'You'd like a cup of tea?' I asked. In my mind I was thinking more of a beer – or ten.

'No, of course not! We've been invited to morning tea.'

'By whom? Where?' I asked, puzzled.

'Curiosity killed the cat, Jack. You'll just have to wait and see.' She turned to Jimmy. 'James, do you think you could find a taxi?'

'Yes, Nicole ma'am,' Jimmy said, moving away to look for a cruising cab.

With Jimmy out of earshot I fell to pieces and started to weep. I didn't mean to – I didn't even know it was coming. I just fell apart. 'But he's my mate – without him I'da been dead. Fair go, you don't let a mate down like this. You just *don't* do it!'

'Pull yourself together please, Jack. James has found a taxi.'

The taxi pulled into the familiar drive leading to Government House. Before I could open my mouth to ask what the hell was happening, Nicole Lenoir-Jourdan said, 'We're having morning tea with Lady Louise.'

'Who?'

'The governor's wife, Lady Louise Cross.'

'How'd you manage to swing that?'

'Manage? One doesn't *manage*, Jack. Occasionally one has to use a little judicious influence.'

'You know the governor's wife?'

'Yes, we met at your ceremony.'

'Does that count?' I asked, surprised.

'Hardly, but in this instance, we're proving useful to each other. Besides, she strikes me as a thoroughly nice person.'

'I see,' I said, but didn't. The morning had already been strange. First I'd discovered Nicole Lenoir-Jourdan could speak German and French, and now we were going to tea with the governor's wife.

Jimmy was seated in the front of the taxi and Nicole Lenoir-Jourdan and I shared the back seat. She turned to look directly at me. 'Jack, I don't know what might happen. You are going to have to leave this to me.'

'Is this about, you know, Jimmy?'

'Perhaps. It wouldn't do to get our hopes up too far.'

Jimmy had remained silent throughout. Now he turned to the back. 'Nicole ma'am, yoh gone done all this foh me?'

'James, don't be silly. The White Australia Policy as we know it, and the parody known as the "dictation test", is plainly wicked legislation that preys on fear and ignorance, deliberately inculcated into the belief system of the Australian people by our politicians. I was born in Russia, but spent a lot of my childhood in Manchuria and early adulthood in Shanghai. In Shanghai I was regarded as a stateless person but eventually obtained Chinese travel papers, so technically I was Chinese. In fact, I feel more Chinese than Russian, and even used to dream in Chinese. But my hair is blonde and my eyes blue so I am excused the dictation test and happily accepted as a citizen of this country. I am ashamed to say that until you came along, like so many others, I chose to remain silent – hidden away on a little island where I wouldn't be confronted by racism, and where my conscience wouldn't bother me unduly when people such as you are refused admission on the basis of a wickedly devised trick!'

*Chinese! Nicole Lenoir-Jourdan Chinese! If she was Chinese, then I was a Hottentot!*

We'd arrived at Government House and Jimmy was looking in his wallet for change to pay the taxi driver. I could hear the butler's feet scrunching on the pink gravel driveway as he approached. There wasn't time for any further questions. Then, just as I went to open the taxi door, Nicole Lenoir-Jourdan said, 'Do you have your harmonica with you, Jack?' I nodded, too confused to think why she would ask me – she must have known I always carry it.

If you're a woman then you must know that women think differently from men. They can be deadset cunning and manipulative.

They can make end results come about by taking the most obscure and circuitous routes most men wouldn't even think of attempting, let alone even think of in the first instance. Patience is yet another weapon they employ, sometimes taking years to achieve an objective – which they never lose sight of. Paradoxically, it has been my observation that having finally achieved what they want, it turns out they don't want it after all. But that's by the by.

If Jimmy had a way of making people see things his way, making them do things they might not otherwise have done, Nicole Lenoir-Jourdan had a way of making things happen without people knowing they were doing what she required of them. That wasn't to say she couldn't be openly persistent and decidedly didactic, as she had been with me when she'd scooped me up off the library floor and decided I was worth the trouble of attempting to educate so many years before.

However, in her role as justice of the peace, a mere witnesser of signatures, she often managed to calm family feuds on the island, prevent cruelty to wives and children, shame the greedy and rapacious into behaving decently, and persuade young blokes who'd got a girl up the duff to walk down the band of gold to the altar. She knew more about land entitlements and fishing rights than anyone on the island, and could untangle a quarrel between two fishermen over a cray lease better than the Tasmanian Fisheries Department ever could, although never by direct interference. Now she was at it again, and I for one hadn't a clue how we'd found ourselves on the steps of Government House for the second time, with the governor's butler hurrying around to open the taxi door for us.

Morning tea took place in the music room, home to two pianos. The butler served Earl Grey tea and hot scones with strawberry jam and cream. After the disastrous session with Cuffe I guess we were still pretty upset, which in my case made me ravenous. Jimmy must have felt the same only more so, and we tucked in while Lady Cross and Nicole Lenoir-Jourdan talked about things women always talk about. You'd have thought they'd known each other for years.

Jimmy kept looking around, and I guess he felt much the same way as I did. This wasn't the sort of place we'd expected to find ourselves. So we munched the warm scones and tried to sip the tea graciously, which was served in little bone china cups that looked so small in Jimmy's hand they reminded me of those cups hanging in the miniature kitchen in the doll's-house museum in Launceston.

Then, to our surprise, two young teenage girls and a woman in her early twenties walked in, the youngest of them carrying sheet music under her arm. Jimmy and I hastily put down our cups and jumped to our feet. All three were pretty in what Gloria would have described as an 'English rose' way. Lady Cross smiled as they entered. 'Ah, there you are, darlings.' She turned to Nicole Lenoir-Jourdan. 'Let me introduce you to my daughters.' She indicated first to the young lady who appeared to be in her early twenties, the eldest of the three. 'This is Diana, then Susanna and our youngest, Karina. Girls, you know Nicole Lenoir-Jourdan, if only by correspondence, so now you've met.' Nicole Lenoir-Jourdan smiled, but didn't offer her hand, and both the two younger girls did a tiny little curtsy, smiled brightly and said, 'How do you do, Miss Lenoir-Jourdan.' Diana reached out and Nicole Lenoir-Jourdan took her hand and they exchanged greetings.

Then Susanna, who looked to be about sixteen, said, 'Thank you so much for the music. I hope we do it justice.'

Lady Cross indicated Jimmy and me. 'This is Mr McKenzie and Mr Oldcorn. You may recall Mr McKenzie recently received the Military Medal from your father, and Mr Oldcorn is visiting us from America.'

'Korea, ma'am,' Jimmy corrected.

'Yes, of course – how careless of me. Mr Oldcorn is a Korean War veteran.' The Cross girls greeted us politely, but once again they didn't shake hands. They glanced at me and smiled and then at Jimmy. The two younger girls then immediately lowered their eyes, while Diana kept her blue eyes on Jimmy, smiling.

*Oh Christ, not the ole black magic again!* Which was what I'd come to call the almost magnetic attraction the various island sheilas seemed to have to Jimmy. I couldn't even bring myself to imagine him and the governor's daughter in a bucking scene.

'Please ta meet yoh, ma'am. James Pentecost Oldcorn, but yoh can call me, Jimmy,' he said in his most mellifluous voice, looking directly at Diana and extending his hand.

'And mine is Jacko,' I added, grinning like an ape.

'Jacko and Jimmy Pentecost Oldcorn,' Diana repeated, accepting his hand, her eyes dancing. Jimmy's eyes remained fixed on Diana Cross, while hers were now sending out signals that you wouldn't need to know Morse code to translate. *Wouldn't that half set the cat among the pigeons!* Jimmy held Diana's hand just a fraction too long before releasing it.

I had this sudden vision of Wendy and me with Diana Cross and Jimmy standing at the altar of St Stephens in a ceremony conducted eccentrically by the Reverend John Daintree. The governor in his flashy ceremonial uniform, epaulets blazing and medals bumping each other out of the way on his chest, having just led Diana, radiant in a gown of at least a hundred yards of white tulle and holding a bouquet of white lilies, down the aisle, with Jimmy waiting at the altar, nearly seven foot tall, in striped pants and tails. Wouldn't that be a turn-up for the books? Then when the Reverend Daintree asked, in my reverie, '*If any man should know of any reason why this man and this woman should not be joined in holy wedlock, let him speak it now or forever hold his peace*,' Cuffe rushed in shouting that Jimmy hadn't passed the dictation test!

I could see the whole thing in my mind's eye. '*Dictation test? What dictation test?*' the Reverend John Daintree would demand to know. Whereupon Cuffe would pull a piece of paper from the pocket of his shabby suit and give it to Helmut, who would read out something in Russian, and the Anglican minister would immediately translate it, then Chinese, Urdu, Maori, Greek and finally Swahili, and each time Reverend Daintree would rattle it off while often stopping Helmut mid-sentence to correct his pronunciation. Then Cuffe would protest that the dictation test was intended for the yellow-skinned nigger in the striped pants and tails. The Anglican minister would dismiss him with a wave of his hand and say, '*Go away at once, you stupid old duffer. Can't you see this is a vice-regal occasion, where I'm burying the past and christening the future in a wedding ceremony of the present!*'

Nicole Lenoir-Jourdan interrupted my daydream by saying to Susanna, 'So you received the music and the translation of the lyrics?'

'Oh yes, thank you. We've been practising like mad. I hope you all approve,' the two younger girls said, almost simultaneously.

Then Lady Cross said, 'Diana's just returned from London where she's been staying with Angela, my eldest daughter. The girls' music teacher, Olga Linley, went over with Diana to study at the Royal College of Music in London, so the girls have had to work out their parts on their own. They've decided Susanna will sing it while they both play.'

I looked at Jimmy, mystified. The old '*Gloria's done it again*' feeling was rising in the pit of my stomach, but this time it was Nicole Lenoir-Jourdan, which just goes to show no woman can be completely trusted.

'The girls wanted a new piece for the original-composition section of the Hobart City Eisteddfod, so they wrote to me at the *Gazette* and we started corresponding.' She said it as if it was the most normal thing possible.

'What, "Johnny, I Hardly Knew Ye"?' I asked. 'It's hardly a new song.'

'No, no, "The Fish Song".'

'"The Fish Song"? – but it's in Chinese!'

'Cantonese actually, not even that – a river people's dialect,' Nicole Lenoir-Jourdan corrected.

'So how did you get the words?'

Nicole Lenoir-Jourdan glanced at Jimmy, who spread his hands and shrugged. 'Hey, man! I don't done nothin', Brother Fish. I jus' sing dem words in chink. Nicole ma'am, she done wrote dem down. She don't say nothin' about no translation foh Susanna an' Karina in dat I-sted-ford.'

Nicole Lenoir-Jourdan, the picture of innocence, then said, 'I do believe I mentioned earlier that I spent much of my late childhood and early adult life in China. After all, among other things I am a music teacher. I ought to know how to put a piece of music on paper – though I must say the melody proved surprisingly subtle.'

'Oh, do play it with us, Jacko?' Karina said. 'Jimmy, would you sing it?'

'I don't know dem words in English,' Jimmy protested.

'No, of course – but we'd much rather you sang them in the original. Susanna and I will play piano. We've worked out parts, but we'll take our lead from Jacko,' Karina replied.

Susanna looked at me, appealing, 'Please, please, will you play the harmonica? You make it sound so beautiful!'

What could a man do? The perfidy of the opposite sex had struck again, but I must say the governor's two younger daughters were wonderful musicians. We messed around a bit trying a few things out and then gave it a go. Karina, who we later learned was twelve, and Susanna took turns to do the dramatic parts with each filling in the backing, which was never obtrusive, never drowning, allowing my harmonica to persist. I'd nod when one or the other was to do a solo and nod twice when it was my turn on the harmonica. Jimmy still believed Jesus had left him with an irreparably broken voice after puberty. All I can say is he owed JC a big apology. When we'd completed the song both Lady Cross and Nicole Lenoir-Jourdan had tears in their eyes, and Diana hadn't once taken her eyes off Jimmy. Even if I say so myself, it was a bloody good effort all round.

Then the girls did it by themselves – Susanna singing the words in English at the piano while Karina took the dramatic instrumental parts. Susanna had a very nice contralto voice that suited the music beautifully, whereas a soprano might have been a little too shrill for the essentially Chinese melody. Listening to Karina without having to concentrate on playing, I realised what a talented young musician she was.

'Dat da first prize, foh sure!' Jimmy said, as we all clapped furiously. 'Dat good, good music, man!' He was right – the song had lost very little in translation, and hearing it in English highlighted how beautiful the lyrics were. Lady Cross and Nicole Lenoir-Jourdan excused themselves and left the music room.

After this we messed around a bit, having a bit of a jam session with the girls, who also played and enjoyed jazz. Diana knew the lyrics of just about everything. I know it sounds bloody corny when I retell it, but Jimmy whispered something to Susanna, who giggled, and next thing the opening chords of 'I Only Have Eyes for You' followed. I picked it up immediately on the harmonica, Karina worked the second piano, and Jimmy started to sing to Diana, who blushed furiously but held his eyes throughout, even when at the end the two younger girls broke up, unable to stop giggling.

Then the butler entered and announced that lunch was being served in the conservatory. Lady Cross and Nicole Lenoir-Jourdan were already seated when we entered the room. 'You'll just have to take pot luck – it's the cook's day off,' Lady Cross announced, as she tossed a green salad and then added a bit of oil and vinegar.

Pot luck turned out to be cold cuts – ham, chicken, a half-carved leg of lamb – and, of course, the salad. I mean, if you give the salad a miss, that's your Christmas food – you can't do much better than that, can you? What's more, there was jelly and ice-cream to finish. During the lunch I asked Diana if she played a musical instrument. 'I'm afraid she's inherited Ronnie's ear,' Lady Cross said, laughing. 'Although she can beat us all at chess, including her father, who gets very cross.'

'Mummy, that's a terribly old pun.' Diana said, laughing despite herself. She and Jimmy had spent most of the lunch talking to each other and you could see she really liked him.

If it hadn't been such a sad day, it would have been a terrific one. On the bus back to Launceston Nicole Lenoir-Jourdan and Jimmy sat together and I had a seat to myself, so I had plenty of time to think. I hated what had happened to Jimmy. I was angry, hurt and humiliated.

The dictation test had been so cynical, sneaky and hypocritical that it was ugly and well beyond being self-righteous. I felt ashamed for my country. Whoever had thought it out must have sniggered behind his hand, dead chuffed with himself, like Busta Gut when he suggested blaming the queen over a damaged parcel.

I simply had no idea what we could do next – the dictation test seemed an insurmountable hurdle. They could simply go on and on in endless languages. It occurred to me that if Einstein had been black and had applied for Australian citizenship he would have been rejected. But then, of course, he was a Jew, historically among the most rejected people on racist grounds anyway.

Then a bizarre thought occurred to me. What if Jimmy and Diana Cross became an item? I mean, not the silly fantasy with the Reverend Daintree, but really? Jimmy Pentecost Oldcorn, Colored Orphanage, Bronx street-gang leader and resident of Elmira Reformatory and the honourable Diana Cross, private school, probably finishing school in Switzerland or tertiary qualifications from some posh English university and Government House, Hobart. What would the bloody government say then? Would the dictation test still apply? '*I'm sorry, sir, owing to your lack of Zulu Miss Diana regrets she is unable to dance tonight.*'

But then I remembered Nicole Lenoir-Jourdan once telling me how important the correct bloodlines were to the English aristocracy, and I felt certain Jimmy wouldn't be the right crossbreed. I felt momentarily pleased with the pun I'd accidentally made, which was no worse than the one made by Lady Cross at lunch. But I told myself forlornly that the Dianas of this world might as well inhabit different planets to the Jimmys – such a conjoining could never take place in a million years. I'd grown thoroughly morose by the time we got to Launceston. What's more, Wendy wasn't home when I called from the telephone box at the airport, so I'd have to go all week without talking to her.

At Launceston Airport we had little opportunity to review the day. I felt pretty scruffy – the starch in my dress uniform had left deep green sweat creases across the inside of my elbows and behind my knees, and the sweatband on my slouch hat was soaked from the bus journey and the hot March day. Other people returning to the island were crowding around, talking to Jimmy and me. Charlie Champion, who owned a dairy farm on the island, cornered Nicole Lenoir-Jourdan about making cheese. He wanted to call his cheese 'Queen Island Cheddar' with a picture of the new queen on the wrapper, but Canberra had said no way unless he obtained a royal warrant. He wanted Nicole Lenoir-Jourdan to write to find out how you'd go about getting one. She explained that being granted a royal warrant wasn't something you could apply for, but was personally granted by the queen. She suggested he refer to his cheese label as '*The choice of all the Champions*'. Charlie called her a genius, and then asked her to write a stinging rebuke to the Minister for Primary Industry, who was dragging the chain over an import licence for some piece of machinery from France that helped to make something called brie. So we couldn't really talk about the day.

It wasn't much better on the plane back to the island, for while she and I sat next to each other, Jimmy preferring two seats with the armrest up, we were forced to remain silent as the plane took off. After it had levelled out the noise wasn't a lot better – we'd copped a seat over the wing next to the engine and had to shout to be heard.

'What now?' I shouted on one occasion. 'It's Mission *Impossible*!'

Nicole Lenoir-Jourdan leaned close to my ear, and said, 'Louise Cross knows Zara Holt.'

'Who?' I shouted back, cupping my ear.

'Zara Holt! They went to the queen's coronation together!' I shook my head, still not understanding. 'Harold Holt, the Minister for Immigration! His wife!' she shouted.

The secret women's business had begun.

# CHAPTER FIFTEEN

## *Secret Women's Business*

God may indeed work in mysterious ways, but perhaps not as mysterious as the female mind – unless of course, God is a woman, which would explain a lot of things. Men, it seems to me, either obey a law, never questioning it, or they break it with intent. Women see it for what it is – legislation or a set of rules usually promulgated by men for what they consider the common good, assuming invariably that the common good has only one gender.

In essence, at the time of which I write it was a man's world, and a man's tacit ownership of the woman he married even extended to her first name. In conventional society a married woman was referred to in newspapers, journals and at official functions by her husband's first name. For instance, 'Mrs Harold Holt, the wife of the immigration minister, will attend the coronation of the queen.' She had not only lost her maiden name but also her given name. In 1954 in Australia there were no women in the House of Representatives, no female judges or magistrates, no female bank managers – in fact, a woman couldn't get a loan from a bank without the signature of her husband if she was married, or her father if she was single. There were no female heads of public-service departments and law firms, no female directors of

Australia's top ten companies, no female vice-chancellors of universities, and only a handful of female academics and medical practitioners. In fact, teaching and nursing were almost the only areas where a woman could rise to seniority, either as the headmistress of a girls' school or the matron of a hospital. The marriage vow 'love, honour and obey' was invariably seen as a one-sided promise with the female partner doing all the obeying – or *else*.

Consequently, women learned that confrontation doesn't work and that circumvention is much more likely to bring about a result that serves their interests. Solving problems the long way round invariably proves the shortest means in the end. 'Secret women's business' is an Indigenous term drawn from more recent times, but it best describes the recognition amongst thinking women at the time of which I write of the power of each other's collective presence and the need for covert cooperation with each other in order to achieve their ends.

At the time we had tea at Government House with Lady Cross and her daughters, women in Australia were at a distinct disadvantage in society. Where they lacked direct influence in a male world, they were forced to resort to alternative ways of achieving a purpose – as women have done for millennia.

Please don't think that I worked all of this out for myself – far from it. Like most men, I had never questioned the status quo. But under Nicole Lenoir-Jourdan's tuition, over a fairly protracted period, I slowly acquired an awareness of the gender inequalities in our society, and how very unfair things were at the time for the female gender.

The day after returning to the island following Jimmy's 'dictation test', I went to the *Gazette* office to see Nicole Lenoir-Jourdan. With the disaster at the Immigration Office the previous day I hardly slept and Jimmy too seemed restless, so we went diving at dawn and brought home half a dozen decent crays. We didn't talk much about what happened in Hobart – after all, we'd been present and the result had been so shattering and terminal there wasn't much we could add. No ifs, buts or maybes – the dictation test was easily explained and so completely lacking in justice with its infinite application and inevitable result that no discussion beyond a series of inwardly expressed expletives became possible. We couldn't even get the day properly off our chests by repeating what had happened. Sue was on night shift and the boys were out at sea for a couple of days. I'd told Gloria, of course, who'd promptly burst into tears, called out 'The bastards!' and rushed over to kiss and hug Jimmy.

Jimmy, for his part, had entertained her at supper with the story of the Cross girls and the translated 'Fish Song', but otherwise kept his thoughts to himself. Anyway, after breakfast I took a nice crayfish over to Nicole Lenoir-Jourdan at the *Gazette*, using it as an excuse to have a bit of a chat.

'How does Zara Holt come into all this?' I asked, after she'd brought me a cup of tea and closed the door to her tiny office.

'Sugar?' she asked, pushing the bowl over to rest beside my cup. Then she smiled. 'I really ought not to be telling you this, Jack. It's what I've come to term *rexposure*.'

'Rexposure?'

She laughed. 'Well, *Rex* is Latin for king, and *exposure* – well, you know what that means. So rexposure is when a woman *exposes* an idea to a male that will enable him to change his mind and perform a given task without being seen to move from his previous position.'

'Like the Chinese not being seen to lose face?'

'Well, yes, but it's not only about pride.'

'But if he is seen by his mates to change his mind,' I protested, 'he's bound to lose face.'

'You're thinking like a male, Jack. *He* isn't *seen* to change his mind – in fact, he doesn't change it at all.'

'I'm still not sure I understand – but then, of course, I *am* a male.'

'Forget rexposure – it's just a silly word I've invented for my own amusement. As you know, I have to deal with a lot of men on the island who often have to change their mind but can't afford to be seen to have done so. Think of it like this. There are rules and there are exceptions.

A man prides himself on dealing with rules, while a woman's currency is in exceptions.'

'Ah, I see – the exception to the rule.'

'No, quite wrong. The exception to a rule becomes fixed, a rule in itself. The exceptions are *not* precedents, they are emotional judgements that bring honour to the rule. They are seen to soften its harshness and give it a sense of charity, and even endow it with a conscience. When a male is able to perform one of these "emotional exceptions" he becomes a hero in the eyes of his contemporaries, and also ends up pretty pleased with himself.'

'So that's how women influence men?'

'Go about *attempting* to influence men. It doesn't always work – men can be stubborn creatures.'

'And you're hoping to get to Zara Holt through Lady Cross, who will try to get her husband to accept Jimmy's case as an emotional exception?'

Nicole Lenoir-Jourdan sighed. 'I admit it's drawing a long bow, Jack. But if we can get Zara Holt, who is a modern gal with a contemporary outlook and, I am told by Lady Cross, a determined woman with definite opinions, we may just have a chance.'

'Do you know how she feels, you know, about the White Australia Policy?'

'Ah, there's the rub. I don't, and nor does Louise Cross. It's not the sort of thing women in polite society talk about.'

'So it could be sudden death? She could simply take her cue from her husband?'

Nicole Lenoir-Jourdan looked directly at me. 'A great many wives of politicians do – that way there are no complications, no moral dilemmas to face. It is a curious condition that the longer an immoral law exists, the easier it is to justify in the mind. "It's what the people want" is the usual political mantra. Justification is a bad habit easily acquired.' She sighed again. 'We can only live in hope, Jack.'

'Hope Mrs Holt is different? What if she doesn't bother to reply?'

'Oh no, she'll reply all right.'

'Okay, so why should she help us?'

Nicole Lenoir-Jourdan looked up, surprised. 'Because one might sincerely hope that she is not a racist and is prepared to make up her own mind about an unjust law.'

'No, no – that's not what I mean. Why should she see Jimmy as an "emotional exception"?' I was beginning to quite like the term.

'Oh, I see. Why Jimmy, and not simply anyone – or everyone? Well, of course, one feels somewhat hypocritical singling out Jimmy, but that's the essential weakness in the emotional-exception argument – it does nothing to change the law.' She gave me a wan smile. 'It's an attempt to solve a specific problem, not to bring about a universal solution. Women know that progress is one small step at a time and seldom occurs in leaps and bounds. As a woman, Mrs Holt would instinctively understand this. She knows she must be given a series of specific and unique reasons why Jimmy is to be that single step, why he can be made to be seen by her husband as the emotional exception.'

She opened a drawer in her desk and produced two sheets of writing paper, which I saw at once were covered with her own neat handwriting. 'It's only a draft, but I've written it on good paper to put it in . . .' she paused, smiling a little guiltily, '. . . the right context.' She handed me the two sheets of paper. 'Perhaps you'll read it, Jack? Please, I'd appreciate your comments.'

I accepted the heavy, cream-coloured pages and noted that the paper was of a beautiful linen-based quality. Then I saw the embossing at the top of the page, through which Nicole Lenoir-Jourdan had struck a line with her fountain pen, and my eyes nearly popped out of my head.

COUNT NIKOLAI LENOIR

*Mrs Harold Holt*
*c/o Mr Harold Holt, Minister for Immigration*
*Parliament House*
*Canberra*

*13th March, 1954*

*Dear Mrs Holt,*
*Thank you for accepting the letter from Lady Louise Cross written on my behalf. It is good of you to respond so promptly, and agree to accept my submission in the matter concerning Private James Oldcorn, a member of the American Armed Forces engaged until recently in the Korean War.*

*Private Oldcorn (soon to be demobbed) has expressed a desire to make his future home in Australia and, in particular, on Queen Island, where we are overwhelmingly anxious to welcome him as one of our own.*

*Jimmy Oldcorn is the guest of Private Jack McKenzie, known affectionately to us as Jacko.*

I looked up, amused. 'You've never called me Jacko in your life,' I accused.

Nicole Lenoir-Jourdan smiled. 'It's what I call you in my head, Jack.'

I continued reading.

*Jimmy accompanied Jacko back to Queen Island on convalescence leave after hospitalisation in Japan, where they were both treated for wounds to the leg received in battle. Each had a bone in one of their legs broken and reset where it had knitted incorrectly due to medical neglect as prisoners of war under the Chinese.*

*They first met each other under the most appalling*

*circumstances in a hospital cave in North Korea. Both were seriously wounded, and Jacko asserts that Jimmy undoubtedly saved his life. According to Jacko, Jimmy saved his life on two further occasions in what became a remarkable and touching friendship between two men of vastly disparate backgrounds.*

*Throughout almost two years of captivity, in the most onerous and heart-rending conditions, against all odds, their friendship flourished and allowed them to survive. Each maintains that had he been 'alone' he would almost certainly have perished.*

*Throughout their ordeal, often when all hope was lost, Jacko would say to Jimmy, 'After the war, when you come home to my island, my mum is gunna make you a cray stew.' This simple promise became the hope that gave them the strength to continue when those around them lost the fight for survival through despair, starvation, disease and torture. When the armistice was declared and prisoners exchanged, Jacko weighed just fifty-two pounds (normal weight 125 pounds) and Jimmy 112 pounds (normal weight 280 pounds).*

*Jacko kept his promise and returned with Jimmy to his island and his mother's cray stew. I confess, the American GI and the Australian soldier, one nearly seven feet tall and the other five feet and five inches, make an improbable if lovable pair, and are both thoroughly decent young men.*

*Almost everyone on the island turned out to meet the ferry from Stanley that brought them home, and there was great rejoicing at the return of our beloved Jacko McKenzie. When it was announced on the evening of their return that Jacko had been awarded the Military Medal for bravery in battle, the cheer that rose from the spontaneous party at the dockside must have been heard on the mainland.*

*Jimmy has proved to be enormously popular on the island, and not only among the 'gals'. I must say he is a truly splendid-looking chap. So, as you can imagine, we were enormously encouraged when, upon inquiry, we were told by Mr Cuffe of the Commonwealth Department of Immigration in Hobart that American ex-servicemen had been placed in Category A as preferred immigrants.*

*Lady Cross will have informed you of the result of our subsequent visit to Hobart, so I have no need to elaborate here.*

*It would be easy to find a dozen good reasons why Jimmy Oldcorn should be allowed to stay, and I dare say the Department of Immigration has heard them all on frequent occasions.*

*However, the most compelling reason I have heard was the anguished cry Jacko made on the footpath outside the Immigration Office in Hobart after we'd been summarily dismissed by the redoubtable Mr Cuffe: 'But he's my best mate – without him I'da been dead. Fair go, you don't let a mate down like this. You just don't do it,' he wept, totally distraught.*

*Is it not equally fair to ask that what is deeply felt as the correct and honourable behaviour between two friends should also be the way two countries that have fought together for the same cause, and that share a deep and abiding friendship, should behave? This especially when a citizen of one has saved the life of a citizen of the other? When both have put their lives on the line for their country? Is it not a question of decency and honour, a matter of being the quintessential Australian?*

*Mrs Holt, I ask only that you do what you can for Jimmy Oldcorn.*

*Yours most sincerely,*

The draft was not signed.

'I thought you were angry when I broke down outside on the footpath!' I said first up.

'I was extremely upset for you, Jack. But it was dashed inconvenient at the time.'

Talk about stiff upper lip! 'The letter's great,' I volunteered.

'I wasn't looking for a compliment. I hoped you might be able to contribute to the content – it's only a first draft.'

I shook my head. 'That's your department. Apart from writing home to Mum from Korea and once to you, I guess I'm not much of a letter writer.'

'Nonsense! Have I entirely wasted my time, Jack McKenzie? When you want to be you can be very articulate. Wendy says you write lovely letters. Besides, you have a job to do.'

'A job?'

'Yes. I want you to write your own version of how and when you met Jimmy, and the subsequent time you spent together as prisoners of war.'

'But that would take forever! I couldn't say it all in a couple of pages . . .'

'No, of course not. We need it as an addendum. Mrs Holt will need something further to give to her husband to read.'

'I dunno,' I said, scratching my head. 'It's pretty blokey stuff. Besides, my spelling isn't too crash hot.'

'You have a perfectly good dictionary and, if you like, I'll look it over.'

'Jeez, I dunno, Nicole ma'am,' I said – because after all these years of referring to her as 'Miss', that's what I'd finally taken to calling her, thanks to Jimmy.

'"Jeez, I dunno"? I'm not sure that's even English, Jack!' she replied. 'Now, hop along. I've got work to do.'

'Can I ask you a question? I mean, may I ask you a question?' I corrected myself quickly. After all these years Nicole Lenoir-Jourdan still had me by the short and curlies.

'You may.'

'The letterhead? *Count* Nikolai Lenoir?'

'My father,' she replied briskly.

'Does that make you a countess?' I asked.

'It makes me a very busy newspaper editor. Can we talk about this at some other time please, Jack?'

The editorial Nicole Lenoir-Jourdan wrote for the *Gazette* that day talked about the dictation test and explained what had happened to Jimmy, but it didn't scream out in angry tones. Instead, the editorial politely asked the people on the island to come into the *Gazette* office to sign a petition saying they wished Jimmy to remain on the island.

I must admit I was surprised at this passive approach. When you own a newspaper, even one as insignificant as the *Queen Island Weekly Gazette*, surely you'd use something like what happened to Jimmy in big block letters on the front page: 'RACISM BLOCKS GI!'

I'd informed Jimmy about the letter to Zara Holt. While Nicole Lenoir-Jourdan hadn't exactly said she was going to go out with blazing headlines, her mention of writing an editorial had led me to assume this would be the case. I'd suggested to Jimmy to 'watch this space!' So when the low-key editorial came out, I confess I was a bit disappointed.

But Jimmy saw it differently, and he proved to be right. 'Brother Fish, Nicole ma'am, she done out-think us. She don't know foh sure how da folk on dis island dey feel, an' now she gonna find out. No pressure – jus' come in nice an' quiet an' put yo' name down iffen yoh want. Iffen she make it big news, she shout an' scream an' carry on – der always someone dey don't want I should stay. Dey gonna put dat newspaper in a big ol' envelope an' dey gonna lick da back o' Her Majesty head an' stick her on da corner an' send it to Can-berra.'

'Mate, they don't get the *Gazette* in Canberra – they don't even get it in Launceston.'

'Don't be too sure 'bout dat.'

I tried to think who such a racist might be. Les Kelly, maybe? No way, I decided – he'd be too pissed to care either way. 'So what are you saying?'

Jimmy smiled and spread his hands. 'It simple, man. When da minister he read dat ed-it-torial, he gonna say, "Hmm, that's a very reasonable approach", it gonna reinforce da emotional exception he workin' on in his mind. Da one his wife gone put der foh him to cogitate.'

'Cogitate! Jesus, Jimmy, where'd you get *that* word?' I held up my hand. 'No, don't tell me. Nicole ma'am?'

Jimmy nodded, grinning. 'I'm learnin' good, Brother Fish.' He tapped his chest. 'I am improving ex-po-nentially,' he said smugly.

I shook my head slowly. 'Watch out – she's got you by the knackers, mate.'

As far as the editorial not being the most effective way to go, I was quite wrong. By the morning following the printing of the *Gazette* there was a long queue outside the newspaper office.

People continued turning up to sign the petition for the next week, until we had 1600 of a potential 1800 signatures. Only the old and infirm hadn't made a showing.

The Reverend Daintree had even penned a sermon about Noah anchoring his ark on Mount Ararat and promptly planting vines. When the first crop of grapes was picked, pressed and made into wine, Noah became drunk and fell asleep in his tent, uncovered. His son Ham saw his father's nakedness, and reported what he saw to his two brothers. When Noah awoke from his wine and found out what Ham had done, he cursed Ham's son Canaan, condemning him to be 'a slave of slaves' forever.

Jimmy nudged me. 'Dat me, Brother Fish.'

The dotty old Anglican minister had then pointed out to the congregation that as far as he knew there had only been one Mrs Noah, and that the laborious study of the Old Testament he'd conducted throughout the past week had shown no evidence of Noah being a bigamist or taking a second wife. This could only mean, according to the good reverend's logic, that Ham was a half-caste and that all of Noah's sons must also be half-caste and that Mrs Noah must obviously have been a black woman. If this was the case then it automatically cancelled out the curse placed exclusively on the children of Ham, as we all came from exactly the same beginning. It was *ipso facto* entirely appropriate that Jimmy Oldcorn should remain among us. But after that the reverend lost the plot and complained that when the bitterly cold south-westerlies blew in over the island it was impossible to get anyone to hew wood for the manse, but that he had sufficient water in the rain tank at the back, thank you very much. He neatly concluded his sermon by thanking Charlie Champion for the half-leg of ham he'd brought over at Christmas, saying it was pink and not black and simply delicious and that on Christmas day he'd enjoyed it with a glass of Madeira wine.

We were just about ready to go with all the stuff we needed when a letter from Mrs Zara Holt arrived. It was short and to the point and seemed to have the right ring to it. Or that's what we told each other, even though it had been written on a typewriter, which I noticed caused Nicole Lenoir-Jourdan to wince. A slightly worried frown crossed her face when she unfolded the letter – she'd waited, not opening it until she'd sent a message for Jimmy and me to come to the newspaper office.

*Miss Nicole Lenoir-Jourdan*
Queen Island Weekly Gazette
*Livingston*
*Queen Island*

*16th March, 1954*

*Dear Miss Lenoir-Jourdan,*
*I received the letter from Louise Cross written on your behalf and by way of introduction. She has become a dear friend since we met when we both attended the queen's coronation in London.*

*The very fact that she has been prepared to lend her support to you in the matter she mentioned in her letter means I too will try to be supportive.*

*Having said this, you will, I feel sure, accept that I must be allowed to make final judgement for myself and in order to do so, I urge you to send me the particulars.*

*Yours sincerely,*
*Zara Holt*

Nicole Lenoir-Jourdan held the letter to her lips and seemed to be thinking. 'Hmm, she'll take him to the top,' she said, after a few moments.

I looked at Jimmy, and he shrugged. 'What does that mean?' I asked.

'She's the right wife – circumspect, clever and conscious of her husband's position without being arrogant. She'll take him a long way.'

'But what do you think about her letter? Is it okay?'

'Reading between the lines, I'd say it was encouraging.'

'Well then, what next?'

Jimmy interrupted before she could reply. 'Nicole ma'am, Brother Fish he done write about da POW camps, him an' me. He say I da hero,' he said, shaking his head. 'He don't write nothin' 'bout da harmonica and how it save our ass more den one time. I ain't com-fort-able 'bout dat.'

Nicole Lenoir-Jourdan smiled. 'I've read the account by Jack and I must say I think it strikes the correct note. I know how difficult all this must be for you, James, but you must trust our judgement. The people on the island have given you their overwhelming support and that's encouraging, but we're a long way off winning this thing and I'd rather gild the lily somewhat than say too little. I'm sure, if it were necessary, witnesses could be found to substantiate what's been said.'

I wondered how the hell we'd go about that or if many of the white American blokes who'd benefited from Jimmy's courage and leadership as prisoners would come forward to give him a rap.

With very few modifications Nicole Lenoir-Jourdan's original letter was sent along with an impressive package that contained the petition, the fifteen pages I'd written, the official press photographs that had appeared in the Hobart *Mercury* showing Jimmy and me standing with the governor and Robert Cosgrove, the Premier of Tasmania, who, by the way, we were later to discover was an ardent supporter of the White Australia Policy, so the photograph may not have been the greatest idea. Nicole Lenoir-Jourdan had written on the back of it 'For interest only, this appeared in the Hobart *Mercury*'. She said at the time that she didn't want the minister to think we were exerting undue pressure or taking advantage of a situation where the governor and the premier had acted in a strictly official capacity. But she also included the official photograph of me receiving my gong. 'It puts a face to the piece you've written, Jack,' she claimed.

We were just about ready to go when Jimmy produced two written pages and handed them to Nicole Lenoir-Jourdan, whereupon he more or less insisted they be included. 'May I read this?' she asked.

'Sure, Nicole ma'am, but yoh cain't change nothin', ma'am. Dat da con-dish-un.' Jimmy said it quietly but in an unmistakable tone of voice I'd heard before and which I knew meant business. It made Nicole Lenoir-Jourdan look up in surprise, not having hitherto seen this side of Jimmy. She started to read and after a while I saw a tear roll down her cheek, and then another. After she finished reading she dabbed her eyes, sniffed and blew her nose real hard. 'Oh dear, yes of course,' she said finally.

'And da "Fish Song", where you done wrote da music an' translate dem chink words, an' Gloria ma'am, her cray-stew recipe – dat gotta go in.'

The good thing was that Jimmy now had a say in the submission to Zara Holt. He wasn't sitting like a shag on a rock while others went to work on his behalf. He had a lot of pride. Lately he'd been going for long walks on his own and I reckon I knew what he had been thinking – that he'd like to crawl into a hole somewhere, disappear and save us all a lot of trouble. I guess he'd been a loner all his life. While I feel sure he knew we loved him, that I was his mate, come what may, love is something you've got to become accustomed to. If you don't get it early in life then it's bloody difficult not to secretly think of yourself as a bit worthless.

Take me, for instance. I didn't lack love as a child. I mean Gloria hadn't dished it out in great big dollops, and Alf hadn't exactly been Australian Father of the Year. But he hadn't been cruel or mean-spirited, and we'd known that Gloria loved us. Moreover, unlike a lot of island men, Alf hadn't taken his Saturday-night drinking out on us. If Gloria hadn't exactly smothered us with affection she'd nevertheless been fiercely protective of her children. She still got teary about having been forced to take me out of school at fourteen. There'd always been food on the table, and I'd had a happy enough childhood. Yet with all this going for me I'd still been pretty sure I didn't amount to a pinch of the proverbial. The Korean War had helped to make me feel more worthwhile and Jimmy had had a whole heap to do with that – much more than the medal, which could have gone to any bloke in our platoon.

Until now, Jimmy had never had anyone in his life to stick up for him or to love and fight for him – except perhaps for Frau Kraus, who had definitely loved him in her own loopy, gobbling-spider sort of way, and I think he'd understood that. But before her it had been the orphanage and afterwards the streets of the Bronx, the reformatory and then the army. There wasn't a hell of a lot of love to share around in that lot. He had a big swag to carry made up of the past, and I'm sure he felt he was being an unnecessary burden to us. Of course, nothing could have been further from the truth. But I'm buggered if I know how you tell a bloke you love him without making it sound like there's something else going on.

After we sent the package off it was only a question of waiting, which, of course, is always the worst part. We had one big problem – Jimmy's visitor's visa ran out in three weeks and the chance of anything happening in so short a time was pretty forlorn. Nicole Lenoir-Jourdan had pointed this out to Zara Holt in her slightly revised letter, which, by the way, had been written on the same notepaper as the draft, but with the embossed bit guillotined off. We'd applied for an extension, but of course if Canberra was going to give us the run-around, they weren't going to extend his visitor's visa for another three months.

Then Nicole Lenoir-Jourdan received a phone call from Lady Cross, who told her that Zara Holt had called and thought it best not to write to acknowledge receiving the package but that she had read it with great interest and felt she might be able to set things in motion.

'What does that mean?' I asked, thinking it sounded like something you did on the dunny.

'It's newspeak for "roger, out",' Nicole Lenoir-Jourdan answered, surprising both of us by knowing a radio operator's term for 'message received and understood'.

I don't know why I was surprised. I mean, I'd known her all my life, only to discover in the last couple of weeks that she'd been born in China, spoke Cantonese, German and French and was a countess – well, probably a countess, she still hadn't told me she definitely was. In fact, she hadn't brought up the subject and I hadn't been game to ask again. If I now suddenly discovered she'd been a secret agent during World War II, sending radio messages to the British about enemy submarines off the coast of China, I shouldn't be a bit surprised. Although, I reminded myself, she'd been on Queen Island during the war.

'Mrs Holt is nothing if not careful, which, if she decides to get involved, is a good thing.' I sensed Nicole Lenoir-Jourdan was a little disappointed at Zara Holt's response. The fact that she hadn't acknowledged our submission in writing, but instead elected to convey a message on the telephone via the governor's wife, was worrying. It meant she was covering her tracks so there could be no evidence of her involvement if her husband didn't take the bait.

I suspected that half the fun in this women's game of 'emotional exceptions' was the interplay in the correspondence passing between them. In those days everyone wrote letters to each other – apart from the back fence it was the major source of gossip in the world. Instead, the exclusive women's club was at work, with Zara Holt and Louise Cross playing the game while Nicole Lenoir-Jourdan, not yet a club member, sat on the sidelines. I wondered if they'd feel the same if they knew she was a countess, which I was beginning to assume she must be more and more.

Then a good thing from a bad source happened. Jimmy received a letter from Mr Cuffe telling him that Canberra had approved a three-month extension of his visitor's visa. He was to go to the Immigration Office in Hobart with his passport so he could complete the formalities.

The time set for his appointment was mid-afternoon, so he'd have to stay in Hobart overnight. I was due to be demobbed in Launceston, so I decided to stay there while Jimmy did the two-day round trip back to Launceston. Wendy was taking time off and we were going to spend a couple of days at the Walsh family fishing shack.

We took the first plane out in the morning. My discharge from the army was not much more than a question of handing in my uniform and signing a few papers at the personnel depot. A bit of a let-down, really, although it's hard to imagine the army thanking you for being in the service – let alone thanking you for something as trivial as putting your life on the line. Wendy and I hoped to be cycling our way to the shack well before lunch. But when I got into the city and called her, she said there'd been a slight change of plan and that her mum and dad wanted to have lunch with us. Would I pick her up at the chemist, as she was doing a half-day because the temporary girl couldn't make it until the afternoon.

This was pretty unusual, as Dr Kalbfell always had his surgery open until after lunch so that people who wanted to see him could come during their lunch hour. He didn't close until three, and had his lunch then before his hospital round.

'What's up?' I asked Wendy after I'd kissed her, and we were walking to the Kalbfell home up the hill. 'What about the surgery?'

'Dad's cancelled his lunchtime appointments to have lunch with us,' Wendy said.

'How come?' I asked suspiciously.

Wendy stopped and turned to me, and with her head tilted towards her shoulder, squinting slightly into the sun, she said, 'It's not him. It's Mum. Well no, it is him *and* Mum.'

'What about?'

'Us.'

'Us? What does that mean?

'The fishing shack.'

'What, she doesn't want us to go?'

'No – what it means.'

'What it means? It means we're sleeping together. What does your mum think – we go down for the fishing?'

'Don't be a smart-arse, Jacko! Sure, they know that. It's just . . .'

'It's just *what*, Wendy?' I said, suddenly angry.

'Jacko, I love you!' Wendy said, distressed.

'But they don't think I'm good enough? Is that it? Well, they're damn right – I'm not.'

Wendy grabbed me and put her head on my chest. 'Jacko, don't say that!' She looked up at me. 'You do love me, don't you?'

I pushed her away. 'Oh Jesus, Wendy, how can you even ask?'

She looked at me. 'Jacko, my dad's going to ask you if you're serious about me.'

It was such a ridiculous understatement about how I felt that I was forced to laugh. 'Serious? You mean so I'd give my life for you? Indubitably, my dear,' I said, using a Nicole Lenoir-Jourdan phrase, grinning.

Wendy laughed, her mood changing instantly. 'Then I can have your medal?'

'All of them – and the one I'm still gunna win rescuing you from the dragon.'

'Jacko! My mum is *not* a dragon!'

I laughed. 'You know that's not what I meant.'

She was suddenly serious again. 'My dad's going to sound pretty pompous.'

'Wendy, your dad *is* pompous. Most doctors are.'

'So my mother is a dragon and my dad is pompous. What does that make me?'

'A vessel full of fire and passion but with an added tincture of rectitude.'

'Jacko, that doesn't sound like you,' she said, though I could see she was pleased by the compliment.

'It's the other me, the Jack McKenzie Nicole Lenoir-Jourdan swept from the library floor at the age of eight.'

'Yes, I've glimpsed him from time to time. Not a bad sort of chap – quite bright, really,' Wendy said, putting on a posh voice and sending me up.

All the same, I was pretty nervous as we approached the house. I'm not sure 'pompous' was the right word to describe Dr Kalbfell. He was a doctor, and in those days doctors sat at the right hand of God.

Mrs Kalbfell met us at the door even though Wendy obviously had her own key. The door probably wasn't locked anyway, but she must have been keeping an eye out for us because the front door swung open as we came up the garden path. You could see where Wendy got her looks – the doctor's wife was still a good-looking lady. She smiled a little nervously as we approached. 'Hello, Jacko,' she said, before turning to Wendy. 'Hello, darling. I'm so glad you could both come to lunch.' She extended her hand to me. We hadn't quite reached the peck-on-the-cheek stage in our relationship.

'Hello, Mrs Kalbfell, thank you for inviting me,' I replied, taking her hand and shaking it lightly.

Wendy kissed her mum, and Mrs Kalbfell then said, 'Daddy is in his study. Perhaps you'd like to show Jacko through, darling.' It was all very civilised, but I sensed it wasn't all sweetness and light in the Kalbfell home.

Wendy gave me a sympathetic look, took my hand and led me down the hall, stopping at a door at the very end. 'Hello, Daddy. I've brought Jacko,' she called out, opening the study door about eight inches.

'Come in!' Dr Kalbfell called. 'I'll see you at lunch, Wendy.' He sounded friendly enough.

Wendy gave me another quick look, then kissed me on the cheek and whispered, 'Good luck.' I entered the study – a reasonable-sized room with a door that led into the surgery that had been built as an extension onto the back of the house. The door to the surgery was open and the two rooms seemed to have spilled over into each other so that the desk in the study and the one in the surgery were both covered in the usual doctor's paraphernalia. There were two leather armchairs in the study and an identical third one in front of his desk in the surgery. The big differences between the two rooms were the basin, the screen that I imagined concealed the doctor's couch in the surgery, and the pictures on the wall. Scottish hunting scenes graced the walls of the study – a perfectly rendered painting of a male or cock pheasant, another of three stags on a hill, one of a gillie knee-deep in grey-green gorse holding up a brace of what were presumably grouse, and lastly a print of a grey hare at full stretch. Hanging in the surgery were two long medical charts showing a male and a female body, the skin missing so you could see all the details – veins and arteries, muscles, heart and intestines. They created the effect of a cold, comfortless and impersonal room. On the wall behind the desk were the two small framed certificates doctors always display to show they're legit. Oh yes, and the carpet on the polished wooden floor in the study was sort of Persian-looking, though at the time I wouldn't have known if it was the real thing, while the surgery floor was covered in blocks of dark-green Feltex.

Dr Kalbfell opened one of the drawers in the study desk and took out a bottle of Scotch and two cutglass whisky glasses. 'A tot?' he asked, and without waiting for a reply he filled a glass almost to halfway and handed it to me.

'I really shouldn't, doctor. I'm cycling down to the Walsh fishing shack with Wendy this afternoon.'

'Doctor's orders!' he said, filling his own glass almost to the top. 'Cheers,' he said, bringing it to his lips rather too quickly and taking a generous swig, then putting it on the desk with a sigh. *This bloke's a drinker – the way he took the first gulp, you can tell every time.* 'The fishing shack. Peter Walsh.' Picking both statements out of the air like that gave neither of them any meaning. Mr Walsh had told me how close the two families had become. I began to wonder.

'Yeah, he's a great bloke,' I said, taking a tiny sip of the Scotch, which wasn't my choice of drink and tasted smoky and harsh.

The doctor took another gulp and plonked his now nearly-empty glass down again. *Pushing it down like that he must be nervous.* 'Look, old man, let's cut right to the chase. The fishing shack – Wendy used to go there with young Harry Walsh. They were *engaged*, you know.'

'Yes, I know.' He was repeating stuff he must have known I knew – in fact, did know I knew.

'Well, dammit man, do you think that's right?'

*Shit, what's going on here!* 'Right? I don't understand, doctor. Mr Walsh gave us the keys. Bluey Walsh is dead. Is this about a suitable time of mourning?'

'You're fucking my daughter in that place!' The word sounded obscene and inappropriate. He drained what was left in his glass and then began to pour a second drink.

With my colouring you blush easily, and I could feel my face burning. '*Sleeping* with Wendy or *where* I'm sleeping with her, doctor? Which is the problem?' His attack had come so quickly and out of the blue that I was grappling for words. Wendy had warned he was going to ask me what my intentions were. He certainly wasn't beating about the bush.

'Well, as a matter of fact, now you mention it, her mother and I don't care for either notion.' He held the bottle poised, pointing at me. 'For godsake, you're not even engaged!'

Here it was at last. 'Oh, is that all! Providing Wendy agrees, we can rectify that,' I said, relieved.

'No, no, that's *not* what I mean.' he said quickly. 'We don't want that to happen.'

'You and your wife, or Wendy?' I replied, suddenly angry.

At the sound of my voice his own became somewhat mollified. 'Dammit, man, you have no prospects whatsoever.'

*So there it is, I'm not good enough.* I wanted to tell him to stop calling me 'man', that I had a perfectly good name, but instead said, 'Wendy's pretty special and I'm pretty ordinary, but I won't always be!' I don't know where that last bit came from – it was just spur-of-the-moment stuff. He was right in this respect – I wasn't exactly God's gift. Then I stupidly added, 'There's good money in cray if you go about it the right way.'

'For godsake, what's the matter with the stupid girl?' he burst out. 'She could have any young man in Tasmania! First she chooses a manic depressive who runs away to be killed, and now a bloody fisherman!'

'Why don't you ask her, doctor?' I said, finding it increasingly difficult to control my temper. *Don't, Jacko, don't let the bastard have both barrels. Stay calm, mate, don't lose it now.*

He'd almost drained the second glass. 'Hmmph! Look here, we've got a bob or two. What do you want? You *are* a fisherman, aren't you? A fishing boat?'

*Gotcha, yer bastard!* I was learning from Jimmy – '*When in doubt bluff it out. Smile, dat da style.*' I attempted to give Wendy's father a cheeky grin. 'Set you back a few quid – forty-footer, Perkins marine diesel engine, radio transceiver, thirty craypots, scallop dredges, fish traps, compass, echo sounder . . . There'll be no change out of 10000 quid, doctor.'

We could probably have done it for less by cutting tea-tree in the bush and making our own craypots and effecting various savings and compromises. In fact, the reconciliation I'd worked up for Jimmy and me starting in the cray business was based on everything second-hand and cutting corners like mad. It had come to a little over 2000 quid, still way out of our reach. The figure I'd given Dr Kalbfell was pie-in-the-sky stuff and was never going to happen in a million years. I was expecting him to say he had a tinnie runabout with a little putt-putt outboard in mind. To my astonishment he walked over to the far side of his desk and, pulling out the top drawer, took out his chequebook.

'Give me a chance to call my bank manager this afternoon,' he said.

Alf hadn't given me much advice in life, but one of the things he'd always said to me was that you never drink when you're making a deal. Wendy's old man's judgement was clouded and he wanted to big-note himself in front of me by appearing to casually write out a cheque for what, in anyone's language, was a large sum of money – write it out in his illegible doctor's hand, rip it dramatically from the chequebook and hand it to me, all without changing expression. What a pathetic twit, but at least the bastard wasn't under-valuing me. I waited until he'd taken the top off his fountain pen before I said, 'Only kidding, doctor.'

'What? What was that?' he asked, not sure he'd heard correctly.

'I don't want your money, sir.'

He paused, momentarily confused, and laughed. 'Of course you do!'

*Pompous prick*. 'Wendy's not for sale.'

'For godsake, man! You've only known my daughter for a little over two months. I'm offering you a fortune to get out of our lives.' He stooped over the chequebook, fountain pen poised. 'McKenzie – MAC or MC?'

'Make it out to Wendy McKenzie, M, small c, big K. It can be her dowry.' I was overreaching by miles. I still hadn't summoned up sufficient courage to ask Wendy to marry me. Her old man was right – I was a pretty lousy prospect. The money I'd accumulated as pay while a prisoner of war was nearly all spent, and while Jimmy and I were talking about going professional cray fishing it was all pie in the sky at that stage. We didn't have the money to outfit ourselves and I didn't even know if he was going to be allowed to stay in Australia, in which case we'd discussed moving to another country. Wendy and I hadn't talked about any of this.

'I see,' he said, capping his fountain pen. 'Well, we'd better go in to lunch.' Just like that, calm as you like.

'Wait on, doctor!' I protested. 'You've insulted me, you haven't even had the courtesy to call me by my name, you've denigrated my social status, you've tried to get rid of me by offering me a bribe and you've disparaged your own daughter! Now we're all going to sit down calmly to lunch, is that how the better classes behave?'

He shrugged. 'Now you know how we feel,' he said calmly.

'*We*? You and your wife?'

'Yes.'

'And Wendy?'

'Wendy? What does Wendy know about life? Wendy's just a silly young girl who doesn't know what she wants. She feels guilty about Harry Walsh going off to war and getting himself killed, and you're the war hero intended to alleviate her guilt.'

'Bluey Walsh didn't *get* himself killed. He died a horrific death at the hands of an American pilot who dropped napalm on us. Do you know what napalm is? Let me tell you, doctor. It's liquid petroleum that covers you in a sheet of flame that penetrates the skin in seconds right down to the bone, and then starts to burn from the inside out. It's almost impossible to stop. Bluey was lucky to die quickly – but he nevertheless died in agony!' I was unaware that I was shouting.

I felt as though I had been hit in the stomach with a pick handle. There was nothing more I could say. What if Dr Kalbfell's version of events was true? My face burned from humiliation just thinking about it. *Jacko the prop holding his daughter together while she overcame the guilt she felt over Bluey Walsh's death. Two and a half months isn't a long time to know the ins and outs of anyone. Wendy was engaged to Bluey Walsh for two years. This bloke's a doctor, he ought to know these things.* I was very close to tears – part humiliation, part anger and more than a good measure of despair. *Think, Jacko. Stay calm. Don't lose your block again – this bloke's trying to make you say something you'll regret.* I swallowed hard, trying to calm my racing heart.

'Wendy was engaged to Bluey Walsh for two years – that's a long time. Why didn't they get married?'

'The boy was a manic depressive – not his fault, I suppose.' Wendy's father was now on his third Scotch and each of them had been doubles.

'A manic depressive.' It was a comment rather than a question.

'No point in explaining – you wouldn't understand,' he said dismissively.

'Mood swings – big highs and terrible lows, the lows sometimes lasting for long periods.' I thought of Rick Stackman sitting on the crane, refusing to go to Korea.

He looked surprised, and then suspicious. 'Oh? You've encountered it? What – in your own family, is it?'

'In the army. It's not uncommon.' If there had been anyone in our family with such a mental condition there would be no chance they would have been diagnosed – just another misfit to adjust to. In all probability there'd been dozens of manic depressives on the Kelly side and a fair few on the McKenzie. On the other hand, I'd read somewhere that artists and poets were prone to the condition, and that definitely wouldn't include our lot.

'Precisely. It was the reason Harry Walsh ran away to fight in Korea. He was in a deeply depressed state after having a row with Wendy.'

*Hence her guilt*. 'I take it you didn't approve of Bluey Walsh?'

'The boy was mentally ill! It's not a condition you recover from.'

'Out of the frying pan and into the fire, eh? Is that what you're thinking, doctor?'

'I think I've made my thoughts perfectly clear.'

'Were you his doctor?'

'Passed him on, not my area – needed a psychiatrist.'

'But you were kept informed?'

'I put him in the hands of a good man, yes.'

'And he let him go to Korea?'

'Of course not. Harry left without informing anyone.'

'I see. But when you knew, or the psychiatrist did, didn't anyone call the army to explain his condition?'

'He wasn't my concern.'

'But nonetheless, it was very convenient?'

'I don't know what you're talking about. I'd referred him on as a patient.' He glanced as his watch. 'And now, I dare say, it's time for lunch.'

I didn't press the matter. I think he was beginning to realise that I wasn't going to be bullied or panicked. I'd gained the upper hand simply by remaining calm. Well, except for the napalm bit anyway. Maybe before I'd gone to Korea he would have intimidated me, but not now. I'd done a whole heap of growing up in the meantime, and I reckon I'd paid my dues and had the right to be my own man. If I appeared to have no prospects it wasn't because I wasn't prepared to work.

Then, apropos of nothing, the thought occurred to me: *I bet the bastard approves of the White Australia Policy*. 'As a matter of interest, doctor, do you agree with the White Australia Policy?'

'Ha! Wendy told me about the blackfella you brought home with you. Jimmy somebody, isn't it?' He smiled suddenly. 'Jimmy crack corn and I don't care!' The Scotch was beginning to get to him.

There was a tap on the door and Wendy's voice called out, 'Lunch, you two!'

'Well we don't want to disappoint the ladies, do we?' he said, his slightly slurring vernacular crisping up the way a hardened drinker can steady himself by concentrating. The bugger still hadn't referred to me by name. The presumption was breathtaking – he seemed quite oblivious to the effect his words would have on me. It was as if he thought that people of my class didn't have the same feelings as those of his own. 'Brutish' was the word that came to my mind. Perhaps he thought we islanders lived in caves on the cliff face.

This silly notion served to help me overcome my emotions and see him for what he was – a man relying on his social status as the sagacious doctor to add effect to his words. It was the insensitivity of the physician telling his patient he is going to die under the mistaken belief that being blunt and to the point is the best way in the end. Or worse, accustomed all his life to doting parents, the approbation of teachers and the sycophancy of patients, he'd assumed his superiority and never learned how to conduct himself in a basic man-to-man relationship.

He 'possessed' (I imagined that was the word he'd use in his own mind) a beautiful daughter – a Miss Tasmania, no less – who had brought credit to his family and was expected to make a good marriage, have nice kids and live a blameless life. It wasn't an unreasonable ambition for an only daughter blessed with looks and intelligence. Instead, she'd taken up with a sometime fisherman, someone smelling of slimy mackerel with fish scales up to his armpits. For her mother this would be the ultimate social humiliation – her daughter married to a descendant of convicts on both sides. Heaven forbid! Can you imagine the whispering at the bridge club! Then there were the children to consider – in all likelihood ginger-haired, their pale-pink skin covered in multiple freckles the colour of rust, the result of the inferior convict blood coursing through their veins. My medal would have counted for little – acts of bravery were usually committed by foolhardy men who got lucky on the day. Not the kind of men to make lasting partnerships built on solid foundations.

Anyway, Wendy's mum would certainly have had a hand in all this. First the nagging, then her planned circumvention, allowing her husband to see me as the emotional exception, maybe even suggesting the bribe to send me packing. Emotional exceptions didn't need to have altruistic motives. She'd have persuaded him it would be a test of my character, worth every penny they'd invested in the rescue of their precious daughter. She'd have convinced him I was bound to fail and Wendy would be saved from a fate worse than death.

Wendy would, of course, be unaware of the circumstances of my departure. With my future as a fisherman secure, I certainly could be relied on not to spill the beans. She might be sad in the beginning, but in the end she'd recover and together they'd reset the course of her future life and it would be plain sailing from there on. They'd even have clear consciences – after all, anyone who'd take a bribe to get lost was not the right man for a precious daughter.

I now found myself in a dilemma. If I stormed out of the house and down the street a distraught Wendy would have to come after me, or worse – be forced to choose between us, me or her parents. There would be a scene and I'd be forced to give her some sort of ultimatum, an either/or, come or stay, which I knew would be foolish on my part.

Then a wonderful possibility occurred to me. Wendy had obviously told them how she felt about me. It must have been that she wanted me for keeps, otherwise why the premature panic from her parents? If this was the case, then I couldn't believe my good fortune.

Perhaps my febrile imagination and sense of inferiority were inventing some of this, or most of it – I could turn shadows into monsters better than most. But if all this was mere conjecture, there was no mistaking the proposition Dr Kalbfell had put to me. Besides, my instincts, which had always served me well, told me I wasn't too far off the mark. If he thought he could bully me, then compared to Lieutenant

Dinh, the interrogator at the POW camp, Dr Kalbfell's devious mind was chocolate fudge wrapped in cellophane.

To walk out of the house in high dudgeon, I decided, would amount to a retreat where recovery would be difficult, essentially becoming a rearguard action. *Swallow your pride. Stay put, mate. Be patient – you can win this battle.* 'Well, I guess lunch was why I came in the first place, doctor,' I answered, even managing to smile.

He swallowed the last finger of Scotch and placed the glass down. Then he actually winked at me. 'Less said the better, eh? Think about it. My offer still stands.' He nodded in the direction of the surgery door. 'You can call me at my surgery any morning except Friday and Sunday, after ten.' He walked towards the door leading to the hallway. 'Oh yes, you've got until Monday. We're leaving for a holiday, a cruise to New Zealand, on Tuesday, and Mrs Kalbfell and I expect Wendy will accompany us. I'd like this matter cleared up before then.'

*Christ! I'll say one thing for him, this bloke can hold his grog.* It had all been worked out in the good doctor's mind, even allowing for the fact that I might initially refuse his offer, then I'd get back to him, mumbling my acceptance in an attempt to conceal my latent greed. By making the deadline just five days away he'd obviously decided to put pressure on me, give me a bit of a nudge to hasten my betrayal of his daughter. Wendy would then be spirited away for a nice little holiday on the P&O boat sailing to New Zealand. Like a game of Happy Families, the ingredients were all there – loving and concerned parents, distraught but dutiful daughter, confrontation leading to a resolution, the storm clouds swept away with nothing but clear horizons ahead. Going in to lunch and pretending that nothing had happened was going to be harder to endure than the Chinese torture in the POW camp.

To my surprise, lunch was a formal setting in the dining room complete with lace tablecloth, Georg Jensen cutlery and bone china. My memory is pretty good, but I can't for the life of me remember what we ate – a big formal meal, certainly, but obviously my mind was elsewhere. I remember Wendy's mum was checking out my table manners. I was grateful for Gloria's early tuition by way of the *Women's Weekly*.

Wendy was her usual bright self and Mrs Kalbfell formally polite, with her old man contributing very little – an occasional grunt or 'pass the salt', so that Wendy glanced at me several times, one eyebrow slightly raised.

'Tell us about your latest visit to Government House, Jacko. When you had morning tea with Lady Cross,' she asked mischievously.

Once again she'd saved my life. This was something I could stretch out and tell in a light-hearted way that would get my part of the conversation over with, and at the same time reduce the tension I felt. Moreover, it balanced things up a bit. If I was good enough to be invited to have tea with the governor's wife . . .

With Wendy promoting me and urging me on, the good doctor grunting and Mrs Kalbfell asking pouty-mouthed questions, unable to restrain her curiosity, we managed to get through lunch passably well.

Directly after lunch Wendy grabbed a small canvas bag with her things. We got the bikes out of the garage and hit the road. It was mid-afternoon when we arrived at the shack.

Because of the busy weekday traffic forcing us to ride single file, we hadn't been able to talk on the way. Now Wendy wanted to know exactly what had happened in her father's study. I was determined not to exaggerate or get overexcited, but to give it to her blow by blow as it had transpired. That way I wouldn't be putting my own agenda forward. I remember we were sitting on an old leather couch, Wendy leaning against me with my arm around her shoulders so I couldn't really see her face. In a strange way this was good. Through the shack window I could see a wide stretch of the river with a small brush fire on the far shore sending up a steady twist of smoke into the pewter-coloured mid-afternoon sky. I could concentrate on the smoke and on what I was saying without having to react to her expressions. When I got to the bribe she gasped, and grabbed my hand. 'Oh, Jacko!' was all she said, but for poor Wendy it was downhill all the way from there. When I got to Bluey Walsh and the napalm she could contain her emotions no longer, and began to howl. I pulled her towards me and held her while she had a good cry. 'I'm sorry, Wendy, perhaps I should have left that part out.'

'No, Jacko – you mustn't,' she sobbed. 'I must know . . . everything.'

She was a bit of a mess by the time I'd related the entire conversation with her father, and I simply held her in my arms and rocked her. We had a fair bit to sort out between us and there was still a good part of the afternoon left, as it was only just past mid-summer and the sun didn't set until much later. 'C'mon, let's take the dinghy and see if we can catch supper. You make a thermos of tea and I'll go dig for river worms.' I knew she'd want a little time on her own to regain her composure. Wendy wasn't one to cry at the drop of a hat, and she was feeling pretty miserable.

We fished for a while and although I didn't even get so much as a nibble she caught a couple of small salmon just the right size for our dinner. 'What about *us*, Jacko?' Wendy asked at last.

'That's the question I haven't been game to ask, Wend,' I said, trying to smile.

'Do you love me?'

'Wendy, you know I do, more than I can say. I can't bear the idea of you not being with me. It's just . . .'

'Just *what*?'

'Well, your dad's right. I have nothing to offer you – I don't even have a job yet!'

'I can feel the little house with the white picket fence and two nice kids coming on,' she said, grinning. 'Jacko, can't you see – it's *you* I want. Romantically silly as that sounds, we'll work out the rest.'

I looked at this most beautiful creature sitting alongside me in the dinghy. Even though her eyes were still a bit puffed-up from crying, she was exquisite. She had a river worm in one hand and a hook in the other and her wonderful green eyes looked at me in a way that, had I been standing, would have made me weak at the knees. Thirty-odd years later she still has the same effect on me. 'Wendy, will you marry me?'

'I thought you'd never ask, Jack McKenzie,' she said, suddenly laughing. 'Yes, yes, *yes*!'

*She said yes.* Overjoyed, I dropped what was in my hands and threw my arms around her and held her tight. Not wanting the moment to end, eventually the question had to be asked. 'What about your parents?'

Wendy gave a sigh of despair then a tiny shrug. 'Daddy's an alcoholic and Mummy's a dreadful snob – both conditions are very difficult to cure. I wish she'd leave him, but she won't. You see, she came from a very poor family and being a doctor's wife is important.'

'You mean my kind of family?'

'She should have been so lucky. Both her parents were alcoholics, and her father interfered with her.'

'She told you all this?' I was surprised. People like us didn't talk about things like that, particularly if we'd managed to escape as Wendy's mum obviously had.

'No, of course not. I found out from her sister who lives in Burnie. I was on a publicity tour there as Miss Tasmania. She came to see me at my hotel.'

'And she told you about your mum?'

'No, not at first. She'd simply come to congratulate me – something good happening in the family, she said. I remember we were together for an hour or so and Agnes smoked twelve cigarettes. I counted them in the ashtray after she'd left.'

'What was she like?'

'Quite nice – very nervous.'

'Did you recognise her? She look like your family?'

'Certainly. She was younger than Mum, but looked older – very thin and worn out. I still write to her, and I've seen her several times. Her husband Cec is an alcoholic, and both her kids have been in trouble with the police.'

'What's he do?'

She laughed. 'He's a fisherman.'

'His surname isn't Kelly, is it?'

'No, Drummond. So you see, the swanky Kalbfells are not entirely what they seem.'

'What I *can* see very clearly is why your mum is panicking over having someone like me in the family.' Wendy didn't reply, deep in thought. She had completed baiting her hook. 'C'mon that's enough,' I laughed. 'Let's go back to the hut and make passionate love, after that I'll cook your hard-earned fish for supper, sir . . . er, madam!'

'No, Jacko. I want to tell you about Harry.' She put down her rod and reached for the thermos.

'Wendy, you don't have to. I don't believe what your father said was true about me being the backlash because of Harry.'

Wendy gave me a grateful look, and handed me the mug of still-steaming tea. 'It was Harry's idea to join K Force. It wasn't the other way around – us having a row, me ditching him and him going off to fight in Korea. I just wanted you to know it was over between Harry and me before he left.'

'You mean he didn't just run away without telling anyone?'

She shook her head. 'That's just Daddy's version.'

'Thank you for telling me, darling.' I was having trouble with the word 'darling' – not that I didn't like it. I did, a lot – it was just that, well . . . it sounded pluralistic, like I wasn't alone any longer.

At last a bite, and moments later I landed a cod much too small for the pan. 'C'mon, stupid, let's go before I'm tempted to throw you back as well,' Wendy said, grabbing the oars and laughing. I unhooked the little fish and placed it carefully back into the river, where it floated motionless for a moment, then, with a flick of its tail, disappeared in a flash of silver.

# CHAPTER SIXTEEN

## *Look Where the Sun Don't Shine*

# Australia Will Continue to Keep Door Shut

## COLOURED PEOPLES NOT WANTED

**(From Our Correspondent)**

**CANBERRA, MAR 26**

**IMMIGRATION Minister Harold Holt is convinced that Asian people understand Australia's restrictive immigration policy.**

He said in Melbourne yesterday that Government would continue to 'Keep the door shut' to coloured peoples.

Mr Holt was answering Lord Hardwicke, who said the Sydney Government could stop the drift from farms to the cities by permitting the controlled entry of coloured farm and domestic workers.

He added that the 'White Australia Policy' was an affront to all coloured nations.

**SUPPORTED BY ALL**

'Australia's policy of restricted immigration,' said Mr Holt, is supported by all political parties and classes of the country.

> The policy laid down was in the interests of Australia and no government found any reason to alter it. 'Realistic people understand its importance to Australia's economic and social needs.' Mr Holt added that Australia's birthrate was climbing steadily. Half a million were born in the last three years. A record number of British migrants were arriving and immigration from non-British countries was at a high level.
>
> Lord Hardwicke, who is visiting Australia in connection with a commercial flotation, emphasised that he was expressing his own views, which did not represent the attitude of the British Government.
>
> MELBOURNE *DAILY NEWS*, 26 MARCH 1954

You can imagine how distressed we all felt. Here was Harold Holt spelling things out loud and clear, and his meaning was unmistakable – his government, and the Labor opposition for that matter, wasn't going to budge an inch. If a bigwig like Lord Hardwicke could be rebuked in such a blatant manner, then what hope had we? We still hadn't heard anything from Zara Holt after her initial telephone call to Lady Cross. The fact that Jimmy's visitor's visa had been renewed had raised our hopes tremendously, but now they were dashed again.

And then, out of the blue, a telegram arrived for Jimmy – and for once Busta Gut was prompt with the delivery.

SUGGEST WE MEET APRIL 5 AT ARMY PERSONNEL DEPOT LAUNCESTON RE YOUR REQUEST DEPT IMMIGRATION STOP SPONSORS MAY ATTEND STOP PLEASE CONFIRM TEL. MELBOURNE MXY 440 OR BY TELEGRAM STOP COL MARK STONE STOP ARMY HEADQUARTERS VICTORIA BARRACKS MELBOURNE

Jimmy made a trunk call to Army Headquarters and a time for eleven forty-five a.m. was agreed. We – that is, Nicole Lenoir-Jourdan, myself and of course Jimmy – caught the Douglas DC3 to Launceston and arrived with an hour to spare. We took the bus into town and picked up Wendy, whom Mr Walsh had permitted to come along. 'The presence of a pretty woman can't do any harm,' he remarked.

When I suggested to Nicole Lenoir-Jourdan that Wendy wanted to come she thought it a good idea. 'Older women like me can be seen as viragos in a situation such as this one; Wendy will ameliorate my presence.' Of course, she was incapable of simply saying, 'Yeah, that would be good', so there was Wendy ameliorating her presence.

Wendy and I had become engaged, not secretly but in a very low-key fashion – no ring or anything, that would have to wait. We made the news public when we returned from the fishing shack, just before her parents were due to go on on their cruise to New Zealand. It was news they definitely didn't want to hear, and they postponed their trip. Wendy wasn't the kind of person who went around defying her parents, so they knew she meant business. Dr Kalbfell threatened to throw her out and Wendy's mum stayed in her bedroom for days refusing to come out. It was an awkward time, with Gloria and our family over the moon and hers sulking and recalcitrant.

In the end Wendy had packed her suitcase and gone to stay with the Walsh family, which made her mum and dad change their attitude in a hurry. Wendy, it turned out, had always been the peacemaker in the family, negotiating the way through her father's drinking and her mother's moods, which Wendy described as becoming much worse as she got older so you never knew what state she'd be in when you got home. 'Sometimes she'll just burst into tears and weep hysterically, and at other times she'll stay in a huff for days,' she explained. Dr Kalbfell put her on sedatives but she complained that they made her woozy. She told Wendy that she believed he was prescribing sedatives so she wouldn't go on about his drinking.

The Walsh family loved having Wendy staying with them, although I know she felt guilty about being away from home. When her parents ate humble pie and visited her at the chemist shop to ask her to return, she made a deal with them: she'd come home if they'd stay away from the subject of her engagement. It was a compromise but not a solution, and it can't have been pleasant. Even avoiding the issue resulted in a lot of tension. Years later she would tell me how her father would get drunk and come to her locked bedroom door late at night, all worked up, and bang his fists against the door and shout, 'I demand you get rid of that cretinous little albino bastard!'

When she told me she made it sound funny. I said, 'Well, I've been an albino when I was also an Aborigine – but I'm definitely not a bastard, and have a birth certificate to prove it.'

Typically, she hadn't told me any of this at the time it was happening – how her father would eventually stop raving and grow morbid and start to weep, sitting with his back against her door sniffing and mumbling drunkenly, drinking straight from a bottle of Johnnie Walker until he passed out. At one o'clock in the morning she'd open the door and, taking him by the legs, pull him along the hallway to her parents' bedroom, where she would roll him onto the bedside carpet, place a pillow under his head and throw a quilt over him. Meanwhile her mum was oblivious to all this, zonked out on the sleeping pills he'd prescribed for her.

Of course, getting married in a hurry was out of the question. We were as poor as church mice, and until I had a steady income I had no way of supporting us. Wendy was perfectly willing to continue working, but there were very few, if any, suitable jobs for women on the island, so we wouldn't even have the prospect of her salary. Life was complicated further by the plans Jimmy and I had made, now placed on the backburner while we waited to see what would happen to him.

We were both working as casual deckhands on the boats, making ourselves available if regular crew were sick or, as was more often the case, drunk. But Jimmy had to watch out for the Fisheries inspectors because he wasn't supposed to work with a visitor's visa. Temporary labour paid poorly, and certainly what I earned as a deckhand wasn't sufficient to support a wife.

At best I was getting back into fishing after all these years, getting the rust out of my system, while Jimmy was learning the cray-fishing game from scratch. If he wasn't going to be allowed to stay in Australia we would have to give up our immediate plans and go elsewhere. I'd spoken about New Guinea, where the colour of a man's skin wasn't a problem and the two of us could start something together. The prospect of our parting company was unthinkable. So this was yet another complication, one with which Wendy and I hadn't really come to terms. Until we knew for sure what was going to happen to Jimmy we were in limbo, and naturally she was anxious to be a part of whatever was going to happen to the two of us.

Colonel Stone looked to be in his mid-forties, his dark hair starting to go grey at the sides. He was a fit-looking bloke and greeted us cordially in what passed as a reception area at the depot. He'd ordered tea and a coffee for Jimmy and when I pointed to his Korea ribbon and asked him where he'd been, he immediately apologised. 'Mr McKenzie, the closest I got to the big stoush was landing on Korean soil on two separate occasions to sort out a problem between the high command in Japan and one of the field commanders. I was posted to military headquarters in Japan as a staff officer and my frequent requests for a job in the field were ignored. That's the problem with the permanent forces – you join up to be a fighting man and you end up pushing a pen.'

But I could see he'd done his bit. In addition to a string of World War II campaign ribbons he had been awarded the Military Cross. 'By the way, this is not the first time I've come across you, sir,' he said to me, with a hint of a smile.

'Me?' I asked, surprised.

He nodded. 'It was when you and a few mates "escaped to the front" and joined the Americans at the beginning of the war, afraid it would all be over before you could fire a shot.'

I groaned, making a face, then asked, 'But how were you involved, sir?'

'Well, the assistant provost marshal in Japan wanted to make an example of you lot. You will recall he sent a contingent of military police to fetch you and your mates and bring you back to Japan.'

I nodded. 'We were . . .' I was going to say 'shitting our pants', but caught myself in time, '. . . bloody terrified we were going to be court-martialled.'

'That was precisely what the assistant provost marshal had in mind. He had already prepared the charge sheets and wasn't too pleased when Colonel Green, your battalion commander, took the matter into his own hands.'

'What a great bloke Green was. *And* a great soldier. Why do the good blokes always have to die?'

I'd told Wendy and Jimmy the story of our escape to the front, and Nicole Lenoir-Jourdan had followed it in the newspaper. In fact, I was to learn that she had been the major source of most of Gloria's clippings for her war journal, ordering the clippings of the war coverage from the *Gazette*'s cutting service on the mainland and handing them to Mum. But I'd only told Jimmy the story of the death of Colonel Green, so I briefly explained it to the others. 'We were in reserve with battalion headquarters deployed in a spot safe from artillery fire in the lea of a ridge line when a freak shell bounced off the hilltop and spun into a tree. A piece of shrapnel from the exploding shell ripped through the tent where Colonel Green was taking an afternoon nap, slicing through his abdomen.' Everyone, including Colonel Stone, winced at the thought of a sharp slice of red-hot metal going straight through your body.

'Yes, well the assistant provost marshal wasn't all that pleased with Colonel Green's decision and complained to the commander-in-chief of Commonwealth forces. I was told to investigate and sort it out. In the end I persuaded the assistant provost marshal that because enthusiasm to fight rather than the reverse was the motivation for the offence, no lasting harm had been done to army discipline, so Charlie Green had done the right thing to deal with it himself.'

Jimmy looked at me. 'Yoh done save his ass, colonel!' he chuckled.

'I owe you big-time, colonel.' I couldn't imagine how different my life would have turned out if we'd been taken to Japan and court-martialled.

'My pleasure, sir,' Colonel Stone replied, grinning. What a crazy thing the army was. Here he was calling me 'sir' when just three weeks previously I would have been standing in front of him to rigid attention, staring at a spot I'd located on the wall behind him and barking out the answers to his questions in monosyllabic bursts. The reminder of the incident in Korea, which seemed to have happened half a lifetime ago, served to relax us all, and it wasn't hard to see why Colonel Stone had been chosen for this particular job in the army. He placed his cup down on the little table beside his chair and reached for a bulging file bound with red tape, and proceeded to open it.

'Private Oldcorn, I should begin by saying that I am not from the Immigration Department, and so have no power to decide on your case other than to try to influence those who do. It is also highly unusual for me to be dealing with the records of a soldier from another nation. However, I received a copy of some of the papers in the submission your sponsors sent in on your behalf, particularly the submission by Mr McKenzie, outlining the role you played while you were prisoners of war together in North Korea. I must say it made for interesting reading. May I congratulate you both – the time you spent in captivity can't have been easy, in particular as you were each carrying a severe wound.'

'There were worse off than us,' I answered.

Colonel Stone looked up at me and smiled. 'Be that as it may, we have checked the details in both submissions and, if anything, both accounts appear to be somewhat understated, which is unusual in a submission like this where sinners are routinely turned into saints.'

'How yoh check dem records, colonel?' Jimmy asked, surprised. 'Wid da US Army?'

'Yes, exactly. We have many affidavits and letters from fellow US prisoners of war that testify to the role both of you played in the various North Korean and Chinese field hospitals and the POW camp where you were held until the armistice.'

'I hope they asked the black blokes,' I interjected.

'No, as a matter of fact they all seem to be Caucasians.' Colonel Stone picked up a sheet of paper. 'This one is from tail gunner Chuck

Ward of New York State.' He began to read. '"Rear Gunner Chuck Ward's B27 was shot down over North Korea. He bailed out and landed in snow-covered mountainous terrain behind enemy lines where he avoided the enemy for two days before finally being captured. He was made to walk a further two days to a field hospital, where his frostbite was so severe the Chinese physician was forced to amputate both feet." He speaks here of the care he received from Private Richard Oldcorn, commonly known as 'Jimmy', of the US 24th Infantry Regiment, US 25th Infantry Division, and Private Jack McKenzie of an unspecified Australian infantry regiment.

> *"I can positively testify that I owe my life to those two men, Jimmy Oldcorn and his buddy from the Australian Army. They were not orderlies on hospital duty and were both recovering from wounds, but they volunteered to dress my feet and bring me water and they fed me by hand such food as was available. They washed me and demanded a second set of bandages from the Chinese and they washed these daily and dried them in the hut, cleaning and changing my dressings morning and evening. They carried me to the latrine and kept me as clean as possible. I do not doubt for one moment that these good men saved my life. Two brave soldiers who took care of a comrade when they were recovering from injuries themselves." Signed, Chuck Ward.'*

The colonel picked up the next sheet of paper. 'Here's another. It's from a Private Ward Brady Buckworth Junior from Georgia,' he said.

*Oh no! The southerner Jimmy nearly killed in the hospital cave. We're gone for all money.* I held my breath as he started to read.

> *'"I owe Jimmy Oldcorn more than my life. In the North Korean hospital cave he taught us to behave like men when we'd been reduced to being animals. He taught us to share when we'd decided it was every man for himself. He made us care for each other when*

*previously we wouldn't have lifted a hand to help the man beside us. I have no hesitation in saying that without his leadership, together with his little redheaded Australian buddy with the harmonica, many a now happily married family man in America would never have come home. Since returning to America I have found Jesus Christ and I am now a born-again Christian and a Pentecostal Evangelist. If this message ever reaches Jimmy Oldcorn please thank him and tell him he made me take a good look at myself, and what I saw I didn't much like. I am certain that the deserved hiding he gave me in that cave was the first step in my salvation. I praise the Lord each day for Jimmy Oldcorn. With men like him, America will always be safe. God bless America!" Signed, Ward Brady Buckworth Junior.'*

I looked at Jimmy, incredulous. 'Praise da Lord,' he said, grinning.

As Gloria would say, 'Miracles will never cease!' Of all the people unlikely to give Jimmy a rap, I would have placed Ward Brady Buckworth Junior about equal with the Kraus twins at the very start of the queue.

'There are dozens more like this, and I must say that together they make an outstanding testimonial,' Colonel Stone said. 'If it were up to me I'd be proud to welcome you to our country, Private Oldcorn.' He paused, and looked at us. 'But it isn't. All I can do is petition on your behalf with whatever influence the Australian Army may be able to bring to bear. Which, from past experience, I am forced to tell you, isn't very much.'

He then went on to explain that he'd been with the Australian occupation forces in Japan in 1946 and for the duration of the Korean War. In that time a number of Australian soldiers had taken Japanese brides. 'It has taken until last year for them to be given permission to bring their wives and, in many cases, children home to Australia,' he informed us. I immediately thought of Catflap Buggins and his little Lotus Blossom, and wondered if she was one of these war brides. 'I was involved in making representations for many of these long-separated families,' Stone said. 'Even now, the Japanese wives can't get permanent residency – they are all on five-year Certificates of Exemption.'

'Exemption from *what*, Colonel Stone?' Nicole Lenoir-Jourdan asked.

'I feel ashamed even saying it, Miss Lenoir-Jourdan. Exemption from the dictation test. The idea is that these women are not actually allowed to become Australian citizens. While they can renew their certificate every five years and – providing they don't commit a crime or get divorced – can stay in Australia for the rest of their lives, they will always remain citizens of their native country.' He leaned back as we took it all in. 'So you see, you're not the only one in the army to run slap-bang up against the so-called White Australia Policy.'

'You mean the policy that doesn't exist?' Nicole Lenoir-Jourdan stated, with more than a touch of irony.

'Correct. Discrimination on the grounds of colour or race is not mentioned in immigration law, and the term "White Australia Policy" does not exist as far as Canberra is concerned. Officially, rejection of someone seeking to immigrate is not based on colour or race, it is based entirely on failure to pass the dictation test. Unofficially, immigration officers are under strict verbal orders to give the test to anyone whom they consider is not white.'

I turned to Jimmy. 'That's why Cuffe asked you about your ancestry.' Turning now to Colonel Stone, I added, 'Jimmy's an orphan and couldn't answer the question.'

Instead of smiling, as I suppose I'd anticipated, the colonel said, 'That might yet prove to be a stroke of luck.'

'What, Jimmy being an orphan?'

'Not knowing his background, yes.'

'The whole thing is so duplicitous,' exclaimed Nicole Lenoir-Jourdan, indignation getting the better of her.

'Maintaining the policy requires a high degree of duplicity,' said Colonel Stone with surprising frankness. 'For instance, in a recent newspaper article, Mr Holt, the immigration minister, makes the usual two points the government habitually uses to defend its position. Firstly, that he is convinced Asian people *understand* our restricted immigration policy – what makes him so convinced he doesn't explain. Secondly, that the policy is supported by both political parties and by all the classes. It's true that both political parties agree to the so-called dictation test, but suggesting that the entire Australian population goes along with it as well is pure conjecture. We have never had a referendum to establish how the nation feels.'

I'm sure we all thought Colonel Stone must have been referring to the column that had appeared in the Melbourne *Daily News* that had so depressed us.

Then Wendy asked the question at the back of everyone's mind, prefacing it with a smile that possessed enough kilowatts to light up the Melbourne Cricket Ground. 'Colonel Stone, you said before that it was unusual for you to be asked to act for Jimmy – I mean, a soldier from a different nation. How did that come about?' It was ingenuously put without any apparent hidden agenda, as perhaps may not have been the case if Nicole Lenoir-Jourdan or myself had pursued this in an attempt to see if Zara Holt or her husband was involved.

Colonel Stone paused to think, scratching his forehead with the tip of his index finger. 'That's a question I had to ask myself, and I can only conclude that someone, somewhere, wants something to happen. Either that, or as is much more likely, they want to avoid being embarrassed. You have to understand, at a diplomatic level the government is very defensive on this issue. For instance, you may be wondering how we were able to get all the affidavits and letters on Private Oldcorn so very quickly.'

'Yes, that had occurred to me,' I said. 'Our army doesn't usually move that fast, and I'm sure that's also true of the Americans.'

'Well, it seems the Americans had the material already documented. Many former US prisoners of the Korean War had mentioned the two of you in their debriefing, and others had written to the Pentagon. As you probably know, the Americans didn't always come out of the Chinese

POW camps covered in glory. Someone at the Pentagon must have seen this story as an opportunity for a bit of positive public relations and decided to collate the information. They then discovered more details – in particular how Mr Oldcorn personally risked torture and possibly death by gaining the confidence of the Chinese communists and exposing their web of informers, thereby throwing into chaos their efforts at indoctrination. With a congressional enquiry about to start on why so many Americans defected to the communists while prisoners of war, this is just the sort of good publicity they were looking for.'

'And then they discovered Jimmy was a Negro!' I interrupted, 'So they put the kybosh on the whole thing.'

Colonel Stone laughed. 'No, that's quite wrong, sir. Ten days ago the American government announced Private Oldcorn is to get a military decoration from the president.' He paused, and grinned. 'That is, when the Australian Government can locate him. The American press has also been looking for him and is becoming very agitated, and Canberra is being bombarded with requests for information on Private Oldcorn's whereabouts. Finally, the US Army is very anxious to parade him for the purposes of publicity and I guess that's how the Australian Army got involved.'

We were gobsmacked. I eventually said, 'But finding him wouldn't be too difficult.'

'Not to us, but a small island off the coast of Australia might as well be on the moon as far as an American newspaper reporter is concerned. They may have heard of Australia but they certainly haven't heard of Tasmania, let alone a dot in the ocean like Queen Island. Private Oldcorn had a Qantas ticket from Japan to Melbourne, but after that he effectively vanished – there are no records of his movements.'

'And that's why Jimmy's visitor's visa was extended so effortlessly,' Nicole Lenoir-Jourdan remarked quietly. 'They didn't want him to suddenly reappear.'

'Yes, I think you all get the general idea,' Colonel Stone said.

Jimmy had remained uncharacteristically quiet throughout this.

'A bit of a turn-up for the books, eh, Jimmy? Now you're a bloody war hero, mate,' I said laughing, with the others joining in.

'Dat funny, Brother Fish. First we got dat chump Ward Brady Buckworth Junior, he gone fine Jesus an' now he for-give me. Now da whole America, dey want to do da same. I ain't no nigger no more – I's a war hero. How come a hero he don't have no skin colour, eh?'

'I'm afraid that's not true in Australia, Private Oldcorn. Your skin colour remains the problem while your potential "hero status" in America is a potential embarrassment for our government.'

'They're gunna give you a ticker-tape parade down Broadway,' I laughed.

'Well, that really put the cat among the pigeons, as you can imagine,' the colonel said. 'So the Australian Government instructed the Department of Defence to follow up on the story and I was given the task of writing to the Americans requesting details of Private Oldcorn's involvement with you.' He paused, smiling. 'Now I'm probably drawing a long bow here, but in 1942 the first shipload of American servicemen arrived to be based in Australia and the customs officials wouldn't allow the Negro soldiers to disembark. This caused both panic and extreme embarrassment because the Australian Government had previously requested that no Negroes be sent. The Americans had officially refused, but in diplomatic circles, as they say, a wink is as good as a nod, and we assumed the matter was settled. So the Australian Government was caught with its pants down when the black soldiers arrived. What I'm trying to say is, could Mr Oldcorn's application for residency possibly have the makings of another such incident?' Then he added quickly, 'This is pure speculation on my part, you understand.'

'I don't think so, colonel,' Jimmy said softly.

Nicole Lenoir-Jourdan smiled. 'There's an old Chinese saying, "When you're defending the indefensible you are a dog barking at shadows."'

'Well, whoever would have thought of that!' I said, leaning back in my chair. 'Jimmy, you could become a "diplomatic incident", mate.'

Colonel Stone laughed. 'If I'm correct, I suspect I've been given this job to avoid anything like that happening.'

'You mean you have to find a way out?' Wendy asked, hopefully.

'*Suggest*. In the final analysis, it's not up to me.'

'I'm led to believe the candidature for the dictation test is made on appearance, and there are no exceptions. Is this not the case, Colonel Stone?' Nicole Lenoir-Jourdan asked.

'Essentially, you're right. But appearances can be deceptive, or at least appear to be, on paper.' He could see we were puzzled. 'This is the decidedly awkward part, Private Oldcorn. I have been authorised to give you a physical examination.'

'What for? Yoh want to see I's med-ic-ally fit? My leg, it healed good.'

'Jimmy's fit as a mallee bull. We dive just about every morning,' I volunteered.

'Hence the healthy tan. Out in the sunshine a lot, eh?'

It was the way he said it, like he was trying to tell us something.

'Where you gonna do dis exam-in-nation, colonel?' Jimmy asked.

'I thought the Gents, Mr Oldcorn. As I'm not a doctor, I'd like Mr McKenzie to come with me as a witness. It won't take long, and I don't mean to embarrass you, but if this wasn't important I wouldn't ask.'

'You say you're not a doctor, colonel – so why would you conduct a physical examination of James?' Nicole Lenoir-Jourdan asked. She then added, 'Is it in your brief?'

'No, it isn't. That kind of thing never appears on paper. I received a confidential call from Canberra two nights ago.'

We were all mystified. What kind of physical examination could the colonel make without him being a physician – or at the very least, a qualified medical orderly? Colonel Stone turned to Jimmy. 'Of course you may refuse, and I wouldn't blame you.' But then he added in a kindly voice, 'In this case, I think you should trust me.'

'Sure,' Jimmy said. 'I ain't got nothin' you ain't seen before.'

Stone rose and walked ahead of Jimmy and me on his way out to the Gents, which must have been down the hall somewhere because he turned to the left at the door. For a moment I was alone with Jimmy, and sufficiently out of earshot of Wendy and Nicole Lenoir-Jourdan and the military officer. 'He's gunna check out your dick, Jimmy – that is, if the bloody thing isn't worn down to a stub,' I whispered, in an attempt to lighten the moment.

'I dunno 'bout dat, Brother Fish. Wendy, she got a nice smile on her face dese days,' he chuckled. 'It spell sat-tis-fact-shun.'

Colonel Stone was waiting for us when we entered the toilet. 'You may be wondering what the hell all this is about. Again, I apologise. But I have to say I've been dealing with these problems since 1946, and nothing surprises me any more. Someone in Canberra, probably the foreign minister, wants this matter settled.' He turned to Jimmy. 'They're obviously concerned you will get back to America and tell them what happened in Hobart. On the other hand the Immigration Department can't make exceptions, even for a war hero. That would create an unfortunate precedent.' I thought of Nicole Lenoir-Jourdan when she'd pointed out to me that a precedent was a law in itself, and not an emotional exception.

'The regulation states, "If the applicant's background and racial history is not available, and if in appearance he is not substantially white, he *must* be given the dictation test." The last two words "substantially white" are the key. That's why I made mention of Private Oldcorn's excellent suntan. I hope you didn't take my remark as an insult.' He paused, then grinned. 'The caller from the Department of Immigration pointed out to me that the report they'd received from their officer in Hobart referred to Private Oldcorn's skin colour as "yellow", suggesting a genetic Negro.'

'I is called a "high yella",' Jimmy said.

Stone smiled. 'Of even more importance is the fact that the immigration official's report states you are an orphan. You see, the law states that if there is no past history available then the subject can, at the discretion of an immigration officer, undergo a physical examination. "Give him a physical examination," the caller from the

Immigration Department said to me. "I'm not a physician," I told him. "You don't need to be," was the reply. "Wasn't that done in Hobart?" I asked. He'd sounded impatient. "*Yellow*, that's what the report says. It could be a suntan – so why don't you look where the sun don't shine, colonel."'

Jimmy and I both laughed. 'Is this for real?' I asked.

'Absolutely! Now, would you mind dropping your trousers and pulling down your underpants, Private Oldcorn.'

Despite the indignity and even the humiliation this may have caused Jimmy, I had to laugh. Fortunately, so did he.

The human buttocks are evidently the area of skin least exposed to the sun, the colonel said, as Jimmy dropped his daks and pulled down his underpants. Under the bluish fluorescent light the skin on his bum looked pale enough to me. 'I'd say that's pretty white, wouldn't you, Mr McKenzie?'

I heard Jimmy take an inward breath and suddenly it was no longer funny. 'Fuck, I'm sorry, mate,' I said to Jimmy.

'Yes, so am I,' said the colonel. 'Please get dressed, Private Oldcorn.'

Jimmy pulled up his underpants and britches. 'It been done before, Brother Fish,' Jimmy said quietly. 'In Elmira Reformatory, dey done do dis to classify yoh. Nigger, chink or white – dat da only three class-si-fi-cation dey got. Sometimes two brothers dey der, one he clas-si-fied white, da udder he a nigger.'

'I don't think I heard that!' the colonel remarked.

'Now what happens?' I asked.

'Well, I put in my report and make a recommendation.' Colonel Stone shrugged. 'After that, I'm afraid it's out of my hands.' He extended his hand to Jimmy. 'Private Oldcorn, good luck. You're the kind of man any soldier would admire and be glad to have at his side in a weapon pit.'

'Why, I thank yoh, colonel. It been nice ta know yoh,' Jimmy said. I knew him well enough to know that when he was upset, he was at his calmest ('*Yoh don't show dem muth'fuckers nothin'*, *Brother Fish*.

*Make sure iffen dey look in yo' eye, dey see da sea o' tranquillity'*). I felt sure the epithet didn't include Colonel Stone, but the humiliation Jimmy had experienced, starting right from the beginning with Mr Cuffe and the impossible dictation test, must be having a cumulative effect. Baring his arse in the men's toilet was just about the last straw.

Turning to me, the colonel shook my hand. 'Mr McKenzie, you're fortunate to have such a friend.'

'He has his moments,' I replied, grinning.

We walked back to the interview lounge and Colonel Stone said goodbye to us all. We were starting to walk towards the exit door when he said, 'Oh, by the way, Private Oldcorn, I understand you are due to be demobbed in a few days. May I suggest you leave it for perhaps another fortnight?'

As soon as we were outside in the sunshine, anticipating what the girls were thinking, I quickly volunteered, 'Jimmy passed his physical with flying colours.' Later I told them separately what had occurred. When I told Wendy, she promptly burst into tears. Nicole Lenoir-Jourdan, who was older and made of sterner stuff, remained silent, then said softly, 'Sometimes, when we reach the depths of despair, we also reach a crisis point in our lives where the weak perish and the strong survive. James is a very strong man, Jack.'

That final sentence about Jimmy not going into the American Consulate in Melbourne to take his discharge from the army for two weeks was perhaps the most encouraging of all the things the colonel said to us. We now had a deadline to look forward to – just fourteen days and we'd know what was going to happen. I guess the Australian Government felt it couldn't hold out much longer and had to locate Jimmy before it appeared totally incompetent in the eyes of the Americans.

Within a week, he received a letter from the Immigration Department in Hobart.

**Commonwealth Department of Immigration**

*Mr Richard Oldcorn*
*Poste Restante*
*Livingston*
*Queen Island*

*10th April, 1954*

*Dear Mr Oldcorn,*
*On behalf of the Commonwealth Department of Immigration I am instructed to request that you appear at this office on April 16th 1954 at the time of eleven a.m.*

*Your two previously attending sponsors may accompany you to the interview if you wish.*

*I remain,*
*Yours faithfully,*
*Clarence Cuffe*
*Officer for Immigration – Tasmania*

We tried not to get our hopes up – after all, anything could happen. Colonel Stone had said that in the past the army had proved to have very little influence over such matters, so there was no point in getting too excited. It was back to Launceston and then the bus to Hobart. We arrived at the Immigration Office on the dot of eleven, and this time there was no waiting and no apathetic receptionist. The legless gobbling spider actually half-smiled and informed Mr Cuffe via her intercom that we'd arrived, and after a few moments Cuffe's voice crackled back and we were instructed to enter his office.

The fat man rose from his seat as we entered, and indicated the three chairs already placed in front of his desk. 'Good morning. Please sit down,' he instructed, his voice slightly less formal than on the previous occasion we'd entered his office. Seating himself, he cleared his throat and said, 'You must understand I have the greatest respect for your war records, but I have a job to do.'

It was a much better plea for understanding than when, on the previous occasion, he'd claimed he was only following instructions. I guess when you're in the public service these terms just slip off the tongue automatically. One thing was new, though – he'd not mentioned our war records on the previous visit, which suggested that he'd been given additional information for this interview and, hopefully, instructed to sort something out.

'I want to apologise,' I said.

'Thank you,' he said formally and a little too quickly, as if he'd expected it. What the hell, I wasn't really sorry I'd physically threatened him, but I wanted to clear the atmosphere before we began the meeting. If something good didn't come out of all this, I told myself I'd most likely do the same again. Fat pigs with power were not my favourite people. I could see Nicole Lenoir-Jourdan had no intention of apologising for drawing parallels between Cuffe's behaviour and that of the Nazis.

'Look,' he continued, 'I'll be perfectly honest with you.' He spread his stubby hands. 'Mr Oldcorn, in my opinion you don't qualify to migrate to Australia. As a Commonwealth immigration officer I am authorised to make a decision based on your physical appearance, noting your racial characteristics. That is precisely the task I carried out last time you were in this office.' He picked up a pencil and leaned back in his chair, tapping the pencil point into the blotter on the desk in front of him and making tiny indentations. 'But now it seems I was mistaken, and I am informed Mr Oldcorn has undergone a *more detailed* examination. I am here to tell you that the decision reached after that examination is that Mr Oldcorn is a borderline case. In other words, the decision could go either way.' He threw up his hands suddenly as if anticipating a question. 'Please, if you think I have the final decision I can assure you that is not the case at all. I am here to ask a few more questions only – the final decision will be made in Canberra.'

*Bloody hell! This thing is up and down like a yoyo! Whenever is it going to end?*

Cuffe continued, glancing down at a file. 'I see here that you are to return to the United States to receive a military decoration from the president, Mr Oldcorn?'

'So I've been told, but not officially,' Jimmy said in a passable Australian accent, his grammar perfect.

'My congratulations,' Cuffe said.

'Thank you,' the Australian version of Jimmy Oldcorn answered politely.

Cuffe turned to me. 'I believe you're in the fishing game, Mr McKenzie?'

'Well, I'm a fisherman, but we – that is, Jimmy and I – hope to go into the cray business together. Providing he is allowed to stay.'

'I see, well, that's most encouraging news. You see, there is a regulation that says that coloured aliens, a category not eligible to immigrate, can be issued with a Certificate of Exemption if they conduct an export business from Australia that is of benefit to the Australian economy.'

There followed a moment of astonished silence between us. Then, quick as a flash, Nicole Lenoir-Jourdan said, 'How very perspicacious of you, Mr Cuffe. That is exactly what James and Jack have in mind to do.'

I looked to Jimmy, who had his hands on his lap out of Cuffe's view. They opened wide at this news, signalling his own surprise, but his expression didn't change. 'That's right. I'm going to see some people when I'm in America. Fish agents – that is, seafood wholesalers.' I don't know if Cuffe recognised the change in Jimmy's grammar from the previous occasion we'd been in his office, but anyway, he looked relieved.

'That's good news.'

'We'll need a year to set things up, maybe a little longer,' I suggested, not wanting to be locked in to promising something rash.

'That will be fine. If Mr Oldcorn is granted a certificate, he will have five years to prove he is a bona fide exporter. If he can't show any proof after that time, his Certificate of Exemption will not be renewed. I must emphasise again, the decision to issue you with a certificate would normally fall to me, but that is not the case this time.'

'But you can make a recommendation – is that right, Mr Cuffe?' Nicole Lenoir-Jourdan asked.

'I am only following instructions,' Cuffe said, pointedly looking directly at her. Oh dear, it was obvious he hadn't forgotten her Nazi crack. Moreover, he was leaving the door open for her to apologise. I knew there was no chance of that happening. Nicole Lenoir-Jourdan had been feeling for Jimmy every step of the way, sharing his humiliation and despair. There was absolutely no way she was going to give Cuffe a mealy-mouthed apology. The stars could jump out of orbit and spin new patterns in the firmament before she'd retract what she'd said about him. She was under no illusions that if Cuffe had had his way, Jimmy, the 'coloured alien', would have been consigned to oblivion by now. I hated the term 'coloured alien' – it sounded like little green men landing in a spaceship.

After the interview, we had a cup of tea at a nearby cafe – Jimmy as usual ordering coffee, which, invariably, after a single sip he refused to drink.

'How dey make dis sheet, Brother Fish?' It had almost become a game.

'Acorns, mate – roasted and ground. You're supposed to add a lot of sugar.'

'Well! What did we think of all that?' Nicole Lenoir-Jourdan asked, keen to get back to the subject at hand.

'I think it lunchtime soon and it gonna be mah spe-ci-al treat,' Jimmy said. 'We ain't gonna talk 'bout dis no more today – ain't no use saying nothin' 'til da man in Can-berra decide.' Jimmy was telling us that we'd spent too much time working on his behalf. He was embarrassed, and had had enough for one day.

'Well, there *is* something rather important we need to talk about,' Nicole Lenoir-Jourdan said, looking at each of us in turn. 'But if you'd rather not talk about it over lunch, then I quite understand.'

Of course we were both immediately curious, but neither of us took the bait. After we'd had our tea, and Jimmy's coffee had grown a dirty grey skin on the top, we asked the waitress, who was young enough to still wear her hair in twin plaits and who'd served us very politely, if there was a nice place nearby to eat. 'Yiz'll be best off at the hotel next door. They do a nice steak di-anne and there's chicken catch-a-tory and Vienna snoot-zil.' We thanked her and left a sixpence in the plate and went next door, where the head waiter, in tails and a starched shirt front, rubbed his hands together as we entered the dining room, welcoming us effusively to the establishment.

'Looks expensive,' I said through the side of my mouth.

'Dat okay. So long da chow good,' Jimmy replied.

Jimmy and I both ordered a steak, and Nicole Lenoir-Jourdan the chicken cacciatore. We tried to find other topics to talk about, but you know how it is. When your head is full of one subject it overwhelms every other thought, and our subsequent conversation limped along, coming to frequent halts. We were dead curious about whatever it was Nicole Lenoir-Jourdan had put on hold at Jimmy's hasty request, and so the tension at the table was palpable. Finally, and even before our meal came to an end, Jimmy said, ''Bout what yoh said when I said we ain't gonna talk 'bout what happen and we gonna have lunch den yoh said dat okay, well, can we talk 'bout dat now please, Nicole ma'am?'

'James, that's just about the most discombobulated sentence I think I've ever heard come from you! No! You'll just have to wait now,' she replied, putting in the boot.

The steak was pretty good, but there you go – it's pretty hard to get a bad steak if you're going to pay seven and sixpence for it. Like I said, when your mind's full of the kind of stuff we'd been going through, the conversation was finally forced to a complete stop. 'How was your chicken?' I asked Nicole Lenoir-Jourdan after our silence caused the clatter of knives and forks to seem positively deafening.

She put down her fork and sighed heavily. 'Very well, I agree to talk.' Jimmy and I both looked relieved. 'I thought we might talk about exporting crayfish to America,' she said calmly.

Both of us giggled. I don't mean laugh. I truly mean giggled. Her suggestion was too absurd for words. 'Nicole ma'am, we don't even know for sure that Jimmy's going to be allowed to stay. Anyway, we don't have a brass razoo between us!'

'Oh, Jimmy will get one of those ghastly Certificates of Exemption,' she said confidently.

'How yoh know dat, Nicole ma'am?' Jimmy asked.

'Women's intuition,' she replied. 'Did you not see the look of relief on the horrible little man's face when I said he showed great perspicacity?'

'What's perspicacity mean?' I asked. The word had been playing on my mind.

'Jack, you have a perfectly good dictionary,' she replied, not wanting to be sidetracked.

Jimmy laughed. 'It mean having mental pen-e-tration, man!' Jimmy said with a grin.

'You'll keep, mate,' I replied. Jimmy had taken to carrying a tiny dictionary around with him, and the bugger had obviously sneaked a look.

'Jack, your problem has always been concentration. Can we keep to the subject, please?'

'Which was about your women's intuition,' I reminded her, showing I hadn't forgotten. 'But even if you're right . . .'

'Correct.'

*Bloody hell! Just at the moment I don't need a lesson in grammar.* 'But even if you're *correct*, we don't own a boat or fishing gear and even if the bank will give us a loan, we'll need a couple of thousand quid to get off the starting blocks. That's if we beg, borrow and steal and virtually buy everything second, third, fourth and fifth hand. To equip ourselves properly, that is, to be competitive, we'll need at least ten thousand quid, which frankly is a bad joke.' I was getting steamed up. 'Finally, we know absolutely nothing about exporting.'

'Ah, but *I* do!'

'Exporting crayfish?'

'Caviar.'

'Caviar?'

'Yes, Jack. The fish market is universal. We worked out of Shanghai, exporting to Europe and America. Caviar is fish – well, fish eggs, to be precise.'

'The virgin sturgeon,' I said, showing her I knew what caviar was. *Christ, what's going to come out next? Is there anything she hasn't done?*

I confess I was getting a bit worked up. Sometimes the smallest things set you off. Correcting my grammar was no big deal – Nicole Lenoir-Jourdan did it constantly, had done since I was eight years old. But I guess we were all feeling the strain, and her latest correction had been the last straw. I was also feeling decidedly sorry for myself but, of course, I couldn't allow myself to admit it. Everything was crowding in on me. There was the problem of Jimmy being able to stay in Australia, as well as Wendy's parents turning nasty and making her sad. And then there was the fact that I was engaged to the most beautiful girl in the world and I couldn't even afford a bloody ring! Not even a diamond I'd seen in a Launceston pawn shop so small it didn't seem to refract light. I was earning bugger-all, and now Nicole Lenoir-Jourdan was giving me my hundred-thousandth lesson in English bloody grammar!

As far as I was concerned we'd basically lied to Cuffe about going into export. I didn't mind that – I'd tell porkies until the cows came home if it would help ensure Jimmy could stay. If Nicole Lenoir-Jourdan had been correct about his getting a Certificate of Exemption Jimmy and I would have five years to get something under way. But in the fishing game five years is bugger-all. Even if we worked our arses off, we might just about make a reasonable living in that time. That is, if our luck held – fishing is as much about luck as it is about good management and the right equipment. How we'd then scrape together the money for a half-decent boat and the gear we'd need to be taken seriously in all-weather fishing on Bass Strait, the Tasman, and the Tasmanian and Victorian coasts was anyone's guess. We certainly wouldn't be anywhere near doing so in five years.

Most fishermen, even those few on the island with a bit of get-up-and-go, have taken half a lifetime to own a boat they can trust in a big sea. Nothing grand – just one that is not only properly equipped for cray fishing but also able to adapt to another kind of catch that will pay for insurance, tucker, fuel bills and the crew's wages in the off-season. Most fishermen never get close and go broke trying, and it's not only because they drown in alcohol on the way. It's the constant struggle – the weather, lack of money, lack of proper equipment, the bloody banks foreclosing, poor seasons, storms, rip-off wholesale fish buyers, Tasmanian Fisheries making new rules faster than you could haul an anchor in a sudden change of wind. It goes on and on until your heart is finally broken.

Nicole Lenoir-Jourdan ought to have known better. She'd been on the island since the early 1930s. She'd seen it all – the hungry families with barefoot kids, their clothes made from sugar bags, the grinding poverty. No jobs available when the weather gets up and goes bad on you, sometimes for weeks, the men sitting on their hands ashore with no wages coming in. She'd been on the island just after the Great Depression – she bloody knew how hard it was to earn a quid from the sea. Now she was talking about the export market where she had expertise in, excuse me, *caviar*! What the fuck had caviar to do with crayfish? Bloody fish eggs in a tin!

'I have a proposition to make to both of you,' she continued. She must have seen the look on my face, because she stopped and turned to me. 'I'm sorry about correcting your grammar, Jack. It was rude and unnecessary – I shan't do it again.' She'd never said that before. To make such a promise was almost more absurd than the ridiculous export idea. English grammar was her passion – she simply couldn't help herself. Then she smiled and hit us with the next bombshell. 'I'd like to go into the fishing business with the two of you.'

It was only just a little past two o'clock in the afternoon, yet already it felt to me as if I'd been up for forty-eight hours. 'Beg your pardon? You? Fishing?' *What can she possibly mean?* Clearly I was not the only one under strain.

'We'll build an export business together. We won't sell locally – cray fetches three and sixpence a pound on the Melbourne fish market; in America we'd clear ten shillings a pound after expenses.'

I was suddenly exasperated. 'Nicole ma'am, have you looked at a map lately?' I stretched my arm to the far side of the table. 'Australia's here.' I then drew my forefinger slowly across the red-and-white-checked tablecloth towards where she sat at the opposite end. 'This is the Pacific Ocean.' My hand finally came to rest next to her half-eaten plate of chicken cacciatore. 'And this is America! Los Angeles or San Francisco, take your pick. New York is on the other side of the flamin' continent. May I ask how we are going to get fresh cray to America, much less New York?'

'Qantas has two flights a week to Los Angeles,' she replied mildly.

Jimmy could see I was getting pretty upset. That's the trouble with being a redhead – when you're steamed up it shows. 'Brother Fish, he cor-rect, Nicole ma'am. We ain't got no dough to do no export business. We ain't got da bread foh a boat, even iffen it gonna be a flyin' boat!'

'But I have.' She said it quietly as if it was no big deal, then, turning to me, she asked, 'If I recall correctly, you said it would take about 10 000 pounds to equip properly for all-weather fishing?'

I nodded. 'Yeah, that's right – might as well be a million.'

She reached down to her handbag on her lap and withdrew a sheet of paper. 'Ten thousand, five hundred and eighty pounds,' she announced. 'That is, with a good transceiver – I'd rather you didn't get lost at sea.'

She pushed the piece of paper over to me. We were silent for a while – I mean, there's not a lot you can say after something like that. I glanced down at the single sheet, carefully ruled with a column down the right-hand side filled with numbers, and on the left she'd written the items we'd require, the very first being 'One 45ft fishing boat'. I glanced at the bottom line where the outrageously large sum, 13 987 pounds, sat squatly positioned between two horizontal black lines.

'Well?' she looked at me querulously. 'Cat got your tongue, Jack?'

'What are you going to do, sell the *Gazette*?'

She drew back in horror. 'Oh, I couldn't possibly do that!' We both looked at her, mystified, and I handed the sheet of paper to Jimmy.

'I . . . I don't know what to say.'

'I suppose your reaction is not surprising, Jack. I dare say it's a lot of money and naturally you're curious as to where it will come from.'

That was probably the understatement of the decade – the century! Fourteen thousand quid could buy a house and a car and was the sort of dough it would take us ten years or more to save. That is, if we got all the breaks, which was highly improbable – fishermen never get all the breaks, the sea makes damn sure of that.

She paused and seemed to change the subject. 'You've been very patient not asking more pointedly about my past, Jack. Thank you for not persisting. After all, I know all about you. James has also been kind enough to tell me most of his personal story. But you know very little about me. If we are to be partners then it's only fair, before you make a decision, that we're completely honest and open with each other. Partnerships are always a tricky business and I would never wish to come between you.' She smiled and looked fondly at us. 'However, I must ask you to keep what I tell you confidential. A woman's life is not the same as that of a man. The world is quick to judge a female who has, as they say, "a past". I've made a new life for myself on the island and if it hasn't been everything a gal could possibly want, it's been satisfactory. I'm fifty years old the year after next – by the way, that's also confidential.' She looked up and took a breath. 'Well, it's high time I stopped dithering.'

We both laughed. *Dithering* was such an inappropriate word for Nicole Lenoir-Jourdan, who had practically run the island since I'd been too small to remember it without her. She and the Reverend Daintree (before he started losing the plot), Dr Light from the cottage hospital, and Father Crosby were the permanent brains – the movers and shakers. Although, in truth, Father Crosby was probably more brawn and bombast than he was brain. The rest of the islanders came and went, sitting on the various committees and as members of the town council, sharing the largely ceremonial role of mayor. But these four were the professionals to whom, from birth until death, in one way or another, we all eventually turned.

Nicole Lenoir-Jourdan, as I've mentioned, performed a number of different roles on the island. As music teacher and the director of the school concert she had brought a smidgin of culture to the community. As librarian she'd taught the disadvantaged and illiterate to read and write. As justice of the peace she'd kept her finger on the pulse of the island's business affairs, protected the vulnerable and changed people's lives, and in the last few years as editor of the *Gazette* she'd steered things in the right direction or stirred the community out of its customary lethargy. She'd made enemies and friends and often the one would change into the other and then revert once more. Nicole Lenoir-Jourdan showed neither fear nor favour, and she couldn't be bought. If all this could be termed *dithering*, then the rest of us might be described as practically flyblown.

But if there were those among the islanders who admired her and those who didn't, she had very few, if any, close friends – with perhaps the exception of the Reverend Daintree. In the old days, before he was in his dotage, she'd spent a lot of time at the manse, and if he hadn't been so old, even then, tongues might have wagged. She still turned up twice a week in the evening to cook something special for him, and I was later to learn that she cooked Chinese meals and that he too had spent some of his early days in China, as a missionary. While she was often the subject of conversation, admiring and otherwise, in all the time I'd known her I couldn't remember any islanders who felt they truly knew her. I was no exception. While I'd regarded her increasingly as a friend, it was still with a sense of wariness.

Jimmy, on the other hand, had seemed to be able to break through her stern, imperious demeanour with apparent ease. I would observe as he pressed on regardless, riding roughshod over her defences, to capture her heart and mind to the point of enchantment. They appeared to understand each other on a different level, and I'd never heard her laugh as often and in quite the way she did in his company. Moreover, while she was interested in his mind, she never corrected his grammar or winced at his pronunciation. She seemed to accept that Jimmy had invented a version of English that was unique, and she didn't tamper with it. He would often disagree with her, but she'd listen without shaking her head in disapproval as she would with me, often before I'd completed the sentence. She accepted Jimmy for who he was, while she had always regarded me as a potential outcome – someone whom she regarded as not yet a finished product.

While I wasn't in the least concerned with their growing friendship, I was now wary of how it might manifest itself in a partnership. The well-worn cliche 'Two's company, three's a crowd' sprang to mind. Fishing is a male business. Boats and fish are, at best, dirty work involving lots of small decisions, some of which can end up saving or losing your life. The sea is always a dangerous place, and on a two-man fishing vessel your partner is an extension of yourself. I never doubted for one moment that Jimmy and I would work well at sea. However, if Nicole Lenoir-Jourdan was calling the shots from the shore there would be the opportunity for tension between us. Her growing closeness to Jimmy had the potential to split his and my loyalty to each other. I told myself that her imperious manner wouldn't vanish overnight, that she was essentially a loner accustomed to making all the decisions. Local gossip had it that there was a constant exit of employees from the *Gazette*, where it was known to be 'her way, or no way'.

On the other hand, there was the Nicole Lenoir-Jourdan of tact and charm, who could twist a real hard case like Harry Champion – 'the choice of all the Champions' – who'd duly received his import licence for the French equipment needed to make brie, around her little finger. Furthermore, the way she'd planned the campaign for Jimmy's Certificate of Exemption had been masterly. Whether he finally received permission to stay in Australia or not, she hadn't missed a trick and her 'emotional exception' concept had showed how very well she understood human nature.

With her guiding us in what still seemed an outrageous idea to export cray to America, we might even have half a chance of succeeding, although I must say I harboured very serious doubts that it could be made to work. If I was being perfectly honest with myself, Nicole Lenoir-Jourdan was a clever and strong-willed woman, Jimmy Oldcorn was a natural and charismatic leader and Jack McKenzie was – well, what the hell was I? I guess a fisherman who read books and worried a lot.

The obsequious waiter, still rubbing his hands together, appeared and asked if we'd enjoyed what he referred to as 'your second course', pointing out politely that we hadn't ordered an entrée. Perhaps next time we came we might like to try the excellent Tasmanian oysters served with cocktail sauce, or the prawn cocktail. He also sincerely hoped we would enjoy our dessert.

He appeared again shortly with our pudding orders – strawberries and cream for Nicole Lenoir-Jourdan, pavlova for Jimmy and crème caramel for me. This gave the head waiter the chance to glide away from our table with a deferential bow, the words *'Bon appétit'* left hovering in the air behind him.

I wondered momentarily if our individual choice of sweets was a good omen or a bad one – whether it meant that, as potential business partners, each of us would make an equal but different contribution to the venture or end up never being able to see eye to eye on any problem. Despite the enormously generous offer she was making, I felt Jimmy and I would have to think very carefully about a business partnership with the dreaded justice of the peace and formidable editor of the *Queen Island Weekly Gazette*.

Nicole Lenoir-Jourdan spooned a single strawberry snow-capped with cream, and held the spoon poised in the air at chin level. 'It all seems so very long ago when, as a fifteen-year-old refugee fleeing from the Bolsheviks, I arrived in Shanghai in 1922,' she began.

# CHAPTER SEVENTEEN

## *The Manchurian Piano Player*

'I was born on a modest country estate on the Volga River near the city of Astrakhan, only a few miles from the border of Kazakhstan, where my family had lived for several generations. My father, Count Nikolai Georgii Avksent'ievich Lenoir, was the eldest of four sons,' she said, smiling, realising his name must seem like a bit of a mouthful. 'In Russia, when you first introduce a nobleman you use all his names. I should also emphasise that at the time, a count wasn't always a title that meant prestige and wealth. At best we were minor aristocracy, and in the salons of St Petersburg and Moscow we would have been dismissed as country bumpkins or, worse still, in trade – and, even more inappropriately, in fish. Unlike the true wealthy and titled our fortunes didn't depend on vast land holdings and the number of peasants we owned, but instead came from the Caspian Sea and, more particularly, from the export of beluga caviar.'

Nicole Lenoir-Jourdan dipped into her strawberries again, half-finishing the bowl before she resumed talking. 'I imagine we were well-off and I dare say, compared to the peasants and the fishermen on the river, we were considered enormously wealthy. At the age of eighteen, as was the tradition in most families like ours, my father entered the

Aleksandrovskoe Military School in Moscow, where he eventually graduated as an officer and as a military engineer.

'It had never been his intention to make a career in the army – as the eldest son he was responsible for running our fishing enterprises and managing the estate. Military training was where young noblemen at the time were euphemistically taught how to be gentlemen, while being trained to be officers in the tsar's Imperial Army. While they may have been young officer cadets, they were almost certainly not, for the most part, gentlemen. The time spent at a military academy was seen as a time when a young man from a good family sowed his wild oats before returning to the family estate to marry and settle down.

'My father's return home from military training coincided with a growing demand in America for beluga caviar. He used his newly acquired skill as an engineer to build a new fish-processing plant on the river near the city of Volgograd, which was said to look remarkably like a fort and was soon known locally as Fort Nikolai. Shortly after returning, he married Celeste Margaret Jourdan, a ballet dancer whom he'd met during his last months in the military academy, at a reception held on Bastille Day at the French Consulate in Moscow.

'I was born in 1906 on the family estate, and despite hopes for a male heir I was to be the only child. I was eight when the Great War broke out and my father joined the Russian Imperial Army as a captain in the Engineers. He was wounded early in 1915 while blowing up a bridge on the Turkish border.' She looked up. 'Curiously, like the two of you, in the leg. He was to walk with a pronounced limp, one leg slightly shorter than the other, for the remainder of his life.'

'Dat too bad, Nicole ma'am,' Jimmy offered, shaking his head in sympathy.

'Rather than be invalided out of the army, he volunteered to work as a military engineer on the Trans-Siberian Railway. With Turkey controlling the Black Sea outlet to the Mediterranean through the Dardenelles, Germany controlling the Baltic Sea, and with the port of Murmansk in the Arctic Ocean frozen for a large part of the year, the Trans-Siberian Railway became Russia's main artery to the outside world with Vladivostok, where my father was posted, its main port. My mother found herself separated from her husband by almost the entire length of Russia. As his was largely a desk job, she insisted, against his will, that we join him.

'The army promoted my father to major, then colonel, and transferred him to become the head of the Port Authority in Vladivostok. Aristocrats, even of a minor kind, were soon to become ubiquitous, but when we first arrived they were few and far between in that part of Russia. We were accepted readily, even gratefully, into the local society. My early life was spent, like most well-bred Russian children, learning to play the piano and, of course, with my mother a ballet teacher, to dance. I was also taught to sing. My mother loved to dance, although my father's gammy leg left her without a partner and my fondest childhood memories are of her winding up the gramophone and dancing with me every morning from the age of seven. By the time I was ten I'd learned all the classic dances as well as the latest steps coming out of America. Naturally, I spoke French, and upon arriving in Vladivostok my mother engaged a Chinese *amah* named Ah Lai, who came from a village near Harbin in Manchuria, to take care of me. Children pick up languages effortlessly, and I soon learned to speak Cantonese fluently.

'I loved Ah Lai dearly and she eventually became more a member of the family than a servant, which was not the way one was expected to treat the Chinese in those days. When I grew too old for an *amah*, she became my mother's *tai-tai amah* – that is to say, her personal maid. With England and France being Russia's major allies, my father was anxious that I learn English as well. A very prim and proper spinster lady, Miss Rosen, was engaged to tutor me for half a day three times a week.' Nicole Lenoir-Jourdan laughed. 'As I recall, she was very pedantic about vowels. "My dear, correctly spoken English is a matter of sounding your vowels clearly," she would say. We would spend the first fifteen minutes of every lesson sounding out a number of words and sentences, with clearly accentuated vowels, she'd prepared in advance. "The clown bounced on the trampoline and burst a boil on his bottom that caused him to become discombobulated" was one of her very favourite sentences. I confess I thought it very funny, and we'd both giggle no matter how many times it was repeated.

'It was a pleasant, privileged and comfortable childhood until 1917, a date I remember less for the revolution that toppled the Romanoff Dynasty and the murder by the Reds of the tsar and his family, than as the year my own beloved mother died. She was an early victim of the flu epidemic that was eventually to spread throughout the world and cause the death of between forty and fifty million souls. I was only eleven at the time, and so Ah Lai virtually became my mother.

'Russia was now divided by two forces – the White Russians, previously the Russian Imperial Army, and the Communists, or Red Army. The White cause finally collapsed on the 7th of February 1920 when the head of the White Army in Siberia, Admiral Kolchak, was killed in Irkutsk. Vladivostok immediately became the destination for the petty aristocracy and bourgeoisie fleeing from the terror of the Red Army. While still in charge of the port my father no longer received a salary, but he nevertheless felt compelled to continue to work. Shiploads of refugees began to arrive from all over Russia and it was important that someone avoid complete chaos. As it was, it was only a matter of time before the Red Army would arrive and, fearing for my life but feeling himself duty bound to remain at his post, my father asked Ah Lai to take me to stay in her village near Harbin. It took several weeks to travel the 250 miles to her village in an ox cart driven by an old Chinaman who'd once had his throat cut by bandits but somehow survived. He could no longer talk other than to make a series of rattling noises, which the ox seemed to understand. He slept with the beast at night while we cooked and camped at the side of the road, which, at the time, I thought was a grand adventure.'

I couldn't believe what I was hearing – on top of everything else, Nicole Lenoir-Jourdan had lived as a gypsy. We were spellbound.

'I spent eighteen months in my *amah*'s *zu ji*, which means the village where ancestors were born, before my father arrived to fetch me. It was immediately obvious that his health was failing and that he was physically exhausted. Moreover, he arrived virtually empty-handed with only a small suitcase that contained a precious icon and a few personal belongings. As he had received almost no salary since the collapse of the White Army, we found ourselves in a most impecunious situation.'

She looked up and saw Jimmy's bemused face. 'We were stony-broke,' she explained. 'My mother's jewellery was all we had – several rings, pearl earrings, a string of pearls and a diamond bracelet, which Ah Lai had placed in a small leather drawstring pouch and kept concealed during our journey from Vladivostok . . .' she hesitated momentarily, '. . . within her woman's private part, in case we were robbed by bandits. These few trinkets and, of course, the icon of Christ on a donkey entering Jerusalem on Palm Sunday were all we possessed.'

I hated loose ends in a story and couldn't help myself. 'What about the estate, you know, the fish factory?' I asked. 'That must have been worth something.'

'Two of my father's brothers died in the war and the third was killed when the local fishermen stormed the processing plant after the communists took over. It is now run as a commune, but curiously it wasn't the last time the family would have a direct connection with it – although that comes much later in my story.'

She pushed the remaining strawberries aside, leaving three uneaten in the bowl. 'My father and I moved into a single room in Harbin, sharing washing and cooking facilities with twenty other families. Water was obtained from a hand pump in the filthy courtyard of the building. My father tried to gain work as an engineer, but with a bad leg and rapidly deteriorating health there was little he could find to do. Refugees are a desperate lot and not given to charity, and no one remembered or cared that he had kept the port open and running for almost two years allowing a great many of them to escape from Russia. Finally he experienced what later I would realise was a mental breakdown, and suffered from a deep depression that made it impossible for him to leave his bed. He talked almost daily of suicide, and I was beside myself with worry.

'Selling my mother's jewellery, together with what possessions my father had managed to bring with him, brought very little. Harbin had become the major destination for the fleeing White Russians and it was awash with jewellery going for a song. Buyers from Europe were converging on the city to snap up pieces worth fifty times what they paid for them. No group of refugees was ever worse equipped to make a living, or could have chosen a more inappropriate place in which to make it. Most had never worked – certainly none of the women and very few of the men, other than in the military, and even this had not been taken too seriously, or the rabble that formed the communists could never have won. Work was what a peasant was born and ordained by God himself to do.'

'Sound like dem Russians, dey don't have no niggers,' Jimmy said. 'In America dat time it da same.'

'Well, yes, I imagine that was true, certainly before the Civil War,' she said, putting Jimmy's somewhat sweeping statement into some sort of perspective. Then she looked at us. 'You will tell me if I'm becoming tedious, won't you?'

'Nicole ma'am, dis a great story,' Jimmy said, while I nodded my agreement. We were beginning to see a Nicole Lenoir-Jourdan emerging we could never have even remotely imagined.

'At that time in Russia it was believed that peasants were not only a lower form of human being but also a different species. The theory was often postulated among the aristocracy that these creatures had developed alongside modern man but with a smaller brain and a much higher threshold for pain, so that they were natural beasts of burden somewhat like an ox in human form. It was commonly thought that when an infant was born with the Siberian winter approaching it was the practice for a peasant family to fatten it up then kill it and pickle it to avoid starvation in the harsh winter months that lay ahead. One such case was reported in a Moscow newspaper in 1906, the year I was born. It was immediately accepted by many of the petty bourgeoisie and the nobility as a universal practice among the Siberian peasants. So it was hardly surprising that after 300 years of being used and treated as one might an animal, the Russian peasants finally rose up against their oppressors. But then again there is a paradox – it was the working classes in the cities that were the first to embrace communism, followed by the miners and finally the long-suffering Russian peasants.

'The only talents most of the fleeing White Russian aristocrats and petty bourgeoisie possessed were for dancing and carousing, while a few like me could play the piano or some other musical instrument prettily, if not truly well. They had never cooked nor cleaned, neither could they perform such mundane tasks as knitting or sewing. They were cultured and sophisticated, but few were truly educated beyond the nicety of manners and affectation. Such refined characteristics were of no possible use to them in a cesspit like Harbin. So they did the only thing they could do – they opened nightclubs, or supper clubs, until Harbin was known to be the nightclub capital of the world, and home to the most beautiful and readily available Russian women in the Orient. Nightclubs invariably lead to other kinds of nocturnal activity, and women who had been born in palaces suddenly found themselves living in whorehouses.'

Once again Jimmy and I looked up in surprise – 'whorehouse' was not the kind of word we expected from the lips of Nicole Lenoir-Jourdan. She must have sensed our surprise because she shrugged, and added, 'Survival, as you both clearly know, is our most powerful instinct, although at the time I was quite unprepared for what it might take to survive the environment I now found myself in.

'I was fifteen years old, and even taking into account the time I'd spent in Ah Lai's village, I had led, until now, a sheltered existence. With my father unable to rise from his bed, I had to find myself a job or else we were simply going to starve. We had sold all my mother's jewellery and retained only the icon, which was said to have been in our family for well over 200 years and which I was determined under any circumstances to keep. By retaining the icon it was as if I retained a small piece of God in my life, and as long as I hung onto it we wouldn't go under.'

She glanced suddenly at her wristwatch. 'Goodness gracious! It's a quarter to three!' she exclaimed. 'We have a bus to catch!'

Her reminder of the time was so abrupt and unexpected that it took a few moments for me to adjust to where we were. I glanced around to see that the dining room was deserted. With the exception of our table, all the tables had been laid for dinner and the staff had long since departed, apart from the head waiter, who stood leaning against the cashier's counter at the far end of the room. I glanced at him and he gave me a somewhat despairing smile. Jimmy paid the bill and left a generous tip, but the head waiter was hard put to even rub his hands together as he wished us good day and, no doubt, a silent 'good riddance'.

Of course, Jimmy and I desperately wanted to hear the rest of Nicole Lenoir-Jourdan's story. But the three o'clock bus to Launceston Airport was usually crowded and, running late as we now were, we'd be lucky to get a seat so that she could continue her tale. Furthermore, the Douglas DC3 to the island was a noisy aeroplane, and there wasn't going to be an opportunity to talk any further until perhaps some time after our arrival.

It had been the most amazing of days. Frustrating, in the sense that we still didn't know Jimmy's fate, but exhilarating in another sense – if Jimmy *was* allowed to stay we might have the money to start a half-decent fishing operation, rather than the prospect of living on the smell of an oily rag for the next ten years. The day's revelations were also worrying, in that the partnership on offer held a distinct possibility of creating dissension among the three of us. Finally, what Nicole Lenoir-

Jourdan had so far told us about her past convinced me that we might be dealing with someone so completely different from the woman I thought I knew that this too might have unexpected consequences. The day had been a seminal one, to say the very least.

As it turned out the plane was as crowded as the bus from Launceston, and we had three separate seats. Mine was on the opposite aisle and two rows behind Nicole Lenoir-Jourdan while Jimmy was well back near the tail. From where I sat I could look at her without her noticing. I was also fortunate that I was seated beside a travelling salesman who was preoccupied for most of the way studying a brochure filled with plumbing fixtures. Had I copped the company of an islander I would have been forced to conduct a conversation, halfway shouting against the noise of the engines, and I was much too overwrought and emotionally exhausted for the usual small talk.

This is probably going to sound peculiar, but I had known Nicole Lenoir-Jourdan from the age of eight and I was now twenty-seven – that's almost twenty years, and I had never truly looked at her. As a small child my eyes had always been downcast when she talked to me and her physical presence had simply overpowered me, and the fear she'd engendered then had left a permanent imprint on my brain. While I now considered her a friend, a subliminal reserve persisted that until now had blinded me from seeing her in any other context but as someone who had always seemed my superior. Not, I hasten to say, in a sycophantic way, but as a teacher and mentor.

Now I looked at her carefully – really looked for the first time. Her face was in profile and in repose. She was by her own admission a woman close to fifty, as slim as a rake, with her natural blonde hair beginning to turn grey. I felt a physical shock as I realised she was still a highly attractive woman and must have once been very beautiful. She used very little make-up – a lick of red lipstick and perhaps mascara. Her hair was cut, not overskilfully, in a bob, while her skin remained clear and firm and, unlike Gloria, who couldn't go anywhere without creating a dust storm around her head, she didn't use face powder. Her eyes, which I couldn't really see, I knew to be a clear deep blue – the colour of sea water looking up to the surface when, as a diver, you are about fifteen feet down with the sunlight reflecting back from a clear sandy bottom below you. I now realised I'd never summed up enough courage to truly look, to observe what lay behind them.

The next question I asked myself was obvious, though I confess it had never occurred to me until this moment. *Why had a beautiful and intelligent woman like her never married*? Was it because no man on the island, with the exception of the Reverend Daintree, had been her intellectual match? But then, *why had she chosen the island in the first place?* Now, it seemed, she was a woman of some means. Why then had she hidden herself on a place she sometimes, in exasperation, referred to as 'This godforsaken island!'?

I'm ashamed to say I even wondered if she might be hiding from someone or something. I told myself it stood to reason that with the kind of looks she must have had twenty or so years ago and with money as well, something funny must be going on. I mean, what the hell was she doing arriving on Queen Island during the Great Depression when poverty and alcohol had reduced the people on the island to little more than gibbering savages?

Then, of course, my imagination began to work overtime. *Maybe there was something dark and ugly in her past that caused her to run away and hide – what better place to choose than Queen Island?* One negative thought invariably leads to another, and I grew concerned once again about going into partnership with Nicole Lenoir-Jourdan – if that really was her name. *What could Jimmy and I possibly be getting ourselves into? She appeared to be telling us the story of her life, but what if it wasn't true, a total fabrication?* I believed the part where she said she'd lived in China. Darkest China was darkest Africa – plus cunning, greed and pitiless evil thrown in. It was Ming the Merciless with fingernails six inches long, inscrutable and cruel, Ming and her, together in a wicked partnership. Maybe the Russian part was also partially true. She'd said the Russian women were beautiful, that they had no means of support. Isn't that a way of saying they were desperate and would do anything to survive? After all, some say a woman's pussy is her last true asset. Maybe she'd been in the white slave trade where she hooked her victims on opium? She spoke Chinese and Russian, didn't she? She'd told us about beautiful aristocratic women finding themselves in whorehouses. Maybe she put them there – a notorious madam grown filthy rich on the carnal desires of licentious men . . .

But then, as usually happens, a gust of further absurdity, the thought of a sixteen-year-old brothelkeeper, let in a blast of clarity and commonsense. I gave myself a severe mental backhand. I'd fought the Chinese – there was nothing mysterious about them, nothing inscrutable. My mind flashed back to the bloke who had rolled me a cigarette then died in front of my eyes, and the soldier who'd held me in his arms and sung 'Swing Low, Sweet Chariot'. There was plenty of mercy, and no Mings with six-inch talons. Only brave young blokes who'd chewed their nails down to the quick and hoped just to get through the day alive. I'd turned Nicole Lenoir-Jourdan into the Wicked Witch of the East.

I looked out of the plane window to cool my thoughts. We were over Bass Strait and it was just after eight o'clock, with the last rays of the sun disappearing behind a dark, flat line of cloud edged with a fiery rim of gold that gave the impression of melting the darkness immediately above it. With the drone of the twin engines I suddenly felt very melancholy, as if I was suspended in time and space, a passing-away of something old, the beginning of something else. *Is this extraordinary day the end of my old life, and tomorrow the beginning of a new path where Jacko would become Jack and I might finally grow up?*

*Jacko* – it was a nickname that carried a lightness about it. It was insubstantial in sound, a bit of a joke really, the name of the monkey at the end of the organ-grinder's chain. Jack McKenzie had a resonance, like a hammer striking bright steel. Maybe Nicole Lenoir-Jourdan was the only one who'd recognised this all along. I turned away from the window and looked to where she sat. She appeared to be asleep. I tried to imagine a girl of sixteen trying to start her life all over again with a bedridden father in a dark, stinking little room in a strange and wicked city teeming with desperate and uncaring people.

When we got back to the island Gloria gave us a message from the co-op that there was a week's work available as crew on a trawler going out at dawn, which would be out to sea until late the following Sunday. Of course we jumped at the chance of some extra money.

Cray fishing is hard yakka and Jimmy and I were often separated and too busy to talk. Nevertheless, we discussed Nicole Lenoir-Jourdan's story at every opportunity. At one stage Jimmy said to me, 'Da only count I knows 'bout is Count Basie. What sort'a count dis cat, her father, man?'

'Like she said, he was an aristocrat.'

'Dat like da queen?'

'Yeah, kinda – it's an inherited title like the English have, you know, like a lord.'

'So now she like, what?'

'A countess, I reckon.'

'Dat good. She ain't Nicole ma'am no more – she now da countess,' Jimmy declared emphatically.

I looked at him. 'You'll have to tell her that, mate. I'm certainly not game.'

'Sure, I do it,' Jimmy said confidently. 'It ain't no good hidin' yo' light under no bushel.' All the reading Nicole Lenoir-Jourdan, shortly to be addressed as 'Countess', was giving Jimmy was beginning to affect him.

We spent a large part of the week discussing her offer of a partnership and what it might mean. I pointed out to Jimmy that it could lead to dissension between us, that Nicole Lenoir-Jourdan was stubborn as a mule and liked to get her own way. We argued to and fro, pros and cons, until on the last day at sea Jimmy said, 'Brother Fish, we done beat da North Koreans, we done beat da Chinese, we done beat da army, maybe we even gonna beat da Aus-tra-lian Government. How come we not gonna beat da countess iffen she make trouble?'

'She's a woman,' I answered. 'We've never beaten a woman.'

Jimmy laughed. 'Dis ain't no wo-man, Brother Fish. Dis one tough she-devil – she tougher den any drill sergeant an' we gonna need her real bad. We don't know nothin' 'bout nothin' export, we ain't got no boat, no bread – only hope.' He thought for a moment. 'As a matter o' fac', we don't know nothin' 'bout sweet fuck-all, 'cept survivin'.' He grinned. 'But dat ain't a bad start. I say we go, man.' From the look on my face he must have seen that I still wasn't entirely convinced. 'She da peace policeman . . .'

'Justice of the peace.'

'She know how to ne-go-shee-ate, she can talk sweet, she know also when to bend, but mostly she a tough cat – she don't take no bullshit from no one, man!' He paused. 'Dat good – we gonna need dat, Brother Fish.'

And so it was decided we'd accept Nicole Lenoir-Jourdan's offer of a partnership – always supposing Jimmy was allowed to stay, of course. Already she was influencing us. We were talking as if it had all been decided, based simply on her assurance that her woman's intuition told her we were sweet with the Immigration Department. That she had got Cuffe's number.

When we got back to the island there was a registered letter waiting for Jimmy. Busta Gut had naturally forgotten to mention it, but Sue had been up to the post office to buy stamps and Ma Gutherie had told her about it. 'I'll take it,' she said.

'Oh no you won't!' the postmistress replied.

'Why not? He lives with us!'

'It's registered, ain't it?'

'So?'

'Confidential. His business, 'fraid I can't do it,' she replied, lips drawn tight.

'They come into port late on Saturday night – that means Jimmy'll have to wait until Monday morning.' She looked at the postmistress, appealing to her common sense. 'It's important, Ma Gutherie. He's expecting to hear about staying in Australia.'

'Won't get it Monday mornin', girl. We closed Monday mornin'.'

'Why's that?'

'I'm goin' in'ta hospital for me varicose veins. They's hurting somethin' awful – comes from standin' all day servin' customers,' she said accusingly, as if Sue was partly to blame.

Sue thought for a moment. 'I don't think so.'

'Eh?'

'Dr Light is much too busy to see you on Monday.'

'What you mean, girl? I've got an appointment – eleven o'clock, Monday mornin'.'

'It just got cancelled.' Sue shrugged, looking sympathetic. 'Sorry.'

Ma Gutherie sighed, and handed her the registered letter without further protest.

'See you Monday then – don't be late, we're very busy on Monday mornings,' Sue called out as she left. She hadn't been born and bred on the island for nothing.

It was with a mixture of excitement and concern that, on our arrival home, Gloria handed Jimmy the letter in the government envelope.

*Private Richard Oldcorn*
*Poste Restante*
*Livingston*
*Queen Island*
*Tasmania*

*21st April, 1954*

*Dear Sir,*
*Forwarded herewith is a Certificate of Exemption No. 54/179 which is valid for a period of five years from the 21st of April, 1954.*

*Please retain this certificate in your possession and sign and return the attached receipt slip immediately.*

*Yours faithfully,*
*C.M.J. Cuffe*
*Commonwealth Immigration Officer*

After all the weeks of anxiety the enclosed certificate was carelessly folded and on poor-quality paper with a badly typed cover note that didn't even address Jimmy by name, but instead began with the ubiquitous and anonymous 'Dear Sir'. It was bordering on being callous, so totally indifferent to the human emotions expended to bring it about, and felt like a slap in the face with a wet rag. But, of course, we threw our arms in the air and jumped for joy and the girls kissed and hugged Jimmy and we pumped his hand with silly grins on our mugs. Gloria produced two bottles of warm beer and we toasted Jimmy. On a whim I grabbed my harmonica. The others followed and we began to play 'When Johnny Comes Marching Home'. Then, with me as the lead carrying the melody for the last line in each chorus, the others broke off to sing, 'When *Jimmy* comes marching home!'

It was already well into Sunday evening and too late to call on Nicole Lenoir-Jourdan, so we hot-footed it over to the *Gazette* office as soon as it opened at eight o'clock the following morning. She was overjoyed – though, of course, she'd predicted it in the hotel dining room a week earlier – and hugged and kissed Jimmy. I'd never seen her hug or kiss anyone before, the only exception being when she'd greeted me at the wharf on my return from Korea with the news of my medal, and that had been sort of semi-official – more a peck on the cheek. 'Congratulations, James. I'm overjoyed for you!' she said, truly beaming.

'Thank you. I owe it all to you,' Jimmy said in perfect English.

'Right on! You did it, Nicole ma'am. You made it happen!' I exclaimed happily.

'No, Jack – *we* made it happen.'

'No, no,' I insisted. 'Getting Mrs Zara Holt involved and your theory of emotional exception, that's what did it.'

'It's not *my* theory, Jack. Women have been practising it since Eve persuaded Adam to eat the apple.'

'Wasn't that the serpent did that?'

'Oh, I don't think so. Eve merely *used* the snake. You see, she wanted to get away from that idyllic, weedless garden after all – there's nothing quite as boring as perfection.'

'And Adam refused to break God's law?'

'Yes. Men like rules – it makes them imagine they're in charge.'

Jimmy and I laughed at the crack, but as usual 'big mouth' had to have a comeback. 'In that case, she must have persuaded Adam that in order to eat the apple God would need to be the one to be persuaded to make an emotional exception?'

'Quite right. Eve knew Adam, like all men, could be talked into thinking that he could have his snake and eat it.'

Jimmy chortled. 'Dat clever! Dat damned clever, Countess.'

Nicole Lenoir-Jourdan drew up sharply, the grin instantly gone from her face. '*Countess*?'

'Dat yo' new name,' Jimmy said ingenuously. 'Yoh ain't gonna be Nicole ma'am no more. From now we is gonna call yoh Countess, because we ain't gonna let yo' light shine under no bushel no more!'

'Jimmy, that's quite preposterous! Imagine what the people of the island will think!'

'Dey gonna think dey got demself a countess, and dat a somebody!'

'I really don't think so,' she said tersely. 'Plain Nicole will suffice, thank you very much.'

But Jimmy ignored the warning tone in her voice, something I could never have done. Instead, he looked surprised. 'Whoa! Dat ain't right,' he protested. 'We cain't have no partner what ain't no countess iffen we gonna be a classy outfit dat gonna sell lobsters to America. In America I gonna tell dem fish merchants, "Hey man, dis crayfish-lobster yo' gonna buy, it come from da private sea belong to da Countess Lenoir-Jourdan o' Queen Island where she da queen o' da crayfish tribe!" Den dey gonna say, "Where dat island, Jimmy?" I gonna show dem da map where it show it da other side da world. "Dis cray, it been flown direct over da South Pole to New York. Dat why it so fresh, man – it cold up der in da air 'bove dat South Pole! Fresh cray foh yoh de-lec-tation, gennelmen!" Dey gonna hear dat, dey gonna flip der lid.'

Nicole Lenoir-Jourdan laughed, despite herself. 'Always providing the price is right. In my experience fish importers are a tough breed.' She looked at each of us in turn. 'Does that mean we have a partnership?'

'Yes, but Jimmy and I agree, only if you may be referred to as Countess,' I said, grinning cheekily, knowing I was chancing my arm.

She thought for a moment. 'Only by the two of you and *only* in private.' For a moment she looked serious. 'Please understand, my privacy is important to me and the past is no longer relevant. But I'm delighted to think we'll be going into business together,' she added, brightening. 'I'm sure it wasn't an easy decision for you to make, Jack,' she said, looking at me.

There you go – she'd seen right through me, as usual.

'May I see the letter?' she then asked. Jimmy handed her the letter, together with the certificate, and she seemed to take it in at a glance. Then she stabbed a finger at the page and read aloud, "Forwarded herewith is a Certificate of Exemption No. 54/179 which is valid . . ." *Which? That* is valid!' she corrected. 'Really, you'd think they'd teach their bureaucrats the rudiments of grammar, wouldn't you?' She sighed. 'But then what can one expect from a horrid little man like Clarence Cuffe!' She glanced once again at the certificate. 'Hmph! Carelessly folded, careless all round – not the sort of thing you'd frame above your bed, is it? But I really am so *terribly* pleased for you, James.' She glanced over to me. 'Cup of tea, Jack? And James, you'll have coffee?'

Jimmy grimaced. 'No, thank you kindly, Countess.' It was the first time he'd used her title with permission, but she appeared not to notice.

'Oh, I have rather a nice surprise for you, James.' She left the room to make tea and returned a short while later with a teapot, three cups, milk and a sugar bowl. Beside them stood a strange-looking glass jug-like device with a chrome lid. It was half-filled with what I took to be coffee that steamed up the top half of the glass container. Next to it was a foil packet nearly as tall as the container. 'I found it in the latest catalogue at Mrs Dunne's and sent away for it. It's a plunger carafe, made in Italy,' she said excitedly. 'And this is . . .' She picked up the packet and read from the back, '. . . "Genuine American Blend vacuum-sealed coffee", ground from beans imported directly from Brazil. As advertised in *Esquire* magazine!' She then proceeded to push down the metal rod that protruded from the lid. 'It's quite ingenious – such clever people, the Italians.' She lifted the plunger carafe and started to pour the hot dark liquid into a cup. 'I say, isn't this rather jolly?' she laughed, pleased with herself.

'Why, I thank you kindly, Countess,' Jimmy said, obviously touched. 'American Blend – hey, dat good.' Later I asked him how it tasted and he gave a long-suffering sigh. 'Brother Fish, it taste like sheet, man!' Jimmy was forever afterwards condemned to drink the countess's coffee, always with due ceremony. 'American Blend' was her permanent gesture of love towards him.

It wasn't entirely her fault that Jimmy disliked her *Esquire* magazine coffee. He'd become accustomed to institution coffee laced with bromide to keep natural male urges at bay. He'd first encountered it when, with puberty approaching, he'd been given it in the orphanage, the coffee disguising the slightly bitter taste of bromide. This practice had been followed at Elmira Reformatory and again in the American Army. I don't recall him ever referring specifically to Frau Kraus's coffee other than in the context of the after-dinner potion she'd concocted to bring about the demise of her husband, Otto.

Over tea and coffee with Sao biscuits spread with butter and fishpaste, I brought up the subject of the story she had started in the hotel dining room a week or so previously in Launceston. 'Will you tell us the rest, please?' I asked.

'Should we not rather be doing an inventory?' she replied. 'The sooner we get started, the better, don't you think?'

'Countess, we got all ears,' Jimmy exclaimed.

'Very well then, where was I?'

'You were alone in Harbin, the city of sin,' I said, then immediately added, 'You were just fifteen and your father was crook.'

The countess looked at me, one eyebrow slightly raised. 'I promised I wouldn't and I shan't, but a Russian count does not get *crook* – he becomes unwell or very ill, the latter being the case at the time with my father. Now let me see, however shall I continue?'

'Jus' like before. It good, yoh use dem words "whorehouse" an' also yoh can say "pussy" instead o' "women's private part" 'cos dat stilted usage and dem two other words dey good light an' shade to punc-tu-ate da story an' give it a sense o' re-ality.' Jimmy's learning programme under her tuition was definitely getting a little out of hand. Although she hadn't troubled with Jimmy's idiolect, on an intellectual basis she was getting through to him loud and clear.

'Oh dear. That doesn't sound like me, I'm afraid. But you're quite correct – colloquialisms do often have that effect on narrative. Shall I continue?'

We both nodded, easing ourselves in our chairs, preparing to listen.

'Well, desperation is the mother of invention and I got a billet in a nightclub, working with the Chinese staff.'

'Excuse me, Countess, what dis billet?' Jimmy asked.

'Oh, I'm sorry, James. It means I obtained a job, a position as kitchen girl. The Russian owners could speak no Chinese and the Chinese servants no Russian, so that the waiters and the cook needed a translator. My wages barely paid the rent for our tiny room, but the major advantage was that I was fed at the club and the cook allowed me to smuggle food back to my father. Had it not been for this, we would have most certainly starved.

'Soon enough, with the continued influx of refugees, all the nightclubs took to hiring desperate young Russian women as cocktail waitresses-cum-hostesses, the emphasis very much being on "hostess". Their job was to persuade customers to drink French champagne at an outrageous price, while their own champagne glasses were filled with soda water with a tincture of cordial added to make it indistinguishable in appearance from the real thing. The girls existed solely on gratuities and the fact that their charms could be purchased to extend further into the night in a nearby hotel room. With an abundance of beautiful young Russian women available at no cost to the nightclub, all but the cook and the cleaning *amah*s were sacked and, of course, they no longer needed an interpreter.

'The proprietor's wife, Madam Olga Kolkoffski, whose husband had previously been a general in the Imperial Army, called me into the office to terminate my employment. I burst into tears at the prospect. "Please, Madam Olga, I need the salary – my father is very ill," I pleaded.

'"Ha! It is the same everywhere. People make up such lies."

'"Oh, madam, it's the truth," I begged.

'"How old are you, Nicole?"

'"Fifteen, Madam Olga," I had not yet learned to lie.

'She seemed to be thinking, then finally said, "Would you like to be a cocktail waitress, child?"

'I was taken aback. "I don't think I could charm the gentlemen into buying champagne, madam," I answered truthfully.

'"Can you dance?"

'"Oh yes, and play the piano."

'"Modern dancing?"

'I nodded, keen to impress her. "All the steps."

'"We'll see. Are you a virgin?"

Jimmy and I both shifted in our seats, but Nicole Lenoir-Jourdan continued her story.

'I was suddenly terribly embarrassed, and when I answered my voice was hardly more than a whisper. "Yes, madam." At that moment the general walked in. He was a large man with a girth that gave him the look of one of those Russian dolls you can't knock down. I suppose to keep the idiom I should say he was a bear of a man, with a blunt, bullish face, a great bulbous whisky nose, walrus moustache and a wild shag of grey hair that looked like scouring wire. In appearance he resembled a peasant and did not seem to come from good stock. Yet, it was claimed, he had been an important general and a personal favourite of the tsar. I curtsied to him as he approached, keeping my eyes glued to the floor. "Good evening, general," I said shyly, trying to conceal the fact that I'd been crying.

'He ignored me and addressed Madam Olga directly. "What's the kitchen girl doing here?" he demanded. "She ought to be with the servants!"

'"I am terminating her employment, Rudi. We no longer need a translator," Madam Olga replied. Then her tone changed. "I thought perhaps a cocktail waitress – what do you think?"

'General Rudi Alexei Kolkoffski looked down at me and grunted. "What do I think? She's got no titties." He pointed a tubby finger at me. "How old?"

'"She's fifteen," Madam Olga said, before I'd had a chance to reply.

'"*Poulet*," he grunted. "A young chicken. Give it to her – at least her barrel hasn't been reamed too large to take a cartridge like the rest of the bitches." Whereupon he walked over to a large cupboard and, withdrawing a key attached to a chain from his waistcoat pocket, unlocked it and removed a bottle of Chivas Regal. He locked the cupboard once more and lumbered towards the door. As he reached it, he turned and said, "Maybe I'll break her in for the establishment, eh, Madam Kolkoffski?"

'I could see he thought this was very funny and he went off chortling to himself, his huge shoulders moving up and down and no doubt his stomach wobbling with mirth. Terrified out of my wits, I observed his departing back, too young to know if he was truly joking. For months afterwards I would have nightmares where his huge and disgusting corpulence lay on top of me.

'"Well you've got the job, child," Madam Olga said. "Do you have an evening gown?"

'"No, Madam Olga."

'"Surely, from your mother?"

'"She's dead, madam. There's just me and my father, Count Nikolai Lenoir."

'"Yes, well, titles don't mean anything any more. I have two countesses on the floor, and the bartender, Petrus Chernikoff, is also a count and not a very good bartender – he keeps overfilling the champagne glasses and forgets to water the gin. The second-hand shops are full of evening gowns. Find yourself one that fits and let me know the price – we'll take it out of your tips."

'"My salary, Madam Olga. How much will it be?"

'"Salary? You won't get a salary, child."

'"But . . . but how will we live?" I asked her tearfully.

'"Tips. You work for tips, my dear."

'I hesitated. "I don't think I could be a hostess, Madam Olga."

'"Why not? You said you could dance, and you're a pretty little thing – the rest will come naturally. We Russians can't afford to be choosy any more."

'I was trembling, but stood my ground. "Thank you, Madam Olga." I could feel the hot tears running down my cheeks. "But I can't," I whispered.

'"Suit yourself, child. But you soon will – life makes us do lots of things we think we'll never do. Take my advice – this place is better than most. Fifteen is not so young – do you have your periods yet?"

'"Yes, madam," I sniffed.

'"There you are, you're a woman now." But I remained firm and I shook my head. "You'll be back," she said. "There are no more fairytales for little Russian girls – the prince does not appear on a white charger to carry her away."

'"No, Madam Olga."

'Just then the maître d knocked on the door. "May I see you, madam?"

'"What is it, Yuri?" Madam Olga asked.

'"The pianist – he's drunk again, madam."

'"Throw him out – he's rubbish! Nothing but trouble, that one!" Madam Olga said, suddenly furious.

'"But tonight – the cabaret?" the maître d protested.

'She sighed. "Can't you sober him up?" she demanded. "It's only seven o'clock – the first show is at nine."

'"I can try, madam, but he's pretty far gone. The vodka's gone to his legs."

'"He doesn't need his legs, he sits down!" she said impatiently.

'"Yes, madam, but last night he fell off his piano stool."

'"Do *something*! she yelled. "Must I do everything around this place!" She was suddenly aware of me standing there, sniffing. "What? You still here, girl?" she shouted. "I thought I told you to go!"

'"I can play all the cabaret tunes, Madam Olga," I said, shaking like a leaf.

'"Don't talk absolute rubbish, child. Now please go, I'm busy."

'I walked slowly from the office, Yuri, the maître d, stepping aside to let me pass. He'd spoken to me on several occasions in a friendly manner when he'd needed to translate something to one of the Chinese staff, but now he ignored me. He'd seen too many desperate refugees come and go and was probably clinging onto his own job for dear life.

'I walked into the semi-dark club, where the air still carried the pungent smell of last night's liquor and cigarette smoke. Small electric lamps with chintz shades sat at the centre of each table and provided the only source of light in the club, except for a red strip of neon across the top of the bar that spelled "The General's Retreat", the name of the establishment. When the cabaret came on, a spotlight worked across a small stage constantly changing colour, which was wholly unflattering to the performers.

'Slumped sobbing over one of the small tables, with his head and shoulders caught in a circle of light, was the drunken pianist. I was too caught up in my own misery to feel sorry for him and started to walk towards the door, a lump in my throat. Then, on a sudden impulse,

I turned back and walked over to the piano, a Steinway baby grand resplendent in brilliant scarlet lacquer. The club was deserted except for the barman, who was polishing glasses and arranging bottles, and the maître d, still in Madam Olga's office. The hostesses usually came in around seven-thirty to do their make-up and change into their evening gowns in time for the doors to open at eight. It had been a while since I'd played but, like you, Jack, I have a good ear for a tune and it wasn't exactly Mozart or Chopin. I sat at the piano and began to play, tears streaming down my face. I have no idea how long I played, but certainly for quite some time.

'"That will be enough!" I suddenly heard Madam Olga say from across the floor. "You have the job."'

'Hey – dat good, Countess. Yoh got some luck,' Jimmy said, happy for her. We'd both been hanging on her every word and I don't know about Jimmy, but I was dead anxious she was going to have to take the job as a hostess. Nicole Lenoir-Jourdan as a child prostitute was more than my imagination could bear.

'I was just a tiny little thing and all the evening dresses I tried on in the various second-hand shops made me look laughable, like a child dressing up in her mother's clothes. Eventually, Madam Olga consulted the redoubtable general. "Hmph, schoolgirl," he grunted.

'"You are a genius, Rudi," Madam Olga exclaimed ecstatically, bringing her hands up to her large breasts.'

Nicole Lenoir-Jourdan sighed. 'So they dressed me like an English schoolgirl in a very short gym frock, Panama hat, black stockings and a pair of button-over black shoes. They plaited my blonde hair and tied it with ribbons to match the colour of the Steinway. I was made to wear bright-red lipstick and a little mascara and kohl on my eyes, my pale cheeks slightly rouged. I suppose it was an improvement on the evening gown, but every time I glanced into the mirror I got a horrid shock and I'd scrub my face for half an hour before taking a rickshaw home in the small hours of the morning. Of course, at the time, I had no idea of the sexual connotations of my costume.

'Anyway, the schoolgirl concept was sufficiently bizarre to take off in quite a big way. I was billed as "Little Countess, the Schoolgirl Maestro" and soon the General's Retreat became one of the leading supper clubs in Harbin. I began receiving *billets-doux*, that is to say, love notes, from male patrons. These usually included a five- and occasionally a ten-dollar bill. Mexican dollars were the stable currency at the time in Harbin and Shanghai, the Chinese currency being practically worthless. One Mexican dollar was worth around thirty-five cents American, or two shillings in English money.'

Nicole Lenoir-Jourdan stopped and felt the side of the teapot. 'Oh dear, it's lukewarm. I'll get some hot water.' She rose and went into the little kitchenette adjoining her small office.

Jimmy shook his head sympathetically. 'Sheet, Brother Fish – dis sad, man!'

I agreed, but I was also beginning to see where Nicole Lenoir-Jourdan had acquired her practical sense of money and the need to look after it. While we didn't know just how well off she was, and might never know, she lived a frugal life for someone seemingly so refined. She drove a little Ford Prefect, and while it was unusual at that time for a woman to own a car, hers was the smallest and cheapest you could buy – hardly ostentatious. While the letterpress printer that produced the *Gazette* must have cost a pretty penny, even second-hand, she certainly didn't flash or throw her money around, and lived in a modest cottage on the cliffs facing out to sea.

She returned with a jug of hot water and offered me another cup of tea and Jimmy another plunger coffee, and seemed disappointed when he refused. Taking her freshly topped-up cup to her lips, she sipped.

'Ah, that's much better. Now, where was I? Oh yes. I soon learned to respond to the overeffusive male patrons between sets. I would sit at the table of a patron who had been particularly generous with a larger-denomination note wrapped in his *billet-doux* and drink orangeade. The fact that I sipped on soft drink while coyly refusing their offers of French champagne seemed to further excite them. I was the real thing, forbidden fruit. I quickly learned to choose my mark – if the promise of a big tip seemed forthcoming I would sit on a patron's lap, slapping roving hands away and pretending to be very cross to the point of tears if he dared attempt to take a liberty.. This seemed to drive them mad with further desire and, if they were sufficiently inebriated, almost tearful remorse. Either way, it invariably resulted in a very generous tip, whereupon I would skip away to play my next set at the Steinway. It was dangerous posturing, but I didn't know any better. I guess God looks after the young and naive.

'My mother had always said that some day I would become a singer – claimed I had a pure soprano voice. So I began to add singing to my repertoire, at first some of the lovely Russian lullabies and folk songs I'd learned as a child. Then I included those contemporary songs that suited a young soprano voice. To a homesick Russian, songs about Mother Russia and songs he'd heard in the cradle created a sensation – grown men would often weep with nostalgia, which opened purses like nothing else.'

Nicole Lenoir-Jourdan looked up with a smile, and Jimmy said, 'She hustling, man! She da sugar chile!'

'Indeed – the more lachrymose the display, the greater the forthcoming gratuity. By the standards of the time I was making a good living as a club pianist and singer. There remained only one setback. Even though we'd moved into better accommodation, two rooms of our own with a bathroom and kitchen we shared with three other couples, my father didn't seem to be getting any better. His deep melancholy seemed to have become a permanent part of him and he would spend hours in bed hidden under the blankets or simply sit staring at the wall, occasionally protesting that he was useless and I would be much better off if he were dead. I felt terribly guilty that I couldn't spend more time with him – the nightclub would often stay open until four a.m. and I'd sleep from six in the morning until one p.m., then do the shopping. It had been suggested to me by the three couples with whom we shared kitchen and bathroom facilities that we jointly employ a cook and cleaning *amah*, and I had readily agreed to this. But my father then decided he couldn't digest Chinese food and I was forced to cook Russian meals for him. This entailed tedious hours of shopping, and after I'd cooked his dinner I would have to be at the nightclub by seven in the evening to rehearse.

'We could now afford a visit by Dr Chung, the doctor who "looked after" the girls at the club. I now realise what he looked after, as Madam Kolkoffski insisted that every girl who worked at the club must have an examination "down there" once a week. Dr Chung was a little man who wore spats resting on highly polished boots, argyle socks, beige trousers, and a mandarin jacket in black. It had the effect of making him appear half-Western and half-Chinese, which was exactly the look he wanted, having once studied at Guys Hospital in London. He was delighted that I spoke Cantonese and refused to charge me for the visit. He examined my father and then reported back to me. "He's got the great sorrow that I cannot cure," he confessed. "But I recommend the opium pipe – at least it will give him pleasant dreams, Miss Countess."

'"Will he get well again, Dr Chung?" I asked him.

'"Sometimes, yes and sometimes, no," he said, spreading his hands, his answer a typical Chinese response. Then he added sternly, "You must not take, you must not smoke opium – it is not for you!"

'While I was aware of the dangers of opium, it could hardly have made my father any worse than he was. In fact, it sometimes appeared to improve his mood – and for an hour or so he'd be his old self again. Opium was readily available from the rickshaw boys who waited outside the club for patrons, and was not expensive. Many of the hostesses in the club had taken to using it to solve their problems. At one a.m. the hostesses were free to leave the club and those girls who had not managed to get a paying partner for the night would take it to go into a dreamlike state where they would forget their fall from grace and their misery.

'Then fairly late one night four Chinese men entered the club, and soon it was buzzing with excitement. The girls hurried into the dressing room to adjust their make-up and straighten their hair. This was unusual – although some of the powerful Chinese businessmen occasionally came into the club, they were afforded no special treatment. If anything, they received slightly the opposite – many of the girls wouldn't go near them. Yuri passed me in a terrible tizz, flapping a white table napkin. I continued playing the piano, but called after him. "What's happening, Yuri?"

'"Oh my God. It's Yu Ya-ching and he's with Smallpox 'Million-Dollar' Yang, Chang Shig-liang and Du Yu-sen, three French Concession gangsters, and we're not supposed to know who they are – but all the rickshaw boys dropped to the ground as they arrived and the Chinese doorman, Wang Lee, nearly had a heart attack." He said this almost in one breath. "I've got to go, Nicole. They drink brandy, and the stuff we serve at the bar is excrement." He hurried off towards the office and passed me a couple of minutes later with the general in tow carrying a bottle of VSOP French cognac, no doubt of a suitably impressive age.

'I was none the wiser, and on a whim I played and sang a folk song Ah Lai had taught me. According to Ah Lai my voice was ideal for Chinese music and she would clap her hands when I sang to her and say I had the intonation and timing just right. I followed the first folk song with another and then, thinking I might be reprimanded, reverted to a popular Noël Coward number. Soon afterwards Yuri came up to the piano panting with excitement. "They want you to sing the Chinese songs again," he said breathlessly.

'"I know several more," I offered.

'"No! Sing the same again! Mr Yu says he's never heard the second song more beautifully sung."

'I had quite an extensive repertoire of Chinese folk songs Ah Lai had taught me. In the eighteen months I'd spent in her village I'd learned all the songs for the region, and several more. So I played and sang the two I'd already performed, then continued with three more.'

'Did you know "The Fish Song"?' I burst out, unable to contain myself.

She laughed. 'Yes, of course. It is known by fisherfolk throughout

China, but there are different versions.'

'But you never said!' I cried, astonished at her admission.

'That would have been extremely rude of me, Jack. "The Fish Song" belongs to both of you.'

'Dat why yoh can trans-late dem lyrics for da governor daughters, easy as pie,' Jimmy laughed.

We were getting away from her story, and while it had been me who'd interrupted her flow I was anxious for her to continue. 'You were singing the Chinese songs – then what happened?' I asked, sounding perhaps a little rude.

'Well, I'd hardly concluded the songs when Yuri arrived with a wine glass holding a hundred-dollar note. "This comes with the compliments of Mr Yu, who hopes you might join his table," he announced. "Oh, you lucky, lucky girl!"'

'Dat like he saying, "Girl, get yo' sassy ass ovah der" – dis cat he a big-time gangsta, who got da bread he gonna spread!' Jimmy filled in.

'Well, something like that. Anyway, Mr Yu was a notorious Shanghai businessman and real Chinese big boss of Shanghai. The other three were known gangsters who, I was later to learn, were referred to as "The Three Musketeers of the French Concession". They were known to be exporting opium, running the sing-song houses – the translated Chinese name for brothels – kidnapping, running gambling dens and various other illegal oriental enterprises, including "collecting taxes" from the coolie boats using the river port. This practice is known in China as "squeeze" and is practised by everyone, from the lowest-ranking house servant to the highest government official. Squeeze isn't bribery as we know it in the West – it's just skimming a bit off the top of everything that passes your way.

'I have to confess I was a bit nervous approaching Mr Yu and his colleagues – I couldn't imagine having to sit on Mr Yu's knee. I brought my hands together and bowed my head in the accepted Chinese manner required when a woman of lower rank meets a dignitary. I was invited to sit down and did so, but not before I had filled their glasses from the bottle of cognac. When Mr Yu and the three gangsters with him realised that I spoke fluent Cantonese they were simply delighted, and we soon got on like a house on fire. "How old are you, Little Countess?" Mr Yu asked. I told him, not expecting any reaction. To the Chinese, a fifteen-year-old girl is already a woman, but Mr Yu knew this not to be the case in the West. "It is too young for a place like this?" It was both a comment and a question – which is very Chinese, as it allows one to respond either way, to ignore or react.

'"I play the piano and sing. I am not a hostess, *loh yeh*," I answered, using the Chinese for "my lord".

'"It is not usual for a westerner to speak Cantonese – even less, to sing Chinese music with a good voice and with all the right intonations?"

'It was another open question. "My *amah* taught me," I answered, giving little away. Yuri arrived personally with lemonade and placed the tall glass in front of me with some ceremony, adding a slice of lemon and placing a napkin beside it. "You will drink brandy with us, Little Countess?" Mr Yu asked.

'"That would be unseemly, and not something a lady would do," I replied, my eyes respectfully averted. He had a deeply lined yellow face with large purple bags under his eyes. Central Casting would have grabbed him for the lead in any feature film requiring an inscrutable Chinese gangster or war lord. But at that moment he was smiling, and had a surprising twinkle in his eye.

'Quite suddenly, Smallpox "Million Dollar" Yang stuck his finger into my lemonade and sucked it. "No gin," he stated in English, smacking his lips.

'Chinese manners are difficult to negotiate. A woman, even an equal in class (and as a despised Russian refugee I was certainly *not* his equal), must be careful how she behaves in front of a Chinese man of substance. I reached over and stuck my finger delicately into Smallpox "Million Dollar" Yang's brandy glass and brought it up to my tongue, trying very hard not to grimace at the ghastly taste. "French Cognac, VSOP," I said in English.

'There was a moment's stunned silence. Then Mr Yu clapped his hands gleefully and broke into a spontaneous chortle, and two of the other Chinese men immediately followed suit, the exception being Smallpox "Million Dollar" Yang. His wide, flat, severely pockmarked face clearly did not accept my return gesture as an appropriate rebuttal. Had it not been for the presence of Mr Yu, I fear I would have been soundly rebuked. However, Mr Yu was delighted. "You must come to Shanghai, Little Countess, and I will look after you!"

'"I cannot, *loh yeh*. My father is gravely ill," I replied. "I thank you nevertheless for the great honour of your patronage."

'"Some time," he said. "You speak English?"

'"Yes, sir – and French, my mother was French."

'"Cantonese, English and French – you will do well in Shanghai." He hadn't bothered to mention Russian, a language of no consequence in the life of the city. "When you come you have only to ask for Yu Ya-ching. I will not forget – you have a brave heart, and good manners." He looked over to Smallpox "Million Dollar" Yang, and then back to me, and said, "Your Chinese name will be 'No Gin'. It will be good joss." Joss, of course, is a Chinese concept of luck, fortune and destiny.

'Smallpox "Million Dollar" Yang broke into a broad smile, accepting the congratulations of the other two gangsters. Mr Yu had cleverly restored his dignity and at the same time he had gained face. I turned to the repulsive-looking gangster and bowed my head. "I am honoured to receive this name from you, Taipan Yang," I said, thus giving him the credit for Mr Yu's perspicacity.

'It was the house custom to leave an empty wineglass in the centre of the table as a not-very-subtle reminder that a gratuity was expected. Mr Yu now produced his thick wallet. "I have a great personal favour to ask, Little Countess?"

'I immediately stiffened. "I am not a hostess, *loh yeh*," I said, unable to hide my anxiety.

'Mr Yu laughed. "And I am not a seducer of schoolgirls." He held out a one-hundred-dollar note, and with the thumb and forefinger of his free hand indicated about four inches. "Please. A lock of your hair."

'I sighed with relief. A hundred dollars for a small lock of hair was a generous offer. My long blonde plaits fell down to my waist and there was certainly more than enough to spare. I signalled to Yuri and asked him for a pair of scissors. When he returned I undid the end of one of my plaits, separated the hair carefully and cut the required length. Then I carefully bunched the small lock of hair, clipped the top with a hairpin and handed it to Mr Yu, re-plaiting the loose hair back in place. Whereupon he placed the one-hundred-dollar note into the wineglass in the centre of the table. Then he looked pointedly at Smallpox "Million Dollar" Yang. "For the privilege of naming her," he said, indicating the wineglass. Smallpox "Million Dollar" Yang grinned and placed the equivalent amount in the glass. Not wishing to lose face, the other two gangsters promptly followed suit.

Four hundred dollars was more – much more – than I could earn in six months, but I somehow knew that I shouldn't take it, even though the urge to grab it greedily and offer my profuse thanks almost overwhelmed me. Seeing the four hundred-dollar notes resting in the glass set my heart racing and I could feel a great thumping in my chest. I was taking a ridiculous risk and stood to lose a fortune. I told myself I would never see the four men again, so why was I being so obviously, almost insanely, stupid? If I walked away without their tip I took the risk of offending them, so they might return the money to their pockets. I had no right to the "face" that leaving the money implied. I was a nobody. Even to the Chinese rickshaw boys, the Russian refugees were deracinated and well beneath other Europeans in China – we were pariahs, poor and thought to be competing with the women in the sing-song houses. If I took the money these four men could think no less of me than they already did. Yet I resisted and walked away, holding my back as straight as I possibly could, feeling quite weak at the knees and inwardly cursing my own stubborn stupidity.

'I returned to the Steinway and played another bracket, which included two more Chinese folk songs. Shortly afterwards I saw the four of them leave, and a minute or so latter Yuri arrived with the glass containing the money and I almost cried from relief.

'"You were magnificent, darling," he said admiringly.

'One of the hundred-dollar notes was missing. "And *you* are a thief, Yuri Petrof!" I replied.

'He shrugged, not attempting to lie. "Pay-back time, darling," he replied tartly. He pointed to the Steinway. "If I hadn't entered Madam Olga's office at precisely the right moment you wouldn't have this cushy job." I guess he had a point – I was learning that in China, everyone takes a cut.

'I was overjoyed, practically jumping out of my skin as I scrubbed the make-up from my face that night. I kept hugging myself, not quite able to believe my good fortune as the rickshaw boy drove me home in the early hours of the morning. Father and I would be able to leave our shared accommodation and I'd make him a comfortable home with our own bathroom and kitchen. I would also be able to afford hospital treatment for him. The "Little Countess" was learning how to survive, and I must say I felt rather pleased with myself as I climbed the rickety stairs to our rooms. I well recall the cacophony of the several hundreds – nay thousands – of roosters in the Chinese city that heralded the approaching dawn, rending the smoky, acrid air and turning it into avian mayhem. As I reached the top of the stairs I felt under my skirt to reassure myself, for the umpteenth time, that the four hundred-dollar notes (three presented to me in the wineglass, less Yuri's cut, and one presented to me earlier, at the piano) and the other tips I'd earned were safely tucked inside my bloomers.

'I inserted my key into the lock in the door of the rooms where we were staying, turning it ever so slowly, thinking to open it quietly so as not to disturb my father. But the door resisted. Then, as I pushed harder, it opened a tiny crack and seemed to bang against a heavy object. I was forced to put my shoulder to the door until it opened sufficiently for me to see a table had been placed against it. I pushed again, grunting with the effort, finally forcing the table far enough away from the door for me to squeeze through the gap. I could see the square-cut ends of the legs of an overturned chair that lay on the table and then, hanging from above, my father's pale, un-stockinged feet, one leg slightly longer than the other. I need not have been concerned about disturbing his sleep – his body was suspended from the neck by a piece of rope that hung from a wooden beam that ran across the ceiling.'

# CHAPTER EIGHTEEN

## *The Strawberry Milkshake Love Affair*

The story that led to Count Lenoir's suicide left me stunned. *Holy shit, what now? What do I say in a situation like this?*

I looked at Jimmy, who sat with his chin resting on his chest, eyes downcast, but as usual he was the first to recover. He looked up at Nicole Lenoir-Jourdan and, shaking his head slowly, said, 'Dat too sad, Countess. Dat jus' too very sad, ma'am,' his mellifluous voice striking exactly the right tone.

'Yes,' was all I could think to say. 'Yes, I agree.' What a lame response.

'Thank you both,' she replied, smiling. 'It all happened another lifetime ago, and I was terribly distraught at the time. But knowing myself to be absolutely alone in the world I was able to see my life more clearly, and staying where I was held little attraction for me. I decided that I must leave Harbin and travel to Shanghai. Perhaps this was a foolish impulse – I had no reasons beyond my recent sad memories to leave Manchuria. I continued to attract patrons to the club and Madam Olga was anxious that I remain, even to the point of offering to give me a small salary. But I was still a child, and children do not see things in such terms. When I insisted that I must go the general lost his temper and said I was nothing but a little . . .' she hesitated, and then said haltingly, 'cockteaser.'

Jimmy laughed, and clapped his hands. 'Ahee! Yoh bet yo' sweet ass, Countess. Ain't no shame in dat word, dat time a girl gotta hustle. Yoh done good!' Then he added, 'Yoh got dat classy red piano an' yoh da best in da music an' singin' hustlin' bizee-ness!'

Nicole Lenoir-Jourdan smiled and looked fondly at Jimmy. 'What a blessed relief. It's taken me thirty-two years to repeat that cruel little word.' She then added brightly, 'And now I have a newspaper to get out at the end of the week. I'm afraid we'll have to leave it there for the moment, as I have a great deal to do. Perhaps you'll both have dinner with me on Saturday night and I'll cook Chinese, and then we really have to start thinking about buying a boat.'

'But you will tell us the rest of the story?' I asked anxiously. 'You can't just leave it there.'

'It all happened so very long ago,' she sighed. 'It's history now.'

'It da his-tory we gotta know, Countess. It da beginning o' our partnership his-tory.'

'Very well – although I must say I'm surprised you both have the patience to listen, after what you have been through yourselves.'

I looked up to see if she was being serious, and she obviously was. What's more, the invitation to dinner was something else again. I couldn't remember if anyone on the island, with perhaps the exception of Reverend Daintree, had ever entered her cottage, much less had dinner with her. We had come a long way in our new relationship.

But the promised Saturday-night dinner wasn't to be. Later that week Jimmy received a notification from the American Consulate in Melbourne to come in immediately to see them. Included in the letter was an air-travel ticket that indicated he was to leave the island in forty-eight hours with the instruction to wear civilian clothes but to pack his kit because he was going back to America to be demobbed. They also included a postal order for twenty pounds. Jimmy cashed it and gave Gloria ten pounds, saying ten was plenty to get him to Melbourne and America.

It was obvious that the Australian Government had lost no time telling their Yank counterparts that they had located their man, explaining that they'd finally found him on a remote island in the middle of Bass Strait. Come to think of it, in a curious way the Certificate of Exemption had not only allowed our government to save face, but also helped the Americans. Though several weeks overdue for demobbing, Jimmy was still officially in the US Army and, of course, remained an American citizen. So he could be used for propaganda purposes by their government while still being in uniform. He had just about everything going for him. He was the token black and the model soldier who had frequently risked his life while in captivity, resisted the communists and behaved in a wholly honourable way. Jimmy was the example they were looking for – a warrior who had honoured his flag and his nation.

Ironically the black boy, the nigger who, until recently, had been considered by much of the American brass as fit only to carry a pick and shovel, was to be paraded by his military superiors as a shining example of the triumph of the American spirit over adversity. Jimmy was proof of the integrity of the American soldier when confronted by the forces of evil. The coloured orphan, delinquent street kid, sent to Korea by the American courts as an alternative to sentencing him to prison, had proved to be the American soldier the nation was preparing to award one of its highest decorations for heroism.

By any standards Jimmy was a hero. He hadn't won his medal with a sudden rush of blood to the head or, as I had done, with adrenaline pumping through his veins in the heat of battle. He'd been awarded this high national honour for being a human being of exceptional character and courage. I was ashamed to think that this hadn't been enough for us. Australia had rejected a man of his calibre, permitting him to remain only while he proved useful and profitable to the country. We would never accept him as a citizen because we based our values on the colour of a man's skin, rather than his character and integrity.

Who were we to judge America? We were certainly no less racist. '*Sorry, mate, you failed the language test. Didn't you know, fluent Gaelic is a basic requirement for immigration to Australia?'* Then, when we'd been faced with the possibility of a huge international scandal, we'd made Jimmy bare his black arse so that we could judge it more than seventy-five per cent white, just to save face. And if Jimmy had endured a difficult, race-tainted childhood in America, then what about our own Johnny Gordon, the Aboriginal forward scout in our platoon? He'd led the way on every patrol knowing he would be the first to die in an ambush, and had done so in my arms on the night I was captured. Johnny could have bared his arse till the cows came home and we wouldn't have given him the right to vote or even move his place of residence from one town to another without permission from a bureaucrat like Clarence Cuffe. This, in a country his ancestors had inhabited for 35 000 years. He didn't have the right in the town in which he was born to enter the local pub through the front door, or to have a quiet beer in the RSL Club as a soldier member who had fought with great distinction for his country in World War II. I could hardly boast that Jimmy was coming to a country where his character and not his skin would be the deciding factor on how he was welcomed and treated.

I am ashamed to say Australians had never marched in the streets for Johnny's rights, as Americans were to do. We'd all rejoiced at Jimmy's temporary acceptance, hailing it as a victory for justice. Justice, my arse! In fact, the very existence of the policy was proof of the defeat of fundamental justice. Furthermore, the White Australia Policy was only possible because of a tacit permission by Australian citizens, myself included, that allowed it to remain on our statute books. I had no right to point a finger at America or South Africa or anywhere that practised racism – we were very much tarred with the same brush.

With all the brouhaha going on in the American press about the collaboration with the communist enemy by prisoners of war in Korea, on their return to America every serviceman who'd been in a POW camp was thoroughly investigated and some were finally prosecuted. I am happy to say that Corporal Steve O'Rourke, 'da man' who'd attacked Jimmy and murdered those two gravely weakened soldiers suffering from dysentery by tossing them out of the barracks at night where they froze to death, got twenty years imprisonment.

We were later to learn that Jimmy's name had come up so frequently during the interrogation that he'd been listed for heroism long before the final prisoners-of-war interrogation was completed. The US had initially decided to award Jimmy the medal for what had happened in the North Korean hospital cave, but there had been so many subsequent incidents reported that involved heroism and personal risk to life that he was to receive a silver oak-leaf cluster to signify that he had won the Soldier's Medal on five separate occasions.

I was later told my own name had come up fairly frequently during the interrogations, and the Americans had recommended that our military might want to do something. Well, we didn't have anything like the Soldier's Medal, only the George Cross, the civilian equivalent of the Victoria Cross, and the George Medal, only slightly less valorous. They certainly weren't going to give either of these to some wanker who played 'Chattanoogie Shoe Shine Boy' on the harmonica! Though a year or so later I was mentioned in dispatches, signified by a bronze oak-leaf emblem attached to the campaign ribbon, adding to the bit of chest fruit salad I'd acquired. Once again I was the dubious recipient of an honour I wouldn't have earned had I been left to my own devices.

We had a bit of an impromptu party at home for Jimmy's leaving the island. At least that's how it began – a few quiet ales with the family, Nicole Lenoir-Jourdan and some of the girls who'd been especially generous to Jimmy. The amazing thing about Jimmy's affairs of the heart – or perhaps of a somewhat lower part of his anatomy – was that the island girls seemed to regard him as a special treat to be shared around. Of course tongues were wagging everywhere, but the gossip, for the most part, was more generous than bitchy – which Gloria contended was a miracle, as the island hadn't yet stopped gossiping about our grandfather's amorous generosity to lonely fishermen's wives. Some of the girls, Jimmy later told me, would beg him not to use a condom. I guess a six-foot nine-inch black bloke didn't come along that often in a girl's life. By contrast, before I met Wendy my puny five foot five inches of freckles and gingerness had largely kept me sex-deprived for most of my post-pubescent life. Predictably, news of the farewell party spread and eventually a couple of hundred people turned up to say goodbye to Jimmy, all laden with grog and supplies. It went all night and would have continued into the morning if Jimmy hadn't had to catch the plane.

Nicole Lenoir-Jourdan drove Jimmy and me to the airport. I sat in the back hugging his army kit and Jimmy sat in the front, the passenger seat pushed back as far as it would go and still his knees seeming to almost touch the roof. On the way we discussed registering a company with the three of us nominated as the directors and Nicole Lenoir-Jourdan as company secretary. 'What shall we call it?' she asked.

Quick as a shot Jimmy, who can't have had a hangover as bad as my own, said, 'Ogoya – dat da name.'

'O'Goya? Goya was a Spanish painter, but I've never heard of an Irishman with that name,' she replied.

'It mean "Operation Get Off Yo' Ass",' Jimmy said.

'Oh, I don't think any of us can be accused of being lazy,' she laughed. 'If we must have an acronym, what about QIFE – the Queen Island Fishing Enterprises?'

'Nah, it gotta be Ogoya. Yoh ask Brother Fish why dat so, Countess.'

'Yes, Jimmy's right – but please don't ask me to explain it right now,' I said. 'It's because of something that happened when we were prisoners of war in the hospital cave.'

'I shall await your explanation with interest, Jack,' she said. 'By the way, if you should get the chance, James, I've taken the opportunity to consult with the Tasmanian Fisheries Act and Regulations Department and several experts they recommended I write to. Between them I've written the specifications for a fishing boat. It occurred to me that it might be cheaper to buy one in America than to have one built here. Perhaps you can make some inquiries while you're there?'

At first I couldn't quite believe what I'd heard. I began to flush deeply, and the sudden rush of blood to my face caused my head to practically lift off my shoulders. Nicole Lenoir-Jourdan had gone ahead and written the specifications for our boat without even consulting us – me in particular, for while Jimmy didn't know a lot about fishing boats, I'd been around them all my life. It was a slap in the face and I could only think it must be deliberate – she didn't trust me, didn't think I knew enough to participate. As my anger rose I told myself this was the beginning of the takeover I'd feared all along. *What the fuck does she know about fishing, anyway? Better end it right now, no more partnership*. Sure, it would be tough without her money, but I wasn't going to live the remainder of my life as the little boy sitting meekly on the library floor.

'Hey, yoh and Brother Fish – yoh been discussin' dis boat behine mah back, Countess?' I knew immediately this was a ploy – Jimmy on a white charger riding to the rescue. Thank Christ for my hangover, or I might have let fly at Nicole Lenoir-Jourdan before he could get another word in, had I the courage. Jimmy laughed. 'I don't mine dat yoh gone talk together. Boats ain't nothin' I knows nothin' 'bout. I gone told Brother Fish jus' one spe-si-fication he gotta know, dis dat da bunk it big enough foh me. Brother Fish, he done discuss dat wid yoh yet, Countess?'

'Well, no, there's been no discussion. It is just that I am anxious to get things going and the opportunity arose when I was obliged to talk to the Tasmanian Fisheries Department on quite another matter we were to run in the *Gazette*, so I grabbed the chance,' she replied.

Jimmy gave a short laugh. 'Brother Fish an' me, we done survive da POW sit-u-ation 'cos we always talk 'bout every-thin', make sure we done both agree. Now we da three mus-ket-teers, it da same.' He said it quietly, but I saw Nicole Lenoir-Jourdan's neck begin to colour.

There was a moment's silence. 'Oh, dear. Do forgive me, Jack!' she cried, immediately recognising Jimmy's quiet rebuke. 'It's just that I am so accustomed to doing things on my own.' She hesitated. 'No, that's being cowardly – making excuses for myself. I don't know what to say other than I'm sorry, and promise not to do it again.' She sounded genuinely distressed.

'S'all right,' was all I could think to say. Not a very gracious reaction, I admit. Then I stupidly added as an afterthought, 'Most of the Fisheries blokes have boarded a few fishing boats in their time, but I doubt they've done a good week's fishing in their lives.'

'Countess, I gonna lose dat letter iffen yoh give it me now. Tell you what. I gonna cable yoh my address in da States an' yoh gonna send me a letter, eh?'

'Yes, quite right. Thank you, James,' she replied in a small voice.

'Yoh an' Brother Fish, you gotta dis-cuss what we gonna need. I don't know nothin' 'bout what's good, so include me out.'

We'd arrived at the airport so, thankfully, couldn't discuss the incident any further. But we'd hardly managed to disengage ourselves from the tiny Ford Prefect when there was great yahooing and laughter as Percy Pig's ute pulled up with eight girls in the back and Dora Kelly behind the wheel. She must have 'borrowed' it while he was away cray fishing. They were all pretty pissed, including Dora, and they crowded around Jimmy, following us into the terminal hugging and kissing him and generally being pains in the arse. In the end, there was only just enough time for the two of us to say our goodbyes. Jimmy laughed as he hugged me. 'Next time when I come back I gonna wear me one dem back-to-front priest collars. See yoh soon, Brother Fish.' He shook my hand. 'Yoh my good brother.'

'Yeah, mate, look after yerself. See ya soon,' I said, trying to sound casual. I remembered how I'd felt after we'd been released as prisoners of war and when we'd been sent to separate hospitals in Japan. Now it was the same feeling all over again. Cory and Steve were my brothers, my own flesh and blood, but I didn't begin to feel the same way about them as I did about Jimmy Oldcorn.

I dreaded the drive back to town alone with Nicole Lenoir-Jourdan. She might apologise again and all I wanted to do was go to the dunny and throw up. Like Alf, I wasn't good with the grog – I was too small and light of frame, a four-beer screamer, and I was only just hanging in. Then Dora Kelly saved me by falling on her arse trying to get back into the driver's seat of Percy Pig's ute. In the name of the family I told her she wasn't fit to drive, and I'd take them all back.

'Will you please call in at the *Gazette* tomorrow, Jack?' Nicole Lenoir-Jourdan asked as we went our separate ways.

'I've got three days on a boat,' I told her. 'I'll call in when I get back.'

'I'd like to make amends,' she said quietly, so the girls couldn't hear.

I guess if you wait long enough there's a first time for everything. But Nicole Lenoir-Jourdan apologising to me was some sort of miracle. 'It's okay,' I replied, this time meaning it.

You're kept pretty busy on a cray boat, going from dawn to dusk and often well after that. You have to have your wits about you most of the time, so there wasn't a lot of time to think about the boat we should have. But I'd been on enough bad boats in my life, ones that had been adapted, more or less, to suit the job at hand. Just about every fishing boat is some sort of compromise because of the usual lack of money. Boats are often inherited, some for two or three generations. Passed from father to son, like people they grow old and infirm – even crotchety. They seldom catch up with the latest technology or are ideally suited to the job at hand. So I knew pretty well what we *didn't* want. Which was, as far as I was concerned, half the problem solved.

Ever since it had materialised that we'd be able to get a proper boat I'd been thinking about it and asking questions. Steve and Cory were by now very experienced fishermen, and a great help. Steve, in particular, had taken his engineer's certificate by correspondence and knew about the correct outboard combinations and ratios and other mechanical aspects. I was confident there were enough people I trusted on the island to ask if we didn't know something. I think this was probably why I'd been blown out of the water when Nicole Lenoir-Jourdan had gone ahead and written up a set of specifications without talking to me first.

Besides, no bastard in the Fisheries Department would have a clue about this kind of practical information, and I wondered who the so-called other experts they'd recommended to her were. Fisheries inspectors only see a boat in terms of safety equipment and, of course, the legitimacy of the catch in the hold. Which is fair enough, I suppose, but any fisherman will tell you that on a boat forty-five foot or less, if you have state-of-the-art safety you can't always have absolute efficiency. A bigger boat wasn't going to happen – the 14 000 pounds Nicole Lenoir-Jourdan was prepared to outlay was a king's ransom anyway. Which brought the next tricky problem to mind. *Was it really her boat, meaning we'd have to eventually pay her the money back?* She'd suggested it was her way of buying in, but what precisely did that mean? Was a loan of the capital the cost of the partnership? Or did we own the boat and gear jointly? I was glad of the three days out to sea so that I could clear my head and sort out the questions I needed to ask her.

When we got back to the island Nicole Lenoir-Jourdan had left a note to say she had gone unexpectedly to Launceston on *Gazette* business. She suggested a belated dinner on the following evening, saying that we'd have another when Jimmy returned. She also mentioned that being in Launceston would give her a chance to get some of the ingredients she needed from a Chinese restaurant she trusted, and she also hoped to persuade Wendy to have lunch with her while she was there. Her note was warm and friendly, and I smiled when she signed herself 'Yours often foolishly, Nicole'. Nicole Lenoir-Jourdan eating humble pie was something I never thought I'd witness, and 'foolish' wasn't a word you'd associate with her.

Again I was glad of the postponement. It would allow me to make notes of the many things that had occurred to me while out at sea, which would show her I knew what I was talking about. I considered doing a bit of an initial sulk, making her work for the information, but decided that the old resentful Jacko was in the past. I had to forget all the past silent recalcitrance. Nicole Lenoir-Jourdan wasn't my teacher any longer – we were equal partners now. If she hadn't quite realised this when she'd gone off on her own to write the specifications for the boat, thanks to Jimmy's tact and firmness she most certainly did now. She'd copped it sweet and we'd avoided our first quarrel by both of them behaving like adults, and it was time I did the same.

Her cottage was surprisingly untidy, but comfortably so – a place for three comfortable-looking cats and a parrot, which seemed to wait until you reached the end of a sentence and then would say in perfectly accented English, 'I beg your pardon. Would you mind repeating that, please?' Moments later, it would follow with, 'You must learn to correctly clip some words and others you shall round.' This was exactly what you might expect from a parrot owned by Nicole Lenoir-Jourdan, but I have to say it was initially most disconcerting. I laughed, and she told me that when she'd been a young girl in Shanghai Sir Victor Sassoon had presented her with the parrot. At the time she was practising her English accent and perfecting her grammar so that she would appear indistinguishable from cognoscenti among the English taipans. This entailed repeating phrases and the peculiar argot of Shanghai's pretentious residents until she sounded as though she'd been educated at Rodean, a famous English girls' school for the upper class.

'I taught the parrot to say those words so that whenever I heard them I would go over whatever it was I was phrasing just one more time. I wasn't to know that a parrot may live for a hundred years, and Vowelfowl has haunted me with that sentence ever since.'

'I beg your pardon. Would you mind repeating that, please?' the parrot squawked. 'You will learn to correctly clip some words and others you shall round.'

In my mind's eye I saw a twenty-something petite Russian countess, disguised as the quintessential English woman with her la-di-da voice, slim as a pencil, dressed in the very latest fashion, stepping off the island ferry. The locals might have noted her smart outfit and strange-looking snakeskin suitcases with a hatbox to match, but they'd be incredulous at the huge red-and-black parrot in its large gilded cage, and piss themselves when the bird repeated the offending sentence to anyone on the dock who opened their mouth. I remember as a child the dock workers talking of how it had taken twenty of them to unload a huge, beautifully made polished wooden crate that fitted together without the use of a single nail. They swore it was bigger than the front room of most fishermen's cottages. It had taken a bullock team and wagon to take it up to the cottage she'd bought on the cliffs facing out to sea.

The incredible thing was that I very much doubt if anyone, with the exception of the Reverend Daintree and now Jimmy and me, still knew very much more about Nicole Lenoir-Jourdan than they'd learned on that first day. She had so completely concealed her original identity, stepping ashore as an imperious young upper-class English woman, that it would never have occurred to any of the islanders to question her. In those days you knew your place in society, and kept it. It was only after the Second World War that the class structure in Australia began to break down, despite the notion fondly held but seldom demonstrated by the working classes that Jack was as good as his master. The islanders would almost certainly have sniggered behind their hands at all Nicole Lenoir-Jourdan appeared to represent. At the same time they would have been completely in awe of someone as grand and prepossessing. Attempting to pronounce her surname with the correct accent would have been seen as putting on the dog to the extreme. Even today she was known as Nicole Len-was-Jo-dan, and very few people had the courage or closeness with her to call her Nicole. I had always, even as an adult, referred to her as 'Miss'. It had taken a barnstorming Jimmy to break down the name barrier and call her Nicole ma'am and, latterly, Countess.

Now I was in this formidable woman's home, sitting on a comfortable if somewhat worn brocaded couch with carved black mahogany dragon-claw legs. The small room had a distinctly oriental appearance. An elaborately woven Chinese silk carpet spread out across the wooden floorboards to encompass the entire room, stopping just six inches short of the skirting boards. Two large chairs that matched the couch held two cats, while a third cat was perched on the armrest furthermost from where I sat. The parrot's cage rested on a tall but compact table draped with a tasselled green-velvet cloth that fell to the floor. Two small mother-of-pearl inlaid mahogany tables held Tiffany lamps, one beside one of the chairs and the other next to the couch where I sat. A large cherry-coloured lacquered cabinet embroidered with elaborate brass hinges that resembled rampant dragons, and a lock formed in the shape of a dragon's head, stood in the corner. Above it rested a huge case ending two or three inches from the ceiling and featuring brilliant yellow chrysanthemums as a design. A window with heavy brocade curtains drawn against the outside light, and what I imagined was the cliff-top view out to sea, was set into the wall to my left. Next to the window stood an upright piano with a piano stool on a brass swivel set into three ebony dragon-claw legs. There were no pictures because, with the exception of the cherry-coloured cupboard, bookshelves occupied every inch of the four walls, stretching from floor to ceiling. I estimated that there must have been several thousand books filling them – so jam-packed were the shelves that some volumes stood in piles on the adjacent carpet. She possessed more books than the town's library. I remarked on the beautifully crafted shelves.

'Yes, they are rather nice. They were the planks that formed the original crate that contained my furniture when I first arrived from Shanghai. I had them cut and polished on the inside as well as the outside by a Chinese master craftsman. If you look carefully on the underside of the shelves, alas you may observe the odd dent sustained from the journey. But when I got here I had Mr Bronson, the carpenter from the co-op, cut them to fit the walls, and he restored the polish and shine as much as he could to the underside. I remember him modestly observing that the crate had been beautifully made, and the shelves it became deserved a better carpenter then he'd ever be to do the fitting and dovetailing. He was a dear man and passed away when you were a small boy, Jack,' she said as she disappeared into the next room.

I knew of Mr Bronson, the carpenter, because he'd carved a crook-looking Madonna and Child for the Catholic church, but Father Crosby had replaced it with the lurid plaster model with the flaming heart after the old man died. As an aside, several years ago I discovered Bronson's original carving in the church cellar, and it is now on display at the Launceston Art Gallery where it is considered a bit of a masterpiece.

I told Nicole Lenoir-Jourdan the story of Mr Bronson's Madonna and Father Crosby and had no sooner done so when the bloody parrot said, 'I beg your pardon – would you mind repeating that please?'

'Oh, do keep quiet, Vowelfowl!' Nicole Lenoir-Jourdan called out. 'He's such an old curmudgeon. I'll have to put the cloth over his cage – otherwise he'll be interrupting us all evening. Excuse me please, Jack, I shan't be a moment.' I could see that this parrot was far from a simple pet that shared her life. They probably talked a great deal to one another, whereas she hadn't even drawn my attention to the three cats lounging about. I guess while a cat may agree to live with you, it's always on its terms.

Nicole Lenoir-Jourdan returned with a second green-velvet drape that she threw over the cage. '*Polly needs a pee!*' the parrot called out.

'Oh dear. I really must apologise, Jack – Sir Victor Sassoon taught him that.' She didn't elaborate, but I tucked the name away for future reference. It was the second time she'd mentioned him and there weren't too many sirs around our neck of the woods – the only ones I'd ever met were the Tasmanian premier, Sir Robert Cosgrove, and the governor, both at the medal ceremony. This Sassoon bloke must have been close to her.

'Let me get you a drink, Jack. Would you care for champagne?'

I hesitated, not sure whether to bluff it out, but decided to come clean. 'I've never tried it,' I said, trying to sound offhand, as if the decision not to drink champagne had been of my own making.

'Oh, then you must!' she insisted. 'I've had several bottles tucked away for just over twenty years and while I turn them religiously, I've never really had an occasion to open one. One cannot drink champagne alone – it's such a joyous, sharing drink.'

Twenty-something years seemed a long time for a bunch of bottles to hang around the kitchen and I wondered how this particular champagne would taste after all that time. I began to question what I had let myself in for. First Chinese food, and now plonk that had been lying around since I was a boy. Then it struck me how sad her last statement was. How very lonely she must have been – in fact, *was*. She hadn't even had someone to share the few bottles of grog she'd had stored away all these years. *Why?* Why had a young woman with the improbable name of Nicole Lenoir-Jourdan arrived on Queen Island looking like someone from the cover of *Vogue* to live a life that had been busy enough, but completely isolated from all she'd previously known?

After removing the Tiffany lamp and placing it on the carpet, she brought the small lacquer table beside the couch to rest in front of me. The circle where the base of the lamp had stood was clean while the rest of the table carried a thin patina of dust. 'Oh dear – I never seem to have time to dust!' she exclaimed. 'Excuse me, won't you, Jack.'

'It's only a bit of dust,' I said. 'Can't harm you.'

She left the room but, instead of the duster I'd anticipated, returned with a silver champagne bucket from which protruded the foil neck of a bottle of French champagne. She placed it down within the clean circle on the table, almost as if that's what it had been intended for all along. Then she removed two champagne glasses from the cherry-lacquered cabinet. 'Darn,' she said, 'the dust seems to get into everything, I'll have to give these a rinse.' She returned a short while later with the two flat wide-brimmed glasses clean and polished. 'Can't put champagne into a dusty glass,' she explained, then added, 'I say, Jack, isn't this exciting? I haven't done this for years. In fact, it's been twenty-two years between glasses of champagne. How time flies.'

If she hadn't had champagne for twenty-two years the dust on the glasses had been allowed a fair while to settle, I thought to myself.

Pointing to the ice bucket, she said, 'You do the honours, please, Jack.' I wasn't to know at the time, but the first glass of champagne I was ever to taste was a twenty-seven-year-old bottle of vintage Krug.

There wasn't any point trying to seem casual about all this – if I messed it up I'd look an even bigger fool. 'I've only seen this done in the movies. I'm not sure I know how . . .'

'Well, now is the perfect time to learn. I do hope there will be many more occasions like this for the three of us!'

I removed the bottle from the ice bucket, where it had obviously stood for some time as it was icy cold to my touch. Drops of water from the melted ice dripped onto the table and the carpet. 'Oh blast! I forgot to bring a napkin,' she commented. 'I really am too, too careless. Never mind, it won't do any harm. And as a matter of fact I don't think I quite know where the damask napkins are kept.' I suddenly realised that Nicole Lenoir-Jourdan was nervous, another first as far as I was concerned. But she wasn't alone – I was shitting myself, not knowing what to expect from the bottle I held. I'd seen champagne bottles explode against the hull of a ship in newsreels at the movies and make a fearful mess and she'd told me this bottle was at least twenty years old!

I removed the foil from the bottle's neck to expose the rounded top of the cork the way I'd seen it done by the maître d in Rick's Café Americain, the nightclub where Humphrey Bogart and Ingrid Bergman met in *Casablanca*. I began to twist the cork, the wet bottle slippery in my hands, but couldn't believe how tightly the cork fitted. Finally I managed to twist it slowly around when all of a sudden it shot out like a bloody rocket, flying up and hitting the ceiling. 'Oh, Jesus!' I exclaimed, almost dropping the bottle.

'Oh, what fun! I'd quite forgotten!' Nicole Lenoir-Jourdan said. Bubbles began to foam from the spout. 'Well done, Jack! Quick, into a glass,' she cried, laughing and clapping her hands as if she were once again a young girl. I poured the champagne, then glanced anxiously at the ceiling where the cork had left a distinct impression. 'I shall think of it as Jack's mark,' she said, her calm now completely restored. 'Oh, what pleasant memories of China the pop of that cork brings back.'

'I'm awfully sorry – I didn't know it would pop out like that. I thought that was only a trick they played in the movies.'

'You did splendidly, Jack. It's really rather dreary and show-off to simply twist and pluck the cork from the bottle. After all, champagne should be a celebration and a properly popping cork is its first hurrah!' Charming wasn't the word! I couldn't help wondering what had happened to the stern, proper woman I'd known all my life.

We toasted the three of us in partnership, and then our thoughts went to Jimmy. 'To James – godspeed, and come back to us soon,' Nicole Lenoir-Jourdan offered, and we clinked our glasses once again. I must say, I was already missing him a fair bit.

While Scotch and brandy might be likened to two irascible old men, different but always difficult and sharp-tongued, I discovered that champagne is like a lovely young woman captured in the first flush of beauty. It certainly didn't take a lot of getting accustomed to. After the first glass I was led into a tiny dining room that contained a table that would only have seated four at the most. It was carefully set but the first thing I noticed was the absence of cutlery; instead, two sets of ivory chopsticks rested on a small porcelain cushion. Thankfully I'd first learned to use chopsticks in Japan and then later in the POW camp. Each place setting contained several bowls, a ceramic cup without a handle and a porcelain spoon. The dishes were a pale duck-egg colour with, at the centre, a brilliant goldfish motif with elaborate ribbon-like fins. Of course, at the time I had no idea of the why and the way of all the small containers. After the Chinese POW camp I'd associated Chinese food with the vile millet gruel eaten from a tin dish and I'd sworn, as long as I lived, never to touch chink food again.

In fact, when Nicole Lenoir-Jourdan had promised to cook Chinese I'd almost gagged at the thought. At the last moment before leaving home I'd considered sending Cory to apologise and say I'd been taken ill and couldn't come. Much as I wanted to sort out the fishing-boat business, I was afraid that I might disgrace myself by throwing up at the table. I was certainly in for a big surprise.

The champagne bucket had accompanied us to the table. 'Not strictly correct but, oh well, that's the beauty of champagne – you can drink it just about anywhere, at any time,' my hostess remarked, as she filled my glass once again.

'What we're having tonight is called chrysanthemum fire pot. It's a bit like a Swiss fondue – you cook it at the table.' She didn't mention, and I didn't know at the time, that it took many hours to prepare.

I hadn't a clue what a Swiss fondue was, and had never heard of food cooked at the table. It sounded a bit barbaric. 'Chrysanthemum fire pot? Fondue?' I asked, somewhat mystified. This was turning out to be a very different sort of evening.

'Oh dear – perhaps it's best shown, and not explained. Come, I need your help, Jack.' She led the way into the small kitchen leading from the dining room.

The first thing I observed was that the kitchen benchtop was covered in dishes containing bits of raw food, all of it cut into small pieces. Fish in one, prawns in another, chicken in a third, followed by pork and beef in two more. Three bowls each contained what Nicole Lenoir-Jourdan called celery cabbage, chopped into three-inch lengths, and what I recognised myself as spinach leaves, while another beside them was half-filled with noodles.

'The vegies are out of the garden,' she said. 'Lovely and fresh. I find vegetables lying around for even a day simply don't taste as nice. Now, Jack, watch me,' she instructed. She moved the small dishes aside to make room and then took two fairly large, flat square plates with the same fish design from a shelf above the kitchen benchtop. Working with amazing speed she arranged each kind of meat, fish and seafood and the noodles in slightly overlapping layers on one of the plates. 'Perhaps you'd like to do the same, Jack, while I prepare the sauce?'

The plate she had arranged looked terrific – what I'd seen as bits of raw food had been transformed into fancy decoration. But I soon discovered it wasn't quite as simple as it looked – pieces kept slipping out of place and the rows I made wouldn't remain straight, while hers looked as if they were glued to the surface of the plate. In the meantime she mixed soy sauce, sesame oil and rice wine into a small bowl, stirred in some beaten egg and served the result in two small bowls. I'd just about completed my own task when she finished but I must say, compared to her arrangement, mine looked like a terrible mess.

Next she poured boiling water from the electric kettle into a pretty teapot, its handle made from bamboo. 'Green tea,' she commented. 'This one is named Dragon Well, sent to me from Hong Kong, and it is quite exquisite.' She glanced at my plate. 'Splendid!' she observed. 'Now, if you will please, Jack.' She pointed to a large brass-and-copper pot sitting on the side of the stove on a stand with a handle on either side. It also had two handles at the top with a hollow brass cone protruding about five inches from the centre. She handed me two pot holders. 'You may need to use these – the cone is filled with glowing charcoal and the stock around it is simmering and should be very hot.'

'The chrysanthemum fire pot?'

'Yes – a truly treasured item in any Chinese kitchen.'

I carried the chrysanthemum fire pot to the table and she followed me with the two square plates, then returned for the various bits'n'pieces, her final trip to bring the pretty teapot. 'Well, doesn't that look splendid,' she said, holding the teapot and standing back from the small table now burgeoning with uncooked food.

'It's the colours,' I replied. 'I mean, it's all raw food and already it looks delicious.'

'Ah, the Chinese are a very aesthetic race – a properly prepared meal is expected to appeal to all the senses. The colours should be pleasing to the eye, the aromas tantalising and the ingredients nicely uniform and cut to be ideal for chopsticks. Knives are not permitted at any Chinese table.' She pointed to the place setting at the far side of the table nearest the door to her parlour. 'You'll sit there please, Jack. An honoured guest always sits opposite the host and nearest the door.'

I moved across and waited until she sat down, unable to stand behind her chair to allow her to sit first, as the *Women's Weekly* and Gloria would have preferred. She brought her hands together, smiling. 'A fire pot is never used by a single person, and so this is a special treat for me as well. Shall we dine, Jack?'

She'd placed the beautifully arranged plate in front of me and the one I'd so poorly prepared she took for herself. We now sat opposite each other with the chrysanthemum fire pot between us to one side. 'You'll have to show me what to do,' I said. 'This is all pretty new to me.'

'You do use chopsticks, don't you?' But before I could reply she added, 'Of course you do, how silly of me. Well then, we'll start with a little green tea.' She lifted the teapot and poured a little of the light-greenish-coloured tea into one of the small glazed-pottery cups and handed it to me. 'It's served very hot but the end result is cool and refreshing and will aid your digestion with the fried food,' she explained. Then, filling her own cup, she lifted it and said, '*Yum sing* – a toast to one's honoured guest.'

'Thank you,' I replied, not quite knowing what to say. I tasted the tea, which I must say seemed rather bland, although the smell was quite pleasant – like the bush after rain. If anything, it was slightly bitter. Certainly nothing to write home about. 'Nice,' I said, not really meaning it.

But of course she wasn't fooled. 'Chinese tea is very subtle. Perhaps one day you'll come to appreciate it.' She brought her tea to her lips and I was astonished at the noise she made – a loud, slurping, sucking noise like a pig sucking from a trough, or a child draining the last drops of a milkshake through a straw. Coming from someone as posh as she was, I was pretty shocked. She placed the cup down. 'The idea is to suck air into the cup at the same time to cool the hot tea. It's quite polite to do it this way – noisy but, like so many things Chinese, really very practical.'

Next she picked up her chopsticks. 'This is really very simple and a rather pleasant way to eat, and the nice part is that you only have to eat the things you enjoy.' She picked up a piece of fish and placed it in a small wire basket with a handle, which she then dipped into the simmering stock. I watched as the stock bubbled around the morsel of fish. 'Fish cooks very quickly – the pork and beef will take a little longer,' she explained, removing the fish from the basket with her chopsticks and dipping it into the sauce she'd prepared. 'Yum!' she said unselfconsciously. Then, after swallowing, she added, 'The Chinese would normally use sole or pike as the preferred fish, but this is a lovely piece of sea bass I got off Jim Blain's fishing boat this morning.' I was beginning to realise that she'd gone to an enormous amount of trouble on my behalf. If this veritable banquet was by way of an apology, then it was certainly working a treat.

Well, I tucked in and I discovered cooking at the table was lots of fun as well as being delicious. We talked about the boat we were going to buy. I did most of the talking, while dripping and cooking and chopsticking away, washing it all down with champagne so that pretty soon my square plate was empty and Nicole Lenoir-Jourdan insisted I eat half of her food, which was no hardship I can tell you. Though I'm afraid I had to give the tea a miss.

Then, when I thought we were finished, I noticed that the noodles and the vegies hadn't been touched. Nicole Lenoir-Jourdan now placed them into the stock and cooked them for what seemed no more than a minute, then ladled a couple of spoonfuls into a bowl and handed it to me. 'Soup is the last course,' she announced, 'The Chinese tend to do things differently.'

The soup, containing all the flavours of the previously cooked ingredients, was wonderful. I know a fair bit about food today, but at that time it was mostly just stuff on your plate you ate gratefully – usually meat and veg. After the POW camp everything home-cooked tasted good. But this was a truly fantastic meal.

'I nearly didn't come tonight,' I admitted, pointing to my empty soup bowl and indicating the empty dishes that lay around me, as my host looked at me querulously. 'Chinese food! I swore I'd never eat it again in my life.' I then proceeded to tell her about the vile millet gruel in the various field hospitals and the prison camp.

'Jack, how very unfortunate!' she cried. 'I could so easily have cooked a roast with all the trimmings.'

I grinned. 'It couldn't possibly have tasted as good as this. Honestly, it was fantastic.'

She smiled, her head to one side. 'You are so very kind – *really* you are, Jack.'

With the help of the champagne, we were getting along like a house on fire. While in the years to come I would eat food cooked by some of the great Chinese chefs of the world, the banquet Nicole Lenoir-Jourdan prepared for me would always be special in my mind. By the end of the feast, having consumed the lion's share of the champagne, I have to say I was feeling decidedly mellow.

'Shall we retire to the lounge?' she suggested, rising and reaching for the champagne bottle. 'Oh dear, it's empty!' She giggled like a young girl. 'I say, shall we have another?' I wasn't going to say yes, but then I wasn't going to say no either. My head was feeling a bit light, but other than that I felt fine, and decided I'd definitely acquired a taste for the stuff. What's more, I didn't have the usual telltale signs of getting plastered. 'Why not?' she suddenly decided. 'This *is*, after all, rather a special occasion. Such a pity James is not with us. Now off you go, make yourself comfortable in the lounge.' She headed for the kitchen with the bucket and empty bottle. Little did I know I would never again taste champagne as good, and it would be many years before I could afford to drink vintage Krug again.

Back in the lounge with my glass replenished and bubbles dancing up my nostrils, life seemed pretty grand. I was still yakking away thirteen to the dozen – whether from the champagne, the splendid meal she'd made me think I'd helped to cook, or the comfortable atmosphere in which an entirely new Nicole Lenoir-Jourdan prevailed, I couldn't say. It was time, I decided, to slam on the verbal brakes and to give someone else a turn to talk.

Emboldened by the champagne, I ventured, 'You said earlier in the evening, when I opened the champagne, "Oh, what pleasant memories of China the pop of that cork brings back". Well, I know Jimmy isn't here, but it could be months before he returns. Would you consider telling me the remainder of your story, right up to when you came to the island?' Before she could answer, I hastily added, 'I have an excellent memory and I promise to tell it to Jimmy exactly as you tell it to me.'

'Hopefully you'll make a better fist of it, Jack,' she replied modestly. 'And yes, you're certainly blessed with a good memory – you've just quoted a throwaway line I used at least two hours ago. I only wish my memory were as good. It seems to be getting worse lately – it's curious how one remembers details from the distant past, yet one can't seem to memorise a grocery list.' She sighed. 'Very well, but you will tell me if I get tedious, won't you? There's nothing quite as exhausting as being cast in the role of polite listener.'

'It's no hardship, Countess. Last time Jimmy and I were blown away!'

She ignored the expression, though I imagined I saw her flinch. 'I'm not sure I remember quite where I ended last time?'

'Your father . . .' I was about to say 'committed suicide', but stopped myself just in time. 'You had decided to make a new start in Shanghai. Did you, you know, meet up with Mr Yu, like he asked you to?' *'As', not 'like'*, I corrected myself silently. I still hadn't grown accustomed to not being picked up and scolded for such grammatical sins. Our dialogue had been peppered with her corrections for so long that they formed a part of our familiarity, and I found myself almost missing them. I poured myself another glass of champagne and noticed hers was still filled to the brim.

'Big Boss Yu? Well, a comedy of errors there, but we'll get to that a little later. Now, let me see . . . ah yes, I packed whatever I possessed, together with my father's papers and a few song sheets I'd acquired from the nightclub, into one small cardboard suitcase. I attempted to sell my father's clothes but the second-hand clothes shop near the nightclub wouldn't accept them, claiming the clothes worn by Russian men were too large for the local Chinese population and there was no market for them among the refugees. I ended up giving them to Ah Foo, the rickshaw boy who'd faithfully waited each night to take me home from the nightclub, often refusing drunken patrons who may have tipped him generously. He said he didn't have any personal need for the clothes, but he could sell them easily enough at the flea market. When I informed him of my intended departure he looked terribly distressed. "Ayee! But who will look after you and take you home safely at night?" he cried.' She paused for a moment, and then said, 'Westerners so often think of the Chinese as people who don't show their emotions and who lack personal loyalty, when in fact they are exactly the opposite. For example, if you've treated your number-one boy well – he is the manager of your household, much like an English butler – should you fall upon hard times, he will accept a cut in salary or even feed you from his own pocket. When I offered my rickshaw boy ten dollars as a farewell gift he refused it. "No, missy. You will need it – the clothes are enough. I wish you good joss." They truly are remarkable people, often contradictory by western standards, but nevertheless an exceptional race.'

'I thought they regarded all Europeans as *gwai lo*?' I asked.

She looked at me, surprised. 'You know what the term means?'

'Foreign devil. It was frequently used in the POW camp by the Chinese guards.'

'Well, yes, I admit *gwai lo* and *gwai mui* are common Chinese expressions to denote European men and women, although I'm not sure they carry the same malice as the translation.'

'I've sidetracked you,' I said, apologising.

'No, not at all – it helps when you ask questions. Where was I? Oh, yes. Leaving for Shanghai. Well, I bought a second-class ticket on the train. By the way, there were five classes available. Second class was far from comfortable, so I'd hate to think how tedious fifth class must have been. We travelled for nearly four days, stopping frequently to pick up coal and take water and, of course, to allow more people into the already overcrowded carriages. I bought food from the peasants on the platforms at the various stations instead of using the second-class saloon, which served mostly European food. Most of the second-class passengers, like myself, were Russian refugees hoping to find a better life in Shanghai. I must say they were a motley lot, overwhelmed with self-pity and constantly comparing stories while, at the same time, lamenting the unfairness that had brought about their downfall.' She paused and glanced at me. 'Self-justification is one of the more odious characteristics among humans, don't you think, Jack?'

I nodded, agreeing, but was forced to admit silently that I'd been guilty of it all my life as she continued the story. 'I was stuck next to a large woman who insisted on telling me her troubles in excruciatingly boring detail. These calamitous circumstances were no more onerous than those of most of the other refugees, but oh how she carried on about them, loudly bemoaning the tragedy of her recent life. Worse still, every few minutes, often in mid-sentence, she'd burst into pitiful wailing and lamentation, beating her ample breasts with her bejewelled fists and commencing a lachrymatory display that befitted a scene in a bad opera, until finally her satin bodice was soaked in tears. It grew so wearisome that when she left to replaster her make-up in the washroom of the next station I hastily moved into a third-class carriage. While it was less comfortable and more crowded, the somewhat better-off Chinese peasants were a much more entertaining and generous lot. I bowed my head and greeted them with the street argot *Lei ho*, which, roughly translated, means "You good?" When they realised I spoke Cantonese their pleasure was quite evident, and a family with several children, the woman suckling a baby, made room for me beside them.' She laughed suddenly. 'I recall, as evening closed in, holding the baby in my arms and singing him a lullaby in Cantonese until he finally fell asleep. But the applause from the other passengers was so raucous the infant woke with a start and commenced to wail at the top of his tiny lungs.' Nicole Lenoir-Jourdan laughed once again at the memory. 'The

Chinese thought this hilarious, and immediately called for a repeat performance. I continued singing for a while and at the end of each song they'd press upon me some small trifle or gift of food.

'I had been practising the new thousand-word Chinese calligraphy ever since Ah Lai and I had been in Manchuria. A Chinese scholar who lived in her village had tutored me in return for lessons in English. I had respectfully written to Mr Yu in the new calligraphy to inform him I was coming to Shanghai and the approximate time I was expected to arrive on the Red Rooster, the Chinese name for the train. His secretary scribe had written back by return mail to say Big Boss Yu would send a servant to pick me up but to be sure to get off at South Station near the Chinese City.'

I made as if to interrupt and then thought better of it. Observing my hesitation, she asked, 'What is it, Jack?'

I was beginning to feel a bit dizzy and decided I'd better lay off the champagne, but felt I still had my wits about me. '*Chinese* City? I thought the whole of Shanghai was a Chinese city? After all, Shanghai is in China.'

'Yes, of course it is. But the largest and wealthiest part of the city was under foreign control. In 1843, soon after its humiliating defeat by the British in the Opium Wars, the Chinese Government was forced to open the port of Shanghai to foreign trade. The British leased a few hundred acres along the muddy flat land of the Whangpoo or Yellow River, where they established the first foreign Settlement. It was not far north of the ancient walled city.' She paused to gather her thoughts. 'Perhaps now is the time to explain Shanghai to you, Jack. Without an explanation, you may have trouble understanding the remainder of my time in China.'

I nodded, happy to hear about such an exotic place. 'Sure, I'd like to hear,' I answered.

'Well then, towards the middle of the nineteenth century the walled city of Shanghai and its surrounding suburbs boasted a town of about 75 000 Chinese, which by the standards of China was a drop in the ocean. But from this unpropitious start, by the 1920s and 1930s Shanghai had become the fifth most important city on earth – the megalopolis of continental Asia with a population of about two and a half million. This increase in population over the previous ninety years had come about because of Shanghai's growing importance as a centre of trade, commerce and industry, and also because it had become a safe haven. Every time an up-country revolt by some misbegotten war lord occurred, the people flocked into Shanghai and its foreign Settlements protected by the foreign rifles and thundering gunboats on the river.

'In the 1850s and early 1860s, for instance, when Shanghai had still not become a great city, the armies of the Taiping Rebellion, led by a general who improbably called himself the "Younger Brother of Christ", butchered an estimated twenty million people. Chinese of every class fled before its hordes, the rich bringing their silver until Shanghai had the richest reserves of silver in the world, and the poor bringing their bedding, birdcages and rice pots.

'By the 1920s, foreigners in Shanghai had consolidated under two administrations – the French in the French Concession and the rest in the International Settlement. Together they occupied some eight and a half square miles, and because of their wealth and military power they were a law unto themselves. The population outside the foreign areas was under a traditional Chinese administration centred in the walled city.

'This occidental city in China came under the twin influences of Queen Victoria's Britain and America's John D. Rockefeller. Both countries saw the opportunity to trade with the Orient from Shanghai, and between the two of them they spread the "Gospel of the Three Lights" – the cigarette, the kerosene lamp and Christianity – while at the same time exporting silk, tea and opium.'

Nicole Lenoir-Jourdan paused. 'You must forgive the history lesson, Jack,' she said. 'But without it, it is impossible to comprehend a city such as Shanghai, with the Bund its business centre and beating heart. This was where the British, American, French, Japanese,

Dutch, Belgian, Italian and Spanish taipans had their great trading houses. We White Russians were there, of course, but only held minor positions – secretaries, doormen, janitors and sometime-engineers in the port authority. The Russian women, many cultured and beautiful, filled the role of the city's nightlife. We were its entertainers. I hesitate to say so, but by "entertainer" I mean everything from a sailor's whore to a taipan's mistress, as well as dancers, singers, musicians and cabaret artists. As refugees without a country, the Russians in Shanghai, with one exception, were regarded as a second-class people. We fitted somewhere between the Chinese and the rest of the expatriate community – a blot on the landscape, so to speak.'

'Who was the exception?' I asked, curious.

'Georgii Avksent'ievich Sapojuikoff, known simply as Sapajou, who was the cartoonist on the *North China Daily News*. He was also the only White Russian ever to be accepted as a member of the exclusive and incredibly stuffy Shanghai Club.'

'His middle name, isn't that the same as your father's?'

Nicole Lenoir-Jourdan looked at me, astonished. 'Jack, you *really* do have a remarkable memory.'

I tell you what – the compliments were flowing thick and fast. I'd had more praise in one evening than I'd received from the dreaded justice of the peace in all my years of growing up. Yet she dismissed or evaded my comment linking the White Russian cartoonist and her father.

'Well, that's probably quite enough history for one evening. This, then, was the Shanghai I entered via the South Gate of the Chinese City on the day of my sixteenth birthday.

'Imagine, if you will, the confusion on the platform as I alighted from the train late in the afternoon. How Mr Yu's manservant, sent to fetch me, would find me in this seething mass of humanity was simply beyond my comprehension. After sitting on my cardboard suitcase for two hours with rickshaw boys and peddlers importuning me and with the evening beginning to close in, I was growing desperate. Then quite suddenly, to the sound of whistles blowing, what seemed like dozens of Sikh and Chinese policemen appeared, wielding batons and scattering people willy-nilly, sending them running for their lives. In about ten minutes the station platform was clear. The only person remaining was me, sitting on my cheap suitcase sobbing and frightened. Fifty or so policemen quickly formed a large circle around me, legs apart with their hands behind their backs and chins held high so that they appeared to be looking into the distance over my head. Quite suddenly one of the policemen, a sergeant, barked a command and they all came to attention and brought their hands up in a smart salute, whereupon the circle opened and Mr Yu, known as Big Boss Yu, appeared.

'"Little Countess, ten thousand regrets – my useless servant has caused you to lose face. You must come with me at once," he said in English.

'I followed him across the deserted railway platform to a big Buick motor car, where the smartly uniformed chauffeur opened the door for me. On the way in I managed to dry my tears. "Why did you ask me to leave the Red Rooster at the Chinese City, *loh yeh*?" I asked when I stopped sniffing.

'"How you are seen will be how you are perceived," he replied. "I will see that you are properly introduced."

'I confess I was too distraught to make any sense of this. "Why do you care about me, *loh yeh*? Am I to be your concubine?" I asked in a small voice.

'He seemed to think this very funny. I was to learn later that he belonged to the old-school Chinese with traditional ways and values and was said to keep ten concubines. He must have thought a skinny sixteen-year-old with blue eyes and blonde hair quite redundant to his needs. "You would make a very bad concubine," he answered me, still amused at the thought, but then added, touching his heart, "You have fire and you are good joss. I have another way for you, Little Countess." It was rare for someone of his standing to take an interest in a white woman, and in particular a White Russian, and his sponsorship was, to say the least, unusual – if not improbable. I was to learn some years later that on the evening he had met me at the General's Retreat he had gone on to a gambling den where he had won a considerable fortune. The Chinese are a very superstitious people and in his mind I had become his talisman.

'We drove deep into the Chinese City and finally came to a halt beside a street so narrow that the big motor car couldn't enter. "The driver will take you to your house," Big Boss Yu said. "I will send for you in a week. In the meantime, you must practise all your songs." He must have seen the expression on my face. "You have nothing to fear here – the hand that protects you has long fingers."

'The house was a small, traditional Chinese structure and, to my surprise, came with my own *gung yun*, or "working person" – a plain-faced, middle-aged woman with a large burn scar to the side of her face, which had the effect of pulling one eye slightly out of line, who was named Ah May, which means "pretty". The Chinese can be very cruel with their humour. I say this only because an *amah* is from a poor and usually large family where, because she is a female child, she is considered a "waste of rice" and not worthy of a name, and is simply referred to by the order of her birth – that is, by a number. She would have received the name Ah May after she'd sustained the burn as some sort of perverted Chinese joke. She must have been waiting at the door because when the chauffeur, Ah Chow, called out, it was opened immediately and, eyes downcast, she silently took my suitcase from the chauffeur and led me into the tiny house. The first thing that met my eyes was, of all improbable things, a Steinway baby grand!' Nicole Lenoir-Jourdan brought her hands to her breast and chuckled at the memory. 'Can you imagine my delight and, of course, with it, bemusement! If I was to be hidden away in the Chinese City it had obviously something to do with singing and piano playing.

'The week passed quickly and I discovered I was free to go anywhere, though until I knew how to find my way home in what was basically a large, unplanned city slum with narrow streets and dark alleys that resembled a teeming rabbit warren, I was accompanied by Ah May. She proved a shy but pleasant companion and was an excellent housekeeper and cook. When I first offered her money to go shopping for food she explained that everything was taken care of, including her salary, and when I pressed a few dollars into her hand I later found it restored to me under my pillow. Wherever I went the people seemed to know who I was. *Gwai mui* were usually treated with indifference on the street, but here, in the Chinese City, strangers would often greet me, calling out a friendly "*Lei ho!*" I wasn't silly enough to believe this had anything to do with my attitude, which was always friendly – I knew it was another sign of the pervasive influence of the powerful Big Boss Yu.

'I became accustomed to giving an impromptu concert almost every time I sat at the Steinway to practise. The narrow street outside would soon become choked with people listening to the strange Western music so different from their own, but when I sang a Cantonese song there would be loud applause. Though quite how they managed to hear the words, I cannot say.

'At the week's end I received a message that I was to be fetched at noon the following day and that I was to bring my music books. Ah Chow arrived precisely on the appointed hour and I was driven to the Bund, quite the biggest and handsomest place I had ever seen. We drove on towards the end of the grand boulevard and stopped at a very large and imposing building that turned out to be the Palace Hotel. The place was simply swarming with flunkeys, brass buttons gleaming on their dark-green uniforms.

'"You must see this person," Ah Chow instructed, and handed me a carefully folded note sealed with black wax that carried Mr Yu's chop. On the outside, written in English, was "Commander Freddy Duncan". "I will return in one hour," Ah Chow said, then added, "I will wait for you if you are not here at that time."

'The car door was opened for me by a tall, imposing-looking man in a long green coat, all braid and gleaming buttons. I immediately took him for a Russian. Some Russian faces are unmistakable. This gave me the courage to say in my native tongue, "I have come to see Commander Duncan. Will you show me what to do, please?"

'This name must have meant something, because he became completely obsequious. "Certainly, miss," he said, bowing so low I thought he was going to hit his forehead on the white marble paving. "Whom shall I announce?"

'Feeling completely intimidated by my surroundings I heard myself saying, "Countess Nicole Lenoir-Jourdan." It was the first time I had ever spoken it aloud – in fact, even thought seriously about it. Being a Russian countess was not anything to write home about in Harbin, much less in Shanghai.

'"Come with me please, countess," the doorman said respectfully. I followed him across what seemed like an ocean of deep, plush maroon carpet to a desk where several of the hotel's guests were being attended to by clerks. The doorman ignored them and walked straight up to the counter and in stentorian voice announced, "Countess Nicole Lenoir-Jourdan for Commander Duncan!" I cringed visibly. Practically the entire foyer would have heard him. Flushed with embarrassment, I didn't know quite where to hide my face, although there was no doubt that the announcement had the required effect. Every one of the clerks behind the desk dropped their pen or whatever they were doing, some halting mid-sentence the conversation they were having with one or another of the hotel guests. They all looked over to a slightly older man who stepped forward and was obviously the senior clerk present. "Certainly, I will call him on the telephone. Do you have an appointment, countess?"

'"I don't know," I stammered. "I have a note." I had lost my previous poise. Gripping my music sheets under my arm, I politely held out the note with both hands in the required Chinese fashion. I must have seemed like a schoolgirl who had committed some infringement of the rules, instructed to report to the headmistress with a note from her teacher.

'The clerk looked at me impassively, refusing to accept the proffered note. "I see," he said, then turned to a clerk beside him and said in Cantonese, "She is a fraud. Pretend to make the call and then when you've done so, return to tell me the commander is not available."

'The clerk nodded and went to a nearby telephone. "He will make the call," the senior clerk said with just a hint of rudeness, not addressing me by my title or even as "miss".

'He had almost turned away. "It is a note from Big Boss Yu," I said in Cantonese.' Nicole Lenoir-Jourdan paused and leaned back. 'Well, you should have seen the look on his face! He turned and snatched the phone from the surprised clerk, who was mumbling something into it, dialled a number furiously and announced me. Evidently the voice on the other end must have told him to send me in, because he placed the receiver down and bowed deeply. "A thousand apologies, countess. I shall take you personally to the commander, who is waiting for you in a private lounge," he said in English.'

I couldn't resist interrupting. 'What a turnaround, Countess!' I cried, a little too gleefully.

'I was tempted to say something that would make him squirm, but even at that tender age I sensed that senior hotel staff must preserve their dignity at all times and could make things difficult for me at some possible future occasion. Instead I smiled, and said, "Thank you for being so helpful."

'It came to pass that Commander Duncan was a bachelor who lived in the hotel, which he part-owned with Sir Victor Sassoon, who lived in England and Hong Kong but visited Shanghai quite often on business. Commander Duncan was the very picture of an English squire. He was every bit as respectable as Sir Victor was rumoured to be reprobate, and at heart was a private banker and very conservative. Sir Victor Sassoon was Commander Duncan's counterpart – a flamboyant and successful entrepreneur famous for his parties. In fact, Sir Victor wasn't thought quite respectable by the standards of the crusty diehards of the British colony, who referred to him privately as "that Baghdad Jew", a reference to his Near East ancestry. They deplored his extravagance and looked askance at his exuberance, while having taken great pleasure in blackballing him from the Shanghai Club. I'm only giving you this background, Jack, because later I was to become very much involved with Sir Victor.

'I handed my note from Big Boss Yu to Commander Duncan, who sat in a large, overstuffed chair and somewhat gruffly invited me to do the same. He opened and read the note, then grunted as he put it aside. "Well, my dear, I am told that you are somewhat of a virtuoso?"

'I wasn't quite sure how to answer him, or whether his information came from the note I had handed him or from a previous discussion with Big Boss Yu. "No, sir," I said shyly, feeling immediately intimidated. "I can sing and play the piano and dance a little."

'He looked at me sternly. "Good Lord, girl – that simply won't do! Here at the Palace we have only the very best!"

'I had no idea what the note contained, but from his reaction he was obviously referring to the hotel's entertainment, so I gave the only reply I could think of. "Perhaps there is a chorus line?"

' "Chorus line? *What* chorus line? What do you think this is – the Follies? The Brighton Music Hall? Eh?"

'It was more than I could bear, and I was on the verge of tears. "I'm sorry. I appear to have wasted your time, commander," I stammered.

' "Nonsense! We have to do *something*, but I'm damned if I know what. Not my kind of thing." He seemed to be thinking, then suddenly reached over for the small bell that rested on the side table beside his chair and proceeded to ring it vigorously. Moments later, with the bell still tinkling away, a bellboy appeared. "Mrs Worthington," the commander shouted above the ringing bell. Just the two words. The bellboy touched his cap and, turning smartly, left. The commander placed the bell down at last. "Well, at least we can teach you the King's English – though I must say, you seem to have made a half-decent start yourself."

'A tall, rather imperious-looking woman wearing a stern grey suit and gloves with a small straw hat perched on the side of her head entered and greeted the commander with a crisp, no-nonsense, "Good afternoon, commander."'

I wanted to tell Nicole Lenoir-Jourdan that this Mrs Worthington character sounded a little like someone else I knew, but thought better of it and let her continue.

'"Yes, yes, sit down, Mrs Worthington," he replied impatiently, not returning her salutation. "You are to teach this girl correctly spoken English." He paused for a moment, then gave the briefest of chuckles. "That is to say, Shanghai guff – though she appears to me to pronounce her vowels perfectly well. You'd hardly take her for a foreigner." He said this as though he was remarking on someone not present in the room.

'"Very well, commander. As you wish," Mrs Worthington said crisply. "I shall do my best – one can do no more." She rose, clutching her black leather handbag to her waist with both hands. She turned to me, a thin smile flickering across her face. "Come along, girl."

'I glanced somewhat in terror at Commander Duncan, who dismissed me with a sweep of his hand. "Go on, off you go." I followed Mrs Worthington and we were about to pass through the doorway when he called out, "About that other business – be here at two o'clock sharp, tomorrow!"

'I had no idea what he meant by "that other business" and turned to ask, "Shall I ask for you, Commander Duncan?"

'"Good God, no! Smithson – dreadful nancy boy!"

'We turned into a small passage richly carpeted in dark blue with a yellow-and-red fat dragon motif that, considering its brash and overwhelming impact, I hadn't even noticed on my way in. "What is your name, girl?" Mrs Worthington asked.

'"Nicole Lenoir-Jourdan, madam," I replied.

'"French?"

'"No, madam. I'm a White Russian – my mother was French."

'"Euh!" she expostulated, as if she'd received a sharp thrust up the bottom. "Well then, I suppose we must do the best we can with the poor clay we have." Then, carrying the analogy further, she said with a note of warning, "I do trust you will prove suitably pliable, Nicole?" I was mortified, and all I wanted to do was to run away from this perfectly horrid woman. "We will now sit in the main foyer and I shall instruct you," Mrs Worthington informed me.

'"What, teach me in the main foyer?" I asked, suddenly terrified.

'"No, no, stupid girl! That will take place at my flat. I shall tell you about your lessons."

'Well, it seemed everything had been decided. I was to have English lessons every morning for two hours or, as Mrs Worthington would say, "You are to have lessons in correct pronunciation – that is, you must learn to correctly clip some words and others you shall round." I was immediately reminded of dear Miss Rosen, and the hours and hours we'd spent together on vowels. "*The clown bounced on the trampoline and burst a boil on his bottom that caused him to become discombobulated.*"

'The following day Ah Chow picked me up in time for my English lesson and returned me home afterwards, and then came back for my appointment at the Palace at two o'clock with, I presumed, *Mr* Smithson (which turned out to be the correct gender). Smithson, as I'd come to think of him, was a rather effete Englishman who, in the tradition of Noël Coward, called everyone "darling". He greeted me in a cursory fashion that seemed to be the norm among the Europeans I'd met so far. "Come along," he said, and led me down a side passage and through a door onto the stage of an enormous ballroom. A grand piano stood in the centre of the stage and three large leather club chairs had been placed on the ballroom floor below and directly in front of it. Thankfully, they were not occupied. "Show us what you've got, darling," Smithson instructed, pointing at the grand piano.

'I looked at him, confused. "What do you want me to do, sir?"

'He brought his forefinger to the side of his mouth and struck a pose with his legs slightly apart, one forward with the toe of his shoe only just touching the surface of the stage like a male ballet dancer. Then he leaned back with his head tilted, his right eyebrow arched, observing me.

"For a start, you will *not* call me 'sir' or 'mister' – I am to be addressed as Lawrence. If you get to know me well enough you may call me Poppy. Now, what do I want you to *do*? Would it be too, too presumptuous of me to ask you to entertain me? You *can* do that, can't you, *darling*?"

'At that very moment three men entered the ballroom. I immediately recognised Big Boss Yu and Commander Duncan. The third man was rather tall, his dark hair slightly greying, and he was walking with a slight limp. Lawrence turned to face them as they prepared to occupy the club chairs. "Good afternoon, gentlemen," he called down, smiling. Mr Yu and Commander Duncan ignored his greeting, but the third man said in a friendly voice, "Hello, Poppy. I hope you have a nice surprise for us!"

'Lawrence shrugged and said tartly, "You may not be the only one to get a nice surprise, Sir Victor." He turned to me and said in an urgent whisper, "For godsake, do something!"

'I walked over to the grand piano where the stool was much too low for me, and started to wind the stool upwards, giving myself a chance to control the absolute terror I felt surging in my breast. I could feel my knees beginning to quake so I sat down hurriedly, the stool not quite right yet. But the moment I touched the keys I felt angry. I'd been humiliated by everyone I'd met from the moment I'd stood in front of the reception desk after being announced perhaps too pompously by the Russian doorman. My first English lesson that morning had been conducted with a condescension that was breathtaking, and my misery was now replaced with a cold anger I'd never felt before.

'I played the introduction and then started to sing at the top of my voice, with all the correct words clipped and the vowels rounded.

*"Poor little rich girl,*
*You're a bewitched girl,*
*Better beware!*
*Laughing at danger,*
*Virtual stranger,*
*Better take care!*

*The life you lead sets all your nerves a-jangle*
*Your love affairs are in a hopeless tangle,*
*Though you're a child, dear,*
*Your life's a wild typhoon.*

*In lives of leisure,*
*The craze for pleasure,*
*Steadily grows.*
*Cocktails and laughter*
*But what comes after?*
*Nobody knows . . .*"

'When I'd completed the new Noël Coward song, which had just come out, I turned trembling to face the three men and Lawrence Smithson, who had left the stage and was now standing behind their chairs. "Bravo!" Sir Victor called, rising from his seat and clapping furiously. The others followed, adding their applause. Big Boss Yu's lined "Ming the Merciless" face was beaming, and even Commander Duncan smiled. "Well, I'll be darned – that took courage!" Sir Victor said, then, half-turning in his chair, he addressed Lawrence. "What do you think, Poppy?"

'Lawrence struck a similar pose to the one before, but this time without the arched eyebrow. "Good!" he pronounced through pursed lips.

'"The eight o'clock?"

'Lawrence thought for a moment. "She's better than a warm-up artist. Why not the ten o'clock, the opening to the cabaret? Of course, I'll need to know her repertoire – it may not be suitable."

'"Splendid, let's do that," Sir Victor said. Then he turned back to me, smiling. 'Wherever have you been hiding all that talent, young lady?"

'"Thank you, sir," I said, more relieved than pleased. Big Boss Yu and Commander Duncan turned to leave and the Chinese taipan lifted his hand to signal goodbye, while the commander grunted and then called, "Splendid vowels!"

'Sir Victor mounted the steps to the stage and I noticed he limped in exactly the manner of my father. "Hello, I'm Victor Sassoon. Do forgive me for popping in – you see, I'm visiting from Hong Kong and, well, I have a share in this hotel and just happened to have an hour to spare. How very fortunate that we should meet, Nicole Lenoir-Jourdan. You're really terribly good, you know." This charming man, who probably knew all the crowned heads of Europe, had taken the trouble to be nice to a sixteen-year-old of absolutely no importance whatsoever. I would always love him for that first meeting. He was the first person, other than Big Boss Yu, who had been half-decent to me since my arrival, and I promptly burst into tears.

'I heard him call over to Lawrence in a calm voice, as if a young girl breaking into sobs when she met him was a perfectly normal occurrence. "Poppy, do ask a waiter to bring Nicole a strawberry milkshake?" Then, turning back to me, he said, "You really *must not* cry, my dear. You were perfectly splendid, and Poppy will want to hear your full repertoire – and so will I.'

'"I've never tasted a milkshake!" I wailed, which I immediately knew was a perfectly ridiculous thing to say.

'"Strawberry's the best," Sir Victor declared, laughing. And sobbing as I was, I instantly fell head over heels in love with him.'

She had told the story of her audition so well I wanted to applaud myself, but there were things happening to my head that shouldn't. 'A bit . . . like me ternight. With . . . cham-pagne . . . first time I've tast—' I said, slurring, unable to complete the sentence, my tongue too thick for my mouth. I was also having a great deal of trouble keeping my eyes open and the room around me was beginning to swim in an alarming manner, dipping and turning and spinning at a faster and faster rate. It happened just like that – one moment I was listening, absolutely intrigued and enchanted by her tale, and the next I was gone for all money. The last thing I remember was a cushion being placed behind my head and my feet being lifted onto the couch.

'Sleep tight, Jack.' Nicole Lenoir-Jourdan's voice seemed to be coming from a great distance, as if carried by a fierce wind during a storm at sea with giant waves pitching the deck, tossing the fishing vessel every which way. I'd disgraced myself. Just when I thought I'd won an encounter with the dreaded justice of the peace or, at the very least, ended up even-stevens, it was the library floor all over again.

# CHAPTER NINETEEN

## *Shanghai Lil and All That Jazz*

Talk about disgrace! I was not a kid any more, twenty-seven years old, a war veteran and would-be professional fisherman and I go and get myself drunk like a schoolboy. I awoke to the sun streaming through the window where the drapes had been pulled back and tied, with one of the cats resting on my chest. The parrot cage was missing. I staggered over to the window and looked out over the cliff face to the ocean. It was a calm day with white caps pushing steadily ashore – a perfect day for cray. Then, to my surprise, I discovered that my hangover wasn't too bad. In fact, relatively speaking it was quite mild – a couple of Gloria's Disprin and I should be okay.

My tongue feeling as if it needed a good rasp. 'Anyone home?' I called out. From somewhere outside the cottage I heard, 'I beg your pardon, would you mind repeating that please?' The bloody parrot again. I walked through the dining room to the kitchen and drank directly from the tap over the sink. Then, wiping my mouth with the back of my hand, I looked around. On the kitchen bench was a plate containing two eggcups, a spoon, a couple of uncooked eggs, two Disprin and half a loaf of shop bread, together with a note.

*Dear Jack,*
*A lovely evening, I did so enjoy myself. Do have some breakfast before you leave. Pot on the stove, frying pan below, butter in the fridge. Call in at the* Gazette *if you have a moment?*

*Sincerely,*
*Nicole*
*PS: Champagne can be treacherous. Take the Disprin!*

Nicole Lenoir-Jourdan was making it easy for me.

When I got home, Gloria didn't hold back. 'Well, well. Look what the cat dragged in! Where were you last night?'

'I got drunk,' I answered.

'Like father, like son,' she said sharply, so I immediately knew something was up. 'We were worried. Cory went down to the pub to see if you were there.'

'Mum, I'm twenty-seven years old, I can look after myself – I've got a medal to prove it.'

'I thought you'd gone to have dinner with Her Highness,' she sniffed.

'I did.'

'Couldn't have happened there – she doesn't touch a drop.'

'French champagne. That's different,' I answered.

'Oh, I *do* beg your pardon!'

I grinned, my head hurting. 'Tastes beautiful, but it catches up with you all of a sudden.'

Gloria, not mollified, replied in an attempt at a posh voice, 'Well, of course, such as us would not know! A bacchanalian evening, was it?'

She would occasionally surprise you with a word like that, one you'd never think she'd know. 'Mum, it was me. I got drunk the . . . er, Miss Lenoir-Jourdan remained sober as a judge.'

Gloria huffed. 'Disgraced yourself, did ya? Trust a McKelly.'

'I'll go around to the *Gazette* and apologise to her.'

'Don't!' she snapped. 'You've been doin' that since you was eight years old!' Then she suddenly changed tack. 'What's this I hear about a partnership?'

*So that was what this was all about.* 'Who told you that?'

'Never you mind. I know what's going on.'

'Well, perhaps you'll tell me. It's bloody Cory, isn't it? Can't ever keep his big mouth shut.'

'As a matter of fact, it wasn't. The whole island's talkin' about it. Father Crosby asked me after mass and I felt a right pillock. Every man and his dog knows and your *own mother's* left in the dark.'

'Mum, it isn't settled. Jimmy has to come back and there are some details yet to clear up. That's why I went over to her place last night.'

'What, and got yourself drunk?'

'That was afterwards.'

'What I want to know is why you want to go into partnership with her? She knows bugger-all about fishing and she's been bossing you around since you were a kid. Don't think I've forgotten how she bad-mouthed me when I took you outta school. What does she know about scrubbing floors and taking in other people's washin' 'til yer hands are red raw!'

Gloria of the elephant memory strikes again – whenever she was stirred up like this, too much mud rose to the surface. 'Mum, I'll let you know when everything's definite, I promise.'

'You be careful, son. She come here outta nowhere like she was Lady Muck! Nobody knows nothin' about that one! And she's got her la-dee-dah nose into everyone's business.'

I should have left it at that, given Gloria the last word, but I felt compelled to come to Nicole Lenoir-Jourdan's defence. 'Mum, she's made an enormous contribution to the island. She started the library, gave us music and singing lessons, the school concert, the band, and she's justice of the peace. Lots of people owe her heaps for the help she's given . . . and the *Gazette* . . . Christ, I should know!'

'You were a happy little boy before she came along.'

'Mum, what are you trying to say? Come on, get it off your chest.'

'She stuck her skinny nose into our affairs, took my little boy. Next thing, you're that unhappy you're running off to war to get yerself killed by them Chinese. Don't think I don't know, Jacko!'

'Yeah, well, that was my decision. Can't blame her if I got myself screwed up.'

'You never was screwed up before!'

'Ferchrissake, Mum, I was eight years old!' I paused, then added hurtfully, 'It was *you* didn't want me to be a bloody fisherman!'

'Ha! Fat lot of difference that's made! What you suppose yer doin' now?'

She had a point. 'You win, Mum,' I sighed. 'I don't want to fight you any more.'

'Just you be careful, son, that's all,' she warned again. Then, turning to go into the kitchen, she added, 'You want breakfast?'

I was just about to say that I'd already eaten, but caught myself in the nick of time. Island rules – passing out drunk is one thing, breakfast in a single lady's home is quite another. 'Cup of tea'll do me fine. My head's hurtin'.'

'Nothin' trivial, I hope?' Gloria replied, which made me laugh.

I had an appointment to go down to the pub when it opened. I'd arranged to meet a bloke named McCorkindale, Paddy McCorkindale, who'd worked with Steve and Cory on a company boat and was supposed to have been on the cray boats in New England. 'He's a bit of a pseudo Yank,' Steve had warned, 'but he's not a bad bloke and he knows his way around a fishing boat all right, so I reckon maybe he's not bullshitting.' Steve usually took a fair bit of convincing with people, so I had my hopes up.

The point was, buying a boat is a tricky business. It's a bit like a marriage – you're stuck with it for a long time. Get it wrong and you're miserable, right and you're set for life. It isn't just a matter of the right fittings and all the correct gear – a boat has a certain feel and way of handling, and no two boats are alike. It's always a compromise – some boats are at their peak performance in heavy seas while others work best when the whitecaps are running to shore.

Old-timers always compare a boat to a woman, and I reckon they're probably right – you've got to know what makes them cranky and what keeps them sweet, how they'll behave under stressful conditions and respond to plain-weather sailing. The idea of Jimmy buying a boat in America was worrying the shit out of me. We could give him specifications until the cows came home and he might find a boat that met every one of them and it could still be a dog. I didn't expect Nicole Lenoir-Jourdan to understand this and Jimmy still hadn't had sufficient experience to be the judge of a good boat – besides, you can only really judge a boat once you've been out on the water with her for a while.

There are three ways to buy a boat. Off the factory floor, which almost never happens; custom-built by a boat builder, which is always dangerous; and second-hand. Curiously enough, second-hand is the best way. If the boat is in great nick and has seen a few seasons in all conditions and has come up trumps, then that's the boat you want. But even then, it has to be a boat you like well enough to marry – which means you've got to have a dalliance or two before you choose her for your wife.

I hadn't mentioned any of this to Nicole Lenoir-Jourdan. I felt I needed to have the facts to convince her, even though I think if push came to shove she would let me have my own way. I admit I was going down to the pub to meet this bloke McCorkindale with a fair bit of an agenda – I wanted him to tell me that an American boat wasn't going to suit our Tasmanian conditions. I wanted to back my own emotional feelings with fact, although I told myself I wouldn't cheat.

He turned out to be a careful, slow-talking kind of bloke who liked to use American expressions such as 'say, buddy', 'you're welcome', 'kick ass', 'goddamn', 'fall' when he meant autumn – words like that. He chewed tobacco and reckoned he'd cultivated the habit from working in bad weather on a cray boat, when the wind would blow a fag straight out of your mouth. He spoke with an affected Yank drawl, but he'd forget sometimes and say the word he'd drawled a moment before in a fair-dinkum way, which is always a bit sus. I bought him a beer but stuck to the lemonade myself, joining him for just the one beer at the very end. He wasn't a bludger and bought his shout so I couldn't dismiss him as a lightweight, and he didn't question me drinking lemonade. I explained I'd been on the piss and he didn't push it like some blokes would, hair of the dog and all that – which, by the way, I reckon doesn't work anyway, or doesn't for me. Chasing the dog after a night out is only getting pissed all over again. About a hundred beers later you feel good, and that's only because you're back where you were the night before and it's going to be the same again the next morning, only worse. If it wasn't for the boats going out a week at a time and the pub being closed of a Sunday, I reckon most of the blokes on the island would be caught up in this spiral.

Paddy McCorkindale told me about fishing out of Nantucket and off Nova Scotia in the winter. 'You reckon we do it tough? Over there the brass monkey is singing soprano for five months a year!' Anyway, without any prompting, he said some of the American and Canadian cray boats were pretty good but wouldn't go too well over here with their reinforced hulls for ice conditions. There were a whole lot of other differences as well, some fairly good, others not. We promised to have another drink sometime and I bought him one for the road.

I was away just before lunchtime and was suddenly ravenous. Greg Woon's pies were unspeakable – only a hungry dog or a drunk would eat them – so I stopped off at Mrs Dunne's to buy four ham sandwiches before calling in at the *Gazette*. Nicole Lenoir-Jourdan looked up from a desk cluttered with bits of cut-out newspaper. 'Cuttings – from the mainland and the big island. I'm foraging for news,' she said. 'It looks like a quiet week. How are you feeling, Jack?'

'I'm so sorry about last night,' I said right off.

'Why, we had a lovely time! You were excellent company, Jack.'

'Yeah, until I passed out. The champagne, I didn't know it was going to hit me like that. One moment I was fine – for instance,

I remember your very last words were: "Sobbing as I was, I instantly fell head over heels in love with him." Then I was out like a light. Anyway, I'm very sorry, Countess.'

She laughed, remembering. 'Ah, Sir Victor Sassoon. It was he who introduced me to French champagne, although he'd only allow me one glass until I was eighteen, which was increased to two on my eighteenth birthday. I recall on one of his increasingly frequent visits he gave me a wonderful party and upped the number to three – one too many for a young lady.' She gave a short laugh, her head to one side, remembering. 'He used to recite a little rhyme he loved to use at a party when a young gal was present:

*"One glass of champers puts a glow upon her cheek,*
*Two is rather helpful to cause Her Prettiness to speak.*
*Three is very interesting and makes a damsel start to flirt,*
*A fourth is most insidious, when a girl should be alert.*
*While five is either promising, or goes directly to her feet,*
*But six is always dull, as she almost always falls asleep!"'*

'Is that why you only had two glasses?' I asked.

'You really are very observant, Jack. I haven't had champagne for years. I seem to recall two glasses, not three, were quite sufficient to enjoy myself while still keeping my wits about me. At first, of course, I was in show business, where a gal has to be very careful of her reputation.'

'Like the general said?'

'Yes, precisely. And then later, when I went into business, a loose tongue was not to be recommended. Especially in a lady, who had no business being in business as far as most Shanghai gentlemen were concerned.'

'Thank you for telling me. May I come back for more?' I asked, rather clumsily. 'I mean, more of the story of your life – not champagne,' I added hastily.

'Oh dear, Jack. I'm not at all sure I'm not raking over very old coals.'

'Please – you can't just leave it at the strawberry milkshake.'

She considered for a few moments. 'Sunday week, afternoon tea. I'll bake scones and we'll have them with jam and clotted cream – I'll ask John Champion to send some in. Did you know he's making a very respectable brie? He really is a livewire – it wouldn't surprise me at all if he doesn't end up doing something rather special for the island.'

'What, "*The choice of all the Champions*"?' I said, unimpressed, then remembered too late that she'd come up with that slogan.

'A good ripe brie,' she scolded, 'is something to be celebrated, Jack. Perhaps, as with the champagne, you could be in for a nice surprise – I'll ask him to send some in. All this talk of food is making me hungry.' She pointed to the brown-paper packet I held. 'I say, have you brought lunch?'

'It's only ham sandwiches. Mrs Dunne's,' I explained.

'Lovely, I'll make tea.' She rose from her desk and walked to the door leading to the little kitchenette but then paused suddenly, turned to me and said, 'Perhaps here in the office you should refer to me as Nicole ma'am and not as, well, you know what. Jack McGinty's ears may be likened to a bull elephant's, constantly flapping, and the walls seem to be made of cardboard. Already the whole island is talking about the partnership, and I'm terribly afraid the gossip may have started the last time the three of us were together in this office.'

Jack McGinty was the printing foreman at the *Gazette*, and a bit of a blabbermouth. I shrugged. 'Since when has anyone been able to keep a secret on the island for more than five minutes? Could have come from just about anywhere. Gloria, er . . . my mum got it from Father Crosby.'

'Trust his nibs to know,' she remarked, and disappeared into the kitchenette.

I opened up the sandwiches and pushed some of the newspaper clippings aside to make room for them on the desk, also allowing for the teapot, milk jug, sugar and cups.

She returned after a few minutes, poured the tea and handed me a cup. 'Jack, I've been thinking,' she began. 'Upon reflection I'm not at all sure it's a good idea to send Jimmy the specifications for a boat.

What do you think?' She must have seen my look of relief, because she immediately said, 'Oh, I see you agree – splendid!'

She'd pipped me at the post again. I'd been just a tad upset about what had happened on the way to the airport and I guess I'd got myself worked up a fair bit stewing over the situation. I had decided that Nicole Lenoir-Jourdan needed a run-down not only on boats, but also on what it was like to be a fisherman. Although it was probably fair to say most of the fishermen on the island were just about illiterate, that didn't make them stupid. I had decided she ought to know how I felt on the subject. In my mind I'd ticked off the attributes of a bloke who can call himself a fisherman, using Alf as my template.

For a start, he had to be a fierce individual with a real love of the sea, so much so that he must be prepared to earn less than if he kept his feet dry. He must have some idea of how to navigate, have a knowledge of first aid, be at the very least a competent bush mechanic – that is, someone who can change a filter, fit or adjust a belt, make up a hydraulic hose and get a stalled engine going, all with the deck pitching like a bronco at the Calvary rodeo. One thing is certain, these things never happen when you're in port or having a smoko in some quiet bay. Oh yes, these days he also has to be an electrician, as transceivers and echo sounders have a propensity to break down – not to mention alternators, generators, starter motors, and so on. Then, of course, like all sailors, he needs to be able to splice a rope, repair a sail (if he has one), fit a shackle, and repair anchor winches, pot haulers and steering devices with whatever material is at hand, most of which is usually inadequate for the job. And all that's just to keep him afloat! After all this is done, he still has to catch himself a load of fish, one of the more skilful, tricky and unpredictable pursuits devised by mankind to fill the universal stomach.

Lying in bed the night after Jimmy left, I had decided I would give Nicole Lenoir-Jourdan this little lecture – then maybe, just maybe, she might show me and people like me a little more respect when it came to writing down the specifications when you were about to buy a bloody fishing boat.

But, of course, I did no such thing. I relayed the conversation I had had with Paddy McCorkindale and then elaborated on my theory on boats and their owners – though, of course, not making quite the same analogies to a woman and marriage. I ended up making the suggestion that we buy a second-hand vessel, pointing out that we'd be able to sea-trial it and, furthermore, that we'd end up getting more for our money. 'There's got to be the right boat somewhere around the main island or even as far up as Eden. Provided they're properly maintained, boats don't necessarily get old. A boat built from Huon pine, for instance, will last practically forever. For the kind of money we're talking we might just be able to get something a little bigger than a forty-five footer if we buy second-hand. There's plenty of good cray fishermen who'll gladly help us sort things out when the time comes to make a choice.'

'That's a splendid idea, Jack. Shall I run an advertisement in the *Gazette*? I'm constantly surprised where my silly little newspaper ends up. Perhaps also in the Launceston *Examiner* and the Hobart *Mercury*. What do you think?'

*Here she goes again, taking over.* 'Great, I'll write the advertisement tonight and bring it in tomorrow.'

That night I wrote the words. The ad needed to be sweet and to the point, so there wasn't much to it:

> *Fully equipped cray boat wanted in good condition. All weathers. Twin donks. Suit crew of 2 to 4. 45 feet plus. Inquiries to the* Queen Island Weekly Gazette, *Queen Island. Tel. Queen Is. 27*

That was the easy part, but what I needed was a catchy headline – and nothing would come. I went to bed with my head spinning, and awoke quite suddenly at about three in the morning. There it was, shining in the air above my head like neon on the Ginza strip! So elegant, simple, amusing, catchy – even a modest stroke of genius.

**Cray**-zy a-**boat** you!

I lay awake until I heard Cory's black Orpington rooster start crowing. Sometimes an idea you get in the middle of the night seems ingenious until the cold light of dawn, when you've either forgotten it or it proves to be gibberish. I reckoned if I lay awake it wouldn't go away, and daylight would tell me if it held up.

I dressed while it was still dark, walked down to the harbour and climbed up to the lighthouse on the rise above, where I could see the fishing boats as they left Livingston. By this time it was coming on light and the fishermen were beginning to arrive on their pushbikes and motorcycles, the engine noises ripping the still, fragile morning air. The gulls swooped down to check me out, squawking at my feet and wheeling above my head, the usual stickybeak opportunists making a bloody nuisance of themselves. Fishing is almost all hard work but it has its moments, and one of them is on a morning like this one with the sea like glass, starting the outboard and putt-putting out of Livingston Harbour just as the sun begins to rise. I could picture Jimmy and me in our own boat, feeling the chill in the little zephyr that always blows across the bow just as the sun is peeping over the horizon. '**Cray**-zy a-**boat** you!' The slogan that was sure to get us the boat we wanted was still holding up, and looked like lasting into the new day. A sliver of the rising sun blistered a few cotton clouds that sat above the horizon and I took this as absolute confirmation that I was onto a certain winner. **Cray**-zy a-**boat** you! *A man's a bloody genius.*

Hardly able to contain myself, I arrived at the *Gazette* office just after it opened at half-past seven. I said g'day to Jack McGinty and noted that he really did have very large ears – the light streaming through a window behind him gave them the appearance of two red ping-pong bats attached to the sides of his head. 'Her Grace is in,' he said, jerking his head towards the door to Nicole Lenoir-Jourdan's tiny office. I knocked, and heard the call to enter.

'Goodness, it's you,' she said, surprised. 'What brings you here so early, Jack?'

I was astounded that she should ask. I'd been so consumed by the composing of our ad that if I'd been told Jack McGinty had been put on red alert, that he was oiling the press for the sole purpose of getting the advertisement into Saturday's paper, I wouldn't have been in the least surprised. 'I've brought the advertisement for the boat,' I said, trying to sound casual. 'It came to me in the middle of the night,' I clicked my fingers, 'just like that!'

Nicole Lenoir-Jourdan looked up over her glasses the way she'd done when I was a kid. 'Hmm . . . in my experience, those flashes of inspiration in the dark are usually better left there.'

'No, you'll *really* like this,' I assured her. I handed her the separate piece of paper on which I'd written my truly amazing headline.

She studied it for a moment, then ventured. 'It's a pun?'

'Yeah, yeah, but it's clever. See how I've picked out the word "Cray" and then "boat"?'

'Yes, I do see,' she said tentatively. 'Quite clever, Jack.'

'*Quite* clever?' I could hardly believe my ears.

'Oh dear, I've hurt your feelings. I am so sorry.'

'You don't like it, do you, Countess? I mean, Nicole ma'am?'

She looked suddenly very stern. 'Jack, the average fisherman can barely write his name. Of course, there are some like yourself and Jimmy who are very bright, but they're in the minority. I'm not suggesting that they lack intelligence – I've seen enough over the years to know that's not the case. But they are, as a general rule, illiterate. That means someone else may have to bring their attention to the advertisement we run. "**Cray**-zy a-**boat** you!", complete with attendant exclamation mark, isn't going to thrill their aesthetic senses to the marrow. Or do you disagree?'

'I reckon it will work a treat,' I said defiantly, determined to defend my work.

She considered for a moment, then said, 'Very well, it won't cost much to find out and I may be wrong – in which case I'd be delighted to apologise. We'll run it as a six-double in the *Gazette* and as a two-inch single in the big-island papers.'

'Six-double?'

'Six inches deep by two columns wide, or two inches by one,' she explained.

In my head I had seen it taking up a full page, which I know would have been ridiculous but these things build up and take on a life of their own.

That night I told Gloria the partnership was a goer and that we were looking for a second-hand boat to buy.

Her first question, of course, was, 'Won Tatts, 'ave ya?'

'Nicole Lenoir-Jourdan is putting up the money,' I replied.

'And where's she gunna get it? Sell that rag of hers, is she?'

'Mum, it's second-hand! A second-hand boat!' I protested, unwilling to tell her we were looking for something pretty special and bigger than forty-five foot. When she saw my advertisement in the paper I'd come clean.

'You know what happened to your father – could never make a go of it with that small boat. Took us a year after he gave it all up to pay the bank.'

I decided to come clean after all. 'It's not like that – we're looking for something decent.'

Gloria would have had a fair idea of what a decent rig would cost. 'Where's her money comin' from, *that's* what I'd like to know.'

'I dunno, Mum. She lives on her own – maybe she's saved her salary all these years?'

'Oh yeah? Then how did she buy that printing press? That would've cost a pretty penny.'

'I don't know,' I sighed. 'I guess it's none of our business.'

'Is if yer goin' to be partners an' all!'

'Leave it go, will'ya, Mum,' I answered, walking away.

'Much too much ya don't know about that one, Jack,' she called after me.

The ad appeared in the *Gazette* that Saturday and I waited for someone in the family to mention it at dinner that night. Nobody did.

'Anything unusual in the *Gazette* this week?' I asked after a while, trying to sound casual.

'No,' Gloria replied. 'Bit about more and more families getting the telephone, and they're putting a switchboard into the post office. Ma Gutherie's goin' to need a girl to operate it. I thought Dora might apply.'

'Anything else? You know, *unusual*?' I cut in hastily, trying to get the conversation back onto the *Gazette*. But they all looked at me, mystified.

'What is it, Jacko?' Sue asked.

'Well, as a matter of fact, only my whole future.'

'What are you on about, Jacko?' Gloria said. 'Nothin' about us in the paper.'

I gave up. 'The advertisement,' I sighed. 'The boat we're looking for.'

'Huh?' Gloria said, rather rudely. 'What advertisement?'

'Wait on,' Sue said. 'Where'd you put the paper, Mum?'

'Over there on the shelf, love.'

Sue left the table to retrieve the *Gazette*, turning the pages as she sat down. Finally, she discovered the ad. '"Cray-zy a-boat you!"' she read out aloud. I must confess, it didn't sound all that great the way she read it out.

'Oh, that!' Gloria exclaimed. 'Bloody stupid.'

'Stupid?'

'I think it's quite clever,' Sue said hurriedly. 'It's a pun.'

'What's a pun?' Cory asked.

'No bloke's gunna read that,' Steve said dismissively.

'Don't make no sense,' Gloria said again.

'Why not? Bloody good headline!' I defended, raising my voice somewhat.

'Jacko, they're fishermen!' she cried.

'That's a poofter headline,' Cory added, picking up on the word 'headline'.

'What the fuck would you know?' I shouted back.

'Eh! You mind your bloody language, Jacko! This is still my house! You're not too old to have your mouth washed out with soap!'

'Well, I still think it's clever,' Sue, ever the peacemaker, said, while Steve grunted and went on eating his dinner.

The ad ran for two weeks and didn't get a single bite – not one bloody reply. I was forced to accept that either there were no fishing boats for sale or the ad was a bummer. It was time to bite the bullet and, weary of clutching a dead baby to my chest, admit I'd been wrong.

Nicole Lenoir-Jourdan was pretty good about it. 'I've prepared another,' she said quietly. 'Perhaps you'll tell me if you approve, Jack?'

**Wanted**
45ft + cray boat
(will pay cash)
All inquiries to:
*Queen Island Weekly Gazette*
Tel. Queen Is. 27

'What can I say? It's perfect, and all in a two-inch single.'

'Thank you,' she said, without any fuss. But I knew she knew I'd got the message in one. She'd made a boo-boo jumping the gun on the specifications for the boat and I'd done the same, thinking I could write an advertisement. We'd intruded into each other's territory and thereby each learned a valuable lesson. The partnership was beginning to take shape.

A week later Busta Gut knocked on the front door and handed Gloria a letter. 'It's from America. Reckon it's from Jimmy, eh?'

'Thank you, Busta,' Gloria said, not bothering to ask him why he hadn't simply dropped it in the letterbox at the gate.

'He comin' back an' all?'

Gloria sighed. 'How do I bloody know!'

'Probably tell yer in that letter, Mrs McKenzie.'

'Maybe,' Gloria said, turning to shut the door.

'Well, ain't yer gunna read it?'

Gloria turned back to face him. 'Firstly, it's addressed to Jacko, and secondly, why don't you mind yer own bloody business, Busta Gutherie? Bugger off!'

'Could be a long time waitin' for the next letter,' Busta Gut said, sighing. 'Mailbag's got them tricky corners – letters get stuck.'

'Then I'll just have to complain to the postmaster, won't I?'

'Ain't no postmaster – only Mum.'

'The one in Launceston!'

Busta Gut seemed unfazed by this. 'Ya'll have to write to the queen.'

The letter from Jimmy was dated ten days previously and was written in the elegant copperplate he'd been taught at the orphanage. '*Brother Fish, dey don't teach much dat place, but dey done teach yoh to write nothin' real good,*' he had said. The letter was written in more or less grammatical English with only an occasional 'Jimmyesque' expression and his way of taking the shortest cut he could find for each sentence. Jimmy's unique expression was essentially a spoken language and didn't carry over onto paper, which, if anything, like the language of people who don't do a lot of writing, was rather formal. He himself would refer to the business of formal writing as, *'I got to chew da pen.'*

*Private Richard Oldcorn*
*Fort Myer*
*Washington DC*

*4th May, 1954*

*Dear Brother Fish,*

*I arrived fit and well but Australia, it a long way to go from. I got a sore ass in that airplane! Over here they treat me like some hero. They sent a full colonel to meet me at the airport and a military police escort. When I first see the provost I think to myself, O'oh, they gone trapped me, man! I under arrest for being AWOL.*

*Ain't no such thing happen. I been treated real special all along.*

*They sent in this tailor man and he make me two dress uniforms fit like a glove.*

*The debrief go all week. I suppose to say this, I not suppose to say that. The man who come from the Pentagon, he reckon the press they going to bombard yours truly. I got to have my wits about me. I know what these mothers want. I know that drill from way back, man. They want a nice polite nigger don't give them no trouble, don't sound too dumb, don't dish no dirt on the white comrades, show he modest and intelligent a natural-born leader. Also, I got to be, the officer from the Pentagon he say, 'circumspect'. 'Do you know what that means, Jimmy?' he ask me.*

*'Yes, sir – cautious, and taking everything into account,' I say. Nicole ma'am use that word once and I done looked it up. Also, I must never lose my temper. Even if the press, they difficult. 'Yes, sir', 'Yes ma'am', all that stuff I learn 1000 years ago when I just a chile. Press don't bother me none. It the protocol for the presentation. It ain't like Government House – they got a whole lot more crapola I got to know on that day.*

*Next week they going to tell the press I arrive here in America. They want me to say that after the POW camp, I found me a remote desert island near the South Pole so I can forget them communist atrocities. They gave me this map and I suppose to show it to the press. I got to point this tiny dot the bottom of Australia and near the South Pole. Only trouble, Tasmania gone get in the way. No problem, they get a new one and, presto! No more Tasmania and an arrow point south that say, 'To South Pole'. I told them, American people, the press, they ain't that stupid. They say, 'Don't you worry – they don't know where Australia is, never mine Tasmania.'*

*They also got me on the Ed Murrow show on the TV called 'See It Now' next week. I big time, baby! 'Hello America – Jimmy Oldcorn, he back from the communist indoctrination – the unshakeable all-American fighting man.' All that crap. I hope the folk from the Colored Orphanage, they watching – and Elmira Reformatory. Maybe the Kraus twins and Frau Kraus? Also on Ed Murrow I going to meet that judge who sent me to Korea. That going to be a big joke. My head going to be swelled the size of the Alabama moon! They shitting themselves that I going to get it wrong. They also teaching me to speak honky English, so I don't sound like some watermelon-pip-spittin' nigger. I don't tell them I can do it any time I want. Don't tell nobody nothing, then they think, 'Hey man, this dude, he a real quick learner.'*

*Man, already I weary of this bullshit! I wish I back on the beautiful island for some peace and quiet.*

*We doing special drill for the presentation at the White House next week so I'm going to write to you about that and meeting with the president. I got to practise hypothetical questions that maybe he going to ask. 'Yes, sir, Mr President, the winters in Korea, they very cold.'*

*The man from the Pentagon, he ask, 'Jimmy, how you get that scar on your face?'*

*'Sir, I got this scar 'cos two white American sonofabitch marines throw me out a travellin' truck – ha, ha, ha!'*

*'No, Jimmy, that's not how you got it.'*

*'It ain't, sir?'*

*'Jimmy, you got that knife scar from that fight with Corporal Steve O'Rourke, the man who murdered the two American soldiers. The story of the murder has already been in the press. He came at you with the knife in the POW camp.'*

*'Yes, sir! That true, sir.'*

*'You remember that good, son – that's what we call colour. That's one of the questions Mr Murrow is going to ask.'*

*'What about the plate, sir?'*

*'What plate?'*

*'The tin plate that broke the knife blade, sir.'*

*'That didn't happen.' He point to the scar. 'You got stabbed in*

*the face! That's what happened, soldier. Now you remember, don't you, son?'*

*'Yes, sir! What happened then, sir?'*

*'You grab him by the throat until he passes out, just the way it happened with the soldier in the hospital cave. You do remember now, don't you, soldier?'*

*'Yes, sir!'*

*'Don't let America down, son.'*

*'No, sir! Yes, sir!'*

*My love to all the family and to Wendy and to Nicole ma'am. Tell Gloria I going to need, soon as I get back, her cray stew – that big black pot all for myself!*

*I must stop now, Brother Fish – this the longest I ever chewed the pen, man.*

*Hoping to see you all real soon.*

*Yours truly, my brother,*
*Jimmy XXXX*

*PS: X – one for each of the girls – Gloria, Sue, Wendy and Nicole ma'am.*

I noted that Jimmy, ever circumspect, hadn't addressed Nicole Lenoir-Jourdan as 'Countess' and had remembered to keep it between the three of us. I was having tea with her on Sunday afternoon and as it was Friday I decided I'd save the letter until then – a nice surprise to go with the tea and scones. Anyway, Gloria wanted to show it to every man and his dog, and she positively preened over the bit about her cray stew. The letter, I knew, would eventually end up in her latest scrapbook together with the envelope plastered with American stamps – one of the American flag, and the others featuring Abraham Lincoln in profile.

Sunday afternoon duly arrived and I had to practically prise Jimmy's letter from Gloria's white-knuckled hands. 'You make sure you bring it back, Jacko. It's private and to us – the family!'

'Well, she *is* mentioned in it,' I suggested.

'Not like my cray stew!' Whatever that was supposed to mean.

We had afternoon tea in the garden, which overlooked the cliff. It was a glorious late-autumn day and Nicole Lenoir-Jourdan had set everything out on a small wicker table with two rather worn wicker chairs. Thankfully Vowelfowl's squawking self was nowhere to be seen. After a while we settled down to talk. That is, she talked while I drank tea, ate scones and listened.

'Well, Lawrence, that is, Mr Smithson, seemed to like my repertoire except that he cringed when, as the very last thing, I sang a Cantonese lullaby. When I finished he said, pout held for several moments, "No, darling, I don't think so. Not the heathen language."

'There was a moment's silence before Sir Victor Sassoon suggested, "Are you sure, Poppy? We always have more than a few wealthy Chinese attend the cabaret."

'Lawrence looked momentarily confused, then said, "Ah! The Shanghailanders will think it's hilarious, and the Chinese will think it's patronising. But if you insist, Sir Victor."

'"No, Poppy, you run the show. I'll leave it up to you. When do you think Nicole will be ready to start?"

'"Two or three weeks. She needs to learn to work a bigger audience, and she's not pitching all the numbers correctly."

'"How shall we bill her?" Sir Victor asked.

'"Hmm, difficult. You are a *real* countess, aren't you, darling?"

'I wasn't quite sure how to answer him – Russian aristocracy was of so little consequence in Shanghai. "I'm a *Russian* countess, Mr Smithson."

'"You will call me Lawrence, please! In that case we must never let that be known." He turned to Sir Victor. "Perhaps 'The Little Debutante'?"

'Sir Victor thought for a moment. "And when she grows up? No, that won't do at all – it's quite obvious the girl has talent. 'The Little Debutante' is much too precious – she can't be stuck with a stage name she'll grow out of in a season. Besides, all the snobs will be asking when she was presented to the queen. Much too complicated." He turned to me and asked, "What would you like to be known as, Nicole?"

'I'd always loathed the way I'd been billed at the nightclub – "Little Countess, the Schoolgirl Maestro". Anyway, at sixteen I felt myself quite grown-up. "I'd like to be myself, sir," then added, "if that's not too much trouble?"

'He seemed to be thinking, then said, "Hmm, Nicole Lenoir-Jourdan. It has a certain cachet – sounds French, and that's not altogether a bad thing." He looked up, and asked, "Why are you Russian and yet have a French name?"

'"My great-great-grandfather was a French instructor at the military academy in St Petersburg, and when Napoleon invaded Russia he elected to fight for the tsar. He was a general in the Imperial Russian Army and after Napoleon was defeated he was given the title. My mother was French and from a titled family, so the two names became hyphenated."

'"Quite a splendid pedigree, my dear – nothing to be ashamed of." He turned to Lawrence Smithson. "Poppy, I think we should let her have her own way."

'It was said without equivocation, and Lawrence must have known the decision was final. "Bit of a mouthful," was all he said.

'"I don't know, Poppy – double-barrelled names are all the rage these days."

'"Please, may I change my mind?"

'Lawrence looked relieved. "So? What's it to be, darling?"

'"Lily No Gin."

'"Are you sure?" Sir Victor asked, looking quite startled.

'"Sounds like you're refusing a drink, darling," Lawrence sniffed. I could see he wasn't impressed. "Lily? Very common. I once had an Aunt Lily – her nose was perpetually running and she smelled of cat's wee. Suffocated when the cat slept on her face."

'We were forced to laugh, but I'd made up my mind. "No Gin is my Chinese name – two words, 'No' and 'Gin', so it's easy to remember both by the Chinese and the Europeans. Lily is the name of my mother."

'"Lily No Gin? Hmm . . . it certainly isn't a difficult name to remember," said Sir Victor, "but if you must be Lily I shall personally call you Shanghai Lil – it sounds much more *show biz*."

'Poppy clapped his hands, bringing them up so that his fingers touched the underside of his chin. "Oh, I say – what an inspiration, Sir Victor!" He turned to me. "Yes, oh dearie me – *yes*! I do so like that, darling. *Shanghai Lil* – we could do something with that."

'"It sounds like a prostitute," I said softly. I knew I was overstepping the mark, but one only gets one chance to name oneself and I, not they, had to live with it – hopefully for a long time. "Big Boss Yu will like No Gin. It was he who named me, gave me my Chinese name."

'That seemed to settle the matter on the spot. I was beginning to realise just how powerful my Chinese protector was in Shanghai.

'I'm bound to say that while Lawrence Smithson was of the same persuasion as Noël Coward – that is, homosexual and in show biz – he didn't sulk or grow petulant for long. He accepted my name, and after ten days of solid piano and singing practice from two to five every weekday afternoon, finally one afternoon he said, "You've done well, darling. You may call me Poppy."

'"Yes, quite – bravo!" chimed in Sir Victor.

'"We open in ten days and . . . " Poppy fell into "the pose", which I had learned happened when he was thinking or upset, although "upset" included a raised eyebrow with one eye shut. This time his right eyebrow was at rest and his eyes were both looking directly at me. "We'll need photographs for posters – and I do think the hair must go, darling. After all, we don't want any of the gym frock and 'Little Countess, the Schoolgirl Maestro' remaining, do we, darling? That would be too ghastly – too *outré* for words."

'I needed time to think. "I'll have to ask Big Boss Yu," I replied, remembering the incident in the nightclub. My comment received the full pose plus arch.

'"Oh dear – oh dearie me. First he names you, now he arranges your hair. How very sweet."

'"Careful, Poppy," Sir Victor warned. "You have to live here – I don't."

'My hair fell almost to my waist and, as many of the songs required me to toss my head about, I mostly wore it in plaits so that it didn't get in the way of the piano keys. If I was going to be a grown-up and lose the schoolgirl tag, then Poppy's request wasn't unreasonable. It was just that it came as rather a shock.

'My mother had always loved brushing my hair, as had Ah Lai. Even when Ah Lai and I were together in her village she would brush my hair morning and night until it positively shone. The locals used to gather around to look at it and occasionally one or two of them were allowed by Ah Lai to touch it lightly. I think she used touching my hair as a return for a favour granted. To these simple village folk, with my blonde hair and blue eyes I was almost like a creature from another planet. Cutting my hair would be the final farewell to my childhood.

'Curiously, I had absolutely no idea how this might be done. My mother had always trimmed my hair and after she died Ah Lai would do it. In Harbin I'd either done it myself, or one of the girls in the club would trim the ends for me. I still had about half of the money I'd been given the night the Three Musketeers of the French Concession had visited the General's Retreat, when Big Boss Yu had christened me No Gin. I would need at least two evening gowns for the show and I anticipated this would take most of my carefully hoarded money. I also felt that as Big Boss Yu was my protector, and because of the lock of hair he'd requested in Harbin, I would need to ask him about cutting my hair. On my way home that night I asked Ah Chow if I might have an appointment to see Big Boss Yu, and he said he would ask.

'The following evening he took me along the Bund to a fairly modest building where Big Boss Yu kept an office. I was ushered into what was not, by Shanghai standards, an overly imposing office. The furnishings, though, were elaborately Chinese – lots of ebony and mother-of-pearl inlay and overstuffed chairs upholstered in an oyster-coloured brocade. Two large, painted scrolls hung on the walls, one of a branch of ripe persimmons and the other featuring a mountain and cliff scene with gnarled trees growing from the cliff face. But what demanded my immediate attention were the seventeen giant grandfather clocks that lined every wall, varying slightly in design though all quite obviously from the same manufacturer. They each registered a different time and the entire room was filled with a cacophony of ticking. Mr Yu sat behind a large ebony desk, the only object on it a wonderfully complicated-looking silver pen-and-ink set designed as two male peacocks.

'I bowed my head. "Good afternoon, *loh yeh*. I thank you for allowing me to see you."

'"Sit down, No Gin. What brings you to see your old uncle?"

'I looked up into his lined face and purple-ringed eyes. It was impossible to guess his age. "It is perhaps a matter of small consequence. They wish me to cut my hair for the new-season show opening at the Palace Hotel. I have come to ask your permission."

'He was silent for a moment, then asked, "Why do you think a man would be concerned about a young woman's hair?"

'"I am aware it is a subject of little concern, my lord. It is only that you requested a lock in Harbin and I thought perhaps . . ."

'But he interrupted before I could complete the sentence. "You are very perceptive, No Gin. I will let you know." With this he offered me tea, which I knew to politely refuse, bowing and turning to go but unable to take my eyes off the clocks. He must have been aware of my curiosity. "The clocks, they tell the time in every major capital city in the world. They are a gift from a Japanese company. I receive a new one every year."

'The following evening Ah Chow drove me to what I took to be a Taoist temple and on the way instructed me to ask for the incense master, telling me that all had been arranged. "At the end you must give him this," he instructed. It was a red-and-gold *li tze*, or "lucky money" envelope with a peach-and-pine design for longevity on the outside, and judging by its thickness it contained a considerable amount of money.'

Nicole Lenoir-Jourdan's story was becoming more and more intriguing, and I wished Jimmy was here to listen to it first-hand.

'I entered into the semi-dark of the building to be met by a young acolyte in a white-and-red robe. I greeted him and asked if I might see the incense master. He nodded as though he had been expecting me. As I passed the altar I bowed three times to Kuan Yin, the Goddess of Mercy. She was very old and made of wood that had once been painted in the gaudy colours Chinese peasants so love. But now only a glimpse of yellow, cobalt and red clung to the dark, incense-stained statue. I had entered a Taoist temple on two occasions with Ah May, my present *amah*, and of course with my first *amah*, Ah Lai, on many occasions in her village, so the surroundings were familiar, although I knew this to be no ordinary shrine.

'I was ushered into a small room and asked to wait, and presently a most venerable old Chinese man wearing an ash-grey robe and a knotted turban of red cloth entered the room. I bowed. "Greetings from my taipan, Yu Ya-ching. I am sent by him, *loh yeh*."

'"You are she," he said, looking at me carefully. "Come." He led me back into the main temple behind an intricately patterned screen, which had also seen better days and was torn and carelessly patched in several places. Here, too, was a smaller statue of Kuan Yin with an incense lion beside it, a curl of dove-grey smoke rising from its mouth. In the customary manner I lit three joss sticks and bowed slowly three times once again, which I sensed somewhat tried the patience of the old man. "What is it you wish to know?" he asked.

'"Will the cutting of my hair cut off my luck, *loh yeh*?" I asked. Then I hurriedly added, "But this is of little importance, my lord. I must know if it will affect the fortunes of my taipan?"

'"I will read the water mirror. Stand still, and look at me," he commanded.'

Before I had the chance to even ask the question, Nicole Lenoir-Jourdan turned to me to explain. 'Reading the water mirror is simply a very close scrutiny of the face, used to decide what divining method the incense master will choose. After some little time looking into the rheumy eyes of the old man, he said, "*Lu ssu* bird!"

'The *lu ssu* bird, also known as the rain bird because it is said to be able to forecast rain, is a tiny finch that was kept in a cage behind the altar. The incense master now reached for one of a number of bamboo flasks each set into a cubbyhole contained within a box-like shelving structure with the cubbyholes facing outwards, much like a wine rack. He opened the lid and I saw the flask was filled with a large number of bamboo slivers, a bit like a container of fiddlesticks, although burned on each sliver was a line of Chinese characters – ancient calligraphy beyond the understanding of any Chinese layperson.

'The incense master up-ended the flask, sending the bamboo slivers scattering to the floor at his feet. Next he lifted the bamboo cage and placed it on the altar, opening the door to allow the tiny bird to hop out. The *lu ssu* bird hesitated for only a moment, then fluttered to the floor, picked up one of the slivers and flew up to rest on the incense master's outstretched hand. He took the sliver of bamboo from its beak and gently placed the tiny bird back into the cage, closing the door behind it.

'Then, searching within his grey robes, he produced a small leather case, opened it and removed a pair of *pince-nez*, which he carefully adjusted on the bridge of his nose. He held the sliver of bamboo so that it almost touched the spectacles and examined it for some time. Then he looked up at me, removed his *pince-nez*, returned them to their case and concealed it, once again, beneath his robes.

'"You may cut your hair, but the left plait must be removed first and immediately destroyed. The right plait must be washed and re-plaited, and this you must give to your taipan. When he returns it to you your good fortune will end."

'"And *his* good fortune, my lord?"

'"It is good for now, but it will sail away across the seas and return again later to his dragonhead."

'I bowed to him, then bowed three times to the Goddess Kuan Yin, and presented the *li tze* with both hands. Jack, you must understand that Chinese fortune-telling is ninety per cent ritualistic superstition. I didn't believe the old man for one moment. What I had done by going to the Taoist temple was simply out of respect for Big Boss Yu. While I was obliged to present my right plait to him, I had already decided to send the left one to Ah Lai, my old *amah* in Manchuria. Then, just as I was leaving, the old man said, "Sadness in your life, death. A man with a limp." I knew he couldn't possibly know of the recent death of my father, or that he had had a permanent limp. I had told Big Boss Yu of my father's death and conceivably his senior assistant, Chang Kia-yin, may have mentioned this to the incense master when he made the arrangements for my visit, but even this seemed a highly unlikely deduction to make. What none of them could possibly have known was that my father possessed a permanent limp. I suddenly felt compelled to follow precisely the incense master's instructions.'

Just as I was wondering how a girl's plaits could bear such importance, Nicole Lenoir-Jourdan said to me, 'Jack, the business of the hair may seem to western eyes a very small thing. You may well wonder why I would include it in the story. But in China it is often the minutiae that in the end are important, and the main thrust of our lives of little importance. There is a Chinese saying that goes like this: "When a single hair of the brushstroke is out of place, the painting is spoiled."

'My visit to the incense master was not to be the end of a long day. Ah Chow next drove me to a hair salon on Avenue Haig on the boundary of the French Concession. It was owned by Madame Peroux, a famous Shanghai hairdresser from French Indochina, who, as it turned out, was French in name and Chinese in appearance. She was delighted when I spoke to her in French. "Such beautiful hair, Mademoiselle Lenoir-Jourdan. It is a shame to cut it – it will never be as good again. How old are you?" she asked.

'"Sixteen, madam."

'"Sixteen years to grow it like this, and I must cut it! How very sad."

'"It interferes with playing the piano," I said, trying to sound practical.

'"No, no, *ma chérie* – I can braid it so." She took my plaits in both her hands and made an arrangement so that they appeared to sit in a circle with a clever twist at the back and all of it on the top of my head out of the way. "No?"

'I laughed. "I look like a Brünnhilde from the Black Forest, madame. No, it has been decided. I cannot change my mind."

'"At sixteen it is no shame to change your mind, mademoiselle. At sixteen it is compulsory to do so at least twice on everything you decide to do. No?"

'"It has been decided by Big Boss Yu, madame."

'Madame Peroux sighed, the magic name putting all further argument aside. "To be a woman, it is a terrible burden," she clucked, then reached reluctantly for the scissors.

'"First the left plait, please, Madame Peroux."

'"As you wish, *ma chérie*." She removed the left plait carefully.

'"Please, madame, will you give it to me now?" I could see the puzzled look on her face. "Now, please," I demanded, holding out my hand and looking at her mirror-image face. She handed me the plait, preparing to remove the right one. I moved my head away and twisted around to face her. "I must destroy this immediately. Do you have a furnace, madame?"

'"You cannot, mademoiselle – impossible!" she declared, horrified at the suggestion. "This is *beautiful* hair – a wigmaker will pay a fortune. You must keep it for your grandchildren."

'I rose from the chair and turned rather rudely to face her. "Please show me the furnace," I demanded.

'"No, I cannot. This is a good neighbourhood – banker Li Ming, the taipan of the Bank of China, lives at number 650. Burning hair will smell bad, and he will complain."

'"I will tell Big Boss Yu – he will fix it," I said confidently, using authority I didn't possess. I walked to the back of the salon and out into a small yard where I expected to find an earthenware stove burning charcoal. In those days small traditional stoves where servants prepared their food were so common at the back entrances of business premises in China as to be considered ubiquitous. As I expected, it was there. I walked up to it, startling the servant standing over it preparing a pot of rice by stuffing the thick blonde plait directly onto the glowing charcoal. The plait seemed to fizz into a shower of coloured sparks, the sound almost as if I was burning something alive. Then it was swallowed up in flames. I had no idea hair was so flammable. I have to confess, Madame Peroux was right – the smell that rose up with the smoke was simply atrocious.

'I returned inside and apologised profusely for my boldness and poor manners. "I have been to see the incense master at the Taoist temple. I had no choice but to follow his instructions or I would bring bad fortune to my taipan." I smiled, attempting to disarm her. "Madame, just one more small favour – before you remove the right plait, will you wash it, dry it and re-plait it and only then remove it, please?"

'I knew the complaint about the smell of burning hair was simply an excuse. Being Asian herself, she nodded, though somewhat grimly, not at all pleased with me. I could well understand her annoyance. Western hair was in Chinese eyes wondrously fine and, unlike coarser Chinese hair, would fetch an excellent price. She was, after all, a Chinese businesswoman and saw the potential for making a fair dollar. She was naturally disgusted to see such an easy profit go up in flames.

'The smell of the burning hair pervaded the salon, and no doubt the entire neighbourhood, so that there was little further conversation between us. She washed and dried my hair, and re-plaited the right side of my head before removing the splendidly shining plait. Then she braided several strands of hair into a small rope and tied one end while repeating the process at the other. She handed me the elegant-looking plait in silence. Then she dampened my remaining hair and snipped away for some time, transforming it into a very smart-looking French bob. Madame Peroux explained that I should return once a week to have it trimmed and re-styled. When I went to pay her she waved me away. "It has been taken care of, mademoiselle." I apologised again, and thanked her for the plait.

'She shrugged philosophically. "I am Chinese, Mademoiselle Lenoir-Jourdan."

'I returned home and stopped on the way to buy a rather expensive box made of persimmon wood with a lucky dragon's head carved into the lid, and placed the plait inside. When Ah Chow dropped me off in the Chinese City I handed it to him. "Please give this to Big Boss Yu. The incense master says it will bring him good joss."

'Ah May opened the door and screamed, then burst into tears, backing away from me. "Aieeyaaa! What have you done!" she cried, unable to control her shaking.

'"I have grown up, Ah May," I replied, holding her to me.

'"The people in the street will mourn for you," she said.

'So much for changing my name on the poster announcing the new season at the Palace Hotel. It appeared at the very bottom of a list of artists who would be visiting Shanghai over the following six months. My inclusion almost required spectacles to read, and stated: "Featuring nightly the delightful new star Lily No Gin as 'Shanghai Lil'." I was to learn that despite his great charm and easygoing ways, Sir Victor Sassoon expected to have his way in all things. He'd only been present for a little more than an hour and the importance of my name on a show poster was of the utmost lack of concern to anyone, yet he'd persisted. It was this attention to detail that made him one of the most powerful and richest men in the world.

'As these things invariably happen, audiences seemed never to hear my stage name when it was announced but proceeded to clap immediately after "Shanghai Lil" followed it. Whether I liked it or not, that was how I was known for the next two years.

'There is always a party after the opening of a new show, and I was looking forward to both with a mixture of anticipation and dread. I had, after all, been locked up in the tiny house in the Chinese City for three weeks. Apart from Poppy and members of the dance orchestra, who were regulars at rehearsals, I saw very few people. The Russian doorman, Zhora Petrov, known to his Russian friends as Georgii, had become a friend and the hotel staff had come to regard me almost as one of their own. But I lacked any real European company except for the dreadful Mrs Worthington with her daily battering of clipped and rounded words. Ah Chow would be waiting the moment I finished rehearsals. I dreamed of some day walking out of the hotel to find no big black Buick waiting for me.

'I forgot to mention that I had been put on a salary – small but not ungenerous considering I was an ingénue. A week before the opening Ah Chow took me to a tailor, where I was allowed to pick the material for three evening *chum sarm*, the traditional Chinese dress for a woman of quality. I chose a glistening black for one, and for the second a red trimmed with gold, the traditional Chinese colours of celebration, and a brilliant peacock blue for the third – all of them in silk, although only the peacock blue carried a sheen to it.

'My mother had always told me that dressing well was about understatement – a beautiful woman is the jewel and not the baubles, bangles and beads she wears. Nothing should distract the eye from her.' At this point, Nicole Lenoir-Jourdan looked up. 'Not, Jack, that I believed myself beautiful, but from a very early age my mother had taught me how to carry myself with a sense of pride. She would say, "Remember, Nicole, less is more. Always remember you are half-French – dress to show yourself, and not your wealth." My gawky figure of a year ago had filled out somewhat, and I think I looked pleasing enough to the eye and, with my new French bob and a little bright lipstick and eye shadow, I felt I looked at least twenty.

'So, of course, opening night was a very exciting occasion. The ballroom was essentially for dancing but it was also a supper club and featured a warm-up for half an hour at seven p.m. and then at ten o'clock "Champagne Hour" – the main show, when the house dispensed free Bollinger to the seated patrons – with dancing interspersed in between.

The warm-up act on opening night was a Chinese acrobatic troupe, while the star of the ten o'clock was, improbable as it sounds, a German *Lieder* singer whose name I forget but who proved a great initial attraction for the German Shanghailanders, most of whom turned up to hear her sing and then promptly left. The German star spoke no English and lasted for only the first week of a six-week engagement, being promptly dismissed by Sir Victor following a tongue-lashing she delivered to the audience in her native German for not devoting to her their undivided attention. I went on as the final act, wearing my peacock-blue *chum sarm*, singing cabaret and playing the grand piano with the orchestra occasionally called upon to accompany me. The idea was to warm up the audience for the late-night dancing that was to follow.

'My very first performance was to a crowd of at least 800 people and I was understandably nervous, but, to my absolute delight, at its conclusion the men rose from their tables and cheered. Mr Coward's "Poor Little Rich Girl", which I did as my final number, brought the house down and was to become an important part of my future repertoire – remind me, Jack, to tell you about meeting and playing it in front of Noël Coward.'

'You performed for Noël Coward?'

'Yes – but more on that later.'

'Sorry, I didn't mean to interrupt. Please, go on.'

'Well, flushed with first-night success I was now looking forward immensely to the party, having vindicated myself to Sir Victor, Poppy, but mostly Big Boss Yu, who attended the show although he declined Sir Victor's invitation to the after-party. Mr Yu had arrived alone, which was unusual – he was a popular and gregarious Chinese taipan usually accompanied by half-a-dozen people of every race. That night he sat alone at a small table with a bottle of Napoleon cognac for company. When I got resounding applause and the men rose from their tables, he did so as well and clapped, beaming at me. So I felt I hadn't disappointed him even though he refused an invitation to come backstage, and left immediately after the show.

'So you can imagine my despair when a serious Poppy approached me in my dressing room. Earlier backstage, he'd hugged me and lifted me off my feet, swinging me around in a circle. "You were wonderful, darling!" he'd gushed. But on this second visit he said, "A word, darling?"

'"What is it, Poppy? What have I done?" I asked, bewildered.

'"Bad news, sweetheart. I'm afraid you're not invited to the party. Your chauffeur will take you home immediately."

'"But Poppy, why?"

'He sighed. "Mrs Worthington. She says you're not quite ready."

'"Ready for what?" I protested.

'"Why, haven't you been told? To be exposed to the public – the nobs, my dear."

'"But, but, what has that got to do with my act?" I asked, distressed.

'"Nothing. Orders, darling. You have to be impeccable."

'"Impeccable? What has to be impeccable? My hair, my gown – *what*?"

'"Your accent. You have to be taken for a young English gal of good breeding. Clipped and rounded, my dear."

'"Who decided this?"

'Poppy smiled. "It came from Sir Victor, but I'm sure he was merely the messenger. He doesn't give a hoot about that sort of thing."

'"Big Boss Yu?"

'He shrugged. "I haven't the faintest, darling. Someone out there is grooming you for something and, whatever it may be, being a Russian countess simply won't do the trick!"

'"But you said it was Mrs Worthington. Was she here?"

'"Don't shoot the messenger, darling – only doing as I'm told."

'Well, of course, all my new-found sophistication went completely out the window and I'm afraid I began to weep like a petulant schoolgirl. Poppy didn't stay to comfort me.

'"That's show biz, sweetheart," he said. "Time to grow up, darling." Then he turned on his heel and left, leaving me to wail into the bunch of flowers I'd received on my debut with a note that said "Sincere good wishes, the Management & Staff". Though, in fairness, I have to add I had also received an exquisite orchid from Sir Victor that I'd hoped to wear with my red *chum sarm* to his party.

'That frightful woman kept me at my English lessons for an entire year before she agreed I was sufficiently clipped and rounded to be allowed among the upper crust of Shanghai society. I was lonely and frustrated but, curiously enough, this did nothing to disrupt my career as a cabaret singer and entertainer. The fact that I never appeared in "public" and no one knew where I lived meant all sorts of rumours began circulating, and Shanghai Lil became a mysterious, romantic woman. I was seen arriving and being whisked away in a big American limousine and then simply disappearing. Newspaper reporters tried to track me down without success, as it never occurred to any of them that I might live in the Chinese City.

Isolation from other Europeans also served to bring me close to the Chinese people again, as I had once been in Ah Lai's village in Manchuria. My Cantonese became fluent and I think I was popular with the locals, who always treated me with great kindness. Even though I was now earning a very reasonable salary, Big Boss Yu continued to support me while making no demands on me whatsoever. He was like a benevolent uncle, always there when I needed something. And while I saw very little of him, I feel sure my every movement was reported back to him.

'Finally, two days before my seventeenth birthday, Mrs Worthington pronounced me clipped and rounded enough to be exposed to Shanghai's elite. In the period I'd been with her she'd fashioned an entirely new background for me, a past life that was appropriate for my impeccable accent. Good school, county manor, minor aristocracy and, most importantly, I had cultivated a mannerism unique to the English upper classes that allowed me to disengage from a conversation that appeared to be getting too personal with just the right amount of polite detachment – the raised eyebrow and almost imperceptible expression of disapproval that Poppy had dreamed of achieving all his life.

'I was ready, although I had no idea for what. Then, coming in to rehearsals the following day, I received a note from Sir Victor, apologising for the late invitation and, saying that he was giving a small party in the tower on the coming Saturday and would I like to come along.

'Well, the party, as it turned out, was being thrown for me – my "coming out", so to speak. It was a splendid affair, and Sir Victor saw to it that I was almost always at his side so that I was never made to answer any difficult questions. That was the first time I tasted champagne. Sir Victor later told me that he'd let it be known that my parents were friends of his family in England, suggesting that they were household names there, and that they greatly disapproved of my being in show business, which made it indiscreet to question me too closely. My clipped-and-roundeds must have been successful, because one of the guests remarked to me in the ladies' powder room, "My dear, being discreet is all very well, but some of us can spot a Rodean accent a mile away." In fact, I can't say I enjoyed the occasion very much. Shopping the next day with Ah May in the Chinese City was a great deal more pleasant.'

She paused, glancing at the table. 'Oh, dear, you've left two scones. It would be a shame to let them go to waste, Jack – you know how quickly they dry out.'

'You've only eaten one,' I said.

'Yes, but I haven't been in a POW camp. You still haven't quite regained your previous weight, Jack.'

'Don't know why. I'm pigging out . . . er, eating like a horse.'

'Time to jump forward a bit, Jack. I don't want to be a bore, but a cabaret act in a grand hotel doesn't change a great deal and I was to spend the next year at it until I turned eighteen. I imagine I had become a household name among the Europeans and the westernised Chinese – that is, of course, only in Shanghai and as Shanghai Lil. Lily No Gin, my original stage name, had long since been forgotten and was now only used by Big Boss Yu and the people in the Chinese City. As for Nicole Lenoir-Jourdan, she seemed somehow to belong to a forgotten past. I'd had several offers to work overseas and Noël Coward had been kind enough to suggest I "come back to England" where he was certain I would be a hit, but I wasn't at all sure I wanted to have a career on the stage.

'Forgive me for jumping ahead momentarily, Jack, by about five years, while I'm on the subject of Mrs Worthington. By 1929 Sir Victor had transformed the Palace Hotel into the magnificent Cathay Hotel and taken up residence in its tower. While I'd given up my singing career by that time I would often play and sing at his parties and naturally I'd sing one or another of Noël Coward's songs, which were becoming increasingly popular. Coward came out to Shanghai on the Orient Express to do a few nights at the Cathay Hotel. As was his wont, Sir Victor threw a lavish party for him in the magnificent tower apartment he'd built for himself. Big Boss Yu and I were among the several hundred guests, and so was the awful Mrs Worthington. At one stage during the party I saw that she'd cornered Noël Coward and that the poor man seemed trapped. Ten minutes later she was still at it and he was looking decidedly embarrassed, so I walked up and said, "Mr Coward, Sir Victor has asked me to sing one of your songs and I wondered if you'd accompany me?" Of course, under normal circumstances, I would never have dared to suggest such an impertinence.

'"Of course, my dear!" he said with palpable relief, excusing himself from the awful woman. When we were out of earshot he said to me, "Who is that simply dreadful woman, darling? She wants me to put her niece on the stage!" I fetched him a glass of champagne and told him the story of my clipped-and-roundeds, leaving him in no doubt about my feelings towards the reprehensible Mrs Worthington. "How perfectly ghastly, I shall write a song about her – it will be your revenge."'

Nicole Lenoir-Jourdan laughed. 'Some years later, after I'd arrived on the island, the song came out and was called "Don't Put Your Daughter on the Stage, Mrs Worthington".'

'Mum loved that song – we played it a lot when I was a kid!' I exclaimed. Then, on a sudden impulse, I added, 'You couldn't sing it now, could you?'

'Oh, I'm much too rusty, Jack,' she protested.

'I haven't played it since I was a kid, either, so we'd be even,' I encouraged.

'Oh, so you'll accompany me? That might be fun.'

Sitting in her cliff-face garden with the whitecaps rolling in as the shadows started to fall on a lovely afternoon, I began to play the opening few bars and then Nicole Lenoir-Jourdan came in, singing in a nice contralto voice.

*'Regarding yours, dear Mrs Worthington, of Wednesday the 23rd,*
*Although your baby may be keen on a stage career,*
*How can I make it clear that this is not a good idea?*
*For her to hope, dear Mrs Worthington, is on the face of it absurd.*
*Her personality is not in reality inviting enough, exciting enough,*
*For this particular sphere.*

*Don't put your daughter on the stage, Mrs Worthington,*
*Don't put your daughter on the stage.*
*The profession is overcrowded and the struggle's pretty tough,*
*And admitting the fact she's burning to act, that isn't quite enough.*
*She has nice hands, to give the wretched girl her due,*
*But don't you think her bust is too developed for her age?*
*I repeat, Mrs Worthington, sweet Mrs Worthington,*
*Don't put your daughter on the stage.*

*Don't put your daughter on the stage, Mrs Worthington,*
*Don't put your daughter on the stage.*
*She's a bit of an ugly duckling, you must honestly confess,*
*And the width of her seat would surely defeat her chances of success.*
*It's a loud voice, and though it's not exactly flat,*
*She'll need a little more than that to earn a living wage.*
*On my knees, Mrs Worthington, please, Mrs Worthington,*
*Don't put your daughter on the stage.*

*Don't put your daughter on the stage, Mrs Worthington,*
*Don't put your daughter on the stage.*
*Though they said at the school of acting she was lovely as Peer Gynt,*
*I'm afraid on the whole an ingénue role would emphasise her squint.*
*She's a big girl, and though her teeth are fairly good,*
*She's not the type I ever would be eager to engage.*
*No more buts, Mrs Worthington, NUTS, Mrs Worthington,*
*Don't put your daughter on the stage.*

*Don't put your daughter on the stage, Mrs Worthington,*
*Don't put your daughter on the stage.*
*One look at her bandy legs should prove she hasn't got a chance,*
*In addition to which, the son of a bitch can neither sing nor dance.*
*She's a vile girl and uglier than mortal sin,*
*One look at her has put me in a tearing bloody rage.*
*That sufficed, Mrs Worthington, Christ! Mrs Worthington,*
*Don't put your daughter on the stage.'*

'Oh dear – what fun, Jack,' she said, laughing and clapping her hands together. She reached over and touched the side of the teapot. 'I'll just pop into the house and make a fresh pot.' When she returned she resumed her story right off, speaking while she was pouring the tea.

'Now, back to the Palace Hotel, 1924. Big Boss Yu had decided against my continuing my singing career beyond my eighteenth birthday – a rather splendid affair with Sir Victor, who was visiting at the time, throwing a marvellous party for me in his Palace Hotel apartment. It was here that I gave my final performance, afterwards thanking the guests, who represented most of the cognoscenti and upper crust of the city, and then announcing my retirement – I must say, to a rather startled gathering. Shanghai Lil, as I previously mentioned, had become a fixture in Shanghai and I think it was taken for granted that I would always be the hotel's professional in-house entertainer. Sir Victor, at this point, was already talking with growing enthusiasm about building the extension to the Palace, to be known as the Cathay Hotel. "It will be one of the great hotels in the world and you shall sing and play on the opening night," he'd promised. So my retirement came as a big surprise even to him – and as a disappointment to me.

'You may well ask why I didn't kick over the traces and go my own way. I could have left Shanghai and started somewhere else – England, perhaps. But it must be remembered I was a stateless person without a passport or travel documents and if I left Shanghai I would be a refugee. I was also a very young eighteen-year-old who lived in alternate worlds where I was a big name in local show biz, yet played no part in the European society of the city. I still lived under the aegis of Big Boss Yu in the Chinese City, where I had become totally accepted as if one of the locals – a *gwai mui*, yet one of them.'

I couldn't stop myself interrupting. 'But surely, Countess, you could have changed that – moved into a flat of your own. You must have been earning a reasonable salary by now?' I asked.

'Yes, of course, Jack. But it may be a little difficult to understand. On the one hand there was the life of the Shanghailander (such a peculiar expression), which I embraced every evening. Although, when you completed your day at midnight this basically meant late-night parties, drinking and imbibing other substances if you were in the wealthy young set.'

'What other substances?' I asked ingenuously.

'Well, there was a lot of morphine and cocaine about at the time. All the young "swinging twenties" people were using it, though it wasn't hard to see that both substances, like alcohol, didn't do much good. Remember, since the age of fifteen, and with the exception of a single year at the General's Retreat, I had been living a Chinese life. Big Boss Yu was, in a very real sense, my guardian – or, put more correctly, he acted in the role of strict but protective uncle. In the tradition of the Chinese he was always to be obeyed, and Ah Chow was always waiting for me after the show. If I wanted to go to a party, usually one thrown by Sir Victor when he visited, I had to let him know and he would undoubtedly refer it to Big Boss Yu. The opportunity to enter any of Shanghai's dens of iniquity simply wasn't available.'

'Did he ever refuse you permission – you know, to go to a party?'

'Yes, but not often. Once, as I recall, when Sir Victor gave a party for a high-ranking visiting Japanese diplomat. Big Boss Yu didn't trust the Japanese even though, judging from the perpetually ticking clocks, he did business with Japan and no doubt with the 30 000 resident Japanese in Shanghai. He never mixed with them and didn't approve of my doing so. In addition he would expect me to refuse an invitation if he himself was attending the same party.'

'It must have been difficult?'

'No, not really. Late nights didn't suit me.'

Having answered my questions, she continued. 'A month before my eighteenth birthday, Big Boss Yu summoned me to his office. "No Gin, it is time to stop playing the goat-herder's flute," he said. I knew by this that he felt I should not continue as an entertainer.

'"What shall I do, *loh yeh*?" I asked.

'Unlike the European taipans of Shanghai, who flaunted their power and opinions and came straight out with whatever was on their minds, Big Boss Yu was old-fashioned Chinese who came from peasant stock and did things the Chinese way. This was to be oblique in all matters – opinions were buried in riddles, directions sounded like polite suggestions and opinions always appeared ambiguous. So it startled me when he said, "Raisins."

'"Raisins?" I asked, thinking it must be some Chinese verbal riddle I was meant to know.

'He was silent, the clocks kicking up their usual racket in the background. Finally he said, "The Sun Maid Raisin Growers of California have a surplus of raisins and I have accepted the agency for China." He looked steadily at me, his purple-ringed eyes deadly serious. "I would be honoured if you would take charge of this project, No Gin."

'I knew immediately this was a test, the beginning of the reason why he had taken me under his wing – perhaps also why he had changed me from Russian to English, the Russians having no business clout in China at the time. "Are raisins a commodity used much by the Europeans here?" I asked.

'"You will sell raisins to the Chinese," he said firmly. "It is a big surplus."

'I was stunned. The Chinese had been very slow in accepting European food and I couldn't see where raisins would fit in traditional peasant cooking.

'"How can this be done, *loh yeh*? The Chinese have never seen a raisin."

'He appeared suddenly impatient. "You must find a way, No Gin."

'He hadn't even asked me if I would accept the task and had simply taken it for granted that I would do as I was told. To show annoyance or anger was unacceptable. At best I was allowed one cautious joke in order to show my lack of conviction for the project – what we in our culture might refer to as a "quip". "Perhaps we can sell them by telling people that eating raisins will bless them with sons," I joked.

'I expected him to smile and then dismiss me – clearly the discussion was over, and I was saddled with the unenviable task of selling raisins to peasants who were often too poor to afford fish sauce for their rice. Instead Big Boss Yu showed genuine surprise and clapped his hands in a gesture of admiration. "I have not wasted my time with you!" he exclaimed. "Raisins will give them many sons! Excellent!" I had inadvertently tapped into a central concern of all Chinese – fecundity and the birth of male children. "I am expecting a boatload of raisins next month," Big Boss Yu said. "It will give you time to graciously resign from the Palace Hotel. You will be working for Yu Ya-ching and for the San Peh Steam Navigation Company. By using his full name, he was telling me that he was now the taipan who would run my life. With this I was dismissed.'

The air had suddenly became quite cool. 'My goodness, it's getting late. Jack, do you mind if we continue this at some other time?'

I'm sure I could have happily listened to her all night, but I nodded – the autumn sun was beginning to set and a slightly chilly breeze was blowing in from the sea. I couldn't believe I'd been listening for nearly two hours. 'Thank you – but you will promise to tell me more, won't you, Countess?'

'Of course – if you wish, Jack. I've come this far. There is simply no point in keeping the remainder from the two of you.'

# CHAPTER TWENTY

## *Jimmy at the White House*

Jimmy wrote several more letters before his return but despite his gregarious nature he didn't really care to talk much about himself. I dearly wished I'd been with him when he received his decoration – not just to share the moment with him, but so I could have picked up all the bits'n'pieces that make such occasions unique. Anyway, over a long period I think I've got most of it in place.

What Jimmy had hoped would be a couple of weeks on the road turned into four months touring with the army press unit, visiting almost every small town north of the Mason-Dixon line. America was in need of a lot of healing, and the media – small-time and big – were insatiable. By the time Jimmy got back to Queen Island it was early spring. He was literally exhausted and not at all eager to talk about the medal ceremony at the White House, which by then seemed such a very long time ago. It took several months for me to piece the story together because when I asked him he'd usually say, 'I's talked out, Brother Fish. It weren't no big deal. Dat occasion it for da Medal o' Honor an' dey done tag me along.'

In fact, this wasn't all that far from the truth. The President of the United States doesn't as a rule present military awards other than the US

Presidential Citation, the award 3RAR had received for Kapyong, and the Medal of Honor, the American equivalent of our Victoria Cross. But President Dwight D. Eisenhower had been a soldier himself and was no doubt deeply concerned about the way the American press was dealing with those prisoners of war accused of collaborating with the enemy. Although this is pure speculation on my part, I don't suppose it would have been difficult for the Pentagon or the brass in charge of public relations to prevail upon Eisenhower to include Jimmy and the other two prisoners of war in the ceremony. One of these was Chuck Ward, the tail gunner who'd lost his feet to frostbite and who had endured his parlous state with great courage when less badly wounded men would have given up in despair and died. The other was a soldier named Jesus Fernando Garcia. Perhaps another reason the president wished to include Jimmy was the fact that Jimmy's regiment, the 24th Infantry Regiment, had fought with great distinction in the assault across the Han River in Korea in 1951.

Jimmy had flown to Washington from the west coast, where he'd barely had time to splash his face in a San Francisco Airport washroom before his American Airlines plane left for Washington. He was weary and dull-eyed from the journey, but coming into the capital he perked up. From the aeroplane window he watched as they crossed the Potomac. While American history, like most of his education, had been somewhat neglected, he knew a little bit about the Civil War. The fighting between the Union Army of the Potomac and the Confederate Army of North Virginia had been one of the more decisive encounters and he seemed to remember Negro soldiers had been involved, fighting, they believed, for the promise of freedom from slavery.

'I done look down at dat river, Brother Fish, where mah brothers dey been once fightin' foh der freedom from slavery. Abraham Lincoln he done give dem der freedom on a piece o' paper, but dat all it been, man! Negro folk in da South dey still not free. Cain't sit in no white part o' da bus, cain't use no white washroom, cain't eat in no white res-too-a-rant, cain't go to no white school an' iffen yoh want to vote, da

Ku Klux Klan dey come make yoh a visit an' yoh ain't doin' no votin' no more iffen yoh want to live to see who da next governor or president gonna be.'

The plane landed at the rather quaint colonial-style Washington National Airport and, as he mentioned briefly in his letter, a weary Jimmy stepped into the terminal to find three military policemen waiting for him, one of them holding a sign with his name on it. 'Brother Fish, I think I done need to change mah pants! Dey gonna a-rrest me. Da muth'fuckers dey done lured me back stateside so dey can put me in jail foh AWOL. Dat judge he done send me to Korea so I got me to stay outta jail an' now I back in America two minutes an' dey gonna a-rrest me an' I's goin' straight to where I been goin' in da first place before I gone to Korea! I think maybe I can run foh it, yoh know, get da fuck out. But den I see da colonel who standin' to one side an' first I gotta salute him 'case dey catch me an' den I got me more trouble foh in-sob-bord-nation. "Welcome home, soldier, and congratulations," I hear dat colonel say. I jump to attention an' I salute. Now it too late to run. He smilin' and den he walk forward an' he gonna shake mah hand. The provosts done do da same. "I is honoured to be your escort, Private Oldcorn," one o' dem, a Negro, says.

'"We'll use a side entrance where my driver's waiting," the colonel says. "Your arrival hasn't yet been announced to the press. This is Washington and there are newspaper reporters stationed in the airport. We don't want one of them spotting you and asking awkward questions." He grinned. "That's the reason for the provosts and my standing to one side. If one of them thinks there's something going on, then these three will say you're being arrested for going AWOL. You'll be billeted at Fort Myer."

'I like dat word "billeted". It don't sound like no jail.' Jimmy laughed at the thought, then grew serious. 'You know, Brother Fish, I been con-dishin' all mah life, so when I step off dat aeroplane I think, maybe when dey see I's a nigger dey gonna be embarrassed an' dey gonna apologise, say dey done make a mistake an' point to where is da bus to da nearest military e-stab-lishment so I can get me mah discharge an' vamoose out da military forces, amen!'

For the next week Jimmy was debriefed, fitted with two new uniforms and taken through his publicity schedule, which began at the presidential ceremony where, afterwards, he was interviewed by the press. Then it was off to New York to appear on Ed Murrow's CBS program 'See It Now'. Thereafter he completed his press and small-town tour throughout the eastern seaboard. 'One time I ask why dey don't send me to da South, and da press officer, he say, "Private Oldcorn, this is a celebration – not a lynching."'

But first Jimmy was put through media training at Fort Myer, which had its own small TV studio where top brass were trained to respond to what was at the time still a new medium. 'Dey done teach me how I gotta re-spond to da TV cam-era. I gotta look always into da camera like it a person. I gotta smile, be modest, I don't gotta wave mah hands. I gotta call Mr Murrow "Sir" and in da other TV interviews, iffen it a woman I gotta say "ma'am". No Christian names – always sir or ma'am. On and on it go – say dis, don't say dat. "Remember yo' a soldier, don't let America down, son. Don't salute da president – he ain't no more the general of da whole of da world in da Secon' World War, he now a civilian." Imagine, a soldier don't salute da president! Dey think, cause I Negro, I got to be some idjit dey got to coach all da way 'case I disgrace da mil-i-tary. Den dey teach me how to speak. Dey don't say, "Jimmy, you speak like some dumb mule-drivin' nigger from da South." Dey say, "Private Oldcorn, the requirement for TV is that your words are pronounced clearly and succinctly." Den my "dis and dat" turn into "this and that" an' dey amazed when, after 'bout one hour, I can say all dem honky words perfect like some chump who done gone to dat Harvard school.'

The big day arrived, where the highlight, as far as Jimmy was concerned, was meeting up with the brave and true Chuck Ward again. 'Hey! Dat one brave soldier – remember, Brother Fish?' I nodded, remembering.

'"Jimmy," Chuck Ward says to me, "I've asked the colonel if you can be the soldier to push me in my wheelchair up to the president." Hey, man, who'd have ever believed it? Buddies, brothers in arms, on da way to meet da president! He got dese artificial feet – he can stand but he cain't walk too far, so I gonna push him up to da dais, den he stand hisself an' get his medal.

'He em-barr-ass me 'cos he tellin' everyone I save his life. "Dat not true, dis da bravest dude yoh evah seen – he save his own life wid his own courage, man!" I tell dem. I feel ashamed, dey done give me da Soldier's Medal an' he got da next one down, da Army Commendation Medal! Far's I concern, he *da man!* It got to be da other way aroun'.'

At eleven a.m. hours the four soldiers to be presented to the president left Fort Myer in army staff cars for the short trip to the White House, Jimmy and Chuck Ward in one car, the other two soldiers in another. Jimmy was always at pains to point out that the ceremony was for Master Sergeant Stanley T. Adams, who'd been wounded three times leading thirteen members of his platoon in bayonet charge against an enemy that vastly outnumbered them, routing them and providing cover for his battalion to pull back.

They entered the White House and followed the great curved driveway to the north portico where the ceremony was to take place. I've seen the north portico, a huge columned porch that forms the north entrance to the White House, which looks like it has been transported direct from ancient Greece. The platform and lectern with the presidential seal were well to the back, with a dozen impressively sized American flags flanked by soldiers in dress uniform immediately behind them. Several hundred chairs faced the dais. These were for generals from the army and air force and admirals from the navy, as well as the congressmen and members of the Senate, past Medal of Honor winners and their families and, of course, the families of the recipients for that day. The press reporters and photographers and TV crews, who had come in some numbers, stood to one side. This was part of the political plan – there was no doubt the press would roll up for a

Medal of Honor presentation, whereas they may not have bothered attending a ceremony for something less. Eisenhower would have an ideal opportunity to get his message across without it appearing to be a blatant set-up.

The four soldiers, Jimmy pushing Chuck Ward, stood to the side of the dais just a few steps away, where an army captain gave them a final briefing and once again emphasised to the two of them in uniform, 'Do *not* salute the president!' The theory, of course, is that you don't salute the man, you salute his military rank.

Then the congressman from Kansas, representing Master Sergeant Adams' home state, announced, 'Ladies and gentlemen, the President of the United States.' The audience stood as President Eisenhower entered from the back of the portico and came to stand behind the lectern.

The moment of truth had arrived for the twenty-four-year-old Jimmy Oldcorn. Left on the doorstep of the Colored Orphan Asylum, where he'd been found by Sister Mary Pentecost, he now stood within the north portico of the White House to meet the President of the United States. He'd come a long way – the orphanage, the Kraus farm, the streets of the Bronx, Elmira Reformatory, the United States Armed Forces and a Chinese POW camp – to finally stand before the president to be honoured by his nation.

The president asked the army chaplain to say a prayer, and then the proceedings began. The president thanked the military brass, the senators and congressmen and women and the past recipients of the Medal of Honor and their families, and began the oration to Master Sergeant Stanley T. Adams. 'We are gathered here to represent America's gratitude to this young man for the almost unbelievable feats of courage that have won our highest award, the Medal of Honor,' he began.

He then went on to describe the master sergeant's valour, leaving nothing out, so that the speech went on for some time. Finally he stepped down from the dais, took the medal and placed it around the neck of Adams, who stood silent (protocol did not allow him to thank the president as it was he who was being thanked by a grateful nation).

The president then returned to the dais and the microphone and said, 'I have another pleasant duty, one that I have personally elected to do. I ask Master Sergeant Adams to indulge me. The Medal of Honor is the only individual military decoration usually presented by the president and, of course, it has no equal. However, occasionally a soldier performs extraordinary deeds when *not* in battle and such is the case with Private James Pentecost Oldcorn of the 24th Infantry Regiment, who was a prisoner of war under the North Koreans and Chinese for almost two years. He was severely wounded in the leg and was on crutches for the first year. Yet so outstanding was his leadership in the various field hospitals, and in the POW camp where he spent most of his time in captivity, that Private James Pentecost Oldcorn has been awarded the Soldier's Medal with silver oak leaf.' He paused and looked up. 'For those of you not in the military, this means we have awarded him this medal five times for five separate occasions where he showed outstanding leadership and risked his life as a consequence. There has been a lot of publicity about a very few men taken prisoner in Korea who did not live up to the highest ideals of their country. But, may I remind you all, there were also men such as Private James Pentecost Oldcorn who make me proud, both as an ex-serviceman and a president, and who represent the true spirit of the American soldier. I now ask my naval aide to read just one of these five separate citations.' The aide then read the citation.

*'Private James Oldcorn was taken prisoner of war in fall 1951 whilst a member of the 24th Infantry Regiment, United States Army. He was imprisoned in a camp on the northern border of North Korea where the conditions were harsh. In 1952, Private Oldcorn, feigning sympathy for the communist ideology, infiltrated the Chinese camp administration and collected the names of prisoners collaborating with the enemy, including those clandestinely informing on their comrades. Even though detection would almost certainly have brought about punishment resulting*

*in death, Private Oldcorn smuggled the list to fellow prisoners who could be trusted. They, in turn, broadcast the list to expose the collaborators, including undercover informers. This action seriously disrupted the Chinese Army's camp spy network, discomforted and isolated the collaborators and gave encouragement by his example to the majority of prisoners to continue to resist. Private Oldcorn's heroic achievement reflects great credit upon himself, his unit and the military service.'*

The naval aide ceased reading and the president then remarked, 'I hope that the members of the press present will see to it that those other four citations, for which there is not sufficient time to read here today, will be made known to the American public.' President Eisenhower then pinned the medal to a very embarrassed, but also very proud, Jimmy Pentecost Oldcorn's chest.

'Den I wheel our good friend, Chuck Ward, to da position, an' he stand on his mechanical legs an' da naval aide done read his citation an' he get his medal an' also da same happen to da other soldier POW, Private Garcia. Now da flashbulbs dey is poppin', TV cameras dey whirrin', an' da reporters dey askin' questions like dey machine-gun bull-ets an' I is tryin' not to use mah hands an' talk real polite, an' journalists dey writin' down stuff wid der shorthand. Den afterwards dey got dis reception in da garden. Natch, da president he mostly been talkin' to the family of Master Sergeant Adams 'cos dat da proto-col, but before he go back into da White House he come over to where I standin' wid Chuck Ward an' his folks. Da one-time general of da whole world, 'cept o' course da Germans an' da Japs – not only dat but he also da Pres-e-dent of da United States of America – he comin' 'cross da White House lawn towards me! He stop an' he say, "Private Oldcorn, America is proud of you and I thank you for being a good soldier and more than that, an honourable man who cared about his brother soldiers." Hey, man, any minute I's gonna wake up an' I back in dat prison camp an' Lieutenant Dinh, he shoutin', "You confess now!"'

It was grand having Jimmy back on the island and, of course, we had another medal party for him, and naturally half the island turned up uninvited. Nicole Lenoir-Jourdan brought a bottle of Krug from her precious hoard and the three of us and Gloria each had a glass. Gloria took a sip from her first glass of champagne and, resting her head on her right shoulder, thought for a few moments, took another sip, then said, 'Well, blow me down – if that ain't something to take away your rheumatiz!'

It seems hardly worth saying, but the boat advertisement Nicole Lenoir-Jourdan wrote brought nearly thirty inquiries: twenty-four from the Hobart *Mercury* and the Launceston *Examiner* combined, and five from the little old *Gazette* – one of them, one of the four finalists. It had taken us all the time Jimmy was away to sort the finalists out. These four seemed almost too good to be true, and three of the owners were willing to come over to the island to enable us to sea-trial their boats. The fourth baulked at the idea of a sea trial, despite our offer to pay for the fuel to get to the island, the wages of one crew member to sail with the skipper and, of course, the provisions for the days out on the Strait.

Arranging to get the three boats to the island to sea-trial them took us another month and proved an ideal opportunity for Jimmy to relax and get over his nightmare tour of America. All three boats were good, and while they had a fair bit in common they also possessed marked differences. Finally we selected a sixty-five-foot boat called the *Janthe* owned by a bloke in his mid-thirties named Michael Munday who'd flown a Dakota during the Second World War. Mike was a fourth-generation fisherman. When I asked him why, if he loved the sea, he hadn't joined the navy, he replied, 'I'm a fisherman, mate. My family have been fishermen for more than a hundred years – it's in my blood. Out here on the Strait and in the Southern Ocean I'm in charge, on my own – no bastard to tell me what to do. In the navy or the army it's all pack drill with some bugger kicking arse for all the wrong reasons.

I reckoned if I couldn't have the sea to myself, the air was the next best thing. Surfing the clouds in a Dakota is almost the same. You're in control, nobody to tell you what to do.'

'So why are you selling the *Janthe*?' I asked him.

'Got an offer to fly for a mining company in New Guinea for six times what I'll make as a fisherman, with a house in Port Moresby and my kids in boarding school in Hobart thrown into the package.' He laughed suddenly. 'Tell you what, though, look after my boat and I'll buy her back from you in five years when my contract's up.'

The *Janthe* wasn't a new boat, but the best of all things, a truly good old one. She was built entirely of Huon pine and, like all the older boats, was both sail and diesel powered. She had belonged to Mike's father who, like his son, had kept it in tip-top condition. She was fitted with a Lister low-revving diesel engine and a Paragon gearbox and they don't come any more reliable. Better still, she also carried a Kelvin Hughes echo sounder; they'd only just come onto the market and I'd not seen one before. Steve had pointed it out in a fishing magazine and we'd all speculated as to when we might get them in Australia. It said something for Michael Munday – something like that on board was not only a tremendous help to find the fishing grounds, but also an essential piece of safety equipment when navigating among the many reefs in Bass Strait.

'What about the echo sounder, hey?' I remarked.

He grinned. 'Wouldn't be there if I'd known I was going flying – cost several boatloads of cray to pay for and a lot of hassle from customs to bring in.'

'I'll bet it makes a difference?'

'You're damn right – I reckon it adds thirty per cent more to my catch.'

I pointed to the huge light mounted high up on the front of the mast. 'Never seen one of those.'

'War surplus, landing light from a C47, a Dakota,' he explained. 'Cost a motser – don't use it often because it'll blind you at 200 yards, but in the big storm of '52 I reckon it saved us.' Most fishing boats have no light and some of the more cautious blokes fit a headlight from a car, but I'd never seen anything like this before. I even wondered if it wasn't a bit of overkill, like extra chrome on a motor car.

The sails too were in tip-top condition as was the gear on board, right down to the thirty craypots and the glass floats. We'd lucked in – Mike Munday was a perfectionist and you'd bet on him being a good pilot. It can't have been easy for him to part with this beautiful boat.

Mike was a big bloke himself and according to him, his father was even bigger, so the two bunks built below deck in the fo'c'sle were each long enough to accommodate Jimmy (just) while I had enough room to swing a cat. The *Janthe* also came equipped with an almost brand-new dinghy with a twenty-horsepower Mercury outboard that hung off the back on davits.

'How come the dinghy's new?' I asked Mike. In an older boat the dinghy, which is usually used for fishing in areas too dangerous to take the bigger vessel, is generally a bit of a battered affair, usually fitted with a donk that's been reconditioned several times. Stupid, of course – a sound dinghy and outboard has saved many a life out at sea. But there you go, fishermen are always strapped for cash and the dinghy is where you cut insurance corners to lower the premium.

'The old one was swept away by a freak wave in that big storm of '52 – torn right off the davits. The insurance paid out,' he replied.

This told me two things: the *Janthe* had not only survived one of the worst storms in the Strait for the past decade, but its owner also earned sufficient from fishing to insure his boat properly.

There was only one problem: he wanted 1500 quid more than we had estimated we would need. I'd given the Countess a carefully worked-out figure to which she'd agreed, but at the time she'd said quite firmly, 'Jack, please don't cut corners. Take everything into consideration, but the figure you give me *must* be the final one.' I couldn't bring myself to go cap in hand to ask for more.

'What about the boat without the dinghy?' I asked Munday, the point being that he'd have no trouble selling the beautiful little clinker-built boat also made from Huon pine and the almost-new Mercury outboard, or he could choose to keep the dinghy himself. 'Put her on a ship and take her to New Guinea with you – the barramundi fishing on the Sepik River is supposed to be tremendous.' We'd easily enough find a good replacement with a reconditioned outboard.

But Mike was adamant. The bugger was about to make 15 500 pounds and he wouldn't budge. 'The *Janthe* is the best cray boat, best fishing boat sixty-five foot or under, in Tasmania,' he asserted. 'Can't have a shit bucket hanging aft, mate.' Then he added, 'She's a proud lady – if you're gunna compromise her I'd rather not sell.' Pretty blunt, but you had to respect him for it.

We told Nicole Lenoir-Jourdan we'd decided on *Four Winds*, a good enough cray boat in different circumstances, just under fifty feet in length. We'd have to fit a new bunk for Jimmy, but even that would be a pretty tight fit. 'Better practise sleeping with your toes curled,' I laughed. All the same, we were pretty disappointed.

'That's nice, Jack,' she said, then added, 'why?'

'It's a good boat – all three we sea-trialled are,' I said, trying to sound enthusiastic.

'It's not what you want, is it?'

'Yeah, all we'll have to do is build in a new bunk for Jimmy – there's just enough room.' I grinned. 'I haven't told him we'll have to break his ankles so they'll grow back both of 'em turned thirty degrees to port.'

But she wasn't fooled. 'Jack, it's been nothing but the *Janthe* all week, and now *Four Winds*? Michael Munday wants more than your budget, is that it?'

I nodded. 'Yeah.'

'How much more?'

'Fifteen hundred pounds.'

'Is it worth it?'

I had to be honest. 'Nah. She's worth more than our budget, maybe

500 pounds more, but that's it. I've had several of the local fishermen and Steve go over her with a fine-tooth comb, and they agree.'

'Let me talk to him, Jack.'

Two hours later Mike Munday came out of the *Gazette* office shaking his head. 'Jesus, I'm a foreign correspondent,' he said, plainly bemused.

'A what?'

'A foreign correspondent – journo for the *Gazette*. What's more, it's cost me 1000 quid!'

I tried hard not to break up, but Jimmy kept a straight face. 'Dat fine, man! Dat a good newspaper!'

'It's a heap of shit,' Mike replied, scratching his head. 'But then I'm not much of a writer, I suppose – always wanted to be, though. But there you go, too busy fishing.'

'What does she want you to write?' I asked, curious.

'It's what she calls a "regular monthly column" – "News from the Islands". File once a month.' 'File' was obviously a new word he'd just picked up from Nicole Lenoir-Jourdan, but you could see he liked the idea of calling himself a journalist.

Mike took the plane back to Launceston the following morning. I drove him to the airport in the Ford Prefect. 'Good luck, Jacko. It's broken my heart, but I'll get the *Janthe* back one day,' he said, shaking my hand as we parted.

'Not if I can help it,' I replied, grinning.

'Oh, by the way, Jacko, if ever you find yourself in a tight spot, big storm or something, and you've got to stay alert, look in the first-aid box – the Bex packets.' It was a strange thing to say – to stay awake wasn't why Gloria took Bex. *To each his own*, I thought at the time.

Later Nicole Lenoir-Jourdan explained how she'd persuaded Mike Munday to knock 1000 quid off his price. 'Everyone has a secret something they'd like to do, but feels that there are more important priorities. Find out what it is and allow them to indulge the dream without disturbing the status quo and they'll usually cooperate.'

'But 1000 quid? That's a helluva lot of cooperation.'

'It's all about perception. In New Guinea they're not going to know the *Gazette* only has 2000 readers. They'll see Michael Munday's name and picture in print. Just as importantly, the people he needs to impress in Port Moresby will be reading about themselves. Munday is a namedropper – he wants a bit of notoriety. He'll make sure the paper lands in all the right places. I've promised him ten copies every month. We all want to be local heroes, Jack. Take John Champion. He dreams of making his Queen Island cheeses and cream the best in Australia. That's his ambition, but it's not his *secret something*. His secret something is that he will receive a knighthood from the queen as a thank-you from a grateful Tasmanian Government.'

'He's a rough bugger – how's he gunna do that?' I asked.

'Well, we're working on it. Some of these things take years. It's a matter of being bipartisan in politics, regular donations and . . .' she laughed, 'making sure your cheese lands on the tables of the governor and the premier every night.'

I was beginning to understand why Nicole Lenoir-Jourdan could get all the dairy produce she wanted from John Champion, a bloke who wouldn't normally give you the time of day. Gloria would sniff when his name came up: 'Hmmph! The school bully, that one.'

So, there it was, for 500 quid more we had what we thought was the best fishing boat in Australia. She didn't need a drop of paint and the hull had recently been scraped and was clean as a whistle. Even the spud sacks that carried the cray ashore when they were taken out of the boat's fish well were washed and neatly stacked, and the gas stove on board was practically new. Oh, yes, only one other thing – we wanted to rename the boat 'Shanghai Lil'. But, as part of the deal Nicole Lenoir-Jourdan had struck with Mike, we were to retain the *Janthe* as the vessel's name. He was dead serious about buying her back one day.

We took Nicole Lenoir-Jourdan out on the *Janthe* for the day to celebrate, making for Hunter Island, about six hours out of Livingston

Harbour. We left the thirty craypots on deck so she would get the feel of a fishing boat going out to sea, and started out early. The idea was to have an early lunch in a sheltered cove at Seal, and then make our way back well before sundown. This trip would also be, we decided, an ideal opportunity for her to tell us more of her story – perhaps even complete it. I'd brought Jimmy up to date, so he too was anxious to hear what happened next. It was mid-spring, and it dawned as one of those magic days you get in the Strait at that time of year.

We laid anchor in the deep, sheltered bay immediately below the light on Hunter Island and took the dinghy to the beach, where I collected driftwood and made a small fire to boil a billy among a group of tall rocks that sheltered us completely from the sun. Jimmy had brought two of the newfangled 'wet suits' from the States and, somewhat unnecessarily, we'd stripped down, climbed into them and in a matter of twenty minutes caught three nice crays. I served the tea in tin mugs and Nicole Lenoir-Jourdan began to talk as we cooked the crayfish.

'Now, let me see – it was raisins, wasn't it, Jack?'

'Yoh got dem raisins up to yoh neck an' ship's comin' in wid more raisins an' yoh don't know if dem Chinese dey gonna eat raisins to make demself a boy chile,' Jimmy reminded her, making her laugh.

'I see you're up to date, James. That's good – we can move right along. Raisins for fertility, but only for male children. It was, to say the very least, a decidedly tricky proposition, but Big Boss Yu loved it. The ship arrived, its hold filled with the surplus product of the Sun Maid Raisin Growers of California. They were unloaded into a huge warehouse Big Boss Yu owned and it took the harbour rats less than an hour to find them. Coolies were paid extra to camp in the warehouses at night to keep the rats at bay, and rat poison mixed with sticky rice was placed everywhere – which, by the way, the rats soon learnt to ignore, much preferring the raisins. Big Boss Yu was most anxious to get going. He had several small steamers that plied the China coast between Shanghai and the ports of Ningpo and Hankow, to name just a few. He also planned to pull his coolie boats operating to Vladivostok to be a part of the raisin fleet.

'This was all very well, but I had to sell the idea to six million Chinese peasants. The first thing I did was to get Sapajou, the cartoonist on the *North China Daily News*, to create a poster for me. It contained four pictures, the first depicting two peasant houses in a typical Chinese village with a childless couple outside each. The second showed the same two couples, one couple eating life-sized raisins, and the other couple eating from bowls of rice. The third picture showed the two couples somewhat older, the first with the husband beaming and four boys and one girl standing beside the couple, and the rice-eating couple with the reverse order – four girls and a puny-looking boy. The inclusion of at least one girl among the boys in one family and a boy among the girls in the other made the promise believable. The final picture showed a strong-looking Chinese juggler juggling a circle of ten raisins above his head along with the sun and the moon. This was to indicate that ten raisins was the minimum number to be eaten by husband and wife each day. The poster, for those who could read, simply stated, "Eat womb-fruit and be blessed with more boys."

'I started in the Chinese City, getting the posters displayed in shops and stalls and selling the raisins in bulk packets at a very low price, allowing the vendors to decide the size and price the market could afford. As we'd expected, the going rate was twenty raisins wrapped in a twist of rice paper for a small coin. I then worked back, calculating the vendor's profit, and priced the bulk packs accordingly.

'We hired the football stadium in the Chinese City and put on a concert free of charge to introduce the marvellous new womb-fruit. We featured acrobats, dancers and contortionists, all of them eating womb-fruit and loudly extolling its virtues before commencing their act. I sang in Cantonese after doing the same. Then we gave away a twist of raisins to everyone who attended. Thirty thousand people turned up, and if Big Boss Yu hadn't had half the Shanghai police force on duty, the distribution would most certainly have caused a riot.'

She must have noticed the incredulous looks on our faces, for she paused to add, 'You may be pondering the morality of such blatant manipulation, but remember those were different times. I imagine I salved my conscience with the thought that raisins were good for them anyway – a lot better than cigarettes, whose advertisers traditionally made the most outrageous promises. One brand I recall even promised a "lucky cough". Another claimed their brand created genuine dragon's breath that made you both powerful and invincible against your foes, and must have led to the untimely death of a great many Chinese.

'In two years we were distributing raisins along the China coast and throughout southern China as far as Qingdao in the north and Shantou in the south, and as far inland as Nanchang. The raisin business grew so large so quickly that Big Boss Yu required more small steamboats for coastal work, and needed short-term finance. To my dismay he brought in the Three Musketeers of the French Concession – the three gangsters, Smallpox "Million Dollar" Yang, Chang Shig-liang and Du Yu-sen – to be a part of his business. This involved two china crockery factories I'd purchased on his behalf and built up to be very profitable. We needed a non-porous product we could send to America in the hold of the raisin ship that was returning to San Francisco empty, as the hold was permeated with the sweet smell of raisins and so couldn't take the cheap cotton goods that were the main export from Shanghai. Crockery was ideal. It didn't pick up the smell and the stickiness that clung to everything loaded into the hold, and could be washed off by the purchaser when it arrived at the other end.

'While I'd helped to build the raisin business, the crockery was something I loved and felt very proud of. I deeply resented that the business was being handed to the three gangsters, and that they stood to profit from my hard work. I had worked for Big Boss Yu without salary as I regarded him as my family and expected to be rewarded finally for my efforts. I had secretly hoped that the crockery factory and export business were to be my ultimate reward.

'As it was, he refused me nothing but gave me very little cash of my own. In addition to my work as the raisin distributor, I was expected to act as Big Boss Yu's social partner. His various businesses were expanding due to the profits from the raisins and he was expected to match the European taipans in lavish hospitality. I now realised why I had been given to Mrs Worthington to be coached in clipped-and-roundeds.

'I was the hostess always beside Big Boss Yu. Of course, at most of these lavish affairs the end purpose was to win friends and influence people – in other words, to raise capital among the European taipans for Big Boss Yu's various business enterprises. Although he never allowed them to invest in raisins, he was building a shipping empire and was getting deeply involved in real estate and construction in the French Concession. I imagine I had the right looks and posh accent to match the snootiest of taipan wives, and spoke French fluently as well. He insisted I dress in the very latest *haute couture* fashion. Madame Peroux did my hair and nails every week. And as I never drank more than two glasses of champagne, Big Boss Yu knew I would be discreet in all things involving his business.

'When the three gangsters joined him we had already built a considerable raisin empire and now I asked for and received a two per cent commission, which may not sound like a great deal but which amounted to a fairly large sum of money. This only came about because I let it be known that I wasn't pleased with the way Big Boss Yu had simply taken the crockery business away from me. Sears, Roebuck & Co., the giant mail-order house in Chicago, had just put in a huge order that meant we could clear all our debts in the crockery business. The order couldn't be filled without my knowledge and Big Boss Yu sold the business to the three villains as being free of debt. He simply told me to hand over the books and the keys to the office. Angered, but unable to do anything but obey his instructions, I went to see him in order to ask politely for some sort of an explanation.

'"*Loh yeh*, how have I offended you?" I asked him.

'"Offended? You have not offended me, No Gin."

'"Then why have you taken the crockery business away from me?"

'He smiled, but I could sense that he was embarrassed. "I have other plans for you, my child."

'Although I knew I couldn't ask him what these were, I asked, "Am I to continue to be worthless, *loh yeh*?"

'"Worthless? That is not so."

'"But it is clear that I am," I insisted.

'"What are these riddles you are talking, No Gin?" he asked, feigning annoyance to cover his embarrassment.

'"Why do I receive no recompense for the work I do, and why do you now make me lose face by taking away from me what I have started and made profitable?"

'"It is the way things are. I need the capital, you lack for nothing."

'"And I must hand over to the new buyers immediately?"

'"Yes."

'"And the order from Sears, Roebuck & Co., that is to be cancelled?"

'"Of course not! What are you talking about?" he cried angrily.

'"It cannot be filled without my personal supervision, *loh yeh*," I said, keeping my voice respectful.'

Nicole Lenoir-Jourdan smiled. 'And that was how I was given a two per cent commission in the raisin business. I would only discover much later that the three gangsters, presumably along with Big Boss Yu, were exporting opium while also conducting a legitimate business.'

Jimmy's and my eyes must have been as round as saucers, because she paused before continuing. 'I'd built the ideal front, and now many of the china vases and pots contained false bottoms where the opium was packed. It was a perfect system – the bottom of the pots were so perfectly sealed and glazed that you would need to break the pots to discover the opium. The Chinese agent in San Francisco, using a code involving certain patterns in the glaze, selected the opium vases and the remainder of the consignment went on to the wholesaler or to the customer. I imagine that a small mountain of broken Chinese crockery must be buried somewhere in San Francisco.

'Then, after five years, disaster struck. The grape crop in California failed for two years running and the huge demand from China had used up the surplus the Sun Maid Raisin Growers possessed. We were about to run out of raisins.'

'But didn't the fact that the birthrate of boys had not increased catch up with you?' I asked. 'After all, in five years this must have become reasonably apparent.'

Again, she smiled before answering me. 'You are right to think that, Jack. But few things in this world are wrought by logic alone. Every boy born was credited to raisins and every girl was the result of eating too few. Superstition, when combined with hope, is a very powerful medium.

'Big Boss Yu had sunk most of his capital into shipping raisins up and down the China coast and had increased his fleet considerably, and now stood to go bankrupt. The Chinese – well, old-fashioned taipans like Big Boss Yu – did not see that natural occurrences such as failure of the Californian grape crop were predictable, and so they seldom carried sufficient insurance against disaster. Everything was put down to luck – bad joss and good joss. Bad joss came about as a consequence of somebody wishing you downfall and, like all Chinese taipans, Big Boss Yu had made lots of enemies.

'Fortunately I had seen it coming, and I had Sir Victor Sassoon to thank for this. While I seemed to have a natural bent for business I knew very little about predicting trends or playing the market. He once explained to me that both trends and disasters are usually predictable. Shanghai, for instance, was under-developed even though buildings were going up at a steady rate and popular opinion thought otherwise. He could see his money safe for the next ten years, and would continue to invest in real estate.

'"But how can you make these predictions?" I asked.

'"The commodity markets," he replied, with absolute confidence. "What do we have that someone wants? How many 'someones' are there? Can we supply it at a competitive price? Is it a long-term need? Who may be in a position to undercut us once we have developed the market?"

'"But what has this to do with real estate?" I persisted.

'"Everything, my dear. Wealth is created at the source of the commodity – that is, in Shanghai. Wealth creates the need to expand, and real estate and infrastructure are the key to expansion. Looking at what southern China can sell to the world at the right price and time will determine if I build a second grand hotel or another giant structure on the Bund. Because we can answer all of the questions I've just posed to you, I know I will continue to be successful. Shanghai is now the fifth-biggest seaport in the world and the chief manufacturing centre in China. We have eighty-two cotton mills and 124 cotton-weaving mills, ship-building yards, twenty china and porcelain factories, paper mills, canneries, leather-making businesses, tobacco and cigarette-producing factories and a host of other exporting industries, almost all of which answer the criteria I've just given you. Moreover, we sit on a throne of silver. We have the greatest concentrated silver hoard on earth. So we have capital as well as product. Finally, we have cheap and, most importantly, intelligent labour – a total of 400 000 skilled workers."

'"Does it work the same way when you import?"

'"My dear child, of course!" He paused, then added, "For example, your raisin business is particularly vulnerable."

'"Why? The Sun Maid Raisin Growers has a huge surplus."

'"And you have an almost limitless market. So far, so good. But what if the Californian grape crop fails?"

'"But it hasn't in five years!"

'"Are you insured if it does?"

'"I don't know – the company accountant takes care of those things."

'"Well, if I know anything about Big Boss Yu you're probably under-insured. Do you have a second and third source of supply?" I shook my head. "Better look into that," he suggested. "Agricultural products depend on good rains, and the weather is seldom predictable. The nature of your market is such that if you cannot continue to supply it, it will almost certainly die."

'Well, I went to see Kwok-Bew, the taipan who owned, among other things, Sincere – Shanghai's biggest department store. At the age of fifteen his family had sent him to Australia to learn about department stores from Anthony Hordern's, and he still maintained several agencies in Australia. He was an old man at this stage and looked frail, but, with an introduction from Big Boss Yu, he received me most cordially and promised to put me in touch with the right people. Then, through another quite unexpected source – a visiting Portuguese dessert and sweet-wine importer – I got the same information in regards to South Africa. After the failure of the Californian grape harvest I knew Sun Maid had sufficient raisin reserves for another year, but I took the precaution of ordering consignments from Australia and South Africa. Big Boss Yu made it known that he wasn't at all happy with the idea, and gave me a thorough dressing-down.

'"Next year California will be good again," he insisted.

'"That is possibly true, *loh yeh*, but we will have used all their surplus and they have to resupply their own markets." But he wouldn't hear of it and refused to finance the raisins from Australia and South Africa, so I was forced to pay for both consignments, which took my entire two per cent commission savings and a loan from Sir Victor at a generously low interest rate. When disaster struck a second year in California I owned sufficient raisins to supply most of the market, but also to make a considerable amount of money.

'I also faced a new problem – the raisins from both countries were different in appearance to those from California. The South African ones were a lighter brown and the Australian ones were almost gold in appearance, made from a seedless grape known as Muscat Gordo Blanco. I was afraid the Chinese would reject them. So it was back to Sapajou for another two posters – "Golden Boy" for the South African raisins and "Double Golden Boy" for the crop from Australia. We priced the South African product the same as the Californian and the Double Golden Boy a little higher, advertising the latter as twice as potent as the raisins they'd previously been eating, and because only one in ten million Golden Boy seeds produced a single Double Golden Boy plant.

'Big Boss Yu had been wrong and I had been right. And while he would never have acknowledged this openly, he was forced to agree that Sun Maid would need to first supply their own depleted and profitable market and so a surplus sold virtually at a loss was unlikely to occur over the next few harvests. I argued that he had too much of his shipping tied up and should sell half his fleet while using the other half to distribute our newly sourced raisins only to the major markets. That is, the bigger cities along the China coastline where the peasants could afford to pay a slightly higher price for the new Golden Boy and Double Golden Boy product. I proved to him that this would result in much the same profit margin.'

'Yo' a very smart busi-ness woman, Countess,' Jimmy said.

'Oh, I wouldn't say that, James. It was a mixture of commonsense, luck and most of all Sir Victor Sassoon. I had, in effect, become his acolyte, learning from the master.'

'How did Big Boss Yu react to this? I thought he regarded Sir Victor as in your past?' I asked.

'Quite right. But in Shanghai it was quite impossible for the two men not to meet constantly and, as Big Boss Yu's hostess, it was almost impossible not to fraternise in public. Besides, I had saved Big Boss Yu from certain bankruptcy and so my good joss was holding. What he was not aware of was that I had become Sir Victor's mistress.'

Nicole Lenoir-Jourdan must have seen the sudden shocked look from both of us. 'Why are you surprised? I was not unattractive and could talk his kind of language and, besides, I'd been in love with him from the age of sixteen. But, of course, even though he was a bachelor, I wasn't able to be seen in public with him and our affair had to be kept very quiet lest Big Boss Yu hear about it. I was in so many ways still naive and knew very little about men – and even less about loving one while being beholden to another. If it had become known that I was the mistress of Shanghai's most powerful European taipan while also a partner of the most powerful Chinese taipan, so great would have been the loss of face for Big Boss Yu that I could easily have lost my life.'

'An' yoh been scared, Countess?' asked Jimmy.

'I was so very much in love that nothing mattered. I'm not sure if I ever thought it through. They say that love is blind, and I was most certainly blind to the danger I faced. The irony, of course, is that I'm sure I wasn't the only gal to share Sir Victor's monogrammed silk sheets. I'm not even sure he loved me in return. He once told me that when you are a billionaire you are at a huge disadvantage in loving a woman, not knowing whether she is with you because she loves you or for what she can gain from the relationship. This I found very sad.'

She looked pensive in reflection so I took the opportunity to place a little more wood on the beach fire.

'I don't suppose I was any different in his eyes,' she continued after a few moments. 'For while I couldn't be seen on his arm, and wasn't kept by him in a private apartment or even given any of the usual expensive baubles, I was obtaining advice that was turning me into a wealthy woman. Which, I must say, he appeared to enjoy. It may even have given him a perverse satisfaction, in an indirect sense, that he was interfering in Big Boss Yu's affairs.

'My success didn't go unnoticed even though, in the Chinese tradition, as a woman I was required to be modest and in appearance reliant on a male. I gave all credit for my success to Big Boss Yu, as expected. As inevitably happens in business, I made enemies. In my case three very powerful ones – the Three Musketeers of the French Concession and, in particular Smallpox "Million Dollar" Yang. By advising Big Boss Yu to terminate importing raisins from Sun Maid, the ship that carried the raisins was no longer available for the export of cheap crockery and, of course, unbeknownst to me, opium.

'It would have been useless to point out that with no surplus raisins available in California the charter ship the Sun Maid Raisin Growers Association used would no longer be calling into Shanghai anyway. It was all my fault as far as Smallpox "Million Dollar" Yang was concerned. The opium trade relied entirely on a carefully created network of foreign Chinese being at the place of destination. San Francisco possessed a large Chinese population and was also the major city from which the Triads operated. They would have to find another ship that travelled between San Francisco and Shanghai on a regular basis. The three gangsters had no sooner created an operation that worked successfully than I had inadvertently pulled the plug on them. In the eyes of Smallpox "Million Dollar" Yang, the youngest and most dangerous of the three, I had deliberately sabotaged their operation. Big Boss Yu would no doubt have been caught in somewhat of a dilemma when he decided to take my advice, but giving up his share of the profits made from the exported opium would have been preferable to being seen to go bankrupt. He was, after all, the unofficial Chinese boss of Shanghai, a position he would never under any circumstances jeopardise.

'Again in the Chinese tradition, I wasn't made aware of the enmity towards me from the three gangsters. I confess that I had taken the trouble to avoid them wherever possible, perhaps still smarting a bit from the fact that they'd taken over the crockery export business. But, as with everyone else, I had always played my role as the polite and respectful hostess and erstwhile employee, and now as a very junior partner in Big Boss Yu's San Peh Steam Navigation Company.

'Sir Victor urged me to take half of the money I'd made and invest it in the security of the British Crown Colony of Hong Kong while starting a business of my own with the remainder. "Money lying around in a bank is making other men rich, my darling. A dollar that doesn't do a good day's work is no different to a human who is lazy, and the end result will be exactly the same – nothing good comes of either. You know about raisins and crockery, but is there anything else that would interest you?"

'Without hesitation, I replied, "Caviar."

'"Caviar, eh? What an extraordinary answer."

'"My family was in caviar for four generations. We were the official suppliers to three tsars."

'"And what do you personally know about caviar?" he asked, lying back against the pillows on the bed with his hands clasped behind his head.'

I don't know about Jimmy, but I'd never imagined Nicole Lenoir-Jourdan as an object of desire. This was silly, because she was still an attractive woman in her late forties and it wasn't hard to see that she must have been a stunner in her twenties. It's just that we so often judge people by the circumstances under which we meet them. It was difficult for me to imagine Nicole Lenoir-Jourdan lying between silk sheets having just made love to one of the world's richest men.

She laughed. '"Know about caviar? Nothing, Victor," I replied, "except what I've read in my father's papers and what he told me as a child."

'"Hmmm. From the Caspian Sea, isn't it?"

'"Yes – that's where my family is from."

'"If my geography is correct, getting it to Vladivostok and then to Shanghai and from there back to Europe . . ."

'"America – that's where the *nouveaux riches* are."

'"Nevertheless, am I not correct – it will have to come three times, perhaps four times as far as if it were sent through the Black Sea?"

'"If I can get the very finest – the golden eggs of the sterlet sturgeon – it simply won't matter," I said to him. "You drink Krug regardless of price."

'"That's true, I guess."

'"If I put Krug and a cheaper though highly respectable champagne in two glasses, could you tell the difference?"

'"Probably not, although there are many who can."

'"Not, I imagine, too many in America."

'"What you're saying is that it's all in the perception – what is thought to be the best *is* the best?"

'"The Chinese peasant wants to believe raisins will give him male children and that Double Golden Boy will increase his chances even further. While caviar appreciation may be at a more sophisticated level, the eggs of the sterlet sturgeon are gold in colour and therefore different. What we perceive is what we believe."

'"And does caviar not require refrigeration?" he asked.

'"Vladivostok has been sending fish to Moscow since 1916. The ice cars exist because my father was an engineer seconded from the army to work on the Trans-Siberian Railway. The Turks controlled the Black Sea when a desperate shortage of fish occurred. One of his tasks was to send fish across Russia to Moscow, so he built twenty ice-making depots from Moscow to Vladivostok. Then he designed a four-axle wooden ice car that loaded ice through its roof hatches. The complete plans for the cars and the ice-making depots are among his papers."

'"Well, it's a madcap idea that may just work with the right social introductions. As you say, everything is in the perception and, as conventional wisdom would have it, it's not *what* you know but *who* you know, and I imagine I'll be able to open a few of the right doors with letters of introduction."

'"When you travel to America will you introduce my caviar to your rich friends?" I pleaded. "That is, of course, if my product is of the very highest quality?"

'He was silent for a while, then said, "Why not? It might be fun. I'll throw a big party." I longed to go with him but knew Big Boss Yu would greatly disapprove. Having an affair with Sir Victor was taking too big a chance as it was, but I was too much in love to give him up.'

We had long since eaten the cray, along with fresh bread and butter, and had drunk another cup of tea. It was getting a bit chilly and a fairly stiff breeze had sprung up. I'd been so intrigued by the story Nicole Lenoir-Jourdan was telling us that I hadn't noticed the change in the sky and the sudden drop in temperature. We had been totally sheltered, but I now realised the extent of the wind – it was no longer a breeze and the water in the bay was becoming choppy. It was just after one o'clock and I decided it was time to get back. 'I don't like the look of the sky,' I said. 'Think it might be time to head home.'

Jimmy looked at me quickly. He'd picked up the hint of concern in my voice. 'It okay, Brother Fish?'

'Yeah,' I said, 'but we'd better get goin' – this time of year the winds on the Strait can be tricky.' I could have kicked myself. It is a ritual for every fisherman out on the Strait to listen to the weather 'scheds' from Hobart Radio. There were three of these a day and I'd tuned into the seven a.m. report, which had forecast a high-pressure zone over Bass Strait. The next had been at three minutes past one p.m. and I'd just missed it, too busy listening to the story to take the dinghy back to the boat to tune in. The third forecast was scheduled for five-fifteen p.m. We were six hours' sailing from Livingston, which was about four hours as the crow flies but due to the myriad rocks and reefs three miles or so offshore and south of the harbour we'd have to keep well out for safety, which would add another two hours. With a bit of luck, a fair wind and, if necessary, the use of the engine, we would be home just after eight p.m., an hour after sundown. I'd only had a few days sailing the *Janthe* and it takes a lot longer than that to become totally familiar with a new boat, so I wanted to be cautious. Alf would always say, '*Mistress Caution is a fisherman's best friend; only fools and drunks take chances.*'

Jack McGinty, the printing foreman on the *Gazette* and a keen amateur weather buff, took barometric readings three times every day, which he passed on to the Hobart Weather Bureau. The bureau, in turn, would give him a complete run-down for the next few hours. If you missed a 'sched' you called Jack, simple as that, so I wasn't too worried.

We went aboard but had a bit of trouble with the winch that hoisted the dinghy, so it was nearly one-thirty when we pulled anchor. I turned the engine key to the heat position and held it for ten seconds so the glow plugs heated to the point where I could push the starter, fire the diesel–air mixture into the cylinders and fire the motor. I was tempted to move out, but nothing wears a diesel out quicker than running it at high revs while the engine is cold. So I waited a further ten minutes, pushed the throttle lever up and, spinning the wheel, moved the *Janthe* out of the lagoon. Fifteen minutes out to sea we hoisted sail. It was now just after two o'clock.

I contacted Jack McGinty and told him we were on our way, and he told me what I didn't want to hear. A low-pressure system was developing and moving over the Strait. Not good news, but not all that unusual. I gave Jack our position and asked him to inform the Listening Watch on Hobart Radio as a precaution.

The *Janthe* responded well to the quickening breeze and I began to feel a little better, although the wind was getting decidedly cooler and the seas were growing. The boat started to rock with a steady rhythm that meant the wind had moved slightly. I called over to Jimmy to take the wheel, and adjusted the sail. But when, an hour later, the rocking progressed to an elongated roll I decided to lower the sail and run only on the engine. Pretty soon the rolling increased even further and the engine revs increased as the boat started to slide down the seas that were now coming from behind.

At three-thirty p.m. the wind was still picking up, the cloud racing from the south-west tearing at the sun, which appeared in brilliant glimpses. As you will have gathered by now, I am not an optimist. Jimmy was a fast learner and had picked up a bit from being out on the various cray boats as temporary crew, but he was still a long way from being competent. Nicole Lenoir-Jourdan was a self-confessed landlubber, despite her background in shipping. She was apt to get violently seasick and I could see she was already growing very pale, trying to hide her distraught expression by turning away from me. 'Better go below, Countess. Take the sick bucket,' I yelled over the wind, and watched as she struggled to get below deck. 'Grab a blanket!' I shouted at her back. It was the best I could do. It was better to have her out of the way, even though being below deck was likely to make her seasickness worse. With Jimmy only half a capable deckie I had more than enough on my plate as it was, and in big seas like this I didn't want her on deck.

Jimmy came into the wheelhouse, his huge frame filling almost all the available space, his head touching the ceiling. 'How we goin', Brother Fish?'

I searched my mind for something positive to say. 'The sea is up our arse and not against us, which means we'll save fuel and get home quicker.'

'Bullshit!' he replied. 'We got trouble, eh?'

'Not yet, mate. It's probably a passing cold front and then we'll have a nor'easterly swell, which will help a fair bit.'

'Yoh done did dis before?' he asked.

'This much, sure. Don't know what's yet to come, mate – could be we're in for a bumpy ride.'

I'd used up all the optimism I had and I hadn't fooled Jimmy. He might not be a good sailor yet but, like so many kids with his kind of background, he was expert at gauging someone else's state of mind. 'Here, hang onto the wheel – I want to check the barometer.' I shifted places with him and showed him how to hold onto the wheel, let her move a bit, go with it and then when it slackened off, correct her to keep on course. I knew from experience that while we were less than twenty miles from shore, in a wrong sea we might as well be halfway to South America. Jimmy may well need to take his turn at the wheel.

By the time we were off Livingston, any hope of getting into the harbour was out of the question. The entrance to Livingston Harbour is shallow with a series of low-lying rocks directly in front of it. Even in calm weather you had to know your way in, as many a visiting sailor had discovered in the past. In these conditions any attempt to enter the harbour would be an act of insanity and we would almost certainly lose our lives in the process. So near and yet so far, but that's the nature of sailing – the sea dictates everything.

I thought for a moment that the barometer must be out of order – it was down to a fraction under twenty-nine inches. I was getting out of my depth – I had never seen the glass so low at sea before. Alf used to keep a barometer at home and I'd seen it lower on land, but never at sea. He would describe the prevailing conditions out to sea at a given reading, and as kids we'd listened, fascinated, as he talked about the changing waves and winds and what a boat must do to handle the conditions. I hoped to Christ that I'd remember a bit of what he'd said.

There was a small natural harbour on the northern point of Queen Island. In fair sailing time it was four hours away, and if I could get through the narrow gap between the island and Navarine Reef it might provide shelter. There was a lighthouse built on the top of Cape Wickham that could be seen at night for ten miles out to sea. Although I hoped at least to have reached the shelter of the small harbour before dark, if we didn't make it the light might guide us in.

With the seas behind us I had to try to slow the vessel. This is done by making a drogue – that is, tying anything you can to a piece of rope and tossing it into the water behind the boat. The craypots were already tied together and I lifted them one by one in sequence until they were all in the water at the stern, the drag they created slowing her somewhat. I did the same with the sea anchor. This gave me just sufficient control to hold the vessel, although we were still tearing along much too fast for comfort and if the waves and the wind increased I would be back with a boat I couldn't steer with confidence.

I took the wheel from Jimmy and altered course to the north-east once we'd cleared New Year Island. It was an hour after sundown and already black as pitch. By now I simply dared not leave the helm. In these conditions helming required all the skill I possessed and then some. With the seas running behind us we were doing in excess of twenty knots at times and this kind of speed required me to be absolutely one with the boat, tuned into her every movement down the huge watery slopes. The slightest movement to one side or the other in the downward plunge required me to turn the wheel as fast as I possibly could in the opposite direction, at the same time applying all the power the diesel could deliver so that the vessel didn't broach.

Perhaps I can explain. When a boat surfs down a wave, if she should remain unchecked in her rapid descent the boat will suddenly veer to port or starboard. This means the vessel is going in one direction one moment, and a moment later has turned ninety degrees to port or starboard. Imagine a motor car moving at high speed and then attempting to negotiate a tight corner on the side of a mountain – it will leave the road and tumble over the edge to oblivion. It is exactly the same with a boat, which will simply roll over and continue to do so until perhaps it rights itself – by which time you are history, anyway.

It had now stopped raining, but to negate this small blessing the wind was now gusting at over a hundred miles per hour. I could quite simply take in the mountain of water that was building up behind us. I'd been in the odd bad storm before, though never in control at the helm, but I'd never seen anything like this. The water simply rose and rose. The *Janthe* was little more than a surfboard on a giant wave. I worked the wheel with all my strength in a frantic effort to keep her straight. I must have been doing around thirty-five knots as the bow dug in and the boat skewed sideways with a terrifying jerk.

I turned on the sounder to measure the height of the waves we were sliding down, although I'd angled the *Janthe* so that we were moving away from the waves halfway between stern-on and side-on. This was a compromise between the safety of a stern-on run down the wave and the possibility of a rollover, which can occur if a boat is struck with sufficient force by a rogue wave, a notorious possibility on the shallow bottom of Bass Strait. The sounder indicated that the wall of water coming behind us was forty feet high. As every seaman knows, if the waves on the Strait are forty feet then it's only a matter of time before you meet up with what's known in the fisherman's vernacular as a 'rouger' – a wave half as high again, or even higher.

We'd gone another hour and were level with Cape Wickham. I made the decision to avoid the gap between the cape and Navarine Reef. What should have been the passage was now occupied by set after set of hundred-foot breakers. The wind had shifted back to south-south-west, so I decided to run for it for a further ten miles before making a turn that would have the effect of putting the sea almost directly on our nose. It was going to be one hell of a punch, but every mile forward would be a mile closer to the safety of the east coast of the island.

'Jimmy, get below and strap the Countess in. See she's wrapped in a blanket – it's going to get a lot rougher before we're through. Then get back here.' Jimmy turned to leave. 'Oh, and tell her there's nothing to worry about,' I grinned, hoping he wouldn't catch on to my concern. I spun the wheel to starboard and headed into the unadulterated mountains of shit that now lay in front of us.

Jimmy grinned back and said something, but he'd opened the wheelhouse door and the roaring of the wind drowned him out. We'd been out for over ten hours and I estimated we'd come more than eighty miles and were at least eight miles from shore. Punching into the waves I needed to see what might be coming at us, so I turned on the C47 light. *Holy shit!* I couldn't believe it! We could see with almost absolute clarity what was coming our way from 200 yards out. I promised myself if we came out of this alive I'd drop a note to Mike Munday to thank him for his 'overkill' Dakota landing light. At least I'd have a bit of warning if a truly big one came at us.

Of course it came. Half an hour later a sixty-foot wall of water came rushing at us. The light allowed me to spin the wheel starboard to meet it head on. I pulled the revs back to reduce our speed and lessen the inevitable collision. The wave struck, but almost immediately the *Janthe* started to slowly climb the slope of the wave (Alf again, watching over us). We reached the top and began to slide down the other side. And so it went – up and down, with each wave seeming to be the one that would bring the boat finally undone.

By this stage the wind was registering sixty knots, with gusts up to seventy-five knots. Technically speaking we were right in the middle of a hurricane on a stretch of water known worldwide for its ferocity. For those who may know little about Bass Strait, it used to be a land bridge to the Australian mainland before the rising seas flooded it. This means it's pretty shallow, so when massive waves roll in from the Indian Ocean on one side and from the Tasman on the other, and warm tropical air from the Pacific Ocean off the New South Wales coast moves down, you have the beginnings of a disaster. The low pressure formed over the Strait sucks cold air from the Southern Ocean and suddenly you've got a hurricane that affects the winds and the tides in a totally unpredictable manner that can be catastrophic. We were now in the dead centre of such a performance.

Jimmy wasn't back yet, and I was beginning to worry. The wheelhouse is the most stable position on a boat such as the *Janthe*. He was down in the fo'c'sle, and if he wasn't strapped in he was in serious trouble. A man of his size – in fact, even someone my size – could be thrown up against the deck beams and easily sustain a cracked skull. If he'd secured Nicole Lenoir-Jourdan she'd be safe, and hopefully he'd done the same to himself in the other bunk. But it wasn't like Jimmy to take the safe option, and I'd instructed him to return to the wheelhouse. The problem was that I couldn't leave the helm.

We travelled just ten nautical miles in the past seven hours and daylight didn't bring any change to the weather. It was approaching seven o'clock on the morning following our departure from Livingston and the conditions, if anything, were getting worse. The speed of the waves was often so fast that the *Janthe* would be suspended in mid-air with only a small length of the rear portion of the boat in contact with the water. We would fall fifteen feet before meeting the water again, and Jimmy was below in all this. I felt a weird sort of panic growing within me – not because of the sea that threatened to kill us but at the prospect of losing my mate because I'd acted like a bloody skipper, telling him to secure the Countess and then report back to the wheelhouse. I could have easily told him to strap himself in for several hours until the storm died down. I could hang on alone another four or five hours before I'd have to take a break from the wheel. I turned the radio on for the seven o'clock weather report.

*'Here is the forecast at 0.700 hours.*

*Situation: A slow-moving high is situated in the Bight and a very deep depression has developed in mid Bass Strait and is moving slowly to the north-east.*

*Here is the forecast: There is a storm warning for all Tasmanian coastal waters.*

*East Coast: Gale-force south-east to south-westerly winds with an increasing high southerly swell.*

*Tasman Island to Cape Sorrell: Gale force winds from the south-west with high to very high sou'westerly swells increasing during the day.*

*Cape Sorrell to Rocky Cape including all of Bass Strait: West to south-west wind changes of sixty to seventy knots extending from the west this morning and increasing to ninety knots in Bass Strait this afternoon. Signed Weather Hobart . . . all ships, this is Hobart Radio. I have traffic on hand for the* Denalis, Western Star *and* Janthe.'

Well, they knew we were out here somewhere, but a fat lot of good that would do. It was pointless trying to get them back – there wasn't anything they could do. So I turned the radio off. I now knew that things couldn't get a lot worse, and we'd survived so far. But life is never like that – I guess it never rains but it pours. I'd hardly completed the thought when the bilge alarm started to ring in the wheelhouse. We were taking water, so I switched on the electric bilge pumps and hoped for the best. I needed to check the engine room urgently. Christ help us if the water was coming in there. The other likely place was the fo'c'sle where Jimmy and Nicole Lenoir-Jourdan were. I couldn't leave the wheel, and was trying to think how I might tie it so that I could go and take a look when I saw Jimmy crawling towards me. He disappeared from my view almost immediately but not before I'd seen that his head and face appeared to be covered in blood. Then there was a banging on the wheelhouse door and I opened it to let him in and nearly passed out with shock – Jimmy's skull was cracked wide open.

'Fuck!' I yelled.

'It leakin' in the fo'c'sle, Brother Fish.'

'Can you man the wheel, Jimmy?' I cried.

'Sure. Can yoh wipe mah eyes, man?'

I grabbed a piece of cotton waste and wiped the blood from his eyes. 'You gunna be all right?'

'Go! It comin' in real fast, man!'

I wasn't sure if he meant the leak in the boat or the blood running into his eyes. I left him to inspect the fo'c'sle. Nicole Lenoir-Jourdan was moaning, but still tied securely to her bunk. 'You okay, Countess?' I called out.

'I've shit my bloomers!' she cried, terribly distressed. The vomit bucket had turned over and I could see she hadn't had much of a time. She must have been really scared to use words like that and despite myself I was forced to laugh. 'You're in good company,' I shouted. 'If all you get is a good shit out of this we'll be extremely lucky.' Not in a million years had I thought I'd ever say anything like that to her. There wasn't any time for further social discourse. The force generated by the continual pounding to the hull as the *Janthe* fell off the tops of the big seas had pushed the caulking cotton between the planks so far inwards that some of it had come out. Now spurts of water were being forced through the holes that had been created.

It wasn't the first time I'd blessed Mike Munday during the storm, but he was about to get another major benediction. Of course, naturally and axiomatically, he had a caulking iron aboard. Working furiously in order to get back to Jimmy, it took me less than ten minutes to plug all the leaks. The bilge pump would do the rest. I left a moaning Countess to contemplate her ruined britches and, grabbing the first-aid kit, made my way back to the wheelhouse.

I had to attend to Jimmy's head. I swabbed what blood remained, which was surprisingly little, and saw that Jimmy's skull had a six-inch crack the width of my small finger. I could see the membrane covering his brain. The first-aid kit contained two crepe bandages that I wrapped around his head, although with the boat pitching and falling this was a task that took some time. There wasn't much else I could do. He was still completely conscious and his big hand gripped me on the shoulder to thank me. The roar of the wind made it almost impossible to talk. 'You okay?' I shouted. He nodded.

I was about to close the first-aid box when I saw the Bex powders. *Fat lot of use they'll be*, I thought, then, what the hell, they just might help Jimmy's headache. I opened a powder to see that it contained white crystals instead. I couldn't believe my luck, or rather Mike Munday's foresight. I suddenly remembered his words: *'Oh, by the way, Jacko. If ever you find yourself in a tight spot, big storm or something, and you've got to stay alert, look in the first-aid box – the Bex packets.'* I'd seen these crystals before – a skipper named Bad Brown I'd once worked with would give us some when we had to work a twenty-hour shift after finding a big cray haul.

The crystals were referred to as 'White Lightning', but in reality they were methedrine crystals – stuff that could keep you going well beyond the capacity of normal flesh and blood. I opened a second packet, same thing again. So I handed a packet to Jimmy and indicated he should swallow the contents, then did the same myself and took the wheel from him. He backed into the corner and sat down on the deck, pushing his back against the planking of the wheelhouse. The poor bastard was in a bad way. I resumed trying to fight an opponent that was getting stronger all the time with a vessel that was getting weaker with every hour that passed. It was midday and in the past five hours we'd gone five miles.

Nothing good ever happens in a storm, and a hurricane is ten times worse. A huge wave caught me unawares and I wasn't able to turn into it sufficiently to take it head on. The bulk of it hit the stern, tearing the dinghy from one of the davits where it hung like a watch on a fob chain. We were suddenly in the deepest possible shit. Without the dinghy we would lose all means of escape. If we had to abandon ship it was our only means of surviving the storm. 'Jimmy, mate, you have to take the wheel!' I shouted. Somehow I was going to have to secure the dinghy by means of a rope, winch it down from the remaining davit and get it into the water. I'd use the Morris line and tie it to the dinghy and then somehow wind the rope around the stern post and then the wheelhouse and secure it with a bowline knot. Jimmy got to his feet slowly and took the wheel.

I was high as a kite and what was clearly an impossible task seemed possible. We were in the middle of a hurricane with a boat pitching like a cork every which way, a seventy-knot hurricane blowing and an inexperienced helmsman at the wheel. I moved out of the wheelhouse, the wind and rain tearing at my oilskins and threatening to blow me overboard. I found the Morris line, secured it to the stern post and pulled it towards the hanging dinghy. Somehow I managed to winch the dinghy down so that I could tie the rope to it and then let it fall into the waves behind the boat.

Sounds simple enough, but the task took me half an hour and I fell frequently so that I was bruised and bleeding from the side of my head where I smashed it against the stern post. I pulled the remaining rope towards the wheelhouse and had almost reached it when I was lifted high into the air and pitched over the side. A freak wave had hit and taken me overboard. By some miracle I still hung onto the rope but I was going nowhere. The *Janthe* was pointed into the waves and there was no possible way I could get back on board.

It was all over for yours truly. I knew, even with the effects of the methedrine, there was no way I could hold on for long. I was going to die – drown, like so many fishermen before me. This didn't seem to bother me – so many of the men on the island died this way it seemed almost predestined. It was the fact that I would kill Jimmy and Nicole Lenoir-Jourdan as well that distressed me most, as they had almost no chance of surviving without me at the helm or on board to get the dinghy prepared if we had to abandon ship. *We should have remained in the lagoon. I should have caught the one p.m. 'sched'. I've fucked up big time!* Gloria was right, we were nothing but a pinch of shit. I'd let everyone down again. Jack McKenzie hadn't made the grade, as usual.

Suddenly I felt my wrist being grasped. Perhaps I was imagining it. It was Jimmy, his grasp strong as an ox. We were both underwater. Instead of feeling grateful, my first thought was *Now we're both gone!* He'd left the wheel and come after me. *Bloody stupid bastard! Fuckwit!* A boat sometimes survives even against the most incredible odds – the storm blows out and it's still miraculously afloat, sometimes even after the crew has abandoned it. Now we were both in the water, good as dead and with Nicole Lenoir-Jourdan strapped to her bunk.

The boat, given its own way, started to turn in order to run with the sea. As a boat turns from having the sea on the nose to having it behind her she must at some point of time be facing side on to incoming waves. If she's hit with a big one she'll roll over, and there were nothing but big ones coming towards us. But, as Gloria so often said, '*Miracles will never cease*' – the vessel turned without being hit and started to run with the sea. With both of us clinging to the rope the next wave hit and lifted us upright to the level of the deck. Quite how Jimmy did it, I'll never know – it would have taken the strength of ten men – but he grasped onto the aft rail with one hand, holding onto the rope with the other. The wave washed over and somehow he managed to get aboard and pull me up on deck. Jimmy was making a regular habit of saving my life.

Somehow I managed to crawl over to where he lay face down on the deck, the wind and rain ripping at his inert form. He'd taken off his oilskins to dive overboard and his shirt clung like a shining skin to his huge body. I dragged him to the stern post, tied a section of the rope we'd clung to into a loop and attached it to the stern post, then wound it over his head and under his arms. I had to hope that the rope tied to the stern post would hold the dinghy and the loop would keep Jimmy on deck. It was the best I could do under the circumstances. He seemed to be unconscious and I hadn't the strength to drag him into the wheelhouse or the fo'c'sle. I'd have another go when I regained a bit of strength. The main thing was to get back into the wheelhouse to maintain some sort of control of the boat and get her punching back into the oncoming seas.

By now the sea was such that every wave was over seventy feet and the wind was gusting at ninety knots, blowing the tops of the mountainous crests. We'd just about reached the end of our tether and I switched on the transmitter to send a mayday.

'Mayday, mayday, mayday all stations . . . this is the *Janthe*. *Janthe*, over . . .'

Within a few seconds a reassuring voice boomed back, '*Janthe*, this is Melbourne Radio. What is your position? Over.'

'Melbourne Radio, this is *Janthe*. Our position is thirty-nine degrees, thirty-five minutes south by 144 degrees, five minutes east. Over.'

'*Janthe* thirty-nine degrees, thirty-five minutes south by 144 degrees, five minutes east puts you eight miles due east of Cape Wickham light. Please confirm. Over.'

'Melbourne Radio, *Janthe*, romeo. Over.'

'*Janthe*, this is Melbourne. What is your situation? Over.'

'Melbourne, this is *Janthe*. Badly injured crew member. Currently experiencing hurricane-force winds. Caulking in fo'c'sle planking leaking and repaired temporarily. Our dinghy is floating and attached. Over.'

'*Janthe*, this is Melbourne. We have your position and situation. We will be listening out for you and will activate search-and-rescue procedures if you fail to make contact by 1400 hours. Over.'

'*Janthe*, Melbourne Radio. Thank you. Over and out.'

'Romeo, *Janthe*. We'll be listening out for you . . . Good luck for now. Over and out.'

At least they would be looking for us in daylight. But even if a spotter plane found us, always presuming they could get one into the air, it might take several more hours before they could get to us, unless they could get a passing ship to come to our aid. But it would be like looking for a needle in a haystack.

At five p.m. I turned on the radio to get the evening 'sched', which was far from encouraging. The low had moved in a nor'easterly direction and joined forces with another low-pressure system that had formed over the Tasman Sea and, in turn, this had merged with yet another just south of Lord Howe Island. It was the recipe for the perfect storm. The wave heights were now reaching over one hundred feet, with the wind sounding like all the tortured souls of purgatory and hell combined. Jimmy was out on the deck, possibly freezing to death. God knows whether or not the Countess was safe, even strapped in – the knocking-about of the waves could easily tear the bunk from its bolts, and she could be badly injured.

The top of our mast was forty-six feet from the deck and the average wave was at least two and a half times as high when we lay in a trough. Normally in big seas you see seabirds, from gulls to mallemucks, with an occasional albatross. They sweep and dive or simply stay right beside your boat, the sheer wind speed passing over their stationary wings sufficient to give them the lift they need. When they're there, particularly the albatross, you feel somehow in contact. But here there were no seabirds to be seen, which is never a good sign.

The methedrine was beginning to wear off and I could feel myself nodding off. I swallowed another 'Bex' not knowing what the effect might be. What the hell, we were gone if I fell asleep at the helm and I had to take the chance. It didn't take long for the white crystals to kick in. I knew I was injured – the little and third fingers on my left hand were standing at right angles to the others, but I couldn't feel a thing.

It was now almost six p.m. and I'd been in constant contact on the radio but there was no sign of an aircraft and they hadn't been able to locate a big boat that could get to us. We were fucked, even though the voice on the other end stayed calm and said they were doing all they could.

I continued as the light faded with no sign of a spotter plane. I'd come almost completely around Queen Island when at around eight that night the wind started to drop from about 120 knots to eighty knots. An hour later it was down to forty. The mountainous swells were still raging, but the birds were back – gulls, mallemucks and gannets, with two albatross, which I took to be a good sign. At last I was able to leave the helm and check Jimmy and Nicole Lenoir-Jourdan. At first I thought Jimmy was dead. The bandage around his head had unwound and disappeared, and the crack in his skull had been washed clean by the waves breaking over the deck. He stirred when I touched him on the hip. 'You okay, mate?' I asked, which was ridiculous, of course – he was unconscious. But I told myself he was still alive.

I then made my way down to the fo'c'sle. The bunk was still intact but, even with the strapping, Nicole Lenoir-Jourdan had taken a beating. Her head was bleeding and she, too, was unconscious. There wasn't anything I could do for her so I grabbed a blanket and went on deck and wrapped Jimmy up as best I could, undid the rope and retied it around his waist to take the pressure off his shoulders. There was simply no way I could get him into the fo'c'sle. The boat was pitching badly in the huge swell and I had to get back to the wheelhouse. Freak waves are not unknown in these conditions.

I radioed through to Hobart to tell them we looked like making it, and after giving them our position they told me that I was three to four hours north of Tussock. We'd come right around the eastern side of Queen Island, approaching Tussock, and miraculously were nearly home. At a few minutes to one o'clock in the morning we came into Tussock Harbour where it seemed dozens of people had come the twenty miles across the neck of the island from Livingston to meet us, along with all the Tussock locals. Cheers from hundreds of people rose, car hooters blasted out and motorbike engines revved as I pulled in beside the dock, hitting it rather too hard. Hands from everywhere grabbed at the side of the *Janthe* to steady her. I switched off the engine, and it was only then that I started to weep.

# CHAPTER TWENTY-ONE

## *Scapegoat for Opium*

The three of us were in a fair mess. Nicole Lenoir-Jourdan received several stitches to her forehead – a future scar she would wear rather proudly. The two fingers I thought I'd broken turned out to be merely dislocated, but to add to my injuries I had several cracked ribs, a cut to my head that required half-a-dozen stitches and a bung knee that, as I grew older, would sometimes trouble me in cold weather.

The moment the *Janthe* had docked Dr Light had come aboard to find Jimmy still unconscious and tied to the stern post. 'Miss Lenoir-Jourdan is below,' I said in between sobs. He rushed below deck with Sue, and two fishermen carrying a stretcher, while I remained helplessly beside Jimmy blubbering like a baby. When he re-emerged he hurried over to Jimmy and untied him carefully, checking that he didn't have a neck injury. I was now wrapped in a blanket trying to control my crying, with Gloria weeping beside me and Steve and Cory hanging onto either arm. 'Is he gunna be okay?' I sobbed, unwilling to move from beside Jimmy. Moments later Sue emerged from the fo'c'sle, followed by the two men carrying Nicole Lenoir-Jourdan on a stretcher.

'Come on, mate, yer goin' ter hospital,' Steve said gently.

'Yeah, you're buggered, mate,' Cory added, as usual stating the obvious.

But I wouldn't budge. 'Is Jimmy okay?' I wailed again, needing their support to stay on my feet.

Sue came over, and in a businesslike voice said, 'It's all right, Jacko. Doc's examining him – taking his blood pressure, checking his airway is clear and examining his pupil dilatation. If they're all okay we'll move him and do the rest when we get the three of you to hospital in Livingston.'

Of course I didn't understand what she was talking about, but the sound of her calm voice brought a measure of comfort. Doc Light got up from where he'd been kneeling beside Jimmy. 'Righto, let's move him.' He supervised while the two fishermen returned to place the still-unconscious Jimmy on the stretcher and carry him off the boat.

Later I learned that Hobart Radio had called Jack McGinty to say we'd survived the storm. They'd given him the estimated time of arrival at Tussock and informed him that we had an injured member of the crew on board and to get a doctor to the small town. Sue, who was now assistant matron at the cottage hospital, together with Doc Light, had driven across the island in the Dodge war-surplus ambulance, and they were waiting with Gloria and the twins when we came in.

All three of us were placed in the ambulance and driven the fifteen bumpy miles across the southern neck of the island to the cottage hospital. Not that I recall the trip – I passed out moments after they strapped me into the stretcher, and was still asleep when we arrived. I woke up just after eight o'clock that morning with Sue standing next to my bed. Everything hurt, but in particular the ribs on my left side, which were excruciatingly painful every time I breathed in. The effects of the methedrine had long since worn off and I was paying the price.

'How are you feeling, hero of the hour?' Sue asked me, smiling.

'Bloody terrible. How's Jimmy and the . . . Nicole ma'am?' I corrected.

'They've both regained consciousness and are out of theatre. They're going to be fine, Jacko – it's you we're worried about.'

She pointed to my hand. 'We were going to wake you and set your fingers but Doc Light examined you and said your pupils were dilated. We were afraid that, like Jimmy, you may have taken a bad knock to the head. But we couldn't see anything, so decided to wait until you woke up.'

'Methedrine.'

Sue had been among fishermen long enough to know that occasionally substances that are not strictly legal are used out on sea. Nevertheless, she looked a bit worried. 'Jacko, you don't use it regularly, do you?' I explained the circumstances in between groans. 'Thank God for Mr Munday,' she said. 'It probably got you home.'

'My left side hurts like hell – worse than the fingers.'

'We haven't X-rayed you, but from the way you're breathing it looks like you've probably broken several ribs.'

'So, where's Jimmy? Why am I in this little room?'

'We're taking you directly into the theatre next door as soon as Doc Light comes in. We've both been up all night. He's gone home to have a shower and a bit of breakfast. Jimmy's in the ward demanding something to eat and Nicole Lenoir-Jourdan is asleep.'

I then noticed how exhausted she looked. 'You'd better get home,' I said.

'Yeah, sure. Matron's already in, but I'd like to attend to you first. It was lucky I was on night shift when Jack McGinty called – he's been at the *Gazette* monitoring your progress for two days.' She smiled. 'You're making a habit of being a hero, Jacko.'

'Hero? No, no, no! Jimmy's the hero!' I started to cough, and thought I was going to die. Cracked ribs or otherwise, coughing hurt like hell.

Sue held me down. 'No more talk, Jacko – just lie still, breathing in as shallowly as you can.'

'No,' I managed to say, 'I have to tell you about Jimmy. I don't want people thinking I'm the hero.'

Sue could see I was distressed. 'Take it easy, Jacko – it can wait.'

But it couldn't. So I told her about Jimmy diving in to save me with a fractured skull when I was washed overboard and was hanging onto the rope I'd used to drag in the dinghy. How miraculously he clung onto the boat when a big wave took us close to the side again, and how he dragged me back on board.

'You sure he's okay?' I asked, suddenly suspicious. 'Sue, don't lie to me!'

She laughed. 'No, honestly – he's fine. But we didn't really know until about three this morning, when he finally came around. There seemed to be only an extradural haematoma and no apparent bleeding into the brain, but we couldn't be absolutely certain there hadn't been any brain damage until we spoke to him.'

I was glad I'd been out to it – with my imagination I'd have resigned Jimmy to being a gibbering idiot with it all being my fault. 'You mean he could have been zonked in the head?'

Sue shrugged. 'You never know. A lot of things can happen if there's an internal haematoma – that is, bleeding into the brain. But fortunately there wasn't. First thing Jimmy said when he woke up was, "How's Brother Fish?"'

I laughed, even though it hurt like hell. Sue, suddenly serious, said, 'Jacko, I've got to get you ready for theatre. Doc Light will be here any moment.'

'You haven't told me about Nicole ma'am. How bad is she?'

'She cracked her forehead, which required twenty stitches. Earlier she was still in shock and kept asking about the two of you, apologising for being so useless in the crisis. I gave her something to put her to sleep.'

Doc Light arrived shortly after and examined my hand. 'Dislocation at the knuckles. I'll give you an injection, but it's going to hurt like hell when it wears off. Sister McKenzie will have told you there's nothing much we can do for your ribs. We'll strap them, although I'm not sure that'll help much – they're going to be painful for some time. We'll need to keep an eye on you, young Jack. If your ribs play up you may have to go to Launceston to be X-rayed. But for the time being the three of you will stay here for the next few days. You're exhausted, and likely to suffer some trauma from the shock of the impacts you've taken.'

By the following morning Nicole Lenoir-Jourdan seemed quite chirpy, and made Jimmy and me go through the whole business blow by blow while she scribbled it all down furiously. By that afternoon the story had been dispatched on the wire service and was to appear as a feature article in newspapers throughout the nation. The report of the hurricane and the story of the *Janthe* had been broadcast on ABC radio. Four boats had gone down in the storm, with all their crews lost, and while we'd evidently been caught in the worst of it, we'd been the lucky ones. None of the boats lost at sea was from the island, as the local fishermen out to sea had been on the eastern side of the island and had all headed for Tussock when the one o'clock sched we'd originally missed had come through.

Of course, I didn't mention the methedrine and the experts were all saying that I had shown unbelievable stamina to remain at the helm for thirty-six hours. If ever we got wealthy enough to do without the *Janthe*, then Mike Munday was getting it back for a song. Gloria had yet another bonanza for her scrapbook, and later when I read some of the articles it was clear to me they'd made much too much of my part in the whole thing. One smart-arse journalist even doubted the veracity of Jimmy's rescuing me.

On the afternoon of our second day in the cottage hospital, the three of us sat in the hospital's garden while Nicole Lenoir-Jourdan told Jimmy and me the final part of her story, which she referred to as 'From Raisins for the Masses to Caviar for the Few'.

'I had gone through my father's papers to find the names of some of the people who might still be working in the production of caviar in what was once my father's family business and was now, I discovered, a commune. After several months of writing letters I finally received one in return from an ex-manager, Pyotr Kuzmich Ivanov, who was in charge of the caviar commune and remembered my father with fondness. Over a period of time we established a rapport and a system of payment, and he would send me only the best. He still worked with Roman Sotnikov, thought in my father's day to be the best caviar salter in Russia, so I knew my caviar would be the optimum – though not always the small golden eggs of the sterlet sturgeon but also beluga, osetra and sevruga. The most delicate caviar is known as malossol caviar, which means that it contains not more than five per cent of the salt from the seas of the Astrakhan Steppe. Malossol is also the most perishable and I wasn't able to send it to America on the long sea voyage, but it nevertheless fetched a good price in Shanghai, and Sir Victor's Cathay Hotel soon became famous for its malossol caviar. The Americans went for beluga, which produces large, loose, glistening dark berries, and I'm sure that's why beluga is now considered the finest of the caviars. I personally think some of the others have a more subtle, delicate flavour, and that the caviar from Azerbaijan is the finest of them all.'

She paused to explain the circumstances that had made going into caviar possible. 'Exporting caviar was really a hobby, one that Big Boss Yu allowed me to indulge in always provided I financed it myself. While it made a nice profit – up until the Great Depression, at least – the supply, like so much happening in the new Russia, was unreliable. This was partly compensated for by Sir Victor, who had kept his promise and introduced my caviar into the very best New York circles so that whenever a consignment arrived in New York it was immediately snapped up. Its very rarity became its greatest advantage. As I've mentioned before, perception is everything. "Kuzmich Beluga", the name I'd chosen to honour Pyotr Kuzmich Ivanov's family, was considered the best caviar in New York, and became the standard by which all other caviar was measured.

'I was still expected to run what had become a veritable raisin empire. Big Boss Yu also set up a business importing frozen fish, which he handed over to me to develop as well. In addition he started a mill to produce cotton and shantung silk, which I also set up for him and supervised. He had come to believe that everything I touched would lead to success, and I dreaded the time when something I'd been asked to control didn't achieve the accustomed expectations.

'I was constantly at his side at all of Shanghai's important business functions and lavish parties, and was his so-called business partner. My impeccable English accent and my increasing business acumen and reputation allowed us many an introduction to local and foreign businessmen. The foreign taipans ran companies that might not otherwise have had dealings with a Chinese businessman whose past business affairs were known to be somewhat clandestine and who had gained control of Shanghai's labour force without ever holding an official position with the government.

'Of course I was aware that Big Boss Yu's business affairs were not always squeaky clean. The Chinese have a different morality to our own. The family and then the clan come first. If either benefits from a business deal or opportunity, then the moral question doesn't arise. It wasn't until Chiang Kai-shek, head of the Nanking Government, secretly recruited members of the Green Gang – a Shanghai Triad secret society whose Chinese name was *Cb'in Pang*, meaning Green Circle Society – to kill communists that I eventually discovered the truth. Nor did I know until later that the Three Musketeers of the French Concession belonged to this Green Gang and that Du Yu-sen, known as Big Ears Du, was its dragonhead, Smallpox "Million Dollar" Yang his "white paper fan" or trusted assistant, and the last of the three, Chang Shig-liang, his second in command.

'Because I had met them in the General's Retreat in Harbin, where Big Boss Yu seemed to be in command, I had always assumed they were simply three gangsters he knew. I thought that perhaps they were sometime collaborators in seemingly legitimate business deals. The English-speaking newspaper, *North China Daily News*, while not condoning communism, was nevertheless highly indignant about Chiang Kai-shek's reputed alliance with the Triads, but such was the power of the gangster leaders that their names were never mentioned. I took little interest in local gossip and it all seemed rather remote from my everyday world of raisins, fish imports, caviar, cotton and silk. That is, until one night when, working back late, I left my office to fetch some papers from nearby "Ticking Clock House", which was the Chinese name for the San Peh Steam Navigation Company.

'I'd been doing paperwork all afternoon and late into the evening and decided to walk rather than wake Ah Chow, who would be asleep in the car waiting to take me home. As I drew closer to the headquarters of the San Peh Steam Navigation Company, I could see what looked to be a devil of a row going on among a group of Chinese on the street outside. I gave them a wide berth and entered the building from the back. The papers I needed were on the same floor as Big Boss Yu's office and, somewhat to my surprise, the lights were on. The stairs leading up to the second floor were rather ostentatiously carpeted, and I didn't call out but walked silently up the stairs to where I needed to go. Arriving at what was predictably known as Ticking Clock Floor, also fortuitously carpeted, I had to pass Big Boss Yu's office. I could hear a loud voice as I passed to get to the small accounts office to retrieve the papers I needed. On my way back, looking into Big Boss Yu's office I noticed that a small sliding grid in the wall was open. It was customarily used to speak through by the accounts clerk and others who were thought too humble to enter the Ticking Clock Room. I crept up furtively and looked in.

'Apart from the Three Musketeers of the French Concession, I was surprised to see the incense master, the old priest who I'd consulted at the temple about cutting my hair. Big Ears Du, who'd hardly said a word that first night in the club in Harbin, was holding the floor, demanding that Big Boss Yu send his people into the International Settlement to kill communists. His Green Gang, he contended, had accounted for twenty deaths the previous night whereas what he referred to as "9X" had only killed three.

'I'd done my best to avoid the three gangsters since that initial meeting in Harbin. Of course, when I handed over the crockery factory to them I'd briefly met Big Ears Du at close quarters again, although it had been Smallpox "Million Dollar" Yang, the youngest of them, who had subsequently taken all the instructions and to whom I'd handed the company accounts. Now, as I watched Big Ears Du remonstrating with Big Boss Yu, I realised how frightening he was. He was tall – not simply tall for a Chinese but truly tall, over six feet, very thin, and his face seemed hewn from granite pierced by small, very black eyes that were too close together.

'While Big Boss Yu, with his purple-ringed eyes, seemed like a Chinese movie gangster, Big Ears Du was truly evil-looking. In his long Chinese silk gown and with his enormous feet in pointed, crocodile-skin European boots that protruded like instruments of torture from the end of his gown, he was the stuff of nightmares. On the carpet beside his chair was a black-silk top hat. When he wore it he was close to seven feet tall – a frightening spectre that made the coolies run for their lives and the better-class Chinese citizens stand aside and bow as he passed.

'He was obviously angry at Big Boss Yu, who remained expressionless, and I wondered what had made Big Boss Yu sell the crockery factory to him in the first place, as there can't have been much love lost between them. I decided it must have been for some or other favour granted elsewhere. Big Ears Du was shouting. "You are the dragonhead of 9X and you are not killing enough communists. We have orders from Chiang Kai-shek and you are not doing your share in the International Settlement."

'"The English newspaper is making a big fuss – I must wait until it dies down. Then we will do our share of the killing," Big Boss Yu replied calmly. Then he added, "What happens in the International Settlement is my affair – you take care of the French Concession, Du Yu-sen! In this business of killing communists we must work together, but each of us must choose the time and method in his own way. I will not disappoint Chiang Kai-shek, who is one of us."'

'Countess, yo' one brave lady, dat foh sure,' Jimmy said with admiration.

Nicole Lenoir-Jourdan smiled smugly. 'I do sound very intrepid, don't I? I have to tell you I was absolutely terrified – so much so that my knees began to knock and I was forced to crawl on all fours down the carpeted passageway until I eventually escaped down the stairs. The row was still continuing in the street and I now realised it must be between guards from two Triad gangs who'd become involved in the argument. The two dragonheads would have assumed the building to be heavily guarded.

'I crept away into the surrounding darkness with my life suddenly and completely shattered. My patron and protector was a gangster and murderer of the very worst kind. I now realised that it was his position as dragonhead of the International Settlement that gave Big Boss Yu so much power. As its gangster boss he had the ability to virtually dictate how the 400 000-strong labour force that worked in the International Settlement would cooperate with the European taipans.'

Nicole Lenoir-Jourdan stopped to catch her breath, which gave me the opportunity to ask a question before I forgot. 'Do you mean to say that General Chiang Kai-shek was part of a Triad? Didn't the Americans back him against the communists?'

'The past has a short memory, Jack. There is a Chinese saying, "It makes no difference if the cat is tabby or black, as long as it catches mice." Pragmatism has always been the deciding factor in any alliance. But, of course, US support of Chiang Kai-shek would happen much later, after the Americans had helped the Kuomintang leader to fight the Japanese. It must also be remembered that Mao Zedong joined Chiang Kai-shek to fight Japan, certainly an even more absurd alliance. War traditionally makes strange bedfellows.

'However, during my time in Shanghai, Chiang Kai-shek greatly feared the emerging communist movement that was rapidly spreading in China, and his murderous alliance with the Triads was one of the ways he devised to keep communists on the run. The Triads was a secret society with literally hundreds of thousands of members, and the communists never knew whether one of them had been planted in a cadre. It was a clever though bloody alliance, and tens of thousands of communist Chinese lost their lives as a consequence.'

'Yoh in big, big trouble, Countess,' Jimmy said, not wanting to change the subject. 'How yoh gonna get yo' ass out dat San Peh Steam Nav-ee-ga-tion Company?'

'Well, yes, indeed, James. I now faced two problems. I was, in effect, working for the Triads, and I was having an affair with the most powerful European taipan in China. I was caught on the horns of a dilemma. If I went to Big Boss Yu and told him I knew he was the dragonhead of 9X and no longer wished to work for him, I would certainly be severely punished. If it was subsequently discovered that I was having an affair with Sir Victor, I could lose my life. Big Boss Yu wouldn't know how much I knew about his underworld affairs – which, of course, was very little, but he wouldn't be convinced. Even very little was too much. If he witnessed me running into the arms of Sir Victor, who was in a position to do him a great deal of harm, he would almost certainly be forced to take some sort of drastic action.

'Powerful as Big Boss Yu undoubtedly was, if it became openly known among the European taipans that not only was he a Triad but also a dragonhead, his legitimate business affairs and real-estate development in the Bund would be severely affected. Big Boss Yu exerted a great deal of influence on the International Settlement and could probably bring a great part of the workforce to a standstill. Nevertheless, his legitimate financial base depended on the goodwill of the Settlement's foreign businessmen. While he might make a fortune in crime he had to launder the money somewhere, and by being allowed to take part in the development of Shanghai he had the perfect mechanism to do so while seemingly growing ever more respectably powerful.

'It was also a matter of face. His reputation as a legitimate ship owner, exporter and importer and property developer was of critical importance to him. While some of his business affairs and sources of income were perhaps obscure, he had never been directly implicated in any criminal activity. He happily promulgated the notion among the Europeans that he was "old school Chinese" – respectable, conservative and even admired for the quaint fact that he kept close to a dozen concubines in luxury. He liked it to be said that he was born in an obscure Chinese village and remained at heart a peasant who, by dint of determination and hard work, had become a great Chinese taipan.'

'But how the hell did he get away with it, Countess?' I asked, perhaps naively.

'Well, except where it affected the Europeans, the foreign-controlled areas had largely turned a blind eye to Chinese corporate crime. Shanghai was a dangerous, corrupt and violent city. Street crime was common, as was the next layer of criminal activity – extortion, armed robbery, drugs, kidnapping and even gunfights between Chinese gangsters and the police, who were understaffed and poorly paid. But as long as it didn't unduly affect the European society, expatriates largely ignored it. While they thought of prostitution and gambling as unfortunate, and such vices were often the subject of editorials in the *North China Daily News*, the municipal authorities quietly regarded both as peripherals to any great maritime port. In this teeming, bursting-at-the-seams city, crime was a matter of fact. But, in truth, the Triads in Shanghai ran an underworld that reached into almost every household, European or otherwise. The young European population was increasingly experimenting with, and becoming addicted to, morphine and cocaine. Both were readily available in Triad-owned nightclubs and dance halls, where marathon dancing had become the latest craze from America. Opium had become as easy to purchase as a bag of sugar, and the Europeans had at last begun calling for a crackdown on the "invisible" gangster chiefs.

'In business terms, with the Triads controlling much of the labour force, this created a quandary among the great European taipans. Nevertheless, something had to be seen to be done, though, of course, only minor tongs, the drug peddlers, thieves, extortionists, confidence men and the like were arrested. The *North China Daily News* kept up its campaign to "catch the big fish" and every once in a while a gangster of some level of notoriety, of which there were dozens, would be brought in. But the big Triad bosses were too powerful and influential to arrest. Outward respectability in the International Settlement was of the utmost importance to Big Boss Yu, unlike Big Ears Du in the French

Concession, and this was not the time, if ever there was one, when he wished to be exposed. Because I ran much of his legitimate affairs outside shipping and real estate, he knew that if I exposed him I would be believed. I also knew he wouldn't hesitate to kill me if it meant protecting his position in Shanghai society.

'I couldn't escape from Shanghai, as I had no papers. As I have already mentioned, the White Russians were stateless people. I was too well known to approach any of the embassies, and sooner or later it would be brought to Big Boss Yu's attention. He would have seen this as a blatant betrayal. Now that I knew he was the dragonhead, the least I could expect for disloyalty was to have my hand chopped off with a *doh*, a meat cleaver, the traditional Triad punishment for betrayal.

'I went to see Sir Victor, entering his apartment using a private lift that could be reached by a small locked door leading directly into a narrow, dark alleyway at the back of the hotel. To the casual user the lift ostensibly stopped at the ground floor, but with the use of a special key it could in fact travel further down the lift well to the door that led into the alleyway. Victor used it when he didn't want to be seen coming or going and, of course, for exactly the same reason, I had the key to both the door to the alleyway and the lift. It was a pointless subterfuge – the Chinese staff always seemed to know one's comings and goings – but once again, perception is everything. If I hadn't been seen entering or leaving the hotel or the tower then I couldn't possibly have been there. No mention was ever made of the unmarked basement destination of Sir Victor's private lift. The door leading to the alleyway had a skull-and-crossbones sign on the outside that read "Danger – Electricity" written in both English and Cantonese. Sir Victor's personal servants, I believed, were very fond of me. I would often delight them with regional delicacies from the Chinese City that they would not have been able to find for themselves, so it was not unreasonable to presume that they would remain completely discreet, even though the Chinese by nature are terrible gossips.

'When I told Sir Victor about Big Boss Yu being the dragonhead, he was fairly sanguine. "My dear, he is an important component in the labour relations of Shanghai and it has been customary to turn a blind eye to what might be some of his more obscure sources of income. It does not surprise me that he is the dragonhead for the International Settlement, just as Big Ears Du is known to be the dragonhead for the French Concession."

'"But how am I to continue to work for him, knowing all this?" I protested.

'"This is China, darling – what the eye doesn't see the heart doesn't grieve over," he answered platitudinously.

'"You're patronising me!" I said, upset.

'"No, that's not true, we all try to avoid dealing with the big Chinese taipans, both here and in Hong Kong, but Triad roots run deep and spread widely – chances are that Big Boss Yu's ancestors have been Triads for over 300 years." He shrugged. "Sometimes one cannot choose one's bedfellows."

'"I'm not dealing *with* him, I'm working *for* him, Victor! Besides, he isn't a bedfellow – he's been a surrogate father to me!"

'"Then you must behave like a dutiful daughter," he replied, remaining frustratingly calm.

'"And if I can't?"

'"Then you'll have to leave Shanghai."

'"And go where? Victor, I'm a stateless person! I don't have a passport. Technically, I'm still a refugee."

'"Of course – I keep forgetting you're not English. I could probably get you into Hong Kong, but you wouldn't be safe there. And without papers it would take a long time to get you to England."

'My heart sank – he was one of the world's richest men, and I felt sure he could have arranged almost anything. He plainly didn't want to get involved, or simply thought of my predicament as a storm in a teacup. "Oh, Victor, I'm so terribly frightened," I said, close to tears.

'He smiled. He had an irresistible smile. "Come to bed, darling," he said, taking me into his arms.

'Afterwards he poured two glasses of champagne and brought them back to bed with him. "Cheers," he said, and after we'd clinked glasses and taken a sip, he cleared his throat. "Are you sure you want to go through with this business of leaving Shanghai, Nicole?" I was about to say something when he held up his hand. "No, listen to me first – then you can comment." I remember thinking how terribly English he was. "You have to be practical, my dear."

'I felt warm and secure after having made love, so I settled down to listen. Victor always reasoned things out with a lack of sentimentality, taking every circumstance and fact into consideration. It was for this reason that his advice, financial and otherwise, while often enough quite blunt, had always been so helpful to me.

'"Practical? What do you mean?" I said, ignoring his demand that I should first listen to what he had to say.

'"Shush! Listen, Nicole," he reprimanded, with just a trace of impatience. "I'm going to ask you a series of questions and you must answer them as honestly as you can. Please don't avoid the difficult ones. Will you promise?" I nodded. "No, that's not enough, you must say it."

'"I promise, Victor."

'"Good. The first is simple enough. How long have you known Big Boss Yu? Please, refresh my memory of how you came to meet."

'"Since I was fifteen. We met in a nightclub in Harbin where I sang and played the piano." I explained the circumstances to Sir Victor to the point where Big Boss Yu had invited me to come to Shanghai. "I think he was intrigued that I sang and spoke Cantonese like a native of China," I concluded.

'"And when you arrived he arranged for you to live in the Chinese City. Did you not think that strange?"

'"Strange? Perhaps, but I was sixteen years old, my father had committed suicide, and I was a refugee. At least he seemed to care about me. I obeyed his instructions and did as I was told."

'"And subsequently? You've never moved into the European area and remain living among the Chinese."

'"It's home. I know the locals, and while at first I was protected by Big Boss Yu that's not necessary now."

'"Have you never felt constrained? I recall on my frequent visits when you were playing the Palace you would go home to the Chinese City immediately after every show. You had no fun as a young person. Did you not long to be free?"

'"Of course, but I didn't know how to be. Big Boss Yu wanted me home, so what could I do?"

'"And your career. You really were very promising – even Noël Coward said so. Were you not terribly upset when Big Boss Yu demanded you give it up? I remember at the party I threw for you on your eighteenth birthday how shocked we all were at the news and how I promised you top billing when I built this hotel."

'"I cried myself to sleep for days. I recall Big Boss Yu had dismissed what was so very important to me as 'playing the herdsman's flute' – a euphemism for doing something entirely pointless."

'"Would that not have been the moment to resist him?" Victor asked me.

'I thought for a moment, then tried to explain – Sir Victor seemed to have no notion of my true position. "Victor, you are reasoning with me as if I was an upper-class English girl, whereas I am a White Russian refugee. But not even that. From the age of thirteen, when my *amah* took me to her village in Manchuria, I have been brought up as Chinese. I sometimes even dream in Chinese. I did what my patron, guardian, surrogate father – whatever you wish to call Big Boss Yu – desired or ordered. I didn't believe I had any rights of refusal – or any rights at all, for that matter. That is the way of the Chinese daughter."

'"Surely there was someone – some European you could have turned to for help?" he persisted.

'"Who, may I kindly ask?" I remember inquiring, a little frustrated. "Poppy? Commander Duncan? The ghastly Mrs Worthington? The best European friend I had at the time, and still have – after you, of course – is Zhora Petrov, Georgii, the doorman here at the Cathay and formerly at the Palace. I knew you, of course, and you were lovely to me when you visited from England and Hong Kong, but you were hardly in a position to act as my protector, even if I'd asked you – though, of course, I'd have done no such thing. I fell head over heels in love with you the first night we met. I made rather a fool of myself by crying and you ordered me a strawberry milkshake. 'Strawberry's best!' you said – and, of course, you were right."

'Sir Victor smiled. "You were just a gawky schoolgirl at the time, though a very talented one." He then leaned over and kissed me on the nose. "Look at you now, a beautiful woman . . . and, if I may say so, at this moment a very confused one."

'"What must I do, Victor? You're perfectly right, I *am* confused."

'"Forgive me for putting you on the spot as I've just done, but if I was right about strawberry being the best then I might just be right about what I'm about to say. As you know, I'm a pragmatist and I'm also a Jew."

'"What has the one got to do with the other?" I asked.

'"Well, quite a lot really." He grinned suddenly. "Why do more Jews play the violin than play the piano?"

'"I don't know," I answered.

'"Because you can't escape with a piano under your arm. That's why pragmatism and being Jewish usually go together. My people have faced persecution and banishment for hundreds of generations. Being able to start from scratch when you've lost everything is an ability we almost take for granted – from riches to poverty and all the way back again. What we have learned is always to be ready for difficult times. We move our assets around the world just in case, we are always looking over our shoulders, reading the signs and portents, preparing for the worst. History shows that every time the Jews become complacent, disaster strikes. So what I am suggesting is that you prepare yourself. It is not yet time to run from Shanghai and there is much to be gained if you keep a cool head. You have proved yourself to Big Boss Yu. He trusts both you and your judgement."

'"He thinks I am his good joss."

'"Indeed, and therein lies your safety. Now let us look at your immediate options. With the collapse of the New York Stock Exchange we are now in the midst of a worldwide recession. Your caviar business has collapsed in the States because many of your former customers are financially ruined. But, curiously enough, Shanghai is one place on earth that will not be greatly affected by the current global economic predicament. We have enough silver deposits and hard currency to see this thing out. So much so that I intend to invest heavily in real estate on the Bund and to build another great hotel I shall call the Metropole. This is perhaps the only place remaining on earth where one's money is safe. In fact, Shanghai is an opportunity to *make* money." He paused. "How much money do you have?" Then, before I could answer, he said, "Did you send any to Hong Kong as I suggested?"

'"Yes, I invested it and I have about 20 000 dollars here."

'"In the bank?"

'I grinned. "I'm a Chinese peasant, Victor. I do not trust banks – nor do I any longer trust shares."

'"But you invested half your Hong Kong money in shares, at my suggestion?"

'"Yes, and I've lost the lot in the crash."

'He looked momentarily crestfallen, although to a man of his enormous wealth the 20 000 Mexican dollars I'd lost must have seemed a pittance. "Bring me your dollars," he grinned. "Where do you keep them – in a shoebox under your bed?"

'"No, in a tin box, buried in a safe place, along with my Russian icon."

'"I'm sorry I've let you down with the shares, darling. Give me what you've got in cash and I'll convert it directly into gold and place it in a safety-deposit box in the Bank of China in Hong Kong, and only you shall have the key."

'"Will you put the icon there as well?" I asked.

'"Is it valuable? Icons vary a great deal . . . "

'"I have no idea. It's been in my family a long time. If nothing else, it has sentimental value." I couldn't tell him it was all I had left of a past life in Russia I'd almost forgotten.

'"I've picked up several very good ones from local White Russians – if it's a good one, it's worth keeping. Certainly I'll take it with me. I'm going to Hong Kong on the Thursday ferry and will be away a week or two. Let me have it, and also the money, by tomorrow."

'"Thank you, Victor," I said quietly, then added, "But I'm still not absolutely sure what you want me to do. Do you want me to continue with Big Boss Yu?"

'"It's not what I *want*, Nicole, it's what appears to be the sensible thing to do. The world is in a mess at the moment, and we don't know how long the situation is going to last. My guess is at least three years. Your raisin business should hold up as you are importing and not exporting. With the caviar gone, your share of the raisin business is important. Not much call for silk shantung in the next couple of years I shouldn't expect, but your fish imports might still work."

'"You're saying I must turn a blind eye and pretend nothing has happened?"

'He seemed to grow a little impatient. I usually grasped his ideas quickly, and now I was making him spell things out. "Darling, if you hadn't overheard the business between the two dragonheads in Ticking Clock House you'd be none the wiser, would you?" He rose from the bed and started to dress. "It's time you used Big Boss Yu for a change. When things get better in a couple of years, I'll help you to get papers to get away from China."

'And so I took Sir Victor's advice. While morally it was reprehensible to continue as if nothing had happened, there was little else I could do. I imagine if I'd continued to persist, Sir Victor may have smuggled me onto a boat to Hong Kong and, with the contacts he had, eventually got me to England. But he hadn't suggested that he do this – in fact, he'd advised against it. I also realised that his advice, while sound enough if one's principles were neglected, was also self-serving. If he was seen to help me escape, Big Boss Yu could make it almost impossible for him to obtain a labour force for his massive building developments in Shanghai.

'I loved Victor Sassoon with all my heart, but I also knew that the love of a woman does not take precedence over a rich man's business affairs or ambition. Besides, while I think he loved me in his own way, it wasn't to the same degree that I adored him. Sir Victor was a confirmed bachelor and I accepted that I may not be the only woman in his life.'

She looked up. 'So you see, I really was more Chinese than European. Few Western women would tolerate such uncertainty in their status or infidelity in a lover, whereas to a Chinese woman it isn't a matter of how many other women are in a man's life, but rather whether you are the number-one concubine.'

Just then a nurse's aide called us in for afternoon tea, so we all traipsed back to the verandah where the ladies' auxiliary had prepared tea and scones for the patients. I took one look and gave the scones a big miss. Sue's scones were the yardstick by which all scones were measured, and these looked hard as cobblestones. With my dodgy ribs all I needed was a severe bout of indigestion.

During afternoon tea I thought about what Nicole Lenoir-Jourdan had told us and whether I might have acted differently in the same predicament. Talk about being between a rock and a hard place! She'd apologised for the morality of her decision to continue with Big Boss Yu, but I could very well see she'd had no choice. Morality doesn't dictate that we get ourselves killed or have a hand chopped off to honour our principles. Like her, I would have shut my mouth and stayed put. When we returned to our seats in the garden, Jimmy, who'd gulped down half-a-dozen scones, urged her to continue.

'It's a good thing that Chinese men are notoriously indifferent to a woman's feelings,' she began. 'I was having difficulty pretending nothing had happened, but as I saw Big Boss Yu on no more than a weekly basis he didn't seem to notice any change in my behaviour. Then about a month after I'd had my talk with Sir Victor, Big Boss Yu called me into Ticking Clock House.

'With even less than the usual lack of ceremony, he declared, "No

Gin, you will take control of the Red Dragon China and Crockery Factory, as well as the export business."

'"But *loh yeh*, we do not own this. Did you not sell to Smallpox "Million Dollar" Yang, Chang Shig-liang and Du Yu-sen?"

'"It was an arrangement. Now I have it back again."

'"But *loh yeh*, with the depression in America it will not be a viable business – we will lose money."

'"No, your joss is good," he said, with the slightest hint of a smile. Then, to my surprise, he said, "You have brought me good fortune in the past, but now things are bad."

'I looked at him, astonished. "But there is a global depression – the markets have collapsed, *loh yeh*. Now is not a good time to have bought the business back. I have run down our stocks of cotton and silk so that we can close the shantung factory until the market improves, maybe in a couple of years' time."

'He nodded. "But you will keep the crockery factory and export business going because I have decided it will be your reward. See – I have all the papers here for you to sign."

'"But it will lose money, *loh yeh*."

'"That will be for you to decide. You are good joss – we have never lost money before. The raisins are still selling well." I couldn't tell him that this was because I'd had the benefit of advice from Sir Victor and others, particularly with the raisins. "Put your chop on these papers, No Gin." It was more of a command than an invitation. I took the papers and hurriedly turned the three pages. The contract wasn't a complicated one and gave me sole rights to the crockery factory and its profits, as well as to the export business. There was only one anomaly. The entire contract was backdated five years.

'"*Loh yeh*, this contract is backdated to when I first opened the factory."

'"That is right, please sign." He was visibly impatient.

'"But it is not correct – I have never earned a single dollar from this business." Then I added, "May I see the books?"

'"It is not in debt," he replied.

'"Why does it not show the names of the previous owners?" I asked, desperately.

'"They are not men of good reputation. I do not want you to own a concern that once belonged to gangsters." Then he added, "I will lose face. You will sign now."

'"I am greatly honoured by such a gift, *loh yeh*, but I must decline as I am not worthy," I said softly, trying to keep my voice under control.'

She turned to us to explain. 'In Chinese, this would be seen as a polite but firm refusal. Big Boss Yu's purple-ringed eyes blazed as he stood up from his enormous desk. "Have I not given you everything you needed? Have I not changed your fortunes when you were nothing but street trash? You have no country, you have lost your ancestors. *I* am your country now. I have fed and clothed and housed you. I have changed you into an English lady from a Russian whore and a sing-song girl! Now I give you a gift from my heart and you refuse it? Sign! Put your chop on those papers!" That's as close as I can get to a translation of what he said in Chinese, but what it amounted to was that he had complete control over me and I had no choice but to sign. So I signed the papers giving me a completely useless crockery business and making me its owner from the very beginning of its existence.

'The gift, in the peculiar way in which the Chinese think, was to be considered an insult – though why, I couldn't be sure. Perhaps Big Boss Yu had lost money and wanted me to know that my good joss wasn't holding up. I imagined I would never know. So I decided to make the best of the situation. Quite plainly there wasn't much of a market left in America, but I'd keep a small part of the business going. Even in times of depression crockery breaks and needs to be replaced, and mine was cheap. The rest of the business I would mothball until better times came along when I could sell it and make my escape. By giving it to me, Big Boss Yu could boast at parties and receptions that he had been generous, giving me the finance to create the crockery factory and export business – the same way he had taken the credit for the caviar business, which, in his own mind, he had also allowed me to own. I had made him a great fortune from raisins, but he never mentioned that I had created and run every aspect of the business while receiving only two per cent of the profits. But that was the Chinese way, and I felt no resentment. My only concern was the backdating of the ownership of the Red Dragon China and Crockery Factory. Even this was pure Chinese lopsided logic. Big Boss Yu may have wanted to dissociate himself from the Three Musketeers of the French Concession. If their names didn't appear on any paperwork involving his business concerns he could never be implicated directly with the tongs or gangsters.

'With the gift of the crockery factory my fortunes began to change for the worse. I had occasion to have lunch with a business acquaintance at the Cathay Hotel as I often did, this time an Australian from Victoria seeking to renew a contract. As raisin importers, we were now of true significance – China had become perhaps the greatest raisin consumers in the world. Afterwards I called on Sir Victor at his apartment in the tower. He was once again leaving for Hong Kong and I hoped to say goodbye in an appropriate way. He'd invited me to come up and I used the lift from the hotel. I had already been seen in the hotel, so going up to see him in broad daylight would not have been considered unusual. After making love and saying our goodbyes I called the ever-faithful Ah Chow, my chauffeur, to pick me up in the new big black Buick that was now mine exclusively, and went down to the hotel entrance to wait for him.

'Georgii Petrov, the doorman I'd befriended since meeting him on my first awkward visit to the Palace Hotel, approached me with a concerned look on his face. "May I speak to you, Nicole?"

'"What's the matter, Georgii?" I asked.

'"Can we go around the corner?" he asked quietly. I followed him and we stood together around a small, curved buttress, the huge doorman with the almost transparent blue eyes towering over me. "Nicole, I don't know how to say this – God knows, everyone is sleeping with everyone else in Shanghai. If you only knew what goes on here – who and when and where – you would be astonished." Georgii wasn't known for his subtlety, but then he said, "You're a single woman and he's a bachelor – so what's the harm, eh?"

'"What are you trying to say, Georgii?"

'"You and Sir Victor. Nicole, all the Chinese staff are talking."

'"That's very unfortunate," I said, my heart thumping. "They know the hotel rules, the three monkeys – see, speak, hear no evil. It was drummed into all of us when I worked at the Palace."

'"Yes, of course, Nicole. But there was an incident last night just as the cocktail hour began and the foyer was full of people. Sir Victor dismissed the Chinese second chef for being drunk, and he later came down into the foyer and yelled out to all the guests that Sir Victor was, you know, 'doing it' to you – only he used the dirty word. There must have been a hundred people who heard."

'"Did he make this announcement in Cantonese or English?" I asked. I knew the man in question, a sullen character who caused trouble among Sir Victor's other servants. Victor had considered dismissing him several times, but he was an exceptional French pastry chef and so had been tolerated.

'"Of course I dragged him out by the collar, boxed his ears and threw him into the street," Georgii said in digust. "But several people followed him out and others were arriving, some of them bigwigs. He wouldn't let up and threatened to tell your taipan, Big Boss Yu. So I ran after him and grabbed him and handed him over to a Sikh policeman, saying that he'd threatened me with a *doh*. He had his chef's cleaver in the bag he carried over his shoulder, so it sounded quite plausible."

'I must have looked like a ghost. "Thank you, Georgii Pavlovich Petrov," I said, using this formal address to show my respect and gratitude.

'He handed me a slip of paper and I glanced at it to see it was his address, though written in Russian it was indecipherable to most Chinese. "You can come at any time, Nicole," he said quietly. "My wife's name is Elizaveta." Then he added, using her Russian familiar,

"Leza will welcome you if I'm not there." I realised to my consternation that while I'd known him and thought of him as a friend ever since I'd arrived in Shanghai, I had never visited his apartment.

'Once I'd thought it over, I wasn't too concerned about Sir Victor's second chef spilling the beans to Big Boss Yu. He was too low a personage to be granted an interview, and could easily enough be discredited. Moreover, he was in police custody and would probably be locked up for a week, or if they took the threat of the *doh* seriously it could be for a couple of months. When he sobered up he'd realise that saying anything about the behaviour of the great English taipan was unthinkable if he ever wished to work for a European household in Shanghai, or even in a restaurant other than a lesser Chinese one. It was the thought of who else might have been in the foyer at the time that troubled me.

'On the way home Ah Chow was unusually quiet – normally he was a bit of a chatterbox. I was rather grateful for this and thought he must have sensed my mood, but when he dropped me off he looked deeply concerned and farewelled me in a very formal manner. Bowing deeply, he wished me a hundred years of good joss and many male children.

'"Whatever is the matter with you, Ah Chow?" I asked, but he simply bowed again and I could see he was close to tears. "What is it, Ah Chow? Have I offended you?" I cried, moving towards the car. But before I reached it he'd driven away. To my surprise Ah May was not at the door to welcome me home, although when I turned the knob it was unlocked. I thought that perhaps she had needed some ingredient for her cooking and had slipped out for a moment, though it was not like her to leave the door unlocked. As I stepped into the darkened house I was grabbed from both sides, and before I could scream a hand closed over my mouth while my arm was twisted behind my back.'

'Jesus!' Jimmy gasped. As for me, I was too stunned to utter a word.

'There were two of them, and they forced me into my bedroom and threw me onto the bed. I struggled wildly, but I was helpless against them. They gagged me using a silk stocking and then tied my hands and legs to the bedposts, again using silk stockings, so that I lay spread-eagled. They then proceeded to cut the clothes from my body, warning me to keep still or I would be hurt by the sharp blade. I lay naked on the bed, weeping and close to hysteria, waiting for them to rape me. To my astonishment they bowed formally as they might to a superior, and left the bedroom. Shortly afterwards I heard the front door close.

'I struggled to get loose but soon knew it was pointless – I was helpless against my bonds, which cut deeper the more I strained. After a while I began to gather my wits. What became clear was that I was being sent a message. It could only be from Big Boss Yu. But what was he trying to tell me? That I was worthless and could be given to any man he wished? That I didn't own my own body and I was his personal property? That if I continued to be Sir Victor's whore he would destroy me? That this was simply the ultimate humiliation, a severe warning that I was not free to do as I wished and that he was punishing me? This last notion seemed to fit best, because it illustrated his Chinese way of thinking. The attack on me was punishment and humiliation that perfectly befitted a warning. I was expected to resume my duties and carry on but relinquish my affair with Sir Victor. Technically and physically I had not been sexually violated. This would be important. Physical harm would have indicated malice when he intended only to warn me, scare me off. It was the mental violation that counted – the demonstration of his power and will over me. I soon convinced myself that this was the case and so I waited for Ah May to return to cut me loose, attend to my wrists and ankles and to bathe and comfort me.

'I was suddenly overcome by a great weariness. I can only describe it as years of weariness – endless, grinding despair. The flight from Russia in the old dumb man's ox wagon, my life in Ah Lai's village, the dreadful months with my mentally disturbed father, the nightclub in Harbin, Mrs Worthington, going directly home after the performance every night, the cutting and burning of my hair, the years working for Big Boss Yu's good joss, building his raisin empire, losing my crockery factory to the three gangsters . . . and the small satisfaction I'd enjoyed with the connection I'd established with my family's ancient glory as purveyors of the world's best caviar until it had been dashed by the collapse of the New York Stock Exchange. I had never had a moment when I belonged to myself, when I wasn't ordered or owned but free to go my own way. I hadn't even visited Georgii Pavlovich Petrov's apartment or met his wife, Elizaveta! I couldn't remember having any real fun from the moment my mother died until I lay in Victor Sassoon's arms for the first time and he had taken my virginity, a gift that was my very own to give. As I lay gagged and tied and naked, an entire lifetime of weariness seemed to weigh heavily upon me. I started to weep for my life, the sad and senseless passing of my young and innocent years, until eventually I must have cried myself to sleep.'

'Dat a real sad story to bear, Countess,' Jimmy said, shaking his head in sympathy.

'I woke up with a start to see Smallpox "Million Dollar" Yang standing naked beside the bed, his small penis erect at the level of my head. In his hand he held a wineglass filled with lemonade, or perhaps it was soda water. I could see the tiny bubbles rising to the surface. He grinned, then dipped his forefinger into the glass and brought it to his mouth and sucked it. "No gin," he said, then he splashed the contents over my face and slapped me hard across the side of my head before repeatedly raping me. "My seed will smoulder within you and destroy the foreign devil's," he spat, then, reaching for the glass, he tapped its rim on the edge of the bed, breaking it, and stabbed the broken wineglass between my legs.'

'Oh, Jesus, no!' I cried, leaning forward with my hands covering my face.

Nicole Lenoir-Jourdan started to weep, softly at first before increasing to a wail like a small child. Jimmy leapt to his feet and, lifting her into his huge arms, began to rock her as one might a distressed child. She clung to him, her arms about his neck and her head against his chest. 'Yoh gonna be okay! Yoh gonna be okay, Countess. Yoh gotta let it come out, baby. All da hurt, it gotta come out. It poison, yoh hear! Yoh cry now, yoh cry real good – der a lot o' sadness an' it gotta go away. It gotta wash out, it gotta be ex-punged. We loves you, baby. Brother Fish and me, we loves you dearly,' he said, his words gaining momentum while the tears rolled down his cheeks.

After a while she calmed down, and Jimmy sat her back in the wicker chair. 'I think we should call it a day, Countess. You're whacked, and need to rest.' It was all I could think to say. Jimmy had said the words I'd like to have said, but that was never going to happen with a McKenzie. Gloria would often say, 'The men on both sides of this family have got emotional indigestion.' I realised how very much I had come to love Nicole Lenoir-Jourdan, how she had become such an important part of my life that I could hardly imagine it without her. But, of course, I'd had to rely on Jimmy to say the right words and to include me with them.

Fortunately Sue had given me a clean handkerchief, which at least I could offer to her, her own having turned into a wet ball she held clutched in her right hand. 'Thank you, Jack,' she said softly, wiping her eyes. Then she looked in turn at both of us, her blue eyes swollen from crying. 'Please, I crave your indulgence. I have never spoken of this to anyone, and if I don't get it all out now I don't believe I shall ever again have the courage.'

Jimmy nodded. 'Dat good. Yoh talk. Yoh do dat, Countess,' he encouraged softly, his voice as comforting as the notes coming from a cello.

I could see she was about to cry again, but then somehow managed to control her tears. 'Smallpox "Million Dollar" Yang stood over me. "If you mention my name to the police, you will not die," he said smiling, as if to reassure me, "but we will chop off your hands." He held up both his hands with the palms turned inwards and with his fingers stretched, then suddenly snapped his hands into fists and pulled them inwards so they appeared to be stumps on the end of his arms. "No Gin, no hands!" he cried and, bending almost double, his hands resting on his knees, he giggled in a high-pitched, almost hysterical feminine voice. Then with a sudden jerk he straightened up and, fierce-faced, pointed to the blood running down my legs. "This is the mark of the white paper fan, so that you will remember to obey your dragonhead." Then he dressed slowly, stretching up each sock and attaching a suspender, then pulling over them light-brown pointed alligator boots, smaller but similar to the ones Big Ears Du had worn that fateful night in Big Boss Yu's office. He placed one boot on the bed beside me and, using a piece of my ruined dress, bent over me and polished it conscientiously, repeating the process with the other boot.

'He was an utterly repulsive-looking man, with his face, neck and shoulders deeply pockmarked so that he appeared to be wearing a hideous tight-fitting hood that covered his face and dropped to his shoulders. No trace of smooth skin showed between the ugly craters that seemed to stretch his face to even wider proportions, giving him the appearance of having a head too large for his narrow frame. His incisors were gold, and when he smiled his eyes returned to deep slits as if they had been ripped into his face. His appendage had sunk like a shrivelled worm under his potbelly and he was almost completely bow-legged, his body bearing all the signs of a childhood spent in abject poverty. He slipped a long black Chinese silk gown over his head and, like his dragonhead master, Big Ears Du, placed a black-silk top hat on his head. Then he turned to look directly at me and, bending, brought his forefinger down to touch the inside of my leg. When he brought it up again I saw a tiny drop of blood on the tip. He touched the tip of his forefinger to his tongue. "No gin," he said, giggling, then turning on his heel he walked from the room.

'I lay on the bed weeping, the silk-stocking gag cutting deeply into the sides of my mouth as my head jerked convulsively. At one stage I thought I heard the front door opening but I wasn't sure. Then a short while later Ah May appeared. She had been crying and was obviously distressed. She looked at me and brought her hands to her face. "Aieeyaaa!" she wailed, repeating the sound several times as she began to cry. "What shall we do, *seal jeh*?" she said, using the Chinese words for a superior who is unmarried. "What shall we do?"

'Her own distress seemed to calm me somewhat. "Help!" I mumbled.

'With tears streaming down her face she attempted to untie the by now very tightly knotted silk stocking that bound and gagged me, her fingers pulling frantically but making no impression on the knots as she panicked and moved from one to the other. "Aieeyaaa!" she wailed again. She hurried out of the room, her small hands fluttering in panic, and returned with a pair of dressmaker's scissors. With dangerously trembling hands, weeping and crying out, she finally managed to cut my gag and bonds.

'She bathed me, rubbed salve into my wrists and ankles and attended to the cuts made by the wineglass. Fortuitously, the jagged glass had cut into the inside of my left leg and not the part it had been intended for. Later Ah May fetched a Chinese doctor who asked no questions but stitched the two larger cuts, bandaged my leg, took his fee and departed almost wordlessly. Ah May told me how she had been gagged and bound in a foetal position so she couldn't move by the two men who had attacked me, and then locked in a large cupboard in the cooking area. One of the men had returned, which must have been when I heard the front door open, cut her bonds and departed so that she could come to my aid.

'I was finally too exhausted to weep and fell into a troubled sleep. I woke early feeling bruised and sore, but mostly dirty. To be violated is never to feel completely clean again and I bathed myself once more, then dressed, and was making green tea when Ah May finally stirred from her narrow bed where she slept in a pantry-like annexe to the kitchen.

'"What shall we do?" I asked her, not expecting an answer. She was *gung yun*, a working person with no rights.

'"It was the tongs," she said in a frightened voice. "There is nothing . . . " She did not complete the sentence.

'My heart filled with terror. What if Ah Chow arrived, as he always did, to take me to my office? How must I act? Would Big Boss Yu call me to the Ticking Clock House? But the big black Buick did not arrive at the appointed hour. Then half an hour later there was a knock on the door. I knew it couldn't be Ah Chow – he would simply have waited in the car until I emerged. Instead of letting Ah May go to the door I did so myself, limping slightly as the wound to the inside of my leg had caused it to stiffen. I opened the door to be confronted by two Sikh policemen and a European police officer. He handed me a warrant. "What is this?" I asked, taking it.

'"Lily No Gin," he announced, then quickly consulted a slip of paper, "also known as Nicole Lenoir-Jourdan, I am placing you under arrest. You are implicated in the export of opium to the United States of America." I was too stunned to answer him. "Come along," he said, without raising his voice. "If you cooperate, we won't need to handcuff you."'

Just when I had thought Nicole Lenoir-Jourdan's story could get no worse, it just had. She sighed heavily before resuming her tale, and I was struck by what an extraordinary survivor she was.

'I was taken to Central Police Station,' she continued, still visibly shaken, 'and later that day arraigned before a magistrate and then returned to the police cells, where I remained for a week while the police raided my offices and went through my papers. I was then charged officially and refused bail by the British judge, a man I had previously met at receptions and the like with Big Boss Yu. Sir Victor was in Hong Kong but I was able to get a message through to his partner, Commander Duncan, who immediately arranged for a lawyer to represent me but did not wish to otherwise be involved.

'The story then emerged for the first time. Customs in San Francisco had discovered the opium in the imported vases and had arrested the local Chinese importer and directed the American consul in Shanghai to notify the Shanghai authorities to make the appropriate arrests at that end. The Red Dragon China and Crockery Factory had been directly implicated. The police had visited Big Boss Yu, who professed astonishment and pointed to the fact that he was not the owner. While he admitted he'd supplied the initial finance to start the factory, he claimed it had been given to me as a gift of gratitude in return for the raisin business I had developed on his behalf. He insisted that he'd never interfered with its operation or received any profits from it, and invited the investigation officers to inspect his books. Moreover, he conveyed that he was deeply disturbed at my corrupt behaviour and ingratitude, as everyone was aware he had treated me as a favoured daughter, and announced that he would have no further dealings with me.

'In reality, the Triad society had managed to get a message to Big Ears Du in time for him to make a deal with Big Boss Yu to return the crockery factory to me. He'd understood that, through the network of agents I'd created along the southern China coastline and with his own ships doing the transport, the raisin business no longer needed my know-how and could be run easily enough by an efficient manager. The fish business was not yet sufficiently big for it to be a financial concern of any great importance, and the cotton and shantung silk mill had all but collapsed with the Great Depression. In his eyes my good joss was spent and I would be the scapegoat for Big Ears Du's opium exports. But in return Big Ears Du had to give Big Boss Yu the satisfaction of punishing me in a more direct way to demonstrate that I had betrayed his trust by having an affair with Sir Victor.

'I was too well known in Shanghai to be murdered at the command of Big Boss Yu. Even had I been disposed of, found with my throat cut in some dark alley of the Chinese City stinking of excrement, this would not have served his reputation as a legitimate businessman and trusted Chinese personality, the so-called "unofficial" mayor of Shanghai. His revenge for what he saw as my betrayal needed to be both personal and public. Smallpox "Million Dollar" Yang was his personal revenge. My conviction as a drug dealer was to be my public destruction, with the intention of sending a clear message to Sir Victor Sassoon not to tamper in Big Boss Yu's affairs by getting involved in my defence. Commander Duncan, Sir Victor's business partner and finance director, clearly understood the implications and, while he did hire a good lawyer for me, arranged it so that the legal fees would be paid directly into the lawyer's bank account without any invoice being rendered.

'He hired an Australian barrister named John Robertson, a man with a very good reputation who, it was rumoured, was headed for the bench. Robertson was a straight-shooting, no-nonsense lawyer who soon became convinced of my innocence, but was not at all sure that he could bring a case against Big Ears Du or Big Boss Yu.'

She paused to explain the challenges involved in mounting a case against Big Boss Yu. 'It would take simply ages to go through the legal ramifications, and I'm sure you'd both find it tedious in the extreme. But there were four factors that made it difficult for John Robertson to mount a case. Both Big Boss Yu and Big Ears Du sat on the Opium Suppression Bureau and the Chinese Advisory Committee on the Shanghai Municipal Council. While it was an open secret in the French Concession that this enabled Big Ears Du to run his narcotics business freely, the same was not true of Big Boss Yu, who cherished his good reputation in the Settlement. Both men were decorated with the Order of Brilliant Jade, one of the highest orders of merit in the Republic of China, which made them virtually untouchable. Both, as I mentioned earlier, enjoyed a Triad alliance with Chiang Kai-shek, which meant no authority outside the Concession areas had the courage to indict them. And lastly, the European taipans had no wish to rock the boat and jeopardise their lucrative business interests.

'However, the American Government wanted something done, and so as to avoid unwelcome scrutiny of the affairs of the International Settlement, a culprit, almost any culprit, had to be found, as long as the matter was cleared up quickly. As John Robertson pointed out, I was the most available scapegoat. The contract giving me the ownership of the crockery factory could only be disproved if he could show that I hadn't been anywhere near the factory for three years and that Smallpox "Million Dollar" Yang had, in fact, been responsible for running it. We both knew it would be impossible to find a Chinese witness who would testify in court that this was the case. The factory staff were all Chinese and feared the Triads far more than they did the law. They would swear on the graves of their ancestors that I had been in control all along and had personally directed the concealment of opium in the special vases.

'Meanwhile Sir Victor, who had returned to Shanghai and had no doubt been briefed by Commander Duncan as well as taken independent legal advice, stayed completely away from me and from John Robertson. Although bitterly upset, I was forced to accept that his huge construction works were a great deal more important to him than a little Russian refugee who, like so many women in his past and probably the present, had shared his bed from time to time. With the very rich, pragmatism is the substitute for conscience. I was emotionally expendable and my case financially supportable, provided always that John Robertson's fees were not traced back to the Sassoon name.

'After bail was refused a second time and I'd spent three weeks in the cells at the Central Police Station, I was placed in the women's section of Ti lan Qiao, the giant prison all the foreign-controlled areas shared with the Chinese authorities. My only support came from Elizaveta and Georgii Petrov. Leza visited me every day with food, and supplied anything else I might need. Georgii would come with Leza whenever he could, and once said that Sir Victor had stopped briefly on his way into the hotel and said gruffly, "Tell her I'm doing all I can."'

'What happened to Ah May?' I asked, with my usual need to tie up the small and, to everyone else, irrelevant details.

'She disappeared. She would have been sent back to her village with the very real threat of death if she returned to Shanghai. It would have been entirely unreasonable to expect her to defy her employer, who, after all, in the original sense was Big Boss Yu.

'And then I missed my period. The following month I knew I was pregnant. John Robertson was doing all he could to get me out on bail or have my case brought before a judge. This occurred on several occasions but always ended in chaos with my return to my prison cell. I was a stateless person and a White Russian and John Robertson explained that because I had no extraterritorial rights, I wasn't liable to be tried by a British judge and was subject only to Chinese law. He cited the clause in the alliance that spelled out the situation:

> '"*Subjects of China who may be guilty of any criminal act towards citizens of the United States of America shall be arrested and punished by the Chinese authorities.*"

'On the other hand, the lawyer for the American Consulate argued that the crime of opium smuggling had been committed through the Port of Shanghai and was therefore a matter for the British/American Legal Alliance established in 1844, and that I must be tried under their jurisprudence. Furthermore, as a stateless person I was not technically a "subject of China". There was much speculation over the issue in the *North China Daily News*. According to Georgii Petrov I had become the major subject of gossip among the cognoscenti, who seemed to be split evenly between those who thought I was guilty and those who didn't. "Those who think you are guilty point to the fact that you are a White Russian and have tried to conceal this with your perfect English accent, therefore you *must* be guilty because you cover your true identity." This ethnic detail was, it seemed, constantly pointed out in the English newspaper, where my stage name, Shanghai Lil, was also frequently used with perhaps the unwritten but implied suggestion that this suited the persona of a drug smuggler – although, I must be fair, the newspaper also asked constantly why a pregnant woman who may well be innocent should be kept in prison because of bureaucratic bumbling. But the American Consulate was insistent that I remain in custody, pointing out that the crime of drug smuggling did not allow for bail.

'Finally, after seven months it was decided that I came under the legal authority of the Chinese Government and would be tried in what was known as the Provisional Court. My trial was set for three weeks from the announcement and I was moved to the Chinese-run Lunghua Prison, south-west of the Bund. Awful as my previous cell had been, at least it was clean and vermin-free. This one was even smaller and stank of excrement and urine, and the hard mattress was infested with bed bugs and lice. I was forced to wrap my head in a towel when I slept so as not to be bitten by the rats that wandered, unafraid, into my cell.

'By the time my trial was to have taken place I was heavily pregnant. Despite Elizaveta's daily food visits I had lost weight, but fortunately the baby was well and the Russian couple had personally paid for a doctor to see me once a week. I was also fortunate that I hadn't suffered morning sickness earlier in my pregnancy.'

I had to interrupt Nicole Lenoir-Jourdan at this point. 'What about Sir Victor? Was there still no word from him?'

'Well, when the decision was made to hear my case under Chinese law, I received another message from him via Georgii Petrov. "Tell her I will fix things, but only under certain conditions." That was all he'd conveyed to the puzzled doorman. Then a week later John Robertson told me what these conditions were to be and presented me with a contract of sorts to sign. I was to make no claims, financial or otherwise, on the Sassoon family in the future, and the child was not to be given the Sassoon name. A settlement of 10 000 dollars would be deposited in the name of Nicole Lenoir-Jourdan in the Bank of China in Hong Kong. Furthermore, I would relinquish any claims on the father of the child, and no future payments or entitlements would be made to me as the sole parent of the child. When I asked John Robertson what I might receive in return for signing the document, he pointed out that the document had come to him from an "unknown" source and that he wasn't free to ask. "That's the problem with the very rich," he explained. "They insist on contracts when it affects them and abhor them when it concerns others. I confess that as a lawyer I'm not happy, but we'll have to accept him as a man of his word." Of course, Sir Victor didn't know about the rape and naturally assumed that I was pregnant to him, which I dare say I may have been. Naturally I signed the document.

'And then while I was in Lunghua Prison, the totally unexpected happened and the Japanese, who some time earlier had invaded Manchuria, attacked the outskirts of Shanghai. The attack was unexpected, that is, for the international community, although not entirely so for the Chinese living outside the foreign-controlled areas who bore the brunt of the attack. The Japanese had been inventing quarrels with the Chinese Government for some time. They'd marched in and annexed Manchuria on a trumped-up excuse, and so the Chinese army, made up mostly of young boys, had prepared trenches across Kiangwan racecourse and thought themselves well prepared. But when the attack eventually came they proved no match for the Japanese artillery. After only a few hours the trenches were piled high with dead Chinese. The village of Kiangwan Chen was razed to the ground, with not a living creature left to be seen. Hundreds of naked bodies, with their flesh torn from the bone, and charred corpses lay in the streets and ditches of the town. In the countryside, where people had attempted to flee, the dead lay in masses among the horses, pigs and sheep.

'Of course I had no way of knowing all this at the time, but later I received the information in a letter from John Robertson that told of how the Japanese made no attempt to bury the Chinese but instead, while banning foreigners and foreign journalists from the battlefield, invited the Shanghai Japanese community on sightseeing tours among the decaying corpses. Some of the local Japanese made it a family outing and fathers, often carrying rusty swords, would take their sons to see the havoc and witness for themselves the scenes of horror wrought against anyone who dared to come up against the Emperor's Imperial Army.

'I could hear the artillery from my prison cell but didn't know what was going on and, unable to sleep, I lay awake, fearfully expecting the prison to be bombed. At two in the morning three female Chinese prison guards entered my cell and told me to dress. What clothes I possessed were hastily stuffed into a rice sack, and one of the female guards opened my handbag. She was going to steal what little money was in it, but I was helpless to do anything about it. One of the guards was demanding in a loud whisper that I put on my shoes. Then I saw my handbag dumped into the rice sack and was grateful to have it returned. It contained my make-up, my mother's pearl earrings and a letter she had written to me from hospital before she died. I was led from the cell by the three guards to a steel grille and door at the end of a long passageway. This was unlocked and I entered a continuation of the passage with two of the female guards, the third remaining behind and locking the steel door. I followed the two guards through a series of zig-zagging damp and narrow passageways ever sloping downwards, some used for sewage disposal and others as water drains. I was frequently required to stoop over, and once to crawl through excrement. With my pregnant tummy this proved difficult. I was aware of the impatient sighs of the two guards, one now leading and the other behind me and both carrying torches. I recall the constant squeaking of rats, and on one occasion a large rat ran over my foot. Finally we arrived at a vertical steel ladder that led up to an open manhole. I could see the stars as I looked up, and was struck by how sharp, clean and bright they appeared. Climbing the ladder proved very difficult and I only just fitted through the manhole. The two guards remained behind to return the way we'd come. I hoped they'd been amply rewarded. In the darkness I was then summarily grabbed and bundled into the back of a van, and driven to the docks.

'An hour later I found myself howling and frightened in a tiny cabin below the decks of a merchant freighter, the *Eastern Star*, moving downriver towards the open sea. During this entire process, from the moment I'd been led out of my prison cell to my being placed in the tiny, bug-infested ship's cabin, not a word had been spoken, and I had no idea where the ship was going. Apart from a brief and very stilted conversation with the captain, I hadn't spoken to a soul on board the ship for the entire four days of the voyage. Ironically, the cargo the freighter carried was cheap crockery – mostly rice bowls – packed in straw in crude wooden crates.

'The captain, the only European on board, was Portuguese and spoke no English, except to introduce himself as Alfredo de Suza and to tell me he came from Angola in Africa. The crew were Chinese, but spoke in the Ningpo dialect I was unable to understand. A plate of food – boiled rice and Chinese vegetables – was silently placed at the door of my tiny cabin at noon each day, and twice a day, in the morning and evening, a jug of water appeared. I remember I used the paraffin in the lantern in my cabin in an attempt to rid my hair of lice, which proved successful but extremely unpleasant, and I must have looked an awful mess.

'We sighted Hong Kong in the late afternoon four days later, and anchored in the harbour. Early in the evening a middle-aged Englishwoman, dressed in a poorly cut woollen checked suit, lisle stockings and sensible black shoes – quite inappropriate for the humid Hong Kong evening – came aboard, having travelled out to the *Eastern Star* in a motorboat. She introduced herself to me as Sister Bradshaw, and said she had instructions to take me to a private nursing home. She was brusque and efficient and paid the captain a sum of money, counting out several large, white English five-pound notes into his palm. "Come along, dear," she said, taking my arm as we slowly descended the ship's ladder to where a Chinese boatman waited in the motorboat to steady me as I came aboard.

'There seemed no point in asking questions, but I did ask Sister Bradshaw in the taxi after we'd come ashore who might have made the arrangements for me. "I haven't the slightest idea, my dear," she replied crisply, explaining no further. I had no choice but to trust her as we continued silently on our way.

'I was close to nine months pregnant when I entered the Happy Valley Nursing Home near the Hong Kong racecourse of the same name. That is, nine months from the time I had farewelled Sir Victor "appropriately" before he'd left for Hong Kong and nine months from the time I had been raped by Smallpox "Million Dollar" Yang.

'I was well cared for by the staff of the nursing home, who addressed me scrupulously and without exception as Countess Lenoir-Jourdan despite my asking them to call me by my given name. It soon became apparent that both doctors and nursing staff had been told not to ask any questions by the inestimable Sister Bradshaw, who turned out to be a midwife specially employed to take care of me and who wasn't a permanent member of the nursing staff. As far as I was concerned she was completely in charge. The other staff soon grew to fear her censorious tongue and to understand that I was a special patient. Only a few days after I arrived at the nursing home, just after two o'clock in the afternoon, to the frequent cheering of the nearby racecourse crowd, I went into labour.'

Nicole Lenoir-Jourdan paused, reflecting. 'It isn't necessary to go into details, but it is important for you to know that a screen was placed halfway across the bed so that I was unable to see the birth take place.' She laughed. 'As any woman who has given birth will tell you, it's not a process where you can assume the role of indifferent observer, but the whole event, excluding the pain, was kept from my observation. After almost twelve hours of labour, at two o'clock in the morning, the baby was born. I was exhausted when the screen was finally removed for me to see Sister Bradshaw holding up my baby, still covered in its birth blood, by the ankles. She slapped its tiny bottom and moments later I heard its first cry.

'"What is it?" I asked.

'"You have a daughter, my dear," she said in her usual brusque manner and without a smile. She really was a cold fish.

'"No! What is it?" I cried, exhausted.

'"A little girl," came the answer again. She then instructed, "No more questions, my dear, you have to rest!" Then she turned to the young nurse and instructed her to replace my screen and give me a sleeping pill to allow me to sleep while I was being "seen to".

'The nurse brought me a glass of water and made me take the pill. I asked again, "What is it?" I simply couldn't bring myself to say, "Is she Chinese?" The young Chinese nurse giggled. "Girl child, velly pretty," she said. Then she replaced the screen. The last thing I recall was my legs being removed from the stirrups on either side of the bed.

'I slept fitfully and awoke at about seven in the morning and rang the buzzer beside my bed. A nurse soon appeared and I asked if I might see my baby. "I've just come on shift, Countess Lenoir-Jourdan. I'll go and ask the day sister – Sister Bradshaw has gone home," she said.

'Nearly half an hour passed and then a doctor entered my room, along with the matron. The doctor carried a pillowcase that obviously contained something. I took one look at them and asked fearfully, "What's happened?"

'The matron took my hand and the doctor, an older and not terribly pleasant man appropriately surnamed Evinrude who'd attended me during my stay, placed the pillowcase at the end of the bed and said, "I'm afraid it isn't good news."

'Before he could say any more, I cried out in a panic again. "What? What's happened? Is my baby dead?"

'"Your baby has been abducted," he said. He didn't wait for my reaction, but continued, "We've telephoned Sister Bradshaw but there was no answer. We sent a man around to her address, but the flat she evidently occupied was vacated yesterday and the Chinese caretaker was given no forwarding address." He cleared his throat. "Because of the special circumstances and instructions we were given when you arrived, we need your permission to call the authorities."

'"Are you suggesting that I know about this?" I wept, too upset to show how appalled I was at the implied suggestion.

'He simply shrugged. "Our instructions were that under no circumstances are we to alert the authorities that you are in Hong Kong. Nor is the birth of the baby to appear on the hospital register." Then he added, in a pragmatic voice, "Unwanted babies are not unusual among the rich and famous . . . the aristocracy. We were told to await further instructions after the birth."

'I was desperately trying to gather my wits together, to stop crying, to think. Tearfully I turned to the matron and asked, "The baby, how did it look? Was it . . . " I hesitated, "Caucasian?"

'She looked at me sympathetically and put her arm around me. "We don't know. Your child was under the supervision of Sister Bradshaw, who, I believe, bathed, prepared and wrapped the baby herself. I shall ask one of the night staff when they come in."

'"The Chinese nurse who gave me the sleeping pill, she said my baby was very pretty – she'll know," I choked.

'"We'll ask her when she comes in tonight," the matron said, removing her arm and pouring a glass of water from the carafe on the bedside table and handing it to me.

'I gulped down the water, my mind racing, stumbling about and confused. Did I want the child if it was the result of being raped by Smallpox "Million Dollar" Yang? Yes, I did! I answered myself almost immediately. Children aren't born evil. The abduction – no, I must call it by the real name, kidnapping – was this done to Sir Victor's instructions? It was obvious, wasn't it? He must have been responsible for making the arrangements to get me to Hong Kong and into the nursing home. But if so, why would he take my child away from me? I'd signed the document. Surely he wouldn't have arranged for the child to be killed simply to protect the Sassoon name? If so, why the document? Was it to be used in the event of an inquiry? I simply couldn't bring myself to believe this was possible. He was a powerful taipan from a rich and famous family, certainly capable of being ruthless, but he was an honourable man and a gentleman. He was rumoured to have had several illegitimate children with Chinese women – a fact he never confirmed nor denied. I couldn't believe he would murder my child or even allow her to go to some institution for an anonymous adoption. Why would he want to take my child away from me? Nothing made sense. If the hospital brought the authorities in, would I not be arrested and returned to Shanghai to face trial?

'"There is another matter," the doctor said, whereupon he reached for the pillowcase on the bed, which, in my panic and despair, I'd forgotten about. "This was left in the newborn . . . in your baby's crib," he declared. From the pillowcase he withdrew the persimmon box with the carving of the dragon's head on the lid. He handed it to me.

'I opened the lid and inside was the blonde plait of hair Madame Peroux had cut from my head when I was sixteen years old. It also contained a note sealed with Big Boss Yu's chop. I broke the seal and read the Chinese characters.

*The good joss will return in one generation.*

'Big Boss Yu had stolen my child, believing she would bring back his luck as her mother had once done.

'"*Please*, do not call the authorities," I begged Dr Evinrude.

'Then, turning away with my face buried in the pillow, I wept.'

# CHAPTER TWENTY-TWO

## *The Curse of the Ticking Clocks*

The latest chapter in the story of Nicole Lenoir-Jourdan had astounded Jimmy and me. I guess it takes a woman to truly understand what it must mean to lose a child. A child dying at birth is a tragedy one might hope to eventually get over. But to know that somewhere you have a daughter, and not know how she is being cared for or even who fathered her, was too horrendous to contemplate.

With the communist victory in China in 1949, the Triads had been hunted, arrested, tried and executed – but, of course, only the little fish were caught. The dragonheads escaped – some to Taiwan with Chiang Kai-shek and the Kuomintang Government, others to Hong Kong. In 1952 Nicole Lenoir-Jourdan had found a mention of the death of Big Ears Du reprinted in the Melbourne *Daily News,* credited to the *Wall Street Journal.*

### Noted Tong Leader Dead

**HONG KONG, JUNE 6**

The notorious Chinese gangster Big Ears Du Yu-sen died in Hong Kong yesterday of natural causes. Born in southern China

> (date unknown) he reigned as the drug tsar and crime boss of Shanghai until the communist takeover in 1949. In Hong Kong he is believed to have been the leader of the secret Triad society involved in drugs, kidnapping, brothels, gambling dens, murder and extortion. Du Yu-sen was never convicted of any criminal offence in Hong Kong, although at the time of his death a factory believed to be owned by him, and concerned with the manufacture of roulette wheels, was being investigated for money laundering by the Hong Kong Police Department.
>
> MELBOURNE *DAILY NEWS*, 6 JUNE 1952

So Nicole Lenoir-Jourdan knew one of the dragonheads was dead but had no idea of where Big Boss Yu had fled or whether he had been captured and executed by the communists, though the chances of the latter happening were extremely unlikely. Like Big Ears Du, he had probably escaped to Hong Kong. She knew that the two dragonheads had established their organisations in Hong Kong as early as the Japanese attack on Shanghai in 1932. Shanghai had been bombed but the attempt by the Japanese to capture it had been repulsed; nevertheless, the attack had served as a warning. The two gangsters had prudently followed many of the European taipans and made Hong Kong a bolthole, which proved a wise decision.

Most importantly of all, she didn't know where her daughter was – or even if she was alive. If still living she would have been seventeen years old when the communists took over. Nicole Lenoir-Jourdan could never return to pre-communist China, as technically she was still an escaped drug smuggler. The communist victory wouldn't have helped her, either. If she had somehow managed to get to Shanghai before the bamboo curtain came down and westerners could no longer enter China, she would have fared no better. The communist government, who understandably saw opium as the root of all evil, would be almost certain to find her guilty. As she was a known associate of one of the two notorious dragonheads, they would not be overly concerned with the niceties of a proper trial. She would be summarily pronounced guilty by the people's court and executed, to become a scapegoat for the second time and for an entirely different purpose.

It was difficult to believe that she'd been caught up in so much suffering and despair – while on the island, she'd always been seen as the somewhat prim and immensely proper English music teacher, librarian and justice of the peace. Now it was 1954 and she was still bound by the same constraints as when she had escaped from Shanghai in 1932 and was unlikely ever to see her daughter or even know which of the two men had fathered her. Somewhere in China, Hong Kong or Taiwan there existed a young woman who was the illegitimate daughter of a Russian countess and an English aristocrat, a man who belonged to one of the world's richest and most illustrious British families; or, alternatively, there existed the half-caste daughter of a consummately evil Chinese peasant and member of the Triads and Lily No Gin, the stateless White Russian refugee. To make matters worse, there was the terrible thought that Smallpox 'Million Dollar' Yang, who had raped her, may have taken the place of Big Ears Du as dragonhead in Hong Kong.

There were only two possible reasons why Big Boss Yu would have abducted her child. The first was that he believed her presence in his life would bring him good fortune, as her mother's had done. The second possible explanation for the abduction was that he wished to demonstrate his infinite power over Nicole Lenoir-Jourdan by abducting and killing the result of her disloyalty to him. But she knew how the Chinese mind worked, and the second reason was the less likely. He would see a female child as worthless. By removing her he would not be punishing her mother. A daughter was 'a waste of rice', and to leave her with her mother would be seen by him as a far more suitable revenge than abduction. Furthermore, he would have known about the rape, and probably instigated it. The presence of any child to have resulted from such retribution would be a reminder of the bitter experience every day of her life. The Countess concluded that her daughter could only have been kidnapped for superstitious reasons.

She was also aware that if the child had survived, her life would have been devoid of love. To a Chinese peasant, especially one who had become as rich and powerful as a dragonhead, any female – his own daughter included – would be seen as unworthy of affection. The child would serve only one purpose – to exist as his living talisman. He would see her in the same way as if she were simply an object. If a female child grew up to be plain-faced, she was condemned to a life of drudgery; if pretty, she became a commodity to be sold as a concubine or a prostitute in a sing-song house. If a half-caste, pretty or not, she would be despised and treated worse than a dog. Nicole Lenoir-Jourdan's daughter's only chance of survival depended on Big Boss Yu's profound and all-embracing superstition. If he believed the child to be the source of his good joss, then she would be safe. Which seemed to be what his message – 'The good joss will return in one generation' – included in the persimmon dragon box suggested.

All these details of Nicole Lenoir-Jourdan's story came to me bit by bit, the result of my usual hunger for even the smallest facts. Whenever an opportunity arose to prise more information I would urge her to continue with the details of her life before she arrived on Queen Island. Sometimes she would simply answer a question and I'd have a sentence or two to store away. It was a bit like attempting to complete a jigsaw puzzle and finding another bit that fitted into the picture.

There were other occasions when she'd talk of her past to both Jimmy and me at length. Her escape from Hong Kong came to us when she invited us to lunch, ostensibly to discuss some aspect of our partnership. It was a lovely afternoon, and after lunch we sat in her garden looking out to sea, where several fishing boats were returning to the harbour. She casually mentioned how the junks of Victoria Harbour, between Hong Kong and Kowloon, had never ceased to fascinate her, and of course I immediately seized the opportunity. 'You've never told us about the time you spent in Hong Kong.'

We must have caught her in exactly the right mood, because she said, laughing, 'Oh, Jack, your wanting to know *every* detail can be quite irksome at times!'

'Me also, Countess,' Jimmy added, to encourage her. 'You in dat nursing home . . .' but he wasn't able to complete the sentence. The subject of her lost daughter always proved a delicate one. We knew she felt guilty that she'd made no effort to find her, even though it was obvious that there was nothing she could do. If she had gone back to Shanghai she would have had no chance of finding the child, and the attempt would almost certainly have cost her her life.

'There's one thing that puzzles me – that Sister Bradshaw. She just doesn't make any sense,' I prompted.

'You're quite right to be puzzled, Jack. There is an explanation, but some parts of it are decidedly open to conjecture. You'll understand it better if I begin right after Sister Bradshaw kidnapped my baby and the dragon box was returned to me.'

She sighed before beginning the next chapter of her tale. 'I have spent the past twenty-two years agonising over my decision not to report the abduction of my child to the police. I made this decision for a number of reasons, which I'd prefer not to go into, except to say that I was confused and frightened and, I dare say, over the years in Manchuria and China I had been sufficiently indoctrinated in the way the Chinese think to know that the child would never be found. Or if she was found, would certainly be dead.

'From the moment I was woken by the three female guards in Lunghua Prison I had no further say in what happened to me. When Sister Bradshaw appeared on the deck of the *Eastern Star*, I simply assumed that it was part of the plan to get me to Hong Kong. As you already know, I had no papers, so I wouldn't have been able to get past customs without questioning and possible detainment. I drew similar conclusions about my arrival at the nursing home – someone was taking care of me, and I was convinced it was John Roberston on behalf of Sir Victor.'

'But why would they then kidnap your baby?' I asked.

'Exactly – they would have done no such thing. You must remember that almost immediately after I awoke from the effects of the sleeping pill I was confronted by Dr Evinrude and the matron, told of the abduction and presented with the dragon box. I was in no fit state to respond other than in sheer terror to tell them not to call the police. I was given a strong sedative and it would have been at least a day later that my head was sufficiently clear to ask questions.

'I asked to see the matron, and, while I don't think she lied to me, she wasn't able to resolve any of the questions I asked. Sister Bradshaw, I was told, was not on the nursing home's staff but was an independent midwife with whom they had a working agreement. She would often refer expectant mothers to the nursing home, where she would oversee the delivery of the baby herself. Her clients were usually well off, and Sister Bradshaw wanted to ensure that if there were any complications during the birth, she would have the help of a doctor.

'I was not untypical of the clients she brought to the nursing home, and the permanent staff there thought nothing more of the matter when she booked me in. They were all suitably impressed when they were given my title, but not surprised when told I was unmarried. "You see, dear, you are not the first unmarried mother to have your baby with us or taken away for adoption. Sister Bradshaw always maintained that what the eyes don't see, the heart doesn't grieve over." She then explained that adoption was a major part of Sister Bradshaw's business, and the hospital had never interfered with her arrangements. The expectant mother would always sign a declaration that she was giving the child up for adoption, with Sister Bradshaw attending to all the details and arrangements for her clients.

'Sister Bradshaw had also impressed on them that under no circumstances was my name to be released or my presence revealed to anyone inquiring about me. This, I was led to believe, was also standard procedure. The matron explained that while the midwife could be a difficult woman to work with, and very possessive of her patients, she was very good at her job. "As long as things progressed normally, we all let her get on with it," was how she put it. "She seemed to believe that only she could satisfactorily deliver a child," she added, not without a touch of sarcasm. "She always took care of the payment to us and left the adoption papers with the office," the matron explained, adding that these details were not her concern. "I dare say management is happy with the arrangement," she concluded.

'"But I haven't signed any adoption papers," I protested.

'"Yes, but I didn't know this until Dr Evinrude and I came on duty." The matron's sense of self-righteous calm was beginning to annoy me. "The night sister and the nursing staff concluded that Sister Bradshaw had taken the newborn baby away with her – it had happened often enough before. She'd make a phone call and a taxi would arrive with a wet nurse in the back and she'd leave with the child. So when I came on duty and was informed your baby had been born and taken away by Sister Bradshaw, I wasn't unduly worried."

'She then explained that the night sister had mentioned that the midwife seemed in a great hurry so that none of them had seen the baby with the exception of Nurse Kwan, who reported that it had been born alive. Dr Evinrude arrived and checked the night register and asked to see the child. He was told what had happened, and only when he informed them that he hadn't signed or sighted any adoption papers had they become alarmed.'

It just didn't seem to add up, and I could see Jimmy was as perplexed as I felt. 'What about the box? Surely the night sister would have found that unusual?' I asked.

'I asked the matron that very same question myself. She told me the night sister had simply thought it was something Sister Bradshaw had left for me.

'With the evidence of the dragon box I was forced to conclude that Big Boss Yu had arranged my escape from prison. The only plausible reason had to be that he wanted the child, and that attempting to obtain it after its birth from a Chinese prison posed too many risks.

'But as it transpired, I was quite wrong. Moreover, I was in a great deal of trouble. The hospital informed me that my stay had been paid for up until two days after the birth and that unless I could make arrangements to stay longer I would have to leave. On the boat to Hong Kong I had discovered that the female guard who'd opened my handbag had not stolen my money. So I had sufficient money to get a taxi and find a cheap hotel and, of course, I had the key to the safety-deposit box Sir Victor had arranged for me at the Bank of China.

'However, it suddenly struck me that I had no way of identifying myself. I carried a rather big and unfashionable handbag that I'd used for documents and the like, rather the way a man would use a briefcase. It was while scrambling through its contents looking for something that might identify me that I found John Robertson's business card. There was nothing unusual about this discovery, as he may well have given it to me on several past occasions when he'd visited me in prison. Fortunately I turned it over to find a handwritten note on the back.

*All arrangements in place H.K.*
*Only in dire emergency call*
*Tel. 6271*

'The female guard must have dropped it into my handbag on the night of my escape from prison.'

'But then how would that explain Sister Bradshaw and the dragon box?' I asked.

'Yoh got yo'self a big, big mis-tery here, Countess,' Jimmy laughed. 'Way I see it, dat card jus' got you out o' big, big trouble!'

'I asked for a phone. A nurse assisted me down a long corridor, and I dialled the number on the card. The phone rang at the other end for some time, and I was just about to replace the receiver in despair when it was finally picked up and a voice said, "Earnshaw!"

'"Mr Earnshaw, my name is Nicole Lenoir-Jourdan and . . ."

'"Good God! Where are you?" the voice demanded. I explained that I was in a nursing home and how I'd arrived there. "You were kidnapped!" he announced, not as a question but simply a statement. "We had a man waiting to intercept you at customs but you never arrived. Give me your address, please, madam." There was some small delay while I got the address from one of the nurses. "I'll have a taxi pick you up in an hour. Are you fit to leave?" His manner was brusque and formal and, well, I suppose, efficient.

'"Yes."

'"Any remuneration, fees, et cetera?" he asked.

'"No, but if I need money for the taxi I have no Hong Kong currency, Mr Earnshaw."

'"Leave it to me, madam."

'"Shall I be coming to see you?" I asked.

'"Those are not my instructions, madam. Taxi in one hour." He placed the receiver down and I realised he hadn't even asked about the baby.

'The taxi driver came to the door of the nursing home and waited for me. I was still a bit weak from the birth, so one of the nurses helped me to the taxi while the driver carried my things. Once in the taxi he handed me an envelope and, opening it, I discovered 300 Hong Kong dollars. We drove for some time up to what is known as the Peak, where many of the more wealthy Hong Kong citizens live. We stopped outside a rather posh-looking apartment block, where the smiling Chinese doorman hurried over to open the taxi door and seemed to be expecting me. The rice sack used in the prison to store my few possessions had been replaced at the nursing home with a small canvas bag, which the doorman carried to the lift. I was taken to the ninth floor. I forget the number of the apartment – I only remember the number of the floor, because nine is generally thought by the Chinese to be lucky.

'I was met at the door by an *amah* and shown into a small but well-appointed flat. She led me into a bedroom where a child's wicker bassinette had been prepared beside the bed. She had obviously gone to some trouble to prepare the basket for a baby she'd anticipated would be a boy, and had decorated it in gaudy Chinese red and gold to celebrate the advent of a male child. "Your baby, *tai-tai*, it is not yet with you?" she asked, giving me the respectful title reserved for a married woman.

'Of course she had not been told about the abduction. In the nursing home, after the visit from Dr Evinrude and the matron and my subsequent discussion with the matron, the subject of my child had not come up. It was as if the birth had never happened and I'd entered the nursing home for a rest cure. The young Chinese nurse who, shortly after the birth, had given me a glass of water and a sleeping pill had laughingly told me I had a "velly pretty baby" and later confessed she had only said this in an attempt to comfort me. She admitted she had not seen its face, as Sister Bradshaw had not allowed any of the nurses near as she swaddled the baby and took her out to wash, so she couldn't confirm whether it was of Asian or Caucasian appearance. After this the staff had simply carried on as if nothing had happened to me.

'The question by the *amah* in the flat was the first time the existence of my baby had been mentioned since, and I could no longer contain my grief and began to weep. "My baby girl is gone," I wailed in Cantonese, in such a way that I must have given her the impression that it had been stillborn. A stillborn child, particularly a girl, is not the tragedy to the Chinese it would be to a western mother. This *amah* would not think to touch me, and made no attempt to comfort me. Quite sensibly, she simply allowed me to cry for my lost child while she made me a bowl of green tea. After I'd calmed down she brought me a plain envelope with my name typed on the outside. Inside was a letter sent from Shanghai by John Roberston. Either the original mailed envelope had been removed, or the letter had been hand-delivered by someone coming to Hong Kong. According to the *amah*, a messenger boy had delivered it the previous day.

'The letter was dated a week earlier and, while I can't remember the precise contents, it informed me that arrangements had been made for me to visit the British colonial administration's passport office. John Robertson had contacted them on my behalf and gave me the name of the appropriate British Government official to call and make an appointment. The official was a friend of his named Rob Henderson, and his telephone number was included. I recall the sentence in John Robertson's letter that said, "I anticipate the outcome will be positive and suitable travel papers will be provided for you to travel to Australia." I confess Australia had never entered my head as a possible destination. All I knew about it was that in the state of Victoria they grew golden raisins, and that a famous cricketer named Don Bradman was an Australian. There had been several Australians in Shanghai, of which John Robertson was one, and they had seemed to be a likeable and unpretentious bunch who didn't often mix with the crowd that formed the social circles I had been obliged to attend with Big Boss Yu.

'John Robertson's letter also said that he would soon send me the papers I would need as a stateless person applying to immigrate to Australia. In the main this would be a certificate that indicated the Chinese Republic had consented for me to remain in China as a refugee until I was accepted by a second country. No doubt the documents from the Chinese Government had required another fairly heavy bribe. "You will also need a reference assuring the Australian Government that you are a person of good repute. A reference from myself and one from my client will be included," the letter said. It went on to say that an amount of money equivalent to, "what my client believes you lost investing in shares has been placed in your Bank of China account, together with the sum agreed to in your contract. The receipt is included." Finally the letter assured me that the flat, *amah* and all my living expenses would be paid for as long as I remained in Hong Kong, and if and when permission came for me to enter Australia the financial arrangements to get me there would be taken care of. Lastly, it suggested that while things were being sorted out I should keep a low profile among the European community.'

'How did you feel about, you know, Sir Victor Sassoon?' I asked her warily.

Nicole Lenoir-Jourdan paused for a moment to gather her thoughts.

'I confess that at the time, and while in jail in Shanghai, I was very upset. I felt he had abandoned me completely. He was deeply involved in real-estate development on the Bund, building the massive Metropole Hotel, and the publicity I was generating while awaiting trial was potentially harmful to him. Even after my escape I told myself that the money he'd spent to bring it about was, by his standards, peanuts. More and more I grew to resent the contract he'd forced me to sign, thinking that he cared nothing for me and simply wanted me and the child out of his life.' She looked at me, her expression softening. 'Over the years I have come to quite a different conclusion. Sir Victor may not have wanted to be openly acknowledged as the father of my child, nor to have any future responsibility for it, but in every other respect he acted appropriately. He was twice my age and could well have abandoned me, and I dare say the whole affair would soon have been forgotten – a bit of a fling with a nice young thing, and no more. Shanghai was the sort of place where the great taipans could get away with anything. An affair with a White Russian refugee who had acquired an English upper-class accent to hide her identity was, in the end, hardly a serious matter. To this day I remain grateful to him. While Big Boss Yu gained considerably from our association, Sir Victor received nothing tangible, and I'm sure I wasn't the first woman to fall in love with him.'

She paused again momentarily, then added, 'One can only speculate how things might have turned out if Sir Victor hadn't come to my aid. With the influence the two dragonheads would undoubtedly have been able to exert over the Chinese Government of Chiang Kai-shek, I would probably have been found guilty and left to rot or die in prison. They were not to know until too late why John Robertson had worked so hard to get me legally placed under Chinese jurisdiction. He knew the Chinese prison officials could be bribed to make possible my escape before my trial ever came up. The expenses involved in achieving this outcome would have been well beyond my own resources.'

'But what if you'd remained under the British justice system? Surely, in the end, you would have been vindicated?' Like other Australians of my era, I had been brought up to believe that British justice always triumphed.

But she shook her head. 'Again, how would one know? Had I not come under Chinese law, bear in mind that the British and American justice systems can only work on available evidence. In this instance, witnesses able to testify that I had not been involved with the Red Dragon China and Crockery Company for the past four years would have been essential to the case.' She paused. 'But think for a moment. The American customs officials had no way of knowing how long the opium smuggling had been going on. The judge hearing my case would have known of my association with Big Boss Yu, and his association with Big Ears Du. It was essentially unimportant who owned the crockery factory. I had started it and it had now been returned to me. Who was to say that the opium smuggling hadn't commenced from the very first shipment to America, when I most certainly had been responsible for the business? I had no way of proving the smuggling operation had not been instigated by me.

'The fear of reprisals from the two Triad bosses would have had every one of the factory workers without exception indicting me in the witness stand, swearing on the graves of their ancestors that I'd owned the factory from the beginning up until the time I was arrested. There were no European witnesses to testify that I no longer ran the business. The factory wasn't large, and it was built on Chinese soil – foreign settlers would never have seen it. It had been four years since I may even have mentioned its existence in conversation with a European, if indeed I ever had. Big Boss Yu did not like to talk about his business affairs in public, and I followed his example. This reluctance to talk about the crockery factory and export business could easily have been construed as my desire to keep quiet about the business for "obvious" reasons.' She smiled widely. 'To use one of your favourite expressions, Jack, I was "caught between a rock and a hard place".'

'Dat foh sure, Countess,' Jimmy agreed, shaking his head.

'I dare say the English judge would have seen through the conspiracy soon enough, but this still wouldn't have proved me innocent. The

Americans were demanding a result to satisfy Washington. They certainly weren't going to be able to bring Big Ears Du or his white paper fan, Smallpox "Million Dollar" Yang, to trial. So the judge would probably have given me the minimum sentence for drug smuggling, which at the time was five years. Of course if this had eventuated my reputation would have been destroyed and, as a convicted felon, there would have been no possibility of my obtaining employment following my release from prison, and even less of being accepted as a refugee by another country in order to leave Shanghai permanently.'

She looked up at me, eager to clarify. 'Jack, this was happening in Shanghai – at the time the most corrupt city in the world, and with a totally venal government in office. If I hadn't been a stateless person but instead a citizen of a Concession nation, some sort of justice may have prevailed. As a White Russian who lived among the Chinese I was of no importance, and once I had lost the support of Big Boss Yu I was just another second-class refugee.

'Sir Victor and John Robertson had conspired to do the best they could under the circumstances, and it had worked. They'd got me out of prison and away from Shanghai. Moreover, they'd been able, with another heavy bribe I'm sure, to get me the correct refugee-status papers to present to the passport office in Hong Kong. It was something I could never possibly have achieved on my own, and I'm sure I owe Sir Victor Sassoon my life.

'Anyway, a week after receiving John Robertson's letter a large packet was delivered containing all the necessary papers and the two references. The reference from Sir Victor, on his personal letterhead, simply read:

*TO WHOM IT MAY CONCERN*

*I have known Countess Nicole Lenoir-Jourdan for a period of ten years. I am aware of her present refugee status and her wish to leave China. I would consider any country willing to accept her as a citizen as being most fortunate. She is of a high moral character and brings with her excellent business skills.*

*Yours faithfully,*
*Victor Sassoon*

'If Sir Victor's reference was somewhat formal, and certainly didn't wax lyrical, it was to prove immensely valuable. I made the call to John Robertson's friend Rob Henderson at the British colonial administration's passport office and he confirmed an appointment for the following day.

'Rob Henderson proved to be a most accommodating and delightful chap. He and John Robertson had become friends when he'd been with the British Consulate in Shanghai and they'd played cricket together and, according to Rob Henderson, had "frequently imbibed far too much ale". He also claimed to have met me on one occasion, though I was forced to confess I didn't recall this. He had received, he said, a long letter from John Robertson explaining my situation and so there was no need to go over it again.

'"Did he explain to you that I was due to have a child?" I asked.

'"Yes, indeed!" He glanced quickly at me. "Obviously that task is now completed – are congratulations in order?"

'"Unfortunately not. I can only hope God might grant me another child at some other time," I replied in a whisper. It was not quite lying, but I knew to tell him the truth was quite impossible. He would be obliged to call the Hong Kong police and the story of the abduction would reach Shanghai and implicate Big Boss Yu. I knew I wouldn't remain alive to be a witness at the inquiry that would follow.

'"Oh, I am so sorry," he said, looking distressed and half rising in his chair. "Shall I get you a glass of water?"

'"No, thank you. I apologise for bringing the matter up – it is just—"

'"Yes, of course. I understand," he said quickly, to avoid any further embarrassment.

'"Please, don't feel awkward – it was simply necessary to tell you. Shall we proceed?"

'"Yes, of course." He cleared his throat. "Officially you are a refugee who seeks to migrate to Australia, and providing you have the correct papers we will apply to the Australian Minister for the Interior for permission." He began to check through my papers, adding as he read, "I'm afraid diplomatic language is somewhat blunt – you will find yourself referred to as a 'white alien'."

'"Do aliens have to be white?" I joked, trying to get my interview back on track after the upsetting business of my baby. "I always thought they were green."

'He grinned. "Whether from this planet or outer space, to enter Australia aliens need to be positively white."

'It was the first time I'd heard of the White Australia Policy.

'"Oh dear," he said, suddenly coming to the end of my documents.

'"What is it, Mr Henderson?" I asked anxiously.

'"You don't appear to have anything that shows you've arrived in Hong Kong."

'So I explained the circumstances of my arrival. "I see, just one moment – I'll see if the senior customs officer is in his office." With that, he picked up the telephone and asked the switchboard for the Customs Department and had what seemed like a pleasant but fairly long conversation with someone on the other end. After he replaced the receiver, he said, "We'll send your papers down to customs and get them stamped. In the meantime you will have to fill out this Australian Form 47, an application for a Landing Permit. I will also notify customs to let them know you've applied to live in another country. In the meantime, I'll issue you with a visa to enable you to stay in Hong Kong for three months. I have only one further question. Are you able to take 500 Australian pounds or more into Australia? You see, Australia, like everywhere else at the moment, has a great deal of unemployment caused by the Depression, and even British citizens are finding it difficult to enter. Australian officials will want to know you are able to support yourself. They will also want to know that you are not a Bolshevik sympathiser."

'"Provided I can obtain Australian currency here in Hong Kong, yes – I can access this amount. As to the other point, the Bolsheviks are responsible for why I am no longer in Russia, so I am hardly a sympathiser." I handed him the receipt showing the deposit in the Bank of China.

'"Good. Now it's only a matter of waiting for the Australians to respond. I shouldn't think there are likely to be any complications," he replied. But I must have looked somewhat concerned, because he then said, "We have a directive concerning White Russians from the Australian Government for when we British officials vet them, as we do in Hong Kong and elsewhere. The directive gives our officials authority to judge whether the references furnished by the applicant are trustworthy." He smiled at me. "I have been following the directive since 1926, first when posted to the British Consulate in Harbin, then in Shanghai and now here. Your references are excellent, and it is generally left to me to decide if you are likely to prove undesirable or otherwise as an immigrant to Australia." He grinned boyishly and, with a twinkle in his eye, said, "I hereby pronounce you highly desirable."'

Jimmy and I couldn't help grinning at Rob Henderson's line.

'Well, that's about the end of it. My Landing Permit came through from Australia six weeks later. Two or three days after, I forget exactly, a messenger delivered an envelope that contained a First Saloon ticket on the Peninsula and Oriental line, as well as a letter from the manager of Lane Crawfords, the great department store in Hong Kong. The letter invited me to visit the store at my convenience, and stated that they had been authorised to allow me to select luggage and any clothes I might need for the boat trip and for my destination. A suggested shopping list was included for me to follow, which contained considerably more than I would have dreamed of purchasing myself and included a range of baby clothes, linen and toys. Actually, the suit I wore to Government House when you received your medal, though slightly altered, was one of the garments I selected. I still have the shoes and evening gowns, although the pretty summer dresses are long since gone.'

It was reassuring to know that after all Nicole Lenoir-Jourdan had been through, at least Sir Victor Sassoon had done the right thing and looked after her from afar. It must have been a terribly sad time. But for me, anyway, there still remained several questions – my usual problem, wanting to tie every knot. I desperately needed to ask her about the magnificently crafted crate that contained all her furniture, and that she'd eventually had remodelled into bookshelves. And then there was Vowelfowl, the plummy-voiced parrot.

In writing this I have put her story together as if all the elements came together at one period in time, whereas, as I have explained, the threads of her story emerged as a result of numerous conversations with her over several months, often with Jimmy present. Sometimes we'd sit down and she'd talk for a while, and I cherished these occasions. At other times we'd simply receive a short snippet in answer to a question. But I am, if anything, persistent, and I'm sure there were times when she thought my constant questioning was payback for all those occasions she'd mercilessly drilled me in the library as a child.

When eventually an opportunity arose for me to ask about the crate and the parrot she laughed.

'You never give up, do you, Jack? The beautiful crate of furniture and Vowelfowl were my final surprises from Sir Victor. On the two-and-a-half-week boat trip to Melbourne, about three nights out to sea one of the officers said to me, "I say, dashed funny that parrot of yours – amusing the ship's crew no end." So much had happened to me since I'd escaped from Shanghai, none of which I had been able to control, that I simply replied, "Oh, good", or some such similar remark. This particular officer had made a pass at me earlier when we'd been having pre-dinner cocktails, and I didn't want to encourage him any further. But the following morning I questioned my cabin steward, who immediately confirmed the presence of Vowelfowl on board. In a later letter to John Robertson I asked him how this had come about, and he replied that the Chinese chauffeur, Ah Chow, had driven up to the doorman of the Cathay Hotel – Georgii Petrov, of course – and dropped off the parrot, declaring it was for Taipan Sassoon.

'As for the great crate, that surprise materialised when I went below deck to see if I could arrange to have Vowelfowl brought outside for some light and air. The baggage master was most cooperative, and as I was looking for a ten-shilling note to tip him, he remarked, "Madam, I've been with the shipping line for thirty years. I've seen every conceivable type of box, crate and container imaginable, but I've never seen anything as carefully crafted as the box containing your furniture. Not a single nail, madam, and every plank is dovetailed and perfectly matched and polished." We walked over to the great box and he pointed to a scratch low down on one of the planks. "It happened in the loading, madam. Do I have your permission to have the ship's carpenter attempt to polish it out?" It was then that I saw, two or three feet above the scratch, beautifully carved in letters two inches high along one of the planks that ran midway along the enormous crate, words that tore at my heart.

*"Thank you for the strawberry milkshake love affair. V.S."'*

Jimmy was silent for a moment, then he said, 'I think dat Sir Victor, he done love you, Countess.' As usual Jimmy had found the right words while I floundered, wondering how to react. All I could think of at the time was how men get screwed up with power and money, and somewhere along the way lose the most precious things to them – the things that in the end matter the most. I later discovered that Sir Victor Sassoon, who had been so concerned with building a monument to power and prestige, had been chased from Shanghai just a few years later by the Japanese. The grand old city of the twenties was then closed to westerners by the communists in 1949. I'm not sure Sassoon returned to see it again.

Well, we had what was now the whole story – except, annoyingly, how Big Boss Yu knew when Nicole Lenoir-Jourdan would arrive in Hong Kong in order to send Sister Bradshaw to waylay her. I simply had to ask, or this singular detail would haunt me forever. 'I still don't know how Big Boss Yu knew you were on the ship in order to make arrangements for Sister Bradshaw to intercept you,' I said finally.

'You never forget, do you, Jack? Well I did begin by saying there was a certain amount of conjecture involved, and I have thought about it myself a great deal since. If I know anything about China and Shanghai at the time – and particularly Big Boss Yu, who was commonly referred to as Shanghai's unofficial mayor – then you may be quite sure he was also the eyes and ears of the Chinese Government. It would have taken a big bribe at a very high level to arrange my escape – not because I was important, but because I was in prison over a matter concerning two dragonheads. Not even a high government official would have accepted a bribe if an all-powerful dragonhead was involved, and in this instance both Triad bosses were concerned. Chiang Kai-shek was probably the only one who could have escaped the retribution that would have resulted.'

'You mean they had to go to him – they had to bribe Chiang Kai-shek?' I asked, astonished.

She laughed, shaking her head. 'No, of course not, Jack! There is a much simpler answer. Big Boss Yu organised the bribe himself.' She could see we were puzzled. 'John Robertson's reason for wanting me under Chinese jurisdiction was because a high Chinese official had approached him and suggested that for the correct amount of money my escape could be arranged, but only if I could be transferred to the Chinese court. The Chinese official would have been approached and encouraged to do this by Big Boss Yu. As they say in the movies, the whole thing was a set-up. It was a typical Chinese solution – everyone got rich and the *gwai lo* was outwitted. It would have been the easiest thing in the world for Big Boss Yu then to discover all the details of the escape, including the name of the *Eastern Star*. But he had no way of knowing the arrangements when I got to Hong Kong, and that's why he had to intercept my arrival by sending Sister Bradshaw to the ship. Big Boss Yu, I'm quite certain, would have shared in the bribe paid by Sir Victor and used his share to pay Sister Bradshaw and the nursing home.

'As I said, all this is only conjecture. Later, I wrote to John Robertson and asked him if he had been approached by a Chinese government official in order to arrange my escape, and he admitted as much. Such a dear man – he was later killed when he was shot down flying a Beaufort bomber over Germany.'

Jimmy and I now finally had the entire fantastic story – or rather, we thought we had. But several years later the three of us were in Hobart to sign a contract for a new boat. We shared a bottle of wine over dinner while discussing the possibility of opening the Asian market for the export of abalone, and took coffee in the hotel lounge afterwards. Hong Kong was mentioned over the coffee, and I don't remember the precise turn in the conversation but it led to one more episode in the life and times of Countess Nicole Lenoir-Jourdan, involving a rather bizarre attempt to ensure the safety of the daughter she'd never seen.

I only hope I can do justice to the tale – the details are important, because, whatever happened, she was never likely to know the outcome of her actions. The incident occurred when she was waiting for permission to immigrate to Australia. She knew no Europeans in Hong Kong except for Rob Henderson, who on two occasions invited her home to his rather small flat to have dinner with his wife and children, but she was careful not to abuse his hospitality. Instead she spent her days wandering around Hong Kong or taking the ferry to Kowloon. Soon she grew to know parts of the city few westerners would have experienced, and her fluent knowledge of Cantonese and the ways of the Chinese people allowed her to move about freely. She had only to enter a Chinese eating house where the locals ate and she'd soon be invited to join in a meal, always careful to pay her share. Pretty soon she became familiar with the lay of the land, and each day would bring more surprises as she explored the island.

It was during a conversation with a group of women in a small marketplace in Kowloon that she first heard about Wang Po, the Abbot of Po Lin (the Temple of the Precious Lotus). She had bought a bowl of steaming *congee* at a food cart where several women were squatting sharing a meal. She asked if she might join them and make a contribution of salted eggs to their food. This caused some initial bemusement that soon turned to merriment – she was, of course, blonde with blue eyes and yet spoke with the perfect rhythms and intonations of their language and was willing to squat with them in the dirt and share their food. They made room for her and she was soon involved in animated conversation when the subject of Po Lin came up. One of the women had visited the temple recently, giving up an entire day's work to travel to Lantau Island, where it was located. She went on to say that at the temple she'd lit joss sticks and made a donation to the Buddha, asking him to release her husband from his fear of heights and to grant him well-paid work in the construction industry. Her husband, while fearless on water, found it impossible to climb up bamboo scaffolding. She explained that she'd already made several donations to the Tao to no avail, and hoped a different God would produce better results. She complained that her husband was treated like a yellow dog working on her father's sampan, carrying cargo back and forth from the junks and ships on Victoria Harbour. The women joined in, laughing at the vicissitudes of life and at a woman's difficult lot, each with her own sad story to tell.

Po Lin Temple sparked Nicole Lenoir-Jourdan's interest from this first introduction to it. She later bought a book that contained several articles on the major points of interest in and around Hong Kong Island. In it she discovered an article about Lantau Island and the seemingly contradictory Buddhist monastery, in the grounds of which stands the Taoist temple.

The peasant women with whom she'd shared lunch had spoken in reverential tones about Wang Po. He was considered the greatest seer throughout all of China, who, in the women's own words, 'no longer counts the years but those who count them for him claim he has passed his 110th year by the Chinese Lunar calendar.' She had at first thought this might be women's talk, but an article authored by a professor of anthropology at Cambridge confirmed Wang Po's venerable status, and quoted his age as being well beyond a hundred years. The article went on to say that he had been given the status of an 'immortal' and that it was extremely difficult to gain an audience with him even though his faculties, with the exception of his failing eyesight, were at the time of writing perfectly intact. The author then suggested that those who held the monastery purse strings could, in the event of a donation of suitable largesse, bring an audience about. She looked at the front of the book to see when it had been printed, and discovered it was only two years earlier.

The concept of two religions living in apparent harmony side by side intrigued her – she couldn't imagine Protestants and Catholics sharing a cathedral, or Muslims and Christians a mosque. The venerated seer was said to wear both the rich purple robe of a Buddhist abbot and the black hat of a Taoist pope. She decided to visit the island, and the following morning rose early and took the tram down from the Peak, then the ferry to Silvermine Bay, from where she rode a rattletrap bus as far as it would take her and joined the other passengers, a throng of peasants, to climb a steep path a further mile up to the monastery.

On a sudden whim she purchased some joss sticks. As she belonged to neither faith, she felt she should be even-handed and burned them at the feet of both the statue of Lao Tzu, the 'source' of Taoism, and Buddha, asking for the safety of her daughter. It was a simple, heartfelt gesture – more to give a purpose to the journey than from conviction. But that night as she lay in bed an idea began to form that seemed at first impossible but was nevertheless enormously compelling. She rose at dawn and ate a little rice and, without waking the *amah*, slipped out of the flat. The first tram left the Peak again at five a.m., having made the first trip of the day up to bring the gardeners, cleaners and other humble folk that arrived each day to attend to the needs of the wealthy. She took the ferry to Silvermine Bay, then once again the old bus, which creaked and bumped and farted blue smoke and finally climbed the last mile, to be among the first of the day's pilgrims to reach the monastery.

Here she bought a red-and-gold packet adorned with the ripe peach of prosperity, and enclosed what by the standards of a normal donation would have been considered a large amount of money, to be used towards the planned construction of a likeness of the Lord Buddha. This monument was to commemorate the life and service of the venerable Wang Po and was to be the biggest and grandest of its kind in Asia. She then walked over to the Pearl Pagoda situated within the temple grounds, where the tomb of the great abbot had been prepared for the time he must eventually leave the monastery to join the celestials. Here she waited for several hours to offer her donation to an elder, with the request that she be granted an audience with Wang Po. The elder took the package, examined its contents briefly, and without changing expression handed it back to her. Over the following fortnight she returned to the temple a further seven times, rising at dawn and always increasing her offering, but to no effect. After each visit she returned to her flat well after sundown, often too exhausted to eat the food her *amah* had prepared.

With each rejection she grew more determined. Prior to her ninth visit she went to the Bank of China and removed a good portion of the gold Sir Victor had placed together with her precious icon in the safety-deposit box. Then, in a nearby market, she purchased a wooden box painted red and gold with the emblem of the pine tree and the peach carved into it, the pine signifying longevity. She placed the gold bars inside the box. Even for the rich this was a significant donation. The following morning, following her usual pre-dawn routine, she returned to the island monastery where she prepared to wait to present her offering to the elder. As if by some predetermined sign, this time she was not required to wait several hours before seeing him. Instead he called out, 'The *jarp jung* woman may step forward!' *Jarp jung* simply means mixed blood. This time, when he opened the presentation box, his right eyebrow twitched and he asked her to wait, affecting a discernibly polite tone.

He returned half an hour later with a request that she follow him into the temple's inner sanctum. In the half-light created by the fragrant haze of burning incense, she saw that the walls contained what seemed to be several hundred small niches, in each of which was placed a gold Buddha. Passing through a small door she found herself in a tranquil, walled courtyard garden. She was led through stands of sacred bamboo to a scarlet bridge that crossed an ornamental lake, where sacred carp swam, flashes of gold among the floating lotus, and a dragonfly poised above a pink blossom. On the far side of the miniature lake she saw a graceful pavilion. As she ascended the arch of the bridge she saw, standing at the far end, Abbot Wang Po in his traditional robe of purple and wearing the black hat of a Taoist pope. His wide sleeves were rolled back to the elbow to reveal arms so thin that they seemed to contain no flesh, although his hands were surprisingly large, with long bony fingers and curved fingernails that gave the impression of being the talons of a bird of prey. He showed no signs of tremors as he tossed scraps from a bowl to the carp agitating the water to the side of the bridge.

He didn't look up as the Countess approached, and when she was quietly announced by the elder he merely nodded his head. The elder bowed and, turning, took his leave. When the abbot spoke there was not a hint of the thin, reedy sound of an old man's voice. 'Do not be confused by the Buddha and the Tao. There is nothing to say we should not take all paths to find God.' At first the Countess thought this was a formal opening remark, but then realised that this religious ambiguity had been her first thought when she'd been told about the island monastery. She almost panicked – had he already discovered her latent scepticism and her purpose for seeing him?

'I am deeply honoured that you would agree to see me, lord abbot,' she said softly.

The old man looked up for the first time and she was startled to see his eyes appeared almost luminescent, his irises the colour of grey pearls. She had forgotten that the article she had read had said that he was losing his eyesight and now, two years later, he appeared to be completely blind. 'The Gods have taken my sight so that I may see more clearly,' he said, as if reading her thoughts. 'Come with me.' He walked without hesitation towards the pavilion, and she followed. Seating himself in a comfortable chair of aged wicker within the pavilion, he motioned towards another. 'You may sit,' he offered. She declined – the idea of sitting beside him rather than standing before him seemed unthinkable.

'I have been told of your numerous visits and I already know you are not Chinese, although this is of no importance – nor is your generosity. What allows you to enter this garden is your determination. I am honoured by such patience and will do what I can to help you. You must tell me why you are here.'

He listened patiently as she explained about the abduction of her child and the reasons behind it and then, choking back her grief, she asked if he could somehow ensure that Big Boss Yu would not abandon her child but care for her until she could take care of herself.

'Are you asking me to send him a warning?' Wang Po eventually asked.

'Lord abbot, I am told it is within your power.'

A wicker pot-warmer stood on a low table within his easy reach, and with practised ease he filled two lidded cups with tea, handing one to her. 'What you ask is not a horoscope, not even a foretelling of fortune or a prediction of an uncertain future. What you ask is conspiracy – you could even call it trickery.'

Nicole Lenoir-Jourdan was plainly shocked. While, of course, he was correct, she had not thought of her request as deceitful. She had lost her daughter because of an evil man's superstition and she was convinced that using the same weapon against him was fair.

'I am sorry, my lord abbot, I have acted wrongly,' she said, fighting back her tears.

He smiled. 'That would be so if you stood to gain wealth or good fortune or love and happiness, or even health and long life, but you have asked nothing for yourself. The life of a child and the sanctity of a spirit I cannot refuse.' He looked up at her, his sightless gaze seeming even more penetrating than if he had been able to see. 'I cannot do anything to return your child to you. Such a deception would become too apparent – this man would see it was brought about by the child's mother and disregard it.'

'Lord abbot, I want only that you ensure her safety,' she pleaded.

'This dragonhead, Yu Ya-ching, you say may be found in Shanghai. I will see that what you want is done.'

As this instalment unfolded at the hotel in Hobart we were all feeling somewhat mellow from the effects of the wine, and I don't know about Jimmy, but I was feeling decidedly ambivalent about the action the Countess had taken. On the one hand her exchange with Wang Po may have been a psychological masterstroke, but on the other it was potentially an incredible waste of money. At the time, the gold she'd donated to the building of the giant Buddha on Lantau Island would have bought a damn good house in Australia. For once Jimmy was lost for words, and I was the one who spoke up.

'But how did you know the old man, the abbot, would keep his word? I mean, he could have just taken your money and left you . . . well, feeling you'd done something to help your daughter.'

She looked at me sharply. 'I can see you don't approve, Jack.'

'Well, I mean . . .'

Jimmy jumped in, rescuing me. 'Countess, dat a sad time for yoh.'

'What you're both suggesting is that I acted in an irrational manner.' She seemed to think about this for a moment, and then said, 'You see, there was a part of me that thought like a Chinese peasant, where choosing between rational thinking and superstition usually means reason is abandoned. Over the centuries Chinese peasants have never had any control over the circumstances of their lives. Often acts of God, but more commonly acts of man, have completely disrupted any attempt to lead a rational and normal existence. Hard work seldom reaps its just rewards or even puts sufficient rice into the family bowl to prevent them from starving. Luck is everything. The throw of the dice or the spinning of a wheel is a better bet in a peasant's mind than a well-contoured rice paddy and a reliable ox. It is for this reason that the Chinese are inveterate gamblers. It is not that they believe the odds will favour them, but that the odds against them are already insurmountable. Because life is purely a matter of luck, they are forever on the lookout for signs and portents and, of course, a talisman is of the utmost importance.

'You may remember that the first time I met Big Boss Yu it was as a fifteen-year-old in the nightclub in Harbin when he asked for a lock of my hair. That night, I was later told, he won a considerable fortune at roulette. Later still I became his living talisman, while the plait of my hair in the dragon box became the actual talisman. With my help he made millions of dollars from raisins, and everything else he touched seemed to turn to gold too. When he discovered my affair with Sir Victor he not only believed I had betrayed him but, in his mind, the talisman – the plait – lost its power. The opium-smuggling operation was discovered by the Americans, and this had the potential to discredit him in the eyes of Shanghai's international community. Unlike his partner in crime, Big Ears Du of the French Concession, Big Boss Yu craved respectability above everything. He needed to be seen as a legitimate taipan. So I became the scapegoat. But he still had to contend with the prophecy the incense master had given him when I consulted him about cutting my hair.'

'What, the message he left in the dragon box when he kidnapped your daughter?' I asked.

'No. It is doubtful even you will have remembered, Jack. The incense master's prophecy, which he had instructed me to tell Big Boss Yu, concerned Yu's joss: "It is good for now but it will sail away across the seas and return again later to his dragonhead." Big Boss Yu's message left in the dragon box, "The good joss will return in one generation", was his attempt to bring his luck back and fulfil the prophecy. I would escape and sail over the seas, taking the dragon box containing the discredited talisman, the plait, with me. By kidnapping my daughter and bringing her back "over the seas" as "the next generation" he would bring back his good luck and thus fulfil the prophecy.'

'So what you're saying is that you had to find a way to reinforce his own superstition with a message from the abbot of Lantau Island.'

'Dat abbot, he da big shaman in all China. Big Boss Yu get his message, he know he gonna obey him, dat foh sure.'

Jimmy and I had met a few Chinese in our time as prisoners of war, and in my experience duplicity wasn't unknown among them. I guess the wine had gone to my head a little, because I added somewhat cynically, 'That is, if he got it.'

'Oh, but I'm certain he did, Jack,' she replied. 'I'd left my details, as requested, with the temple, and eight days later I received a hand-delivered note in very businesslike calligraphy.'

*"Pavilion of the Four Seasons, Palaces of the Four Winds,*
*Shrine of the Dragon Mother, Hollywood Road,*
*Hong Kong, 7 a.m., Thursday."*

'The coming Thursday was two days hence. I should explain that the Shrine of the Dragon Mother is one of Hong Kong's best-known temples. Every morning its courtyard is crowded with early-morning worshippers anxious to burn joss sticks on their way to work. Many grab a hasty breakfast from the food carts that stand against the walls of the shrine. Vats of steaming rice porridge bubble away, there are salted eggs, roasted peanuts and custard tarts. Most Chinese have a sweet tooth, and there are dozens of other dishes on offer to feed the hungry crowd.

'I was keen to allow myself plenty of time to get to the shrine, as I had two trams to catch to reach my destination. On a whim I decided to wear my mother's pearl earrings to bring me good luck, although a moment's reflection would have told me it was too late to affect the outcome of anything. That's when I discovered one earring was missing. I'd been so relieved to find that the prison guard hadn't stolen my money on the night of my escape that it hadn't occurred to me to look for the earrings. And then, of course, I thought it may have been stolen in the hospital. I knew it was pointless making a fuss – I couldn't prove anything anyway – but I confess I wept at the discovery of the loss. I only tell you this because the fuss of discovering the earring missing caused me to miss the first tram, and so I had to hurry. I finally got off the tram from Causeway Bay and took a short cut through the Central Market, which was already throbbing with early-morning preparation.'

The Countess stopped talking. Jimmy had ordered another bottle of wine, and to my surprise she held out her glass. 'Allow me briefly to paint the scene of the Central Market. Even in Shanghai the markets were never as exotic, and by taking a shortcut I was rewarded with a sight few people, even those who lived in Hong Kong, would have experienced – walls of glass tanks filled almost to overflowing with live fish, eels and crabs of literally hundreds of varieties; baskets of squawking poultry stacked to the roof-beams; carts of freshly butchered meat, offal and bones dripping trails of blood as they trundled loudly over the cobblestones; and the squeals of live pigs, who seemed to know their imminent fate, cutting through the tremendous cacophony, adding to the mayhem. This was no place for a sensitive western stomach, and the rubber-booted workers stared at me as I dodged the carts and the carelessly spraying water hoses to find my way to the crowded ladder street that led up to the lower end of Hollywood Road.

'Inside the shrine, the crowd was fighting to reach the feet of the Goddess seated on the dragon throne. The interior was in permanent twilight as huge coils of incense, some the size of a small wagon wheel, choked the shadows with smoke. Pigeons in their hundreds strutted the rafters and, like the market I'd just passed through, the shrine was a confusion of jostling, shouting people seeking just enough luck to see them through the day.

'I had visited before at a quieter hour and knew that behind the shrine, through a moon gate, stood five pavilions, one for each of the four winds and one located in the centre. It was too early for sightseers, and the central pavillion was empty but for a slight figure, a Buddhist nun, wrapped in a saffron robe. She approached me without hesitation and I could see from her face that she was a woman in her middle age, or perhaps a little older. Her saffron robe was old and faded, and she wore scuffed sandals on her broad feet. She bowed to me in the manner of a Buddhist devotee, and I noted the triangle of three small scars on the crown of her shorn head – part of her initiation into the realm of pain, where three small cones of incense are placed on the scalp, lit and left to burn down to the bone in a process that takes an hour, during which showing any sign of weakness is forbidden. These scars were her badge of office and they commanded respect in any company – even a dragonhead would not dare to dismiss her from his presence.

'"I greet you, *tai-tai*," she said, showing me the respect of a married woman of status.

'"I greet you, *seal jeh*," I replied, giving her equal status as a single woman.

'"I am a disciple of Wang Po, Abbot of Po Lin. I have visited the one intended and now have for you, on the instructions of my abbot, the master of wind and water, a second copy of the scroll I delivered to Yu Ya-ching."

'"It is not necessary – the abbot gave me his word," I replied, though I confess I was secretly thrilled at this apparent confirmation of Wang Po's promise. From her begging bag she removed a scroll and handed it to me with both hands, bowing as she did so. I accepted it in the same manner and saw that it contained the monastery's chop or seal, which was absolute confirmation that the scroll was genuine. With trembling hands I broke the seal to unroll the narrow piece of parchment, only to be confounded by the ancient characters of its text, which were quite beyond my ability to read. Immediately to the side of the final character on the scroll was a second seal acting as a "forbidden mark" or, in western terms, a full stop, so that no other words may be added. As custom would have it, the second seal is also the personal chop of the sender of the message – in this case, the most revered Abbot of Po Lin.

'The nun had been expecting my confusion and, smiling, took the scroll from me. In a quiet, even voice she began to read.

*"'He who is known as an 'immortal' and is the master of wind and water, the sage who reads the palaces of the moon and who interprets the twenty-eight constellations that foretell the affairs of mankind in an ancient almanac, the commander of the five elements, Wang Po, the ancient and venerable Abbot of Po Lin, sends Yu Ya-ching this message.*

*"I have heard, in the wind and over the trembling water, of a* jarp jung *girl-child who alone holds the key to your future life and fortunes. If harm should come to her by your own hand or by those who obey you, then a hideous fate awaits your lineage, and your ancestors face eternal damnation. This fortune-bringing child must be given all the privileges afforded to a male child of your direct lineage. In exchange your health and longevity will be assured and the Gods will smile upon you, and the good fortune of your house and clan will be assured."*

'The Buddhist nun came to the end of the reading, bowed and handed me back the scroll. I thanked her and asked permission to ask one question. She nodded, agreeing with a smile. "Was there anything peculiar about the office of Yu Ya-ching?" I asked.

'She smiled again, immediately realising the reason for my question, but showing no offence. "There is no deceit, *tai-tai* – it was I who delivered the message to Yu Ya-ching, the one with the many ticking clocks in his office, each with a different time on the face."'

The Countess took a small sip from her cup. 'So there you have it, gentlemen – I had my confirmation. There is simply no way she would have known about the clocks had she not been in Big Boss Yu's office.' Coming to the end of her anguished story, she sighed deeply. 'I shall never see my precious daughter. Nor know which of the two men fathered her. But I am certain that my donation to the monument to honour Abbot Wang Po, the "immortal", is the most important investment I have made in my life.'

# CHAPTER TWENTY-THREE

## *Dr Whisky*

I guess the time has come to tie up the bits'n'pieces that have gone into this rather ramshackle story. The path a life takes inevitably meanders, and in the telling of its story some elements are seen as important, and others not. I've talked about the events I thought might be interesting, leaving out the subject of 'earning a living' – that day-to-day grind that earns us all a crust. Not that the thirty-two years building Ogoya Seafood Company into one of the nation's biggest fishing fleets, with canneries the world over, wasn't an interesting time or immensely rewarding. As Jimmy often says, snatching a few bars of an old number and altering the final word, 'No, no, they can't take that away from us.'

The near-wreck of the *Janthe* was an early warning that life on a fishing vessel is never easy or predictable, but, of course, I always knew that. In the early years of Ogoya we had our good times and bad – but then, who doesn't? Looking back I couldn't have wished for better. I married Wendy a year after the three of us went into partnership. With me spending most of the time at sea, it was a bit of a struggle at first. I imagine it must have been a lonely time for a young bride who hadn't been brought up in a fisherman's family, and so didn't know what to expect. As was the case for all young couples at the time, there was precious little money about, and our first few years together was a time of rented accommodation, second-hand furniture and scraping and painting, most of it by Wendy, who could make something pretty out of something I saw as junk. She would tend to a battered old chair and before you knew it friends would be saying, 'Where'd you get that great-looking chair?'

Wendy has put on a pound or two – or kilos, as it is today – but she's still the most beautiful creature I ever laid eyes on. I often stop to watch her moving about, bringing in flowers from the garden or simply stacking the dishes in the dishwasher, and I shake my head in wonder that she chose me, Jack McKenzie, the freckled kid from the Queen Island family that wasn't worth a pinch of the proverbial. Can you imagine what might have happened if, standing at the bus stop in Launceston, I hadn't suddenly realised that Jimmy was going to be the number-one big-time romantic hit on the island, and had not rushed across the road to buy condoms from the chemist? That day, the day I first met Wendy, was one of the most fortunate of my life.

Most couples have their problems, yet I can honestly say ours have never been too big to be solved by a kiss carried over to the other side of the bed and the cuddle that invariably results. But you can't have everything and, although we tried, no kids came. I had all the tests, as did Wendy, but the results were inconclusive. Perhaps with today's technology and know-how they'd find the reason.

Jimmy hasn't married, although there were a few kids on the island with very impressive year-round suntans. He looked after all of them, and their mums have never gone without. Most of his kids were eventually accepted into university in Hobart, and have made something of their lives. One of them became the youngest skipper in Ogoya's fishing fleet. That was the thing about Jimmy – even the island blokes who married the girls who'd had one of Jimmy's kids loved him. If the subsequent kids of these couples were bright enough, they too went on to further their education at Jimmy's expense. To have had one of Jimmy's children was considered a status symbol, because it had evidently taken some planning. In the early days some smart-arse fisherman whose sister was proudly pregnant to one James Pentecost Oldcorn might have a go at him, and Jimmy would flatten him. They'd have a beer, discuss the perfidy of a woman determined to become pregnant, agree that the guilty party's offspring would be looked after and be mates forever.

Now, about the fishing, canning and export business that today forms Ogoya Seafood Company Pty Ltd. Left to our own devices, Jimmy and I would never have made it past owning the *Janthe* and making a reasonable living from the sea. If Nicole had simply bought the boat and left us on our own I'm not sure what might have happened – certainly nothing like what did. Jimmy might have taken the business further – remember the tomatoes, Radiator Charlie's Mortgage Lifter? He was an organiser and he had plenty of ideas, whereas I was a details man, so maybe we'd have ended up a bit more than a couple of fishermen with a good boat. But it was Nicole's business acumen, developed in China while she worked for Big Boss Yu, that enabled us to build what some people refer to as 'a vast seafood and fishing empire'. And while Jimmy and I can hold our own in any boardroom in the world today, she taught us most of what we needed to know to get started.

For the first few years Nicole and Wendy ran the business onshore and Jimmy and I took care of the *Janthe* – and then another boat, and another, and another, and so on, as the business grew under Nicole's direction and with Wendy's organisational ability. In those days not too many women ran a business, and main-island and mainland suppliers – salesmen, fish wholesalers and suchlike – thought a couple of women in charge would be a pushover. The good-looking sort, she'd be the bimbo – after all, pretty women are stupid, aren't they? The older one, well, c'mon, she was a music teacher and a librarian turned bloody journalist – what would she know? We had to laugh. Mike Munday was far from the last guy to walk out of the office ruefully shaking his head, wondering what the hell had happened.

Nicole started the export of cray tails to America, and had to go cap in hand to the bank in Launceston to beg for a sixty-day letter of credit or a loan to get us through one predicament or another on more than one occasion. The first five years were really hard going. Getting our product fresh to Sydney to catch the Qantas Super Constellation flight to San Francisco was a bloody nightmare, dependent on a factory boat that always waited until the last of the other crayfish boats brought in their catch before leaving for Melbourne, or it might be delayed by a sudden storm or some other mishap on the Strait. Often we'd miss the connecting flight from Melbourne to Sydney and have to dump the lot on the Melbourne market for a quick sale, not even earning enough to pay the crews and our sub-contractors.

Fishermen from Tasmania to Eden thought we were bloody crazy, and there were times when I wondered the same myself. We were so often forced to use the *Janthe* and *Sans Souci*, our second fishing boat, as security for a loan, that they became known as Pawn 1 and Pawn 2. On several occasions we came within forty-eight hours of the bank foreclosing on us. Often, after we'd used up all of Nicole's considerable powers of persuasion, I'm ashamed to admit our last card would be the 'Miss Tasmania Factor'. Wendy would get dolled-up and go into the bank or the supplier to whom we owed money and turn on the charm – and then, if necessary, the waterworks. It's got to be a bloody hard bastard that will turn a tearful and still very beautiful former Miss Tasmania down when all she wants is an extra week of credit.

Somehow we pulled through, though it was invariably to Nicole's credit. She was not merely good at business; she simply never gave up. I often wondered if she secretly believed she'd lost her daughter by not trying hard enough and was determined not to be on the losing end again. She could draw blood from a stone, make a bank manager beg for mercy, and get blokes to whom we owed money to eat out of her hand as a result of her incredible persistence and persuasive powers.

The big turning point for us came five years in, when one bright spring morning the *Gazette*'s foreign correspondent from New Guinea, in the form of Michael Bloody Munday, turned up and wanted to buy the *Janthe* back. He'd completed his flying contract with the mining company and had the cash, and then a bit, to settle the deal on the spot. He seemed to be of the opinion that, while there was no contract or paperwork to prove it, we had a gentlemen's agreement to sell the *Janthe* back to him.

Of course we could have told him to go jump in the lake, but that had never been our way. There'd been many a contract in the early days that had been no more than a handshake, and some of them still stand to this day. Mike Munday believed, though incorrectly, that we'd shook hands on the return sale of the *Janthe*. The matter needed to be urgently resolved, and with as little bloodshed as possible. I still believed that we owed our lives to him, in the first instance, for the way he'd fitted out the boat with the aircraft landing light and the caulking iron, but more importantly, for the methedrine stored in the Bex packets. You don't kick a guy like that in the crotch.

Jimmy went to work on him to soften him up and then turned him over to the Countess. Mike emerged out of the *Gazette* office scratching his head as he had done when he'd sold the *Janthe* for less than his asking price five years earlier. 'I've just bought an army-surplus Gooney Bird and I'm now flying a regular crayfish run from the island to Sydney,' he said, confused. 'How the fuck did that happen?'

Nicole helped him to start up a charter company, negotiating the purchase of an American Air Force surplus Dakota and doing all the paperwork with the Department of Civil Aviation. She then put him on a contract where we paid him for his charter services. We also gave him three per cent of the profits of Ogoya for ten years, after which the *Janthe* would become his again, but only in return for a twenty-five per cent share of Munday Aviation, as Mike rather grandly termed his fledgling one-aeroplane airline. The three per cent cut of Ogoya's profits Mike received would not have amounted to more than beer money for the first couple of years, but by the end of the ten years he'd done pretty nicely.

But then, so had we. Munday Aviation became an Australia-wide operation as well as the principal charter aircraft for mining exploration throughout the Pacific Islands and Indonesia. It was claimed that Mike Munday could land an aircraft on a sixpence in the middle of the jungle or on a mountain top, but that he always made sure it would cost someone a few bob for him to do so. He became a very wealthy man, and our purchase of twenty-five per cent of his company in return for the *Janthe* proved to be a very good investment indeed.

Nicole always denied that she'd been overly shrewd in negotiating the terms for the sale. It was, she claimed, a part of the original deal, so that Mike would know that we'd back him in his new aircraft venture and that one day he would regain ownership of the marvellous old boat. When the time came to hand her back to him, twenty-five per cent of Munday Aviation was fifty times what the *Janthe* was worth. Mike never batted an eyelid – he had his beloved boat back, and felt he'd done well out of the deal. 'Mate, Nicole Lenoir-Jourdan made the deal in my interest. Anyway, I would literally never have gotten off the ground if she hadn't organised the whole shebang.'

With the Dakota getting our cray to Sydney to catch the Qantas flight to San Francisco as regular as clockwork, things began to pick up. We only had one problem. The cray season ends on the 1st of September each year, when the crayfish lose their old shells and start to grow new ones, and restarts again in November, so for two months a year we had to convert to a regular fishing operation. As we had no overseas market we were competing with every man and his dog to get fresh fish to the mainland. Furthermore, the wholesale fish buyers did us no favours with the prices they paid. Jimmy commented that while the tuna we often caught was worthless on the local market, Americans ate a great deal of it, canned tuna being almost a staple food in the big cities. He claimed that on his medal propaganda tour of America tuna-fish sandwiches and salads had almost been a lunchtime necessity for the media personnel, particularly the women.

Inspired by Jimmy's insights, Nicole leased the machinery for a small factory to can fish. As it turned out, the tuna caught in Australian waters was of a very high quality and we were soon sending shiploads to America. In the meantime, the indefatigable Countess discovered the fresh tuna market in Japan. Jimmy was sent there to investigate and returned with the news that, providing it was of the highest quality, they'd take all the product they could get at prices we could hardly believe possible. We then had two highly profitable ways of compensating for the crayfish breeding and moulting season.

Tuna, like most ocean fish, can be elusive. To combat this challenge we purchased a Piper Cub that Wendy learned to fly, and she became our fish spotter. She'd be up at dawn and became an expert at finding a school of tuna. She'd radio back the coordinates to our fishing vessels, and once in the area the echo sounders on the boats would do the rest. Wendy would then put in a day at the office. She loved flying, and eventually we developed a fleet of small aircraft as a subsidiary of Munday Aviation.

Until we organised the export of fresh tuna to Japan, Mike Munday had been forced to find other work during the cray moulting season and gained a contract with a mining company in the Northern Territory. Eventually, with a little help from his friends, he purchased three more US Air Force surplus Dakotas. He continued to build this part of his business while still getting our fresh tuna to Sydney for export to Japan during the cray off-season. He would always explain his phenomenal success by saying, 'I was working both ends of Australia, so why not the rest of the world?' Then he'd add, 'Wherever we decided to open for business in Asia there would be a local Chinese family that wanted a partnership. With Nicole Lenoir-Jourdan on my board, and with her knowledge of the lingo and how to deal with the shrewd buggers, getting set was almost easy.'

All this was achieved over a ten-year period and, as I said, not without a good few very hairy moments, a tremendous amount of hard work and even, at times, sheer luck. 'We had good joss,' Nicole would reason when things went well. And the harder we worked, the luckier we got. But she also added a touch of heavenly intervention and insisted that every boat in the fleet carry a small statue of Buddha and Lao Tzu, the founder of Taoism. On one occasion I mentioned this quaint practice to Gloria, who suddenly grew very silent. 'What's up, Mum?' I asked.

'How big?' she snapped. In her old age, and with our success, she had gained the prominence on the island I suspect she'd always craved and was now somewhat of a matriarch.

'How big?' I repeated, not sure what she meant.

'Them heathen statues!' It seemed a curious question but I told her how they were all positioned in the wheelhouse of the boats so as not to get in the way, and were no more than nine inches high.

Soon after she visited the company headquarters with an equally ageing Father Crosby in tow. At that stage we had eleven working vessels and a factory ship, and Gloria and Father Crosby delivered a dozen statues of the Blessed Virgin, all of them standing ten inches high.

'They've all been sprinkled with holy water blessed by the Holy Father himself,' Father Crosby declared, bringing his palms together in a pious gesture.

John Champion, who by now had put Queen Island cheese on the national map, had quarrelled with Reverend Daintree's successor, Reverend Unworth, predictably known as Reverend Unworthy, and, like Gloria, had gone over to the Catholics. Ever the big-noter, he had visited the Vatican on a tax-deductable cheese-making, machinery-buying trip to Europe and returned with a small bottle of holy water, which he'd presented with a great deal of fuss to Father Crosby.

This grand event had taken place a good five years earlier, from which moment every new child, boat, building or object of any importance had ostensibly been sprinkled with what the non-Catholics on the island referred to as 'the Pope's piss', so that by the time we received the statues of the Blessed Virgin, Father Crosby would have needed a bathtub full of the stuff to have met all the past sacred sprinklings. He even sprinkled a generous drop on the coffin of

Reverend Daintree, whose last eccentric request had been to be buried by Father Crosby. This resulted in the biggest funeral ever to take place on the island, and Gloria ever after maintained that the Anglican minister had finally seen the error of his ways, and if he hadn't quite asked for the last rites this had simply been an oversight on his part and he was henceforth to be declared a good Catholic.

Anyway, the Blessed Virgin joined the other two celestial images in the fishing fleet to form a trinity of protection. I feel sure the Abbot Wang Po, master of wind and water, wherever he sits in the pantheon of Gods and Goddesses, would approve.

While I'm dusting the cobwebs from the corners of my mind, I need to say that Jimmy, Nicole and I all had a problem in common – from time to time we each suffered from some sort of depression. When these bouts occurred we would absent ourselves for a few days, and sometimes weeks. Even Nicole would need to break away and be alone for a period of time. Today we know this affliction as post-traumatic stress disorder. I realise now that I'd first encountered it in Japan, when Rick Stackman climbed the crane and refused to go to Korea with K Force. As they say in the vernacular, 'it was a bastard of a thing' when it happened – you couldn't explain it and there was no name for it, and I sometimes felt that people might think I was carrying on. Wendy knew better, and had her own name for it – she called it 'Jacko's sadness'.

After Ogoya started to prosper, I had the idea that I might try to find some of my mates from Korea. If these bouts of depression were troubling Jimmy and me, then I figured they too might be having a bad time. If any of them was doing it tough and wanted or needed a job, we'd make a place for them in the fleet or find something they could do ashore.

Finding Rick Stackman took a fair bit of effort, but eventually I tracked him to northern Queensland, where he lived as a virtual beachcomber in the Daintree. I flew up to Cairns, hired a four-wheel-drive vehicle and eventually found him cooking his breakfast one morning outside a bit of a hut set beyond the tide mark on a deserted beach. He'd pretty well lost the habit of conversation and, in effect, told me to bugger off. I left him my card, told him to call me if he needed any help, which I admit was bloody presumptuous on my part, and did as he'd less than politely requested. A month later he turned up on the island, and asked for me. 'In trouble is yiz? Need a good man to get yiz out the shit, do yer, Jacko?' Rick really took to the life at sea and eventually skippered one of our boats until he retired to go rock fishing.

Over the years we brought a few more of the mob together, such as Catflap Buggins, who'd married his Japanese Lotus Blossom and had six lovely kids. Today an ageing but still graceful Lotus Blossom and her kids own a business that franchises sushi bars in shopping centres throughout Australia. Catflap passed away twenty years ago from a heart attack. The priest referred to him dying peacefully in bed as a good man should, but Lotus Blossom, hiding her grin behind her hand, told me he'd died 'in the saddle', doing what he did best.

John Lazarou, 'Lazy', my frustrating but loyal weapon-pit partner, was Greek, and turned out to be a natural-born fisherman. He too ended up captaining one of our factory ships. He'd always managed to create a fair bit of chaos on land and I still don't know how he hadn't got himself killed in the war, but he was different as the skipper of a fishing boat. I think Greeks are a bit like that – give them something they love to do and you'll find no one does it better. Lazy's heart had never been in soldiering. He'd only joined the army because he hadn't wanted to work in the family cafe in Gympie and he thought going to Korea with K Force was the lesser of two evils.

Even Ivan the Terrible ended up manager of our first fish-canning factory, and later, when we moved into Asia, he supervised building canning plants in Thailand, Indonesia and Singapore and travelled extensively, acting as our international production coordinator.

I found Ian Ferrier, the D Company radio operator with whom I had shared that first night on Hill 504 in the Battle of Kapyong, panelling for a country radio station. I hauled him out of there quick smart to run the radio operation for both our fishing fleet and Munday Aviation. He'd married and had four kids, whom Ogoya put through university.

Best of all I found Dave McCombe, the bravest of the brave, who had carried one end of my stretcher across the icy paths in the mountains of North Korea when we'd been taken prisoner. He had cradled my bootless feet within his army jacket and in the warmth of his armpits to save them from certain frostbite and amputation. I still remember his last words to me, as I was dragged from the prison cage we shared with the South Koreans: 'Jacko, don't die, don't let the fuckers win!'

I'd discovered through the War Memorial archives in Canberra that Dave had survived captivity in Korea, and I knew more or less where to look for him. He'd taken over the family wheat farm in the Mallee, in north-western Victoria, but in 1968 he'd been wiped out by the long drought and been forced to put the property on the market. Dave had no aspirations to be a fisherman – he's the sort of bloke who needs a lot of space and dust under his big RM Williams boots. Anyway, with a bit of a loan and what with one thing and another, he was able to remain on the land. He's a proud man and he paid every cent back to me. So we bought another 5000 acres adjoining his own property and one of his three sons now runs it for us. It's good wheat country and has been another good investment. Christmas last year, Wendy flew me over in the company helicopter and we visited the McCombes, staying with them for a week in the old family homestead.

I fear I digress, my mind jumping around like a jack rabbit. Where was I? That's right, we're twelve years in, and suddenly abalone was the next big thing in the fishing industry. We had a bit of space booked on Qantas for a shipment of tuna to Japan when two of the tuna boats broke down three days out to sea and it looked as though we'd miss the flight. One of the other boats had brought in a load of scallops and a ton or so of abalone to feed the cray we kept in a harbour tank to top up supplies. We didn't want to waste the Qantas cargo space so, purely on a whim, Jimmy tossed in the abalone and the scallops. Well, the Japanese went crazy and cabled back to say they could take all they could get of both, but especially the abalone.

And so the abalone 'gold rush' began. The price of abalone soared and kept going up. In 1968 we were getting one dollar per pound exporting to Japan using our own licences and those of the fishermen we employed, who got the going rate of ten cents a pound for their abalone. It doesn't sound like much, but a good diver could make 300 dollars a day, and fishermen who'd always done it tough didn't know what to do with all the money they were making. If only all this had happened in Alf's time.

The metric system had arrived but the fish wholesalers were slow learners and fishermen hate change, so cray and abalone were still paid for by the pound. Every fisherman with a five-dollar fishing licence from Tasmania to Eden hocked everything he had to buy a Briggs & Stratton motor, used to drive a twin-cylinder Clisby compressor hooked up to Nylex premier garden hose, a twenty-foot boat with an outboard motor, and a regulator, weight belt, wet suit and flippers. He was then fully equipped to go into abalone diving. In 1969 the Tasmanian Government was forced to restrict the number of licences to 120 so that abalone fishing didn't get totally out of hand.

In 1970 Japan discovered the superior green-lip abalone, which proved to be a bonanza for Ogoya Seafood Company as the east coast of Queen Island – our very own backyard – possessed an absolute abundance of green-lip, and we were getting three dollars a pound in Japan. The demand for abalone in Japan increased and the price doubled, so that a good abalone diver on the west coast could bring in 3000 pounds of black-lip abalone a day, and make up to 600 dollars a day.

By 1974 licences became transferable and came with twenty-eight quota units. One unit enabled the diver to fish for 600 kilos of abalone a year. A single licence plus full quota units sold for 20 000 dollars. We owned our own licences and over the years bought all the quota units we could, for whatever the going price. We were soon running, and continue to run, a very big diving operation. Today, in 1986, a licence with twenty-eight quota units is worth four million dollars, and is still rising – heaven knows where it will end. The large and useless shellfish with the beautiful mother-of-pearl interior Alf had fed to his cray catch to keep it healthy before sale is now worth a king's ransom.

It was at about this time, 1974, that we decided to trial abalone on the Chinese market. As China itself was closed to westerners, this meant going to Hong Kong. This wasn't something we'd previously planned – in fact, it was a move we'd avoided, for Nicole's sake. After all, Hong Kong contained for her only bitter memories she wouldn't want to revisit.

It had all happened in the small town of Bermagui, on the far south coast of New South Wales, in 1974. It was unusual for Jimmy and me to be in the same place at the same time. He'd been spending a lot of time in Japan and I wanted to catch up with him. A local fisherman was selling his abalone licence and I was going up to put in a bid for it and suggested Jimmy come along for the ride. Wendy flew us up in the Cessna and arranged to pick us up again the following day, her last words being, 'Enjoy your boys' night out!' Anyone who's ever been to Bermagui won't fault it for being a nice little village, but it has a snoring problem – 'sleepy hollow' would be an exaggeration. So the Horseshoe Bay Hotel where we were staying wasn't exactly jumping.

As we were having a beer or three on the pub's verandah we'd watched the sky change colour as the sun set and then the moon rise, a thin melon slice that did nothing for the dark. I was feeling restless, I don't know why – perhaps a bout of 'Jacko's sadness' was coming on, though I dismissed the thought immediately. Jimmy was with me, and we were two mates with a few, all-too-rare, precious hours to spend together. But I no longer wanted to remain drinking at the pub. There was something about the sound of the surf rolling in, crashing every minute or so on the rocks at the end of the beach with an explosion, that was getting on my nerves. Earlier I'd glanced at the chalkboard menu behind the main bar and there'd been nothing I particularly fancied. 'Let's find a greasy spoon in town,' I suggested to Jimmy, hoping the walk would settle me down.

We set off down a dark street behind the hotel, the exploding surf roaring in my ears. In the distance a car's headlights coming over a rise flashed suddenly and disappeared, momentarily lighting up the streetscape. Then I lost it. Something snapped and I was back on Hill 504, looking down at the battle below with grenade and mortar explosions momentarily lighting the grim scene. The sound of a lone bugle floated up from Kapyong Valley like a funeral wail. *So many dead, so many dying below*. Then a series of horrific images flashed before me: Ted Shearer slumped in the weapon pit beside me, his heart sliced by shrapnel; Johnny Gordon lying lifeless, his dark hand resting on a patch of moonlit snow; Doug Waterman, the Irishman in the POW camp, turned to the wall dying of shame; the Chinese soldier with his arm hacked off at the shoulder rolling two cigarettes with his good hand, then lighting them and handing one to me before dying quietly, his sputtering cigarette stuck to his bottom lip. Everywhere the dead lay around me. I could feel myself beginning to shiver and wondered if I was dying. A song filled the air.

*'Some of these days you're gonna miss me, honey*
*Some of these days you're gonna feel so lonely . . .'*

'Hey, Brother Fish, yoh okay?' Jimmy's hand was on my shoulder.

'Yeah, yeah – fine, mate,' I answered, trying to snap into the present.

'Dat a black woman, man!'

'Huh?'

'Singin'. Ain't no white woman can sing like dat.'

We were standing outside Le Marlin Café. A large, free-standing sign at the door announced: 'MADAM AND THE RAGTAG JAZZ BAND'. The amplified voice coming from inside hit me like a smack in the mouth. There was only one person in the world who sounded like that, a voice that was etched into my brain forever. 'That's no black lady, mate – that's the immortal Pat Brand!'

It was hard to believe the hallucination of a few moments back wasn't continuing. She was in full flight belting out the song, pushed along by a band pounding out a rhythm like an oncoming steam train and adding to the excitement with lines of four-part harmony. We eased our way inside just as the pianist finished his solo and raised his bowler hat to the cheers of the crowd packing the room.

At the end of the set we attempted to squeeze our way to the front. Jimmy, a head taller than anyone in the place, said in his deepest voice, 'Excuse me, sir; excuse me, ma'am', while I followed directly behind him. Pat Brand stood signing cassette tapes as we approached.

'Ma'am, God he done make a *big* mistake. How come yoh ain't been born'd black?' Jimmy asked, laying on the accent thick as peanut butter.

Pat Brand looked up, clearly delighted. She stood on tiptoe and grabbed Jimmy around the neck, who obligingly lowered his head sufficiently for her to give him a big kiss. 'That's got to be the greatest compliment I've ever had!' she said, gushing at the bastard.

'I've waited nearly thirty years to do that!' I exclaimed.

'Ma'am, allow me da pleasure of intro-du-cing Brother Fish,' Jimmy said, laughing.

'Brother Fish?'

'Jack McKenzie. I fell in love with you in 1945 at Puckapunyal,' I explained.

'Dat God's truth, ma'am. Brother Fish, he done tol' me 'bout yoh in da POW camp in North Korea.'

That really got us all going. She was now Pat Thompson, had married some lucky bugger after the war – kids, the whole works. She was only just making a comeback, playing small gigs like this to break herself back in for the big city venues, she said. We talked for a while but then the band started coming back and she excused herself. 'Better get back to work. Will I see you afterwards?'

She sang a couple of numbers, and as far as I was concerned she'd lost none of her former glorious voice. She was in the middle of a song when I could contain myself no longer, and out came the harmonica.

*'Frankie and Johnny were lovers*
*Oh Lordy how they could love*
*Swore they'd be true to each other*
*Just as true as stars above . . .'*

Pat invited me to sit in with the band, and over the next hour I swapped solos with the beautifully inventive trumpet player. I could see the band didn't mind – in fact, from their looks of appreciation from time to time I reckon they quite liked the addition to the music. I wasn't trying to show off – I was just another muso, adding my small contribution to the jazz. Afterwards the bass player, who also had a heart-melting voice, asked me if I'd like to join the band. Nice compliment.

After the gig we had a few drinks and talked for an hour. When the time came for Pat to leave I wasn't game to kiss her. Stupid, I know, but for nearly thirty years of my life too much anticipation and imagination had gone into the very thought of kissing her, thoughts that often extended well beyond the kissing stage. Furthermore, I felt, if only in my mind, that I'd be being unfaithful to Wendy. But she came over, put her arms around me and planted a kiss on my lips. 'Thanks for hanging in, Jacko,' she whispered. I didn't know if she meant playing with the band or if she was referring to the years I'd spent dreaming about her. It wasn't a passionate kiss, but it completed something – put something inside me to rest. What's more, I reckoned she'd blown away any hint of 'Jacko's sadness'.

Back at the pub we sat on the verandah until well after the bar had closed. The place was silent, and the surf rolling in no longer worried me. Even the pale sliver of moon that now hung overhead seemed to be appropriate, as if something old had ended to make way for something new. I know I'm sounding mawkish, and God knows I love Wendy with every bone in my body, but Pat Brand's name had been invisibly tattooed upon my heart for so long that a single chaste but lovely kiss was, somehow, the perfect resolution.

Jimmy, reading my thoughts, said, 'Dat's good, Brother Fish. What happen tonight, it good.' Jimmy's 'dis and dat' vernacular had softened over the years, but he slipped right back into it when he was relaxed, or when he was fooling around or courting some lady.

'Yeah. Who'd have thought, after all these years?' I replied.

Jimmy was silent for a while, then he said, 'The Countess's daughter, she forty-two years old.'

'What made you suddenly think of that?' I asked.

'It ain't *suddenly*, Brother Fish. Sometimes I think of that little girl, she don't know who is her mama, or her daddy – she jus' like me. She don't have no love when she been growing up. What happen to her? Is she alive? Has she evah had good joss? Did Big Boss Yu, he listen to da great shaman an' done treat her right? Man, sometimes I lay in mah bed an' it done drive me crazy. I only know'd about it twenty years – Countess, she been concerning herself crazy foh forty-three years, man!'

'Well then, let's go and find her,' I announced, as if it was somehow the simplest thing in the world to do. I don't know how such a bloody stupid notion came to me, or why – perhaps it had something to do with meeting Pat Brand after so long, which was ridiculous, of course. If I'd wanted to meet her desperately enough, it wouldn't have been that difficult to have done so years ago. Whereas finding Nicole's daughter didn't fall within the realms of possibility. How many people in Hong Kong? A million? More? In Taiwan? Four million? It was one of those things you say but later would give anything to take back.

There was a silence and I desperately wanted to say, 'Stupid idea, of course', but the words didn't come.

Instead, Jimmy said, 'Thank you, Brother Fish.' So that was that. I knew from long experience that once Jimmy had decided to do something there was no turning back. We went to bed soon after and it took a fair while for me to fall asleep, my mind racing over how we were going to tell Nicole.

In the morning we had a leisurely breakfast before seeing the local lawyer named Don Pertano, who was handling the silent auction for the abalone licence. He was grossly overweight and of a rubicund complexion with a black pencil moustache that seemed at odds with his large frame. He kept us waiting half an hour despite the fact that we had an appointment and there appeared to be no one in his office. Even then the Ogoya Seafood Company was big time in the fishing industry, and I guess the chip on his shoulder had been exposed. When we were finally ushered into his office it wasn't hard to tell what he was thinking from the way he looked at Jimmy. It also wasn't hard for Jimmy to tell what *I* was thinking, either: *We don't do business with this bloke*. He told us what the last bid was, which was way over the top, and I asked for the name of the bidder, the usual practice to ensure that we were not being gazumped. He refused to answer. 'Private bidder – bloke doesn't want his name mentioned.'

'We'll be off, then,' I said, not arguing, and Jimmy and I both rose to leave. Normally I'd have given him a serve, but the trip to secure the licence suddenly wasn't important any longer.

'Wait a mo!' he called, plainly surprised. But as far as I was concerned it was all over red rover. We had lunch at Le Marlin Café, where they played a cassette tape of Pat Brand singing, and we had a salad and cold roast beef, cray being the specialty of the day.

Halfway through lunch a bloke who looked to be in his mid-fifties walked into the restaurant. It only took a second to know he was a fisherman: Sunday best, light-coloured sports jacket with his yellow shirt turned over the lapel, chocolate-brown pants, slightly scuffed cheap brown shoes, hair cut short and combed in a fifties quiff stuck down with Brylcreem, skin the usual mottled patchwork of sun spots. We had a hundred deadset replicas of him on the island and he could have been Alf. If I hadn't learned how to pull things together a bit with the right haircut and gear, I'd be in the same parade.

He came over to our table and introduced himself. 'Doug Twentyman. Mr McKenzie, could I have a word?'

'It's Jacko,' I said, extending my hand. I indicated Jimmy. 'And this is my partner, Jimmy.'

'How yoh been?' Jimmy said, standing up to shake his hand.

'Take a seat.' I gestured to a vacant chair. 'Twentyman – that's an old fishing family round these parts, isn't it?'

'Four generations, man and boy. Me grandson'll be the fifth.' He grinned. 'If he turns out to be as big a mug as his dad and his grandpa.'

'Beer, or a glass of wine, Doug?'

'Yeah, beer'd be nice,' he replied.

We chatted while the waitress went to get the beer – the usual stuff, weather, boats, the fishing season. The beer came. 'Cheers.' We raised our wineglasses, Doug his beer. 'What can we do for you, Doug?' I asked, now that the formalities were over.

'It's about the ab licence with Don Pertano,' he said.

'We're out of there, Doug,' I replied. 'He may be your lawyer, but he couldn't lie straight in bed.'

'Yeah, Safcol bloke come in yesterday, same thing.'

'Same thing?'

'Walked out, got in his car and drove off back to Eden, tyres spinnin'.'

'So what are you saying, Doug?'

'The flamin' lawyer. He don't know nothin' about fishing . . . fishermen.'

'Why are you selling? Didn't you say you had a son in the game?'

'Smashed the ute, broke his leg. I'm too old to dive – asthma.' Like most fishermen, he was a man of few words.

'Broken legs get better.'

'Yeah, right, but we can't fish 'til it do. We can't use all our quota units.' Then he added the real reason. 'They say the ab licence price is gunna fall, can't keep goin' up.'

'Does your son like fishing?'

'It's all we know, mate.'

'So you'll take the twenty grand or so and do what?'

'Dunno – maybe buy a bit of a dairy farm.'

'Know anything about cows?'

He grinned. 'If they didn't have horns I wouldn't know the arse end from the head until it mooed or farted. But we're grafters – we'll learn.'

We'd seen it all so many times before – three generations of a fishing family scratching their arse in the hope of finding the Christmas-pudding sixpence. The abalone licence was the first opportunity, and probably the last, they'd ever had to make a buck. But they panicked over the imagined possibility of the bottom falling out of abalone, like everything else always does for fishermen. Along comes the smart-arse lawyer or con man: 'Sell, mate, it can't last. Give me ten per cent and I'll do the deal for you, no problems.' What was on offer was more than they'd ever see again in their lives.

'What's Pertano on – ten per cent?'

'Nah, fifteen.'

'Did you sign a contract?'

'Yeah.' He pulled a contract out of the inside breast pocket of his coat, and handed it to me. I read through it quickly. Thank Christ there are still some stupid lawyers around – the contract stipulated that the licence alone was for sale, and made no mention of the quota units. The licence was worthless without them. Admittedly it was a technical point, but a good lawyer would make mincemeat of a careless operator like Pertano. He didn't know the fishing industry, which was pretty unusual, Bermagui being a fishing town.

'How long's this Pertano bloke been in town?' I asked Doug Twentyman.

'New. Come in about two months ago. Says he was in Melbourne.'

I pushed my chair back and ordered another beer for Doug Twentyman. 'Okay, Doug, here are your options. Sell the licence and your quota units and go dairy farming – it's only slightly more risky as an industry than fishing. Don't sell your licence and keep the number of quota units your son can handle himself when he can dive again, but sell the rest. Safcol will buy them, or we will.'

'Mate, what if the abs go bottom up?' he asked again.

'The abalone industry won't – there are a few million Japs who'll crawl over broken glass to get the stuff, and we haven't even started with the Chinese. Your abalone licence and quota units are going to increase enormously in value – if you hang on long enough you could end up a millionaire.'

'So, what do I do?' he asked, looking confused.

It's no wonder these poor bastards get taken for a ride. They're ripe for the plucking. 'Mate, you've got to make your own decisions. Go home and talk to your son.'

'Nah, he'll go along with me.' Then he asked, 'Jacko, will *you* buy the licence?'

'No, keep the licence and half the quota units – that's your superannuation,' I answered, but could see he didn't know what that was. 'That's what will take care of your old age. Sell the other half to us, or to anyone else if you have to. But if you don't need the money, keep the lot – the price of an abalone licence is *not* going to go down.'

'What about my son's leg? It's broke bad, and he can't fish for a year.'

I was trying not to become impatient. 'We're bringing a boat up here with divers. Your son can come on the payroll as a deckie until he can dive again. That way we'll be more or less within the law and we'll take a small percentage of your quota for the diving operation and buy the rest from him at normal prices. When he can dive again you can make up your own mind what you want to do with your quota units.'

'What about him, the lawyer bloke?'

'Withdraw the sale. If you want to sell some of your quota units in twelve months we'll buy them from you at the going price at the time.'

'He reckons he's got expenses over and above.'

'What, Pertano? Greedy bastard. Tell him to sue you. By the time it gets to court your son will be making plenty and you can settle out of court. When that time comes, give me a call.'

'Do yiz want a contract?'

'Later maybe, when you decide what you're going to do. In the meantime, let's shake hands on the deal.'

After he'd gone, Jimmy laughed. 'Why you gone do dat, Brother Fish? Twenny grand yoh got da whole caboodle!'

'Mate, I kept seeing Alf. My dad died when he was around Doug's age, leaving us without a brass razoo to our name. He'd worked like a dog all his life and had nothing to show for it. The middle men, the fish merchants in Melbourne, were all driving around in Chevvies and Packards and living in mansions and we could barely put food on the table. Gloria had to take in washing. We're the bloody middle men now and I've got a house on the island big enough to turn into a rest home for the elderly. It's too late for Alf, but it's time to look after blokes like Doug Twentyman and his family. The poor bugger even looks a bit like my dad.'

Jimmy smiled. 'Dat good. Anyhow, we gonna do jus' fine wid his abalone quota units.'

On the plane back to the island we told Wendy the plan to try and find the Countess's daughter. At first she wasn't all that enthusiastic about the idea. Let sleeping dogs lie, blah, blah, blah – that sort of argument. But Jimmy got to work on her.

'Wendy, yoh gotta see it from two direction – da chile and da mama. Da chile, she want to know who is her mama. Da mama, she want to know how her chile she doin' in life. She can't say dat to no one, but what she thinkin', every day of her life, is dat she is guilty.' Then he clinched it, perhaps a bit unfairly, by saying, 'Don't one day pass when I don't think somewhere in America der a black lady who my mama. How she doin'? She lookin' in trash cans or she doin' okay?'

The three of us chose an invitation to afternoon tea at Nicole's cottage to talk to her about the prospect of exporting abalone to China via Hong Kong. Seated in the garden, she listened carefully as I outlined the potential of the Chinese market, first having done all the sums and worked out the details. Like everything we put to her, I knew she'd think about it before venturing an opinion.

'We'd be dealing with the Triads,' she said at last. 'They control most, if not all, of the fish imports to Asia, with the exception of Japan.'

I was ready for this. 'As you know it's the same in Japan, where we're already dealing with the agents of Yoshio Kodama, the godfather of the Yakuza. It's either working with them or forfeiting business with the Japanese.' I shrugged, trying unsuccessfully to look matter of fact. 'I guess it's the same with the Chinese. We'd need your expertise – it's not something Jimmy and I could handle on our own,' I said.

A silence followed that seemed to last about ten years. 'Jack, I'm sixty-seven years old and I woke this morning, as I do every morning of my life, with a knot of fear in the pit of my stomach. It's always the same waking thought – *today they are going to come for me*. I'm not even sure who *they* are. The past? Big Boss Yu? The CIA? The Triads? For goodness sake, Big Boss Yu would be in his mid-eighties by now, if he's not dead. Whatever happened with the Triads is long past. Even Smallpox "Million Dollar" Yang would be in his late-seventies. I tell myself I have nothing to fear from the Americans. The trumped-up evidence against me would have been long since lost in the Chinese court system, and besides, my case wasn't ever within American jurisdiction. So why the deeply ingrained fear of being found? When I came to Australia all I wanted to do was to find a safe place to hide. I looked on the map and saw Queen Island, a speck of a place in the middle of Bass Strait. I've never been able to shake the original fear. Ridiculous, I admit, emotional nonsense to be sure, but it all amounts to terror at the prospect of ever going back to find my daughter.'

As usual, Nicole had cut through the preliminaries and gone straight to the heart of the matter, realising that finding her daughter was behind the so-called business proposition to export abalone to the Chinese. I could see Jimmy was about to say something, but she continued. 'If I'm being honest with myself, it's the fear of what I might discover. Several times in the past I've almost summoned up the courage to leave the emotional safety of the island to try to find her. But I always end up making excuses. I tell myself I don't even know her name. If she survived she'd be long past wanting to know who her mother was. She probably doesn't even speak English. She would bitterly resent me. She would have a life of her own that I'd only disrupt, without adding anything to it. I've convinced myself we would have absolutely nothing in common.' She paused, visibly distressed, then said quietly, 'Or I'd discover she is dead and died in a horrible way. Or worse, she is a prostitute or living in abject poverty. But, in the end, it all boils down to my own innate cowardice.'

'Countess, she gonna want to know who is her mama jus' the same I want to know who is my mama. That don't evah go away. That a hunger inside yo' heart. I ain't never gonna find my mama to sat-is-fy my hungry heart, but you can try to find yo' daughter.' He paused and looked at her almost angrily, and then demanded, 'Yoh gonna try to do that, or yo' gonna wake every mornin' 'til yoh die, like yoh jus' said?'

By not comforting or reassuring her but by taking her daughter's point of view, Jimmy had hit the jackpot – it was precisely the right aggressive approach. Nicole looked at Jimmy, then with her eyes downcast she whispered, 'Yes.' That was all. Just the one little word, but it had taken forty-two years to say.

She rose from her wicker chair. 'I shan't be long,' she said quietly, visibly upset, and disappeared into the cottage. We looked at each other. 'Well done, mate,' I said quietly to Jimmy.

'She's terribly upset,' Wendy cried. 'I must go in to comfort her!'

'No! Leave her be,' Jimmy said firmly. 'Dis thing she gotta cry out alone.'

Wendy sat down reluctantly, and for a moment I thought to encourage her to go in after the Countess. But then I realised Jimmy wasn't being bossy. In order to say what he'd said, he'd had to reveal a sadness and longing within himself I'd never seen before. He wasn't being harsh – instead he was being sensitive to Nicole's feelings.

She appeared half an hour later and we could see she'd tried to conceal the effects of her tears by applying a little make-up. She carried a wooden box about twelve inches long, four inches deep and six inches wide, and placed it on the table among the afternoon-tea clutter. It was made of a light-coloured wood with the head of a dragon carved into the lid. It was the first time we'd ever seen the dragon box.

'Open it, Jack,' she instructed, and I did as she asked. Inside, it was lined with red satin, upon which a thick blonde plait lay, running the length of the box and then almost all the way back again. It was nearly two feet long and looked as if it had been washed and brushed only moments before to a lovely sheen. Jimmy and Wendy rose to stand behind my chair. Nicole lifted the plait from the box. 'I washed and brushed it and then replaited it only a week ago. I do so from time to time, though I can't imagine why – I always end up crying my eyes out.' Where the plait had lain was a small folded card with the top section of a broken seal of red sealing wax resting on the edge and at the centre of the top fold.

'May I?' I asked, while Wendy held the magnificent plait of hair. Nicole nodded and I lifted the card out and opened it to see a line of Chinese characters across the centre.

時来風送滕王閣

I knew, of course, what they said: '*The good joss will return in one generation.*' 'Will we be taking the dragon box back to Hong Kong with us?' I asked.

Nicole smiled. 'I feel rather foolish saying this, but I'd feel safer if we did. If ever we can return it, I think that might mean something to me.'

At Kai Tak Airport we were met by a chauffeur driving a Rolls Royce and taken to the Mandarin on Hong Kong Island, at the time a pleasing blend of modern luxury and traditional elegance. We each had a suite that came with its own butler and maid. Even though we were doing pretty well and money was no longer a problem, I remember feeling a little out of place. You never quite forget where you come from, and shaking the poor boy out of your head isn't all that easy to do.

When we arrived at our suite the butler asked if he could unpack our suitcases. After freshening up following the long flight I came out of one of the two bathrooms (Wendy had her own) to find my shoes had been polished, my slacks ironed and the creases ironed out of a recently unpacked shirt. The shirt, socks and underpants I had been wearing had been taken away to be laundered, and a new set lay neatly folded on the bed with a shoehorn, for godsake, placed beside my socks.

We all travelled for Ogoya a fair bit and, now that we could afford it, stayed in good pubs wherever we found ourselves in the world. But the Mandarin was something else. Nicole claimed that although the hotel was comparatively modern, its service felt very similar to that of the Cathay Hotel Sir Victor had built in Shanghai, and she felt very much at home. She was soon chatting away in Cantonese with all the staff and didn't look a bit frightened now she was here, although Wendy, who'd sat beside her on the plane, said she'd been rather quiet. In a way, considering what had taken place the last time she'd been in Hong Kong, so far this was somewhat of a triumphant return.

It wasn't going to be too difficult to get to the local fish importers, as the Australian Trade Commission official had set us up with several appointments. The problem was going to be getting to the right Triad family as part of our other mission to find Nicole's daughter. It wasn't as if we could simply pick up the telephone directory and look up Yu Ya-ching. There might be a hundred such names, but Big Boss Yu's would not be among them. There was only one way to contact a Triad boss, and a rather frightening one at that. If we could get a message to him it would have to be delivered by unseen hand, and if a meeting was arranged it would be at a place and time nominated by the recipient.

We'd had two photographs taken of the dragon box, one showing the carved dragon's head and another showing the open box with the plait of hair inside. A separate photograph captured the original note with the calligraphy. Nicole purchased some bright-yellow parchment and had one sheet fashioned into an envelope of sufficient size to take her message and the three photographs. She'd had a chop made – that is, a seal – from a small block of polished granite about half the width and slightly taller than a matchbox, with one end containing the carved seal. Its design was a replica of a simple plait lying within a circle, cut into the granite so that when hot-waxed and stamped the design showed in relief.

With a message as confidential as this Nicole dared not take the contents of the letter to a calligrapher, and knew she needed to write it with her own hand and that this must be apparent to the receiver. She spent almost three days composing and preparing the note and used up a couple of dozen sheets of parchment in the process, burning each of her mistakes in the bathroom basin and washing the remains down the drain.

The message had to be carefully thought out so that it contained not the slightest threat and, at the same time, made it worthwhile for the recipient to respond. This was not an easy task – deception is the mainstay of the Triad secret society, and a message correctly phrased requires a deep knowledge of the culture of the brotherhood. Even Nicole was not familiar with this secret protocol, so she simply had to use the language of respect familiar to the Chinese in the context of such a letter. It was her very lack of deception that she was counting on. Her message was therefore simple, direct and unique.

*My Lord, may the recipient of this message be blessed with many sons to honour and magnify his name. May he be blessed with a long and illustrious life, his luck remain golden and his clan prosper above all others. If the Lord Yu Ya-ching has not departed to take his place in the palace of his forefathers then this message is intended for his eyes alone. If by the grace of all Gods he now resides in the*

*Western Heaven, then this dispatch is addressed with the highest respect to his eldest living son or he who wears the robes of dragonhead.*

*The reader does me great honour and receives my humble gratitude for deigning to receive it. I am known by the name Lily No Gin, and it has fallen upon my unworthy shoulders to return dutifully the dragon box according to the two sacred prophecies:*

*'It is good for now but it will sail away across the seas and return again later to his dragonhead.'*

*'The good joss will return in one generation.'*

*Destiny also allows me to humbly offer great good fortune to the esteemed family of Yu Ya-ching of far greater magnitude than that of the propitious venture of Double Golden Boy raisins.*

*In return I ask only moments of your precious time, and to be allowed one question. May all Gods bear witness that the information I seek can in no way compromise or disturb the peaceful virtues of the clan Ching, but only enhance its immortal name.*

*I swear upon the name of my lineage that this message will remain only between the sender and the receiver. I will come to the place, and at the time, of your choosing to seal this covenant for all time.*

*I may be contacted at the Mandarin Hotel by the name Miss Nicole Lenoir-Jourdan.*

*Lily No Gin*

The next challenge was to deliver the message by 'unseen hand'. This was done by attempting to find an establishment frequented by Big Boss Yu, or his family, or one that was popular with his white paper fan or the golden sash, his Triad general. We had nothing to go on except that, status being important, a Triad boss would need to be seen in the most exclusive and expensive public venues. As wealthy Chinese invariably eat out, the logical choice was a restaurant. We made several inquiries about the names of the most exclusive and expensive restaurants in Hong Kong under the pretence of taking a wealthy, conservative Chinese businessman to dinner. We finally selected the Golden Phoenix, a millionaires' 'club' with a restaurant appropriately named Great Shanghai. We were told that, given two days' notice, it would serve any dish available in China. Some years later when we travelled frequently to Hong Kong on business, we discovered that in the restaurant's private dining room 'forbidden species' were served at a banquet if the diners were of sufficient importance and the host was known to the establishment. Furthermore, far from forbidden love was available for the after-dinner gratification of guests from Hong Kong's most beautiful, accomplished and expensive escorts.

Our dinner at the Great Shanghai was a splendid experience at which Nicole selected all the dishes and was plainly to be seen as the hostess. At the conclusion of our meal it was the Countess who paid and left a gratuity for the maître d that if rolled into a bundle would have choked the proverbial horse. She also ordered a bottle of 100-year-old Napoleon cognac. We waited in the reception area while, armed with the brandy, she asked to see the maître d privately.

She returned in a surprisingly short time and, while we said nothing in the taxi back to the hotel, once back in her suite we wanted to know what had happened. Her answer was disappointing. 'He didn't even glance at the name on the envelope. Its colour may have alerted him, for he simply took it from me, together with the brandy, and bowed. Not a word was exchanged between us.'

It was now a question of hope. As an evening out to dinner it had proved to be the most expensive meal for four people for which the company had ever paid, and I think it probably still holds the record.

Suddenly we were all scared. If there *was* a response to the yellow envelope Nicole would be on her own. Up to this point the mission had involved all of us. I dared not think about what might happen, and the worst part was that we wouldn't be able to do anything to protect her. If she was summoned and never returned, what then? We'd go to the police, but whether or not they'd be able to do anything was another matter. Wendy started to get cold feet and I can't say I was feeling all that good myself about the possible outcome.

Five days passed and no message came, and we'd retired to bed that night beginning to doubt anything would come from our efforts. Our talk at dinner shifted to our appointments with fish importers. Then at seven a.m. the following morning, apparently the phone in Nicole's suite rang. She awoke and answered it, still confused from her fitful sleep but somehow knowing this wasn't her wake-up call. She'd been unable to sleep, feeling acutely the disappointment of what was increasingly looking to be a failed mission. She knew that this was her last and only chance to find her daughter – if this door closed it would remain so forever. Finally, in desperation, she'd taken a sleeping pill in the early hours of the morning, and her head now felt as though it was filled with cotton wool. 'Hello?' she said sleepily.

'The bonesetter's shop at the gates of Ling Nam, today at twelve . . . lunchtime. Bring the box.' She was momentarily dumbstruck. '*Waieee!*' the voice barked, demanding a response.

'Yes, yes – today, twelve o'clock, the gate of the walled city. I understand. Thank you,' she replied in Cantonese.

There followed a moment's pause, then, 'You take taxi. No own driver. You come alone . . . bring the box.'

The fact that the messenger had twice asked for the dragon box filled her with hope – he had obviously been told to stress its importance. She was too overwhelmed to stay in the hotel, so she dressed hurriedly without putting on any make-up, and then scribbled a note and left it at the front desk, instructing the desk clerk to deliver it to me at breakfast. It simply said that she'd heard from 'our fish contacts' and that while she might be back by mid-morning, not to expect her until mid- or even late afternoon.

She later explained she'd had an urgent need to be alone and that, given the chosen venue of the meeting, she'd realised she would need to dress differently or she would be highly conspicuous in the walled city. She wore a simple cotton dress she could discard and went shopping, taking the dragon box with her in a roughly woven shoulder bag she'd purchased on our first day in Hong Kong, buying one for Wendy as well. The bag had a substantial flap secured with a wooden toggle and, while not very elegant, she'd explained how it stopped *larn jai*, street boys ('who can steal the gold from your teeth while you're speaking'), from snatching their handbags. She'd demonstrated how it was slung around the shoulder in such a way that no arm would be strong enough to snatch it away.

She left the hotel on foot, immediately finding herself swallowed up in the early-morning press of mainly *amahs* heading for the ladder streets of the Central District. It was seven-thirty a.m., and while this might not seem early in a western city, the Chinese eat late, stay up late and rise late, so the central business areas don't get going properly until mid-morning. Soon Nicole found herself among the mass of pedestrians, the crowd noises mixed with the remorseless screech and whine of Chinese music played over tinny transistor radios. She climbed up a set of steps to a higher level, leaving the throng of jabbering Chinese *gung yun* behind her, and stopped to look over Hong Kong Harbour. She recalled how breathtaking the harbour view had been even to her tortured soul forty-two years ago, coming down from the Peak in the tram on her way to Lantau Island. Back then it had given her hope that she might be successful and be granted an interview with the venerated Wang Po. But now, so many years later, the harbour seemed to have quite the opposite effect – the sky was masked by a dense curtain of cloud, made worse by smoke from the factories of Kwun Tong, behind which a burning sun was already turning the day into a furnace. In the growing heat she was aware of the smells – the food carts in Wan Chai, salt fish from the squatters' camps in North Point and carried on the hot breeze, the reek of Aberdeen. The harbour below her was leaden in appearance, except for a patch across the water at Tsim Sha Tsui, where it gleamed like beaten tin.

She walked on and came to a market of cheap wares, and stopped at a clothes stall. To the surprise of the woman who owned it, she purchased a *sarm foo* – the drab jacket, wide-legged trousers and black canvas slipper-like shoes of a working-class woman. She asked the woman to keep watch while she changed behind the hessian screen that formed part of the stall, then paid the woman and handed her the Australian summer cotton dress she'd been wearing. The woman showed neither surprise nor gratitude, and simply accepted the dress. As Nicole walked away she heard the woman laugh and call out, 'That one's up to no good!'

She had made a wide circle coming from the hotel and now headed back, but as she approached she decided she didn't want to go in. She'd be forced to explain everything to the three of us, when 'everything' was in fact a phone call that lasted no more than a minute. The rest had simply been her emotional turmoil. The terminal for the Star Ferry across to Kowloon was only five minutes' walk from the Mandarin Hotel and she decided to have a late breakfast there – it was now almost nine-thirty and she had been walking for two hours. But when she arrived at the terminal the prospect of breakfast no longer appealed, and she decided to take the ferry across the harbour and wait on the Kowloon side until it was time to take the taxi to the gates of Ling Nam.

On the ferry she bought a mug of scalding tea, which helped settle her stomach and nerves. All morning long a single phrase from a Chinese village song she'd learned as a child in Ah Lai's village had been driving her crazy: 'Bamboo door face bamboo door; wooden door face wooden door'. She remembered it was used to indicate the matching of partners in a marriage – the rich should not stoop to partner with the poor, and the poor should not aspire to partner with the rich. It also referred to racial purity, and served as a folk treatise on social standing and pedigree.

As a White Russian in Shanghai Nicole had always been somewhat intimidated by the rarefied world of the taipans, the upper echelons of big business. Yet she reminded herself that Sir Victor had been among the most powerful of them, and she hadn't felt intimidated in his presence. Big Boss Yu had been the dragonhead and he hadn't frightened her either, except when he'd made her the scapegoat for the opium smuggling operation. If the folk song was indeed a subliminal message from her past, intended to warn her not to attempt to get involved with someone above her station, then it was wrong. She was suddenly angry with herself. The Triads was a secret society of criminals of the worst kind, and while she was frightened by them she told herself she had no reason to feel intimidated. As the chairperson of a fishing empire that was big by any standards, she was a taipan herself. She stamped her foot on the deck in a physical gesture of defiance, spilling some of the hot tea over her trousers, but it drove the silly lyric out of her head.

On the Kowloon side of the harbour she'd found a shop selling expensive silk and bought a sufficient length to wrap the dragon box, and with it a piece of heavy gold cord with a tassel attached to either end. The simple act of wrapping the dragon box, with some help from the proprietor, made it no longer the curse and comfort it had been to the Countess for so long. It signalled that the box was soon to be taken from her, and that this meant a conclusion – although she didn't yet know what this ending might be. She still retained a sense of being Chinese – if not in her blood, it was nevertheless in her heart and a part of her past culture. The return of the box, thus fulfilling the incense master's prophecy, had always accorded in her mind with finding her daughter. Wrapping it finally in the trappings of a fortunate gift, she was wrapping forty-two years of hope into its return. The fact that they'd responded to her offer suggested that Big Boss Yu was still alive or, at the very least, that his family valued the return of the box, and this fuelled her hope of finding her daughter.

She still had an hour and a bit to kill before catching a taxi for the twenty-minute ride to the walled city and she was suddenly ravenous. Not far from where she stood she could see the Peninsula Hotel. In contrast to the Mandarin Hotel's modern deference to the past, the Peninsula Hotel was the opulent past itself, elegant and snobbish, the grand dame of the Far East who welcomed only those who were sufficiently wealthy to pay for her patronage. Now it seemed to beckon, an oasis in the middle of the roiling, jabbering, smelly human struggle around her.

Ignoring the white-uniformed door boy who gawked at her passing, she crossed the lobby to the first-floor elevator to the surprise of several people watching. Perhaps they were thinking that the blue-eyed woman dressed as a peasant was returning late from a fancy-dress party. It was to the credit of the maître d on the mezzanine balcony – probably the most pleasant, expensive place to have breakfast in Asia – that he didn't bat an eyelid and simply escorted her to a table.

At this moment Nicole was about as far from the dirt, sweat and infamy of the walled city as it was possible to be. Ling Nam is often referred to as the dirty footprint of China in the centre of the British colony. All that is vile, brutal or treacherous in the colony is said to emanate from this human cesspool, a walled city withheld by the empress when she had grudgingly and under some duress approved the lease of the Kowloon Peninsula to the British merchants grown rich on the opium trade to China and the subsequent export of tea and silk. Even now it belongs to China and, as a sovereign protectorate, is beyond the reach of British law. Within its verminous and hostile perimeter one is beyond the reach of police protection and said to be even out of the sight of God. It is here that illicit business finds a haven, where every vice and perversion is catered for in the walled city's whorehouses, opium dens and illegal gaming parlours. Triad gangs, illegal immigrants, snake-boat operators, murderers, kidnappers, white slavers and numerous black and devil cult societies, some said to involve human sacrifice, all prosper in Ling Nam, perhaps the toughest and most desperate place on earth.

After a silver-service breakfast of coddled eggs, paper-thin slices of sesame-seed toast and a pot of Earl Grey tea, with slightly less than half an hour to spare, Nicole left the Peninsula, and the liveried commissionaire summoned a cab with a white-gloved hand. The taxi driver glanced in his rear-view mirror as she mentioned her destination, and she was careful to tell him to take her only to the gates and not beyond. Within moments she was headed east along the broad stretch of Prince Edward Road towards Kowloon City.

While she was aware she might never return, she told herself that at least she had finally summoned the courage to try to find her daughter. She was numbed by the prospect of what might lie ahead in the next hour or so, but she knew nothing could change her resolve – there was no turning back. At two minutes to noon the taxi halted a block from the gates of the walled city. She stepped from the cab to be confronted by the last of numerous official warnings they'd passed on the way – a large sign warning the public that entering Ling Nam unescorted and without a permit is done at one's own risk. Once inside the gate, she crossed the swarming street to what could only have been the bonesetter's shop, for a yellow skeleton hung from a beam that stuck out above the entrance to the run-down building. The grimy window was filled with assorted human bones and faded anatomy charts. As she reached the broken curb of the littered sidewalk in front, a tall, emaciated Chinese man stepped from the shop's doorway. He was wearing voluminous shorts cinched around his wasted gut by a leather belt. Heavily veined hairless legs protruded from the shorts, so thin that the veins gave the appearance of thick vines twisting around a yellow sapling. His dirty singlet was rolled up against the mugginess of the day and rested under his chin. His hair was pure Harpo Marx and seemed charged with electricity, which gave him a desperate rather than frightening appearance.

'You come taxi?' he demanded, his voice hoarse with suspicion, peering left then right as half-a-dozen taxis wove through the incessant honking and roar of traffic. It was the unmistakable voice she'd heard earlier on the telephone.

'Yes, I am alone. I came by taxi and I have the box,' she replied, anticipating his next question.

He continued to scowl and, with a gesture that she should follow him, turned and led the way through a labyrinth of dirty shopfronts and putrid-looking dwellings. On they continued through the maze of passages, most no wider than outstretched arms that seemed to be roughly leading into the chaos of the evil-smelling city centre. Her canvas shoes were wet from stepping over open sewers and she was constantly confronted by illegal electrical appendages bunched and strung at head height, many crackling with a warning of danger. Every drain they passed was infested with audacious rats and cowering, scrofulous dogs. Mangy cats jumped from her path.

The centre of the walled city took no more than ten minutes to reach. It consisted of little more than a depressing, greasy, cobbled square lined with a variety of eateries. Dog meat was a feature of every menu, and rows of skinned canine corpses hung from the open shop windows, dripping blood. Her senses had grown immune to the smells and chaos pressing around her, and she simply focused on the dirty rolled singlet below narrow, bony shoulders moving ahead of her. They passed crowded tables, drawing little attention. She was thankful that she had thought to dress as a working woman.

Finally they crossed the square and entered a lane only wide enough to walk single file. It was a place that had never known sunlight and was the first lane they'd entered where there were no people – only overstuffed cardboard boxes filled and spilling over with garbage, and crawling with rats. Deep within the darkened alley the messenger turned, and she saw he was holding a dirty cloth stretched between his sinewy hands. A silent scream rose in her throat as his hands reached for her neck. He was almost close enough for her to bring her knee up into his crotch. Then a sudden roar overwhelmed everything, shaking the walls of the alley, and so loud she was forced to look up at the narrow strip of sky. She saw the silver underbelly of a passenger jet so low she could make out the lines of rivets along it. The messenger was suddenly right up against her and she could smell his foul fish-oil breath. The absurdity of the jet coming in to land had claimed the split second that would have changed everything. Instead of her throat, the filthy cloth wound clumsily over her eyes and she felt the messenger's hand twist her around so that he could knot the cloth at the back of her head.

He was behind her now, urging her forward with sharp prods from his forefinger, clucking his tongue, anxious, she felt, to be rid of her. His hand on her shoulder stopped her. 'Down,' he grunted, warning her of steps to come. His bony fingers pinched her elbow as he guided her downwards, then it was flat going again and they seemed to pass through several doors, each opening and closing behind them until only the soft tread of her canvas shoes could be heard. They passed through yet another door and she noticed the heavy, cloying smell of opium smoke. Then, without warning, her escort pushed roughly past her to open a final door. Speaking in gutter Cantonese, the language of the underling and the thug, she heard him say, 'No driver, only taxi. She has the box. Nobody follow.' She was pushed forward, and the door closed behind her.

Several seconds passed, and then a voice with an American accent said quietly, 'You may remove the blindfold – there is nothing to fear.'

The Countess silently cursed her shaking hands as she snatched at the rag around her head, but it had been tightly knotted and in her panic to remove it her fingers became frantic, plucking at the knots ineffectively.

'Allow me,' the American voice said. She caught a waft of expensive cologne as he untied the dirty rag, and she was suddenly blinking into the shadowy candlelight. A young man moved to stand in front of her and she saw that he wore a white robe. She guessed it concealed a lounge suit as she could see the bulge of a necktie under the collar of the robe, and from its hem protruded perfectly creased trousers and highly polished and expensive shoes.

The young Chinese man with the perfect American accent stepped back to join two other men, one of them seated so she could only see his legs, the remainder of his torso lost in the gloom, while she could barely make out the outline of the standing figure. If asked on some future occasion to describe either man she would have found it quite impossible, whereas the younger man made no attempt to hide his face. He bent down to say something to the seated man, and then stepped forward from the shadows. He had a pleasant-looking face that seemed to her to be without guile. His short hair was brushed back from his brow without the use of pomade, and he wore thinly rimmed spectacles that gave him the overall appearance of a mid-echelon office worker destined perhaps for higher things.

'I must apologise, Miss Lenoir-Jourdan. This is not a pleasant place to come, or to do business, but in this instance it is necessary.'

'I understand, and am grateful for this opportunity to meet you,' she replied quietly. The softly spoken and calm-looking man, who appeared to be in his mid-thirties, gave her confidence.

'Let me introduce myself. I am Sun Lu-ching, Lord Ching's eldest son. Or if you prefer my western name, it is Edward – Eddie Ching. I returned from the States yesterday to conduct this business. It is my father's express wish that the dragon box be accepted by me. He is no longer young but he is present to witness its return.' He turned towards the standing figure in the shadows, and added, 'With him is his white paper fan. In normal parlance you could say he is our lodge secretary, and it is important that he is also in attendance.'

The Countess realised that Eddie Ching must have been born after her escape, and she wondered if Big Boss Yu considered that the kidnapping of her daughter was the reason for his having a son in his fifties. 'I am greatly honoured that *loh yeh* Yu Ya-ching is present. May the contents of the dragon box bring him many grandsons to sit on his venerable knee.' The shadowy seated figure gave the slightest of bows from the waist, but did not speak.

The overwhelming stink of the oppressive cellar made it difficult to breathe. Two branches of half-burned-down candles, the stands holding them buried in spent wax, threw a flickering light over a small altar upon which stood an image of Kuan Kung, the heavily armoured God of War. A thick bunch of joss sticks burned cherry red at his winged feet. Curls of incense smoke rose undisturbed, somewhat obscuring rows of decorated pennants beyond which she could just make out what appeared to be racks of some sort of bladed weapon. To the side of the altar stood a fish-head drum of the kind used in the dragon dance at every Chinese festival.

'Your message was received and as carefully read as it was composed. We congratulate you on your understanding of our ways, and thank you for your considered choice of expression.' Eddie Ching paused. 'We see no reason why, if you bring us a business proposition of significant importance, we would not be interested, providing always that what you want in return does not compromise us. My father has told me of your business acumen. Perhaps you will now tell us what you require from us and then, if we are able to meet your request, what you propose to bring us in return. But first, have you brought the item?'

Nicole slipped the bag from her shoulder, undid the toggle and withdrew the silk-wrapped box. She moved to give it to Eddie Ching but he stepped to the side and pointed to the altar. 'Please, be so kind as to unwrap the box, open it, and place it on the altar.' She suddenly realised that they may have thought the box contained some form of danger and she may be seeking revenge, prepared to sacrifice her own life.

She did as she was told, and Eddie Ching moved to the altar, examined the opened box briefly, then picked it up and carried it into the shadow towards the seated Big Boss Yu, who she suddenly realised was in a wheelchair. She heard a soft cackle as he inspected the plait and, for a fleeting second, glimpsed his black-ringed eyes and white-bearded face, creased in a smile. She had re-lined the box with silk and taken the plait to a hairdresser who had prepared it so that it looked like spun gold on its bed of rich crimson. Eddie Ching returned the dragon box to the altar and closed its lid. 'The Lord Ching is pleased with the return of the box,' he said, then added in a businesslike tone, 'Now, what is your request?'

'It is a simple one, Sun Lu-ching. I wish to know if my daughter is alive and, if so, how I may contact her.'

Eddie Ching smiled. 'We have correctly anticipated your request. But what have you to offer us?'

Nicole was feeling a little more confident – Eddie Ching was a smooth combination of velvet glove and iron fist, something she understood. 'I have to respectfully add that if my request cannot be met we will not enter into a future business arrangement.' She paused, then added softly, 'It is a matter of principle.'

'I understand,' Eddie Ching replied. 'On the other hand, we will not gratify your wishes unless we are impressed with your business proposition. It is less a matter of principle than it is of stubborn pride.'

The Countess realised that he knew about the kidnapping. 'I am in the fishing and wholesale seafood business and am in a position to supply abalone and crayfish to you to give you control of this lucrative market in all of Asia, the exception being Japan.'

'You can guarantee this?' Eddie Ching asked.

'We have sufficient licences and long-term leasing arrangements, as well as the boats and infrastructure, to make you the major Asian supplier for the next twenty years.'

'Consider this business closed and, for the moment, completed in good faith. You do of course understand that if we meet our end of the bargain and you do not substantiate your end, the consequences will be onerous?'

'I have tasted the dish of your clan's wrath and it has poisoned my life,' she replied simply.

Eddie Ching made no attempt to reply, but instead said, 'Please bow three times to our God, Kuan Kung.'

'With permission, may I ask one more question?'

'Of course.'

'What is my daughter's name?'

'Lily – Lily No Gin, the same as yours. My father wished to perpetuate exactly his good joss.'

'Thank you, Mr Ching.'

'The way back is fortunately easier than the way you arrived. I must congratulate you on your intelligence and the initiative you have shown to dress in the manner you have.'

Even in such dire circumstances she was still the old Nicole Lenoir-Jourdan, and Eddie Ching was not going to be allowed to get away with such a comment. 'Do not patronise me, Mr Ching,' she said sharply in English. 'We are potential business partners, each with something to gain. I expect to receive normal business courtesy from your organisation.'

Eddie Ching drew back in surprise, and she heard a cackle of laughter from the shadows. 'I did not intend to offend you, madam,' he apologised, then suddenly smiled. 'I am suitably chastened, and look forward to our business relationship.' Eddie Ching, she decided, had a cool head. He had recognised the courage it took to be assertive under her compromised circumstances. He produced a spotless handkerchief. 'I'm afraid I must blindfold you once again,' he said, apologising. 'I will contact you at your hotel to discuss future business arrangements after I hear that you are satisfied we have kept our side of the bargain.'

He thanked her for coming, and she turned, blindfolded, and bowed in the direction of the wheelchair in the shadows. 'Thank you, Lord Ching,' she said, and was surprised to hear a grunted '*Ho!*' in reply.

Less than ten minutes later Nicole found herself in the back seat of a taxi, threading its way through the traffic along Prince Edward Road towards Kowloon City and the Star Ferry. The driver, who glanced uncertainly into his rear-vision mirror, must have wondered why the strange *gwai mui* dressed as a *gung yun*, a working person, suddenly burst into tears.

Our reunion at the hotel was highly emotional. The three of us had gone down to the lobby directly after lunch and positioned ourselves on a set of chairs directly facing the entrance. It was a few minutes to three o'clock when Nicole finally came through the doors, and we all leapt up simultaneously, shouting out our greeting, oblivious to the fact that we were drawing attention to ourselves.

'Oh, thank God you're back!' Wendy cried, running up and hugging Nicole tearfully, then suddenly drawing back and saying in a surprised voice, 'What on earth are you wearing?'

We all went up to Nicole's suite and waited while she showered and changed. We ordered afternoon tea and, when room service arrived, sat back and got a blow-by-blow account of the day's events. Despite the harrowing experience she'd so recently been through she was ebullient, certain that Eddie Ching would soon arrange for her to meet her daughter.

'What's her name?' I asked.

'Lily No Gin, of course. How incredibly silly of me not to have thought this through – Big Boss Yu was, after all, trying to replicate the good joss he believed I originally brought him.'

'What if she's in the telephone book?' I asked, grinning. Nicole looked at me, astonished, and we all laughed – but it was one of those laughs you'd rather not have. She might have been under our noses all the time. Wendy ran to get the telephone directory and I think we were all relieved to discover that among several variations of Gin, none had either a 'No' preceding it or an 'L' as the first and only initial.

We had another anxious wait to see when Lily No Gin No. 2 would turn up. The Chings had promised to keep their end of the bargain, and Eddie Ching knew the terms: no daughter, no deal. But suddenly I was troubled by another concern: if Lily No Gin No. 2 was dead, or they didn't know where to find her, or she'd been sold into prostitution years ago, what was there to stop them from substituting any mixed-blood female in her forties down on her luck? I imagined that Hong Kong would have dozens, perhaps hundreds, of such women – after all, Caucasian expatriates had been coming and going in Hong Kong for a very long time.

How would the Countess be able to identify her daughter? Her baby had been kidnapped moments after birth, which presented a perfect opportunity to substitute an imposter. She wouldn't need to know anything about her mother – there'd be no hearsay, no shared history to question her on past events, nothing at all. There wasn't a single question Nicole could ask her to verify the fact that the woman the Triads produced was genuinely her daughter. All an imposter would need was a thorough briefing from Eddie Ching about her childhood – any cock'n'bull story would do. How the hell would we know the difference? The Triads were the masters of deceit, and now Eddie Ching would think all his Chinese New Years had come at once.

I mentioned my new-found fears to Wendy when we got back to our suite, and she turned pale. 'Thank you, Jacko – there goes my good night's sleep!' she cried. 'Have you spoken to Jimmy about your concerns?'

'How could I? We all left together.' But then I added, 'I'm not sure I want to. In many ways, finding Nicole's daughter is a substitute for finding his mother. He can't ever hope to know who his mum is – there are no possible leads he can follow. She left him on the doorstep of an orphanage. That's like placing a piece of garbage in the rubbish bin rather than throwing it onto the footpath, because it's the right thing to do.'

'That's not fair, Jacko. His mother may have been desperate at the time – you don't know the circumstances.'

'Of course, but that's the problem – neither does Jimmy. He doesn't know if she was an alcoholic, or a junkie and just didn't care, or, as you say, if she was a good woman in a desperate situation doing the best she could. He can invent anything he likes, but he doesn't *know*, and he knows he never will. Even knowing the worst is better than not knowing at all.'

'So what are you saying? Finding Nicole's daughter is going to help Jimmy?'

'Didn't you hear him on the Cessna flying back from Bermagui, and when we were persuading the Countess to try to find her daughter? I thought I knew every aspect of Jimmy, but I've come to realise that a kid who's never been loved never gets over it. The hurt never goes away. Finding the Countess's daughter is like trying to stop the hurt that's been mounting inside him since he was knee high to a grasshopper. It's not just Nicole he's concerned about – it's also her daughter. Think about it – Jimmy is in exactly the same position as Lily No Gin No. 2. Like him she has no history, no past. I know this probably sounds weird, but by helping to give her back her past he'll somehow share in it.'

'So what are we going to do, Jacko?' Wendy had become distressed and I was sorry I'd brought up the subject.

'Nothing. What *can* we do? Hope it all works out – what else?'

'Oh, Jacko, don't let it be awful. After all she's been through, don't let it turn out badly for her!'

Two days went by and we were all in the foyer waiting for Nicole to come down from her suite so that we could leave for Lantau Island to visit Po Lin, the place where she'd met with Wang Po. We were all excited about seeing the biggest Buddha in Asia, the one erected in his memory and to which the Countess had made a considerable contribution. She was seldom late – punctuality was a part of her character. But it was now twenty minutes beyond the time we'd agreed to depart. Wendy was about to go back upstairs to see what might have happened to delay her, when the lift doors nearest to us opened and she appeared. We all stood, ready to leave, but she signalled with her hand that we should sit down. She smiled nervously as she approached.

'She called, half an hour ago, and will be here in about an hour,' she announced. We all jumped up and surrounded her, offering our enthusiastic support. 'I have to be carrying a single rose.' She looked around, trying to locate the florist shop at one end of the foyer.

'I'll get it,' I said. 'What colour?'

'Oh dear, she didn't say. Any rose will do, I imagine.'

'Wendy, what colour?' I asked.

'White,' she said without hesitation. Of course, the florist had roses of every other colour but white. I later learned that white is the Chinese colour for death and finding a white rose outside of a funeral parlour in Hong Kong is just about impossible. I settled for a yellow rose, the colour of friendship.

Of course there were two immediate questions we were desperate to ask Nicole. Firstly, had the phone call been in Cantonese or English? Secondly, was Lily No Gin No. 2 of mixed blood or Caucasian? Of course, we couldn't ask the second question.

'She speaks perfect English, though with a slight lilt that probably comes from speaking Cantonese,' Nicole replied, answering the first question. Then, with downcast eyes, she voiced our unspoken one. 'I didn't ask her the question you've probably all got in your minds.' She looked up again to face us. 'I decided a long time ago that it really doesn't matter. She is my child, regardless of who her father is.' She paused, then added, 'We didn't speak for long. She sounded very nervous, and I confess I wasn't really in control myself, so she said she'd be over in an hour and a half and we could talk then. I'm afraid the trip to Lantau Island will have to wait, unless, of course, you'd like to go on your own?'

'Countess, we ain't goin' nowhere,' Jimmy said, and then pointed to a group of lounge chairs close by. 'If you want, we can sit over there.'

'Actually, I'd very much appreciate it if you were all with me when I meet her. I must say I feel rather nervous, even tentative.' The moment she said this I knew she, too, was worried about the possibility the woman would be an imposter.

Wendy ordered tea and scones, and the next hour seemed to last forever. We were all trying, in my case unsuccessfully, not to look at the hotel entrance while we made small talk. Then Wendy said, 'For goodness sake, we're all talking polite rubbish. Let's just sit and watch the entrance.' We laughed, because she was right, of course, and suddenly we were chatting like we normally would, so that we were unaware of the approach of the woman who suddenly stood in front of us. As it turned out, she'd entered through one of the hotel's side doors.

'Miss Lenoir-Jourdan?' she asked politely.

We all broke into wide smiles and Jimmy brought his great big hands together and clapped, so that people at nearby tables turned to see what the fuss was about. Thank God for strong Russian genes. Except for her dark hair, which she would have inherited from Sir Victor, the woman standing in front of the Countess was a younger version of herself – the same brilliant blue eyes, an identically shaped nose, just a trifle too long to be called petite, high cheekbones, firm chin and wide brow. She also wore her hair in a bob, not all that different in the way it was cut from Nicole's, who'd been to the hotel hairdresser the previous day. They were unmistakably mother and daughter, and both realised it at almost precisely the same moment and simultaneously burst into tears.

Jimmy and I leapt to our feet but Jimmy got to Lily No Gin No. 2 first and led her gently to his seat next to Nicole. Wendy, too, had risen quickly from her chair and was on her knees beside the weeping Countess with her arm around her, though not offering much comfort as she was weeping herself. Jimmy stood behind Lily No Gin No. 2's chair, not touching her but with his big hands resting on either side of her slim shoulders. He was grinning like an idiot, but then I realised that he was also crying, great tears running silently down his smiling face. I was pretty choked up myself but, as usual, was stuck for the right words. 'What, no embrace?' I asked awkwardly, reaching in three little words a new height in the art of the inappropriate comment.

Both women, perhaps initially too overcome or shy to fall into each other's arms, now rose and embraced, and a torrent of further tears followed. For once in my life I'd got it right. I tried to imagine what it must be like to know absolutely nothing about your mother. Lily later explained that she had never been told a single thing about Nicole. As a small child she'd asked Ah Yuk, the *amah* given the responsibility of raising her, where she'd come from. She was told the highly improbable story that shortly after the Japanese attack on Shanghai in 1932 she'd been found newborn and naked in a horse stall at the Kiangwan racecourse.

It was at Kiangwan racecourse that the main Chinese defences had been dug in, and it had borne the brunt of the Japanese artillery attack in 1932. Most of the young soldiers defending it had been killed, and in the process the Japanese guns had demolished the racecourse and the stables behind it, killing all the horses but for one pure-white mare in the only stall miraculously left standing. Trapped in the stable and surrounded by artillery fire, the mare had been driven crazy with fright and the interior surfaces of the stable had run red, the mare's whiteness turned crimson from her own blood. Lily was told that people who came to bury the dead said that the horse's great heart could be seen exposed where its flesh had been ripped from its chest in its desperate attempts to break out. Yet the newborn child found naked at the crazed animal's feet was unharmed. The mewling infant and the terrified horse had been the only survivors among the tens of thousands of Chinese killed when every house in the village surrounding the racecourse was razed to the ground. Big Boss Yu was the owner of the mare and so, according to the story, he'd taken the matter of the 'horse child' to a famous soothsayer, who concluded the infant had sprung from the mare's exposed heart. The soothsayer told him that the horse's child was not a *gwai mui*, but was white-skinned with the round eyes of a horse because the mare had been pure white in colour. He'd also told Big Boss Yu that the horse's child was a gift from the Gods and would bring him great good fortune. And so Big Boss Yu had taken the white-skinned, round-eyed infant into his esteemed household.

When things had settled down a bit in the hotel foyer, Jimmy proposed lunch on the balcony. It was here that Lily suddenly said, 'Oh dear, I was so excited I quite forgot to show you my proof.'

Jimmy laughed. 'Ain't no better proof dan your lovely face, Lily. Der ain't no mistakin' your mama is sittin' der beside you.'

Lily No Gin No. 2 dipped into her handbag. 'I was given this by Yu Ya-ching when I won my scholarship to university. "It belonged to your mother," was all he said.' From her handbag she produced a single pearl earring.

'Oh my goodness!' Nicole exclaimed and seemed quite overcome, her hands clutched to her breast. When she recovered sufficiently she said, 'You shall have the other one with my love, my darling child.'

Over lunch Lily told us the story of the white mare and how she'd acquired her Chinese name, then laughingly added, 'I wonder if you'd mind very much calling me Whisky?' We all paused and waited for an explanation – it was, after all, a very peculiar nickname. 'At school, with a surname like "No Gin" and the Chinese name *Baht Mar*, which means "white horse", the name of a famous brand of scotch, it was almost inevitable that I became Whisky No Gin.' Apart from the Countess, we all laughed at this simple explanation.

'Oh, you poor darling,' she exclaimed. 'Children do so hate that sort of thing.'

'Well, yes, of course I was teased a great deal at school. But as I grew older I became accustomed to it, and now, well, it's my name, and I'm simply known to my patients as Dr Whisky.'

'That a good name!' Jimmy exclaimed. 'Dr Whisky? It got *panache*.' I could see Jimmy was greatly taken with Whisky No Gin.

It was the first time that 'Whisky No Gin', or plain 'Whisky', or even 'Dr Whisky', as she would variously become known to us, mentioned that she was a doctor of medicine. Over lunch she told us briefly about her life. Of course, it has taken a long time and many trips to Hong Kong to get the whole story, particularly of her childhood. I hope to encourage her to write it down, as it is a remarkable story of survival and determination that deserves to be told. But at our first lunch together, for our benefit she briefly outlined the forty-two years of her life.

She had spent her first five years in the compound of Big Boss Yu, whom she seldom saw and who, as far as she could recall, never spoke to her. In 1937, with the certain invasion of the Japanese, they left for Taiwan and then, after the war, did not return to Shanghai but went instead to Hong Kong. Whisky attended school in Taipei, where Big Boss Yu insisted she learn English. She must have been a bright child because at the age of thirteen, when they'd arrived in Hong Kong, she sat for a scholarship to a private girls' school attended by both expatriate children and the wealthy Chinese. The gain of face Big Boss Yu had received from this success, along with Wang Po's injunction to give her all the privileges of a male child, had overcome his predisposition not to educate her beyond primary school. She eventually became head prefect and the captain of the school lacrosse and hockey teams, and when she sat for her 'O' levels won a scholarship to the University of Hong Kong to study medicine.

I don't know why we all assumed she was single – perhaps because we'd always thought of her in the singular. But when she told us she was married to an Englishman named John Forsythe who worked for Jardine Matheson as an accountant, and had a twenty-year-old son, Mark, who was in his second year of medicine, I think it came as a bit of a surprise. We learned that her husband was a man of sixty-two and on the edge of retirement, and of course we eventually met him and Mark. Nicole later found out that her daughter's marriage had been a difficult one, although Whisky didn't pretend that her husband was entirely to blame.

'When one has experienced my sort of background one's emotions are always a contradiction,' she explained to her mother some years later. 'You want passionately to be loved, but don't know how to reciprocate. Loving is a learning process and I'd never had any tuition in the subject. John comes from a rigid, upper-middle-class English family, and with his father in the military he spent most of his childhood at boarding school, so he is almost as emotionally crippled as I am. While Mark has changed that somewhat for me, his father is perhaps too set in his ways to change and a mother's love for a child isn't transferable to her husband.'

It was sad to think that this lovely woman, like her mother, had lived such a sad life. That's the problem with real life – it seldom turns out the way you want it to. Mark turned out to be a very nice young bloke, and loved to spend his holidays on the island – mostly out on the fishing boats. With such a busy practice, and her dedicated work with the poor, unfortunately Whisky seldom found the time to visit, although Nicole grew to love her dearly and, in the end, mother and daughter became very close.

The business arrangement with Eddie Ching who, after returning to America for a year, returned to Hong Kong after the death of Big Boss Yu two days after his eighty-ninth birthday, prospered. At seventy the Countess retired and spent the next seven years travelling to and from Hong Kong to see Whisky and her grandson and to supervise the building of the Lily No Gin Children's Hospital in the New Territories to take care of the needs of the poor. The No Gin Trust set up by her is endowed with ten million US dollars and, along with Whisky, who runs the hospital, and Mark, a paediatrician, Nicole presides over the hospital board. John Forsythe died of a heart attack last year and Whisky now spends most of her time working in the emergency ward of the hospital, often not returning home for three or four days at a time. At fifty-four she is no longer a spring chicken, but Jimmy, who sees a lot of her, says she's a driven woman and sometimes he has to drive over to the hospital and haul her out for a decent meal.

Jimmy and Whisky have grown very close since John Forsythe's death, and I know he's very fond of her. For once the charismatic James Pentecost Oldcorn has hit a brick wall with the opposite gender. Whisky, in the parlance of today's pop psychology, is too damaged for a relationship, and has put all her emotions into getting to know and love her mother, and into the care of neglected, disadvantaged and sick children. As she says, in her pragmatic medical way, 'I understand the sick children with whom I work. Superficially they suffer from the diseases of neglect, but psychologically I share with them the symptoms of emotional neglect. I don't suppose I can change now.' I always think this a great pity because Jimmy also suffers from the same symptoms – if anyone can understand Whisky, Jimmy is the man. But there you go. I guess when the heart is emotionally damaged in childhood it becomes the hardest of human afflictions to cure as an adult.

Jimmy is the chairman of the No Gin Trust and Eddie Ching is also a member of the Trust and the hospital board. His family recently donated four million US dollars to the establishment of a new research complex under the joint control of the University of Hong Kong and the hospital, to be named the Yu Ya-ching Children's Diseases Research Centre.

I explained earlier how we were forced to work with the Triads and the Japanese Yakuza if we hoped to export abalone, the fish-importing industry in Asia being totally in their control, however, you may wonder why Nicole would appoint Eddie Ching to the hospital board and also make him a member of her trust fund. He is trusted and even respected in Hong Kong business circles, where he is known as a charismatic and highly regarded entrepreneur, just as his father once was in Shanghai. All I can use in Nicole's defence are her own words: '*A poor parent is not fussy where the help to save the life of their child comes from, as long as it's available.*' China simply doesn't work the same way as the West, as Jimmy and I discovered so long ago as prisoners of war.

Jimmy took over working with Eddie Ching when Nicole retired, and for the past ten years has spent a great deal of time in Hong Kong, living there for almost half the year. 'Sometimes, Brother Fish, what dey do don't make no sense. But always, in da end, it Chinese logic an' it work out. Those dudes dey crazy, but crazy like a fox. Yoh know what I mean?' While Jimmy loves the complexity and convolutions of doing business with the Chinese, I'm rather glad Wendy and I run the island side of the business with the help of Jimmy's various children, my K-Force mates who joined Ogoya and their children, and, of course, the islanders.

As I come to the end of my story there is so much I need to wind up. Gloria died quietly in her sleep ten years ago. She was the first of the Kellys since Mary the Great to make it into the big time as the matriarch of a family who went from being a pinch of the proverbial to one of the most successful in the land. Father Crosby buried her with a full Latin mass, and has a brand new church to show for it. In its nave is the beautiful carving of the Madonna and Child brought back from the Launceston Art Gallery to where it belongs. Sue, now retired, never married, but does a great deal of charity work on the island, and the new operating facility at the cottage hospital is named the Matron Susan McKenzie Theatre. The twins Steve and Cory are still fishermen, happy each to skipper one of the company fishing boats. Cory spends his free time at the pub and has a long-suffering wife, Jane, while Steve spends his free time in his shed restoring vintage cars and has a long-suffering wife, Melissa. Between them they have eight rowdy kids, who Wendy and I love to death. Father Crosby is in an old-age home in Launceston for Catholic priests who refuse to die. I visited for a few minutes yesterday to take him a bottle of Irish whiskey. 'You're your mother's boy, you are and all, Jacko. Will you not be thinking of coming over to the true faith now?' he asked me. Mike Munday is the Reg Ansett of mining exploration and air surveying, and Munday Aviation is now a worldwide operation that can still land a plane on a sixpence anywhere you like, but it's going to cost you more than a few bob.

---

## THE GALLIPOLI BAR – 1986

When this story began I was seated where I am now, at the Gallipoli Bar in the Anzac Hotel in Launceston, waiting for Jimmy to arrive from Hong Kong. It is the thirty-third anniversary of our return from Korea and, alas, the saddest of them all. The Countess is dying in Launceston Hospital. She has recently been diagnosed with cancer and, at her age of seventy-nine, it is inoperable. Thank God she claims to have very little pain. When Wendy and I visited her yesterday she was quite bright, giving us specific instructions on how she is to be buried. She wants her grave to be in her wild garden overlooking the cliffs, with nothing in sight but the whitecaps rolling in all the way from South America. There are to be no orations, but I am to play the harmonica and Jimmy is to sing 'Don't Put Your Daughter on the Stage, Mrs Worthington'. I'll bet Noël Coward never envisaged a six-foot nine-inch American Negro with a voice as deep as Paul Robeson's singing his song at a funeral service.

Two days ago I put a stepladder in the back of the ute and drove around to her cottage, climbed up and took down the beautiful board bolted to the wall above her bed.

*Thank you for the strawberry milkshake love affair. V.S.*

When the time comes it will be set into the lid of her coffin.

I am to be the unfortunate owner of Vowelfowl. Nicole informs me he has his birthday on the first of January, and next year he will be sixty-six. The old bugger is going to outlive us all. Thank goodness Jake, Cory's eldest son, loves him like a brother, even though his own vowel sounds are anything but rounded.

Jimmy is bringing Whisky and Mark down with him from Hong Kong. He and I will have a quick beer to continue the tradition we started thirty-three years ago, and then we'll all visit the Countess in hospital.

I suddenly feel a large hand on my shoulder. Jimmy has arrived looking a little the worse for wear, his suit crumpled and his tie loosened – not his usual immaculate self.

After going through the scene of trying to catch a taxi at the airport, and, for the thirty-third time, toasting our friendship and our traditional 9th of August reunion, he produces a soft pack and a lighter and places them on the bar. He lights up and takes a short, sharp drag, then places the fag into the lip of the glass ashtray and blows the smoke out through his nostrils. He turns to me and says, 'It's been a long journey, Brother Fish.'

'No longer than usual. I'm the one can't sleep on planes – you always look like you've just stepped out of Johnny Chang's tailor shop in Kowloon.'

'Nah, not da trip, da journey.' He picks up his glass. 'Our Countess,' he says, his voice low and gentle. 'Hell, man. I done love her so much.' Jimmy, his beer halfway raised to his mouth, is crying, softly, without a sound – just tears running down his 'high-yella' face.

We finish our beers in silence. 'Let's go, mate,' I say, feeling pretty choked up myself. I go to pay the barman but he waves his hand.

Jimmy dropped Whisky and Mark off at the hotel where Wendy and I are staying and they've gone ahead to the hospital, so he and I leave from the Anzac together in a cab.

Nicole is very weak and seems even more frail than she looked yesterday. Jimmy bends to kiss her. 'How ya doin', Countess?' he asks.

'You look a mess, James,' she replies, her voice hardly above a whisper.

'Bad trip,' Jimmy says, explaining no further.

Then Whisky speaks up. 'Mother, I have something to say.'

Nicole looks at her precious daughter through deeply hooded eyes, 'Better say it quickly, darling – there isn't a lot of time left.' Even now, she is still able to joke.

'I've learned how to do it,' Whisky says, her eyes filling with tears.

'Do what, darling?' Nicole asks, her voice only just audible.

'To love. James Pentecost Oldcorn and Dr Whisky are getting married. Please, please, stay for the wedding tomorrow,' she sobs.

At two a.m. in the morning, on the hour Whisky was born, the Countess can't hold on any longer. I take out my harmonica and play the opening chords and Jimmy starts to sing 'The Fish Song' in his deep baritone voice as the Gods, ours and the others, lift her good, good soul up and away from us.

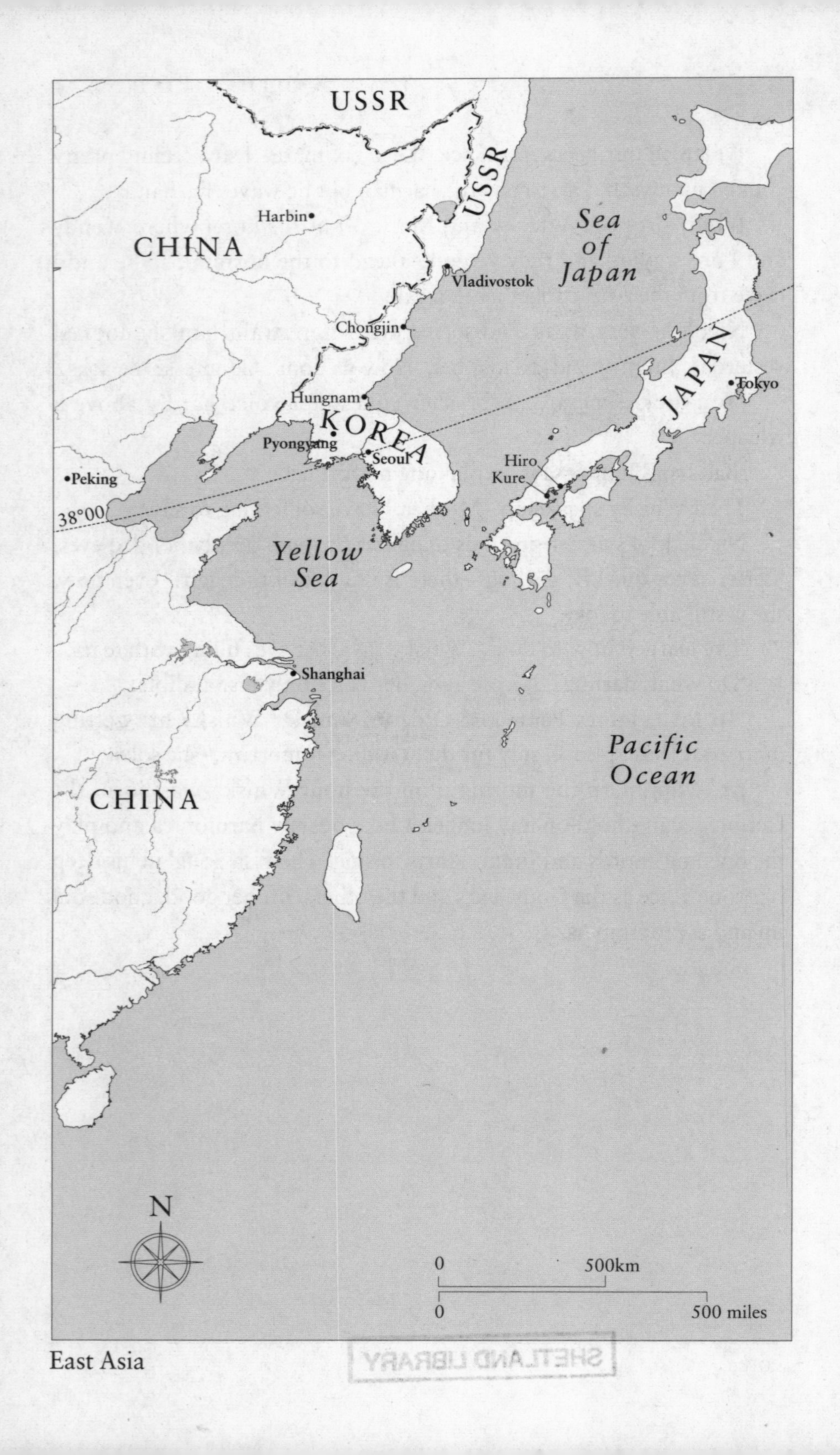
USSR
USSR
Harbin
CHINA
Sea
of
Japan
Vladivostok
Chongjin
JAPAN
Tokyo
Hungnam
KOREA
Pyongyang
Seoul
Hiro
Kure
Peking
38°00
Yellow
Sea
Shanghai
Pacific
Ocean
CHINA
N
0
500km
0
500 miles

East Asia

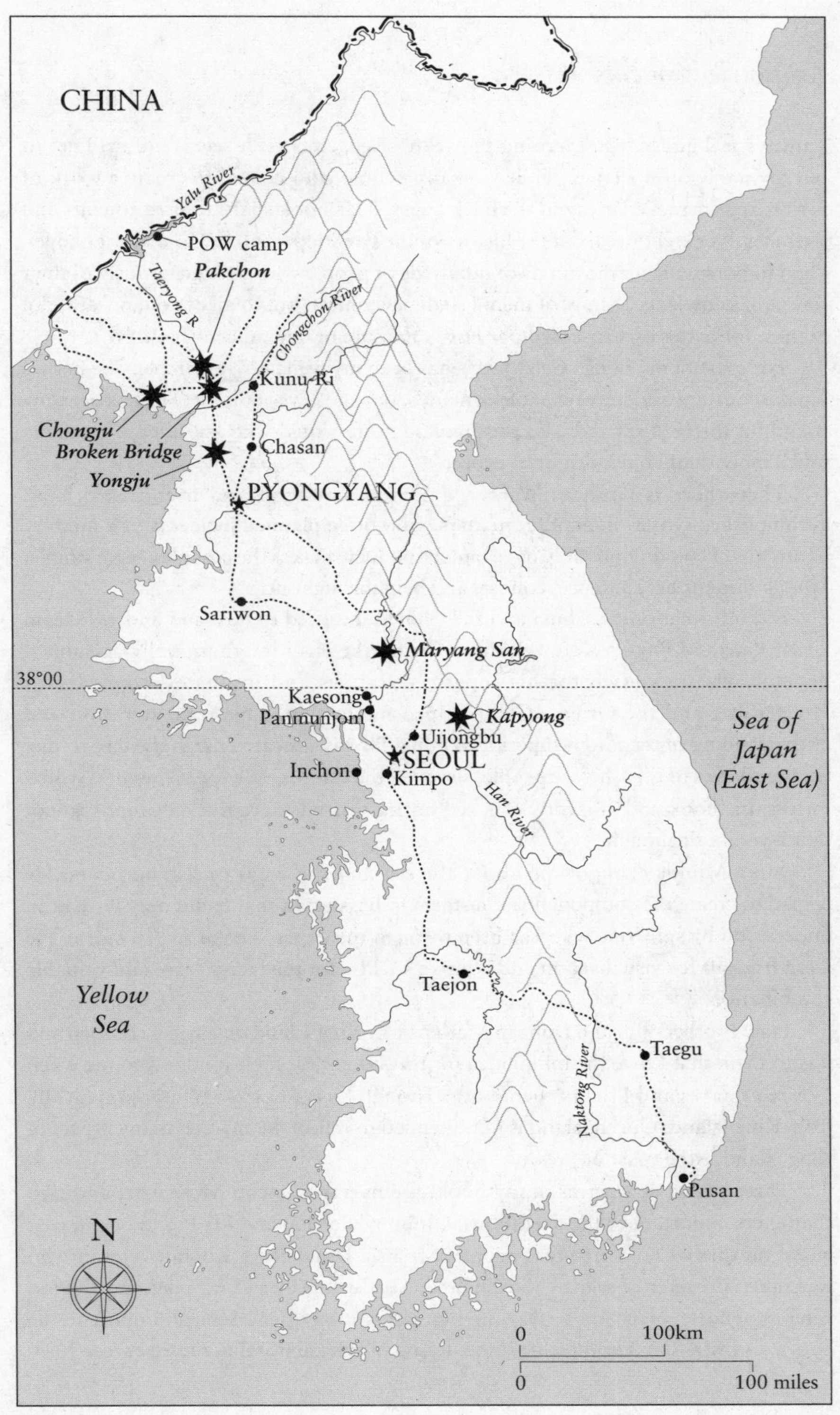

CHINA
Yalu River
POW camp
Taeryong R
Pakchon
Chongchon River
Kunu-Ri
Chongju
Broken Bridge
Chasan
Yongju
PYONGYANG
Sariwon
Maryang San
38°00
Kaesong
Panmunjom
Kapyong
Uijongbu
SEOUL
Inchon
Kimpo
Han River
Sea of Japan (East Sea)
Taejon
Yellow Sea
Taegu
Naktong River
Pusan
N
0
100km
0
100 miles


Korea

## *Acknowledgements*

I always feel guilty when writing the acknowledgements. It seems unfair: I get to put my name on the cover while so many people who helped to create a work of fiction appear tucked away in the back pages. This book spans four continents and stretches over eighty years of the history of the twentieth century. To make it happen I had to borrow from the minds of hundreds of people who gave generously of their time and knowledge. Many of them I shall never meet, but to all of you, my grateful thanks; for better or worse *Brother Fish* is the sum of our collective minds.

For most of my books Celia Jarvis has been my principal researcher. She knows I make constant and unreasonable demands, but she never fails me. She has been my friend for thirty years and is a consummate professional who has always given me much more than I have a right to expect.

Then there is Graham Walker, a Vietnam veteran and friend who is an accomplished writer on military matters, who often planned incidents of a military nature that I couldn't possibly have understood. He makes the complex seem simple. I thank him for his guidance, counsel and help throughout.

For information on China and the Chinese I turned to husband and wife team Geoff Pike and Phyllis Kotewell-Pike. Geoff Pike is an internationally acclaimed novelist who is known for his superb narratives and intimate knowledge of Hong Kong and the Orient. Geoff helped me factually, his transliteration and understanding of the idiom superior to mine. Phyllis educated me in the day-to-day ways and lives of the Chinese people, supplied the Cantonese expressions and words I use in the book and diligently checked my narrative for accuracy. I simply cannot thank you both enough.

Mike Munday taught me about the sea and the ways of fishing boats. He helped to create the components of a storm in Bass Strait that could only have been understood by someone who has been through the experience of such a storm. He has a true gift for visualisation and is also a stickler for the facts, a rare and valuable combination.

I met brothers Jim and Duncan McKenzie of King Island on a trip to Borneo and it is to them that I owe the initial idea for this book. For their kindness to me when I visited their island I thank them both. Though I have borrowed topographically from King Island, Queen Island is not intended to reflect on anyone or any aspect of King Island, either past or present.

Three of the characters in my book, the narrator, Jacko McKenzie, and two characters important to the overall story, Johnny Gordon and Pat Brand, are in part based on the lives of three real people: Mr Eric Donnelly, a Korean veteran who was taken prisoner of war by the Chinese; Mr Cecil Fisher O.A., poet and Korean veteran, whose poem 'Anzac Day, Living with Granny (Cherbourg)' I quote in the book; and Mrs Pat Thompson, some events of whose notable music career form the basis of my character Pat Brand. Thank you all for allowing me to mould hard-won truths, songs and poetry into my fiction, helping to give it veracity and depth.

The following Korean veterans generously told their stories for my benefit and I am most grateful to you all: Lieutenant Colonel Alfred Argent; General Sir Phillip Bennett A.C., K.B.E., D.S.O.; Major General David Butler A.O., D.S.O.; Mr Keith Cameron; Mr R. (Nugget) Dunque M.M., W.O.1; Keith R. Everle; Mr Max Everle; Major Len Opie D.C.M., R.F.D., E.D.; the late Brigadier Noel 'Chick' Charlesworth D.S.O., Mr Keith Langton; Mr Ivan Petty; Colonel David Manet M.C.; Colonel Colin Townsend D.S.O.; and Mr Frank Willard. Others who gave of their military expertise were Mr George Bindley, Dr Robert A. Hall, Mr Sam Hilt, Brigadier Kerry Mellor, Mr Roy 'Zeke' Mundine, Mr Bruce Olsen, and Mr Peter Gilbey.

There are the people we pestered more than once and who gave unsparingly of their time: Ms Melba Butler, Executive Director, Harlem Dowling-West Side Centre for Children and Family Services, N.Y., U.S.A.; Mr Graham Earnshaw – Tales of Old China, Shanghai; Mr Anthony J. Harrison – fisheries historian, Tasmania; Mr Rob Henderson – historian, P&O; Hugh Spencer – music history; Mr Charles Updike, genealogist, N.J., U.S.A..

Material from the Australian National Archives on the White Australia Policy was greatly aided by advice from Mr Al Grasby A.M., Australia's Minister for Immigration 1972–74, and Dr James Jupp A.M., Director, Centre of Immigration and Multicultural Studies, A.N.U..

Those who helped with pertinent information are: Australian War Memorial Library (especially its store of personal accounts) – Canberra; Ms Margaret Aldrich – Princeton University, N.J., U.S.A.; Mr Ian Barnes-Keoghan – Bureau of Meteorology, Hobart; Mr Mark Bolourchi – Caviar Club, U.S.A.; Mr John Brooksbank – Hobart Marine Radio; The Help Desk – The American War Library; Mr Anthony Bruno – Crime Library, U.S.A.; Ms Elaine Camroux McLean – Library Enquiries Team, Foreign & Commonwealth Office, U.K.; Mr F. 'Jack' Casey – President, Korean Veterans Association, Vietnam Veterans Federation; Mario Cordoma – Cordoma Grape Marketing; Mr Owen Denmeade – religion; Dr Anthony Freeman; Mrs A. Gliksman; Dr Michael Gliksman; Mr James Graham; K.T. Jackson; Ms Killy Lau – calligraphist; Dr Irwin Light; Mr Nick Mauger – Qantas Customer Care; Mr Thomas McCarthy – historian, Correctional History, N.Y., U.S.A.; Mrs Lexie McClenaghan – author; Mr Bill McKenzie – drug & alcohol counsellor; The Mitchell Library; Ms Ann Parker – Senior Advisor, Government House, Hobart; Ms Kaye Paletz – New Jersey State Librarian, Law; Tasmanian Museum & Art Gallery; Ms Jovee Tiee – Tri-Counties Genealogy & History Centre, N.J., U.S.A.; Mr Stewart Williams – President, Parrot Society of Australia; Mr Geoffrey Valentine – abalone diver; Ms Heather Wade – Archivist, Booth Library; Chemung Valley Museum, N.J., U.S.A.; Mark Woodhouse – Archivist, Elmira College, N.Y., U.S.A.; Mr and Mrs Victor and Yana White – Russian advisors; Ms

Libby William – Department of Fisheries; Messrs Morrie, Kevin and Paul Wolf – cray fishermen, Lower Channel; Ms Carol Wonders – horticulture; Tippy the cat – lap sitting and typing %3#*& (example only).

The Penguins: A book is a long and arduous process. A year is about average to make one happen, six months is stretching things, three months is lunacy and two months is chaos. My book family at Penguin have had just two months to get this book out for Christmas 2004. I cannot begin to thank them. My thanks for her patience, help, advice, wisdom and for not panicking, Clare Forster, my publisher. Then there were Bob Sessions, Julie Gibbs, Anne Rogan, Lyn McGaurr, Katie Purvis, Carmen de la Rue, Tammie Gay, Tony Palmer, Nikki Townsend, Deb Brash, Peter Blake, Lyn Amy, Beverley Waldron, Gabrielle Coyne, Dan Ruffino and Sally Bateman, my publicist.

To my new editor Rachel Scully, who carried my novel and her pregnancy for almost the same period of gestation, my sincere thanks. One's editor is literary mother, father, friend, counsellor, teacher, mentor and partner, and Rachel has been all of these.

Finally, my own partner, Dorothy Gliksman, who was the first to see what I wrote and to correct, punctuate and offer suggestions. She put up with me, fed me, protected me from the telephone and allowed me to work undisturbed for months on end. She is also one of my very diligent proofreaders. No author could possibly ask for more from a partner.

## *List of Sources*


Adam-Smith, Patsy, *Prisoners of War: Gallipoli to Korea,* Viking, 1992

Allen, Fred C., (ed.), *Handbook of the N.Y. State Reformatory at Elmira 1916, The New York State Reformatory at Elmira 1926, New York State Reformatory Employee's Book of Rules 1930*

Appleman, Roy E., *United States Army in Korea, South to Naktong, North to Yalu (June-November 1950),* Office of the Chief Military Historian US Army, 1960

Barth, Brigadier General G.B., *Tropic Lighting and Taro Leaf July '50–May '51,* U.S. Army, 1955

Berens, Robert J., *Limbo on the Yalu and Beyond,* Southern Heritage Press Inc., 2000

Chinnery, Phillip D., *Korean Atrocity! Forgotten War Crimes 1950-53,* Airlife, 2000

Cunningham, Cyril, *No Mercy, No Leniency, Communist Mistreatment of British and Allied Prisoners of War in Korea,* Leo Cooper, 2000

Dannen, Fredric, 'Partners in Crime', *The New Republic,* 1997

Dennis, Peter & Grey, Geoffrey (eds), *The Korean War 1950–53, A Fifty Year Retrospective,* The Chief of Army's Military History Conference 2000, Army History Unit, Department of Defence, 2000

Farrar-Hockey, Anthony, *The British Part in the Korean War, Vol.II.* H.M.S.O., London, 1990

Farrar-Hockey, Anthony, *The Edge of the Sword,* Frederick Muller, 1954

Flynn, George Q., *The Draft 1940–1973,* University of Kansas, 1993

Gallaway, Jack, *The Last Call of the Bugle, The Long Road to Kapyong,* University of Queensland Press, 1999

Green, Olwyn, *The Name's Still Charlie,* University of Queensland Press, 1993

Grieve, Ray, *A Band in a Waistcoat Pocket,* Currency Press

Hall, Robert A., *The Black Digger,* Allen & Unwin, 1989

Hanlon, Thomas J., *Treating the Problem Cases in the Psychopathic Clinic at the Elmira Reformatory 1934*

Jackson, K.T., *Encyclopaedia of New York City*

Jager, Handy, *A Fisherman – What is He?*

Knowles, Patrick, *A Rifleman's View of the Battle of Kapyong,* Australian War Memorial PR83/150

Lane, Rev. Francis, *Twelve Years in a Reformatory,* Elmira Reformatory, N.Y., 1926

Manchester, William, *American Caesar: Douglas McArthur 1880-1964,* Hutchinson of Australia, 1978

Morrow, Curtis J., *What's a Commie Ever Done to Black People? A Korean War Memoir of Fighting in the US Army's Last All Negro Unit,* McFarland Publishers Inc., 1997

Newspaper archives: *The Age, Sydney Morning Herald, The Mercury, The Examiner*

Odgers, George, *Army Australia, An Illustrated History,* Child & Associates, 1988

O'Dowd, Ben, *In Valiant Company, Diggers in Battle – Korea 1950–1953*, University of Queensland Press, 2000

O'Neill, Robert, *Australia in the Korean War, 1950–53, Vol 2., Combat Operations*, Australian War Memorial and Australian Government Publishing Service, 1981

Palfreeman, A.C., *The Administration of the White Australian Policy*, Melbourne University Press, 1967

Parker, Robert, 'Bat on Chaps, Bat On', in David Chin, *Korean History Project*, Australian War Memorial PR 4036

Qantas Airways, *From Wagon Wheels to Wings*

Rishell, Lisle, *With a Black Platoon in Combat, A Year in Korea,* Texas and A&M University Press, 1993

Ritchie, John, *Australian Dictionary of Biography*, Melbourne University Press, 1993

Saddler, Stanley, *The Korean War, An Encyclopaedia*, Garland Publishing, 1995

Schnieder, Eric C., *Egyptian Kings: Youth Gangs in Postwar New York*, Princeton University Press, 1999

Smith, Lt Col. Neil C., *Home by Christmas, The Australian Army in Korea 1950–1956*, Mostly Unsung, 1990

Summers, Harry G. Jnr, *Korean War Almanac,* Facts on File, New York, 1990

Thompson, Pat (nee Brand), *She's a Fat Tart, Ain't She*, Ginninderra Press, 2002

Wilson, Stewart, *Dakota, Hercules and Caribou in Australian Services,* Aerospace Publications, 1990

**Websites**

Australian Bureau of Statistics, Australian War Memorial, Budweiser, Catholic Encyclopaedia, Christian Web Host Inc, Gangland Net, New York State Library, Quaker Organisation, Organised Crime Registry-U.K, St James Church, Tom Newton – K9 History: The Dogs of War, Trade & Environment Data Base – American University Washington.